MW01489902

MONSTERS IN LOVE

VOL. 1: LOST IN THE LABYRINTH

DARKLIGHT PRESS

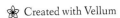 Created with Vellum

CONTENTS

DARKHEART
VIVIENNE HART

BELFRY
DEE J. HOLMES

THE DEN
ATLAS ROSE

BLOODED LABYRINTH
S.J. SANDERS

BESPELLED BREWS
ELLE CROSS

STALKING TAMARA
NOVA BLAKE

MY VEILED PURSUER
OPAL FAIRCHILD

THE MINOAN BRIDE
C.M. NASCOSTA

PUBLISHER'S NOTE

Dear Monster Lover,

Monsters in Love is an ongoing anthology series. Each volume is limited edition, and will be available for purchase for three months in digital and print format.

We are creating a special edition *Monsters in Love* anthology to be available on all major digital book markets. It is set to release March 7, 2023.

Please consider preordering on all three major retailers: Apple, Barnes and Noble, and Amazon (link will be available in June). We would love to see our monsters dominating on the *USA Today* Bestsellers list.

When you do, please upload a digital copy of your receipts HERE, or enter this link into your favorite browser:

https://bit.ly/monsters-in-love-GWP.

Doing so will reserve a digital gift-with-purchase for you, to be fulfilled starting in June 2022, when the Amazon link goes live.

Preorder Here: Monsters in Love: A Monster Paranormal Romance Anthology

Releasing March 7, 2023

Future Monsters in Love anthology volumes and release schedule is listed below. We thank you in advance for preordering in support of our stories.

Monsters in Love vol 2: Lost in the Dark
Releasing September 2022

Monsters in Love vol 3: Lost in the Forest
Releasing March 2023

Monsters in Love vol 4: Title to be announced
Releasing September 2023

Monsters in Love vol 5: Title to be announced
Releasing March 2024

Thank you for all your love and support. Your preorder lets us know that you want to read more of our work.

FOREWORD

Please note that this anthology features a diverse range of stories that span from sweet to spicy, and all the delicious flavors in between.

They may contain the following themes, tropes, and triggers:

Abduction, Assault, BDSM, Dark Themes, Fighting, Graphic Sex, Heat, Kink, Menage, Power Exchange, Reverse Harem, Size Difference, Slave Auction, Trafficking.

Please proceed with caution.

FINDING HER MINOTAUR

EVANGELINE PRIEST

AUTHOR'S NOTE

Finding Her Minotaur is a steamy romance crossover story that is part of my Obsidian City: Love and Monsters world set in the Obsidian Rift universe featured in my paranormal romance stories with my Legion and Intergalactic Republic universe featured in my sci-fi/alien romances.

The tone is sweet, though there are some dark themes that are mainly off the page, and ends in a non-cliffhanger, happily-for-now.

Featured tropes include: size difference, grumpy protective males, sunshiny females, heat-induced, graphically-described sex between consenting adults.

Potentially triggering themes include: abduction, trafficking, forced drugging, slave auction, and assault.

CHAPTER ONE

KARIS

"CALL US AND LET US KNOW WHEN YOU GET THERE SO WE KNOW YOU'RE ALRIGHT! LOVE YOU, KAR-BEAR."

I had let my mom's phone call go to voicemail when I struggled with unearthing my suitcase from the belly of the bus. As I listen to her message now, my heart crumbles into even tinier pieces.

I play it again, her slight southern accent drawing out the "you," as if she could hang on to the digital connection of me just a while longer.

God, I wish I let her.

Instead, I flew halfway across the country, then took both a bus and a train into New York only to find out that the love of my life decided that he needed a break from us so he can spend his immediate future upstate impressing his new friends.

The same friends we were supposed to be sharing our new apartment with.

Funny how he didn't bring any of these issues up two days ago when I gladly transferred money to his cash app for my half of the down payment for the apartment.

So, now I'm basically homeless and have less than $100 in my bank account. The twenty dollar bill that my dad slipped into my hand for snacks is now $5.22, thanks to my overpriced latte and the damned box of condoms that I thought was a good idea to buy.

I should've bought a sandwich instead. Would have satisfied me better and longer than Liam ever could have, that's for damned sure.

Okay, options. Who do I know in the city? Answer: No one.

All the contacts I have are Liam's contacts, and they all thought that abandoning a girl in a new city would be an acceptable idea.

Bright side: My phone battery is full, and I have my charger in my backpack.

I can always call home...

If I tell my parents that I need money, they would send it to me immediately —well, once I walk them through how to use their app on their phone—and it would hit my bank account within minutes. They would welcome me back home without question, and say that everything happens for a reason Kar-bear, and this is the Lord's will.

My stomach twists at the thought. I do not want to reinforce my parents' need to look for signs from God in order to make every. little. life decision.

I made such a big deal about heading out on my own and being in love and how Liam is the one and how much I trusted him and so they needed to trust me, too.

God, just thinking of him makes me see red.

Liam didn't even have the decency to tell me in person he no longer wants to be with me. He let me come all this way, and by the time my phone finally got a signal, his text came through.

I'm still fuming over the text message heat rising into my cheeks, but now that reality is sinking in, I'm realizing that I'm alone in a city that I don't know. I can easily become a statistic, and I hate Liam even more for putting me in this position.

Fuck Liam.

Raised voices cut through the red haze of Liam's elaborate death and torture that I'm fantasizing for him. Looking around, I don't see anyone in obvious distress. Tourists are scuttling about like good little ants, checking out the various announcement boards on their way to their terminals.

It's only at a second glance that I see a barely lit alcove off of the corridor. Had that been there before?

There is a man wearing a hoodie and baggy pants, towering over a petite woman. It looks like a lover's quarrel the way he is all in her space, but it still makes me feel uncomfortable to take a discreet picture. My parents wouldn't raise their voices at each other even if they were on fire, so seeing a couple fight always triggers me.

I try to ignore them, turning my attention back to my phone when I see the man yank the woman's elbow when she tries to walk around him.

How dare he put his hands on her!

Just as I practiced in my self-defense classes, I plant my feet firmly on the ground, trigger the release on my asp baton, and call out in a voice supported by my diaphragm so it can carry. "Hey! Get your hands off of her."

The man looks my way and freezes. His hood is up, so I can't see his face clearly at this distance, but I swear I see a flash of glowing red eyes and scales for a moment before his face becomes a nondescript scruffy-looking guy again. He takes in my stance and my asp, then bolts away.

I retract my baton. It's not exactly legal here, but I would rather be cited for carrying a non-regulation weapon than be dead.

The poor girl is shaking. She is shorter than I am even with her platform heels. She reminds me of a porcelain doll with her creamy skin and delicate stature. Up close, I see that her blue eyes are contacts and she may not be a natural blonde.

"Are you okay?" I ask.

She looks at me as if she's waiting for something.

"What?" I ask. "Oh god, do you speak English?" Panic rushes me as I try to scrape together the bits and pieces of conversational French and Spanish that I took in high school and college.

Maybe I can download a translation app on my phone...

"Yes, I can. I'm sorry, I can't believe you saw me, let alone helped me," she says, her voice high and sing-songy like a trilling bird. "Thank you so much."

Rage against the man came over me once more. I'm taller than the average woman and I do not look like anyone's version of frail or delicate. I take pride in being able to hold my own bussing tables and balancing huge trays at my old restaurant.

She oozes vulnerability, and whoever the guy was knew it. "So, is he a boyfriend or something? Is he going to cause any trouble for you in the future?"

"No, he's not a boyfriend. I don't know him at all, but I've seen him around now and then." She crosses her arms, shivering despite the muggy air.

"You have a stalker? Girl, no offense, but you need to watch out. I'm not trying to be mean, but guys like him can put you in their pocket and walk away and no one will even know."

Instead of the anger I expected, she ends up laughing. "Yeah, I normally have a couple of other people with me, but I wanted a little me-time on my day off before going back to work. Besides, we don't have good reception there."

She shows me the phone in her hand.

I swallow a groan. Being aware of my environment has been drilled into me since I started middle school. It isn't fair, and I should have the right to feel carefree and safe no matter what, but as my parents would say, *that's the way of the world.* "You know better than to go out alone again, right? At least not be distracted on your phone alone in public?" I say, somehow sounding a little like my mom.

Her face lights up in a brilliant smile. "No, I swear," she says. "My name is Adalyn Wilde."

I shake her proffered hand. "Karis. Karis de la Cruz."

"Well, if you're free, Karis, I would love to treat you to a drink or a meal or something. I don't work for a few more hours, and I was going to grab a meal before my shift starts."

"Is there a restaurant nearby?" I ask. The food court is in the opposite direction and I don't see any restaurants in this area.

"It's in the lower level," she says. "Just through this door." She points to a drab metallic door with a flat panel where a door latch would be.

"Was the door always there?" I muse more to myself than her.

She laughs in that sing-song way of hers. "Blends in with the wall, doesn't it? But don't worry..." Her voice trails off and her already large eyes widen as she looks past me. "Oh no," she gasps, grabbing my hand and tugging me toward the door. "Run!"

I glance behind me, looking for this source of danger that scares Adalyn. There's nothing there. "Wait, what's wrong?"

She fumbles at the panel, fitting her hand over the pad. It lights up in an array of colors. The latch clicks, but before the door opens, a sort of seizure overtakes Adalyn's body.

I want to help her, but I can't move. Something locks my entire body in a vice. Any semblance of coherent thought slips from my mind.

Something large and invisible lifts Adalyn's contorted body up in the air. Her phone clatters to the ground at the same time a call tries to connect. A single word, Bronn, flashes on the screen.

Through the microphone, a gravelly voice says, "Adalyn?" before the display shatters.

Bile threatens to claw up my throat as I'm suddenly weightless and buoyant. A harsh vice wraps around my middle and around my wrists. I can't even cry out.

The contents of my bag spill across the floor. My cell phone lights up with a cheery text from my mom. "Love you, Kar-Bear! I know you're having so much fun! Text us back when you arrive at your new place!"

Tears blur my sight as I desperately fight to reach my phone and the last connection I might have with my mom. Black shrouds the edge of my vision, until all I see are pinpoints of light and then nothing.

CHAPTER TWO

BRONN

My comm display turns black as the connection cuts off. I don't like it. Adalyn is flighty, but she wouldn't reach out to me unless she needed something. For some reason, the girl is afraid of me, and would rather ask anyone for help with her problems before coming to me.

That she did tells me something is gravely wrong.

I dial Mrs. Roads, and she answers before the ringtone sounds. "Yes, sir?"

It grates me when she calls me 'sir'. I run this hub of the Nexus; my men who answer to me barely address me as their urso or leader. Taurines are a practical lot. Rank means nothing. We follow those who earn our loyalty and respect, which usually translates as the one who can win in a fight.

I remain undefeated.

"Is Adalyn working today?" I ask. I double-wrap my tone with care. Mrs. Roads is a treasured Dame. It would not be appropriate to upset her needlessly.

I have a hard enough time keeping the soldiers from locking horns when their chosen female is with another paramour. An upset Mrs. Roads would tip the scales into chaos.

"No, sir. Adalyn is on a personal day, which usually means she's getting some beauty treatments done." There is a pause. "She usually calls, though. And I believe she expressed she would be at lunch to chat with the girls. Sort of a brunch date, and I do not recall seeing her. It's not like her to miss an appointment, client or otherwise."

I know this as a fact. Adalyn is sweet and submissive. A darling in the house. She is always careful to avoid upsetting anyone. Considering her long list of clients, she is precious indeed if she can so skillfully manage so many male egos. And many Taurine egos among them.

A sour feeling settles into the pit of my stomach. If something happened to that girl...

A hint of worry tinges Mrs. Roads's unflappable demeanor. "Is something amiss, sir?"

"No, nothing," I say in what I hope sounds like a soothing tone. I am more used to speaking to a troop of soldiers and not honored females. "Just checking in on her schedule. Is she free this evening?"

"Why? Are you finally availing yourself of our hospitality discount?"

I balk at the idea. If ever I were to avail myself of a partner, she would not be house-bound. Counter-culture as the thought may be, I dislike sharing my chosen partners.

I do not want to offend Mrs. Roads, so I sidestep the question. "I have heard some chatter around the Nexus, is all. Please keep a close eye out for any suspicious activities. We are looking at anyone incoming within the next rotation. When is her next client expecting her?"

"This evening. A Lupus from House Darkclaw."

The hackles on my neck raise. Though we are technically allies, the Lupines and other wolfkin shifters had been a major nuisance for the past hundred years with their endless skirmishes at the borders of others' territories. They made it difficult to maintain order.

"Thank you. Please forward the client's information to the guard on duty. They will need to postpone any arrivals by at least one solar day. Will that cause much upset at the stable?"

Mrs. Roads huffs. A clear image of her ramrod-straight spine and starched suit appears in my mind. "Do not worry, sir. I will handle the roster and scheduling. This is nothing out of the ordinary. The stable's security means more than a few ruffled feathers."

I nod in approval, though she can't see me. A bull with half her sense would do wonders among my ranks. "I will send more guards to the house to increase patrols as a precaution. Please call for backup if any of the clients become disrespectful in any manner."

She huffs again, this time in challenge. "I will be certain to do so, though it will be my pleasure to remind them of house protocol, especially regarding the Dame. Will that be all, sir?"

"Indeed. You are the pride of the stable."

"Remember that when next we meet for the budgeting committee."

As soon as the line clears, I send a message to the relief unit commander that he and his men will go in a day earlier than planned to head off a threat. I also make it abundantly clear that if any of the house guests so much as look at Mrs. Roads with disrespect, he would be free to pluck out the offenders' eyes and haul them off-property.

My next message is in coded text to my second-in-command, Tag. "*Gather your most discreet and elite soldiers. Potential extraction mission.*"

He answers back. "*Wet work?*"

"*High possibility.*"

"*Off world?*"

"*Yes.*" Adalyn's last ping shows on my screen. Earth. Of course. A non-extradition, non-inducted planet. Perfect setting for the scum of the galaxy to operate, especially as it is a natural hub with many portals. "*Terra Prime. We've already lost ten minutes triangulating her last coordinates.*"

Tag responds. "*My team is ready. Boots on the ground in five.*"

"*I will see you in one.*"

The scent hits me first as Earth materializes before my eyes. Terra Prime, being as raw as it is, allows many natural states to proliferate. Sewage clashes with the sugary scents wafting from a nearby food vendor. My stomachs clench at the noxious odors.

I make sure my cloaking armor is on. The last thing we need would be for a hysterical mob impeding this investigation.

My second-in-command is already here. Tag looks to be a nondescript human, forgettable at first glance thanks to our armor's optical deflection field. The disguise wouldn't get past true security scanners, but is good enough for what passes as technology on Earth.

Which is how my second is virtually invisible among the stream of smaller humans despite his height, mass, and set of horns. Tag, unfazed by the locals, straightens to attention when he spies my approach.

I tilt my chin to him in acknowledgement. "What do we see here, Tag?"

Tag was a younger Taurine, but his austere temperament was shaped in a landscape of war. He follows order and discipline to a near-religious zeal that I respect. He recites his initial observation in a clipped tone, each word precise and necessary.

In the end, he shows me a crushed unit in the palm of his hand. "This seems to be the end of Ms. Adalyn's tracking. Her last known logged location."

I take in the scene. The framework of this section of tunneling hides key components of a deflection field as well. Before I can ask, Tag says, "The deflection field was deactivated when my team and I arrived. I reactivated it to see that it was not malfunctioning and kept the field on to minimize curious persons."

Tag narrows his gaze at the flow of humanity at large, and so I know he means the uninitiated natives.

"I took the liberty of calling in a forensic team, too," Tag continues. "While my team is tracking down a promising scent trail, these investigators are making sure we miss nothing."

Tag nods to a young Taurine analyzing the portal. "Report," he commands the bullock.

The investigator stands at attention, heels together, chest out. Everything about him was shiny. He will not last long in the field. "Sir! The doorway was opened and connected to a portal. No signs of entry or exit. Sir."

Rage simmers in my chest, a warm feeling that constricts my ribs. Poor Adalyn. I can only imagine her panic. She had been so close to safety. Her call had even connected with mine.

Tag's face is neutral. "You know what would happen if we do not retrieve her."

"The possibility is moot, and so we do not need to speculate," I say.

"We do not need to speculate. The other houses will lash out. Adalyn is the prime aurochs's daughter—"

I hold my hand out to squash his words. We don't know what kind of spies may be listening. Besides, I do not need to be reminded of her pedigree. An aurochs's daughter or no, she is under my protection and should have been untouchable.

"House Nighthold can withstand threats," I say.

"We are strong but one house against a swarm will eventually fall."

Tag says the truth, but I refuse to poison my thinking with any possibility of failure. To lose a precious gift like the one Adalyn represents would cost House Nighthold. Once others doubt our ability to protect our stable, it would leave the females open to being poached and taken—if the females even choose to stay.

"Then let's not allow for that possibility," I say. "What are you holding?" My second looks like he had bits of random debris in his hand.

"The investigation team found these. They were scattered closely to the scene with the same scent signatures that overlaps with Adalyn. It could be related." He presents the collected bits of personal items and an empty bag.

I pluck the bag from his hand, holding it aloft between my thumb and forefinger. An offensive odor clings to one strap. I've smelled it before, and grit my teeth against the memory. Viper pheromones mingles with the wet, dank musk of old dirt.

"We found these items near Adalyn's broken comm unit, along with this device. Bring the device here," Tag calls out.

The bullock from the forensic team shows me a unit similar to Adalyn's. "The humans call it a mobile phone," the forensic investigator informs me.

I raise my brow at him before he retreats to the rest of his team to analyze more data. The unit in my hand is a more primitive model than what we carry, but its purpose is still obvious. I tap the screen. "It seems to be locked."

Tag looks at it for a moment and fiddles with the settings. "I believe the power is low. Here, I have a spare charger." He slaps a charger around the phone, and after a moment, it glows to life. Tag hands it back to me.

Text messages float across the screen. I scroll through them, hoping for a hint of something. Nothing. "This is unfortunately a dead end. What do we have—"

The screen lights up once more, cutting off my words. I see that the notification is for a message from someone labeled "Mom." From my interpretation of the jumble of hieroglyphs, Mom is full of hearts and tears yet is laughing.

Another message chimes through with text this time.

Karis!!! Found the picture from Parents' Day! Adding it to the church family directory, so if you hate it, speak now or forever hold your peace!

A picture arrives next, and what I see there steals my breath. Three people stand together, an older couple who frame a young woman. Based on their respective coloring and physical traits, the couple is not biologically related to the younger female, and yet this Mom refers to this moment as being from "Parents Day" and will submit the image among a family directory.

Tag's voice interrupts my reverie. "Is everything all right, sir?"

It takes strength of will to tear my gaze from the female to meet my second's. "Whoever took Adalyn also took this young lady. I am positive." I hold the image out to Tag, who studies it. "The poachers had a very successful moment indeed."

An urge to punch Tag in the face ripples over me when it seems like he is taking a little too long studying the woman named Karis. I shake my head to clear it. "They must be celebrating their victory right now."

Tag scoffs. "Let them celebrate. They will have their guard down. When we find them, they will regret the day they ever touched these females."

"Indeed," I say. The promise of blood rang in my ears.

I swipe at the image. The picture shifts as if on a carousel and I'm startled to see that there is an image of Adalyn. There is a stricken look on her face as she sees a male I recognize too well.

I shove the phone at Tag. "I know where they are. I'd suspected who might have taken her, based on the pheromones, but now I know."

A violent snarl rips from Tag's mouth when he sees who has Adalyn.

I take the phone from him and tuck it into my breast pocket. I place the other personal items found around the scene into the bag, which I sling over my arm. Karis will want these.

"We're on the move," I tell the forensic lead investigator, trusting them to wrap things up discreetly here as I head toward the nearest transport portal. Tag falls in line beside me.

"At most they have a thirty-minute lead," Tag says. "Realistically, closer to about fifteen minutes."

"We all know what can happen and how quickly they can disappear in that hellhole, even within one minute." We need to get them back. Fast. "Contact your team, and tell them to meet us at the Minotaur's Labyrinth."

CHAPTER THREE

Karis

The covering over my head is scratchy and smells. It reeks of the sweat and tears from previous prisoners. Or maybe I'm projecting.

I try not to think of just how many heads this cloth has covered.

I still can't speak. Whatever muscle stunner my abductors used on me affected my tongue as well. Just as well, I talk way too much when I'm nervous.

Right now, I'm plenty nervous.

I don't know why they bother with a head covering since they did something to my eyes, so I can just barely see anything past a black haze. It's as if I'm trying to see through a tinted car window.

It does nothing to curtail the sounds I've heard, though. It's what I expect from people who have been kidnapped. A lot of crying, a lot of whispers, all kinds of torment.

And the worst part is that they all sound female. I can't pinpoint Adalyn's voice though, so I have to hope that she is the one that huddles close to me.

I wish I could speak to her. The way others are crying and whining, I should be able to verbalize something however, my body is still frozen.

"Karis, is this you?" Adalyn's soft voice carries through my hood.

Well, that answers my question on her location. I can't respond, so I try my best to nudge her shoulder.

"I hope it's you. Don't be afraid help is coming. I know it is."

I don't know what to believe, since the very idea of being kidnapped is unreal to me. It's all supposed to have been a cautionary tale, something out of urban legends. It's not supposed to have happened in the middle of the day with plenty of onlookers around.

The heavy, plodding steps of boots cut through the sounds of despair. My heart races, knowing that they belong to our captors.

"Someone is coming," Adalyn says.

A gate with rusted hinges groans as it opens. Someone with an obsequious tone and slippery cadence speaks first. A second man responds in what sounds like grunts and...hisses?

It's frustrating because I can't understand any words, however, the tone transcends languages. A deal is happening and we are the products being bought and sold.

A few grunts later, rough hands grab my shoulders and the covering comes off of my head. I was face-to-face with a black smudge of a figure, so whatever happened to me is still affecting my vision.

Someone presses something cold against my neck. If I could move away from it, I would have, but I'm still somewhat paralyzed. Great.

It still feels like I'm looking through a black veil, but slowly, the world clears in front of me. The first thing I see is a strange creature. He wears a black tuxedo suit jacket complete with tails and a pocket square. No shirt, though, so his lean torso is bare. All the better to display the layers of gold necklaces festoon his neck.

Oh yeah, the bottom half of him is that of a goat. Small horns that curve backward over his obnoxiously beautiful curly hair complete the look and confirms that I'm descending into madness.

"Yes," goat man says, sniffing at me. "This one is perfect. She'll fetch us a lot. She must be first."

I realize I understand his words where everything I heard before was gibberish. I work my jaw, trying to figure out if I could talk or not.

"Where—?" I squeak out. It takes great effort, but I inhale and try again. "What—?"

"Oh good. She hasn't lost her ability to speak. Sometimes the venom works differently depending on what species. The females from Terra Prime are more fragile than others." The goat man peers at me. "But, you're not originally from Terra Prime, are you?" He gives me a sly smile, as if we somehow share an inside secret.

What's that supposed to mean? From the context, I gather that Terra Prime means Earth. But, something is getting lost in translation.

The snake creature looms behind him with the red eyes boring down on me. "No, she's not," he hisses at me, a forked tongue darting out in the air. "She may reside on Terra Prime–Earth," he says, as if spitting something gross from his mouth, "however, she is not Terran."

Snake man wiggles his tongue at me and curls it back into his mouth. He tips his head back as if savoring what he tastes. "She is something else. I can't identify where. Regardless, I have fulfilled the letter of the contract. I have not touched a native Terran. Otherwise, we would have ignored her."

The goat man rolls his eyes. "As if you would have left her since you took this one." He points to Adalyn, who shrinks into the corner of the cage.

The snake leers at her cowering form. "This one is a message."

The goat man brays an obnoxious laugh. "You are a fool to continue this feud with the Taurines. I will not be culpable when they catch up with you. And they will catch up."

"I would like to see them try," the snake man snarls. He lunges at Adalyn in a lightning fast strike and wraps her in his coils, sniffing at her. "Yessss," he hisses as his body undulates around her. "I'm going to enjoy squeezing you... just as your tight little body squeezes around me."

Rage flares over my body. "Put her down," I seethe. Anger must have given me strength. My voice finally returns. "Put her down. Now."

Goat man stares at me curiously. "Agreed." He snaps his fingers and two large minotaurs appear. One grabs a hold of the snake man while another one pulls Adalyn from his grasp and lays her back down next to me.

"You know the rules, Serge," the goat man says. "You may be a little princeling among your people, but these are tributes now. And tributes are property of the Minotaur's Labyrinth. If you want them, you will need to win them at auction just like anyone else."

Labyrinth? Minotaur? This has got to play into some kind of drug-addled dream.

With another snap of his fingers, more minotaurs appear as if they linger in shadows until called upon. They herd us down a cavernous hall. Bas-relief sculptures and other interesting carvings decorate the walls. I would have loved to check out some of the artwork if I weren't a tied-up prisoner.

"Don't worry," Adalyn says. "Bronn will find us."

That name clicks into my memory. "Bronn? That was the person you were trying to call on your cell phone, right?"

She nods. "Yes. Don't be afraid he will find us."

It seems Adalyn is trying to convince herself as much as me. I'm not about to burst her bubble. If she believes this Bronn person is coming, then I'll let her. It's no different from my parents believing every kind of platitude about all things working out for the good.

Adalyn's mantra that Bronn will find us is a lot better than having her break down into some kind of inconsolable mess. Lord knows I need a bit of reassurance as well. Especially when the guards slot us into individual cages.

They leave me for last, but instead of a cage, I'm being escorted into a separate room. The goat man is already there and positions me in the middle of the room.

What now?

Goat man's eyes narrow at me. He slowly walks around me, his cloven hooves clip-clopping so I can mark his progress until he stands in front of me once more. He's only a little taller than me, and if I focus on his face, I can barely see the short horns that curl into his hair or that the lower half of his body is that of a goat. His lashes are annoyingly full and curly, and I decide to hate that about him, too.

At least he doesn't intimidate me as much as the minotaurs. He looks at me as if I'm a walking pile of money. The minotaurs...though they don't touch me, their gazes make me feel dirty. At least the non-drugged ones.

"Don't look so scared, dove. Nothing can harm you here. You are the Labyrinth's now. A tribute, so to speak...and you will make the house so very, very happy."

I open my mouth to speak, but a yelp comes out when goat man stings my arm with something. "What was that?" My words slur together.

Great. Am I going to pass out again?

"Just a little something-something to make you even more enticing than you already are." He beams at me like a proud parent, the curling grin of his face not quite reaching his eyes.

True fear curls into my stomach. I was wrong to favor him over the minotaurs. His pretty appearance and sensible words made me forget that evil comes in all forms.

"Now, let's get all these troublesome clothes off, shall we?"

CHAPTER FOUR

Bronn

The Minotaur's Labyrinth used to be the premier hub in the Nexus, boasting the best Venus House the galaxy had to offer.

Now it is a cesspool, overrun by gangsters and thieves, trading flesh for profit rather than pleasure. The ever-shifting nature of the labyrinth makes it ideal for mercenaries and scum to hide from the law.

It's been a while since I traveled these paths through the black market that the Minotaur's Labyrinth has become. Not since I was a new cadet ready to take on the world and the universe. A few rounds in this place is a meat grinder for the soul.

You either develop skin as thick as rawhide or this beat will chew you up and spit you out and keep you as lost and broken as the people who choose to make this place their home.

It's no wonder that this is usually the proving grounds for most young Taurines who wish to move up the ranks with an eye on being stationed on the Nexus.

Though the various paths and alleys are made to shift, I've learned the patterns and timing long ago—it's not the sort of thing you forget—and soon I stare at the Viper's Nest, a patchwork of building fronts, it changes names as frequently as another slumlord gains power.

I know it as the Hollow, one of the few known stable wormholes in this sector of the galaxy, and an easy dumping ground for prisoners and other undesirables of society. After years of turmoil and other threats to the stability of the Nexus and the Intergalactic Republic at large, the entire Labyrinth became a sort of self-governed prison.

The gaudy black and red lights that form the words "Viper's Nest" flicker in rhythmic patterns. Something is going down. I'm no longer up to date on the various codes. However, having coded signals present at all means that something big is happening now.

I jerk my chin toward the Hollow. "Take your men and go around back and hold."

Tag confirms with a crisp hand gesture to the men and under his command. In silence, they wend their way through the crowd of lost and sorrowful souls.

"That's the Hollow, isn't it?" Tag asks, more for confirmation rather than genuine curiosity. When I nod as an answer, he follows up with another question. "Do you know who runs this place now?"

"I have a suspicion," I say. My mental catalog of criminals grows larger by the day, but I will never forget their faces. Not until I can erase their existence. "I may not know who is in charge of the Hollow now, however, I know the type. They would be the kind to stab you in the back or smile to your face while someone stabs you in the back in order to slip a knife in between your ribs. No mercy."

Tag seems to like that as a slow smile lifts the corners of his mouth. "No problem. I don't intend to show any either."

It's worse here than I thought. Within moments of entering the Viper's Nest, I spy the heads of multiple clan leaders. Some are trying to hide behind their lackeys, however, there are many who are glad enough to flaunt their status. With enough clan leaders like this, there is only one treasure in the universe that would bring such disparate creatures and rivals together and keep them from ripping each other apart on sight.

An announcer calls out, "Time!"

As if under a spell, the raucous noise fades to a murmur befitting a temple service rather than a den of debauchery. Everyone shuffles to their seats. All attention is on the central stage that is yet empty.

I tap the comm device on my gauntlet, only it's dead. A blocking device must be suppressing any outside communication. I figured that would be the case. The underground world of the Minotaur's Labyrinth was a safe enough hideout for the criminal element, so these extra measures only confirm the growing suspicion in my gut.

Tonight, they are hosting a slave auction. Not just any slave auction either. With all this interest and safety measures? The slaves they're featuring are Grade A Prime Meat: fresh, ripe females who are dosed up to bring on a heat cycle.

The house will probably want to make everything as secure as possible.

A reverberating gong vibrates through the air. From the depths of the stage, a satyr appears. He's far from his native woodlands. The way he struts on stage with his tailored suit jacket and nothing else tells me he's no stranger here.

"Welcome, honored guests." His voice carries among the crowd. The stage slowly rotates so that he can have a 360 degree view of the audience. A nice touch when you don't want to have your back toward a potential enemy. "We will show each lot and there will be a bidding. The house decides what bid to accept—and it is not always the highest bid. Our word is final. If you don't like it, you can take your complaints to the House."

That threat should keep them all in line. It is easy enough to eject any troublemakers into the Hollow—an endless void. No beginning. No end. A fate worse than death.

The emcee continues. "We will have a clean exchange tonight. This is your only warning. When the lot is sold, the house will hold it in trust until we seal your contracts. Once you transfer your credits to the house, and you have your contract in hand, then and only then, are you able to claim the lot. At that point, the house no longer lays claim to it nor will extend any protections toward it. You will be on your own."

An appreciative murmur rumbles throughout the crowd, with several of the males savagely grinning. They caught the hint in the emcee's words. Once the lot is under new ownership, the house will turn a blind eye to any poaching, should any allegedly occur.

The satyr gives a sly smile, tut-tutting the crowd with a wag of his finger. "Remember. Until the moment of the exchange, any lot is still the property of the house and as such, you will respect our property." He snarls the last word, which the labyrinth walls echo in a cavernous yawn. A reminder of the fate of those who misbehave.

Anger simmers within me at how he speaks of the slaves imprisoned here. I slide among the shadows, moving silently toward the Taurine guards that are bound to this house. Cuffed, collared, and pierced, the labyrinth and the ruling house owns them now, mind, body, and soul.

Each guard has a small section to oversee. I take the Taurine at the closest to the back, binding him with restraints and leaving his unconscious body tucked into a pantry. I take off my jacket, wrapping it around my hips. In the low light of the arena, it would pass as the loin covering that the others wore. His cuffs barely fit around my wrists. I refuse to wear the nose or ear piercings. No one would look too closely at me, anyway. Their attention would be on their prize.

I weave my way back among the crowd, moving in the slow, zombie-like way of a captive Taurine.

"Now then. The first lot is a treasure. A diamond in the rough that even we did not want to part with. However, as the saying goes, 'the gods giveth and the gods taketh away.'"

The satyr sweeps his arm to the side as a pillar of black smoke flumes from the stage next to him. The stage lights cast a stunning contrast against the pitch black gloom that hovers within. It looks like magic. Except, I know it hides a portal and if you know where to look, you can see the outline of one forming.

Where it originates is the mystery that I intend to solve.

When the blackness disappears, a lone figure stands in the middle of the circular stage. It's not Adalyn.

This female is taller, leaner, and she holds herself as proud as any queen. Though she trembles, she does not lower her gaze as the satyr presents her before the crowd. The diaphanous cloth that drapes strategically over her body does nothing to hide her glorious brown nipples or the triangle of her sex. Her golden bronze skin gleams like burnished silk, offering a striking contrast to the long blue hair that tumbles down her back and curls around the generous rise of her breasts.

Karis.

She is perfect. And she is mine. Twin heart beats roar to life within me at the sight of her. As plainly as I know my name and rank, so, too, do I know that the softer beat, the shadow beat, is one that pulses from our entwined souls. If I were to place my ear against her chest, her heart would echo mine.

My mate.

The urge to hide her body from view pulses through me, but I stay rooted to where I stand. This needs to play out. I cannot afford to trigger the labyrinth's defense systems.

And so I wait, letting the discipline of my training take over. Memorizing every lecherous glance and smirking face, filing them away into my mental catalog. Once she is safe, I will hunt each one of them down and gift her their charred remains.

CHAPTER FIVE

KARIS

The spotlights break my trance. Pinpricks shoot down my left arm, and I welcome the bite of pain.

Hello, nerves, nice of you to regain sensation.

I still can't tell my body to run—not like I can get far—but I can sort of curl my fingers, so I'll count that as progress. The goat man is playing some kind of announcer, and I realize belatedly that beyond the circle of light on me, there is an audience.

They are little more than silhouettes, many of which seem to have horns. I'm not so sure I want to see the crowd. Especially when the white noise turns distinctly feral. Hisses, growls, and grunts; at one point, there is a sustained roar, low and almost...territorial. Others challenge him down, adding their own bestial responses to the cacophony.

I wish I could pretend that they're all arguing about something among themselves. Politics, perhaps, or how wonderful their food is and could they have more? The way goat man prances on stage, though, working the crowd, pointing at one shadowy figure after the other, disabuses me of that fanciful hope.

Especially when there is one final low growl that is followed by a hush for a full second after. Goat man's eyes darken with unrepentant excitement, a triumphant grin breaking across his face as he slashes his finger toward the one who made that last offer.

"Sold!"

The goat man clip-clopped over to me as a dark mist surrounds the stage once more. He runs his fingers down my hair, patting my cheek as if he's proud of me. It takes all of my strength not to flinch from his touch.

"I knew you would garner the highest price." He giggles to himself. "That's why I needed you out first, while everyone's pockets are nice and deep. And now, they'll all fight for the privilege of emptying their wallets of every last bit of credit on the rest."

I calculate the amount of slaves being held in the cages I saw. Even if the buyers have deep pockets, there is no way that every single slave will be sold tonight.

If there were leftover girls, then they might be here for who knows how long. And who knows what kind of lascivious desires they will have to satisfy?

A single tear rolls down my cheek.

He takes it and licks it off the tip of his finger. He shivers. "It's almost a shame that you have to leave so soon. I didn't even sample the goods. At least I have a chance with that friend of yours," he says, wiggling his eyebrows. "Serge took advantage of the early buy-out offer for her, and he likes an audience."

There is no way I will allow Adalyn to be taken and victimized. It's a good thing that the goat man's attention shifts to something behind me because I'm sure he would have seen my eyes narrowing with anger.

"Perfect timing. Cyril, take her to the waiting area. Go the back way. I don't want her buyers taking her before payment is in hand. And this should go without saying, but do not sample the merchandise! She is bought and paid for."

A large hand wraps around my upper arm. The grip is firm but gentle. This touch is different, so unlike the rough treatment I endured earlier. I sneak a glance up, way up, and don't recognize this guard. He looks different from the others, too, though I can't place how. His bullish profile is as alien to me as the rest, stern and aloof, even. Yet, there's something about him that makes me feel safe.

Cyril, on the other hand, makes me cringe. "Don't worry boss, she'll be intact," then under his breath he adds, "more or less." Even though the minotaur doesn't have human facial features, that predatory smile is universal enough.

Figures that no matter where I am in the universe, I always seem to attract the creeps.

I'm grateful that this new guard moves me in a way that has me tucked firmly against his body, his hand moving from my upper arm to my opposite shoulder. Flanked this way, he escorts me into the mist, not waiting for his partner. Instead of walking off stage as I expect, we are now in the back of the house again, with its circuitous halls that look identical.

My heart pounds with every step. How am I going to get Adalyn out of here? How am *I* going to get out of here?

The room he leads me to is barely bigger than a closet, but at least there is a place for me to sit. The new guard moves me so I can sit. Cyril leers at me from the doorway.

He swaggers in, crowding me. When he reaches out to touch me, I shrink away from him reflexively. He pauses in mild surprise.

Oops, I gave away that I'm no longer completely frozen. Maybe I can make a dash toward the door—

The new guard grabs Cyril's arm, twisting it up and pinning it behind the creep's back quicker than I would've thought possible given his bulk. Like following steps to a graceful dance, the minotaur sweeps Cyril's legs out from under him. Cyril's knees crunched as they hit the ground. Before he can utter one sound of protest, the new guard grasps Cyril's horns and twists his neck.

I swallow a scream as Cyril slumps over.

The guard steps over the lifeless body and nudges it aside with his boot. My sluggish brain realizes in that moment the contrast of this new minotaur's boot and pants to that of Cyril's—and his lack of a uniform.

This new minotaur's clothing is crisp, maintained, and something out of a science fiction movie's interpretation of space military heroes. Even with his chest bare—I assume he did so to blend in with the others—I can see him more at home standing on a starship deck shouting commands like, "Engage!" and "Fall back, it's a trap!" than cavorting with the horrible people who called this place their home.

The minotaur kneels in front of me. Clear blue eyes look at me from a broad face, a stunning contrast against his rich, reddish-brown fur. What I wouldn't give for those cheek bones...

Some blood splatter glistens along his jaw, marring his otherwise perfect face. I reach out to wipe it away before I realize what I'm doing. I stare at the blood on my fingertips.

The minotaur takes a cloth from his pocket and gently takes my hand and wipes it clean. He inspects my face, and I try not to squirm. Satisfied with whatever he saw, he pulls away.

I stop him, taking the cloth from him and wiping away the offending speckles of red from his fur. When I finish, I hand the cloth back to him with a smile that I hope translates my gratitude.

He speaks words I cannot understand, but at least it differs from the grunts and growls of the other people I've encountered here. "I'm sorry. I can't understand you," I say.

He tilts his head in a decidedly animal gesture. Nodding as if weighing out a decision, he reaches into his pouch and pulls out something that looks like a small flashlight.

What is he going to do with that?

He lays it against my neck and pushes the button. It feels like a lightning strike. The shock of it makes me gasp. "What the hell?!"

"I am sorry for the temporary pain. I would normally ask for permission before touching someone under my charge, but the communication barrier prevented me from doing so."

I rub at the sting at my neck, grumbling. "A little warning would help next time." My gaze meets his at the realization that I understood his words. "Oh wow. I understood what you said." Pain forgotten, I throw my arms around him in a hug.

"Indeed," he says. He pats at my arms awkwardly.

Oops. I forget not everyone is a hugger like my family. I lean back before this minotaur regrets trying to rescue me. "You do not know how horrible it's been, only understanding that goat man and his crew. Thank you." I stick my hand out to him. "My name is Karis. Karis Gloria de la Cruz, but please call me Karis only my mom calls me by my full name, and only then when I'm in trouble, and I'm sorry for snapping at you, and for rambling since I tend to do that when I'm nervous. I'm sorry."

A slight frown creases his forehead as he stares at my proffered hand. I help him out by grasping his hand with both of mine. His brow furrow deepens as he stares at his hand between mine. "You may call me Bronn. I am the urso of House Nighthold. I am not sure when this snapping occurred. And you apologize for things you do not need to apologize for."

"Bronn?" I say. The memory of Adalyn's mobile device flashes in my mind, along with the deep voice that answered the call before it was smashed. "Adalyn's Bronn? The one she tried to contact?"

His mouth quirks. "I am not Adalyn's," he says. "And not only did she try, but she did indeed contact me."

"Thank God! Adalyn swore up and down that you would find us. At first I thought she was crazy, but you know, being in this nightmare world is crazy." I pause, and then add, "I'm not dreaming, am I? This isn't some drug-addled trip? Please tell me you're actually here to rescue us?"

A smile broke across his face as a deep chuckle rose from his chest. "Yes, I am here to rescue you."

Heat radiates from my stomach and stretches all over my body. God, Bronn has no business being this handsome. I bite my lip to hold in my sigh. Swooning over my rescuer is the last thing I need to be doing.

He unsnaps something at his waist and wraps it around me. It's a jacket, warm with his body heat. I stick my arms into the sleeves, which are only comical because they're so long, they can probably fit over my legs. An insignia on the front of the jacket catches my eye. It looks like an intricate circular logo: part spiral loops, part computer circuit board. Seeing it tickles something in the back of my mind, as if I've seen it before.

"If you are well enough, we must leave. Quickly." He gathers me in his arms. "The paralytic and other poisons they gave you should wear off soon now that I have given you the nanotech boosters. But we will be faster if I carry you."

I want to protest—after all, I don't want to feel like a burden—but he's right. I may be able to move again, but my feet are still numb.

Besides, when I'm this close to him, he can't see me make a fool of myself trying not to ogle him. His chest is massive, with muscles that ripple and flex with every move. It shouldn't feel this comfortable to be nestled against him like this. I can't help but rub my cheek against his warm fur. I stop before he thinks I'm weird.

Bronn walks out the door, confident in his directions. I've already lost count of how many times he's turned. I would have been a liability trying to keep up with his fast, long-legged strides.

Soon, we were at a familiar T. On one side is a set of double doors. Beyond them should be the docking station that leads to freedom. On the opposite end of this hall is the gated paddock that leads toward the prisoners.

Bronn heads toward the double doors.

"Wait! We can't leave."

He freezes. "You wish to stay here?"

My face twists in disgust. "God, no! But we can't leave. Not yet. Not without Adalyn and the others."

Understanding dawns on his face. "Of course. Do not worry, we know about the others."

We? I look down at the jacket I'm wearing. That and Bronn's precision actions, of course he's part of a 'we'. He's probably part of an elite unit. Heck, I hope he has an entire army with him.

I have to ask how Adalyn can get someone like Bronn and the 'we' he rides out with on my personal speed dial.

"Are there a lot on your team?" And did they come with tanks and guns?

"A handful."

A handful? Why so few?

"Because it is easier to hide the tracks of few rather than many," Bronn says.

Oops, I must have said my thoughts out loud. Well, might as well keep going. "This place has like an entire army guarding it," I tell him.

"An army?" Bronn says. "I counted less than fifty on their payroll."

"Well, fifty is still more than five," I counter.

Bronn's laugh erupts out of him in a roar that sounds like colliding boulders. "Taurines are an army of one. A lone Taurine can fight against a battalion of soldiers single-handedly. I think I can handle a bunch of untrained, drunken louts who are used to preying on weak, shackled prisoners. If I am feeling generous, I will allow my men to partake in some of the fight."

A mewling cry reaches our ears. *Adalyn?*

All the humor leaves Bronn's face as he turns toward the cry and charges through chained paddock gates.

CHAPTER SIX

BRONN

I have her. Karis. And she is one of us.

The injection I gave her produced a generic profile of her blood history, and even that general scan shows she is part Taurine and part...something else. Maybe she has a shifter gene, like Adalyn, or has some other human-presenting bloodline like many other races...?

How in the world did she end up on Terra Prime, of all places?

When we return to Nighthold, we will complete a full scan of her biological record to see her origins. There have been many colonies scattered all over the Intergalactic Republic. We have lost countless souls and generations of potential mates from our registrars before we created the Nexus, a central hub of portals that connects us all.

Finding someone like Karis and her lineage is as impossible as myths and legends. And yet, here she is. More telling is my body's reaction to her. Every beat of my heart pulses with my need to protect her and shelter her from harm.

Especially since this damned place injected her with something that would speed up her already present heat cycle. Even now, she is changing, the scent of her clawing my reason to shreds. It's subtle now, but soon, it will become insistent. If she's been raised as a human on Earth, she's likely never experienced a heat cycle before. The conditions on Terra Prime don't allow for it, or so the theory goes since they are not common in uninitiated humans. Yet, when the human females are taken off world and in the presence of potential mates...

I will not allow her first heat to be in the bowels of this hellhole.

I glance down at her. Her focus is purely straight ahead, toward the troubled cries. Considering her ordeal, I am grateful she's calm. It's already hard enough restraining myself so as not to tear this place apart brick by brick until the labyrinth fully folds in on itself.

I have to get the word out to Tag. I take apart the guard's gauntlet and adjust it to my own. With a few quick taps in old code, I can send and receive messages to Tag. I punch in a few numbers for coordinates and add a simple command: "*Get ready.*"

I have to find the holding cell where they have Adalyn. The satyr hinted potential buyers had a way to check out the lots for an early buy-out option. I need to find it. The cavernous wall echoes too much, and relying on the sound will take too much time.

"The cage where they put Adalyn is one in the back. One of the first ones, the farthest from these dressing rooms." Karis trembles as she looks at one of the closed doors. I want to know what causes her additional fear, but I file that away for later. "Whatever happens, please don't leave me alone. Please keep me with you."

She must be some sort of mind reader, because I had every intention of keeping her in one of those rooms until I can ensure her safety. The haunted look I see on her face changes my mind. "I will keep you, Karis."

Her beaming smile is all the happiness I will ever need.

I move us through the dark. I am both relieved and also sick that so many of the cages are full. Most of the prisoners are in some sort of trance, like a waking sleep. I tap each gate with my pilfered comm unit as I pass each one, sending Tag their coordinates so he can coordinate an exit.

Sounds of people grappling grow louder the deeper into the pens we go until I hear a sharp slap and a trilling cry. Rage narrows my vision, and I charge toward the sound, with Karis slung over my shoulder.

A large Naga with red and gold scales has wrapped his coils around Adalyn. His fangs are already dripping with venom. Without a word, I slip Karis onto the floor, take the broken gauntlet I'd stolen from the guard and slam it into the viper's mouth before he can strike Adalyn.

I pry his jaws apart until I rip his head off of him. The rest of his coils fall away from Adalyn. It is a slight comfort for me to see that his cock is still in its sheath and so he hadn't violated Adalyn further.

In the aftermath, I notice the Naga had the markings of a prince. No matter. The outcome would have still been the same. I'll take the repercussions when they come. For now, my worry melts seeing Adalyn whole.

She launches herself into my arms and together, she and I back away. Adalyn flings herself at Karis next. "I was so scared they were going to ship you away before he got here. I told you Bronn would find us, didn't I?"

"Yes, you did," she says. She looks at me in a way that makes me feel like I can destroy worlds. For her, I would.

Glowing lights wrap around a cage up ahead before winking back to darkness. Another one glows. And then another.

"What's happening?" Karis asks.

A portal opens just on the other side of us. It is limned with blue light and ripples like a reflecting pond in the middle of the air. The watery outline barely transmits Tag's image, let alone his words. "Bronn. Now."

"No," I shout back. Alarms sound throughout the labyrinth, and the walls groan from the pressure of too many wormholes. At least the defense system will have a hard time pinpointing me and swallowing me down into the endless void.

I throw Adalyn to Tag. More cages light up as the occupants are being whisked away to safety.

Tag's eyes grow wide. "Sir! This portal isn't stable. We don't have time."

"I will not leave until they all are safe. Cut transmission of this portal. Divert energy to the remaining cells. Only after they are all transported out, do you open another one at the docking station. That will buy us some time. We cannot stay here. They will easily pin us."

I don't wait to see if Tag complies. Scooping up Karis, I run through the stables, backtracking the way we came in. The double doors to the docking station are up ahead, and I charge toward them.

Two labyrinth guards turn in from the main hallway. Their drugged state makes them slow to react, and I easily weave around them. The satyr is right behind them, and I barrel into him. He launches backward, bowling down a motley group of beasts who have the misfortune of being behind him.

"You!" the satyr snarls at me. "Put her down! She's our property."

Karis clings to me desperately, her fear tempering the anger that pulses within me. I don't pause. Instead, I push ahead toward escape despite every molecule in my body telling me to answer the challenge of the enemies at my back and destroy them.

Soon, I tell myself.

I charge through the double doors, the portal barely visible. Tag's faint voice is fading fast. The connection glitches, but I vault into the shimmering blue.

CHAPTER SEVEN

Karis

We land in a heap. It is not the back alley of the club nor are we surrounded by Bronn's men or the freed hostages.

Instead, a blanket of stars stretches over us. The sky is so black that it looks solid. "Where are we?" I ask.

Bronn looks around. "We are still inside of what we call the Minotaur's Labyrinth. This section is closer to where we need to be, with more stability to open a portal, so that is good. This portion also lacks the emergency defense mechanism present in the Hollow."

"You mean the one that goat man kept threatening about the House swallowing anyone who steps out of line?"

"Yes, that's the one."

I can feel the other shoe about to drop. "That's good, huh? Then what's the bad?"

His forehead crinkles, and his mouth quirks as if he's about to say something, but changes his mind. "Since we are still in the labyrinth, they can still track our location."

Of course. "How are they able to track us when we were spit out at some random location?" I ask.

He spares me a look. "I will answer your question, but we must be on the move." Before I can ask what he means, he hauls me over his shoulder.

"Yeah, I'm not in love with this position. I feel like I might get sick all down your back."

With barely a grunt, he shifts my body so that I'm slung in front of him. Bronn picks up the thread of our conversation, as if picking up lost girls and trampling through an overgrown forest is an everyday occurrence that is not worth remarking upon. "You asked how they can track us, though we were transported to some random place," he says. "The Taurine guards can guide the satyr and his minions the same way that I know where we are in this labyrinth."

The way he holds me, and the cadence of his speech, is comforting. For the moment, I can forget that there are flesh traffickers after me and I'm in this surreal underworld where myths like a Minotaur's Labyrinth is an actual place.

"Taurines are native to the winding ways of the labyrinth. It used to be a portion of our home world that's since been destroyed. This was the only bit that our ancestors could save. It has since grown to be an underbelly of sorts, where only the exiles and outcasts of society go."

"Great," I say. "Sounds homey."

The corner of Bronn's mouth lifts into a charming half-smile. His entire demeanor changes with just that slight change. Gone is the dour, no-nonsense authority figure—though if I'm honest with myself, is still kinda hot—instead, he looks younger and more approachable. And the way his hair curls over his forehead and into his eyes, tempting me to brush it away for him as his hands are currently fully occupied...

"The leftover bits of the labyrinth, what's cobbled together today, were originally meant for prisoners; it is not meant to support a full on colony. There are too many of us to be housed on one colony, so we are scattered throughout the galaxy. A central station that we call the Nexus monitors a truly stable wormhole that allows us to travel to each hub. I lead the hub of House Nighthold."

It's a good thing he can't see me. My face is a dead giveaway for my moods, and right now it's an embarrassing beacon for how attracted I am to Bronn right now. "And where is that hub located?" I ask.

Focus on the nice rescuer's words. Stop trying to calculate how much he weighs, or approximating girth based on palm sizes...

"Partly on the Nexus, partly in Terra Prime, and another part...elsewhere. It balances between three or four worlds depending on the time of year."

"That seems so hard to navigate. I can barely keep up with Daylight Saving and multiple time zones."

Bronn laughs, a warm, inviting sound that makes me melt. "For Taurines, it is natural to navigate their own territories. Especially here, on what was once our home world."

I desperately scour my short-term memory to piece together what he had been saying. Flipping past the torrid mental images of riding him or being railed by him, I settle on the last thing I recall. "So basically, any native, regardless of the generational gap, can sense their way around here because it's their native soil. It's how you instinctively know where you are? And how the Taurine guards can track me?"

"Not track you, per se. Just know where you are. Which is why, if we cross paths with them, the Taurines need to be taken out first. It won't be easy, since the labyrinth will want to protect them as much as us."

"If it were up to me, I'd take out goat man and his little rape-y cronies." I nestle into Bronn, seeking his warmth. God, he smells so good. He is all my favorite things wrapped up in one powerful body. With him, I forget to be scared. "Most of the guards were doped up. That Cyril you killed was one of the few exceptions. Most of the rest I saw were empty dolls. Like they were nothing more than robots. Cut the goat man off, and whoever he serves, and maybe those guards become less zombie, more normal."

Bronn's chest rumbles as he ruminates on my words. They may be silly thoughts, but he doesn't trivialize them. "You may be right, Karis. I did not think about the probability that the guards could be victims. Your perspective is wise."

My heart soars at his praise. "Will your team be able to pinpoint our location, too?"

"Unfortunately, no. I left my communication device in the Viper's Nest. There is an old transportation hub in one of the temples. It was one of the original gateways. There are only a select few that can activate it. The problem is, the location is not exactly secret, so it will be logical of a hunting party to assume that is a potential exit point."

Knowing my luck, they would already be there, waiting for us. "Is that where we're going now?"

"No, we are going in the opposite direction. At least for a little while."

"And then what?" I ask, not sure if I really want to know the answer.

"And then we wait. While we rest for the night, those who hunt us will probably perish. The labyrinth is not kind to outsiders. Too many secrets. Too many traps."

A night. With Bronn. Alone. Under the stars.

He looks at me curiously. "Are you unwell? Are you having trouble breathing?"

I realize belatedly that I was holding my breath. I let it out in one long exhale. "Oh, don't mind me, just thirsty."

Thirsty? What the hell kind of answer is that?

Without breaking stride, Bronn unclasps something from his utility belt and hands it to me. A water flask. Of course.

I accept the offer and sip, since that's what you do when a kind gentleman hands you a bottle of water after you tell him you're thirsty. "You know where all those pesky traps are, right?"

Bronn grins down at me. A near-feral gleam tinges his gaze. "Of course. I spent my training years patrolling this territory. Some traps I placed here myself."

I blink at him. "If we stumble into any of the traps you've set, I'll be so mad."

Bronn throws his head back and laugh. He really should do that more. The sound of it warms me and fills my heart to the brim. "I promise you, I shall avoid them all. Come, we are nearly there."

BRONN

"I want to make it perfectly clear that I can walk," she says after awhile. Following her mind is as circuitous as the ever-shifting landscape of the labyrinth, and I find myself marking the boundaries and pathways as I would anything else I would explore.

I know you can walk, I say to myself, *but I prefer feeling your hot body against mine, especially when you smell so sweet and enticing.*

I swallow down my words. She just lived through the humiliating experience of being auctioned off and had to witness me killing one Taurine who couldn't control himself around her mating pheromones, and a Naga who tried to force himself on Adalyn. She doesn't need to witness yet another male who cannot control his base impulses.

Especially as her heat intensifies. Every time she sighs, every time she bites her lip before she says something clever, I think I will go insane. The worst part is she does not know her every little move makes her so enticing.

Focus, soldier.

"You mean to say that you can walk without tripping on brambles or bleeding over thorns? If you can, by all means, I will let you walk all on your own."

Silence. I scowl, berating myself. My words were too harsh, it seems, and now she withdraws me. How many times must I remind myself of my tone around females?

"Okay, now that you put it like that, you're right." With a huff, she adds, "But if I'm an inconvenience or heavy or anything, just let me go, okay? I don't need you breaking your back because of me."

Even though it is safer on the move, I pause. Grasping her by her hips as modestly as I can, I hold her out in front of me so I can look her squarely in her eyes. "Do you doubt my virility?"

Her forehead crinkles in that cute way that makes me want to kiss it.

"What? No! I–"

"Do you think that something as small as you would exhaust me in any way?"

"Well, no, I–"

Her cheeks flame in a riot of pink, and it is only through supreme discipline I don't drop my gaze to see if she blooms pink elsewhere.

"Good. Then enough. If carrying you were a burden, I would have found another way to transport you. As you are not, this conversation is moot. Agreed?"

"Yes, but–"

I tsk. "Agreed?"

I don't move until I see her nod. "Good. Now say you are not a burden."

She scowls at me this time, and I love every moment of her withering gaze. "I am not a burden."

"Good, I'm glad we agree." I cradle her in my arms once more. I do not get to feel the rise of her sweet backside under my hand in this position, but she can at least find some comfort pressed against me. And, if she ends up with more of my scent all over her, then win-win.

She is rigid for a moment and I brace to hear more of her sharp words. But she melts against me, and sighs, inhaling deeply. She nuzzles more of her face against my chest and murmurs some words I can't hear. I want to ask her, but her body relaxes completely, and soon, the rise and fall of her steady breathing matches the twin heart beat within me.

She is asleep.

Joy expands in my chest, and I increase my pace. A shelter is only a few steps away. Even now, I see the knot of brambles open for me.

Perfect timing, as a portal tears open somewhere nearby. I see a fleeting glimpse of the blue-limned light that shows a wormhole.

They're too late. I slip Karis into the welcoming haven of the brambles. With a silent apology, I tear the offending dress from her. Swaddling her in my jacket once more, I adjust it until it covers her to her knees. I encourage the brambles to close while I scatter shredded pieces of her cloth in random directions.

The hunting party follows the false trails, and I return to the safety of the temporary nest. In a few hours, the labyrinth will reset, and this trail which seems to have veered away from our target location, will once more connect to the temple at the heart of the maze. From there, it's an easy walk back to the Nexus.

Meanwhile, as Karis sleeps, I can strategize how I may find rest when her body is ripening for her heat. This will be a long night.

CHAPTER EIGHT

BRONN

There's noise outside. The fools have finally made their way back here. The way they stumble in the dark, I am not bothered.

They are not walking with purpose, so they do not know our location.

With the way they are arguing, the males are likely to kill each other before the labyrinth can take care of them.

"She's mine, or have you forgotten?" The slimy voice must belong to the buyer.

"Until your money is in my hand and my signed contract is in yours, she still belongs to me!" the satyr snarls.

My hand covers Karis's mouth as her eyes fly open. I press my lips against the delicate shell of her ear.

She freezes, eyes wide. I hate seeing her fear. What did the satyr do that causes this reaction? Stupidly, recklessly, I press my lips against her brow and kiss the crinkles away until they are smooth.

I ignore the curious way she looks at me. Instead, I press my finger to my lips, a universal sign for silence.

And we need silence. One of the party is a hunter, and there are a couple of Taurine guards. Drugged or no, they are still bound to serve their master.

I place my hand against her stomach, holding her still. Karis flinches once, but relaxes under my touch, moving closer to me. Good.

The brambles are thick, and I won't allow them to open. But they're still thorns, and if they think to set this part of the labyrinth ablaze, there is little protection I can do that won't give away our location.

I bet they will not, though. Not on a whim. There would be a lot to risk burning parts of the labyrinth unnecessarily. They move away, but I am still overly cautious. I refuse to take chances with Karis here.

"They have moved away, but their absence could still be a trap. We should stay quiet and hidden, at least for a while longer," I say.

Karis nods, shifting her body again, and I press down reflexively so that she knows to keep still. She nuzzles the side of my face with her cute nose. I am a horrible person for being aroused by every little move she makes while she is probably scared out of her mind.

And then a hot little tongue licks against my earlobe. I must be imagining things. It happens again, and this time it's sucked between luscious lips.

I gaze down at her, wondering if I'm hallucinating, and her sly smile is answer enough. Without breaking eye contact, she places her elegant hand over mine and pushes it down her body. I follow her lead until I am cupping her sex.

I find her wet and open for me, and gods, I want to see her.

"Karis—"

She sucks in the rest of my words into a soul-searing kiss. Her mouth opens beneath mine and there is that tempting tongue once more, searching for me. I yield and taste her sweet offerings.

Her hand curls over mine once more, directing my fingers inside her as she spreads her legs wide in invitation. I press inside of her, the hot, slippery feel of her so addictive. I add another finger, then another, reveling in how she stretches for me. More would be required for her to accommodate me.

I do not want to injure her. Even if a heat-induced mating overrides her pain receptors to feel only pleasure, overzealous rutting males have damaged a female in the height of her heat. Caution and self-preservation are secondary to her need to mate.

I would die a thousand deaths before I inflicted any injury upon Karis. Yet, I know that the fastest way to end a heat cycle is to fill her so thoroughly with seed that she is satisfied.

She moves her hand to circle the pearl of flesh nestled above her entrance.

I pull away from her so I can watch her pleasure herself. Watch her movements as she arches and swallows her moans. See her body trembling as pleasure overtakes her body.

Her muscles tighten around my fingers. I thrust into her faster, matching her quickening pace until she claps her other hand over her mouth and comes.

Slick gushes over my hand, and more pours from her when I remove it. I rise to my knees, the tops of my horns grazing the brambles above me. Resting on my haunches, I tear open my pants, my cock rising from my hips now that I am no longer restrained.

I smear her liquid heat over me, pumping my hand in a slow and steady up and down motion. Her gaze locks onto my actions, following along as if hypnotized.

"Do you want this, Karis?" I ask.

She nods, eyes transfixed on what I hold in my hand rather than my words. I bend toward her, lifting her chin so I can see into her eyes. Her pupils are dilated, but she focuses on me when I ask her to. "Answer with your words, please."

"Yes," she says. Then adds, "Please."

I smile at that. "That's my good girl."

She stifles a strangled moan as she shifts her hips, a small orgasm rippling over her. I do believe my little mate likes praise. Noted.

It is a good thing the hunting party has left the area and is well away from here. I want to hear more of Karis's pleasure noises.

I settle between her legs, reveling in the feel of her wrapped around me. Nuzzling into her neck as she sighs in pleasure, I tell her how good she is, how beautiful she looks, how I will enjoy tasting every bit of her body...I'm not sure how much she hears, but I keep talking.

Even as I leave a trail of kisses down her neck...and as I lave one breast and then the other, paying special attention to her nipples...and as I taste her taunting heat, dragging my tongue over her seam and delving into her core... and as I finally suck her clit, swirling my tongue over her in circling motions that echo the way she touched herself...I don't stop praising every bit of her until she is desperately gripping onto my horns, mindless to anything else but her pleasure as she unravels, commanding me to fill her.

She can't take me, not completely, not yet, so I push her legs up so her knees are to her chest, and slide my cock along her drenched folds.

"Yes! Please! Faster!" and I piston my hips to meet her demands, bearing down on her clit.

A primal scream rips from her throat as she comes for me. I let out a growl of satisfaction when the first rope of cum jets out of me and splashes across her chest. I enjoy seeing her marked with evidence of my claim. She swipes at some that land on her breast, and sticks her fingers in her mouth, sucking them clean, licking her lips for every drop.

More cum shoots out of me, rope after rope, until I am wrung out, and she is awash with my fluids. I massage it into her skin, between her legs, inside her core, until there is nothing left.

Bright-eyed and eager, Karis rolls to her knees and crawls toward me. She isn't winded in the slightest. In fact, she seems even more energized. I now understand the awe and wonder in males' voices when they describe servicing a female in heat. Staring at Karis now, I see it.

I have never backed away from a challenge before, but damn, do I want to. I don't know how much of my control I have left. Especially when Karis looks at me like that. Touches me like this. And swallows me down.

CHAPTER NINE

Karis

I wake, sore, achy, and, strangely, energized. I feel good. Damn good, and I haven't even had coffee yet.

I stretch and realize that the warm bed I thought I laid upon is actually Bronn, who is sleeping so soundly that I'm sure he would be embarrassed, knowing I am awake and he isn't.

I wonder why he's so tired...

The blur of last night's activities flash like huge alarm bells in my mind.

Oh.

God.

We had sex last night. Lots of sex. Copious fluids level of sex.

And I couldn't get enough. Wouldn't leave him alone. I took advantage of him and forced myself all over him.

I bury my face in my hands. I'm a horrible person.

"Who is a horrible person?" Bronn's grumpy voice breaks through my reverie. He sits up in one fluid motion. His muscles taunt me, and I curl my fingers into tight fists so I'm not tempted to touch what doesn't belong to me.

"I am," I say glumly. "I'm so sorry about last night."

Bronn cocks his head to the side. "For placing your finger in my—"

"No!" I say, cutting him off before he finishes his sentence. My face already feels like it's on fire. I don't need to relive details from last night. "I mean, maybe? Was that too forward?" I wonder out loud more to myself than to him.

"I was surprised, but I thought I made it obvious how well I liked what you did."

He did indeed. Many, many times.

His heavy hand rests on my shoulder. "Is there something else, Karis? You seem upset. I did not do anything to hurt you? You will tell me if I did."

His voice is insistent, and I look at him. Worry creases his brow, and a little light retreats from his eyes, as if he is bracing himself for what I may tell him. "Hurt me? Of course not. I mean, we didn't even..." *have intercourse*, but those words die in my throat. There were enough body parts put into various holes that to deny we had sex seemed like splitting hairs for no reason. "Anyway, no, you did nothing wrong," I say, flailing my hands as if to ward away his words. I'm not good at articulating what I want to say when I want to say it.

"Then what is it? You are upset. You cannot deny this, and as I am the only other person here, I must have been the one to upset you. Do not feel you need to shield me from my mistakes. I can handle it."

He looks like he's about to face a firing squad, and I can't help but laugh. I place my hands on either side of his face. "You did nothing wrong." I pronounce each word slowly so he can hear me. "I am not upset at you. I was upset with myself. That's all."

Bronn looks at me as if truly confused. "Why?"

"Why?" I cover my face with my hands. He's really going to make me say it.

Bronn draws me against his chest, a gentle hand on my shoulder. "Yes, I really am going to make you say it."

Dammit. If I weren't so nervous, I wouldn't be blathering on with barely any control over what words tumble out of my mouth. At least nestled against him like this. I don't have to look at him. I take a steadying breath, and it seems Bronn does the same.

"I'm upset at myself because I forced myself on you, and made you do... things. And I'm so sorry." I stop talking because if I keep going, I'll likely start crying.

"Is that all?" Bronn asks tentatively. His chest rumbles and his body shakes all over.

Gods, what have I done?

"I know one apology can't cover everything, but I'll try really hard to—are you laughing?"

That flips a switch in Bronn. He throws his great head back and laughs a deep belly laugh. The kind that has tears leaking from his eyes.

I stare at him with various degrees of shock and awe. He's usually so reserved, so proper, even in the few hours of knowing him, I know that laughing his ass off isn't a common occurrence for him. I am unnervingly turned on by the way his entire demeanor changes when he smiles.

He is striking for sure, but when he smiles and certainly when he laughs as he's doing now, his entire face glows.

My heart stutters at the sight of him, so happy. And then it sinks in that he's laughing at something I said. I narrow my gaze. "I didn't realize I said something amusing."

Bronn sobers up, at least attempts to. "I did not mean to laugh. Truly. I was just so relieved. I was expecting something heinous or dire. Look, look, I am serious now."

I cross my arms over my chest. "You're about to die laughing again!"

His mouth twists to maintain a straight face before succumbing to the inevitable. "I am sorry. I am not laughing at you, though. I am laughing from relief and happiness."

As if I wasn't confused before... "Because you're so happy I forced you to be with me?"

Fire blazes in his eyes as he reaches a hand out to tug on my chin. He waits until my gaze locks onto his. "You force nothing, my sweet mate. Hear me well. From the moment I saw you, I wanted you. I knew you were mine. I carry your heart beats within me. I want nothing more than to have you mount me and take all of me inside of you. That is what my happiness stems from. It is from knowing that my mate hungers for me as well. I have never dared to hope for such a thing happening to me."

I barely breathe. His words wash over me, the intensity behind them searing into my soul. One word stands out like a beacon. *Mate.*

"So you force nothing. You are always welcome to me whenever you need. In fact, I will insist that whenever you need sex, you get it from me. Are we clear?"

"Crystal," I say, then launch myself at him. I don't care that my kisses are sloppy or that Bronn somehow maneuvers me, so I end up straddling his face.

His silver tongue can do more than just say pretty words that turn me on.

He even plunges the thick head of his cock into my pussy, stopping when he meets resistance. "I cannot wait until I can be fully sheathed within you," he says. His shallow thrusts timed with his quick fingers over my clit makes me come around his throbbing hardness. My body takes him in deeper, fluttering around him. "That's it, my good girl. Soon, you will take all of me."

I come again at his hot words, and with a grunt, he spurts inside me, filling me so full, I'm gushing liquid in not too long. He loves working the excess into my skin. Something about marking me with his scent. I'm just happy that I don't feel sticky.

Bronn gathers me up onto his lap, searching my face once more. "While we rested, the labyrinth reset itself. We are now a few paces from the temple."

"One of the first portals," I say, like an eager student. Some of his information sunk in, despite being overwhelmed with lusty hormones.

He rewards my answer with a forehead kiss. "Exactly. It will be just a few paces and then a few minutes to activate the portal. Then, we will arrive at the Nexus. There we will see to your health properly."

"Why do I have a feeling like you're preparing me for something?"

"Because I am," he replies. "The Nexus can be overwhelming for those who are uninitiated. It is easy to get lost. But know that I will always find you, okay? You can always ask any Taurine guard to page for me, and I will be at your side in moments."

He must feel the same thing I am. That once we step out of this little nest we created for ourselves, everything will change. Real life will intrude, and we will have to adjust to a new normal.

Or at least, I will. This is all normal for Bronn. I'm the one that's the outsider. The new girl. I'll be the one who tries to fit in.

Again.

But I don't want to spoil the moment. He is happy and nearly done with this bit of his mission, which should have ended hours ago. I plaster a smile on my face and place a chaste kiss on his stern mouth. "No need for the pep talk, chief. I got this, and will follow your lead."

Bronn cradles me once more, the brambles and thorns curling back to reveal an exit. "As a beginner, I had to touch the thorn, maybe even let it prick me a little. Now, it's second-nature for me to will the vines open or close."

He lets me try on a small curl of thorn. It wraps itself around my finger and then lets go.

"It likes you," he says. Even though Bronn has repeatedly told me this is merely technology, older one at that, it's nothing short of magic to me.

Especially when the landscape has completely changed from last night. Before, we were walking through a densely overgrown forest knotted with thorny brambles everywhere that formed a sort of hedge maze.

Now, the way before us looks like the heart of a mature rainforest jungle.

"The labyrinth really shifted overnight. One of these days, I'll need to figure out how this is mechanically possible," I say.

Bronn squeezes me. "I will be happy to arrange your education." Something draws his attention away. A blur of movement makes me gasp.

He's already running before I can shout, "Look out!"

A black pile of fur and claws lands where we had been just moments before. It is a four-legged beast with three sets of eyes, a long, baboon snout, and a gaping maw full of teeth that looks like jagged knives.

I describe what's after us to Bronn. "I knew they had hounds with them," he mutters under his breath. He takes something out of his utility belt—a small steel ball the size of a marble—and flicks it over his shoulder without a backward glance.

The ball bursts open on contact, and spreads a wide net with fine filament in the air. The hound is caught in the trap, along with the two others that had been in some kind of invisible stealth mode.

The temple is straight ahead. Its architecture reminds me of a Mayan temple with four sets of stairs leading up to a plain building that looks like a covered pavilion. Thankfully, there aren't as many steps here.

"The portal is located just on the platform. You will see it when you crest the stairs."

"And?" I ask. He makes it seem as if I would do this alone. "You'll be charging up those steps with me, too, right?"

"Yes, but only after I am sure our pursuers are neutralized. I cannot let them know how to get to the Nexus."

Well, hell, when he says it like that, neither can I. "Just throw me down, I can run up from here."

He gives me a side eye, but at least it's accompanied with a little smile. "Just touch the portal. Tag will be manning the connections. Do not go until you see him."

I don't intend to go into the portal until Bronn's with me, but I keep that part to myself.

Bronn tosses me toward the temple, and I land squarely on the smooth paver stones that lead toward the stairs. I dash up it and slap the portal.

The area between the slabs of stone lights up in a familiar blue light. Shadows recede from its glow, whereas the desiccated vines that cling to the walls swell and bloom.

"I knew you were something special," a familiar voice says.

I whirl around to face the goat man. His Taurine guards flank him. Out of the corner of my eye, the portal is still trying to connect. I refuse to let someone like him figure out how to leave.

"And I know you're just some creep in a cheap suit."

His face turns vicious. "Take her!"

The guards rush toward me. I back up until I hit the wall, then grasp a nearby vine. I imagine the type of nest that Bronn created for us last night. While the guards were seconds away from reaching me, a knot of vines lay on top of me, swelling and growing as it pushes the Taurines away.

"Karis!" Bronn's voice booms.

"I'm fine!" I say behind my shield of vines.

"Get rid of him!" Goat man screeches as he backs away from Bronn. The Taurines jump on him, and I seethe at the imbalance.

I direct the vines outward until one reaches goat man's leg. Goat man trips, falls and gets part way into the portal as it is being activated.

"Push him in," Bronn says, and I do.

The goat man disappears into the void. His endless cry is replaced by a thunderclap, and a shimmering wall of rippling water fills in the space. "Sir! Finally!"

Tag directs his team to subdue the Taurine guards. Bronn tells them to take them in for reprogramming. They need our help, not our punishment.

Then the rest of the team apprehends the various nets. Tag was impressed that there were so many survivors.

"For now. The dead don't talk and I need answers more than I need vengeance. At least for now." He looks at me. "Come, let's take you home."

CHAPTER TEN

BRONN

Tag is waiting for me in my office to debrief on this mission that technically never happened. Just a day ago, I sat behind my desk with a call from Adalyn. Now, a solar day later, I have found not only her but also my mate.

My hand moves of its own accord to rest just below my heart. It's where I feel Karis's shadow beat. The pulsations are soft and calm, so I know she's at peace.

I ignore the knowing smile of my second in command when he sees me wearing only my regulation pants. He had seen Karis wearing my jacket when we arrived, and the state of her dress, or lack thereof. I'd given him a hard stare but said nothing.

"If you wish to give voice to your observations, speak now. This will be your only moment, after which you do not get to speak on it any further." I consider my words. "Watch what you say regarding Karis. I find I have no humor where she is concerned."

Tag raises his hands in mock surrender. "I was not going to say anything. I may laugh to myself and cover it with a cough. Or give significant glances, but I had not planned on saying one damn thing." He grins, eyes wide with fake innocence.

I snort as I make my way to my desk and settle into my chair. The familiar comfort of being in my office with my house in order once more is a relief I cherish. "This is your moment. Do with it as you wish. Except remark on Karis."

Tag stands, arms behind him at rest. "No worries, sir. Anyone with a lick of sense can feel your claim on her. Only a fool would test that "

My heart swells at the thought, and I reach for her shadow beat once more. It does not stop me from wanting to be near her or keeping her within sight. Even now, I fight the urge to walk out on Tag and find her. Mark her so well that no other bull would question that she belongs to me.

But my duty as the urso roots me to my chair until I hear from Tag and see what his team has uncovered. I may need to authorize extra assignments and rotations to manage an unseen threat. Ones that may harm Karis or the future of House Nighthold.

Soon, though...

"Do not mention such things to her, at least not at this moment. Karis has been uninitiated, raised with human sensibilities. Talk like this troubles her." Indeed, she has a hard enough time being able to voice what she needs. It will be quite the treat to train her to open up, in more ways than one.

"Understood," Tag says, interrupting my lascivious daydreams of rutting inside of Karis.

"Is there anything else?" I ask him.

"No, not at all," he says, his lip smirking as if he can read my thoughts. "It is interesting to picture you with a piercing."

I cock my brow at him. Piercings are optional, especially when in the field. But I do like the idea of all those who look upon me to know that I am already claimed.

"Thank you for your report," I say pointedly. "Now I am sure you have a lot of paperwork to file, so don't let me keep you."

"No more than you." A shadow passes over Tag's face as he thinks about something. "Will there be a new assignment at the Minotaur's Labyrinth? There is a void in leadership now."

I shake my head. "The satyr was no leader. At best, he was a puppet, a henchman doing the house's bidding. With the name 'The Viper's Nest' I assumed it was part of a Naga syndicate, but now I am unsure."

Naga princes rarely do grunt work for anyone. Even if they are low-ranking, a prince is still a prince. I say so to Tag.

Tag scowls. "That Naga prince that poached Adalyn and Karis. The rest of my team went back to sweep through and see if we might have missed anyone. The Hollow is under new management. No one has claimed it yet, but all traces of the prince and his crew are gone."

Not surprising, but I'm still not convinced that the Nagas had control over the hollow. "Something does not settle well with me about this. It is like we are seeing trees, but missing the forest."

"Agreed," the younger Taurine says. "Do you think it could be a Taurine?"

That thought had been in the back of my mind. "It's one possibility. After all, it was originally our homeworld before it became a penal colony." One that our ancestors abandoned to its fate.

I do not want to say much more because I dislike speculating. Outside of the Nexus, Taurines are often used as muscle-for-hire. Enforcers, berserkers, juggernauts...positions that would leverage our brute strength. Few outside of our fold would actively harm our own people. Sure, there are house skirmishes, but we fight to defend our homes and territories.

We do not enslave and sell our own people...do we? It is unsettling to think about.

We settle on a dry account of a report that would be on record as a routine part of our rounds in our territory. I give Tag the unwieldy task of ensuring all of Adalyn's delayed guests at the stable are in an amenable mood.

"Where is your lovely new mate now?" Tag asks as he prepares to leave.

I do not correct my second. Though she has not accepted me as a mate, I have already declared that she is mine. The rest is just paperwork.

I tap on my console where a scrolling account of Adalyn and Karis's movements has been updating every few minutes. "Adalyn insisted on treating Karis to a spa day. Karis pounced on that idea." Her eyes had softened to a dreamlike trance. I could not resist encouraging her to take Adalyn's offer. "I told her not to wander off too far."

"Adalyn or Karis?" Tag asks.

I give him a flat look that says, *what do you think?*

"I see. Let's see if Karis can follow your orders any better than Adalyn does."

"That would be a miracle. Regardless of where she wanders, though, I will always be able to find her."

KARIS

When I stepped through the portal and into the Nexus, I was not prepared for how homey it looked. I was expecting either an ultra-utilitarian space station or a spaceship transport pad that features in all those science fiction shows where the cast treks across the galaxy on bold quests.

What greeted me looked more like the reception area of a posh hotel. Rich woods, polished marble floors...there were even framed images along the walls.

The images changed after a while, so they had to have some kind of tech behind them.

I felt overwhelmed and slightly panicked until Adalyn skipped toward me, plastering herself to my side, and demanding why I was not in a spa at that very moment.

First, I was taken aback at how Adalyn, small, adorable, smiling Adalyn, could command with such force as she did to Bronn, of all people. After I got over that shock, the second one came seeing all the bulls within earshot who were easily twice–thrice?—her size tripping all over themselves to do her bidding.

After an hour-long shower followed by a bunch of beautifying treatments I can't name, Adalyn presents me with my lost backpack, a change of elegant yet comfortable clothes and takes us to the Waystation. It reminds me of a speakeasy nightclub in the roaring twenties.

Here Adalyn treats me to the meal she intended to share with me the day before. She has a client in a few minutes, and this was the most convenient place for her.

"So the Nexus is all interconnected to various hubs. And, we're in space?" I ask.

"The Nexus is more like a space station," Adalyn says. "This is one hub of the Nexus, which Bronn oversees." She says it with glowing pride. I mention how it looks so different to my expectations, and Adalyn giggles. "That's Bronn for you. The rest of the Nexus is different based on the house's urso. Here, let me show you."

She taps on the table, and it glows. It's like a computer interface that I can eat off of. I flip through various images of the Nexus. Overall, it looks like a labyrinth, but instead of decaying stone and rundown streets, or a surreal landscape of twisting hedgerows and blood thirsty thickets, this is straight out of a computer game.

Soft and sedate decor hides a whole load of sleek tech and modern amenities. Like this table. It even let me message my folks via email. I send them a lame excuse that my phone broke, and I would need to replace it.

Believable enough. My parents answer me, assuming I had been delayed in transit. They say they wouldn't have worried about me for another few hours yet.

What felt like an eternity for me was only a few hours for my parents.

I chat with them for a few minutes more before telling them I need to get going.

"Where is the rest of the Nexus?" I muse out loud. All the talk of houses seem like entire worlds and planets.

"In the heart of a wormhole," Adalyn answers. "It's how the Taurines could scatter throughout the galaxy, looking for a home that can accommodate us. And then, well, someone eventually realized that the Nexus itself can be our home."

It makes sense now. "Why need one planet when you can be on many at the same time?"

"Exactly!" Adalyn says. "The older generation tried to cling to bits and pieces of our ancestral home. There are many who still seek to claim it. But honestly, I'm of the opinion that home is where you make it."

"Agreed," I say. My heart tugs thinking of Bronn, of who he is in relation to the magnitude of this place.

He's practically the president of this country, and he left to rescue Adalyn.

And found me.

Good lord, what a mess? What would have happened if we stayed in that labyrinth?

Or had gotten him killed?

I would have ruined all of this...

Adalyn needs to meet her clients, but she makes me promise to meet her again for dinner tomorrow. I plaster a smile on my face, and tell her I'm looking forward to it.

"I can find you a comm so that you can talk to Bronn?" she offers, not wanting to leave me alone.

Funny thing is that I prefer a little solitude, at least to help me process... everything. All this external chatter has been trying on my nerves. "Don't worry about me. Bronn told me how to contact him."

Adalyn beams at me. To her, Bronn makes the universe spin. "Well, let me give you some privacy and I'll get a little of my own."

She skips away to wherever she's needed, flanked by an army of guards.

No one's taking chances with her.

I collect my things from the hostess station and head toward the engineering bay. With every step, I tell myself that Bron is in his element here. He has his network of people and places he has to go. If I stay here, I would just be a distraction for him.

The Taurine who works the portal is confused at my presence, and even more so, at my request. But I channel a bit of Adalyn's energy and repeat myself, this time with zero question in my tone. "Please connect me to this portal," I say with authority wrapped in kindness as I hand him the card with the coordinates Adalyn uses to gain access to Earth.

"I will let Bronn know where you are," he says.

"You don't have to," I say. "He already knows." That's more or less true. Bronn knows everything. Sometimes, the timing is delayed.

When the familiar shimmer of the portal appears, I wait for the go-ahead signal from the engineer before stepping through.

Somehow, I will adjust to a new normal knowing that space stations exist, aliens are real, and that I crave the touch of one alien male in particular, and it's for the best that I walk away from him.

EPILOGUE

I find myself on the same train platform as I arrived. Though it's been a couple of days for me, it's only been a matter of hours here. The Taurine engineer manning the portals offered to take me back to my parent's house. There is a direct drop and everything. But I opted to go back to the city.

It's a matter of pride. After all, I intended to be a tourist for at least a week, and dammit, that's exactly what I'll be. And I don't need Liam or any of his connections, either. Especially not after I figured out how to reverse my payment to Liam, so now I'm pretty flush with cash.

And the first thing I do is book a hotel with a spa. It's Adalyn's favorite place, so it's pricey, but worth it to me. After the taste of it earlier, a full on spa day tomorrow would likely kill me with pleasure.

That would be a good way to die.

First things first. I need to hail a cab.

I look at the long queue of worn out tourists waiting for their turn to dash into a taxi. Maybe I can just walk to the hotel from here...

"Do you need a ride, miss?"

As skeevy as the words are, there is a tinge of dry humor that makes me turn rather than run away from whoever says it.

Instead of the person I expect, I see a large man whose suit is custom-tailored to accommodate the pronounced V of his torso. My smile falters at the sight of this stranger. However, the way one corner of his mouth lifts as if laughing at some inside joke lights something up inside of me.

And, though he doesn't have an impressive set of horns balanced on top of his head, I would know those startlingly blue eyes anywhere. "Bronn?" I barely dare to breathe, in case I'm wrong.

His face breaks into a dashing grin, one that reminds me of a delirious night surrounded in a nest of brambles and thorns. "Do you need help to find your way home?" The deep velvet rumble of his voice trails over my skin like a caress.

"Bronn!" I throw myself into his outstretched arms. He crushes me against him, and I welcome the ache in my bones. "What are you doing here?"

"Following a lost mate who seems to have wandered off on her own when I asked her not to."

My face heats, but I don't care. Bronn is here with me. I pull back to study him. "How?"

His head tilts to the side. "Impressive technology coupled by the willing delusion of human psychology that aliens don't exist makes me look like an average, nondescript human."

I scoff, drinking in his appearance. "No amount of technology or delusion can make you look 'nondescript'."

His team needs to do more research on what the average human looks like, because it isn't this. Then again, no one has even looked our way standing here in the middle of a highly used walkway. The flow of traffic streams around us as if we are part of the scenery.

Flames dance in his eyes, enough to make me blush even harder. "You make me forget myself. I would mount you right here against this building." He blows a sharp whistle, and a sleek black sedan appears at the curb. As if it's a normal occurrence, Bronn carries me aloft, shifting me so I'm cradled against him. With his free hand, he lifts my luggage with ease, passing it off to the driver, who takes care of it.

Nestled against him in the backseat, his hands span my hips. He presses me closer until I can feel every vein and ridge on his cock. "What are you doing here?" I ask.

His eyebrow lifts as he shifts his hips in a delicious dance. "I hear this is called foreplay and I intend to get you dripping wet."

I throw my head back into a delirious laugh. He nuzzles my neck, my heart racing. "No, I meant here. Looking like this."

"What? Do I look so awful?"

Of course, he doesn't look awful. He looks like a gorgeous male, with his smooth brown skin and powerful body. "No, of course not. You're beautiful no matter what form. I meant why? What is all this? How are you here?"

"Why? Because you are my mate, and when I said 'don't wander too far,' you went and did just that. 'All this' is to blend in so humans do not panic, causing me to delay my reunion with the aforementioned mate. And I am here thanks to technology that is beyond my scope to explain." Bronn pauses, as if mulling over what he said. "I believe that answers all your questions."

I swallow my laugh. He is right. He did technically answer my questions. I cock my head to the side, surveying my very human-looking Taurine. "So this isn't permanent, right?"

He slowly shakes his head as he assesses me.

"Good, because I miss those horns."

He grins. "It pleases me that you prefer my natural form. This is camouflage, not a shift." Bronn dips his head a little. "Feel."

I run my fingers over his head, through the thick thatch of hair, to find the base of his horns. It's a trip to feel them under my hands while they are invisible to my sight. "There you are," I coo.

A rumble vibrates in his throat. He is sensitive there. The memory of him lapping me up while I gripped his horns must be on both of our minds. He licks his lips as he grinds me against his thickening cock. "Here I am. Always. For you."

I tremble as a small flutter of an orgasm teases at my core. "Always?" I say.

In answer, he lays me out on the seat, tearing open my pants as if they offend him. My panties are next, shredding them from my body in his desperate desire to taste me. He groans, deep and long, when he can finally delve his tongue along my seam.

"Always. There is nowhere in the universe where I cannot find you, so do not test me. You are mine. My gift. My home. My everything. Now lay back and take your tongue lashing. You ought to be disciplined for misbehaving."

My giggles turn into an extended sigh as he adds fingers to my dripping heat. "Yes, sir."

Follow Bronn and Karis in *Mounting Her Minotaur,* which will be the first book in the series Obsidian City: Love and Monsters, releasing June 2022. It is available for preorder HERE. You can also paste this link into your favorite browser:
https://books2read.com/mountingherminotaur

For more monster romances, check out A Cherry on Top, a serial story set in the underworld of Obsidian City. New episodes are published on Radish and Patreon, and once complete, will be available as an ebook on all digital retailers.

For more stories in the Obsidian Rift universe, click HERE to read *Blood Tithes,* part of the Obsidian City: Vampire Accords series.

You can also read "Blood Oath" a ménage paranormal romance with omegaverse tropes. It's part of the *Fates and Mates* anthology offered for free HERE, or enter this link into your favorite browser:
https://evangelinepriest.com/links

ABOUT AUTHOR

Evangeline Priest writes love at first bite paranormal romance featuring growly alpha heroes and women strong enough to tame them. She writes "monsters in space" science fiction romance as Eva Priest. Try out The Legion universe, starting with *Hunted,* HERE.
{https://evangelinepriest.com/book/hunted-the-legion-savage-lands-sector-1/}

She is usually within reach of coffee, chocolate, or a bowl of noodles.

Join her VIP community on Patreon where she shares NSFW art, excerpts, cover reveals, and featured stories each month.

For more news on releases, you can sign up for Evangeline Priest's newsletter HERE or enter this link into your favorite web browser: (https://evangelinepriest.com/newsletter).

| patreon.com/evapriestwrites
tiktok.com/@evapriestwrites
instagram.com/evangelinepriest
facebook.com/evapriestwrites
twitter.com/evapriestwrites

CURSE OF THE CYCLOPS

CLIO EVANS

AUTHOR'S NOTE

Hello, my little monster loving creature.

This story has the following:

Size differences, fated mates, MMF threesomes, monster love, praise kinks, sub/dom dynamics, tons of orgasms, and more.

As always, please proceed with caution.

Enjoy this kinky sweet monster romance story!

CHAPTER ONE
CAMBRIDGE CREATURE LIBRARY

DAPHNE

I glanced at my text message again as I bounced on the balls of my feet, trying to keep my blood pumping. My coat was warm but not warm enough to keep me from feeling like my heart was going to turn to ice. Not that it wasn't already.

It's a secret library. The password is 'Epistêmê'.

How the fuck did I say that? I hissed between my teeth again and finally caved, descending down the steps to an ancient wooden door. The wood was dark and riveted, and the handle elaborate wrought iron that spiraled out into metal vines.

At the center of the door, there was a sign. I stared at it as I crept closer, scowling.

Cambridge Creature Library.
Enter if you dare.
Knowledge is power.

HUMANS: BEWARE

The last part was a *little* extra.

Who knew that there was an underground library in Cambridge? I'd been here for over a month studying at the college, buried in my Anglo-Saxon, Norse, and Celtic courses. I had always loved medieval history, literature, and languages— and studying here in Cambridge had been a dream come true. It was far from my small hometown in the US, but I had found the complete independence to be refreshing.

My parents had made a point of calling me once a week to check-in and update me on their boring lives. It usually involved the neighbors, rumors from the golf course, or the adventures of Pookie (who was a hairless dog that perpetually had her tongue sticking out). I loved both of them dearly, but their path was very straight and narrow, whereas I preferred to tumble head-first down mountainous roads. I loved going to new places and meeting new people.

My obsession with books had never gotten me into trouble until possibly now. I had caught wind of a special book one night at a pub. My friend, Catherine, had shared all her secrets with me, swearing that I could *never tell anyone* because it could get her in trouble.

It had been the most bizarre conversation I had ever had. She told me about a secret library that no one knew about that had a book called 'Creatures of History and Their Curses'. Not only did it tickle my curiosity about history, but I also found myself wondering about the word 'creatures'. *Creatures* led me to think it meant mythological beings, which would be interesting.

Too interesting for me not to check out.

Overall, it was a weird conversation. Catherine had kept calling me a human, which I was, but...

What an odd thing to say, right?

What had really got me was her mentioning that the book hadn't been studied in at least a century. As a certified book whore, I had to see it in person. What was it about? No idea. How old was it? Also, no idea.

But, it was secret and never seen by humans, so that meant that I— a human — had to lay eyes on it, come hell or high water.

Catherine had told me I'd have to work to get to it but that I would always regret it if I didn't. She'd been wasted, but her conviction had been... convincing.

Aside from having a fictional addiction, I also had a curiosity that had gotten me in trouble many times in my 25 years. That curiosity had also given me plenty of adventures, though.

My phone buzzed again in my hand, and I glanced at it.

Don't let the dragon trick you.

My eyes narrowed, a little alarm bell going off in my head. One that I ignored.

She must have been at the pub again, although it was a little early for such an outing.

I snorted as I put the phone back in my pocket and reached out, grasping the knob. I tried pushing it, but it didn't budge.

Would a password really work?

"Epistêmê," I whispered, knowing full well that I had probably butchered the pronunciation.

Regardless, I heard a click and found myself pushing open the door to the Cambridge Creature Library.

I was immediately greeted with the musky scent of books and earth. I stepped inside, my bones thawing as warmth hit me.

I had to blink a few times to get my sight adjusted.

I was standing in an arched entryway. The walls were stone, the dappled gray leading up to marbled molding. The floors were an odd black and white checkered, running out into the next room.

The silence was deafening. I let out a soft breath, one that practically echoed, and left the entry space.

"Whoa," I whispered, my head tipping back in awe.

The size of the room didn't make sense to what I had seen outside. The ceiling was at least twenty feet above me, the walls lined with thousands of books.

Hundreds of thousands of books. I couldn't even see the back of the library.

In front of me, there was a massive oak desk. A candle flickered on top of it amongst stacks of dusty books, the wax rolling down like tears. There was a cup of coffee that was steaming still, the scent wafting through the air. At least a hundred coffee rings stained the top of the desk, proof that someone was here regularly.

I moved closer, my heart pounding.

There was something extremely odd about this library. Everything looked untouched even though it was obvious *someone* was here.

"Hello?" I asked softly, still looking around like a child in a candy shop.

This was magnificent. The library of my dreams. Yes, it *was* creepy, but the shock at the number of books squashed the weird factor.

Now, to find the ancient book.

I sucked in a breath, looking back at the desk. A book was split open, the yellowed pages holding the sweeping ink of an illustration. I moved closer, studying the colors.

It was a drawing of a crimson dragon guarding stacks of books. I leaned in, studying it closer. The ink was vibrant, the red scales glistening. Its teeth were bared, smoke curling out of its nostrils. The illustration felt *alive*, which was a testament to the artist's talent. Some of the ink was iridescent, decorating the page with gold, royal blue, and emerald green.

"Hmm." I reached out and ran my fingers down the side of the page. Parts of the drawing were raised and felt good against my skin.

Maybe *this* was the book. It was fantastic.

I lifted the page and turned it, gasping at the next drawing.

I took a step back, my cheeks turning hot.

The next drawing was not anything I could have ever expected. It was of a woman, her legs spread as a monster lapped at her. Holding her was another monster, his claws clutching her neck.

She looked like she was having one hell of a time, but WHY was that in this book?

Alright, you puritan, I scolded myself. I stepped closer, swallowing a giggle as I studied it closer.

Jesus, she really was having a good time. The two monsters looked like Cyclopes. Except they weren't anything like the egregious ones that I'd seen in shows and books growing up. Their bodies were muscled with hard abs and even harder cocks.

"God, that's like ten inches," I muttered, shaking my head. "And what is that...." I drifted off.

The one holding her— his cock had a knot before reaching his balls.

She looked a lot like me, which was startling. Like me, she also had brown hair and curves. Her thighs were thick, her nipples taut. The artist hadn't attempted to hide her, including her rolls and stretch marks.

My eyes narrowed, my hands flattening my clothing for a moment.

The difference between her and me was that I would never, in a million years, manage to entice someone to be like *that* with me. Let alone two of them.

Sure, I'd had my fair share of sex. And I'd had a couple of failed relationships too. But, at the end of the day, the kinks I secretly yearned to explore would stay dormant.

I raised a brow, trying to ignore the way the heat seemed to go straight to my core.

The librarian here had to be kinky as fuck. Who just left a book out like *this* with their coffee at the front desk of an establishment??

"Hello?" I asked again.

This time I heard movement and looked around wildly, trying to figure out which direction it was coming from.

Behind the desk, there was an entrance to the first row of shelves. It reminded me of a doorway, even with a crimson velvet rope stationed in front of it.

There was even a little sign next to it.

"Hello?? I'm here to check out a book," I called, amplifying the volume of my voice.

I let out a dramatic sigh as soon as the movement stopped.

Well, I wasn't waiting around.

I had things to do, places to be. I'd grab the book and be out of the weird library before anyone noticed a thing.

I snuck past the desk, looking around and listening for more movement. The library was quieter than a tomb, a suppressing cloud of silence.

My footsteps echoed across the checkered floor, and I paused at the sign, frowning.

Enter if you dare.
Knowledge is power.
HUMANS: BEWARE

I scowled again.

Part of me hoped to meet the librarian of this place because I had questions about *why* they were so dramatic. The sign was silly at best and did nothing but make me more curious.

Also, why 'HUMANS'? As if the librarian wasn't one.

Find the book and then leave, I told myself.

I unclipped the red rope and slipped past it.

As soon as I stepped forward, my entire body stiffened from a jolt. I dropped the rope, stepping closer to the books in shock. My entire body was tingling, my blood heating.

I heard shuffling again and spun around.

Well, *now* there was someone— but not what I was expecting.

His back was facing me, and my mouth dropped. How tall was this guy? Since when did libraries have linebackers employed? He had to be over seven feet tall, his shoulders impossibly wide. He wore a black turtle neck that reminded me of a blanket and charcoal pants.

His hair was blonde and drawn back into a bun.

"Hello??" I asked as he lifted his cup of coffee.

The giant spun around, his coffee cup flying.

The porcelain crashed, and I covered my mouth, stumbling back.

The monster from *that* book had jumped out of the pages!

We stared at each other. Then, finally, my brain caught up with me, and I let out a window-smashing scream— turning to run.

I immediately slammed straight into a wall.

Except it wasn't a wall— it was a massive chest.

One that was covered in tweed and smelled like books.

One that belonged to yet another monster.

CHAPTER TWO
BEWARE OF HUMANS

ANDREW

"DID YOU NOT READ THE SIGN??" I thundered, picking up the human woman.

Her bright blue eyes stared at me, her scream dying. She had dark brown hair pulled back in a loose braid, her cheeks bright pink from either the wind outside or...

Her scent hit me, and it took every ounce of control to not throw her across the room.

Of course, there was no way I could anyways. She had stepped into the barrier. We were safely sandwiched between two rows of books, with me blocking her from the maze behind me and the invisible wall blocking her from leaving.

Adam was still staring at her from his desk, his mouth wide open and purple eye even wider. He was as horrified by her presence as she was of ours.

"What...what...*Fuck*. What are you?" she whispered.

I blinked. Her feet still dangled in the air, her body slowly relaxing.

The longer she stared at me, the more...curious she seemed?

Who was this woman?

"Why in the seven hells are you here, woman?? Did you not read the 'HUMANS: BEWARE' sign?" I seethed.

Her cheeks were crimson now, and I felt a lusty heat swell up inside of me.

That was *not* a natural reaction.

I immediately set her down like she was a jar of poison, taking a step back from her. The bookshelves towered to either side of us, creating a narrow hall. She was trapped.

She didn't hesitate to turn and run, and I didn't try to stop her as she slammed straight into the invisible shield.

She stumbled back and then ran for it again, banging on it. Kicking it. Cussing at it.

She reminded me of an angry little cat.

"You can't escape. *Gaea*, help us," I sighed, rubbing my face with my hands. "Adam, get over here, please."

Adam was still staring at her like a ghost.

"ADAM!" I snapped.

He jerked and then moved, coming closer.

"Let me out!!" the human wailed. "Please! This was a mistake!"

"It's too late," I sighed.

And it really was.

This library was a labyrinth, one that had been kept for the last 50 years by Adam and me. We had stumbled in together one night and had activated the curse.

We hadn't left these walls in a long time. I hadn't seen the sky, hadn't seen the world in what felt like an eternity. Our only link to the outside world was our fairy friend, Catherine. She kept us updated on the state of the world and also helped us stay up to date on language changes.

The Cambridge Creature Library had been a legend to us. We had done everything we could to seek it out, not knowing what would happen the moment we came in.

We were bound to this place until our soulmate found us. I had resigned to that being forever.

But now...

The warmth in my chest felt foreign. A flicker of hope that I didn't want.

The woman had quieted again, her body still stiff.

Adam finally spoke. "Little dove," he crooned, stepping closer to her. "We won't hurt you. I know we're creatures, but we won't cause you any pain," he promised gently.

He had always been a lot nicer than me.

"Unless you want us to," I muttered, crossing my arms.

She shot me a dark glare over her shoulder, and I couldn't help it— I smirked. I reached up and stroked my beard for a moment, thinking about all of the possibilities that should not have been in my mind.

"What is this place?" she whispered. "Why did Catherine tell me to come here??"

"*Catherine*," Adam and I said together, equally surprised.

"Yes," she breathed, reaching into her pocket.

She drew out a little rectangle, and I gasped as it lit by itself.

Was this one of those devices the fairy had told us about?

"Well, now I have no signal. I'm stuck between two monsters. There's an invisible wall. I really fucked up this time, didn't I?"

She was talking to herself, furiously tapping at the device. She finally blew out an irritated sigh and then chucked it.

Adam and I watched it fly through the barrier, clacking as it landed on the floor.

She immediately tried to lunge for it again, smacking into the barrier. She rubbed her forehead, stumbling back again.

I'd forgotten how ridiculously stubborn humans could be.

I groaned, annoyed. "Don't be a fool, woman."

Adam was still on the other side of the barrier. He picked up the device and then brought it with him, stepping into the labyrinth entrance. He met my gaze for a moment, his expression haunted.

I hesitated for a moment and then refocused on the human. "There's a way out of this," I said quickly.

Her gaze reminded me of lightning now, an expression of determination. "How?" she asked, tilting her chin up.

"We have to go through the labyrinth. If we survive, then we will all be able to leave. Adam and I have been here for fifty years," I said.

"FIFTY?"

"Yes," Adam murmured. "What's your name, little dove?"

"Daphne," she mumbled, still rubbing her forehead. There was a red circle from where she had smacked it twice in a row.

Her cheeks turned pink again as she looked up at him.

I frowned. She was confusing. One moment she was furious, and the next, she was determined, and now...

Her scent hit me again, and I took another step back. My mouth watered, my cock already threatening to harden. I even felt my form threaten to shift, which frightened me more.

I hadn't turned into my full cyclops form in ages. I was a monster, an ugly one at that, and had learned through trial and error how to at least remain in a better functioning form. One that wasn't fifteen feet tall with bulging muscles and blundering movements.

I drew in a breath, controlling myself.

"I'm in shock now, I think," she said, leaning back against one of the book-shelves.

"We are too," Adam said, grinning foolishly.

She looked up at him again and smiled a little. "So you're Adam," she said. She then looked at me, "And you are...?"

"Andrew," I answered curtly.

"Adam and Andrew. Okay," she breathed, nodding. "Okay. Well. I have a pretty strong imagination. That's nice of it to give you good names."

I raised my brow, narrowing my eye. "Human, we aren't imaginary. Creatures are real. Dragons, cyclopes, Minotaurs. You name it, and it's probably out there. It's just that we stay hidden from your kind."

She snorted, which frustrated me more.

I stepped toward her again, determined to make her understand. She had to believe we were real. She couldn't live under the belief that the journey we were about to take was fake.

I expected her to shrink as I stepped closer to her, but she didn't. Instead, she straightened her spine, looking straight up at me. The top of her head barely reached my chest.

I leaned down, breathing in her scent fully. I planted one of my massive hands on the shelf above her. "We are *very, very* real."

She stared at me for one beat...for two. Finally, her brows drew together, crinkling her forehead. "No. I must have fallen, and now I'm dreaming of that freaking woman getting tag teamed by the two of you in that book," she said. "She even kind of looked like me too. Except she was missing the tattoo that I have on my ass. I like it when my lovers kiss it."

Adam sucked in a breath, letting out a groan next to me.

"That drawing was pretty hot," she added, grinning.

It was my turn to truly feel shocked. Her brazen announcement made my cock harden, my moan escaping.

"Woman. How do I convince you this is real?"

Her hand reached out, splaying across my chest. I froze, my heart hammering from her touch. She then patted me like a dog, smirking.

"The only way I'll believe it is if you can make me cum."

"*What?*" I growled, stunned.

She giggled and then slipped past me, moving down the row of books.

I looked at her, to Adam, back to her, and then down at my cock.

"Fuck," I breathed.

Adam was just as bewildered as I was. "Andrew, what do we do?"

"I don't even know," I said. At this point, I was fighting the deeply rooted desires that had decided to spring up.

We watched her pause and pluck a book off the shelf.

"Daphne," I growled, marching up to her.

She turned to look at me, but then her gaze fell to my cock. "Do you really have a knot, Mr. Dream Cyclops?"

"Would you say these things to someone real?" I growled.

She shrugged. "If I were drunk enough, probably."

"Okay. I'm real."

"Yes, you're real," she mocked.

I was about to snap a response when a growl echoed through the library. The first stab of panic hit me as reality sank in, and I didn't even give the human time to process it.

I picked her up, threw her over my shoulder, and then looked at Adam.

He gave me a nod of assurance, and the two of us took off, diving straight into the library maze from hell.

CHAPTER THREE
REALITY

DAPHNE

I'd convinced myself this really was a dream until now.

Andrew slammed me up against one of the shelves, protecting me from the burst of flames that spewed from the dragon's mouth. I buried my face against his chest, holding onto him for dear life.

Apparently, Cyclopes were heat resistant. Also, apparently, they could run pretty damn fast.

Also, apparently, their erections lasted a lifetime.

Hard or not, he was now my protector and the only thing keeping me alive.

I heard Adam shout, and another burst of flames hit us. Andrew groaned, his grip around me tightening.

I was caught between death and a sexy monster.

Sexy?

I really was going crazy.

I wanted to believe this was a dream, but the cut on my forehead from falling into one of the shelves was too real. The blood dripping down my face was definitely not made up.

And Andrew's hard-on was one hundred percent not a fantasy.

The fire died, and I was immediately tossed like a doll, then caught by Adam.

He was a lot more gentle with me, holding me like a baby as he ran down the rows of books.

"We just have to get to one of the stopping points, then we'll be safe," he grunted.

I nodded, burying my face against him. He smelled like books and tobacco, but in an aphrodisiacal way. I found myself breathing him in, wondering what he would taste like if I kissed him.

Fuck.

What the fuck was wrong with me?

Ever since the initial shock had worn off, all I could think about was sex. With monsters. With one-eyed hunky librarians.

My life was at risk, we were being chased by a dragon in a book whore's fantasy of a library, and all I wanted was what I had seen in that drawing.

"Your scent is intoxicating," Adam groaned as he took me around a corner.

We were bathed in shadows, and he became still, pressing me into another shelf so he could protect me if there were more flames.

He wasn't as forceful as Andrew was. His hands were massive, but his fingers were gentle. He leaned in for a moment, his nose brushing my neck.

I shivered against him, letting out a moan. He immediately covered my mouth with his hand, silencing me.

We heard the shifting of a massive body again, the clack of claws on the checkered floors. The deeper we went into the maze, the more and more lost I felt.

But the two of them seemed to know this place at least.

"Your human finally came, but I won't let you go," a heavy voice snarled.

I squeezed my eyes shut, trembling.

Adam held me, his nose still pressed into my neck.

"I won't let you escape with her. I will kill her, and you will never leave my side. Your job is to protect the knowledge here. You can't abandon me...."

The voice sounded closer, the claws becoming louder.

I opened my eyes, looking over Adam's shoulder to the entrance of the shadowed row we were in.

Red scales glistened, a massive body slinking by. The dragon paused for a moment but then kept moving.

It took a few minutes, but finally— the dragon disappeared.

Adam let out a breath, drawing back to look at me. He lifted a finger and swiped away a tear from my cheek. "Little dove, you're safe," he whispered.

We both stared at each other, and I became painfully aware of the fact that my legs were around his massive hips. He had me pressed against the shelves, the shape of his cock pressing into me.

I let out the smallest whimper, and before I knew what I was doing, I ground my core against him.

He breathed out a hiss, falling forward and catching himself against the wood. "Woman, you're tempting a monster."

I was fully aware of what I was doing, and I couldn't stop myself. I studied him, focusing on his eye for a few moments. The purple in his iris was luminescent, burning with lust.

"Adam."

We both looked up to see Andrew. He jerked his head to follow him, his gaze lingering a little too long on us before he disappeared.

Adam grunted but then readjusted me, carrying me like a baby again. He followed Andrew down a couple of rows until we came to a door. Andrew went through it quickly, and we followed.

We were now in a small room, one that had more books and a few chairs.

And a bed.

Adam set me down slowly, breathing a sigh of relief.

"That was close," he mumbled.

I nodded numbly. If I hadn't been wet before, I was now.

Andrew moaned, placing his hands on top of his head. "This is our bedroom. We're safe here for a little while, and then we will need to get on the move again. The walls will change, the library will reorganize itself. The dragon won't come after us next. I'm certain it'll be a couple of the harpies."

My mind was swirling as I registered his words.

Andrew and Adam had a few differences in appearance. They were similar in size, although Andrew was even taller, and he had short dark hair and a beard. His eye was bright green, his lashes long. He wore charcoal colored pants and a dark tweed blazer over a hunter green sweater.

He was hot, and I found myself wondering again about how it would feel to do bad things to him. I wondered what his beard would feel like against me as he sucked my clit.

"I'm very confused by everything right now," I blurted out.

I went to one of the plush chairs and attempted to pat off the dust before plopping on the bright red velvet cushion.

"You are, according to the powers that be, our mate," Adam said, looking directly at me.

"Mate?" I echoed.

"Yes. Creatures have mates. Cyclops, especially, have soulmates. Andrew and I are lovers, but we are also destined to have a third. You are that person for us," he explained.

I studied the two of them, heat creeping up the back of my neck. For a moment, I imagined them doing things to each other and felt my pussy clench.

They both grunted, and Andrew covered his face again.

"We can smell your arousal," Adam said softly.

"I can see yours," I mumbled, looking down at both of their cocks.

I could see the shapes beneath the charcoal slacks they wore. I whimpered a little, unable to stop thinking about them.

"Is this some type of spell?" I asked.

"If it is, then we are also bewitched," Adam said, cocking his head.

At some point, his blonde hair had unraveled from the bun he had worn earlier. It now fell in a glorious wave. His eye was purple, and there was a kindness there that made me feel...

Curious.

I was curious about what it would be like to be with them.

The desire was becoming almost unbearable, growing and growing. I had been wet for a while now, the heat pulsing in my veins.

I was a grown woman, I reminded myself. I made my own decisions, and that included who I had sex with. When it came to relationships— I had always been the committed type, but that didn't mean I didn't know how to have fun.

And if that drawing from the book did them justice, then being tag teamed by the two of them would be a lot of fun.

"We need a plan," Andrew said, interrupting my thoughts. "We need a plan to get out. The dragon will keep coming after us until we make it to the end. We're barely at the beginning at this point. Adam and I know the labyrinth very well. We've just never been able to use the exit because we didn't have our 'soulmate' with us."

"But now that we do, we can all three get out," Adam said, smiling. "It would be nice to see the sky again. I miss watching the sunset."

My heart melted a little. I realized fully now that these two had literally been trapped here for half a century.

"Tell me about creatures," I said softly, studying both of them. "I have so many questions. Like why don't humans know that you're real? How is the soulmate thing even possible? Those are things I read about in my books, but they're not real. And yet, here I am."

"Humans have always feared creatures," Adam said. He moved to one of the chairs a couple of feet from me and took a seat, relaxing.

Andrew chose to pace the room instead, his forehead wrinkled from scowling.

"There was a certain point that collectively, creatures started to hide from humanity out of fear of them. It's ironic. But many monsters have perished due to the silly beliefs of humans. Many humans have been wrongly accused of being creatures too," Adam said. He was studying me intently now, which caused a blush to turn me pink again. He stood up suddenly, crossing to me. "I just realized that your forehead is still bleeding. Let me heal it for you, little dove."

"Adam, have you already committed to her then?" Andrew snarled, glaring at me.

Adam raised his brow but ignored Andrew. He cupped my face and tipped my chin up. "Fate doesn't lie," he murmured.

My eyes fluttered closed, my throat tightening. My heart felt light, my head even lighter.

His touch felt good. Warm and gentle. His fingers slid to the cut on my forehead, and I felt a stabbing heat, followed by a flood of pleasure that swarmed every part of my body. My breath hitched, a moan escaping.

"I want you," I gasped, my eyes flying open. "I don't know what this is. It's crazy, insane. But I want you."

Adam withdrew his hand, a shadow falling over his face. "I fear that if I take you once, I will never be able to take another again. Also, I will not take you unless you accept Andrew as well. He is my mate, after all, little dove."

Andrew's presence fell over me, and I realized that he had stepped behind the chair. I looked up, swallowing hard as I tipped my head back.

The two of them towered over me. One of them felt safe, the other dangerous.

Andrew braced his hands on the back of the chair and cocked his head. "You really want to give yourself to two monsters, Daphne?"

The answer should have been no.

The answer should have been not in a million years.

But between the rush in my blood, their scents, their appearances (which should have been frightening but turned me on instead)— I found myself nodding.

"Verbal consent, human," Andrew said gruffly. "A simple nod will not do."

"I want both of you. I want what that girl in the book had. Maybe if we do it, then our heads will clear, and we'll be able to get out of the labyrinth faster," I whispered hoarsely.

"We'll escape the labyrinth, but you will never escape us if we do this," Andrew said plainly. "You will be mated to two cyclopes. What of your family? Your life?"

"My family is boring, and my life isn't that exciting," I whispered. "I study at the college. I would still want to do so."

"But what of the rest of your life? What happens when a lad seeks you out, and his cock can't fill you?"

I was out of my god damned mind, but I couldn't stop the thoughts rushing through me.

The heat in his gaze had me burning from the inside out. I parted my lips, my words faltering. "I...I don't think I'd want anyone else."

"Oh?" Adam chimed in. He leaned down, breathing in my scent at the crook of my neck.

A breath escaped me. I felt like I was about to cum now. They weren't even touching me, but the tension of being between them like this was driving me to the edge.

"You'd be joining the world of monsters, little dove," Adam murmured. His fingertip traced the line of my cheekbone gently, sending a shiver down my spine.

"Now that I know it exists, how could I not?" I whispered.

Which was the truth. My world had changed the moment I'd stepped foot in this place. I would never be the same again, even if I didn't end up with two monster boyfriends.

"I came here for a book, but now my life has changed," I murmured.

"What book?" Andrew asked, frowning.

"*Creatures of History and Their Curses,*" I said.

Adam snorted, his hands falling to my thighs. He spread them slowly. "Tell us about it, little dove. We're librarians, after all."

CHAPTER FOUR
JUST A TASTE

Adam

I was toying with her, but it couldn't be helped.

My cock was pulsing, aching to be free. Andrew was in the same state as me, even though he was doing his best to hide it beneath the tough exterior.

Daphne was a miracle. She didn't know yet how much we would cherish her. She didn't have an understanding of how much Andrew and I would do to keep her safe.

Even though Andrew was an ass, I could already see the cracks in his demeanor. He was doing his best to keep her at arm's length, but he would fail.

How long had we been together in this dusty place? Cursed Librarians, stuck roaming the countless rows of books. Every day, we would maintain the library while plucking tomes here and there. I had found my own stack of reading and had learned much.

The crimson dragon, although evil, had a nice collection. One that did deserve to be coveted, even if his methods were madness.

The interesting part was that aside from the first meeting, where we had been given our cursed duties, we rarely saw the dragon. He kept to himself, and sometimes I wondered if he left the library. There would be days, months even where we wouldn't hear a thing from him.

Then there were the other creatures in this library too. Also cursed, with different duties. They didn't interact with Andrew and me, though, keeping to themselves.

How Catherine had found our mate was beyond me. But both Andrew and I knew that she had sent Daphne to us.

The moment I had seen her, I had known.

I had been shocked. She had slipped into the library without either of us noticing. It wasn't until she'd entered the labyrinth that her presence had overwhelmed the two of us.

Now, the clock was ticking. We were safe in our makeshift bedroom for now, but we would need to move soon before one of the other creatures came after us.

We *would* get out.

I was determined to see the colors of sunrise again. I craved to sprawl out beneath the stars, to lie in fields with morning dew, to dance in the rain.

I missed the outside world. A world that I hadn't cherished until Andrew and I had been stolen from it. I yearned to see all of the wild changes that Catherine had spoken to Andrew and me about.

I knelt in front of Daphne, spreading her legs so that I could tease her while she attempted to explain the book she was after. Andrew was listening to her intently while I was focused purely on making her scent rise again.

The moment we'd had while waiting for the dragon to pass had nearly broken me. If I weren't a gentleman, I would have ravished her there.

Fucking her against the bookshelves would have been magnificent, but I didn't want to scare her.

I didn't want her to run away from us.

But now, she had made it clear that she wanted us. She willingly spread her legs, her moan interrupting the words she poured out.

"I...ah, fuck...I don't know. The book sounded magical, and Catherine was pretty cryptic about it. I love books, so I had to see it. And a secret library?? Like what kind of— ah, fuck, Adam—" She bit her bottom lip as my hand grazed the apex of her thighs. Her fingers dug into the arms of the chair, her hips thrusting. "What kind of bibliophile could resist a secret library? I simply couldn't."

I would need to rid her of these pants.

It was interesting seeing a woman in pants. Catherine had told us that women didn't wear dresses as much, and I appreciated that evolution very much. It meant that I could see her curves. I wanted to sink my teeth into her flesh, to taste her core.

"The book is one I've never seen before," Andrew said. "But perhaps we can keep an eye out for it on our adventure. Are you certain you want this?"

I glanced up at him and smirked. He was fighting himself very hard, but he would lose.

"Yes. For the love of god, yes," she gasped.

Andrew's hand lifted, and he slid it around her neck, forcing her to continue to look up at him. "I have an appetite for obedience, Daphne. I have a thirst for seeing my lover beg. For making them ache for me. Do you understand, human?"

I unbuttoned her pants, and she automatically lifted, allowing me to pull them free. I blew out a hiss.

She wore black lace around her pussy, and her scent was mouth-watering. I could taste her even though my tongue had yet to touch her. Her thighs were beautifully plump, her skin striped here and there.

Andrew would have a pretty time with her.

"I understand," she rasped as she slid a hand down to her pussy. I grabbed her hand before she could touch herself, passing it to Andrew. He leaned in, capturing both of her hands and forcing them above her head.

Andrew chuckled, his eye darkening as he caved in to his lust. "If at any point, we are too much, you must tell us. Do you understand?"

"Yes," she whispered, whining.

"Adam, make her cum."

"Yes, sir," I whispered gleefully.

She squealed as I tore the lace, freeing her completely. She was beautiful, her pussy bright pink and slick. I lifted her legs and placed them on my shoulders, sprinkling kisses on her stomach and inner thighs until pressing my nose against her core and breathing her in.

"Fuck, she smells good, Master," I mumbled.

"Master?" she echoed.

"In our everyday life, we are equals," Andrew said, explaining one of our relationship dynamics. "But when it comes to sex, Adam obeys me. I am his Master, and he will do whatever I ask. You will obey me too, Daphne," he said, the last sentence a soft command.

I looked up as I buried my tongue into her, watching her entire body respond. Andrew slipped his massive thumb into her mouth. "Suck it, angel," he urged. Her lips formed an 'o', the suckling sounds delightful.

His eye met mine, and I felt my entire body shudder.

I would need him to fill me later, but now— my role was to bring our new mate to climax.

I began to lap at her, burying my tongue into her slick heat. I forced her legs open as wide as possible and then moved up to nibble at her clit.

Her thighs immediately clamped around my head, her cry lighting up the room.

"Here, let's get this clothing off," Andrew said.

He began to strip her as I lapped at her, enjoying the pressure of her thighs holding me in place. The next time I looked up, I was blessed with the sight of her beautiful breasts being freed. Her nipples hardened, her chest bright pink as she drew in ragged breaths.

"Fuck," she gasped. "I've never... No one has ever made me feel like this."

I chuckled as I forced my tongue back into her. She tasted like heaven, and I intended to show her that she would be worshiped like a goddess.

I drew out my tongue, my chin wet from her. I lifted my hand, slipping the first finger inside of her.

She groaned, her hips bucking.

"Don't stop sucking my finger," Andrew growled, giving her cheek a soft slap.

The shock on her face had both of us enthralled. She wasn't untouched, which I was thankful for, but the way she responded was like she'd never experienced pleasure.

"How does my finger feel?" I asked, stroking her inside.

She moaned, and Andrew pulled his hand free to allow her to answer. "Good. Fuck, it's so big. It's already so big. I want more."

I chuckled as I added my middle finger. She gasped, letting out another cry.

"I think we should move to the bed," Andrew murmured gruffly.

I nodded and removed my fingers as I lifted her on my shoulders, shoving my tongue into her again. Her scream echoed around me, her hands gripping my hair. I stumbled to the bed, laying her down as carefully as possible— all while ravaging her like a starved monster.

As soon as her back hit the mattress, she lifted her hips and began to hump me. I groaned, my cock throbbing.

I felt Andrew behind me. He spread my legs, reaching around to undo my pants. Within moments, I was stripped, and his hand was stroking my cock.

"Let her see it," he commanded.

I moaned, withdrawing from her pussy. She gasped, her cries turning to pants as she lifted her head. Her eyes slid to where my cock was, and they widened.

"Fuck. It's so big. You have a knot. Fuck," she whispered. "There's no way that'll fit inside of me."

"It will," I groaned.

His strokes were lazy, teasing me.

"You have yet to make her cum, Adam. I'm disappointed."

I growled, leaning back down to take her with my mouth with a newfound determination. I *would* make her cum.

Andrew continued to stroke my cock, his other hand gripping the back of my head. He held me to her pussy now, her cries rising like a wave.

"Fuck. I'm close," she wailed.

I groaned and lifted a finger, pushing it inside of her ass.

Her scream was rewarding, her confused cries drowned into a moan as she immediately came. Her entire body clenched as her orgasm overtook her, the gush flooding my tongue. She was a glorious little thing, her ass and pussy tight.

To take one of us would be a feat, but it could be done.

Taking both of us, however, would be almost impossible.

CHAPTER FIVE
HARPIES ARE RUDE

DAPHNE

I was still reeling from the most intense mind-shattering orgasm I had ever experienced in my life. Adam withdrew his tongue and his finger but kissed my stomach. He pinched my belly, and I lifted a lid to glare at him, but then I realized...

He loved every soft curve I had. The look on his face was one of reverence, his mouth kissing every part of me with a diligence that was flooring.

Andrew rose above him, studying me with a satisfied smirk.

"I think we'll leave this here for now. We need to get on the move. If you want another orgasm, you will need to get dressed and come with us. Adam, if you want a release— you'll need to do the same."

I wasn't sure about Adam, but I'd never been this motivated in my entire life. Adam grunted, planted a kiss on my mouth, and then rolled off the bed with a groan.

"Not fair," he mumbled, pulling on his pants quickly.

Andrew winked at me and gathered my clothes, bringing them to me.

My entire body felt like jelly as I sat up and moved to the edge of the bed. Andrew leaned down, gripping my jaw as he planted a full kiss on my lips.

He left me breathless and back to having an ache between my thighs.

"We have to keep moving," he whispered. "But the next stopping point, I will fill you."

The promise stunned me but also motivated me to get dressed again. The three of us were ready to continue after a few minutes, with Adam grabbing a bag and packing water with some snacks.

Time was beginning to melt together, it felt like, and I found myself wondering how long it had been since I had eaten.

"We'll eat at the next stop," Andrew said.

Before I could respond, I was swept up by him.

"I can walk—"

His glare silenced me.

"We'll move faster if one of us carries you," Adam chimed in, smiling at me. "Alright. Are we ready? I'm certain this is the last time we will be in this room."

"I hope so," Andrew muttered.

I glanced over his shoulder as he stepped back out into the library. We were greeted with deafening silence and the familiar musk of dusty pages.

The shelves *had* changed, which was mind-boggling. The heavy oak shelves had changed to stone and were shorter than before. I looked up at the ceiling and realized that it had changed too. Now, natural light shifted through the space— coming from windows that I could not see. The ceiling had a painting that was the same as the illustration of the dragon in the book I had seen. The difference was, now the books around the dragon were on fire.

This place was bizarre.

The silence was edged with tension as the three of us moved down the row. Adam moved ahead of us, leading the way. His shoulders were massive, almost brushing the shelves to either side of us.

There hadn't been a moment in my life that I had thought I would end up in a scenario like this. Being carried by a Cyclops in a hellish library after having one of the best orgasms of my life.

I held onto Andrew and peeked over his shoulder.

My blood turned to ice.

Staring at us from the end was a creature with tawny wings for arms, raptor claws for feet, and the face of a Gucci model. Somehow, the last part was the most disturbing. Its body was covered in feathers, and there was a rabid look in its eyes.

It was a harpy.

"Andrew," I whispered.

"I know," he huffed, his pace quickening.

Adam seemed to know too. Our pace turned from a brisk walk to a light jog. Their footsteps lost stealth, turning into heavy pounds.

I continued to stare at the creature as it stalked us, following. It grinned at me and opened its mouth, letting out a terrifying screech.

Andrew cursed as we shot out into a path that went down between hundreds of rows. He took off running, and I buried my face into the crook of his neck.

I was terrified and would admit it to anyone.

"Grab the human!"

Andrew was suddenly shoved as a body slammed into the both of us. We hit the ground, and I rolled from his grip.

"Adam!" Andrew yelled.

I scrambled to my feet, looking around wildly. Adam was moving towards me when wings suddenly hugged my entire body.

"Human—"

Two burly hands ripped the wings apart, revealing none other than Adam. His face was twisted in rage, his eye burning with an intensity that made me squeal.

The harpy screeched louder than a stereo at a frat party, and I was yanked free. Adam shoved the creature back, the two of them diving into a fistfight.

To my right, Adam was pummeling the harpy against one of the shelves. To my left, Andrew was battling the harpy that had tackled us.

That left me defenseless, which I became painfully aware of the moment I decided to look up.

Another harpy, one with phthalo blue feathers and the face of a god, was balanced on top of one of the shelves— staring right at me. He grinned, craning his neck like an owl.

"Lost, little human?"

All of the sounds around me were lost to the rush of my blood and the hammer of my heart. I swallowed, my chest swelling with panic.

His head cocked the opposite direction, unnatural in the way his neck twisted. *"You look like you'd make a delicious snack. How about you take a harpy mate instead of the two of them?"*

As if now was the time to flirt. I knew that I shouldn't, but I still laughed.

The laughter cut through the other noises, and I realized that all had gone silent.

I looked over at Adam and Andrew and realized that they had knocked the other harpies unconscious.

The two of them were immediately at my side, glaring up at the flirt.

He chortled, a weird sound gurgling from his throat. *"Your rejection will not be taken lightly. You will not make it out of here alive."*

I scoffed, glaring at him. "You're a fucking—"

Before I could finish my sentence, Adam scooped me up and ran. The harpy screeched and lifted from his perch, dive-bombing us like one of those birds that hung out in grocery store parking lots.

I heard a sickening snap but didn't bother to look back, knowing that Andrew was pummeling the creature into the pretty checkered floors.

I buried my face against Adam as he ran, focusing on his scent.

There were a few things that I had learned in my short time in the library. One, cyclopes were real. Two, harpies were real. Three, the world was a lot crazier than I had originally thought. And four...

I wanted to be in another room with Adam and Andrew.

I wanted them to touch me, to fuck me. I wanted the promise that Andrew had made to be fulfilled.

I had never felt this alive in my entire life. Even with the looming danger, the crazy dragon, and the ridiculous curse— all I could think about was how good that orgasm had been. Giving Andrew the control had been...

What I'd always wanted. All the dark, dirty desires that thrived in my soul had been brought to the surface just by his touch. The idea of being touched by him, of being worshipped by Adam... Hell, even the idea of being in a threesome was completely exhilarating.

"I can't hear your thoughts, little dove, but I'd like to," Adam drawled, stepping into cool shadows.

His steps slowed as he moved down the row. I lifted my face, looking up at him.

"Are you scared?" he murmured.

"No," I whispered, heat rising in my cheeks. "No, I'm not scared at all, which is the scary thing."

"Even of all the monsters in this place? Of me? Of Andrew?' "

"No. I might be crazy, but I want both of you. I..." The heat became almost unbearable. My heart hammered in my chest, my blood pumping. I felt like I was in a confessional— if the priest was a massive cyclops with a violet eye.

How long would it take until that was me?

Adam came to another door and kicked it open, bringing me inside. It was yet another lost room, one that was filled with oddities. There was one window that allowed light to surround us. More shelves, more books, and then jars and baubles here and there.

Not one speck of dust covered any of it, which was unnerving in and of itself.

There was no desk this time, but there was a plush chair with a blanket folded in the seat. The floor was marble, aside from the rug at the center.

Adam slowly let me down, and I wobbled for a moment, gripping him. He made sure I was okay before offering me a smile.

"Are you certain you want this?" Andrew's voice speared the room.

I looked up to see him step in, closing the door softly behind him.

In the light, I could see that he had suffered some bruises and scratches. Nothing major, but still a blunt reminder that the three of us were fighting for our lives right now.

"Daphne," Adam murmured, cocking his head as he looked down at me.

Both of them were too damn hot to be monsters.

"I want both of you," I said hoarsely. "I... I don't know what the hell is wrong with me but, I need you. I need this. It's a hunger."

"We feel it too," Adam said softly, offering me a gentle smile.

In contrast, Andrew's face darkened. His green eye blinked, his gaze falling to the floor for a moment. His muscles were still teeming with energy left over from the adrenaline, and I could see that he was fighting himself.

"You promised," I challenged, crossing my arms.

There was a moment of silence, and I realized that I had really just thrown the gauntlet down.

Adam grinned, stepping past me. His hand came to rest on my shoulder for a moment. "You've done it now, little dove."

"Come here, Daphne," Andrew said, looking down at me.

The moment his gaze fell on me, my stomach burst with butterflies. I felt my breath leave me as if I had been punched, the feeling of anticipation melting into something entirely more forbidden. Something that I had been told over and over growing up I shouldn't feel.

Lust.

Not the Hallmark kind.

The kind that you read about in the dirtiest of romance books. The kind that you found in the corners of the internet. My pussy gave a light flutter, my words dying on my tongue.

"Daphne," he said again, his voice a lot deeper. A lot rougher. "*Come. Here.*"

CHAPTER SIX
PROMISES

Andrew

All of her resistance melted beneath my words. Her body snapped forward, closing the gap between us. The air sizzled as if we were in the center of a storm, the taste of desire stinging my tongue.

I would have her. I would cherish her just like Adam, but I would show it in a *very* different way.

We had been waiting for her for so long. She didn't know. She didn't realize how important she was to the two of us.

She was more than just freedom. She would break the bonds that had tied us to this cursed library and be the guiding light to a life that all three of us could share.

Fate might have been cruel sometimes, but fate was also purposeful. The little human woman had stumbled into our world, crashing it like a bright star.

I wouldn't let her get away.

Daphne closed the gap between us, and I met her obedience by tipping her chin up and forcing her to meet my gaze. I enjoyed the flicker there and how it wasn't fear staring back at me.

It was pure lust.

She *did* want this.

I would give her everything she could dream of and more. The thirst to breed her was becoming more and more pressing with every moment that passed. I wanted to fill her with my seed, with Adam's seed. Hell, I wanted to fuck him while he was buried deep inside of her womb.

My cock hardened in my pants, and I gripped her face.

"Daphne," I murmured, stroking her soft skin. She smelled delicious, and I couldn't help the hunger I felt in being this close to her.

It was a very ancient desire and one I would never act on, but I found it interesting that she made me feel this way.

All of a sudden, I wasn't an ancient monster. I was a fresh, lustful cyclops pup— thirsting for something so fragile and so strong, something that was my salvation and my ending.

"Yes, Andrew?"

Hearing her say my name made me shiver. I licked my lips, leaning down to whisper in her ear. "Can you be a good girl for me?"

"Yes," she wheezed, letting out the smallest whimper.

I leaned in closer so that I could take her earlobe between my teeth, giving her a gentle bite.

I expected a yelp, but what I got was a groan. Her hand shot up, curling in my shirt. Her little fingers wound around the fabric, pulling it taut.

I looked up to see Adam. He was sitting in the chair, his cock out and his hand already stroking.

"Undress yourself for us," I said, drawing back from her. "I want to see all of you again. Every curve, every beautiful part of you."

Her skin blushed again. She froze for a moment, and then I watched all of her shyness peel away. It was like watching a flower bloom in the spring. Her eyes became heavy, her lips drawing into a sly smile. She looped her fingers under her shirt and then slowly drew it up and over her head, revealing her body. Her skin was soft, her curves even more so. My eye fell to her breasts and the way that they shimmied as she moved.

She licked her lips as she undid her bra. Adam grunted in appreciation, shifting so that he could stroke his cock even harder. Her gaze found him, falling to his cock.

"Fuck," she whispered.

"You're going to suck it, but not yet," I said, crossing my arms. "Did I tell you to stop?"

"No," she breathed, her lower lip quivering.

"Then you've just earned your first punishment."

"Punishment?" she echoed.

Adam snickered, enjoying her innocence. She was definitely an adult, and this wasn't her first time, but I knew damn well that no human man could ever match my abilities.

Once she rode us, she would never want a human again.

She unbuttoned the top of her pants and slid them down, kicking them to the side. Her thighs jiggled, and I fought another moan, biting into the side of my mouth.

I wanted to sink my teeth into every part of her.

"Underwear off, please."

Daphne stuck her tongue out, causing me to snort.

Adam blew out a breath. "Honey, if I were you, then my ass would have been bright red by now."

"Her ass is about to be," I muttered, glowering at her.

She snorted as if she didn't believe me.

"Come here," I commanded, my tone becoming darker and darker with every moment that passed.

She paused but then came to me.

"Turn around."

She did as I said, turning.

I paused for a moment, studying the curve of her ass.

I stepped closer, and she tensed as my cock brushed against her. Even through the clothing, I knew that she would be able to feel the hard outline perfectly.

The heat between us became an inferno. I leaned in, not touching her anywhere else on purpose.

"You will submit to me," I whispered. "You will submit to me. You will obey every command I give you. If it becomes too much, then you will say the word 'red'. This will immediately end what is being done. Do you understand?"

"Yes," she whispered.

Her entire body shivered.

I swept her hair to one side, exposing the curve of her neck. I pressed my lips there, tasting her as my mouth trailed all the way down to her delicate shoulder. I breathed her in, savoring her scent.

Fuck. I wanted to bury myself inside of her and watch her swell with my seed.

I watched Adam while doing this, enjoying the way his cock stiffened even more. His cock was at least 12 inches now and thick. I could see a bead of precum glistening in the golden light of the room.

"Watch him," I whispered. "I want you to see what this does to him."

Her breath hitched as my hand came around. I cupped her breasts, pinching one of her nipples. She cried out, her body arching. Her ass rubbed against my cock, her hands flying to grip my wrists.

"I'm going to make you cum once before I enter you to make sure you are wet enough for us. I don't have any of the proper help, so we must make sure your body is ready," I said. I continued to sprinkle kisses down her neck, enjoying her tremors.

"Please," she gasped.

"You're so eager," I murmured. "So eager to give yourself to a *monster*."

"Yes," she rasped. "*Yes.*"

"Tell me what you want."

"I want... I want this," she said, her hand sliding back to grip my cock.

My eyes fluttered, my body immediately reacting. Before she could truly grip my staff, I grabbed the back of her neck and pushed her forward—bending her at the waist. I had a perfect view of her ass now and the way my bulge fit between her cheeks.

"Stay like this," I grunted, gripping her hips.

I slid down behind her, kneeling so that I could get a good look at her pussy. She let out a moan as I ran a finger down one of the lips, her entire body shivering again.

"Fuck," she moaned. "Andrew..."

"He's just getting started, little dove," Adam chuckled.

"Adam," I said, "Come give her mouth something to do."

She started to raise her body, and I smacked her ass, the sound echoing through the room. Her skin immediately flushed, her cry following the clap.

"I told you not to move," I growled. "Move again, and your ass will pay the price. Only Adam may move you."

"Fuck," she gasped again.

I paused for a moment, watching the internal battle inside of her. She stiffened for a few moments before relaxing again. Accepting us.

I smiled to myself, tracing my finger across her pussy. She was already dripping, her muscles spasming from every touch.

I leaned to the side as Adam cupped her face, drawing her lips to his pulsing cock. She immediately opened her mouth, taking him.

His eye closed, his head tipping back as pleasure shot through him.

I hummed to myself, pleased to see *him* being pleased. He was my mate, and soon she would be too, so watching him this way made me feel content.

More than content. It made me feel euphoric.

I gave her a moment to adjust to him before licking her. Her entire body froze, her yelp drowned by Adam's quickening thrusts. The sound of his cock hitting her throat was music to my ears, and I wasn't surprised to hear her cry out as I buried my tongue deep inside of her.

I took a moment to rid myself of my pants, freeing my throbbing cock. I then wrapped my arm around the front of her thighs, offering her more support so she wouldn't topple over as the two of us had our way. I began to thrust my tongue in and out of her, rubbing her clit with my free hand.

She pulled off Adam's cock for a moment, gasping for air. "Fuck. Fuck— this is insane. Fuck!!"

Suddenly, I was lifting her entire body up into the air, swinging her around so that her legs sat over my shoulders and her pussy was a feast for my mouth. Adam came up behind her, offering her more support so that if she fell back, she would never hit the floor. I felt his hard cock brush against mine and moaned as one of his hands held ours together, stroking the shafts.

Daphne came, her entire body arching. Her fingers dug into my hair, gripping me as she cried out. Her cream spilled onto my tongue, her body shivering.

I reached up, slowly shifting her body down. Her legs wrapped around my hips, her head falling against my shoulder with heavy pants.

"Fuck," she whispered hoarsely.

I chuckled, "Just had to get you wet, lass. Now, who do you want first? I think Adam has been patient, no?"

Adam's breath left him, his eyes glistening with appreciation.

Daphne nodded, looking from me and then to him. She gave him a shy smile, her body flushing with heat.

I lifted her again with ease, turning her around so that her back pressed against my chest. She let out a nervous laugh, "You pick me up like I'm nothing."

Adam smiled at her, leaning forward to touch her face. "That's because you're our little dove," he chuckled, brushing his mouth against hers.

She let out a moan, melting into him. I watched them, my pulse picking up. Her legs wrapped around his hips, and he leaned in, kissing her neck, her shoulder, down to her breasts. Her head fell back, pressing against me.

Fuck.

"Adam," I whispered hoarsely, my cock pulsing.

He raised his violet eye, winking at me and smirking.

Bastard.

I was his Master, but he knew damn well what he was doing. I moaned and closed my eyes, sinking into our mating bond so I could feel everything that he felt. Every touch of her skin, the taste of her essence, the feeling of *us*.

"Please," she whispered, letting out a breathless pant. "I want to feel you inside of me."

Adam growled, "And you will."

He continued to trail kisses, watching me the entire time. I tightened my hold on her thighs, spreading her further.

"Are you going to fuck her or not?" I growled.

"I was waiting on your command," he teased.

I glowered at him. "Adam," I snarled, "Make our human scream."

CHAPTER SEVEN
ONE EYED SNAKE

D<small>APHNE</small>

I gasped, gripping Adam's shoulders as he pressed the tip of his cock into me. I moaned as he eased in, "Fuck, you're so big."

And he *was*. He wasn't even two inches in, and I already felt like I was being speared. He paused, drawing in a breath. "Look at me, little dove," he whispered.

I looked at him, deep into the violet of his eye. At the way the colors swirled from a deep royal purple to fresh lilac flecked with gold. I dug my fingers into his muscles as he eased in more, his moan rising.

"Fuck, she's tight, Master," he gasped.

"You'll fit," Andrew growled behind me.

Adam continued to push, leaning in to kiss me. I broke the kiss to cry out, arching against the two of them.

"It's so much," I cried.

"How does it feel?" Adam asked softly, lifting a finger to wipe away a tear that had escaped.

"Good, good," I whispered. "Like hell and heaven. *Fuck.*"

Adam grunted and then stopped, letting out a hiss. "It's too much," he said. "I'm not even halfway in."

Not even halfway?! I made a strangled noise, trying to process.

There was still the knot too.

"Hmmm," Andrew hummed, "The only solution is to use our magic, but we cannot without being mated to you."

"Then fucking mate me," I rasped, twisting my head to look up at him.

He shook his head, "I didn't want to rush this. What if we leave here and you don't want us?"

"Listen," I growled, "I already said that I wanted this, right? Mate me so you can do your magic thing and then— AHH!"

Andrew's teeth sank into my shoulder, pain interrupting my words. I gasped as heat immediately flushed through my body, followed by the soft tingling of something. It was like getting high, floating on clouds, opening up a present. I moaned, sinking into the feeling— something that really could only be described as magic.

It was like rope wrapping around my soul— but I wasn't being restrained. I was being protected, cared for, bound to a creature that would give his life for me...

Mated to a monster.

I opened my eyes and realized that Adam had also sunk his teeth into my other shoulder, although there wasn't a sharp pain. Instead, there was just more pleasure. My body burned, my breath turning to pants as every touch became wondrous.

Adam's cock pushed into me more, spreading me wide. I writhed against him as heat pulsed through me, crying out.

"Good girl," Andrew rasped, brushing kisses across my shoulder and neck. "Such a good girl. Can you take more, gorgeous?"

"Yes," I moaned. I wanted more, needed more. I wanted to know what it would feel like for his cock to be inside of me entirely, filling me up—*fuck*.

"No knot," Andrew said.

My blood continued to sing as Adam eased into me more until finally, he was fully inside of me aside from his knot.

"Are you ready, little mate?" Adam asked.

"Yes," I moaned, "Make me scream like he told you to."

Adam growled and pulled back before thrusting inside of me, all of the gentleness melting away. Andrew's grip on me tightened as Adam set a heavy pace, his massive hand sliding up to grip my neck. I sucked in a breath just as he squeezed, shocked by how good it felt to give complete control to both of them.

"Harder. She can take it," Andrew breathed out.

Adam obeyed, and I realized that at this point, I was basically singing. My lungs burned, tears slipping down my cheeks as wave after wave of pleasure began building until finally—

Adam let go of my neck, thrusting into me hard. I came, raking my fingers down his shoulders with a cry.

"Fuck," Adam gasped, "You're beautiful when you cum, little dove. I can feel you squeezing around me. *Gaea, help me.*"

He roared, letting out an inhuman sound just as he began to cum. I held onto him, floating on cloud nine as he filled me.

Adam moaned, raising his eye to look at me. His hair fell around him in wispy waves, his cheeks bright red. I studied him for a few moments and then grinned like an idiot.

I had a mate.

I had *two* mates.

"You liked that," Adam chuckled, brushing away a tear.

"I fucking loved that," I laughed.

Andrew chuckled and then surprised me by carrying me towards the chair. Adam was already grabbing the blanket to put on the floor.

Andrew let me down, and my knees immediately buckled, hitting the soft blanket. He knelt behind me, pushing my torso forward until my ass was up in the air.

He ran his hands along my body, and I shivered, biting my bottom lip.

I wanted him. *Needed* him.

"Please," I gasped.

"You're so good with your manners," he chuckled. His hands continued to rub circles on my ass cheeks, his palms rough. "Say it again, mate."

"Please," I whispered.

"*Again.*"

"Please!"

His palm struck my ass, the sound crackling through the room. I was met with sharp pain, but it melted into something more sinister. A feeling that dripped with lust, filling me with all types of dirty thoughts.

"I know what you want," he said softly. His hand slid down between my thighs, and I moaned. "I can hear your thoughts, your desires. You've never been commanded this way, have you?"

"Never," I squeaked.

"And now you're mated to two Cyclopes. Poor little human," he drawled, his finger rubbing my clit. "I think you'll find that you'll enjoy this predicament."

He moved behind me, and I felt the tip of his cock press against me. I shifted my hips back, sheathing myself on him just a little.

He hissed, his hands grabbing my hips. "That's cheating," he groaned.

I twisted my head so that I could look up at him, gasping, "Sometimes it feels good to cheat."

He chuckled and then buried himself to his knot inside of me. I cried out, my spine arching.

"Oh god, you're huge," I moaned.

Andrew laughed and began to fuck me, his cock even larger than Adam's. I screamed as he thrust over and over.

I wanted him to use me, to cum inside of me.

He leaned over me, his hands planting to either side of me and his chest against my back as he continued to rut into me.

"You feel like heaven," he groaned. "Fuck, angel. You're a miracle, and you don't even know it."

The magic in our mating bonds began to thrum, my blood singing. A shadow fell over me, and I realized that Adam was now kneeling in front of me. I looked up with a ragged cry as Andrew's knot pushed into me.

"Oh my god," I breathed. "Oh my god, I'm being stretched so fucking much. *Fuck.*"

Adam cupped my chin, "Does our mate feel good inside of you? Do you like his knot?"

"*Yes,*" I said, squeezing my eyes shut as another orgasm ripped through me.

Andrew groaned, pressing his forehead against my back. "*Gaea,* you do feel good. More than good."

His knot was now inside of me, and to my surprise, I felt it swell even more.

"What's it doing?" I gasped. "It's getting bigger."

"I'm about to cum," Andrew grunted, "And it's to make sure every drop stays inside of you."

I cried out, writhing beneath him and pressing my face into my forearms. It didn't hurt— in fact, it was the exact opposite. Every moment he was inside of me was another moment I was in excruciating rapture.

Andrew gave another thrust and then let out a savage growl. I gasped as his hot cum spilled inside me— and there was a lot of it. He held me to his body, his cock and knot pulsing.

Adam ran his fingers through my hair, and I looked up at him. He gave me a soft smile, a loving one.

I started to try and move, but Andrew groaned, and Adam stopped me. "Hold on, little dove, you have to stay still. His knot is still in you," Adam said gently.

"What does that mean?" I whispered.

Another wave of pleasure crashed through me, taking me by surprise. I came hard, my entire body tensing.

"Fuck!" I screamed.

His knot and cock continued to pulse, the feeling keeping me on edge. My mind became a puddle, barely coherent enough to ask any questions.

"Fuck... you feel so damn good," Andrew moaned.

"I keep cumming," I cried.

"That's part of this," Adam crooned gently. "Look up at me, little dove."

I did. He gave me a slow smile, eyes glimmering with something I couldn't quite place. "I'm so proud of you," he murmured. "Look at you, you did so well. You took his knot like such a good girl."

Fuck. I shivered, his words warming me. He continued to stroke my head lovingly, all while Andrew pressed kisses along my spine.

"Sorry, love," Andrew gasped, "You're stuck with me for at least an hour."

"AN HOUR?" I cried. I started to pull away, but Andrew and Adam both stopped me.

"Love, you're knotted to him. You won't be able to get up until his knot goes down," Adam explained carefully.

Andrew's arms came around me, and he lifted me gently, holding me to his chest as he laid back.

Now, I was sitting on top of him but still very much attached.

Adam knelt to the side of us, sweeping my face to the side to look into his eye again. "You're so beautiful," he murmured.

Fuck. Tears sprang to my eyes, surprising me.

This was crazy, but...

It was all I wanted.

"Don't cry, little dove," Adam sighed.

Andrew immediately sat up, his arms circling me again. "I'm sorry, Daphne, we should have explained more about this. I'm so—"

"No, it's okay," I whispered, twisting so I could look at him. "I think I'm in shock, but I'm also really happy. And you feel good inside of me, everything feels right. Although I'm worried about being in here for so long...."

"They won't find us in here," Adam assured me. "After we leave here, we should try to get past the dragon. If we can do that...then we can escape. And then we'll be free."

CHAPTER EIGHT
DRAGON

Our human mate handled everything better than I could have dreamed.

She was still seated on Andrew, her thighs spread and her head tipped back. Andrew was still lost in the bliss of being knotted to her, and I knew that it was torture to try and cut their pairing short.

A typical mating would last at least three hours, but we didn't want her to be scared. Also, I would worry since, as of right now— we were still trapped in the library labyrinth without the resources we needed.

Once we escaped, we would have an all-day knotting. One with me, one with him. Fuck. Maybe even he could knot me as I knotted her. It would be a glorious, cum filled mess. One that would allow us to worship her the way we both wanted.

"Lean back," Andrew commanded her gently. "You'll lay back on my chest. I'm going to try and free you. Adam will help."

Daphne moaned and nodded, leaning back. I sucked in a breath, my cock hardening at the sight. I had the perfect view of Andrew's knot spreading her pussy, both glistening from some of the cum that had leaked out.

I leaned in, running my fingertips over his knot.

"Fuck," Andrew gasped.

Both Daphne and Andrew moaned in unison.

I chuckled, leaning in further, blowing a breath on his balls.

"*Adam*," Andrew snarled. "I swear to Gaea, I will fuck you senseless if you tease me right now."

I snorted, "And I'd like that."

"*Adam*," Daphne moaned.

Grinning, I reached up and pressed my palm against her abdomen while running my fingers along where his knot rooted inside of her. Andrew hissed from the touch, his balls squeezing.

It took a few minutes of coaxing, but finally, his knot popped free. Cum immediately spilled out of Daphne as she rolled to the side, dripping from here.

"Hold on, little dove," I said, reaching for her.

She let out a moan but pried one eye open to look at me.

"Spread your legs so I can clean you up," I said, smirking.

Daphne shook her head, "Haven't you had enough of me?"

"Never," Andrew and I both said.

Andrew chuckled, sitting up with a groan. "Let him clean you. I can't have my seed dripping from you as we fight a dragon."

Daphne muttered a string of words that neither of us caught, but she spread her legs. I leaned down and splayed my hands over her thighs, enjoying how soft she was.

I couldn't think of a better meal.

I immediately began lapping everything up, my lips tingling from their mixed essences.

"Fuck," Andrew sighed next to me. "We need to get out of here so we can have more time for this. I'd like to fuck you while you eat her out," he growled.

Daphne cried out as my tongue touched her clit. "I thought you said you were cleaning me, not making me feel like this again."

"Mmm..." I looked up, drawing back for a moment to lick my lips. "Do you want me to stop, little dove?"

Her head shot up, and it took everything in me not to grin in satisfaction.

"If you stop now, then I will surely die," she said.

Andrew snorted. "Well, we can't have that, can we? Finish her up. I'm going to check on the library. After this, we will confront him. I'll be back in a few minutes."

"Okay," Daphne moaned, already lost to my tongue again.

My little human squirmed with every lick, her voice rising again. I loved watching her reactions to the pleasure, how she writhed like I was torturing her.

She was everything I could have ever dreamed of. Her taste was now mixed with Andrew's, which was even more enjoyable.

I pulled her body closer to me and then moved my mouth up to her body, to her lips. Her arms wound around my neck, our tongues clashing. She moaned, her voice melting into me.

I reached down between us as we kissed, stroking her clit. She immediately bowed up, her body arching beneath me. I drew back, letting out a breath as I watched her face.

"Torture," she gasped, her eyes squeezing shut.

I chuckled but didn't let up. I wanted to watch her come, even though her body was trembling. Her arms wound around me tighter, her nails digging into my skin as she cried out.

It was the most glorious thing to witness— watching her cum from my touch. She melted beneath me, her breaths turning into quiet pants.

I leaned back, licking my fingers. "You're beautiful, little dove. A miracle. I can't tell you how much you mean to us."

Daphne opened one eye, her expression softening. "You're really charming, you know that?"

I smiled and scooped her up, enjoying her squeal. "Let's get you dressed. One more fight, and then I hope we can escape."

The three of us were completely dressed and ready.

We huddled in a small circle, talking through our plan.

Andrew and I, ideally, didn't want to shift into our complete forms— as it was dangerous for Daphne.

"If we have to shift, you need to hide," Andrew said, giving her a hard look.

She started to protest, but he cut her off.

"Daphne, we're monsters. I can't guarantee that we will sense that it's you. I don't want to hurt you. I would never forgive myself."

She fell silent, scowling. "What do we have to do to get out of here?"

"Defeat the dragon," Andrew answered.

"By defeat, what do you mean...."

"Kill him if we must," I answered softly. "At the very least, make sure he can't stop us. Once we get to the end of the labyrinth, which is where he will be waiting, the exit will be right there. Once we tell you, you will make a run for it. We will make sure that you aren't eaten."

She shivered but nodded, her expression hardening. "What about the two of you?"

Andrew and I exchanged wary glances. "We will follow you when we can."

"And then after, we can go get a drink at one of the pubs," she mumbled, her cheeks flushing.

She wasn't happy with this plan, and quite frankly, neither was I.

What if she was hurt? What if one of us were? What if the three of us got separated?

Andrew's heavy hand settled on my shoulder, and he gave me a light squeeze. "All will be good, mate. The three of us will make it out of here."

We stared at each other for a beat, and then I nodded, giving Daphne a soft smile. "And then we'll go get that drink, love."

"Adam is going to carry you, and I'm going to lead the way. We'll get to the end of the maze, and then you'll hide while we confront the dragon... Okay?" Andrew asked her, cocking his head.

She nodded. "Okay. Let's do this. I'm ready to be out of this place, although I do wish I could explore it more."

I understood what she meant. This library was a treasure, after all, and there were many books I would miss.

But it would be worth it to be free again.

"Alright, come here," I said, reaching for her.

Daphne let me scoop her up, drawing a little chuckle from me. She was already starting to grow comfortable with us carrying her, which made me happy.

Andrew came up to the two of us, cupping both of our faces. She let out a whimper, her body melting against me. He leaned in and kissed her, and then me.

Fuck.

He knelt his forehead to mine for a moment, breathing in our scents. "I can't wait to start our new life," he whispered.

I swallowed hard and looked up at Daphne. Her eyes glistened, her cheeks flushed.

"Let's go slay the dragon."

CHAPTER NINE
ESCAPE

DAPHNE

I would have never found my way to the end of the maze.

Without Adam and Andrew, I would have surely been lost. I watched the last of the shelves approach us, and my stomach twisted as they both slowed.

This was it.

We were almost there, almost free.

I had walked into this maze a single college student, and I was leaving mated to two Cyclopes. My entire world had changed.

The sound of claws scraping echoed around us, sending a shiver up my spine. Adam held me tighter for a moment and then held his finger to his lips, reminding me to stay silent.

I gave him a nod. He slowly set me down, careful to make sure our movements were barely audible. He gripped my hand for a moment, and I knew that he was nervous.

Andrew was ahead of us, standing in the shadows as he peered out into the open.

I knew the dragon was there.

The maze, I realized, had led us back to the entrance of the library. I could see the desk if I squinted hard enough.

"The three of you might as well come out," the dragon's voice floated around us. *"I know you are here."*

Andrew straightened, and I fought a gasp as he stepped out of the maze. Adam gave my hand one more squeeze and then left, following him out.

"We need to talk," I heard Andrew say.

My heart began to pound in my chest. The dragon wanted them to stay, to guard his knowledge. The books in this library were a vast treasure, but...

"We can't stay here forever," Adam said.

I crept a little closer, trying to see them. I could see all three now, the dragon, Adam, and Andrew.

"Bring your human."

"No," Andrew growled. "She is our mate, and we will not put her in danger."

"Keeping her from me will put her in more danger. You've left her unprotected in the mouth of the maze. One flame from me would destroy her."

Fuck. He had a point.

You know that I speak the truth, human, the dragon's dark voice curled through my mind like wisps of smoke. *Come out.*

You'll hurt us, I responded back, my heart pounding.

I promise I won't kill you.

I heard Andrew and Adam continuing to argue, and I felt the seconds counting down.

The dragon was...was what? Giving us a chance? After trying to kill us a couple times.

A shuffle behind me had me spinning around, and I gasped, seeing the harpy bastard that had tried to snatch me up earlier.

Fuck, now I had no choice.

He started to move towards me, but I was already running, popping straight out of the mouth of the maze and back to where everything began.

Where I'd first met my Cyclopes mates.

Except for this time, the picture in the book I'd seen on the desk was...more real?

A magnificent crimson dragon hulked in front of Adam and Andrew, his massive wings stretching around him. He had a long neck and a long tail, scales that glistened in the soft lighting, and eyes that burned like massive gold coins.

His tongue flicked out, his teeth baring.

Adam and Andrew immediately jumped in front of me.

"God damn it," Andrew cursed.

It was the three of us against the dragon.

"What do you want?" I asked, staring directly at him. Fear iced my blood, but...

Maybe, we could talk our way out of this. Make a bargain with the scary book whore dragon.

"Because if you want librarians, you've got one. I just would need to be able to come and go as I please."

Andrew and Adam both hissed at me. "Daphne, no!" Andrew bellowed. "She will not be working for you!"

The dragon shifted his massive body, his muscles rippling as he moved closer. I was tugged behind my monster boyfriends, but I could still feel *him* looking at me.

"*I have two librarians. You are taking them.*"

"I'm freeing them because they've been your slaves. Not librarians," I snapped, my anger starting to simmer.

Andrew tried to block me, but I slipped between their two huge bodies, planting myself between them and a creature that could destroy me within a breath.

"You're a fucking coward," I said. Yep, my temper was definitely hitting now. "A fucking *cowardly* dragon. You want librarians to help you keep all this wonderful knowledge, but you just imprison monsters! It's insane! I'm their mate, and they should be able to have a life outside of this place! One with me!"

The dragon blinked heavily, and his head swung towards me, smoke curling out of his nostrils. Andrew's arms came around me, and he yanked me back, letting out a growl.

"You call them mate, and yet you've never seen them in their real form. Would they still call you mate if they lost control? If they became what they truly are?"

"Daphne, don't—"

"Yes. They would," I snapped, glaring at the beast.

A low chortle clinked in his throat. *"I'll make a deal with you, human. If they can keep themselves from devouring you, as is their true nature, then I will let the three of you leave without any harm or any curses."*

"Daphne," Adam wheezed next to me. "Daphne, don't do this."

"Deal," I said immediately.

I was determined to prove this snotty bastard wrong. I spun around, looking at Adam and Andrew.

Andrew's eye was burning with anger and a hint of fear. Adam already looked defeated.

"I'm your mate," I whispered. "I trust both of you."

"You shouldn't," Adam murmured, swallowing hard. "You shouldn't trust us. We're monsters."

"She already made the deal," the dragon snarled, shifting his heavy body.

I felt the air thrum around us, plucked by what could only be described as magic. Goosebumps rose over my skin, and I watched Adam and Andrew start to shift before my eyes.

They both took a step back, their low growls becoming a lot scarier than I'd heard before.

Fuck.

This could have possibly been the worst idea I'd ever had.

The dragon chuckled behind me. *"They won't know you once their darkness takes over. They will hunger for you, hunger to devour your pretty little bones. Good luck, human. I'll enjoy your screams from my treasury."*

I let out a gasp as the dragon lifted up, leaving me alone in the circle with my two Cyclopes mates.

Their clothing ripped now, their muscles bulging. I took a step back, too stunned to speak.

I had to remind them that I was theirs.

I watched Adam's turtleneck split, and he stumbled back, letting out a ferocious snarl. His bright eye blinked as his teeth sharpened. He grew and grew until I was faced with a fifteen-foot monster.

Andrew held on a few moments longer, giving me one dark look. *"Don't run. That will make us hunt you. Hide, if anything, Daphne. We will fight our inner beasts."*

Adam released an ear-shattering scream, one that tore straight into my heart. I listened to Andrew and didn't run, but I moved to the desk, slipping beneath it as Andrew began to shift too.

I heard his yells, his enraged growls.

My heart pounded in my chest, the mate marks stinging on my shoulder. I could feel their pain, and it hurt me too. Their hunger was something that would be almost impossible to control.

But I had to trust that they'd find a way.

Silence filled the library, and I curled up into a ball, listening intently.

"Human," an unrecognizable voice spoke. *"Must eat."*

A heavy footstep. Heavy enough to make the desk rattle around me.

"Close," another voice spoke, deeper. *"Find. Devour."*

I squeezed my eyes shut, my thoughts rushing. I couldn't run even if I wanted to. I opened them, seeing the foyer to the entrance of the library. I stared at the heavy wooden door, the temptation staring back at me.

If I got to that door, I knew that I would lose them. If I left without them, I wouldn't get them back.

I could put everything behind me. Go find a nice young guy that could give me average sex and a normal life.

That didn't appeal to me. Not one bit.

I had to make them see me and defeat whatever monster was telling them to eat me.

Suddenly, the entire oak desk was lifted into the air. Two shadows fell over me, and I let out a squeak, looking up.

Holy fucking shit.

They were both naked, their clothes in shreds on the floor. They both towered above me, impossibly big. Their muscles now bulged with layers of skin, which had changed colors too. Now they were both a soft gray, contrasting greatly with their green and purple eye.

Andrew, and I knew it was him because he had a green eye still, threw the desk across the room. I winced as it crashed, the sound of wood splintering echoing around us.

Look at them. I should not have felt the way I did, but from this angle, I had a perfect view of their insanely massive cocks.

Before, they had been big. But this? This was different.

An idea started to form just as Adam started to reach for me. I got onto my knees and reached for his shaft, running my hand down the top.

He froze, letting out a snarl.

His cock began to harden, the length and thickness making me swallow hard. There was physically no way for me to take that thing, but maybe I could distract them...

Andrew immediately snatched me up, his one hand fitting around my torso. I fought the urge to scream as he lifted me into the air between them.

"Mate," I said urgently, trying to remind them. "I'm yours, Andrew! Remember me!"

"*Fear,*" he growled.

"Mate! I'm your mate. Look at me. I belong to you," I said quickly. My heart beat hard enough to fall out of my chest.

Adam let out another noise, one that made me want to cry, but instead, I just let out a breath.

Andrew breathed in my scent, his nostrils flaring. I watched in horror as his jaws parted, showing me the rows of teeth.

Fuck. I was really about to get eaten.

I squealed as his teeth dug into my clothing, tearing them away like strips of paper. My shirt fell apart, my bra straps snapping.

Of course, he'd start with the tits.

He let out a low growl, and I braced myself, accepting my fate.

But then, his tongue slid over me, the tip flicking over my nipples.

The mating bond on my shoulder burned even more, but not with pain.

With pleasure.

Adam let out a low grunt behind us. "*Remember,*" he growled.

"*Mate,*" Andrew snarled.

I gasped as he lifted me, giving Adam the chance to tear away the rest of my clothes. Then, I felt his tongue dart between my legs.

Oh, fuck. *Fuck, fuck, fuck.*

I couldn't help it. I let out a throaty moan, trying desperately to ignore the pulse in my pussy.

A dark chuckle rumbled through Andrew's chest, and his nostrils flared again, breathing in my scent.

"*Wet. Ours. Eat, in a different way.*"

Andrew continued to hold me up in the air like I was nothing, leaving my legs dangling. Before I had a chance to say anything, Adam came up behind us, and I felt his tongue touch me again.

"Fuck," I gasped, heat spearing my core.

His tongue began to move between my legs, stroking my pussy. I started to writhe but was bound by my Cyclops's fingers, held in place as my other mate drove me crazy.

"*Cum*," Andrew growled. "*For mates.*"

Did the dragon know this was what was going to happen? It was a funny thought, one that made me question whether or not he was actually evil...

I cried out as the tip of Adam's tongue pressed into me, spreading me wide.

Andrew's grip tightened enough to keep me from wriggling free. My moans echoed through the hush of the library, my cries growing louder. I found myself wishing I could take one of their cocks, even if it meant I would not live to see another day.

Adam gave one last thrust with his tongue, and my orgasm unfurled, overcoming me like a wave against the shore. My entire body seized, trembling with pleasure.

Andrew lifted me higher, and they both lapped at me, tasting my cum.

And then, they both began to shift.

I was left in a daze as I was slowly lowered to the floor, watching the two of them slowly turn back into the Cyclopes men that I knew.

Andrew let out a moan. "Fuck," he gasped, falling forward. I was swept up into his arms now, by Adam too.

The two of them cradled me, and Adam let out a soft cry.

"Little dove," he crooned. "That was..."

"Amazing," I whispered.

"Terrifying," they both said.

I let out a soft laugh. "I think it worked out."

Andrew shook his head. "Lucky little dove. Somehow we came to an understanding once we smelled you."

"Thank god because I thought I was about to get eaten. But, I did get eaten... just in a different way."

Adam snorted. "Little dove, I'll eat you any day."

"Are you free now?" I asked, raising my head.

Andrew and Adam shared a look, both hesitating.

"All we can do is see. We can try to walk out...."

"If we pass into the foyer, we will know," Andrew said. "But uh...our clothing...."

"Maybe I can text Catherine now," I whispered. "And ask her for clothing."

Adam nodded.

With that, the three of us got up. I grabbed my phone and my torn shirt, trying to slip on what I could that would cover something. I opened my phone, doing a little happy dance.

There was a signal now.

I sent Catherine a quick text and then looked around.

The dragon was gone, the desk was turned over, and at the center of the floor, there was a book. The same book I'd seen when I'd walked in. I went to it, picking it up to look at the spine.

Creatures of History and Their Curses.

I let out a laugh and then turned, tucking the book under my arm. "Alright, let's go before he comes back."

Farewell, human, a dark voice said.

Goodbye, dragon, I responded.

The three of us stood together for a moment, staring at the doorway. We then went to the foyer.

Adam and Andrew both stepped through.

We all let out an audible sigh, and tears sprang to my eyes.

"We did it," I whispered.

"We're free," Andrew said in shock. "We're free. All because of you."

The door to the library swung open, and Catherine popped in, giving all three of us a series of happy hugs. I listened to her talk, answering her questions as we changed into clothing.

Even as she chatted with us, all I could think about was one thing.

I had come to this library to find a book, and I'd found a new life. An adventure. One that was worth living, with two monstrous mates, a dragon, and books. I'd lived my own story, and this was just the beginning.

"Are you ready, little dove?"

I looked at Adam and Andrew and nodded, grinning. "Let's go get a drink."

The four of us left the library, stepping out into the crisp sunlight. It was as if no time had passed.

When I looked back, the door was gone.

"Shit," I whispered.

Catherine winked at me. "It'll come back. When it's needed. When someone's mate comes along. It's magic that way."

I started to ask more questions, but then I looked at Adam and Andrew.

The two of them stood together, simply staring up at the sky.

Joy filled me, and I went to them.

"Aye, it's as blue as I remembered," Andrew whispered.

Adam swept me into his arms, holding me and the book. "Our little human mate. Brave enough to face down an ancient dragon. I love you, little dove," he said.

I cupped his face, kissing him. Andrew pulled the two of us close, and I turned, kissing him too.

"I love you both. I had a moment where I thought I would run, but...I had to stay. I want this with both of you."

"I love you as well," Andrew said. "Both of you. More than life itself. But I can't wait to build one. Together."

"Together," we all agreed.

CHAPTER TEN
ONE YEAR LATER

DAPHNE

Looking back on how I met my monsters, I realized that maybe the great dragon had meant for us to happen. I wasn't sure, and I wasn't going to paint him as a hero, but sometimes I was left wondering if the curse was one meant to be broken.

At some point, the book that I had taken from the library had disappeared. I'd asked Catherine about it and had received a cryptic 'it went where it needed to go, more than likely'.

Which was a bummer because I never got to really read it.

But, regardless, I couldn't complain. I was beyond happy. We'd survived the maze, the dragon, and had found our happily ever after.

"You're thinking, little dove," Adam chuckled, drawing me into his arms.

The two of us were in a massive bed, enjoying the lazy Sunday morning. We'd flown out to my parents, who had immediately put the three of us up in the 'guest house' and were all meeting for mimosas in a couple hours.

Andrew came through the bedroom door, a massive blanket wrapped around his shoulders. He came carrying glasses of water, which, thank god— being tag teamed by two cyclopes made a girl thirsty.

"I think your parents were in shock," he grumbled.

I grinned like a fool, taking the water for Adam and me.

"Of course, they were," Adam chuckled. "They didn't expect their girl to end up with two mates. Any parent in their right mind would be worried, especially given our size."

Adam found the whole thing hilarious while Andrew was worried about winning over my parents.

"Oh my god," I laughed. "Andrew, you shouldn't worry. They'll support me no matter what. Plus, you already won over Pookie. She is the true head of the house."

"I think that dog is a demon, but I still like it," he said, crawling back into bed.

I giggled and drained my cup, then plopped back down between the two of them.

"Can you believe it's already been a year?" I asked.

"A good year," Adam said, setting the cups down and then turning over. He propped himself up on one elbow, looking at Andrew and me.

"A very good year. Although I'm still confused about how the Internet works. It comes from the sky, and it gives you access to all knowledge," Andrew said. "Do you know how much I've learned from the Wikipedia?"

"Do you think the dragon would stop cursing monsters if we gave him wifi?" Adam asked, laughing.

I snorted, shaking my head. "Who knows? I'm just glad the three of us are free."

Andrew hummed, and his hand slid up my thigh, resting on my stomach. "I'm ready for us to be on our honeymoon."

My pussy gave a tug, and I moaned.

We were one week out from our wedding, which meant only 8 days until the three of us were in our cabin in Fiji.

It turned out that Adam and Andrew had a shit ton of money, which we all agreed would go to big life things like buying a house big enough for the three of us.

Plus more.

He smirked, his hand sliding back down. "I'm looking forward to watching your belly swell," he murmured.

Adam groaned, "Fuck. Don't get us worked up again."

"You can just watch," Andrew teased.

I laughed, swatting his chest. "And we'd all like that."

"One more round and then we will try these fancy mimosas," Andrew said.

He made me squeal, lifting me. I laughed as I straddled his chest, looking down at him. Adam let out a soft moan, his hand already sliding down to his hardened cock.

There was no better way to start the day than to be taken by two monsters.

Thirsty for more monsters? Check out The Creature Cafe Series, starting with Little Slice of Hell.

ABOUT THE AUTHOR

Hello Creatures 🥰

My name is Clio Evans and I am so excited to introduce myself to you! I'm a lover of all things that go bump in the night 🌙, fancy peens 🍆, coffee ☕, and chocolate 😋

IF you had the chance to be matched with a monster- what kind would you choose?!

Let me know by joining me on FB and Instagram. I'm a sucker for werewolves to this day 🌙🐺

P.S. Join my Newsletter by clicking here! I won't spam you, but I will offer you fun rewards for being one of my monster loving creatures.

Clio's Creature Newsletter

🅰 amazon.com/Clio-Evans/e/B09FG93N8M

▐● patreon.com/clioevansauthor

♪ tiktok.com/@clioevansauthor

📷 instagram.com/clioevansauthor

f facebook.com/Clio-Evans-Author-107243805025580

DARKHEART

VIVIENNE HART

BLURB

ABOUT DARKHEART

Thanks to an unexpected inheritance, witch Annie Winslow has returned to Haven's Hollow for the first time in seven years. Once a beloved vacation locale, the town became nothing but a bad memory after Annie suffered her first heartbreak. Now stuck with a dilapidated manor and a foreclosure deadline, Annie must figure out how to rescue her family home from a greedy property developer, who just happens to be the man who broke her heart all those years ago.

Bound to Mabon Manor for centuries, gargoyle Lucien Lafitte wants nothing more than return home to France, and he needs Annie out of his way as he attempts to break the spell that ties him to the property. But when he discovers the developer's plans to demolish the manor—thereby killing Lucien in the process—he begrudgingly teams up with Annie to save the home they reluctantly share. Tension between the two soon flares into heat, but can they set aside their differences long enough to find the answers they need? Or will the clock run out before they can save everything that matters to them?

CHAPTER ONE

ANNIE

I fling open the living room's ratty velvet drapes, trying to get enough light to see what I'm working with. Unfortunately, the action unleashes a tsunami of dust that immediately attacks, sending me into a coughing and sneezing fit. Out of the corner of my eye, I spot a spider the size of a tealight scuttling away from the commotion and into a dark corner, where it will undoubtedly lurk, biding its time until it has a chance to murder me in my sleep.

I run a hand over my face and sigh.

What in Wicca has Aunt Celeste gotten me into?

With another cough, I make my way across the room and open the curtains on the other picture window, letting in a weak stream of light that reveals a billion dust motes fluttering in the air and window panes too filthy to comprehend.

I add to the mental shopping list I've been making since I got here: food, all the cleaning supplies, maybe an industrial dumpster. Or a bulldozer. For a split second, I consider enchanting the supplies I do have to tackle the work for me, à la The Sorcerer's Apprentice, but I discard the idea almost immediately. For one thing, it wouldn't be a good use of magic, and for another, I'm vaguely horrified at the idea—however unlikely—of being overrun by an army of militant mops.

Instead, I brush off my hands and head back outside to collect my bleach, my cats, and my suitcases. I have my work cut out for me.

Before I go to my car, I wander back to the enormous iron gates that guard the driveway and try to assess the outside of the home. It doesn't look any better than the brief peek I got of the interior. My house, the thing that's brought me back to this town after seven years away, is a hideous eyesore. Admittedly, until today I hadn't been inside since I was a kid, but it definitely didn't used to look like this from the outside. At least, I don't think it did. I remember it looking sort of spooky and elegant, not dilapidated.

Standing here, hands on hips, all I can see of my new inheritance is disaster. It's quite the welcome to Mabon Manor: my family's ancestral home, and as of two weeks ago, my new property. Great-aunt Celeste lived here when she was younger, but in the last ten years that Mom and I visited Haven's Hollow—before I banished myself from it—Celeste lived in town, in a sort of assisted-living, studio-apartment-complex for senior citizens. I always knew the house on the bluff belonged to her, but it was never really on my radar. Mom always rented one of the lakeside cottages for us when we came to town, and because no one actually lived in the manor, we stopped bothering to visit it when I was about nine.

It's clear to me now, though, that Celeste wasn't paying any attention to it either. It's foreboding and run down, a neo-gothic haunted house if ever there was one. There are turrets and roof pitches, with gargoyles and grotesques tucked in the various nooks along the eaves. Ivy is making a valiant effort to cover every wall, the rose beds are more thorn than flower, and from what I can see from here, the hedge maze in the back is a giant, overgrown nightmare.

Oof.

The winding driveway is as shabby as everything else, but at least there's still enough pavement left that I was able to park close to the house, so I can unload all the stuff I brought. With another sigh, I go to the car and drag in all my belongings, including three suitcases, various brooms and buckets, and two cranky Ragdoll kitties.

I open the carriers as soon as I'm finished bringing things inside, and the cats react just as I expect. Mr. Biscuit leaps on the old settee in the parlor, sending up more plumes of dust, and immediately gets to work kneading the ancient damask fabric. Purrsnickety, his much-grumpier twin sister, yowls and hides under an end table, glaring at me as only an irritated feline can.

"Yeah, yeah, I'm sorry," I tell her. "I know you aren't happy about spending several hours in the car, but I have a can of ocean whitefish with your name on it for dinner. To atone."

She just blinks at me and flicks her tail, which is about as close to forgiveness as she gets.

My watch beeps, reminding me that it's already 3:00PM. I need to head into town and at least pick up some food, and I want to do that before it gets too late. I quickly set up a litter box and put out water and kibble for their highnesses, then grab my keys and head down the winding drive from the bluff into the town proper.

ANNIE

Haven's Hollow.

A place almost as familiar to me as my mother's ancient Airstream. Maybe more, in some ways. I take a deep breath, enjoying the unusual crackle of the air as it wafts in the open window. This town is special, and I didn't realize how much I missed it until I returned.

Driving here brings back a flood of memories. Most of them good, though the bad ones are really bad, which is why I stayed away for so long. With a shake of my head, I banish the negative thoughts. Chad Alder doesn't deserve to occupy any space in my mind. I won't give him the satisfaction.

Instead, I pay attention to the view, trying to track the changes to Haven's Hollow.

It looks pretty much like I remember, though with some obvious updates. A quaint town tucked along a lake in the dip of the mountains, with cute shops and cobblestone alleys. Fun for tourists, pleasant for residents. A good place to take a vacation or raise a family. It's pretty, and the magic that naturally infuses the place feeds the witchy part of my soul.

I note the business names as I search for a parking place: Fur and Purr Veterinary Clinic—good to know—Silver Serpent Metaphysical Treasures, Outdoor Outfitters, McCray's Realty. I spy a small grocery market called Haven's Pantry on the corner and manage to find a parking place relatively close to it.

I lock the car and stroll down the sidewalk, planning to reacquaint myself with old businesses and learn the new ones before grabbing groceries, when a shout catches my attention.

"Annie? Annie Winslow?"

I glance up to see a tall figure with poker-straight posture barreling down on me. Moments later, I'm engulfed in a hug that smells like apple blossoms.

"Haven?" I say, voice muffled against her shoulder. "Is that you?"

She takes a step back, hands still on my shoulders, towering over six feet in her heels. "Annie! I haven't seen you in years. What are you doing back in Haven's Hollow? And why didn't you tell me you were coming?"

I grin as my teenage-era best friend comes into focus. Her white-blond hair is long and straight, tucked behind one ear so that the ever-so-slightly-pointed tip of it peeks out. Her ice blue eyes are still startling, but the expression on her face is one of warmth.

"Hi! I've missed you, you weirdo. What if it hadn't been me and you'd just assaulted some stranger?"

"Eh, I'm basically the town's Welcome Wagon. It would have been fine."

Naturally. Nothing ruffles her. "Anyway, I just got back," I say. "I inherited Mabon Manor."

"Of course!" Haven hooks an arm through mine and tows me down the street. "Make time for coffee," she orders. "You have to tell me everything."

Typical Haven Bishop behavior. A descendent of the town's founders, she is the most organized, efficient, natural-born leader I've ever encountered.

When she makes a decision, everyone else just falls in line. Honestly, I think she was born to be a military general.

She tugs me down a few doors to a place called Queen of Tarts; when she opens the door, a smell like heaven wafts up my nose. Vanilla, cinnamon, sugar, and something citrusy—lemon?—combine to make my mouth water.

"My god, it smells good in here," I mutter.

Haven nods. "Welcome to the best bakery and café in the world," she says. We take a booth in a corner, and a few moments later, a pretty waitress with wild, colorful hair and a bohemian-style dress strides up. Bracelets are stacked up and down her arms and she has multiple piercings in each ear and her left nostril.

"Hi, Haven," she says with a twinkly smile.

"Hey, Oaklyn," Haven says. "Meet my friend, Anya Winslow. Annie, this is Oaklyn Drake. Assistant manager here. Makes a key lime pie you would die for."

I shake hands with the waitress as Haven places our food order. "Two fritters. And a black coffee for me. Annie?"

"Just orange juice," I say. "After all these years, I still can't stomach coffee." OJ this late in the day is a little weird, but it sounds like it'll pair well with fritters.

Haven shakes her head conspiratorially at Oaklyn. "What self-respecting adult doesn't drink coffee?"

"Got me. I can't get through a day without it," the waitress says.

Oaklyn goes to retrieve our food and Haven leans back in her seat and grins at me. "I can't believe you're back."

"Yeah. I just got to town a few hours ago. I guess maybe you heard that Aunt Celeste passed away? I never really thought she would; can you believe she was 97?" I shake my head in wonder. "Anyway, she left me the manor, and between you and me, it's not in great shape."

As if that's a secret. Anybody who glances at the place could figure that out. It looks like if you sneezed hard enough, the whole thing would tumble down. "I came here to check it out and decide what on earth to do with that monstrosity. I'm not really sure I want it, and even if I do, I don't know if I can afford to keep it, especially considering the repairs it needs. Like possibly a full renovation. Which would take a long time. Which would mean staying here for months. Not too sure about that."

Haven rolls her eyes. "Give the place a chance. Don't let one bad smell ruin your nose."

"What the hell does that mean?" It seems Haven still has the occasional tendency to mix metaphors—or simply make them up to suit her point.

"It means Chad Alder is a dick and you shouldn't let him get to you. He's not worth it, and besides, it's been ages."

Ah, Haven. Like the true best friend she is, she knows me well, even after years apart. And she's never shied away from tough love. "I had this thought..." I trail off and she tilts her head at me.

"Spill it."

Oaklyn returns to drop off our drinks, and I wait until she's gone before continuing.

"Well," I say. "This might sound crazy, since I have no experience and don't even know if I want to stay here, but I was thinking maybe I could turn the house into a bed and breakfast. The income could help me pay off the repairs, and I think maybe it could do well? This is a tourist town, after all. Maybe people would want somewhere cute to stay?"

Haven lights up with a grin. "I love that idea! Keep this on the DL, but the town council has been looking for ways to increase tourism, and part of that is offering more lodgings, a project I am stuck overseeing." She rolls her eyes. "Anyway, Mabon Manor would be great for that! And selfishly, I'd love to have you around all the time. I've missed you, Annie. You should have come back sooner."

I reach out and give her hand a squeeze. "I've missed you too. I know shouldn't have stayed away as long as I did. It was stupid, but...well, you know what Chad did to me. It was a real mind-fuck and it's taken me this long to figure out that I was punishing myself and not him."

She squeezes my hand back. "I totally get that. Not that I have any time for men these days, or mind or body fucks of any kind. But I know he messed you up."

I take a sip of my juice, which tastes freshly squeezed. "You really think the B&B thing is a good idea? I'm not too sure. Maybe it's better to just sell the place and get on with things."

"I think it's a fantastic idea." She reaches into her bag and pulls out a card. "I have a reno of my own in the works, and this is my contractor. He does good work. Give him a call and at least get an estimate before you decide to turn tail again."

I stick my tongue out at her. She knows why I left seven years ago without a backward glance. But she might also have a point about not letting Chad chase me away from a town I used to love. I meant what I said: it was dumb to let him win, but I only figured that out recently.

"Thanks," I say, tucking the card into a pocket. "I don't know how I could even afford to renovate, but it's good to have options. I plan to head to the bank tomorrow to see if a loan is even feasible."

"Lauriel works there," Haven says. "I'll tell her to expect you."

At that moment, Oaklyn brings back our fritters, and I take an absent-minded bite, mind still on the mess that is my new home. But my focus is quickly shifted to the flaky pastry and apple-cinnamon sweetness in my mouth.

"Ohmygod," I mutter around a mouthful of decadence.

"I know," Haven says smugly. "Like I said, Oaklyn makes good stuff, including great pie when she takes a turn at the ovens. But the real secret is that the owner of this place is an incredible baker. She won't cop to it, but I'm positive she has some siren in her somewhere. There's no other explanation for how alluring her foods are. She has to be infusing them with magic, whether she means to or not. I can practically smell it." She sniffs her fritter before nodding and taking a big bite.

I'd actually believe that. No matter how many generations her family has been intermarrying with humans, or how diluted her blood is, the elf in Haven is strong. From the piercing features to the pointy ears to her devotion to the magical town her ancestors founded, it just runs through her. If anyone could smell magical shenanigans, it would be her, even if she is mostly human.

"Who is this magical baker?" I ask. "I might need to make her my new best friend."

Haven leans in conspiratorially, elbows on the table, totally unthreatened at the idea of losing her BFF status. "Her name is Libra Cartwright, and she's a bit of a mystery."

I raise an eyebrow at that. Nobody remains a mystery where Haven is concerned. She's a freaking bloodhound.

"Came to town a couple years ago, opened the best bakery on the planet, and barely talks to anyone other than Oaklyn and the other employees. Keeps to herself, exercises a lot, rides a motorcycle. An interesting mix of tough-girl exterior and like...I dunno, somebody's grandma." Haven shrugs her slim shoulders.

"Wait until you try her applesauce donuts. And her pumpkin bread should be a sin, but she only makes it in the fall, so you have to stick around if you want to experience that particular mouthgasm."

I'm a sucker for all things pumpkin, and she knows it. She's dangling it like a carrot to make me stay and it might work. If I were a horse, anyway. I'm not a particular fan of carrots, but the metaphor stands. Good pumpkin bread is worth a lot of hassle in my book. And it could be fun to celebrate Mabon at Mabon Manor—get the place all decked out for autumn. I could follow that up with a Samhain celebration. Hmm.

"So," Haven says, setting down her fritter. "Backtrack a minute. Celeste left you the manor, instead of your mom? What's that about?"

I cock an eyebrow at her. She knows my mother. "Of course. Aunt Celeste was ancient, but she wasn't senile. She knew better than to expect Mom to do anything with the property."

Haven grins. "How *is* your mom?"

I roll my eyes. "Same as ever. Last I heard, she was on a tropical cruise somewhere with her three boy toys in tow."

"Boy toys?"

I nod. "Mm-hmm. I think they're around our age. Don't get me wrong, she looks great for 54, but I think she's a little old to be gallivanting around the world with a stable of stallions."

"I don't know, I think she might be my role model." Haven waggles her brows and I snort.

"I can't think of two people with less in common than you and Linnaea Winslow."

"Don't count on it," Haven says. "You haven't seen me in seven years. Maybe I've changed."

"Sure. You're totally the type to shrug off all sense of responsibility, blow where the wind takes you, and dance naked under the moon as you assume 'the goddess will take care of all things.'" I put the last part in air quotes.

Haven chuckles. "Fine, you got me. I pay all my bills and never go anywhere. And as I mentioned, the mayor roped me into one hell of a town improvement project, because he knows I'm responsible, so I won't be hopping on a cruise ship anytime soon." She huffs a tiny sigh, the closest Haven ever really gets to complaining.

"The mayor, huh? Who exactly is that these days?" Her family has always run Haven's Hollow, so it's not as weird as it sounds that the mayor randomly assigned her some massive project. I have no doubt they're related.

"My cousin Griffin. He has some ideas about increased tourism that are actually pretty good. Stuff involving the lake."

"Ah. That makes sense." The lake is the lifeblood of Haven's Hollow, and the town is rife with lore about it. It's supposedly the source of the magic that drew so many of our ancestors here generations ago, and that still pulls magical folk here now and again. You don't see many pure elves or pixies or anything these days, but the stories say they used to live in the woods and mountains around the water.

Plenty of the residents here, while all primarily human, have a little something extra in their blood. It doesn't apply to my ancestors—the witches came here from Europe—but a large part of the population of Haven's Hollow has a tiny trace of magic in their backgrounds, no matter how faint, like the elf lineage in Haven. According to stories Celeste told me, there even used to be ceremonies honoring the town's magical ancestors, but those seem to have become a thing of the past. It's kind of a shame, because I bet that could be a tourist draw.

Anyway, I think the once had an official name—I'm sure Haven would know —but I've only ever heard it called Lake Eerie, a joke that stuck around long enough that everyone just calls it that now. It's fitting; there have been rumors for years that the lake is haunted. I've never seen ghosts there, but that doesn't mean anything. Eerie is huge, settled in the lap of the mountains and surrounded by a forest. Who knows what could lurk there?

"I live there now, you know," Haven says.

"At the lake?"

She nods. "I built a house there three years ago. I love this town, but there's something peaceful about the water that drew me to it. I treasure the quiet, foggy mornings. You have to come by. It's a pretty good house, if I do say so myself."

"Of course. I'd love to see it." I glance at my watch and realize that we've been lingering here way longer than I thought. "Crap. I have to go. I need to get groceries and get back to the manor and the cats before it gets dark."

"Sure. Just let me give you my number before you go." We swap phones and add ourselves to the other's contacts, then I skedaddle to the little corner market I saw earlier.

The sun is setting by the time I get back to the house, and it's dark once I have all the groceries put away. It's a miracle the refrigerator still works, but like everything else, it's covered in a blanket of dust and grime. I do my best to clean it, along with the countertops and sink, but I suspect it will ultimately have to be replaced. Which is fine; I prefer something more energy efficient anyway.

I collect the cats and make my first foray to the second story, where the bedrooms are. I don't relish the idea of sleeping in a pile of dirt, but fortunately I had the foresight to bring fresh linens and pillows with me. It won't help with a mite-filled mattress, but at least my body won't actually be touching it.

I examine the five bedrooms on the floor and select the one that seems cleanest, which also sports an enormous canopy bed, complete with fanciful carved posts and curtains all around. On one hand, that means that more dust could rain down on me from above. On the other, it fulfills all of my childhood princess fantasies.

I'll take my chances.

"All right, cats," I say. "Let's change these sheets and get this room as clean as we can for the night." Naturally, they ignore me. Biscuit goes to explore the closet and Snicket immediately hides under the bed.

I roll my eyes and strip off the old linens. Just as I'm about to fluff out the new mattress pad, I hear a huge thump above me.

"What the hell?" I freeze and listen closely; there are more faint sounds that seem to be coming from the attic. There's no way anyone could have broken into the top floor, because it's way too high up. We're talking four stories and a rickety exterior. It would be impossible. Which points to one thing.

Dammit.

I flop down on the bed with a dramatic sigh. It would seem the house doesn't just *look* haunted, it actually *is*.

"Well, cats. It looks like we have a ghost."

CHAPTER TWO

My family has a history with hauntings. It's as if the Winslows just won't let go of that last thread of existence or something. Maybe it's Celeste banging around up there, waiting to impart some useful knowledge to me. Like why she never sold this place when it was still worth something, or what the hell I should do with it now that it's mine.

I know a banishing spell or two, but I'm hoping it won't come to that. Maybe I can get the ghost to quiet down, or finish its final business and move on. Though honestly, I'm filthy and exhausted, and the last thing I want to deal with is an excitable ghost, even if it is certain to be some long-lost relative who's simply happy someone is living in the manor again. I was really looking forward to a shower and about twelve hours' worth of sleep.

I heave myself up, turn on my phone's flashlight, and head to the stairs. The lights are on for the first three floors, but I'm not sure what's happening with the attic. I think it has a separate breaker box that's turned off. Besides, it's a giant, cavernous space with lots of nooks and crannies, so I feel like the flashlight will be necessary.

As far as I remember from childhood, the home's layout is fairly typical. The main floor has the kitchen, the formal living and dining rooms, a family eating nook, and the parlor. The second floor is all bedrooms, while the third is a huge library and two studies that would essentially function as his-and-hers offices. Plus bathrooms scattered about. I've never been into the attic or the basement, though, and I wasn't planning on tackling those areas any time soon. But this ghost has forced my hand.

I clamber up two flights of stairs, armed with my phone, wondering what I'll find. True to form, it's basically a horror movie. The attic is dark and ominous, all creaky floorboards and rustling critters. I try the light switch, but as expected, nothing happens. I shine my meager light around the corners, but something is wrong. Ghosts emanate a faint luminescence; they don't glow, exactly, but that's the closest description. In this dark, I should be able to see a ghost perfectly well.

But there's nothing but shadow.

I continue swinging the phone around, and when I get to the large picture window that faces the back of the property, I see it. It illuminates in pieces: a talon here, a wing there. At least eight feet tall, enormous and terrifying.

It's no ghost, that's for damned sure.

There's a creature—a monster—in my attic.

Holy shit.

I shriek and stumble back toward the stairs, while a low, chilling voice shouts, "Trespasser! Stop!"

I ignore that with every bone in my body and flee down to the third floor, to the welcome light and dusty furnishings. But the thuds behind me tell me that my pursuer is close at hand. Almost without thinking, I summon my magic, ready to throw some sort of barrier in between us.

In a few seconds, the monster emerges and I get a closer look at it. Huge, with a pair of enormous leathery wings that must span fifteen feet when fully extended. Muscular chest and legs, limbs that end with talons, a tail swishing around in irritation. Its skin is an interesting blue-gray color and it has long hair with little braids woven in. His—it definitely seems male—face is interesting, with surprisingly human, patrician features. He has full lips, an aquiline nose, and solid black eyes, iris and all. His ears are even pointier than Haven's and he has a shallow cleft in his chin.

What the fuck is this thing and how did it get in my house?

"Don't come any closer!" I shout, hand lifted so I can cast at a moment's notice.

The monster simply stares at me, unperturbed by my warning. "Leave this place," it orders in a gravelly voice.

I take a deep breath; my heart is racing 400 miles an hour and I'm about one second away from hyperventilating. I thump a hand to my breastbone, trying to calm my speeding pulse. One shouldn't cast spells in a panic if it can be avoided.

"Who are you? What are you? Why...are you?" I ask in a stumbling rush.

He lowers a brow, his features turning stern, and unfurls his wings with a mighty flap, becoming ten times more terrifying, which is saying something. "I am Lucien Lafitte, gargoyle and protector of Mabon Manor!"

Say what now?

"Excuse me? The what?" I say, trying to process that.

He frowns, as though supremely irritated by my presence. "I am the house gargoyle."

Okay, what the fuck? Since when does Mabon Manor come with a gargoyle? How is this something Celeste failed to mention? *My house is equipped with a straight-up monster.* I was prepared for ghosts, but this is really pushing the limits of my sanity.

"I don't understand." I press a hand to my forehead.

"It's quite simple. I'm the property's guardian. It is my duty to banish interlopers such as yourself."

That gets my attention, and I rear back in a mix of terror and indignation. Exactly how would he banish me? Tear me apart with those claws? Fly me straight to hell, which is most likely where he came from? "Interloper? I own this place. You're the one who should leave."

He crosses giant arms across an equally giant chest. "Ridiculous. Celeste Winslow owns this property."

I summon more magic and stand my ground, ready to fight if I have to. Monster or not, hell beast or not, he's not about to tell me off. "Uh, hate to break it to you, buddy, but Aunt Celeste is dead. She left the manor to me."

"Nonsense. Celeste is a healthy young woman." There's something almost foreign about the way he speaks. Not an accent really, but more the cadence.

I snort. "What are you talking about, you lunatic? Celeste was 97."

"That can't be."

"I don't know what to tell you." I shrug. "Look, I don't know what year you think it is, or if you're crazy, or what, but you need to know two things. I own the house. And I'm a witch, so if you even think of hurting me, I'll enspell your ass before you can blink."

He pauses, a thoughtful look passing across his interesting face. "Celeste is dead? I suppose this is possible. It has been some years since I have seen Celeste, and it is so hard to keep track of time." He fixes his black-eyed gaze on me. "Who precisely are you? Do you have proof of ownership?"

"I'm Anya Winslow, and of course I do, not that I need to prove anything to you." I can't believe I'm talking a *freaking gargoyle*—that gargoyles are real, living creatures!—and Celeste never once bothered to tell me. My mind is reeling, and I'm struggling with what to say. How do you casually chat with a gargoyle who just chased you out of your attic? And more, how do you get him the hell out of your house?

"You're a Winslow?"

I nod and he takes a small step back, his posture relaxing. I finally notice his outfit, which is weirdly old-fashioned. He's wearing boots, black pants with leather lacing, and a loose white shirt open at the neck. Very pirate casual.

"If you are a Winslow, you have nothing to fear from me. I apologize if my presence startled you. No one informed me that a new owner had arrived. You will not need magic to defend yourself. I will not harm you."

Yeah, there seems to be a lack of informing going around. I take a deep breath, feeling a little better now that he's not looming at me. Still, I'd prefer that he not be here at all.

"You said you're the home's protector?" I ask, trying to process what he told me. He nods. "That's great and all, but I won't be needing your services.

There's nothing to protect me from but dust and dilapidation, and I can handle those. Thanks, but you're free to go."

He laughs, but it's a dry, humorless sound. "I haven't been free to go for centuries. I'm bound to this property whether I like it or not. Whether *you* like it or not. I live here and I always will." He looks down his nose at me. "If you intend to live here as well, I suppose we'll have to find a way to adapt to one another."

Super. That's just the news I was hoping for. Every minute I spend at Mabon Manor makes me want to leave this place and never come back. I definitely should sell the thing and run away.

I rub my temple at the spot where a headache has suddenly formed. "Where did you come from, anyway?" I mutter.

"France."

I roll my eyes. "That's not what I meant. Like, how did you get in the house? And what do you mean when you say you're bound to the property? It case it wasn't clear, Aunt Celeste never mentioned you to me, so I wasn't exactly expecting you to appear in the attic, all menacing and yelling and terrifying the shit out of me. I had no idea this place came with a roommate."

"I can see that. Once more, I apologize if my presence startled you. Truly, I mean you no harm. I only raised my voice because I thought you were a trespasser. I serve the Winslow family."

"What in the world does that mean?" Do I have some sort of gargoyle servant at my behest? Because that's just...weird.

"It's a long story," he says.

I gesture to the stairs. "Then let's go to the kitchen for some tea." I'd prefer wine, but I don't need to make this headache any worse. Maybe tea will at least calm me down and help me feel better. "You can tell me everything."

L UCIEN

I watch the new Winslow girl as she makes tea. She's nothing like Celeste, the last Winslow I knew. Celeste was rather prim, with short hair and a terse manner. This one is young and pretty, with long curls the color of dark honey, and wide blue eyes and freckles that lend an air of innocence to her appearance. But the way she faced me down upstairs suggests a certain amount of steel in her spine. She also strikes me as talkative. Not my favorite trait in a human. Not that I have many—humans are irritating.

She glances over her shoulder at me. "Want some? It's valerian root."

I shake my head. "No, *merci*."

She turns and leans back against the counter, arms folded across her chest. "Do you even drink tea? Or eat? I didn't know gargoyles were real before tonight, so I don't know much about your kind. I mean, obviously, the ones on buildings are technically real, but I meant, like, real living beings. I'm assuming there are more of you, right? Like a gargoyle species? Although, aren't you a grotesque rather than a gargoyle? Or do you have a water spout I haven't noticed?"

I blink at her chatter. "Ah," I say, fumbling in an uncharacteristic manner. I usually know exactly what to say, but then again, I'm rarely bombarded with so many questions at once. Further, I haven't spoken to anyone in...well, it must be decades at this point. I'm rather out of practice.

"I can eat if I choose to, but I'm fine at the moment. Yes, gargoyles are a species, though there aren't many of us here in North America. No, I do not have a spout—your architects simply got the name wrong."

"What do you mean?" She gives me a curious look, her blue eyes large and intrigued.

I sigh. "We creatures who inhabit the eaves and serve as protectors for families and buildings have always been gargoyles. But there was some confusion —in a translation, I suppose—that misnamed us as grotesques. We are all gargoyles, regardless of the rainspout. Someone may have found us grotesque in appearance and named us that as an insult. I neither know nor care."

"Huh." She nods. "That's interesting. I'd like to know more about gargoyle history. Where you all come from, how many of you there are, that kind of thing. Do you have families? Tribes? Clans? I have so many questions."

I frown. Is there no limit to her curiosity? "We are a private species. We prefer not to share our stories with those not of our kind."

"Um, okay." She wrinkles her nose. "Kinda rude, but whatever."

"I do not mean to be rude. It is simply our way."

The kettle whistles and she turns back to the stove to finish preparing her tea. "Anyway," she says. "What's the deal with you being...what did you say? Bound to the house?"

"Yes. How much do you know about the history of the manor? Or the Winslow family? Mary Winslow in particular."

She joins me at the table and blows on her tea. "Pretty much nothing. I didn't grow up around here, because my mom is the 'footloose and fancy-free' type. We moved around a lot. Until today, I hadn't set foot in this house in close to twenty years." She shrugs. "Can't say I'm much of a genealogy nerd."

"And Celeste never told you about me or the curse?"

She leans forward, eyebrows raised. "Curse? That's the first I've heard of it. Tell me everything!"

I sigh again. "It's not some romantic story. I was born in a small village in France, and I was initially affixed to the tiny cathedral there. When it was deconsecrated and torn down, the part of the building I was attached to was shipped here. Mary Winslow had purchased it for the home she was constructing. This was in 1796."

"You've been here since the beginning, then?"

I nod. "Yes. Once Mabon Manor was built, I officially became the protector of the home, and by default, the family within it. But I failed in my duties and was cursed as a result. It's my own poor luck that I happened to be watching over a family of witches."

"Wait, go back. You're a living being. How can you be physically attached to a building?"

"You truly know nothing about gargoyles?"

She shakes her head cheerfully. "Not a damn thing. Believe me, meeting you gave me the fright of my life. But now that you're not being all scary, I have to admit you're kind of fascinating. Tell me all the things."

"Well, while it's true that I am alive, I am only mobile when the sun is set. During the day, I am stone. This is true for all of my kind. When my clan assigned me to the cathedral, the builders affixed me in my stone state. I was able to move around at night, of course, but was bound to my post during the day. The same still holds true all these years later, but with this building instead."

"So you only 'come to life,' so to speak, at night?" She makes air quotes with her fingers.

I shrug. "That's one way of looking at it."

"So that's why I didn't run into you this afternoon while I was cleaning. You were literally out on the eaves, still as a statue." She giggles, as if this is a clever joke.

"I'm not a statue," I grumble. "I'm a gargoyle. It's very different. I wasn't carved from some lump of stone by a lowly human."

"Eh, tomato, tomahto." She absently waves a hand in the air. "I'm going to ignore the 'lowly' comment so you can continue the story about the curse."

"I have told you the story." Why is she so hungry for information? She knows the gist of what happened. Why is that not enough? Bah, humans.

She makes a face. "Not all of it, you haven't."

"What else do you want to know?"

"Uh, like every single detail! What happened, how you failed, why she cursed you, the details of the spell. All of it." She sips her tea and stares at me expectantly, her cornflower eyes unblinking.

"You're a chatty thing, aren't you?"

"I prefer gregarious. Or vivacious. Or just plain friendly." She points at me. "Now talk."

"We need to add demanding to that list of adjectives," I mutter. I do not know what to make of this girl. She is young and too energetic. Her presence here disrupts the peace to which I have grown accustomed.

"How long do you intend to stay at Mabon Manor?" I ask her.

She frowns and fiddles with her teacup. "I'm not sure. I need to talk to some people. I have this wild idea..." She trails off and I wait, but she doesn't continue the sentence.

"What is your idea?"

"Well, it's very expensive to maintain a home this size, especially one that needs this much work. If I'm going to renovate it and make it habitable, I'll need a lot more income than I have now. So I'm thinking I might turn it into a bed and breakfast. I could convert one of the studies on the third floor into my bedroom and use the rooms on the second floor for guests. I'm actually going to the bank tomorrow to see if I can get a loan. That will help me decide for sure what to do."

I lean back in horror. The idea of strangers constantly roaming about the house is unthinkable. Unfathomable. "You cannot."

She blinks at me. "What do you mean?"

"The house is for Winslows only. You cannot let a parade of strangers stay here."

"Uh, I can if I want to. I own the house, remember?"

"That may be, but I live here as well. Surely my opinion counts for some-thing in this matter?"

"Well, I have to admit, I hadn't planned on factoring in the opinion *of the house gargoyle*, since I had no idea you existed," she says, her tone thick with sarcasm. "But if you have a stash of money I can use to cover the cost of reno-vations, then sure, we can talk about it."

"I have no money," I protest. "No one has ever paid me for my work. It is an unappreciated...vocation."

"Well, if you can't contribute to the reno, I don't think you get a vote."

I inwardly shudder at the idea of workmen swarming around the house, updating it into some soulless modern dwelling. "Why must you renovate? What is wrong with the house as it is?"

She laughs. "Have you seen this place? Like really looked at it? Everything is covered in six inches of dirt. The draperies are moth-eaten, the carpets are shabby, the furniture is old and lumpy. There are cracks in the walls and ceilings, shingles are missing from the roof, and the grounds have gone feral. The electricity is ancient and wonky, which means the utility bills must be a nightmare. The plumbing clunks and clanks. And that's just the beginning. *Everything* needs to be cleaned, updated, and upgraded."

"But the manor is beautiful," I protest.

"It is, and I don't want to change that. I'm not talking about destroying the character of the house. I love me a neo-gothic mansion. But it needs work."

I look around, trying to see what she sees, but all I can see is the place I've called home for more than 200 years. I can't imagine altering it.

"No," I say, and she rolls her eyes.

"We can come back to this later. You're supposed to be telling me about the curse," she prompts.

Merde. Humans have not become less irritating in the last few decades. "Very well. As I said, I was shipped here in the late 1700s when Mary Winslow built the house. She was a widow with two daughters. Alice was nine, and Abigail only two. People were a bit suspicious of a woman of means living in such a large home with only two children, but Mary lived a quiet life and the townspeople mostly left her alone.

"As soon as I was installed on the manor, I became its protector, a fact of which Mary was well aware. She was not simply enamored with French architecture. It turned out it was not a coincidence she had shipped me here; she wanted a gargoyle to look after the her and her daughters, and as she couldn't find one in North America, she simply sent for a European one.

"All went well for the first few years. Mary became known as a local healer, trading and her poultices and salves. Of course, she was a witch, but people didn't know that there was anything magical about her cures. Only that they were effective, and therefore she and the girls were tolerated, despite the way they kept to themselves in their huge, strange house."

"I sense a but coming," Anya says.

"Indeed," I murmur.

"Haven's Hollow may have been founded on magic, but during this time, most of the folk had gone and the population of the town was almost entirely human. Religion and closed-mindedness were the hallmarks of that era, and though the country's witch trials were more than a century past, people still looked on women like Mary with suspicion. The rumors that she and Alice —and to a lesser extent, Abigail—were witches simply couldn't be quelled, though Mary didn't do much to stop them. Mary was a good woman and a strong witch, but she was also too proud for her own good. If she'd been more subtle, tried harder to blend in with the others, things might have been different..."

"Something bad happened," she interjects.

I nod. "One night, the town came for her. Not a mob with pitchforks, but a handful of self-righteous men who couldn't let this woman be. They were fueled by hatred and ale, and they broke in, fully intending to kill the Winslows, justified in their actions by the rumors of witchcraft. Fortunately, they arrived under the cover of darkness, so I was active. I did what I could to intercede, but there were six of them against me and they were armed...

"In the end, no one ever saw those six men again. I made certain of that. But before I was able to stop them all, they managed to kill Alice. I was cornered in a room with Mary and Abigail at my back, defending Mary from men who would violate her before murdering her, but two broke away from the pack and strangled Alice before I could stop them. My only consolation was that they didn't bother to violate her before they murdered her."

"Oh, no," she gasps. "That's awful."

"Yes. Mary was heartbroken and, understandably, had no gratitude that she had survived. She would have been willing to die if it meant saving Alice, and she blamed me for not protecting her daughter. As punishment for my failure, Mary cursed me, forever binding me to the manor. In most cases, a gargoyle can leave its post if it reaches an accord with the property's owner. But that is not true for me. I am unable to leave these grounds unless I can rectify my mistake—not only save a daughter of Mary Winslow, but earn her forgiveness so that she chooses to set me free. An impossible task, given that poor Alice has been dead for centuries, as has Abigail. I will never be able to save Alice. I will never be able to leave. I will forever be at the mercy of the whims of the Winslows." I can't keep the bitterness out of my voice.

She fiddles absently with the ruby pendant around her neck. "I don't even know what to say. That's a hell of a tale. I'm sorry?"

I exhale slowly, trying to release the tension that built up as I recounted my past. "That's enough for tonight," I say as I stand. "I'll be in the library if you need something. But I suggest you get some rest, Anya Winslow."

"My friends call me Annie."

"We may be bound, but we are not friends," I tell her. "*Bonne nuit*, Anya."

I turn and leave her to her tea. I have work to do.

CHAPTER THREE

Annie

Given my intense level of fatigue and the valerian root tea, I expected to sleep soundly. I was wrong. I spent the night tossing and turning, repeatedly waking up and wondering where I was. The old mattress was murder on my back, the cats were being space hogs, and Lucien's tale—and casual dismissal of me—haunted my thoughts. The snatches of sleep I did manage to catch were marred by weird, disturbing dreams.

Now it's 8:00 AM and I'm grumpy.

My plan is to go to the bank as soon as it opens and see what I can do about a loan or refinancing or whatever would be required to fund the reno. Maybe afterward I can pop over to Queen of Tarts and get a donut or something. Donuts make everything better.

I shower the best I can, given moldy tiles I don't want to touch and water pressure as strong as a sick kitten, then dress in my favorite outfit: my pleated magenta skirt, a simple white top with a black moto jacket over it, and a pair of black ankle boots I spent way too much money on.

I let my waves air dry and put on enough makeup to be tasteful but not over-done, then add a pair of simple earrings that complement the necklace I never take off. I'm pretty pleased with the overall effect; I'd give me a loan if I worked at the bank.

I kiss the cats goodbye and head out. I can't help but peek around the back of the house before I leave; sure enough, a huge stone gargoyle hunches under the pitch of the roof, overlooking the mess of the hedge maze. It's crazy to think that grouchy thing was in my house last night, telling me stories of curses while I sipped tea.

Life is weird.

I head into town and find parking, then stroll down the sidewalk on Main Street. The First National Bank of Haven's Hollow is an elegant brick building with trailing purple and red flowers spilling out of symmetrical window boxes in the front. I take a deep breath and open the door, the heels of my boots clacking against the shining marble floor.

The first person I see is a pretty mixed-race woman with auburn hair and a trim gray suit, sitting at a polished mahogany desk. I recognize her immediately; she's one of Haven's many cousins and she and I got into trouble more than once when we were all teens.

"Lauriel," I say as I approach her desk.

She looks up and a smile blooms across her face. "Annie Winslow! I heard you were back in town! Haven said to expect you. How are you?"

I grin back. "I'm doing all right. How about you?"

She waggles her left hand, where a diamond glints. "Got married three years ago and have twin babies at home. Life has never been better. Now let me guess why you're here—it's about Celeste and Mabon Manor, right?"

I nod and she points to the guest chair at her desk. "Have a seat." I do as instructed and she leans forward. "What exactly can I do for you?"

"Well," I say. "I guess you know I inherited the house when Celeste passed. But it's in bad shape. I need a loan so I can renovate everything. I'm actually thinking of turning it into a B&B. But even if I don't, I can't sell it in its current state. It has to be repaired."

She purses her lips. "I had a feeling you might say that. And sure, if you want to apply for a loan, we can do that. But first I need to make sure you're aware of the full situation Celeste left you with, because I'm not sure a loan will help."

My stomach drops. That doesn't sound good. "Okayyyy," I say, drawing out the word.

"Yeah." She nods. "When Haven called yesterday, I made a point of looking at the paperwork. The will, the deed, all that. And I have to tell you, it's a little strange."

"In what way?"

"Well, the good news is that the will is solid. You definitely inherited the manor. But it looks like Celeste refinanced the place decades ago and never kept up with the payments. It should have gone into foreclosure, but...it didn't."

"Wait, what? Are you sure?"

She nods. "Positive."

"How did that happen? Did the bank just overlook the lack of payments?" Is that even possible?

Lauriel shrugs. "I doubt it. And it gets weirder. The interest has been piling up all these years, on top of the original loan. It's a mystery how she managed to avoid making payments, though I have my suspicions. But the point is, now that ownership has changed hands, the full loan amount is due in fourteen days. And Annie, it's nearly a hundred grand. If you can't pay it off within two weeks, the bank will foreclose and auction the property."

I lean back, stunned. "What? How is that not illegal? I've never heard of anything like this. It's literally insane."

She shrugs. "Neither have I. But this is the first time I've ever looked into the estate of a powerful—if not often practicing—witch. My gut tells me there was a spell in place to prevent Celeste from having to make payments, thereby allowing her to retain ownership. As to why she refinanced in the first place, or why she left you with the burden of only two weeks to make the payment, I have no idea. It's not a very kind thing to do, but maybe she had a reason?"

This is crazy. Why would Celeste have taken out a mortgage on a house she didn't live in? A house that the family has owned since day one? What could she have needed that money for? And why leave it to me without telling me about this bonkers caveat that can't possibly be legal? Why would she leave me a house she knew I was going to lose?

Maybe she was senile after all.

"You could talk to Jim Hampshire," Lauriel suggests. "He's the best lawyer in town and he might be able to find some loopholes. But if I'm right and there's a spell at play, it's probably air tight. Though you would know more about that kind of thing that I would."

I run a hand through my hair. "But Lauriel, I don't have a hundred thousand dollars."

She gives me a sympathetic smile. "I didn't think you did. And that's not even the worst part. The local property developer has his eye on the manor. He wants to knock down the house, rezone the land, and make a mixed-use development. Including Mini Golf on the Bluff and Grand Tetons, a very classy beer-and-wings chain." She rolls her eyes. "One of those skeezy places where the waitresses have to wear tiny uniforms and all the menu items are double entendres. The logo is a suggestive pair of mountains."

Ugh. What a horrible idea. "Well, I completely hate that."

"Speak of the devil." She points discreetly at the door. "Said property developer just walked in."

I glance over my shoulder and my heart sinks as I take in the sight of him. Blond hair, hazel eyes, dimples. Blue suit with a red tie. Evil dressed up in the bland good looks of a newscaster. My ex and the enemy of my life: Chad Alder.

I turn back to Lauriel. "No. NO."

She makes a sour face. "Unfortunately, yes. He's got the money and the connections to buy the place if it goes into foreclosure. I'm so sorry, Annie, but things don't look good."

"What the hell am I gonna do?"

"I wish I knew. But I can tell you this much. Miller Higgins, the bank president, doesn't have a drop of magic in him. He moved here from out of state a few years ago. He's golf buddies with Chad and wouldn't believe in an enspelled mortgage if you worked the magic in front of him. He's dying to sell to Chad, so you won't get any help here." She opens a drawer and slides a fat manila envelope across the desk. "These are copies of everything I could find on the house, the mortgage, the will, etc. Maybe you'll spot something useful."

I slip the envelope into my bag and stand up. "Thanks. I appreciate it."

"Sure thing. Let me know if there's anything else I can do."

I nod and move to get out of the bank before Chad spots me, but this is clearly not my day. I'm only feet from the door when he steps out of line and intercepts me.

"Annie Winslow?" He moves in for a hug and I deliberately drop my purse.

"Whoops!" I bend down to pick it up, avoiding his embrace. "Chad. I go by Anya now."

He grins, looking like nothing so much as a used-car salesman. "Nah, you'll always be

Annie to me. I can't believe you're back in town. I thought I'd never see you again!"

"One can dream," I mutter. "Look, I'm kind of in a hurry."

"Oh, come on. Surely you can spare a couple minutes for an old flame? We should get coffee and I can catch you up on all the things you've missed around here."

"I'm pretty caught up, and really, I need to go."

"Seriously, though, I'd like to talk to you. I'm planning on buying the Winslow property out on the bluff."

"I've heard."

He beams. "Yeah? Isn't it great? You should come by my office and I'll show you the plans. It's gonna be excellent."

I stare at him. "Yeah, it's awesome how you're trying to buy my family home out from under me and tear it down."

"Aw, come on, don't be like that. It's not like you care about the place. You're the one who ditched this town, remember?"

"Chad, what on earth makes you think you have any idea what I care about? You don't even know me."

"Sure I do," he says, his eyes twinkling. "I know you better than most, babe."

I make a face like I just sucked a lemon. "Ew. Never call me that again. My name is Anya. Not Annie, and sure as hell not babe. And since you can't seem to take a hint, let me spell this out for you. You don't know me, we're not friends, and I don't support your plan to ruin my life again. I'll be fighting you on this property development thing."

He shrugs, unperturbed. "It's your funeral. Miller showed me the terms of the loan. There's no way you can afford to pay it off."

I straighten my spine and glare at him. "You don't know anything about me or my finances. So you can kindly fuck right off." I march out the door and onto the sidewalk, out of his sight, and then lose the wind in my sails. I feel aimless, like a piece of driftwood caught in the current, just tugged wildly in all directions. I wander down to Queen of Tarts and text an SOS to Haven.

There's a new woman at the counter today, and she's freaking stunning. Long, dark hair, chocolate chip eyes, dusky skin. Pouty lips and cheekbones that could stab a man. Delicate tattoos of moons and stars—whole constellations and galaxies—decorate her fingers.

"Welcome to Queen of Tarts," she says in a perfectly husky voice. "What can I get for you?"

"Do you have anything that can save me from getting screwed by a complete asshole?"

Her dark eyebrows shoot up and she chuckles. "Not specifically, no. But I'd recommend the cherry Danish. It might help your mood."

"Sold. I'll take four."

"You got it." She slides them onto a plate and I take them to a corner booth to wait for Haven, who arrives a few minutes later.

"Hey, Libra," she calls to the beauty queen at the counter, who nods in response. That must be Libra Cartwright, the mysterious granny-biker siren who owns this place. Haven slides across from me, grabs a Danish, and takes a huge bite. "I'm starving," she mumbles. "What's going on?"

I recount everything that happened at the bank as Haven devours her share of the pastries. At one point she pauses me to get a giant cup of coffee, but otherwise, she's silent as I tell the tale.

"Wow. So what you're saying is Celeste totally fucked you over. And opened the door for Chad to do the same. Again."

"Chad," I mutter. "More like choad." Haven snickers and I consider what she said. "It sure looks like Celeste is screwing me with this, but why? Why would she set up the spell that way? It doesn't make sense."

"I don't know," Haven says, "but she must have had a reason."

I give her a look. "Can you think of any possible reason to do that to someone you like? A relative, no less?"

"Not off the top of my head, no. But like you said, Celeste wasn't senile. And she wasn't out to punish you, so there has to be a purpose for this. You just need to figure out what it is."

"Hell, maybe she was losing it. She was 97, after all."

"Not when she put all this in place. There's a reason," Haven says again.

"Come on, this is hopeless. I only have two weeks."

"Then why are you wasting time here? What happened to Celeste's things, by the way?"

I shrug. "Apparently, there wasn't much. All her furniture was rented with the condo, and as part of her will, she donated stuff like dishes, blankets, and clothes. I got her small jewelry collection, and her remaining personal effects were delivered to me in a box that I haven't opened yet."

Haven stares at me, her ice-blue eyes wide. "And your first thought at finding all this out wasn't to rush home and see what the hell is in that box?"

"I didn't have any thoughts other than I hate Chad Alder and I need sugar!"

"Well, you've had sugar. Now go home and figure out what Celeste was up to before Chad screws you again." She stands up. "I've gotta go, but trust me, you've got this. Call me later and tell me what you find out."

NNIE

As soon as I get home, I change into sweats and wind my hair up into a floppy topknot. Then I grab a boxcutter and tear into Celeste's box of personal effects. I check each item carefully, searching for any hint of a spell, or at least useful information. There's a packet of handwritten letters and postcards Celeste received from various friends; an ancient flip phone; a beautiful antique silver hairbrush and mirror; some heavy candlesticks; a little pile of hand-sewn doilies, hankies, and other small linens; discontinued perfume that smells like violets; and miscellaneous other old lady stuff. Nothing with even a whiff of magic, and no notebook helpfully labeled "This is why I decided to screw over my grand-niece."

I blow a loose strand of hair out of my eyes and sigh. Biscuit, who was sitting on top of the dresser, notices my distress and wanders over to bonk his head into me, so I give him scritches and cuddle him to my chest. "Can you think of any reason this could be happening?" I ask him.

He just blinks and purrs, which is weirdly comforting. If I had to, I could let the bank take this house and all its shabby furnishings. The cats and I would be just fine. Of course, that would mean letting Chad win, which is an infuriating idea. It's been years since we were together, but the anger has never really faded.

I was 16 when I met Chad, a handsome high school graduate with dreams of getting his MBA. Of course, I only visited Haven's Hollow in the summers and on holidays, but we kept in touch all year long, counting down the days until I'd be back and we could be together again. It went on like that for three years, years when I was convinced we'd get married and have babies. I was madly in love as only a teenager can be, but my naïve dreams all shattered when I was 19.

Naturally, I had been faithful to Chad all those months we were apart, and I assumed the same was true for him, even though he was off at college. After all, how many times had he told me he loved me? That I was beautiful, that he couldn't wait to see me again, et cetera, et cetera, barf?

Of course he was cheating on me. The entire time. With lots of other girls. Like, *lots*. Then, when I was crying my eyes out over my broken heart, I discovered his parting gift to me was an STD. One easily cured, thank heaven, but still. Seven years later, I'm still royally pissed about that. That and the fact that he was stealing from me the whole time. Five dollars here, a missing ten there. Just whatever small bills he could find in my purse or bedroom. Not a huge amount, but enough. He is a Grade A Dick. USDA Prime Asshole.

Because of him, Haven's Hollow became the place of my own personal tragedy, the place where he and his family still lived, and the place that I never wanted to return to.

That irritates me now. That I let him take this town from me. I could have been visiting Celeste and Haven and everyone else all these years, and instead, I was hiding from fucking Chad.

That's on me, I guess, but the rest of it is definitely his fault.

I suppose, in retrospect, there are worse things he could have done. But lying, cheating, stealing, and infecting me with his little, unfaithful dick have been enough to keep my fury fires burning all these years. And there is no way I'm letting him take my house and turn the property into some tacky restaurant where the servers have to carry shot glasses in their cleavage or something.

I'm taking back Haven's Hollow and I'm keeping Mabon Manor.

Somehow.

I heave myself up off the floor and head upstairs to the big library, which I've yet to explore. If there's useful paperwork about this whole thing, maybe I'll find it in there.

The library is like something out of a TV show...or a witch's mansion, I guess. Enormous, with wall-to-wall shelves, sliding ladders, and nooks and crannies. There are two big wooden study tables set up in the middle, complete with those traditional green banker's lamps. A stained-glass window depicting a dragon takes up the far wall, and cushy chairs are tucked in the corners.

Somehow, the dust and dirt that settled over the rest of the manor haven't touched this room, which means there's a spell in place to keep it clean—presumably to protect the books. I have no idea why the same spell wasn't applied to the rest of the house, but there are dozens of possibilities. Maybe the spell can only encompass one room, maybe it only works on books, maybe the witch who originally cast it was weak or crazy or only cared about the library.

All I know is, there must be a thousand volumes in here and I'm glad I don't have to clean and restore them. A handful are already out on one of the tables, lying open as though someone was just reading them. Lucien, I presume. I wander over and idly run my fingers over the spines, investigating the titles: *Basics of Cursework, Spells and Their Inverses, Garden Witchcraft, Working with Crystals.*

Ah. It seems Lucien has been doing research, trying to break Mary's curse. I know he wasn't anticipating me and we startled each other, but I didn't expect an hour of my presence to drive him to try to undo a spell that he's lived with for two centuries. Am I really that bad? He seemed kinda put out with me, but I didn't think it was enough to send him packing. Oh, well. If he wants to break the curse and leave, it's more than fine by me.

With a shrug, I walk along the perimeter of the room, investigating the shelves themselves. Unfortunately, there's no card catalog in here and it doesn't seem like anyone put good Mr. Dewey's system to use, so if there's a method of organization in place, I can't figure it out. There are books on everything. Spellcraft, of course, but also gardening, history, art, cookery, home repair, mysteries, romances, myths and legends, and loads more. I could spend a decade reading and not get through all the titles.

Given the situation, it seems like the best place to start is with the witchcraft books. Maybe, if I can figure out which spell Celeste used on this whole mortgage thing, I can figure out how to fix it. I grab *Spells and Their Inverses*, since it's already out, then plop into one of the armchairs and get to reading.

L UCIEN

The instant the sun sinks below the horizon, I rise from my crouch in the eaves and stretch, joints popping in relief. The joy that comes from moving after being frozen all day is impossible to describe. I extend my wings to really work out the kinks, then clamber through the attic window that has always served as my entrance into the manor.

I'm heading toward the library, as is my nightly routine, when I remember Anya. I pause, uncertain. Hopefully, she's out for the evening, or at least occupied so she won't interrupt my work. I can't imagine she would object to me reading the various books in the house, but then again, humans are fickle, temperamental things. With a frustrated sigh at the wrinkle her unwanted presence has caused, I continue down the stairs and into my favorite room in the house. It's dark, the shelves casting long shadows, and I light the lamps. It's not until I've turned on three of the four that a small noise alerts met to the fact I'm not alone.

I turn, tracking the sound, and find Anya sprawled in one of the chairs, snoring lightly. Her hair is pulled up in a messy bun, and her mouth is wide open with a tiny bit of drool in one corner. She's a pretty girl, but an ugly sleeper, and I can't keep the smile from tugging at my mouth at the silly picture she makes. A book has fallen to the floor near the chair, and I creep closer to look at it.

Spells and Their Inverses. One of the ones I've been reading. I frown; doesn't she know library etiquette? If someone has left their book open, they obviously intend to return to it. Do not touch. I pick it up and take it to the table farthest from her chair. I don't care if I wake her, but the longer she sleeps, the less opportunity she has to bother me.

I manage a solid thirty minutes of research before Anya snorts loudly and then gurgle-chokes herself awake. She sits up coughing and blinks, clearly confused about where she is.

"Good evening," I say.

Her gaze darts to me and she clears her throat. "Hi. I think I fell asleep."

I raise a brow. "Clearly."

She scrubs a hand across her eyes and brow, shoving fallen curls out of the way. "What time is it?"

"I have no idea. I don't wear a watch."

"Right." She shifts and pulls a rectangle out of her pocket. "8:37. Phew. I was afraid it was midnight or something." She stands and stretches, her shirt rising enough to expose a sliver of smooth skin. I refuse to notice it, or how attractive she actually is. It's simply been a long time since I've seen a lovely girl. That's all. I clear my throat, but she doesn't notice.

"I'm starving. I wonder if Haven's Hollow has a Thai restaurant?" She taps at her rectangle, and I realize it's some sort of phone. Hmm. Times have changed since I last interacted with humanity. I need to get caught up on a few things.

"Score! Soup and spring rolls, come to Mama." She taps the phone a few more times. "Are you hungry?" she asks.

I shake my head. "I have no real need for food. I can eat it if I choose to, but it seems an unnecessary mess to me. Besides, I'm working."

"I see that. Trying to break the curse, huh?"

"I can't see how my work is any of your business."

She rolls her eyes. "Technically, that's my book, buddy. And my library." Her gaze sharpens on me. "How long have you been reading these books?"

"I haven't harmed your precious property, if that's your concern."

"No, it's not, Mr. Cranky. Ugh, why are you so prickly? It was a simple question."

I stare at her, hoping to quell her, but she just stares back.

I sigh. "I'm not cranky, I'm busy. And you are interrupting me."

"Oh, no. The horror of having to have two whole conversations in what... ten years? Twenty? I can see how that would really hamper your progress."

"Sarcasm is the lowest form of communication."

"At least is counts as communicating! Which is something you could really work on," she says. "Anyway, I was asking because I'm curious how familiar you are with the contents, especially since there's no card catalog."

"I've been reading in here for decades. I'm quite familiar with the collection," I say.

"Excellent. Have you seen anything in the spell books about mortgages and deeds? Refinancing, bank loans, that kind of thing?"

I shake my head. "No. Most of these books are quite old. They tend to predate concepts like refinancing."

"Damn. I was afraid of that." She purses her full lips in annoyance.

"Why? Are you hoping to refinance the manor?"

"No, nothing like that. I don't think I could if I wanted to. I just need some info about a spell."

Curious. "What else can you tell me about it? With more detail, I might know where to look."

She shakes her head. "It's fine. Besides, my food will be here soon. I'm going downstairs to eat. You're welcome to come if you want—I ordered extra."

"Thank you," I say stiffly. "But as I said, I'm busy here."

"Suit yourself." She shrugs and leaves the room, and I can't help but wonder about the questions she asked. She told me it would be expensive to repair and maintain the house, but I can't see her trying to use magic to fix it. From what I understand, magic has rules that must be followed, consequences if it's misused. The witches I've known have mostly used it for healing and personal protection—things that help others or provide defense. Nothing that supports selfishness or laziness.

Plus, based on her litany of required updates, it would take a lot of power to get this place up and running, and I have no idea what kind of witch Anya is. She doesn't have the gravitas of Mary or Celeste, or even Rose, Celeste's mother, which makes me think she might lack their skills, but it's hard to tell with Americans, especially one as young and modern as she is. She's so chipper and friendly, even when I try to discourage it—I can't get a handle on her at all. On top of that, she's oddly likable, which makes me uncomfortable.

I can't afford to like her.

One thing is certain: I cannot allow her to turn the manor into a bed and breakfast—at least, not yet. The idea of strangers crawling all over the home like insects is enough to make me ill. I only have two choices—find what Mary Winslow stole from me two hundred years ago, or come up with a way to stop Anya Winslow in her tracks. Preferably both.

I cannot (and would not) harm her, of course, but there must be some way to change her plans. In time, I suppose I could get used to sharing the manor with her. But I will never adapt to sharing it with an endless stream of strangers, humans who would no doubt fear me and spread malicious rumors about my kind. It would force me to live in hiding, and my life is sad and empty enough as it is.

I'm still working—to no avail—when Anya returns an hour later.

"You really don't like me, huh?" she says.

"Hmmm?" Engrossed as I am in my research, I barely hear her.

"Well, I've been here a day and you're already desperately searching for a way to break the curse. Presumably so you can leave. Am I that bad to be around?"

"What?" I put down the book. "This has nothing to do with you."

"No?"

"Of course not. I've been researching ways to break the spell for years."

She sits across from me, a curious expression on her face. "Why? I mean, I understand that being cursed is no picnic, but as curses go, it doesn't sound so bad. You just have to live on and in this house, right? Is it so terrible?"

I shake my head in irritation. "You do not understand."

"Then explain it to me."

"I was taken from my home, against my will. Transported across an ocean. Forced to serve as protector to strangers in a strange land. And cursed so that I could never leave, never see my home or family again, doomed to always live in the shadow of my greatest failure."

She blows out a slow breath. "Okay, when you put it that way, it sounds bad. I'm sorry that happened to you. I didn't realize how unhappy you are. Of course, I barely know you, so it's understandable..."

I sigh. Her tendency to ramble is irritating. All I want is peace and quiet so I can continue searching for a counter spell.

"Well, if it helps, you might get your wish sooner than you think," she says.

I look at her sharply. Has she found a way to free me? "What do you mean?"

"It turns out Aunt Celeste worked something wonky with the deed and mortgage. I have two weeks...nope, make that thirteen days to come up with nearly a hundred thousand dollars, or else the house will be foreclosed. There's a property developer—who's a real dick, I might add—already lined up to buy the place. He plans to demolish the house. There's no way I can get the money in time, so as soon as the house is gone, *poof!* The curse is broken and you're free of my family forever."

"What?" I ask in horror. "The house will be demolished in less than two weeks?"

"Well, probably not. It would have to transfer ownership and stuff like that. But within a couple of months, yeah."

"We cannot let this happen!" I yell.

She blinks at me, no doubt startled by my uncharacteristic outburst. "I agree, but there's not much I can do about it. I don't have the money. And I have to say, this is not the reaction I expected from you. I thought you'd be happy to be free."

"What are you talking about?"

"Without the house to physically hold you here, you can go. Return to France or whatever."

"You don't understand. If the house is demolished, I will not be set free. I will die with it, forever bound to Mabon Manor in whatever form it takes. I will crumble into dust."

A horrified expression settles across her face. "Are you serious? You're bound so tightly to the house that if it goes, you go too?"

I nod.

"Well, hell, that's a problem. Unfortunately, probably not one I can use to extend the timeline on the payments. Imminent death of house gargoyle isn't a common or believable justification."

I lean back and run my hands across my face. Time is the one thing I've always had on my side. Now my future looks bleaker than ever.

Anya purses her lips and glances around the room. "You said you're familiar with these books, right?"

I nod. "Most of them. I haven't read them all, but I have a good idea of most of what's here. Of course, that doesn't count the books in the attic."

Her blue eyes widen. "There are more books?"

"Yes. Several trunksful, in fact. I haven't gotten to them yet, since they're in storage."

"All right. That complicates things a little bit, but I'm not ready to give up."

"I don't think we have much hope," I point out.

She grins. "Oh, Luc, there's always hope."

"Don't call me Luc," I grumble, but she just laughs.

"Don't worry, Luc. I have an idea."

NNIE

"Here's my proposal," I tell him.

He sighs, like he always does when I speak, but nods. "Yes?"

"Let's help each other with our problems. You help me look for a way to alter the spell

Celeste cast. And I'll try to help you break the curse and get home."

"You think you can find something in these books that I cannot?"

I shrug. "I don't know. But you have knowledge of the library and I know about spellcraft. As a witch, there could be things in the books that stand out to me, things you might not have noticed. And your familiarity with the books might help us find something on...I don't even know what to call it. Bank spells? Mortgage magic? Or like...anything that could help us save the house."

He's quiet for a moment, apparently considering my idea. But then he must come to the same conclusion I did—what choice do we really have?—and nods in that annoying stoic way of his.

"Very well. We shall work together."

"Good." I stick out a hand and he reluctantly shakes it.

"However," he says. "If we succeed in saving the manor, I will still protest your plans."

"If we find a way to break the spell Mary put on you, will it really matter? Won't you leave? Why would you care what I do if you're back in France?"

He considers that. "Perhaps we should make a second bargain. We will focus on saving the manor first. And once that is achieved, you agree not to open it to strangers until after my curse has been broken."

I nod. That seems fair. "Agreed. Is there anything else you can tell me about the curse? Any details at all? Who knows what might be important."

He rubs a hand absently over his chest. "I do not know the name of the spell she used. Only that she stole my heartstone."

I look at him curiously. "What's a heartstone?"

"It is...a part of me. My equivalent of a heart, you could say, but more than that. Also my soul, I guess you could say? Without it, I am incomplete. After she took it from me, Mary hid it somewhere, but I have searched the manor a hundred times and never found it. It must be here; it is the thing that physically connects me to Mabon Manor. But I cannot find it. In order to break the curse, we need both the correct spell and the heartstone, not to mention Alice's forgiveness. It must be returned to me before I can leave."

I think about that. "You know, the spell may not be the important factor here. It's hard to say for sure, but any general disenchantment might suffice. The heartstone might be the key to all this."

"You don't think there's a specific spell we need to find?"

"I'm not sure. Maybe. But if the spell were difficult to break, I don't know why Mary would have gone to the trouble of hiding your heartstone so well. It seems to me she took that precaution because the curse itself might be a simple one."

"Do you think you could break it?" Luc asks.

"Probably, if it's a simple disenchantment. Of course, I won't know for sure until we find the heartstone. And I don't have any idea where to look for that."

He looks at me helplessly. "I've been searching since the day Mary died. I have turned the manor upside down. Perhaps it is enchanted to be invisible."

"Ugh, maybe. That would make things harder. Let's put that on the back-burner for a second. Finding the heartstone won't matter if the house sells and you end up crumbling to dust, all because of that shithead Chad Alder."

"Who?"

I huff. "Chad Alder. Local property developer. And my ex. And a world-class dickbag."

"I take it he broke your heart?"

I roll my eyes. "Let's not be dramatic. I was young and didn't understand heartbreak. But yes, he hurt me in more ways than one."

Luc frowns, his handsome features turning grim. "Maybe the solution is to simply remove this Chad Alder from the equation. If he is not around to buy the property, the problem is solved. Besides, if he hurt you in the past, this would be a form of protecting you. That is my job."

I stare at him. "What exactly are you proposing?"

He shrugs in a remarkably elegant, Gallic gesture. "Whatever it takes to...*discourage* him." He flashes his fangs in an unsettling smile.

"You're not talking about killing him, are you?" I ask warily.

"Not if we don't have to. But no sense in taking it off the table if it is our only resort. It would be an efficient solution."

"Luc!" I shriek. "We are not killing anyone!"

"You humans," he says with a sniff. "So sensitive."

"You gargoyles," I counter. "So bloodthirsty."

"Not at all. We are simply not bound by human laws and sensibilities. We do what must be done. And stop calling me Luc."

"Look, if there's a way to get rid of Chad that doesn't involve *murder*, I'm all for it," I say. "But that doesn't necessarily fix the problem. Someone else could buy the property and tear everything down. We need to either adjust the timeline of Celeste's spell or find a way to raise a ton of money in a matter of days."

"Have it your way," he mutters.

"You know what?" I say, standing. "It's been a really long day and I'm tired. I'm going to bed, and I'm going to start fresh in the morning. Or maybe sleep in and plan to work through the night with you. I'm not sure. All I know is that I'll work better once I've had some sleep."

"*D'accord.* This sounds like a sensible course of action. Like something a gargoyle would do," he says pointedly. "*Bonne nuit,* Anya."

"Call me Annie," I say over my shoulder as I leave, mostly because I know it will annoy him. Something I'm very much starting to enjoy.

CHAPTER FOUR

Annie

I spend the next seven days cleaning and organizing, as well as casting "reveal" spells in each room in case Luc's invisible heartstone theory is correct. No success on that front. In the evenings, Luc and I pore through the library, searching for answers to both our problems. Although we're getting along well enough, settling into a companionable rhythm and verbally poking at each other, our success rate is crap. Since nothing is forthcoming in the library books, I decide to tackle the trunks before we run out of time.

After my morning cleaning binge and final "de-invisibilize" attempt, I shift my focus to getting some decent lighting in the attic. I finally track down the breaker box that controls it, which helps, and then I drag a couple of standing lamps up there as well. If Luc is right about there being trunks of books up here, one or both of us is going to need to go through them.

I dust my hands off on my jeans and wander over to the large window that Luc must use as an entrance and exit. I can't see him from here—he's perched above me—but from here I can take in the view he gets every day before he turns to stone. This spot provides an excellent view of the hedge maze; when it was in good shape, this was probably a cool shot, since it's essentially an aerial perspective. But the maze is tragic now, so overgrown that the lines are no longer clear. It's a shame, because it's one of the coolest features of the property. But probably not one I can keep.

The idea of getting the grounds in order is overwhelming; dealing with the house is intense enough. I should probably take out the maze entirely and put in something else. A formal garden? A tennis court? A pool?

Probably not a pool, since I wouldn't want to deal with the liability of having guests at the B&B drown or anything. But using the space for something visitors could enjoy might be a great idea. Something lower maintenance than a giant-ass hedge maze that would require almost daily trimming and shaping.

Ooh, maybe an herb garden. Then I could make my own tisanes for the guests. That could be fun. I give the maze one last look and then return to the trunks to see which ones have books in them.

"Holy crap," I mutter when I'm done with my survey. "Twelve? Twelve trunks of books? Dammit, Winslows. Why do we love reading so much?"

It's a lot to go through, but on the plus side, the more resources we have, the more likely we are to find a solution.

I'm still standing there, trying to figure out where to start, when Luc comes clambering in the window—evidently the sun set while I was goggling at all the freaking books. Watching him come in is like watching someone try to shove a sectional through a keyhole—even though it's a big picture window, he's so huge that he barely fits. His wings are folded back and he has to contort himself just to get inside. I bite my cheek to keep from laughing, but a few giggles escape and he frowns at me.

"What's so funny?

"Nothing! Definitely not you folding yourself into an origami gargoyle just to get inside. Why not just use the door?" I shake my head and point to the trunks. "I did an inventory. Twelve trunks of books."

His black eyes widen. "That many?"

"Yep. We need to find a way to divide and conquer, or else we'll never get through it all. Oh, by the way, I finished my reveal spells on the house today. You know, just in case your heartstone was magically concealed? No luck. I can keep trying, though. A more powerful spell with something to ground it might work better."

A startled expression drifts across his elegant features. For a monster, he actually is very good looking. And his body is banging.

"Really? You did that for me?"

"Of course. I said I would help."

"You did, I know. You have kept your word and I appreciate all you have done. Thank you." He looks puzzled. "I just...I am surprised that you, as a Winslow, would be willing to aid me."

"What does being a Winslow have to do with it?"

He mutters under his breath while refusing to meet my gaze. "Nothing."

Wait, is he being shy? Or coy? Who is this person, and where is the grouch I'm used to?

I tilt my head and stare at him, trying to figure out why he won't look at me. If he thinks a Winslow witch won't work with him... "Have you *never* asked for help with this before? From anyone?"

"No..." he trails off.

"You're telling me you've lived here with, what? Nine, maybe ten, generations of witches and it never occurred to you to ask any of them to help you break the curse?"

"Why would they help set me free?" he shouts in exasperation, throwing his taloned hands in the air. "Then they would lose my protection. Besides, it would be asking them to go against an ancestor's wishes. I would not ask them to do that. I wouldn't have asked it of you, either. But then you suggested our partnership."

I flail my own hand in the air, waving off his suggestion. "Piffle! I'd never even heard of Mary Winslow before you told me your story. What do I care if her curse is broken? I'm closer to you than her, so why wouldn't I try to help out? And no offense, but I don't need you to protect me, especially against your will."

He looks bemused, a small smile curving his generous lips. "You are an unusual girl, Anya Winslow."

"I'm not a girl, I'm a woman. Fully grown and independent." I arch a brow at him, daring him to contradict me. My life may be messy, but I have things under control. Mostly.

He nods. "I suppose that is true, even though you seem very young to me."

"Yes, well, twenty-seven *is* young compared to two-hundred-and-whatever, but I'm not a kid."

"I'm more than 400, but I take your point."

"Good! And I'm perfectly normal—you're just out of touch, ancient one."

"Is that so?" he says.

"Yes. Another thing. Would you please stop calling me Anya? I told you to call me Annie."

"*Oui*, but you also said that is what your friends call you."

I sigh and roll my eyes. "Is it so hard for you to imagine that we might be friends? We live in the same house and have the same goals. We're working together! We've been hanging out every night for nine days! Unless you dislike me for reasons you've yet to mention, I think it's okay to consider us pals, *mon ami*."

He looks like he's fighting back another smile, probably at my terrible French accent. "I apologize if I have offended you. It's only that I have never befriended a human before. Few of my kind have. Gargoyles do not tend to mingle with humans, even though we often occupy the same spaces. This relationship is new to me."

"I'm not offended. Just pointing out the obvious. And what's the deal with gargoyles not befriending humans? It hasn't been *that* hard."

"It just...isn't usually done."

I narrow my eyes at him. "Is this because gargoyles look down on humans? Consider us 'lesser,' even though your kind serves and protects mine?"

"I didn't say that," he protests.

"That doesn't mean you don't think it," I point out.

"It's not that I think humans are lesser. Just different. It's as if someone asked why you hadn't befriended more trees. I doubt the thought occurred to you."

I snort. "That is *not* the same and you know it. Trees aren't sentient. We're talking about two species who can cohabitate and communicate." Another thought occurs to me. "Can humans and gargoyles cross-breed? What would that even look like? Granted, I don't have a lot to go on, but based on you, gargoyles are huge. Could a human woman even carry a half-gargoyle baby?"

He looks horrified—again—which is basically his normal expression every time we talk. Or when I talk *at* him, which is mostly what we do. "That has never happened. Could never happen. I admit there may have been a few friendships over the years, but never relationships of that nature. I assure you."

I give him a long up-and-down look and waggle my eyebrows suggestively. "Why not? You're built all to hell and back and have a pretty face. We could give it a go."

His slate-blue skin actually turns a little pink as a blush washes over his face. "I...what...you..." he splutters and I burst out laughing.

"Luc, I'm teasing you. Don't get your knickers in a twist." Well, I'm *mostly* teasing. Though I am curious what it might be like. And it's been a while since I had any hands on me other than my own. I could use the fun.

"It's been many years since I've spent time with a human, and even then, it was only Celeste. She was more...reserved in her conversational choices."

I grin. "Times have changed, buddy. These days women earn money, make choices, and occasionally tell dirty jokes. You're gonna have to get used to it and work on not being offended by every little thing."

"I was not offended. Merely surprised," he says, looking as prim as a gothic governess.

I need to change the subject and stop considering the naughty things we might do together, if only he would relax for five minutes. "Speaking of things that might surprise you: I'm thinking of demolishing the hedge maze."

To my credit, he does look a little startled by the idea. "Why?"

I walk back to the picture window and he follows me. It's dark now, but there's enough moonlight to see the maze. "Look at it. It's a disaster. I can't even imagine how much work it would take to get it in shape. And then the maintenance...surely there's something better to do with that chunk of land."

"I suppose. But that maze has been here as long as the manor itself. Mary had it built. It's hard to imagine this place without it."

I look at him and grin, suddenly struck by an urge. "Let's go walk it."

"Now?"

"Why not?"

"It's dark and that maze has been abandoned for at least forty years, maybe more. You really want to stumble around in there?"

"We'll bring flashlights. Besides, it's not like we can go in the daytime. You're stone."

"That's true," he says. "But you could go without me."

"Well, that's no fun. It's something we should do together. I want to explore the maze at least once before I tear it down. Please? As my friend?"

He raises one of those patrician brows at me. "Hmm. I see you're already playing the friend card. Next you'll ask to borrow money."

I goggle at him. "Lucien Lafitte, did you just make a joke?"

He looks as startled as I am. "I suppose I did. Huh." He glances back out the window. "You know, I can fly. I can just take us to the center of the maze any time we want to go."

I stick my tongue out at him. "That's cheating and you know it. Come on, I really think we should do this." I stare out at the full moon, hanging low and fat in a dark sky. I don't know what this compulsion is, but I feel like if I don't go to the maze now, I'll always regret it.

"But the trunks," Luc says. "There are so many books up here, plus the ones in the library. We're pressed for time as it is. Why waste it on this ridiculous endeavor?"

I turn to him and reach for his shoulders, which I can barely touch, he's so tall. I meet his dark gaze and speak as seriously as I can. "Please, do this with me. I don't know why, but this is something that needs to happen, and it needs to happen now, under the full moon. Call it witch's intuition."

He gazes back for a moment and then lets out a slow breath. "All right. If you think it's important. As your friend, I will accompany you. But if we're doing this, you need a flashlight and I need a machete."

"Uh, do you *have* a machete?"

"I'm sure there's one in the garden shed," he says.

"Right. Of course. Because that's normal."

We head downstairs, grabbing two flashlights out of the utility closet—better safe than sorry—along the way. Despite Luc's pronouncement that he can see in the dark, I'm not taking any chances of tripping over a root and breaking an ankle. We head outside and Luc leads me around the back, where sure enough, there's a dilapidated shed that's sure to be infested with tarantulas or corpses or something awful.

"I'm not going in there," I say.

He rolls his eyes, looking surprisingly human for a moment. "Fine. Wait here."

He returns a few minutes later, rusty machete in hand. "Hopefully this isn't too dull to cut through a hedge."

I glance at his talons. "I suspect you could just tear your way through if you wanted to."

His eyebrows shoot up. "That had not occurred to me."

"You know," I say, "for someone who is essentially a monster, you're awfully benign."

"I'm not a monster!" he says, utterly indignant. "I'm simply a different species. No more monstrous than a tiger or a vulture."

I think about that. "Okay, that's a fair point. I apologize if I offended you. It's just that gargoyles are sort of monster lore for humans, and until a few days ago, I had no idea your species was real. Anyway, I didn't mean monster in a negative way."

"Is there any other way to take it?" He still sounds huffy.

"For what it's worth, I like monsters. Horror movies, haunted houses, spooky books—those have always been my jam. I love Halloween. As long as they aren't spiders, monsters are cool to me."

He looks a tiny bit mollified. "Well, I suppose that's good. Not that it matters, as I am *not* a monster."

"Okay, okay, comment withdrawn. Now can we get a move on?"

"What's wrong with spiders?" he asks as he leads me to the entrance of the maze.

"What's right with them? So many eyes and legs, and they scuttle. And lay egg sacs that erupt into thousands of baby spiders. And sometimes I see news reports of people who have spiders living in their ears, and I swear to everything that is holy, I would kill myself if that happened to me. I cannot think of a more horrifying thing in the world."

He glances over his shoulder at me, a "you are strange" expression on his face. "There are so many worse things in the world, though. Crime, murder, rape."

"Yes, thank you for filling me in on all the things women must fear. I'm aware of these horrors, you know. And for your information, I'm street savvy, I'm a witch, and I can defend myself. But not against spiders." I shudder. "They're so *scuttly*. And sneaky. Just waiting in the dark to crawl on your face and bite you. Ugh."

We reach what Luc insists in the entrance to the maze, although it could have fooled me. I guess, if you look closely, there's a spot where the hedge is slightly thinner. But it doesn't count as an opening.

"Have you been in the maze before?" I ask him.

He nods. "Not in a long time, though."

"How long?"

He shrugs. "More than a hundred years, I think. Back when Rose owned the manor. Celeste maintained the maze for a while once she took possession, but eventually she let it go to seed."

"Super. So you probably don't have the route memorized or anything."

"No, of course not. Besides, wouldn't you consider that cheating? It's not so different from flying to the center."

"Yeah, I know. I was just checking." I wish I knew why I felt so compelled to do this. Hacking through bushes in the dark is just dumb. But I can't back down now. Every fiber of my being insists that this is important.

He lifts the machete and chops his way through the opening; I follow close at his heels. He notices immediately.

"Are you frightened?" he asks.

"Not really. I know, intellectually, that this is just a hedge on my property and it's unlikely that anything will happen to me. Or at least it was unlikely, until I said that out loud and jinxed myself. But it's a little spooky, out here in the dark, all hemmed in. Sticking close to you makes me feel safer."

In the moonlight, I can see the surprise dance across his face. "Really?"

"Is that so strange? You're big and strong and technically my protector. I feel safe with

you."

"I am humbled and honored. And I must say...I am sorry that I was not more welcoming when you arrived. I was out of practice interacting with humans, and I lacked patience with you."

I wave that off. "It's fine. I sometimes have that effect on people when we first meet. I have a big personality and some people need to adjust to it. But everyone comes around eventually. I'm irresistible." I grin at him, and for the first time, he really grins back. His teeth are even and white, glinting in the moonlight. Even his fangs look nice in this lighting.

"You know, that might be true," he mumbles, then starts cutting at the hedge again before I can ask what that means.

It's hard work getting through the maze, and I'm not really doing anything other than struggling not to fall down. But despite the effort and the dull tool, Luc handles it admirably. He's as strong as about ten human men, muscles bulging, and doesn't seem to be sweating or out of breath. I've never been into brute force before, but there's something about watching him hack and slash that I enjoy. It's kind of hot.

Three hours—and many wrong turns—later, we finally make it to the center of the maze. It's a circular clearing with a statue in the center. Weirdly, this area is not overgrown at all. The circle is perfectly preserved, covered with soft grass that looks like it was just mowed. The statue in the center is polished marble, as pristine as the day it was carved. There's no hint of moss, lichen, or water damage anywhere on it.

"This is bizarre," I say.

Luc sets down the machete and stretches, while I ogle him discreetly. "What do you mean?"

"Why isn't this as messed up as the rest of the maze? There's not a blade of grass out of place. It's like someone came in here earlier today and tidied up."

He looks around, taking in the strange scene. "You're right. That is odd."

"More than just odd. Unnatural."

I walk over to the statue and squat down to read the inscription on its plinth. There are only two words. "Alice Winslow. Holy shit, is this her grave?"

"No," Luc says. "I'm certain of that. Mary gave her a witch's burial. She burned Alice on a pyre and scattered her ashes over the bluff."

"Then what is this? A creepy enspelled memorial?"

He shakes his head and shrugs. "I don't know. But now that you mention it..."

I stand and turn to him. "What?"

"There's an old map of the manor and grounds in one of the books. I never paid much attention to it, because I'm the last person who needs that information. I know where everything is. None of the Winslows I have known have ever mentioned this statue as being important. But this place was marked on the map with an X, as if it might have some significance. I don't know what, though."

I tilt an eyebrow at him. "What, like a treasure map?"

"What do you mean?"

"You know, like X marks the spot? Yarr mateys, thar be treasure here?"

"I have no idea what you're talking about," he says.

I shake my head. "How can someone your age be so out of touch? Especially when you dress like a pirate?"

"Pardon?" He looks baffled.

"Never mind," I mutter. "It's not important."

I step back a few paces and reexamine the scene in front of me. Perfectly preserved circle in the middle of an overgrown maze. A statue of Alice untouched by time. An old map that marks this spot. Could it be?

"Luc, are there any shovels in that garden shed?"

"*Certainement*. Why?"

"Could you fly out and get a couple? I think we need to do some digging."

"Sure." He unfurls his massive wings—honestly, they truly span at least 15 feet—and simply lifts into the air. He may be a grumpy gargoyle, but damn, he has an excellent body with some very handy skills.

He's back moments later with a pair of shovels. "Where are we digging? And why?"

I point to the base of the statue. "Right there. The spot that Alice is essentially watching over. If my hunch is right, Mary left something there."

CHAPTER FIVE

Lucien

This expedition is turning out to be more interesting than I'd anticipated. Then again, the whole evening has been unusual. The fact that Annie has been spellcasting to help me...it's hard to fathom. I never thought a Winslow witch would go out of her way for me.

That's why I initially decided to humor her with this maze trek. It seemed silly when we're so short on time, but she was so certain that we needed to do this that I felt obliged to help her. I must admit, over the past several days, I've grown accustomed to her spontaneity and sense of humor. For the first time in recent memory, I've actually had fun. She deserves the credit for that, and so I will help her, even though I have no idea what we're doing in the maze under a full moon.

I follow Annie's instructions and begin digging at the base of the statue, and to my surprise, she takes up her own shovel. I assumed she'd let me handle the physical labor, but she seems intent on digging up whatever might be buried here as quickly as possible. I suppose I must get used to her surprising me, as she keeps doing it.

With the two of us working, it doesn't take long. We find a long metal box buried about a meter underground, and I heave it out of the dirt. I attempt to open it, but despite my best effort, I cannot pry off the lid.

"It's locked," I tell her.

She narrows her eyes at it. "Not just locked. Magically sealed. I don't think there's any normal lock you couldn't break." She takes the box from me and waves her hand over it, whispering an incantation under her breath. The latch releases and she pops open the lid, revealing piles of yellowing paper.

"Oh my god," she says, examining them.

"What is that?"

"Savings bonds. Piles of them. Luc, these must be worth a fortune."

"Define 'a fortune.'"

She looks at me. "I don't know offhand, but a lot. Enough to pay off the mortgage and probably tackle the reno besides."

"Is there anything else in there?"

"There must be," she mutters, riffling through the box. "Mary didn't put these here."

She collects all the papers into a neat pile, revealing one final item: a dull, gray-blue stone the size of her fist with veins of silver running across its surface. What to her probably looks like a normal, if interesting, rock. But to me, it's everything. My breath catches as I stare at it.

"*Mon Dieu*," I whisper. "You found it."

She removes the item from the box and hands it to me. "This is your heartstone?"

I nod. "I can't believe it. I'd begun to think it was lost forever. It still needs to be reinserted into my body, but to even hold it after all these years..." A wave of sheer joy pours through me; I can't remember the last time I was this elated. Possibly never. All because of her. "Annie, thank you. *Merci beaucoup*. This is everything to me."

She closes the box and recasts the sealing spell. "We're saved. Both of us."

I nod, and then on impulse, lift her by the waist and twirl her around. She laughs, a bright, tinkling sound, and madness comes over me. I lean forward and plant a smacking kiss on her lips. She tastes like spun sugar and starlight. It's dizzying and delicious and I want to keep doing it for the rest of the year. The rest of the decade. Maybe the rest of forever. But I restrain myself.

After a moment, I set her back down and she blinks at me. "What was that for?"

I shrug. I can't really explain it to myself, either. A little more than a week ago, she was an annoying hindrance. Now she's Annie, my friend and savior, a vibrant woman who is the first human who has ever been willing to help me. A beautiful witch who smells like vanilla and apricots, who refused to be put off by my cold shoulder, who genuinely seems to like me, despite my faults. She's a miracle.

"Do it again," she says, and it's my turn to blink.

"What?"

"I want to see something," she says. "Kiss me again."

ANNIE

I'm staring at Luc in anticipation, taking in his dark eyes and full mouth, his elegant features, the confusion apparent in the tilt of his brows. When he kissed me, it was like my whole body ignited, a wildfire of passion jolting through me. I've never felt anything remotely like it.

I need to know if it will happen again.

Tentatively, he leans down and lightly presses his lips to mine. I grab the back of his head and pull him closer, deepening the kiss, the connection, sliding my tongue along the seam of his lips and tangling my fingers in all that long, dark hair. Bright heat sears through me once more, each nerve ending alive and dancing with excitement.

Luc parts his mouth and glides his tongue against mine, his rich taste flooding my senses. When he finally pulls back, he stares at me, his black gaze hypnotic.

"Whoa," I breathe. "That was unexpectedly...intense."

He releases a slow breath, like he's as caught off guard as I am. I stare back at him for another moment, lost in those eyes, and then I leap. I literally throw myself at him, trusting him to catch me, and fasten my mouth to his. He tastes like aged wine, dark and smoky, and when I nibble his lower lip, I feel his fingers flex against my ass where he grips me.

He growls, so deep in his chest I can feel the rumble, then tears his mouth from mine. The look in his eyes has gone feral, a Luc I've never seen.

"How far do you want this to go?" he asks, his voice fierce.

This is the moment. The moment I can back away, call things off, and celebrate what we found tonight. Or I can dive in and see what he's like unleashed; what all those muscles and unusual body parts will feel like against my skin.

I skim my tongue along my lips, still tasting him there. My body is on fire: nipples hard, wet heat pooling between my thighs, every muscle taut and quivering. There's no doubt about what I'm going to say.

"I want it all," I whisper, and it's like flipping a switch.

Gone is the cool, distant, aloof gargoyle. In his place is something molten, all heat and desire and dominance. He wraps my hair in his fist and pulls my head back, feasting on my neck, sucking and licking all the exposed flesh. He blows a hot breath in my ear, sending shivers through me, and then spins me around, pulling my back against his chest.

He points one talon and hooks it in the neckline of my shirt; with a yank, he tears all the way down the shirt and through my jeans. My close fall off in tatters, leaving me in nothing but a bra and thong. With another groan, he slides his hands between us and cups my ass again.

"Take off the rest," he commands, and I scramble out of my underwear.

He makes a satisfied sort of grunt and then slowly slides a hand around to the front, cupping my belly and then drifting lower.

"Are you wet for me?" he whispers, again blowing hot air into my ear.

Somehow, despite the fact that all we've done is kiss, I don't think I've ever been wetter. I swallow hard and manage to speak. "Why don't you find out for yourself?"

He chuckles and slips a finger into my underwear. I'm acutely aware of the vicious talons that top his fingers, just how sharp and deadly they can be. But somehow, the danger just makes it all hotter.

His finger glides against my moisture and he makes an appreciative sound. "So hot and slippery." With exquisite slowness, designed to kill me, he drags his claw across my clit and applies the slightest pressure. I squirm against him and he clucks his tongue. His left hand comes around my chest, banding me to him, and his agile tail coils around my legs, effectively rendering me immobile. Then he flaps those massive wings around to the front, hemming me in. Trapped in a cave made of Luc. Yum.

"Uh-uh," he murmurs in my ear. "We do this my way."

He presses his finger harder against me, just enough to make me pulse and wiggle under his touch.

"Mmm," he says. "Someone likes that."

He adjusts the pressure again and again, lighter then firmer, over and over, but that's it. It's enough to get me hot but not get me off, and he knows it. He chuckles against my ear, his hot breath giving me tingles.

"Tell me what you want, Annie."

"I want you to make me come," I say on a gasp. "Touch me more, please."

"Mmmm," he says. "I'll see what I can do. But no rushing. I want you to savor it."

Slowly, slowly, slowly, as wicked as can be, he slips his clawed finger inside me. He glides his other hand down my belly and strokes my clit again, all while his finger swirls deep within me, teasing the sensitive flesh inside.

I suck in a breath at the sudden intensity, then hiss when he slips a second finger in, stretching me just enough. He gently pinches my clit, making me throb even harder, and moves his fingers faster inside me.

I wouldn't have thought I could come from just this, but if he keeps it up, I absolutely will. "My god," I moan. "That's so good. Never stop."

He laughs, a dark, wicked sound, then leans in and nips at my neck. It's not hard enough to break the flesh, but the sudden bite of it, combined with his nimble hands, is enough to suddenly send me over the edge. I cry out in surprise as the orgasm rushes through me, my clit throbbing and more creamy wetness spilling down my thighs.

I'm surrounded by him; he's around me, over me, inside me, supporting me as I shudder and gasp through the throes of pleasure. He slows his strokes, dragging it out, and then purposefully removes his fingers and drags his hands up my torso, leaving damp trails in their wake. He cups my breasts, tweaking at my nipples and bringing on a new rush of sensation. When I touch myself, it usually takes a long time for me to come a second time, but being with Luc is a whole new realm of sensation. I can already feel the first orgasm subsiding and a new, sharper one building in its place.

And Luc knows it.

He uncoils his tail and slides a knee between mine, opening me slightly. And then he slides that tail all along my thighs, until the pointed tip is resting against my opening. With exquisite precision, he presses the tip against my clit and holds it there, applying a steady pressure. At the same time, he rolls my nipples between his fingers and sucks on my neck, his cock pressed into my ass crack and twitching.

"Luc," I moan. "I need you inside me."

"You can have your wish. All you have to do is come again." His tail flicks against my clit, slow then fast, over and over, slipping and sliding around, and after a few moments, I feel the pleasure building in an unstoppable wave. God, I have never felt anything like this. I can feel it building all through my body, sharpening in my nipples and low in my belly. I clench my thighs and trap his tail right where I want it, the tip rubbing me exactly like I need it to.

"Fuck," I breathe, and then it hits me, intense pleasure like the force of a tidal wave. My knees buckle, but he catches me, his tail still working my clit. I'm spasming hard against it, and he can feel it, because his cock gets even harder against me.

He slides to the ground, pulling me with him. "Take off my clothes," he orders, and I scramble to obey, desperate to see what he looks like in the moonlight. Once his pirate garb is gone, I take in the view. He's huge and muscular, his wings fanned out beneath him. His cock is shaped mostly like a human one, though it's longer and thicker than any I've ever seen, standing tall and proud.

I'm curious about it—what it feels like, what it tastes like—but Luc has grown impatient.

"Ride me," he demands.

I straddle him and take a deep breath, trying to force my muscles to relax. He's enormous, but I'm dying to take all of him in. It takes a minute and a few bounces, but eventually I loosen up and slide all the way down, grinding my hips against him. I stay put for a moment, tightening my inner muscles around him, loving the way his cock flexes deep inside me.

I rock against him, slowly at first, getting a feel for him. He's lying flat on the ground, eyes closed, mouth contorted with pleasure. Knowing that I've done that to him brings on a rush of power and pleasure, and he groans as my wetness floods against him. Without opening his eyes, he reaches up with perfect aim and captures my breasts in his hands, thumbs flicking at my nipples.

I bear down on him, hard, and then pick up the pace, sliding and bouncing. Impossibly, I feel him swell inside me, and then he gets so hard it's unbelievable. It's like nothing I've ever felt.

"Ahh," I moan. "That's incredible."

He grins and opens his eyes. "During the day, I have to turn to stone. At night, I can control it."

So that's what's happening: he's literally rock hard inside me. But with none of the roughness of stone; his skin is silky and hot. Good god. I could get used to this.

I grind against him until we're both sweating and panting. He rears up, shifting the angle inside me, rubbing against my sensitive inner spot. "Oh, fuck," I moan and he picks up the pace, thrusting frantically.

"I want to feel you come around me," he whispers in my ear, and that shivery bit of heat is all that I need to send me collapsing over the edge again, the orgasm pulsing through me. My tremors set him off; he gives a final roar and then I can feel him twitching and spurting inside me, hot and thick. It sets off another mini-orgasm, and we rock together until all the aftershocks finally pass, flopping into a tangled mess in the old hedge maze.

"Wow," I finally manage as we roll apart and I slump onto my back. "I did not see that coming. No pun intended."

He looks as ravished as I feel, clothes missing and his glorious hair all tangled. He meets my gaze and chuckles. "I can't say I foresaw that either. As far as I know, a gargoyle has never coupled with a human in all of history."

I smirk at him. "Well, I do like making history. But there's no way this hasn't happened before."

He props himself up on one elbow, completely comfortable at being naked in the grass. "Truly, I've never heard of such a thing. When you mentioned it earlier, I was honestly stunned by the prospect. Now that I've experienced it, I have to admit that both our peoples might be missing out."

I cuddle against him until I finally find the energy to stand and collect the tattered remains of my clothes. "Given the fact that this maze is prickly and I'm basically naked, I'm gonna need you to fly me back to the house," I tell him.

He stands and flaps his wings open, then scoops me into his arms. "Happy to oblige. You're a rare delight, Annie Winslow."

ANNIE

I wake up early the next morning, sore in all the best ways, and with a grin on my face. The sun is up, which means Luc is back at his post, which kind of sucks—I'd like him here in this ridiculous canopy bed with me, making me come until I can't remember my own name. But since I can't have that, I'll shower and head to the bank, cash in these bonds, and deal with this dumb mortgage thing.

Celeste must be behind this; it's the only thing that makes sense. She must have known about the bonds—not to mention Luc's predicament—and set out to make us work together. Somehow, she figured we'd help each other and find the box before the deadline. Which means she must have known his heartstone was there too. It's odd that she never returned it to him, but I'm certain she had her reasons.

Celeste was a sly old fox with a small gift for foresight. Her setting all this in motion sure makes more sense than the idea that she was deliberately out to get me. Celeste and I stayed in touch up until the end, and I think she wanted the best for me. She just had a sneaky way of going about it. Sure, she gave me the house, but she gave me more than that. A home, a new career, a new purpose. A friend with a hell of a lot of benefits. That old lady knew what she was about.

Whatever her exact plans, I'm thankful for the way things have turned out. I'm about to own this house free and clear, and I got hit with the best sex of my life. Who knew gargoyles had so many moves? Luc is stacked in all the right places, all big and proportionate and strong. Yum.

At the bank, I make a beeline for Lauriel and open the box on her desk. "Check this out."

She gives a low whistle. "Where did these come from?"

The real explanation is way too complicated. "Celeste left them for me. It's taken me this long to go through things and find them. They're valuable, right?"

She nods. "I'm not an expert, but I think you have close to half a million here. Plenty to cover the loan and stop the foreclosure."

I grin. "That's what I thought. Oh, I can't wait for Chad Alder to discover that his plans for cheesy commercial expansion are about to go up in smoke."

Lauriel chuckles. "Serves him right. I'm assuming you want to create an account and deposit all this, right? And then make the payment?"

"Yeah, if I can."

"Of course. It'll take a little while to get everything set up, especially since this we're dealing with high value bonds and not cash. I'd recommend getting a safety deposit box and putting some of these in it."

I nod. "I was thinking the same thing. I've decided for sure to turn Mabon Manor into a bed and breakfast, so I'll need money for the renovation."

"You're gonna go for it? That's great! What made you decide?"

"Well, like I said, it was initially my best plan to keep the property. The reno is going to be costly, so I needed a way for the house to sort of pay for itself. I figured a B&B in a charming town would do the job. Now it looks like I don't actually need the income—for a while, anyway—but I do need a way to occupy my time. I think running the Mabon Manor Bed and Breakfast could be really fun. And if it turns out I hate it, I could always stop. But the truth is, I've missed Haven's Hollow. I want to stick around."

"Sounds like a solid plan to me," Lauriel says.

"Worth giving it a shot, right? Haven gave me the name of her contractor. Once I own the house free and clear, I'll give him a call. I have a lot of ideas for the house and the grounds."

She smiles at me. "I'm glad you've decided to stay and make this place your home. I know Haven has missed you these last few years. So have I."

"It's really, really good to be back. I can't believe I let that asshat Chad keep me away all this time. We should grab coffee or something when you have free time. Or! I noticed a wine bar a few blocks down. Maybe we could grab a drink? My treat, as a thanks for your help."

"I'd like that," Lauriel says. "I'm awfully busy with work and the babies, but my husband owes me a night off. I've been dying to try Wallow and Wine."

It takes two hours to get everything squared away, but Lauriel assures me she has it handled. It will take a few business days for everything to get processed, but Mabon Manor is mine.

TWO WEEKS LATER

Lucien

This close to dusk, I can actually feel the sun starting to set. I can't move yet, but there's a sensation on my skin and in my bones, a prelude to freedom. It's been centuries since I've seen another of my kind, but I remember the complaints I used to hear from other gargoyles, the chagrin at being born a creature of the night. A creature who is forever unable move about during the day. It has never truly bothered me, for I have never had much to live for.

But now, stuck up here while Annie meanders around the yard, I realize that everything is different. *I* am different. She told me the other night that she changed her mind about destroying the hedge maze. According to her, we christened it and it's special, and there's no way in hell she's ever tearing it down, which I appreciate. She wants to restore it and make it a feature of her bed and breakfast. I don't think she knows much about gardening, but she's out here now, under my gaze, puttering around pulling weeds and making notes about how to spruce up the grounds.

I feel the strongest longing to join her, to tackle these projects as a team.

She is the only human I've ever felt connected to, something that surprises me as much as it does her. When I met her, only weeks ago, she seemed an annoying child. Now I see her as the vibrant woman she is, the sunlight to my endless nights. I don't even mind any more that she calls me Luc. *Mon Dieu*, I might even like it.

These past two weeks have been like something from a dream. Instead of going straight to the library each night, an endless dismal existence, I seek her out. We talk, we laugh, we tumble into her bed and search for new realms of pleasure. Now that I have found this new life, I never want to give it up. Never want to give *her* up.

As I watch, she stands up straighter and turns toward the driveway. I hear it too, the low hum of an engine. It stops and I hear the car door slam. There's a tension to her now that I can see from here, and I wonder who has just arrived.

A man comes around the corner; he's slightly shorter than average, with bland features, light hair, and a navy suit.

Annie holds herself stiffly, and shifts the rake in her hand so that it's between them. "Chad. What are you doing here?"

Ah, so this is the infamous Chad. The one who hurt her and sought to destroy my home. He's lucky I'm unable to move, or I would forcibly eject him from the property. Maybe toss him over the bluff.

"Hey, Annie." He leans in to hug her, but she sidesteps him, using the rake as a buffer.

"Not long enough. Stop trying to hug me like we're old pals. And I've told you, my name is Anya, not Annie. Why are you here?" she asks again.

"Miller Higgins from the bank called and told me that you paid off the loan. Apparently, you own the property now."

She crosses her arms over her chest. "Miller Higgins needs to keep his mouth shut. He had no business calling you."

"*Au contraire.* I have something I want to discuss with you. Can I come in?"

"No. I'm busy. We can talk out here, but make it fast."

"Aw, come on, Ann. No need to be so frosty. Our breakup was ages ago. Let's be mature adults and try to be friends. Invite me in for coffee."

Annie hates coffee, I think. *He should know that.*

"Hell, no. What part of 'I hate you' are you not understanding? The last time I saw you, I told you to fuck off. Take the hint, Chad. We will never be friends."

"Why not? Why can't you let bygones be bygones?"

"Because you suck. I shouldn't have to explain that. You have sixty seconds to tell me what you want and then I'm going inside and you're getting the hell off my property."

His smarmy expression finally fades and he glares at her. "Damn, who knew you'd turn out to be such a bitch?"

She rolls her eyes. "We're done here." She turns to go inside, but he catches her shoulder and spins her around, causing her to drop the rake. At the sight of his hand on her, anger boils in my chest.

"Get your hands off me," she snarls, but he ignore her.

"You're going to listen to me one way or the other," Chad says.

She twists, hard, and manages to dislodge his grasp. "Get away from me."

"Not until you hear what I have to say. I want to buy the property from you! I'm prepared to pay more than it's worth."

She has her arms wrapped around herself now, a defensive posture if ever there was one. "It's not for sale. Build somewhere else."

"There isn't anywhere else!" Chad bellows. "The town has strict guidelines for new buildings within city limits. Out here on the bluff is the best place for my development."

"I don't care! Your problem is not my problem." She turns to go in the house, but he grabs her again.

"I'm making it your problem." He wraps a hand around her upper arm, and even from here, I can see his fingers turn white as he squeezes.

"Let go! You're hurting me."

"Then stop being a bitch and listen to what I have to say!"

"Chad, I don't care about your development. Accept it."

I can see his chest heaving as his anger builds; clearly, he doesn't react well to Annie's dismissal of him. He reminds me of the men who invaded the manor all those years ago, all bluster and ire. I strain to move, to intervene, but the sun has me trapped here.

"You have to at least hear me out! I'm entitled to that much."

"Fine," Annie says, her voice low and calm. "Let me go and I'll listen to what you have to say."

He relaxes his grip and she shakes him off, but he doesn't back up. He's still in her face, still menacing her, and I cannot abide it.

Why is the sun taking so long to set? I'm stuck up here, impotent and helpless, while that asshole manhandles my woman. I use all my willpower to try to move, but it's useless. I'm frozen in stone, once again unable to aid someone under my protection. Maybe this is my real curse, my real failure in life. Yes, I want my heartstone back and I want the freedom to leave the manor, but truly, if I cannot protect those who reside here, what is my purpose? Why do I exist, if all I do is fail the Winslows and spend my nights lamenting my fate? What kind of wasted life is that?

No. I will not fail. I will not let harm come to Annie now that I've found her.

"You don't care about Haven's Hollow, Annie. You never have. This was never even your home. It's mine, and I have a right to make it a better place. I'm offering to make you very wealthy, and all you have to do is sell me something you don't even care about. Then you can go and do whatever it is you want in life!" Chad is aiming for a reasonable tone, a sales pitch, but his face is flushed with frustration.

Annie manages to take a step back from him. "I do care about this house. I live here. I'm turning it into a bed and breakfast. I'm not going to sell you the manor, Chad."

I can see the rage cross his face, turning his features ugly, but luckily, Annie sees it too. She backs up another step and lifts her hands just as he lunges for her. Her magical barrier holds, stopping him in his tracks.

"Listen to me, Chad. You need to take a deep breath, calm down, and get in your car. This conversation is done. You need to go."

"No! You can't just tell me to leave. We have to figure out a deal. I'll pay you more! My investors are counting on this!"

That's when it hits. I feel it the second the sun slips beneath the horizon, casting dusk upon Mabon Manor and loosening my shackles.

I'm free.

ANNIE

I'm holding Chad back with magic, but with the way he looks, I'm not sure how long it'll last. I've never seen him so furious, stomping around like a toddler who didn't get his way. This entitled asshole thinks he can intimidate me into selling my house...just because he wants it.

Fuck that.

Chad springs and collides with the barrier, but he's undeterred. He charges it again, his face contorted with fury. Not only did I stand up to him about the house, I'm standing up to him physically, and he's like an enraged bull intent on taking down the matador. What an entitled, small-dicked little shit. What did I ever see in him?

He squares his shoulders and lunges again, and this time, he manages to push through. I stumble back to regroup, but I'm not fast enough. Chad's hands are on my neck; his face is red and his eyes are wild.

He's squeezing, cutting off my air, and little black dots begin to dance in my vision. I tug at his hands, but they're strong and immobile, and I frantically try to think of another spell before I pass out.

As I struggle, growing weaker by the second, there's a flurry of motion out of the corner of my eye. I'm able to look up just enough to see Lucien *explode* off the eaves, plummeting straight down like a blue-gray rocket. He lands behind Chad with an audible thud that actually shakes the ground, and yanks him off me with one mighty tug, then plants himself between us. He rears up to his full height, wings expanded, talons exposed, tail swishing. I've never seen him like this and there's only one word for it: magnificent.

"What the fuck?" Chad shouts.

Luc responds with a massive growl. He flaps his wings, and I know the resulting gust is enough to knock Chad on his ass. I giggle at the thought.

Luc roars again, and this time I peek around him to see Chad backpedaling, only to stumble over the rake I dropped.

"What the hell is that thing?"

"This is Lucien," I call, voice a little raspy. Fortunately, Luc interceded before Chad managed to do real damage, though I'll be wearing his finger-prints as a necklace for a few days. "He's my roommate and he's not happy about your presence here."

Luc glances at me. "Are you okay?"

I nod. "I'll be fine."

He stalks forward. "To say I'm not pleased about your presence here is an understatement. Time to go, Chad Alder. And never return. Or else I throw you over the bluff and let the vultures feast on your corpse." I don't know if we even have vultures in these parts, but as threats go, it's a good one.

Chad turns ashen. "But Annie and I have business," he says weakly.

I can't see his face, but I hear Luc's snarl. "Your business is concluded. Never set foot on this property again."

"You should listen to him!" I call. "Lucien is very casual about murder. Defending me from it, of course. But also committing it."

"What?" Chad squeaks.

"You almost choked me to death, you fucking psycho. Get out of here before Lucien pays you back in full!"

Luc growls again. "This town is Annie's now. You don't belong here anymore. It's time to move," Luc tells him.

"But my house, my business...you can't kick me out of a town!"

"Are you sure about that?" I ask. "You've just been given an order by an eight-foot-tall monster who does not like you. You really wanna take your chances against him? Or me when I take pictures of these bruises and press charges?"

"But it's not fair—" Chad starts, only for Luc to interrupt.

"GO!" Luc bellows, and that's when something occurs to me.

"Wait," I say, and Luc turns to me.

"You can't honestly want anything else to do with him?"

I laugh. "Of course not. But I owe him a little something." I step around Luc and raise my hands again, already chanting the spell under my breath. It would be stronger if I had herbs or crystals to ground it, but in a pinch, this will do. I direct the spell at Chad, who is still frozen with indecision, torn between his fear of Luc and his determination to get this property.

"You must leave and not return,

and never bother me.

Why you left, you'll never learn.

As I will, so mote it be."

I can see the moment the spell takes effect; his features go slack with bewilderment

and he scuttles to his car, tearing down the driveway much faster than is safe.

"What did you do to him?" Lucien asks.

"Nothing much. Just a little aversion and memory spell. It will make Chad want to leave Haven's Hollow and never come back, but he won't remember why. Can't have him blabbing about gargoyles at Mabon Manor."

Luc grins at me. "What an excellent use of magic."

I smile back. "I thought so. Thanks for your help with him. I thought I had it under

control, but I didn't expect him to break through that barrier. I don't know if he would have actually done it, but he could have killed me in that blind rage." Now that the adrenaline is fading, I'm realizing what a close call I just had. Holy hell.

Luc's expression turns sober. "I will always protect you."

"I know. It's your job."

"No," he says. "It's my choice." He leans down and kisses me, sending my brain and body into a tailspin.

"Mmmm," I murmur when we break apart. "How are you so good at this?"

He shakes his head. "It's not me. *We're* good at this."

"That we are. Take me inside and show me just how good?"

"With pleasure." He sweeps me up and carries me to the parlor, depositing me on the old couch there.

"You called me a monster again," he points out.

"I know, and I'm sorry. I just did it to scare Chad. I don't think you're a monster, and as I've already said, it doesn't even matter, because I *like* monsters."

"Well, I like you. Very much. And I don't mind being seen as a monster if it gets rid of miscreants like Chad Alder."

"I very much like you back, my big, scary, sexy gargoyle. Now take off your pants," I demand with a giggle, leaning forward and tugging at the laces.

Before I can get his trousers off, he leans forward and scoops under my butt, hooking his hands in the waistband of my sweats and tugging them—and my undies—off in one swift motion. I don't manage more than a squeak of surprise before he's on his knees in front of me, a wicked gleam in his black eyes.

Without preamble, he pulls me to the edge of the settee and shoves my knees apart, exposing my hot, damp flesh to him. He leans forward and drags his fangs against my inner thigh, a teasing threat that makes me shiver. Then he lunges and fastens his mouth against me, and my eyes literally roll back in my head at the rush of sensation.

His mouth is even hotter and wetter than I am, and his tongue is magical, flicking and stroking against my clit. I buck against him, demanding more pressure. He laughs against my skin, tickling me in the best way, and then shifts so he's able to get a finger inside me. He swirls it, expertly stroking my G-spot, while never relieving the pressure on my clit, sucking and lapping at me like a wild man.

I manage to flutter my eyes open enough to see that he's undone the laces on his pants and is stroking his huge cock while he works me over. It's the hottest visual: a giant gargoyle so overcome with desire at pleasuring his woman that he has to touch himself.

His cock is rock-hard, the tip is glistening, ready to slip inside me and fill me up. I can't hold back; the orgasm rams through me like a freighter, and I frantically thrust against his mouth as I come. He licks it all up, making appreciative noises all the while. And then he lifts me and spins us so that he's sitting on the couch and I'm sprawled across his lap. He impales me with perfect, smooth aim and I gasp at the sudden sensation of fullness.

Aftershocks are still ripping through me, milking his cock, and he groans and kisses me hard. I can taste myself on his tongue, which makes me even wetter; I pinch my own nipples to try to rein in the second orgasm that I can already feel building.

His hips are pistoning under me, pushing us hard and fast, with nothing slow or sweet about this. I tip my head back and moan, lost in all the sensations. He takes advantage, locking teeth and lips against my neck, getting the sensitive spot just above my shoulder. I don't understand why I always come when he bites my neck, but it happens every time, and this is no exception.

I stop fighting the orgasm and let it take me under, drowning in the pleasure of it. It hits me in powerful waves that make my whole body clench as my clit pulses with it again and again. Just when I think it's about to wear off, Luc shifts beneath me, a grinding new angle that makes me shudder with pleasure.

"Fuck," I moan, collapsing against his chest as I ride the waves.

He growls with approval and tips over with me, swelling even bigger inside of me as his own orgasm rips through us both.

When I catch my breath, I lift my head and meet his gaze. "Honestly, I think we get better at that every time."

He huffs a little laugh. "I think you might be right." He gives my butt a squeeze and I feel him twitch to life inside me, a quick recovery one of the impressive features of his gargoyle physiology. "Let's do it again and make sure."

LUCIEN

I watch the sun's slow march across the sky, appreciating the cascade of colors it paints on the horizon. I've come to appreciate a lot in recent weeks, finding small pleasures in things as simple as a sunset or a purring cat.

I give all the credit to Annie. Before she arrived, I was barely living my life, singularly devoted to breaking my curse. And yet, I had no real plan for what I might do if I succeeded. Return to France, yes, but then what? I am a gargoyle, suited to one purpose and one purpose alone. I would simply have been assigned to some other building, perhaps some other family.

Life would not have been so different, save for the view from my perch. Who knows where I would have been stationed? Here, I'm pleased to look at the maze. It has a new meaning to me now; it is the place of my salvation.

My thoughts turn to France again, and if I could shake my head, I would. I have no idea if my village still exists, or where my friends and family are. For all I know, the entirety of my clan might have been shipped away to various continents. There is no way to know what might await me back in Europe, but I have been fixated on returning for so long that I never stopped to consider these things.

Here, I know exactly what I have: what the Americans call "a new lease on life." A woman I adore, a newfound sense of purpose, a joy in living rather than merely existing.

The sun sinks below the horizon, and I rise from my crouch and slip inside the window. I don't know what the future holds, or whether Annie will ever be able to return my heartstone, but even if she does, one thing is certain: This is where I belong.

ANNIE

I'm sitting in the library, waiting for Luc to reanimate and puzzling over his heartstone. It's resting on the table in front of me, along with a pile of books. Finding it was the first major hurdle, but not the last one. I still have to reinsert it into his body and figure out how to undo the spell that was placed on him.

The cats followed me, curling up in their usual spots: Snicket in a far armchair and Biscuit in the middle of the table, where he can supervise.

I start with a crumbling old book I found at the bottom of one of the trunks. It's labeled as the journal and grimoire of Mary Winslow, so it seems like the best place to find answers about her magic.

I flip through, searching for the night of the attack and Mary's response to it. If she wrote anywhere about the curse, it would be here. I finally land on a passage that catches my eye.

The men who came that night will be punished, by one means or another. There are spells that would suffice, but I suspect Lucien will take matters into his own hands. His remorse over the loss of Alice is plain, but I find I cannot forgive him any more than I can forgive John Marshall, Elias Smith, Josiah Alder, Jacob Adams, Edwin Gray and Robert Turner.

The name Josiah Alder leaps out at me. I'd bet dollars to one of Libra Cartwright's magical donuts that he's an ancestor of Chad's. Which means that family has been fucking with mine for centuries. I don't know what Lucien and Mary did to those men, but they deserved it. And Chad got his too. Ugh, good riddance.

I keep reading, but the next few passages are about craft.

It has been my experience that bloodstones such as garnets and rubies work best for binding rituals, while sea stones (aquamarines and the like) are beneficial when treating ailments of the lungs. Earthstones such as diamonds and quartz are useful for purifying and blessing the land, ensuring healthy crops and a bountiful harvest. Poultices with sage help to purify the body, while rosemary and mint may be used to draw out infections. I find that both amethyst and lavender temper ailments of the mind.

It goes on for a few pages, her personal Wiccapedia. Interesting enough, I guess, but nothing I couldn't find in any basic spellbook. Unfortunately, I don't find anything about the specific curse she placed on Luc. With a sigh, I set the book aside and try the next one. I'm still reading it when Luc makes his appearance. He sits down next to me and I lean close, letting him drape an arm across my shoulders and inhaling the scent of him. It's deep and woodsy, but also aromatic, like pine trees and coffee.

"I'm researching your curse," I say. "Nothing yet, but I'm just getting started. It would be a lot easier if she could have just forgiven you. Or if I could do it for her."

"Annie," Luc says slowly. "How long has that been happening?"

"Hmm?" I look up and see him staring at his heartstone on the table. The stone that is now glowing with an eerie red light.

"Whoa," I say. "That's new."

"No idea what caused it?"

I shake my head. "I haven't cast any spells, so it's nothing I did. It's glowing all on its own. Tell me again what Mary said about the curse? The only way to break it?"

"Just that I would be cursed until I saved her daughter and earned her daughter's forgiveness. But of course, I couldn't save Alice. And Abigail never forgave me, either. She grew up poisoned by her mother's bitterness."

I think about everything he's told me. His duty as protector, his inability to save Alice from the men who strangled her, his desperate need for forgiveness...

"I think I understand," I say slowly. "Technically, every Winslow woman since then is a daughter of Mary. She was Celeste's ancestor, my grandma's, my mom's, and mine too. And yesterday, you helped save me from Chad, when I really thought he might hurt me or worse, from the fate that Alice suffered. Plus I totally forgive you for what happened with her. You weren't to blame—that's on those horrible men. I think...I think you saved one of Mary's daughters and earned your absolution. I think that's why the stone is glowing. It's letting you know that the curse is ended."

"Does that mean you can give it back to me now?"

"In theory, maybe? I'm not sure. I sort of thought that once the curse was broken, you'd automatically reabsorb it or whatever."

"Okay, so is it simply a matter of using the right spell to return it to me?"

I shrug. "I don't know. Every instinct is telling me the spell isn't really the important part. There are plenty of ways to break a binding. It's much harder to create one than to break them." I pause and think. "Wait a second, Mary's grimoire said something about that. Her preferred method for binding spells..." I grab the book and read over her craft notes again. "Blood-stones such as garnets or rubies work best for binding rituals."

Luc points to my necklace. "Rubies like that one?"

I blink at him in wonder and unhook the pendant I always wear, a small ruby charm. "My mom gave this to me when I was 10. It's a family heirloom, but I've never thought that much about it. But now that you mention it, I'm wondering if there's more to it."

I set it next to the heartstone, and almost instantly, the ruby begins to glow with the same eerie red light.

"*Mon Dieu*," Luc breathes.

"That charm has been in my family for generations. Maybe it was originally Mary's? Maybe it was the stone she used in the binding. But what are the odds that I would have it now, just when we need it most?"

I pick up both items and can instantly feel the magic coursing between them, like an electrical buzz. They're definitely connected in some way. I close my eyes and try to completely relax, letting myself feel the tone and cadence of the magic in each item. Spells are often like fingerprints, with an energy unique to themselves. But I can't sense any difference between the heartstone and the ruby, suggesting that the magic in each stems from the same source.

I open my eyes.

"Luc, this is it. It wasn't that I needed to find the right spell. I just needed the right charm. The other half of the *original* spell."

Was this Celeste's doing? She knew where the heartstone was, so she probably knew the pendant was connected to it. Did she ensure Mom gave me the necklace all those years ago, because she knew this day would come? That I would feel compelled by the full moon to go wandering through the maze and find the box?

Still holding both objects in open palms, I begin to chant, using the strongest releasing spell I know. I can feel the energy shifting from the heartstone to the pendant, setting the heartstone free of Mary's magic, and I know with every ounce of my being that this is going to work.

"*Binding magic, come undone.*

Set your victim free.

What was two, return to one.

As I will, so mote it be."

I keep the chant going, transferring the energy, and the heartstone begins to float.

Mr. Biscuit, who is still sitting in the middle of everything, goes wide-eyed and lifts a paw. Luc gently moves the cat as the stone lifts out of my palm, hovers for a few seconds, and then begins to drift toward him as he watches in awe. We both stare as it picks up speed, zooms toward his chest, and then *poof!*, disappears inside him.

He grunts and presses a palm to his sternum, pain contorting his features. "It hurt when she ripped it free, but it seems returning it is no less agonizing." He hunches and breathes slowly, taking deep inhalations to manage the pain. After a few beats, he sits up, his face suffusing with joy. "You did it! I can feel it settling back into place. And the pain is subsiding."

I sigh and lean back, drained by the intensity and focus required by the spell. "I'm so glad. You never deserved to be trapped here. Now you can finally go home." I fasten my necklace back on, now that it's returned to its normal, non-glowing ruby state.

"Home," Luc says pensively. "Do you want me to leave?"

I shoot him a quizzical look. "What? No, of course not. This last month has been amazing. Despite everything we've been dealing with, I've loved spending time with you. Getting to know you. But I also know how anxious you are to get back to France. To others of your kind. And you were pretty clear about not wanting to be here when I turned the place into a B&B, what with all the workers and mayhem. Besides, we had a deal. You held up your end."

"If I wanted to stay, would you change your plans? About the B&B, I mean. Now that you no longer need the money."

I blink at him; it hadn't occurred to me that he might not go back to France the absolute second he could. "Uh, I don't know. If I'd thought there was a chance you might stay, I'd have consulted with you more about the whole thing. Since you were leaving, I didn't see the point. I mean, I know how you feel about the B&B idea, but I also thought it was moot, since I wasn't going to do it until you went home."

"That doesn't really answer my question."

"I know I don't need the money the way I did in the beginning, but I still need a job. Something to do with my time. And Haven's Hollow relies on tourism, so I think it's actually a smart business idea." I meet his gaze, which is intent. "Luc, I'm excited about opening the Mabon Manor Bed and Breakfast. Restoring the house and the property, celebrating holidays, becoming part of Haven's Hollow again. I don't want to drive you away, but I also don't want to give up on my plans. So I guess I don't have an answer."

He smiles at me, a big bright grin that shows off his perfect teeth and gleaming fangs. "I don't want you to give up your plans either. I would never ask you too. To be honest, I was simply curious what you would say. I suppose I can get used to work crews and guests. After all, I got used to you. And it's not so hard to stay out of sight of humans when I need to."

"Are you...what are you saying? What about France?" I don't dare get my hopes up.

He gives one of his Gallic shrugs. "I might return one day, to visit. Perhaps you would even join me. But Mabon Manor is my home." He tucks a finger under my chin and meets my gaze. "You are my home. We have just found each other and there is no way I will leave you."

"Are you serious? You're staying? This isn't a joke?"

"Not a joke, *mon coeur.*"

My heart gives a little thrill. I'd been preparing myself for his eventual departure, maintaining that everything between us was casual. Friends with benefits and nothing more. Not willing to admit to myself how I was feeling. Or how devastated I would be when he was gone.

"You're really going to stay?" Tears are threatening, and touches my face tenderly.

"Yes. I'm staying. After all, with people coming and going, you might need some extra protection around. And I've developed a soft spot for the hedge maze."

I give a watery laugh. "I'm going to convert one of the third-floor studies into a bedroom and keep the other for the office. That story will be just for us. Our room, our library. Well, us and the cats. The visitors can use the first two stories, but those will be only for us. We'll make a good home here, Luc. Together."

"I know we will. I can't wait to see what you do with the place. But I should tell you something. I don't think we're friends anymore."

"No?"

He shakes his head. "The way I feel about you isn't friendly. I love you, Annie Winslow. I intend to spend the rest of our time together showing you exactly how much."

I laugh. "That works out nicely, Lucien Lafitte. Because I love you too. I can't tell you how glad I am that you're staying. I'd have put on a brave face and let you go, but it would have broken my heart. Real heartbreak this time, not that silly teenage stuff."

"I will never break your heart. I will spend all my life being worthy of it."

He leans forward and gives me a long, deep, drugging kiss, and I send a silent thank you to Aunt Celeste for somehow giving me everything I ever needed, even when I had no idea what that was.

THE END

Read on for more about Darkdream, book two in the Monsters of Haven's Hollow series...

Libra Cartwright has done everything in her power to leave her past behind, but a new town and a new name can only get her so far. When she learns her ex is out of prison, she panics, because she's knows he'll be out for revenge—against her, the woman who put him away.

Callister, the King of Nightmares, has never met a human he couldn't terrify, feasting on the delicious taste of fear. But the nightmares he finds inside Libra are more intriguing than most. Fascinated by her darkness, he transports her to the Nightmare Court, where he shows her just how seductive and powerful dreams can be. But Libra can't hide forever, and the real world is about to come knocking...

Releasing in Fall 2022, as part of the Monsters in Love Volume 2: Lost in the Dark anthology.
Preorder a copy HERE.

You can also type this address into your favorite web browser:
https://books2read.com/monstersinlove2

While you wait, check out my other books!

Zella Unlocked
Aura Awakened
Forest of Frost: Sugared Plums and Poisoned Apples
Lustre
Queens of Thorns and Stars (with Elle Cross)

ABOUT THE AUTHOR

Greetings! I'm Vivienne, and I write all things magical and mysterious, from fairy tales to alien romance to futuristic whodunits.

I've been writing fantastic tales since I could hold a pencil. Captivated by fanciful stories from a young age, I gradually began to create my own worlds filled with fantastic creatures and monstrous beasts. Now a USA Today bestselling author, I'm still sending my characters on as many wild journeys and dark adventures as I can.

In addition to spinning a good story, my loves include chocolate, reading good books, traveling, and taking as many bubble baths as possible. When I'm not writing, you can find me roaming around the southern U.S. with my husband and two very fluffy cats. I'm the redhead in pajamas.

For a list of my books, click here. To find out more about me, and to subscribe to my mailing list, please visit my website.

BELFRY

DEE J. HOLMES

BLURB

Enter the Lands of the Spreading Dark, where demons creep beneath the streets and love lingers in the darkest of places...

When Isabelle DuNorde's true love is thrown to the demons, she becomes determined to save herself and her little sister from her town's increasingly unstable bishop. But when the bishop's deadly condemnation lands on her sister, Isabelle has to follow her into the same demon-infested tunnels that killed her love.

Hunted through the dark labyrinth beneath Windhaven, Isabelle and her sister are rescued from certain death by a massive, bat-like creature. Broad-shouldered, with large ears and claws and fangs, he leads them to safety. Protected by the strange demon, Isabelle discovers her love might not be lost after all—if she's strong enough to fight for what matters and to face the true evil in Windhaven.

PROLOGUE

Isabelle DuNorde crept quietly down the steps of her family's cottage, careful to avoid the middle stair that creaked. Silly to be sneaking out of her own home, but she'd promised her love that she'd meet him in the fields that morning, and her mother did not approve—she wanted more for her daughter than a 'simple farmer.' Ridiculous. Who could be a better fit for the daughter of a baker than one who tended the grain in their fields?

Yet if Isabelle was caught, she'd be put to work and told to cast her eye in more suitable directions.

Directions she had no desire to pursue.

Her heart was spoken for—and as far as she was concerned, there wasn't a better man than Thomas. It had been too long since she'd seen him, and she refused to wait another day. After all, today was the harvest feast. The time when the remains of the old year were stored and seeds were laid for the new.

It was also when the men of Windhaven made promises to their loves.

Today, he'll ask me to marry him. Her heart swelled with certainty, and she crept down another step.

The scent of baking bread filled the small building, and her mother's voice melded with the clatter of cooking trays and rattle of wooden spoons against bowls. It used to warm her toes and invite her to ease into the small space and help prepare the morning's orders.

But those days had faded.

Her father had disappeared, and so had the family she'd known.

More and more, she felt as if she'd lost her mama as well that cold winter's day. Only instead of vanishing into the dark forest surrounding the town of Windhaven, her mama was slowly eroding into flour and benedictions.

She glanced into the kitchen at the figure bent over their iron stove and pressed a fist to her stomach.

They used to laugh over sweet buns.

Now, Mama chastised her while kneading the Chastry-approved loaves—and their revered bishop claimed daily sugar consumption led to sin. And sin fed the demons beneath the Chastry, instead of filling the bellies of Windhaven's workers. So sweet buns were saved for special occasions, and their bread had to be made with solemnity of mind and body.

No more smiling over raisins or leaving treats for the mice.

Isabelle reached the bottom step and hesitated.

Had she given up too soon? They'd already lost her father—and her sister deserved to know their mother as she'd been. Warm and always ready with a hearty laugh, not this woman with her hair scraped into a tight bun and her mouth pinched at the corners.

Letting out a breath, she started toward the kitchen—

"Don't you dare," a voice hissed at her.

Isabelle spun around to find her younger sister, Emmanuella, crouched among the cloaks hung beside their front door. "Emmi," she whispered, keeping her voice as quiet as possible. "What are you doing?"

"Stopping you from guilting yourself into working another day." Emmi smirked.

Isabelle gaped at her sister.

"Don't pretend, Belle. You've worked every day with Mama for the past fortnight." Chin tilting uptight, Emmi held out Isabelle's cloak. "It is my turn to make those damn rolls—"

"Mind your words." Isabelle sent a worried glance at the kitchen.

Her mother would tan their hides if she heard Emmi cursing in their home, or anywhere, truth be told. And then neither of them would have a break from the kitchen for a month.

"She can't hear us over her chanting." Her sister rolled her eyes. "Go, Belle. You deserve a break. See Thomas, enjoy the fields...just make sure you're back in time to get ready for the ball. If Mama does my hair, she'll pull it so tight my eyebrows will mate with my hairline."

Belle shook her head. "Whose child are you?"

"Dunno." Emmi shrugged. "Maybe the demons that dwell beneath the Chastry snuck into Mama's bed one night? It would explain my love of sweetbreads and sugared frosting." She grinned mischievously. "But we both know I'm your sister and I say all the things you think."

Smothering a laugh, Belle wrapped an arm around her sister's shoulders. "I pray it's not so."

Dimples flashed in her sister's cheeks. "And yet I adore frosting."

"You're incorrigible." Tugging on her cloak, Isabelle gave her sister a stern look.

Even as a baby, Emmi had always been full of spirit. Her sister had been too young to be as affected by their father's disappearance, and Isabelle had done what she could to fill the space left behind. But it seemed the more their mother turned to the Chastry, the more Emmi rebelled.

A dangerous practice. Especially in these fallen times, where every week carried fresh tales of demons snatching people from their beds.

She might not believe everything the Chastry claimed, but the demons were real.

The monsters had claimed too many of their neighbors, she wouldn't let them take her sister.

She cupped her younger sister's face. "I will go see Thomas if you promise to behave. I mean it." She kissed Emmi's forehead. "Mama will ban you from the ball if you don't, and I refuse to go without you."

Emmi let out a long-suffering sigh. "Fine. I'll be good and make boring rolls."

"Thanks be." Isabelle grinned and slipped out the door.

Drawing in a deep breath, she let the crisp morning air wash over her. Gods, it had been too long since she'd enjoyed a day away from the kitchen.

Unable to keep a smile from her lips, she hurried onto the cobbled streets and headed for the stone arch that marked the edge of town. The sun had barely risen above the mountain tops and the night torches were still lit, and yet she knew Thomas would already be in the fields. Today might mark a festival, but to reach that celebration required a lot of their farmers.

A chill wind whipped along the street, tugging on her cloak, and she held the sides closed. The lanterns framing the street sputtered out and the ground trembled beneath her feet.

The demons returning to their lairs, her mother would say.

Or reminding us they're hungry.

Isabelle pulled her cloak tighter and walked faster, trying to ignore the sensation of creatures scratching and crawling beneath the road. The bishop claimed the demons couldn't pass beyond the Chastry, yet she'd swear they'd spread beneath all the streets. No one wanted to be caught on the streets in the dark, because the demons came out at night. That's why the lanterns were lit at twilight and only extinguished at dawn—and why every person in Windhaven was told to stay inside despite the lanterns.

Passing underneath the arch, she searched the fields for Thomas. An easy enough task, given most of the grains had been cut and he stood tall in the distance.

Shoulders broad enough to belong to a fabled minotaur.

Arms heavily muscled from plowing fields.

His physique rivaled any member of the city guard, and she'd swear he could have sat in place of any of the statues of the golden age's great kings that once sat in the town square. Yet it was his ready smile that had her running the final stretch and throwing herself into his arms.

"My Belle!" He spun her around as if she weighed no more than a feather. "You got away."

"Of course." She wrinkled her nose at him. "You expected otherwise?"

He lifted his brows, brown eyes twinkling with warmth. "Perhaps."

"Wretch." With a laugh, she kissed his nose. "I missed you. I'm sorry I haven't been able to get away—Mama has been... Well, you know. But today, we have the whole day together. And later at the ball we will..."

Her words faded as she realized it had been a long time since they'd been alone together—her certainty might be misplaced. Thomas had never promised her marriage. Was he even planning to announce their union at the ball? He was older than her by a handful of years, and handsome enough to give the sun pause. There had to be more than one lady seeking his affections—ladies who'd already reached their majority.

"Belle?" His head tilted and a lock of sun-kissed brown hair fell in front of an eye.

Stomach twisting, she bit her lip and whispered, "Tonight is the ball."

"So I've heard." He pushed his hair out of his face and rolled his shoulders. "I was thinking I might not go."

Not go?

Her jaw dropped. "But you... but I..."

"Oh. You were thinking to attend, were you?" His face split into a grin and he pulled her into his embrace, spinning her around before returning her feet to the ground. "As if there's anyone else I would wish to take. Or any reason aside from you that I would go."

She swallowed hard and met his gaze. "You have not seen much of me lately."

"Belle." His expression sobered and he framed her face with his hands. "I only meant to tease. There's no other woman for me, and there never will be. It's you, love. It's always been you. I am a humble farmer. I spend my days in the fields and my nights tending the livestock. It's not a glamorous life—nothing like you'd have in the Keep. But if you will have me, we'll announce our union at the ball, then it's mere months until the spring tyne."

"You beast." Pure joy filled her being and she wrapped her arms around his waist. Beaming up at him, she soaked in the strength of his arms and the sheer love in his eyes. Her mother thought she could do better than this man? Folly. Pure folly. She loved this man, and love was all she needed to have a good life. "Of course, I'll have you—terrible sense of humor and all. There's no other man for me, and there never will be."

From her position comfortably reclined against a haystack, Belle stretched her arms and smiled up at her sweetheart. As the sun had risen, he'd taken off his jacket and scarves until he toiled in a linen shirt—and she could see every line of his muscles through the thin fabric.

"If you're still warm, you're welcome to take that shirt off," she said, sending him a wicked look beneath her lashes. "A wife should know what to expect from her husband."

In fact, she'd like to do a great deal more than look.

"Belle..." Wiping sweat from his brow, he shook his head. "Stop tempting me. I mean it." He pointed his scythe at her. "I won't give the Chastry any reason to deny our union. When we announce our intentions tonight, and when we join the rest of the couples pledging to each other at the spring tyne, there can't be any cause for question."

"Come now," she said, crooking her finger in a silent plea for him to join her. "Who would protest?"

His gaze traveled past her and his mouth flattened. "I can think of one."

"Huh?" Getting to her feet, Belle turned and found an armed patrol passing the field.

Armor bright in the afternoon sun, the men all focused in their direction. The figure in front, with a bold plume of red adorning his helm, lifted a hand in silent greeting. The esteemed captain. Who her mother had invited to tea on more than one occasion over the past month.

"Oh. Right." She forced herself to wave at the guards until they passed

"He's interested," Thomas said, voice low. "Jaston is the captain of the guard. You'd have a life of privilege in the Keep. Servants. It would please your mother to take such a suitor and—"

"Bite your tongue," she snapped. "I want none of that."

"Are you sure?"

Eyes narrowed, she slowly turned to regard him. "Are you trying to be rid of me, Thomas Marr?"

He flashed her a grin. "Never."

"Good." She gripped the front of his shirt and tugged. "Because I'll have to do terrible things to you if you decide to throw me over now. You had your chance. You failed to use it."

"Tragic." His hand slid up the back of her neck.

Her breath caught.

She slid her hands up his chest, stretching up on her toes until her mouth hovered a mere hand's breadth from his. But instead of a kiss, he rested his forehead against hers. "I suppose I'll keep you, if only to spare the rest of the town your violent wrath."

She blew out a frustrated breath.

He laughed. "Spring isn't so far away."

"It's far enough," she muttered. "Yet they deny us even a kiss."

As he returned to his work, she found herself staring past the fields at the forest. The narrow trees this high up the mountain shouldn't form much of a barrier, yet they sat tight together, preventing her from seeing much beyond the length of a horse.

There were towns beyond those trees. Cities. Or, there had been. Despite what the bishop claimed, she wanted to believe those places hadn't fallen to the Spreading Dark.

She wondered if people were happier there.

If there were places where one could live without the Chastry watching every breath, where they could kiss and laugh and love without judgment. Where demons didn't scurry beneath their streets.

How could trees be worse than demons?

Even with the mist and shadow, the trees didn't feel as dangerous as the tremors at night. And she'd overheard the butcher talking in hushed tones about people leaving Windhaven for the forest. Mama claimed the woods killed Belle's father, but whenever her mother made that claim, she looked at the belfry—the highest tower in the Chastry, where the deacons rang the bells for mass, and the only part of the church they could see from their cottage—and not the forest.

Despite the sun, Belle shivered.

"Here, love." Thomas placed her cloak around her shoulders, then his hand slid across her stomach and he pulled her gently against his chest, warming her back while they both stared at the forest.

His chin rested on the top of her head. "Do you want to leave Windhaven?"

She jerked with surprise and half-turned, staring up at him in shock. "I didn't say that."

"I know." His mouth curved into a rueful smile. "But I'm fairly certain we were sharing that thought. Dreaming of a world where you can kiss without judgment..." At her nod, he squeezed her waist. "I'm not supposed to talk about it, but my father has been meeting with others. There's talk of traveling through the forest to see if Finch or Goldbreak still stand."

Oh, Gods.

An actual city?

Fire lit inside her at the thought, so fierce she couldn't understand how the sun wasn't beaming from her fingertips. "I would love that! Yes!" Grinning madly, she bounced with glee. "Papa told me about other lands, how he drew maps for merchants and lords before..."

Before he married and had children.

Before he had me, and my sister...

She covered her mouth with her hand and stared at Thomas, her joy crumbling like a stale biscuit. "I... I can't." Her throat worked, and she let her hands fall from his chest to hang limp at her sides. "I want to. But I can't leave Emmi. And she won't be able to leave until her majority."

Which would be five years after Belle's.

A fortnight was one thing, but five years? She couldn't ask Thomas to put his entire life on hold for that long—just as she couldn't leave her younger sister alone in that cottage with their mother.

Lips trembling, she met his gaze. "Y-you could go. Get settled—"

"Belle..." He cupped her face. "I—"

"You... you could send for me when you're ready," she whispered. "I'd wait as long as it—"

"I'm never leaving you behind." He brushed his lips across hers.

The faintest touch, and yet a thrill ran from her mouth all the way to the tips of her toes. Gods, but she loved this man. They'd made promises to each other, and she knew in her heart the vows spoken over grain and soil were more binding than anything before an altar.

"Who cares what the Chastry says," she said, pressing a light kiss to the corner of his mouth. "We love each other and—"

Bong.

The Chastry's main bell rang, its deep knells signaling that the afternoon drew to a close. *Demons bite my ankles.* She sent Thomas a rueful smile. "I have to go home and get ready for the ball. I promised Emmi I'd help with her hair, and Mama will never let me hear the end of it if I don't."

He kissed the tip of her nose. "Of course. But before you go."

Bobbing his eyebrows, he made a production out of pulling a small package from the pouch tied to his belt. He held out a small square of folded parchment, tied with a cord of woven straw.

"For me?" she asked quietly.

At his nod, she took the tiny package and carefully untied the cord, making sure everything could be reused. Inside the parchment was a bed of dried moss. And past the moss...

She gasped as she uncovered a silver ring.

As if the silver had been woven together to resemble a wreath of grain, the strands shimmered in the fading light. It slid onto her finger as if it had been forged just for her. She supposed it had. It must have cost months of wages to purchase such a beautiful piece.

A promise ring. He'd gotten her a promise ring.

Simple and elegant and exactly what she'd have chosen.

"Oh, Thomas!" She threw her arms around his neck. "It's perfect. I love it. I'll wear it around my neck until our union is approved. I'll count the minutes. Thank you, thank you, thank you."

The bell rang again.

"Damnation," she muttered.

"Go." He nudged her toward the village. "Get ready. I'll see you at the ball!"

His laugh followed her all the way home and up the stairs. She dressed as if in a dream, barely aware of her gown—grateful that she'd hung the garment out the night before. It was green—Thomas' favorite color—and she couldn't wait to see his face when he saw her.

"Belle?" Her sister opened the door. "Mama says—"

"Emmi! Isn't it gorgeous?" Belle spun in a circle, then admired how the ring shone from its place on the thin gold chain her father had given her for her twelfth birthday.

Even in her simple mirror, a square of polished tin, the silver band glowed.

"Soon I'll be able to wear his ring on my finger and..." Her words dried as she took in her sister's stark expression. Her sister's mouth was a flat line, her eyes devoid of their usual sparkle. It was an all too adult expression for one so young. "Emmi? What's wrong?"

"Mama wants to see you," her sister whispered. "Right now."

Belle swallowed hard.

She held her sister's gaze, silently asking what it was that had upset their mother—normally Mama loved the harvest tyne ball. But all Emmi could do was lift her hands. If the problem wasn't Emmi's latest hijinks, then Belle shuddered to think what was the matter.

Whatever it was, she'd face it. Take the brunt of any disapproval and do what she could to spare Emmi.

Giving her sister a nod, Belle hurried down the stairs.

Her mother was waiting at the bottom, her brows drawn together so tightly they nearly formed a single line of disapproval. "Isabelle," she snapped. "What are you doing with that cheap ring around your neck? Take it off immediately."

"What?" Eyes wide, Belle stepped back and stared at her mother. "No. This is Thomas' ring and—"

"Don't test me, girl." The crack of her mother's boot-heel against the wooden floorboard struck with the force of lightning. She pointed a shaking finger at Belle. "You're not to throw your life away on a farm boy. You will put that ring away and pay attention to Captain Jaston at the ball—"

"No!" Fingers tight around her ring, Belle retreated another step. "Mama. You know Thomas and I are sweethearts. We've made promises. We're going to be married at the spring—"

"No," her mother bit out. "You won't."

Belle gaped at her mother.

Behind her, she heard Emmi suck in a breath.

She held a hand out, low at her side, a silent plea for her sister to hold her tongue. Whatever demon had possessed her mother to say such things, she wouldn't let that ire be turned on her sister. There had to be some kind of mistake, some strange mischief afoot. "W-why are you saying this, Mama? I know you wanted a life at the Keep, but you know Thomas is a good man—"

"Not anymore." Her mother's mouth was hooked with distaste. "Thomas' father has sinned. The family will be shamed. To protect your sister and this house, you must return that ring and deny any promises."

Sinned?

Oh, Gods.

Her heart hammered against her chest, and a rushing sound filled her ears, so loudly she wondered if the mountain wind had gotten trapped there. She held the ring so tightly she felt the woven pattern imprinting itself on her palm. "Mama..." Her voice cracked. "Tell me. Please. What has happened? The Marrs are good farmers who tend our fields. They're *good* people."

"They have sinned, Isabelle." A glacial wind had more warmth than her mother's expression. "They will be punished."

Punished?

The earth trembled beneath Belle's feet, and for once she couldn't tell if it was demons or her bones quaking in terror. It was frowned upon to talk about leaving the town, but it wasn't a sin. Or, it hadn't been. Surely the bishop wouldn't hold Thomas' father to blame if he'd broken a new creed? The Marrs had served Windhaven for generations.

It had to be a public shaming, followed by a sermon on why leaving was temporarily banned.

Please, Fallen Gods of Gold and Scale, let it be a shaming.

It wouldn't be the first time the bishop had opened the Harvest Ball with a public shaming, as if to remind all of Windhaven why events at night were rare moments of celebration to be treasured.

Yet her mother's face said otherwise.

Barely able to breathe, she pushed past her mother and onto the streets. She should have been running for the edge of town, but her limbs were frozen, her feet unwilling to do more than stumble a few steps.

Daylight had fled and the lamps were burning brightly—always bright, especially in the twilight hours, when the demons were most prone to hunt. She felt them scurrying beneath her feet. Claws. Scraping like iron nails against stone. And they all seemed to be going in one direction.

Voices echoed from behind her.

Heart sinking, she turned slowly to the square. She'd barely made it past the edge of her cottage, and she was close enough to the square to hear. And to see. The lights were brighter there, the shadows of many figures stretching along the rooftops as if reaching for the stars.

They'd already gathered.

Picking up her skirts, she ran for the square. Her slippers, made for dancing on the Keep's polished floors, provided no protection from the jagged cobblestones—Belle didn't care. She barely noticed the pain as she raced past the tailor and the butcher, gripping the lamppost on the corner to swing herself onto the next street at pace.

Chest burning, she burst into the square in time to see Thomas' father and a handful of his friends being dragged before the bishop—who stood with not one, but four city guards in full plate mail.

She stumbled to a halt, unable to process what she was seeing.

So many guards? And was Ser Marr in chains?

Dear Gods, they didn't use chains for shamings. Nor did they let people bleed freely from obvious wounds.

Clad in his gold and white ceremonial robes—Chastry colors, to honor the fallen golden gods and hearken their return—the bishop stood upon a wooden dais, a scroll clutched in one hand and harsh lines framing his mouth. Two guards stood on either side, torchlight dancing across their polished armor.

Set before the Chastry, in the middle of the square, the dais was only used to punish serious sinners. But that couldn't be possible. Ser Marr and his friends were farmers and tradespeople, hard-working folk who helped keep Windhaven turning from season to season.

This had to be a mistake.

A terrible mistake.

She began pushing her way through the crowd, trying to reach the dais and find Thomas.

"*Sedition.*" The bishop's voice sliced through the crowd and silence claimed the square. Everyone around her drew still, as if collectively holding their breath, and even the wind vanished.

Except for the demons.

Their scratching increased, as if the bishop's pronouncement drew them near.

"Salacious lies," the bishop continued, words dripping with disdain and celestial judgment. "Roland Marr, you have been found guilty of the grievous crime of luring the good people of Windhaven to their deaths in the woods. There is no future in the woods, no hope. Only death at the hands of the monsters that, even now, draw closer to our village—"

"Liar!" Thomas threw himself at the dais. "Leaving is no sin! My father has done nothing—"

"Silence." One of the guards slammed the pommel of his sword into Thomas' head, while two others restrained him. Unarmed and bleeding from a cut above his eye, and it still took a guard gripping each arm to hold him back. "If you want to stand by your father, then you can suffer the same fate."

"No!" She rushed forward. "Thomas—"

An armored arm caught her middle, driving the air from her lungs. "Be quiet, Belle," a cruel voice hissed in her ear. Jaston. The captain of the guard. "Or you'll share their fate."

"I don't care." She struggled in his grip. "Let me go. Thom—"

Jaston clamped a hand over her mouth. "I said *quiet*."

All she could do was watch as the guards forced Thomas to his knees beside his father. Past the townspeople and the guards, she met Thomas' gaze. His eyes somehow grim and yet full of love, she felt him begging her to stop, to save herself from what came next.

No, no, no.

She went limp in Jaston's hold as the iron door set in the square's cobble-stones, right front of the Chastry entrance was pulled aside—so heavy it took four men to move it. The rest of the crowd moved back, afraid to get close as the guards shoved all the prisoners to the opening.

There was nothing Isabelle could do. She had no weapons, no resources. Nothing that would save them.

"If you truly repent your sins," the Bishop intoned. "You will be spared."

Then Thomas, his father, and their friends were cast into the depths beneath the Chastry—where the demons lived. Haunting screams filled the night. Sounds that had nothing to do with repentance.

In all her seventeen years, not one sinner had ever returned from the depths.

"Let this be a lesson to you all," the bishop cried, voice resonant, as if on the brink of breaking into song. "Vigilance. Piety. Demons hunt for your weakness. You must deny them at every turn, lest you become their pawn. The Golden Dragons will return, if only we have strength to endure."

They were supposed to want the return of the dragons above all else, but Belle couldn't care.

Couldn't feel anything past the screaming in her heart.

Frozen from the inside out, she said nothing as Emmi led her home and up to her room—she didn't have the will to brush away her sister's tears. Too numb to even cry, all she could do was curl onto her bed and pretend to be asleep. She lay there for hours, until her mother went to bed and the house was still.

Then she rose.

Creeping into the attic, she opened the box full of her father's belongings—ink, parchment, candles and maps, a cartographer's arsenal. There were some half-drawn sketches of Windhaven, and scrolls showing lands beyond their borders. All the things her father had spent his life crafting. He'd had a plan. Had known of other places, other ways.

Was that the truth of why he'd disappeared?

She yanked out a map, held it tight.

Gods forsake her, she'd done nothing while the love of her life was thrown to the demons. Hadn't been able to save him—or offer anything useful. All she'd done was stand there.

Her gaze lifted to the attic window.

The small circular pane was set right beneath the eaves, yet Belle could just see the belfry glowing bright against the night sky.

Her eyes narrowed.

The map crumpled in her grip.

Damn the bishop and his guards to the spreading dark. She was done with their lies. Their cruelty. Thomas and his father were no more sinners than she was—and they wouldn't be the last good people to fall under cries of 'sin.' The bishop wouldn't stop with them.

Well, neither would she.

The next time the bishop turned his gaze on a loved one, she would be ready.

CHAPTER ONE

ONE YEAR LATER
FALLEN 1:10
FALL HARVEST

T he sun had barely crested the mountains and the lamps were still burning when Isabelle DuNorde took measured steps along the twisting alley that ran from the back of the Chastry through rows of cottages to the town's lesser well. She meticulously counted each step and marked each turn on her piece of folded parchment. Each line adding detail to her map of the town—and what lay beneath.

Walking softly, she kept an ear out for the guards.

And, more importantly, for the scratching beneath the cobblestones.

The demons were quiet this morning, with only a faint scrape of claws to guide her, yet the town remained silent enough to confirm her suspicions: another tunnel lay beneath this alley. It stretched all the way from the Chastry to the well, yet more proof their Bishop lied.

Not that she had anyone to tell.

Blowing out a soft whistle, she noted the tunnel on her map and then carefully returned her notebook to its hiding place in her sleeve.

She'd spent the past year methodically finishing her father's charts, completing his life's work. She wondered whether that work had gotten him killed, but the only person to ask was Mama, and the only result would be an order to stop—and Isabelle couldn't stop. Some nights as she lay alone and aching for her lost love, tracing those lines in her head was the only thing that kept her from falling apart.

Well, that and her sister.

Emmi would have loved this project, but her sister never knew when to hold her tongue.

Her sister's life was worth more than company on cold mornings.

And why Isabelle needed to finish this map.

As soon as Emmi was of age, they were getting out of Windhaven. A map shouldn't be necessary for that, but the more the bishop tightened his grip on the town, the more Isabelle feared it might be.

She pushed strands of pale hair from her face and studied the stone path as it wound past the well to the forge and beyond. She wanted to track the tunnel further, to see if it spread beyond the town's outer wall, but the blacksmith's chimney belched smoke and the crackling of the forge drowned out the quiet scrape of the claws beneath.

She blew out a frustrated breath.

Gods of Gold and Scale, this work is taking an age.

Still, stopping for the day was probably for the best. As summer slid into autumn, the townspeople had been told to stay indoors at dawn and dusk. It gave her a window in which to work each morning—but also made that work increasingly risky. If she got caught, she'd draw even more attention from the guards and might lose any chance she had of escaping with her sister.

The sun was brighter now and the lanterns were sputtering out for the day. The townspeople would be up soon, and Mama would expect to find Isabelle in the kitchen, ready to prepare dozens of Chastry-approved buns.

Tasteless lumps that they are.

Ensuring her parchment was concealed and her pencil hidden in her hair, she reluctantly turned toward home.

The ring of iron horseshoes on cobblestones echoed down the alley.

Her shoulders tightened.

Fingers fisted in her skirts, she forced herself to keep walking. Sound carried in the morning streets. The city guard could be in the square, or circling the wall. There was no cause to look over her shoulder or hurry down the alley like a thief caught with stolen wares.

Oh, Gods. Let it be a false—

"Isabelle," Jaston's polished voice dashed her hopes. "You rose early this morning."

Be calm.

Be charming.

Do not show your feelings.

Coaxing her lips into a smile that would never match her eyes, she turned to regard the Captain of Windhaven's guard. Clad in brightly polished armor, his bold plume of red dancing atop his helm and his horse's white coat brushed to a fine sheen, he looked every inch the brave knight coming to pay tribute to his lady.

How looks can deceive.

Behind that easy smile and golden armor was a damned vulture circling its prey.

Unfortunately, she was the rabbit.

She swallowed hard and willed cheer into her tone. "Good morning, Captain Danilo." She shifted her gaze to the two guards flanking him on either side. "And to you both as well, brave Sers."

"What brings you out so early, Isabelle?" Jaston's outward expression didn't flicker, but a thread of steel laced his words. "You know the bishop has advised people to stay inside."

"Oh, you know..." She waved a hand and mentally flailed for an excuse. *Come on, think.* His eyes narrowed and her stomach flipped with worry.

Desperate, she latched onto the one thing he wanted to hear—the one thing she least wanted to say. "Ah... with the ball tonight, I was too excited to sleep, Ser. I thought to get an early start to the day, to have time for preparations..."

Forgive me, Thomas.

His silver ring burned from where she had it hidden against her breast.

Jaston's mouth split into a wide grin, the kind that made Isabelle want to scrub herself in a boiling caldron. "Ah, pretty Belle. You know how much I look forward to this evening."

Behind him, the pair of guards chuckled.

"Of course, Ser," she said demurely.

"Your mother has told you that I expect you at my side tonight." Jaston urged his horse forward until the massive warbeast was beside her and he loomed overhead. Her skin crawled as he stroked her hair. "The woman at my side must be the fairest in the room. But that cannot be at the expense of your safety, Isabelle. You must abide by the bishop's warning."

"My apologies, Ser." She lowered her gaze as if chastised.

Her mother wanted this match—had effectively told Isabelle she expected her to abandon Thomas' memory and allow the captain to court her. Isabelle wanted none of it. Her mother saw only status and protection, while she saw the marks on Jaston's servants and the way they scurried through rooms like scared mice. Foolishly, she'd thought he'd tire of her and choose one of the many willing women in Windhaven, not redouble his efforts.

Gods.

She'd rather set her hair on fire than dance with this man.

But she had to play nice until she figured out a way to discourage Jaston's pursuit—without making the lives of her mother and sister worse. No matter what, Emmi's wellbeing had to come first.

Tipping her chin up, she shielded her eyes from the brightening sky. "I thank you for the reminder."

"You'll thank me for more than that, Belle." He bent down, close enough for her to smell pork and oats on his breath. His mouth curved into a smile cold enough to grace a marble statue.

She couldn't understand why the other girls fawned over this man, with his cruel mouth and hard gaze. In the days after Thomas' death, he'd visited almost daily, bringing flowers and promises of a future she wanted no part of. She'd begged him to leave, but that only spurred him on. A creature as terrible as the demons below, who hid his truth beneath armor and the feigned role of protector.

He twirled a lock of her hair around his finger. "So pale. So fine. Such hair must be a sign of your purity and grace."

Or simply the result of my grandmother in my blood.

There were dozens of people in this town with pitch black hair that were a hundred times purer than her—she hardly said her prayers every night or thought of the bishop with respect.

And, most sinfully of all, she was planning to leave.

But she couldn't say any of those things. Couldn't pull away or push him off his horse and laugh as he tumbled ass over tea kettle. Instead, she made herself smile up at him.

"How kind," she managed.

"Tonight, Belle." He tugged on her hair and she winced at the sudden pain. "Look your best."

Oh, Gods.

He means to ask for my hand at the ball.

Her throat closed. She feared she'd be sick all over the stones if she tried to make a sound. Thankfully, he didn't appear to require a response. With a wave and a flick of the reins, he and the other two guards carried on down the alley. She stood there, hands fisted in her skirts, heart pounding and a false grin stretched across her face, until they disappeared around a corner.

Then her knees gave out and she sagged against the grocer's cart.

"Please, Gods, no," she whispered, one hand covering her mouth while the other reached for the silver ring hidden beneath her dress. In the year

Thomas had been gone, she'd never once taken it off. The simple band warmed her palm, even as tears slid down her cheeks. *I can't do it. I cannot accept his hand. No matter how terrible that might be for my family.*

Agreeing to bind herself to another man would cut her soul to ribbons. Gods. It had only been a year since Thomas had been taken from her.

Not enough time to heal—if she ever would.

Emmi swore she'd find love again, and her mother said she was being a foolish girl and that she was too young to waste her beauty in mourning. Hurry up, Mama said, and choose another—and by another, her mother most definitely meant Jaston, the most eligible bachelor in town.

Isabelle would rather live with the rats—an increasingly likely prospect when she refused Jaston that night.

But what else could she do?

Emmi wasn't old enough to leave town, and there was no more Thomas to stand between her and the captain's desires. In truth, she should be surprised he'd waited a year to make his move.

My love, I need you. She pressed the ring against her heart. *Show me what to do...*

Awareness skittered over her skin.

Something was watching her.

Breath catching in her chest, she forced herself to her feet and searched the alley—but there was no one in sight. No figures stood in windows, judging her from inside their warm cottages. Yet she couldn't shake the sensation. Slowly, her gaze lifted above the rooftops to the belfry.

The tower stood against the sky, all weathered gray stone crowned with a sharp spire.

None of the deacons walked the ramparts or rang the bell.

She must have been imagining things—she'd been doing that a lot since Thomas was taken. Feeling eyes on her only to find nothing around. Finding herself staring at the belfry, as if it held the answers to her heartache.

Perhaps it did.

The stark tower should have been imposing, and yet its steady presence soothed the raw edges of her grief. As if the lone pillar stood against the blue sky just to remind her it was possible to reach beyond your means, like a compass that pointed to dreams instead of the north.

Every time she studied the belfry, her breath seemed to steady and her resolve to escape Windhaven grew.

Her fingers tightened into fists. Her chin lifted.

Enough tears. The demons could eat her flesh before she'd agree to marry bloody Jaston.

She scrubbed her face dry and marched toward her cottage with renewed determination. There had to be a way to escape Jaston—and she'd damned well find it. She'd spent the past year studying paths and patterns, surely she could navigate this situation. She had an entire day. She'd solve this puzzle. Jaston would give up. Isabelle would remain free. Then as soon as Emmi reached her majority, they'd leave.

Her love had died in Windhaven.

Isabelle wouldn't choose another just to have a body in her bed—nor would she make a future in the town that killed him.

CHAPTER TWO

The rolls were finished, and so was Isabelle. She felt as if she'd been rolled in seeds and baked in the stone oven alongside the day's bread by the time she escaped the cottage and her mother's watchful eye. Gods. If she had to hear about Jaston's fine chin one more time, she'd shave her head and live in the trees.

In truth, that might be her only remaining option.

And if it wasn't for her sister, she'd gladly take such a life. But she had Emmi to protect. What she didn't have was any semblance of a plan for getting rid of Jaston's affections.

Get some air.

Figure it out.

Brushing flour from her skirts, she tipped her face up to the afternoon sun and drew in a deep breath.

Fallen Gods of Gold and Scale, what was she to do?

Unable to remain still, she started walking. She wove around carts and townspeople, letting her thoughts wander. Sending her unwanted suitor packing by informing him she'd rather wed his horse was guaranteed to land her entire family in difficulties. Isabelle might struggle to find care for her mother these days, but she couldn't put Emmi in danger.

Rejecting the beloved Captain of the Guard?

Not the best plan.

Like her mother's Chastry-approved rolls, that was a recipe for a chipped tooth—or worse. Unfortunately, Belle hadn't found another solution, no matter how hard she'd kneaded the morning's dough.

Think, think, think.

The sun heated her back as she moved inextricably toward the farm. Even now, a year after Thomas and his father had been cast down to the demons, she was drawn to the place. Whether it was the relative quiet of the fields or a way to remain closer to Thomas' memory, she couldn't say.

Probably both.

She waved at the miller as she passed, then a group of washers gathered around the tubs, scrubbing bedding for the Keep. Her gaze lingered on the red cloth hanging beside the miller's door, a subtle marker that they too wished to leave Windhaven. Along with the three washers, all of whom had cloths hanging from the backs of their aprons.

It was tempting to walk over and unload her worries, to take solace in those who felt as she did.

But that could put them all in danger.

And right now, she had enough trouble.

So, she carried on past them until she stood by the worn wooden fence that separated the Marr's farm from the rest of the fields. Or, what had been the Marr's farm. At one time she'd known that thatched cottage and brightly-painted barn as well as her own room. The buildings, with their dark-stained wooden frames and plastered walls, had exuded warmth, and always offered a place to shelter in a storm. Now both buildings felt foreign.

With a sigh, she propped her elbows against the rough pine fence.

In the first months following Thomas' death, she'd spent hours curled on his bed. Then the structures had been donated to Chastry-appointed nobles, who wouldn't live there, but also wouldn't suffer trespassers.

Belle thought it should have gone to Toby, the young farm hand who'd been apprenticing beneath Ser Marr. For a time, it looked like it would. Then Toby disappeared.

Those who worked the fields today did so at the bishop's bidding, under the management of his nobles. She was no expert, but even she could see they had no love for the work—and no real talent for it, either. They were likely cooks or footmen from the Keep, forced to do necessary work.

Since all our farmers are dead.

She blinked furiously against the heat in her eyes.

She'd shed no more tears over this stretch of land—or anything else the bishop had taken. No. Life in Windhaven had been hard before Thomas died, but now it was nigh unbearable. She'd quietly finish her map, and find a way to use the knowledge she'd gained to break free—

Something touched her arm. "Belle?"

"Ah!" She jumped and spun around to find her sister had joined her. "Gods, Emmi, you gave me a fright."

"Because I look like a ghost?" Flour dusted her sister's nose and streaked her copper hair. "The new grains are terrible, aren't they?" She wrinkled her nose and gave herself a shake, sending up a halo of dust. "If I were a ghost, I believe I'd find a better place to haunt. Maybe I'd lurk around a traveling caravan or explore the old ruins. Definitely no bakeries."

Belle failed to keep a smile from her lips. "Logical as always."

"Never say so." Emmi elbowed her, then propped herself against the railing in a mirror of Belle's pose. Eyes uncommonly serious, she appeared to study the farm. "Don't you find it hard being here?"

"Yes," Belle whispered. "It hurts."

But I can't stay away.

Standing side-by-side with her sister on the edge of the farm, she blinked back another unruly tear. Her fingers closed around the silver ring, and her throat flexed. How could she possibly explain that, as much as it hurt, the pain of being here kept the memories alive?

"I miss them, too," Emmi said quietly. "Did you know that I thought Toby would be my Thomas?"

Belle kissed the dusty top of her sister's head. "I suspected."

Heart aching, she wrapped an arm around her sister's shoulders and gave her a squeeze. Gods, what a tangle their lives had become. She wanted her sister to find that pure love she'd had for Thomas—but not the grief that followed. "When we're free of this place, we will find love."

Emmi gave a soft laugh. "You know I know you're lying, right?"

"What?" Belle started.

"You don't have any intention of finding love again, and I know it." Emmi rested her chin on Belle's shoulder. "But I'm wily and tenacious and am going to make sure love finds you."

"Hah..." Belle's attempt at a laugh emerged as a strangled sob.

Her sister pulled away and stared up at her, concern knitting her brows. "What is it? What happened? You were so quiet this morning, and I just knew something was wrong."

"It's nothing." Isabelle shook her head. She couldn't drag Emmi into her troubles with Jaston. Her sister was like a bottle of black powder held too close to a flame when it came to the captain, all too ready to explode at the drop of a handkerchief. "I am just—"

"If you say sad, I am going to strip naked and run screaming down the road."

Her jaw dropped. "You wouldn't dare."

"No?" Emmi's chin jutted out and she kicked off a slipper. "Mama sent me out here to collect you, so we could get ready for the fete. I figure if I'm already naked, there's one step accomplished."

"Stop." Isabelle caught her sister's hands before she could untie her overskirt. "Please."

"Then *tell* me." Emmi's voice broke. "I can't help if you won't tell me."

"I can't," Belle hissed. "It's too..."

The clatter of iron horseshoes against stone had her swallowing her words. She slowly lifted her gaze to regard the trio of riders trotting along the edge of town. Jaston and his guard, their armor bright with warning. Jaston lifted a hand, and the ground seemed to tremble beneath her. Or maybe that was her body, quaking with horror at the thought of those hands touching her skin.

She gripped her sister's shoulders.

Emmi twisted around to stare at the guards. "Demons suck buns," she muttered. "It's that jackass, isn't it?"

"Hush," Belle whispered between her teeth, her lips curving into what had to be a failed attempt at a smile. She forced herself to lift a hand and wave at Jaston. His answering smile was a flash of white teeth that reminded her of a fox in a henhouse, while his eyes were sharp as a hawk's, searching for weakness. "For the love of the fallen gods," she hissed, "smile and wave."

For once, Emmi didn't argue.

If her sister's wave resembled a washer working on a stubborn stain, the guards didn't appear to notice.

In silent agreement, they held their respective poses until the guard had passed the turn for the farm and continued along the western border of central Windhaven. As the figures grew smaller, Belle sagged, a mix of relief and dread churning through her middle.

He's going to demand my hand tonight.

Cupping her hands over her mouth, she tried to catch her breath.

"Oh, Belle," Emmi whispered. "The bastard announced his intentions, hasn't he?"

Unable to muster a lie, Isabelle gave a miserable nod. "He does not care that I don't want him."

"I imagine that's the appeal." Emmi snorted. "He's a bully."

When had her sister gotten so wise?

"I don't know what to do," she confessed.

"Hmm." Emmi chewed on her lip. "He knows you despise him and he likes it—you can't reason with that kind of man. So... we go? Stuff my majority. We could leave for the woods tonight—"

"Too dangerous." Isabelle shook her head. "We can't."

Jaston might expect her to make just such a move—he and his guards had been awfully present today. Besides, the miller and others weren't ready yet. She couldn't put their plans in jeopardy. "We have no supplies prepared, and no way of gathering any without being noticed. Besides, leaving with someone still considered a child? The guard won't stop hunting us."

"Fine, fine." Emmi crossed her arms. "But you're marrying that horse's ass over my rotting corpse."

Isabelle sucked in a breath. "Don't speak of such things."

After the past year, she couldn't even *think* of losing her sister.

Still, Emmi was right. Isabelle truly could not marry that horrid man. Lying with anyone other than Thomas felt like a betrayal. But Jaston? That would be so much worse. "You're right. I can't." She ran her hands over her hair and searched the shorn fields for inspiration. "But we cannot reason with him or appeal to a better nature. We don't have the funds for bribery..."

"We can't even try sugar buns." Emmi slanted a glance at her. "You could get ugly real fast?"

Isabelle couldn't help it, she laughed. "Oh, is that all?"

"I know, I know." Emmi stuck out her tongue. "You're too pretty for your own good. That ass wants the 'prettiest girl' in the town." Her sister smacked her lips together with exaggerated distaste. "He's always talking about your hair and figure. Ugh. It's like you're a prize horse and not a person."

"Neigh." Belle puffed out her cheeks, then lifted her gaze to the sky. "Perhaps if I smelled like a horse, he'd look elsewhere..."

Wait.

That was it.

Her eyes snapped to her sister. "You're right, he wants a prize—not a person. So, what if I am no longer a prize to covet?"

"Oooh." Her sister's eyes resembled saucers. "That's *brilliant.*"

"Yes, yes is it." A true smile shaped Isabelle's lips, and she straightened with renewed resolve. No one could spend years keeping Emmi out of trouble and not learn a few tricks of their own. "I will simply have to disgrace myself at the ball. Not anything terrible enough to endanger you or Mama, but just enough to make Jaston reconsider his intentions."

Maybe even turn his attentions elsewhere.

Fragile hope burned in her chest.

Emmi grinned mischievously. "Lucky for you, I'm an expert at this."

"The gods have blessed me," Isabelle said with a laugh. She held out her arm. "Come then, my sister who is an expert at public disgrace. Let's go home and you can teach me your ways while we dress for the ball."

Laughing over their schemes, they returned to the cottage and readied themselves for the Harvest Tyne. Their mother joined them for a time, ensuring necklines were modest and their hair was styled in a Chastry-approved manner. When mother brushed Isabelle's hair, just as she had when Isabelle had been little, tears once again threatened to fall.

"There," Mama said. "Aren't you a beauty."

Isabelle nearly confessed everything.

She missed the mother she'd known. She longed to be swept into a hug and told everything would be alright. But as much as she wanted to believe her mother would stand beside her, the words caught in her throat. Mama had grown even more devout over the past year. Every word was a hymn or chastising phrase. Every action designed to please the bishop.

If he approved of her marrying Jaston, her mother would move mountains to make it happen.

"Thank you, Mama," she said softly. "I will be down in a moment."

"Don't dally." Her mother walked to the door without a backward glance. "It is sinful to be late to our Bishop's celebration."

Emmi made a face as she followed.

Belle forced a smile for her sister's benefit. She waited until her mother and Emmi were downstairs, then she pulled out what she considered her safety kit. Folded parchment map. Flint. Twine. And a roll of waxed cotton that could be used to create a small torch.

She carefully secured the items in her corset.

Ever since Thomas had been cast below, she'd been prepared to suffer the same fate. And while she planned to counter Jaston with simple fumbles and minor offenses, this ball could be no exception.

CHAPTER THREE

N ight had fallen and torches lined the roads.

Isabelle would have been struck by the novelty of walking the streets in the dark, swept up in the magic of flames warming the sides of buildings and the stars twinkling above. Except she was about to embark on the social equivalent of warfare, and dread sat in her throat like a frog.

Keeping close to Emmi, she followed her mother and joined all the towns-people walking in the same direction: toward the Keep.

They flowed down the streets, a stream of attendees.

Emmi reached up and took her hand—Isabelle held tight without shame.

When she'd been young, she and Emmi had skipped down the streets, singing songs and delighting in the pageantry of it all. She remembered the people around them laughing and joking, swapping tall tales. But revelry had fled with the years. Now, Mama marched as seriously as a soldier drilling on a field. And the people around them walked with careful expressions and spoke in hushed tones.

Sure, there was a smile here, a laugh there.

Yet the overall feel was somber.

Ominous.

They turned a corner and her heart beat faster. They'd almost reached the Chastry and the Keep lay just beyond. While shorter than the Chastry, the Keep's sprawling footprint more than made up the space.

Giving Emmi's hand a squeeze, Isabelle released her grip and stepped slightly behind her mother. Careful not to draw attention, she tugged at her dress, lowering her neckline from proper to almost-scandalous.

Well, scandalous for their current year. Three years ago her neckline would have been considered acceptable, possibly conservative.

How things had changed.

What they ate, what they could safely speak in public, all seemed to be tightening around them. More than necklines had changed when it came to style in Windhaven. She felt strange in her formal dress. Old-fashioned, with long sleeves and high waist. A style that had gone out of fashion with the old gods, but that the bishop was determined to resurrect.

Even Mama had seemed shocked when the bishop had described "acceptable" dress for young ladies. Isabelle and Emmi had been forced to take apart multiple older gowns to match the style—which limited their options when it came to fabric and colors.

But Belle didn't mind.

In fact, she rather fancied her combination: green in memory of Thomas, steel gray for bravery, and red for courage.

Tonight, she needed all the courage she could muster.

Emmi had cobbled together a dress in similar hues, though her sister had more green, with just enough red left for trim. Surprising no one, their mother wore subdued tones of brown and ochre.

They reached the square and flowed with the others around the Chastry. With every step her insides tied themselves into tighter knots. Struggling to keep a placid expression on her face, she quietly greeted their neighbors and acquaintances, with a special glance for her co-conspirators.

She nodded at the blacksmith.

"Good eve, Miss Isabelle," he rumbled.

"Ser Braww," she replied, pleased to note the red scarf at his throat. "You're looking well."

"Come now, girls." Mama ushered them along, pushed ahead toward the line of people waiting for their turn to enter the Keep. Her mother huffed, clearly displeased with their position. But Belle welcomed the four wagon-lengths between them and the doorway.

She focused on breathing, on readying herself for what was to come. Her whole life she'd done what she could to please her mother in public, to behave at events and maintain a perfect reputation.

But not this evening.

Awareness tickled the back of her neck.

She turned around, and her gaze followed the sensation to the belfry. Nothing moved beyond the torchlight glimmering along the brass bell, yet she felt a presence as she often did. If her father's spirit or Thomas' or a single scale of the lost gods resided in that stone tower, she would take any support they offered—she needed it, for what was to come.

"Bless me, Belfry," she whispered. "For I am about to sin."

"Come, Isabelle," her mother announced. "Keep up."

Respite over, she held her head high and walked into the Keep beside her sister and mother.

Despite her worries, Isabelle couldn't help but marvel at the inside.

The stone block of a building had been transformed into a space of magic and mystery. The very air seemed to sparkle, glowing with the light of hundreds of tiny candles set within faceted glass jars.

Fall's bounty had been twisted into fantastical constructions. Wreaths of vine and tiny gourds hung along walls, pillars of the same framed the great hall's heavy stone columns. Yet none of those held a candle to the display covering the far wall: a massive autumn dragon woven from branches, shafts of wheat, and strips of shimmering fabric.

All in shades of gold, the dragon circled the stained glass window and loomed above the bishop's seat.

"Whoa," Emmi whispered.

"It is extraordinary," Belle said.

They were ushered into the interior receiving line. Everyone attending this evening—and that was the entire town, to be sure—were expected to be formally introduced to their host, the Chastry's Bishop.

And to pay homage to him.

Her wonder fled as her gaze landed on the man.

At one time they'd had a baron, who'd ruled these lands with his family. Now, they had Bishop Vaqueln. A man so dour, his face would probably shatter if it ever adopted a smile. And what an unnerving face it was. Narrow and pointed like a beak, his eyes small and close set across the bridge of a hooked nose. Harsh lines framed his mouth.

In his ceremonial robes of white velvet embroidered with thick gold—the colors of the fallen gods—he looked more like a bird of prey than a leader sent to save them from folly.

Beside him stood Jaston, dressed in his autumn finery: tight white breeches and an ochre velvet doublet with subtly puffed sleeves and threads of gold trim, which complimented the bishop's robes. Jaston's gaze landed on her and his top lip hooked into a smirk, as if he already considered her his property.

Gods have mercy

Emmi elbowed her and hissed, "Don't let him win."

"Never." Isabelle spoke carefully, barely moving her lips. She tipped her chin and steeled her insides.

It was time to damage her reputation.

Their family was called forward and she stepped on her hem to lower her neckline just a little further, then intentionally stumbled on the single step to the bishop's raised platform, repressing her usual grace. She curtsied as expected, but kept her back stiff and held her skirts unevenly as she dipped low. Small things, to be sure. Yet the bishop's mouth tightened at the corners and a thrill of triumph ran through her.

It was working.

The spirits must be looking out for her.

She sent a tiny prayer to her guardian belfry and rose from her curtsey at the bishop's bidding.

Now came the Captain of the Guard.

She recited thanks for Windhaven's protection along with her mother, careful to let no feeling bleed into the words. Then she offered her hand to Jaston to kiss. Holding it limp, she gave no reaction as he pressed his lips to the back of her hand. The narrowed angle of his eyes told her that he'd expected more. Good. Let him be disappointed. She kept her expression placid and quietly slipped away when another group of young ladies approached—if he thought she'd cling to him like a vine, he was very much mistaken.

Without so much as a backward glance, she eased into the crowd, confident in the knowledge that he'd be trapped at the bishop's side for at least another hour as they greeted all the attendees.

Giving me time to remove the bishop's approval of our union.

She squeezed Emmi's arm and mouthed, *Wish me luck.*

Her sister grinned and winked. "You've got this."

Bolstered by the support, Isabelle set about doing as much minor damage to her reputation as she could in an hour.

Moving between pillars of woven branches and glimmering lights, she greeted neighbors and made a calculated series of social mistakes. She complimented the Yang sisters on their brightly-hued dresses—though the bright yellow was considered a summer color—and brushed a woven pillar with her shoulder, getting tiny pieces of dried vine and leaf in her hair. She danced with Ser Morris and laughed at the same brewing joke he told every year—even though the bishop had suggested ale should be spoken of seriously.

A glance at the figure sitting in the raised throne confirmed the bishop had noticed the laughter, and he wasn't amused. His eyes glinted with warning, and for a moment, a skull sat where his face had been.

She blinked and the image vanished.

I'm imagining things, that is all.

Yet, she hesitated.

Throat tight, she ducked behind a pillar and tried to catch her breath. What if her guardian spirit was sending her a warning, trying to tell her she was in danger? Gods above, she didn't want to go too far. And these days it was so hard to know when minor irritations would transform into sin.

But would one inappropriate laugh and a handful of compliments be enough to discourage Jaston?

Not a chance.

She straightened her shoulders.

No more quaking behind a pillar or imagining skulls for faces, she had work to do. So what if the bishop had taken note of her social blunders—that was good. She needed him to notice. Instead of hiding like a scared little mouse, she needed to finish the job. Make sure he rescinded approval and forced Jaston to turn his attentions elsewhere.

Anywhere else.

"Psst." Emmi appeared at her side. "You're doing great, sis."

"Thanks," Belle muttered. "Not sure I'm cut out for social disapproval. I can't think of what to do next."

"This is why I don't follow rules." Her sister snorted softly. "And why I'm here to help. When in doubt..." She nodded at platters of tiny bowls of soup being circulated by servants.

Right. Food.

There were hundreds of ways to fumble social niceties when it came to eating, especially at the ball. "Thanks, oh wise miscreant." Isabelle grinned at her younger sister and gave her a quick, one-armed hug. "Now, please try to be better than me for the rest of the evening?"

"Maybe." Emmi's dimples flashed, then she vanished into the throng.

Shaking her head, Isabelle followed suit.

She made her way to a platter of neatly cut pork pies, garnished with perfect dollops of apricot jam and bright sprigs of parsley. Her stomach rumbled and she repressed a grin—apparently misbehaving was hungry work. And she could raise eyebrows while enjoying a snack.

"This looks wonderful," she said, snatching the largest piece from the tray with her bare hand and popping it directly into her mouth.

The servant gaped at her. "Mm... miss?"

"Delicious." She spoke around a mouthful of pastry and meat.

The servant seemed to pale before her eyes. She cringed internally, but made herself continue. As terrible as she felt for those working on the day of the ball, needs must. Normally, young ladies took a sliver of embossed parchment before allowing a servant to place a treat—normally the smallest on the tray—on the paper. That way their bare hands never touched food.

They also never spoke with their mouths full.

Oh well. Tonight, she was in for a penny, in for a pork pie.

The poor servant was still staring at her in obvious horror. "M-miss, there is paper for—"

"No need," she said blithely, and snagged another piece.

Mmm. She didn't need to fake her delight. It had been too long since she had a real meat pie—months since she'd had bacon. This whole misbehaving strategy was surprisingly tasty—

A hand grabbed her arm.

She was whipped around, and Jaston's face filled her vision. "Jaston, I—"

"Be silent and smile." His mouth was a flat line, his eyes cold as the outer wall in the depth of winter. His fingers dug cruelly into her forearm and her back as he pulled her into a dance. "I don't know what you think you're playing at, Isabelle. But you'll stop now or regret it."

She forced her lips to curve upward into a bland smile. "I have no idea what you are talking about."

"Don't play the fool with me," he snapped.

They whirled across the floor.

Her hair threatened to fall out of its pins as he whipped her through a series of vicious turns. Pale strands tangled across her view, but did nothing to blur her view of his anger. Her knees wanted to quake, but she refused to crumble into defeat in the middle of the ballroom.

"I have been enjoying the evening," she said defiantly, tilting her chin.

"The bishop had noticed your little activities, and suggested you might not be a wise choice for a wife." He spoke through clenched teeth. "I assured him it was nerves, and that you would prove your worth."

"What if I don't want to?" She tried to spin free.

He yanked her closer and spoke softly. "You'd better change your mind. Or your family will pay the price."

Please, Gods, no.

She'd done all this to avoid such a fate, convinced he'd never argue with the bishop. How wrong she'd been.

"Why—" Her voice broke. "Why do this?"

"Because you're the fairest girl in the town, and until tonight your reputation has been beyond reproach." He pulled her flat against his chest. "You're the prize female, and I'll have you."

"Some prize," she hissed, "when you have to threaten a family to claim it."

"Threaten?" He laughed in her face. "No, darling. You're confused. I'm the Captain of the Guard and the most eligible bachelor in Windhaven. Only a female who's demon-touched would reject my offer. And if she's been influenced, so too is her family. It's only right to remove that danger."

She was going to be sick all over the ballroom floor.

"So, Belle," he said. "What will it be?"

Swallowing back the bile in her throat, she met his gaze. She had no choice— and the smug tilt to his lips and gleam in his eyes announced he knew it. He'd always planned to force her; it might even give him pleasure. There was nothing else she could do.

At least, not right now.

She carefully considered all the ways she could murder him in his sleep and said, "Very well, I will marry—"

"No!" Her sister's small form barreled out from between a pair of skirts and threw herself between them. The force knocked them apart, and Isabelle tripped over her skirts and landed on her rear. Tangled in her dress, she struggled to get to her feet. It should have been easy, but it was as if fear had sucked any strength from her limbs.

Please. Please don't let me lose Emmi.

"Begone, flea." He swung at Emmi.

Smaller than Jaston and easily twice as fast, her sister dodged his attempts to grab her. She ducked under his arms and pummeled his chest with her fists. One strike swung upward and caught the corner of his jaw. "You're a bloody monster! You leave my—"

"What is the meaning of this display?" The bishop's voice sliced through the room, like a sharpened scythe through grain.

Jaston wiped blood from the corner of his mouth. "Nothing, Eminence. The girl is confused."

"Many apologies." Mama scurried forward. "Emmanuella. Stop this at once."

"It's my fault. I tripped." Trembling with fear, Isabelle staggered it to her feet. "Please..."

"My bride-to-be was overcome with delight at my offer," Jaston said, a vicious edge to his words. He watched Emmi like a mountain wolf did its prey. "This foolish child—"

"No!" Emmi pointed at Jaston. "He's forcing Belle to marry him to protect us."

"Hush, child." Mama's face was tight with displeasure. "You're overwrought."

"No," Emmi said defiantly. "I'm not."

Isabelle needed to say something, to do something. But her tongue was frozen and she couldn't seem to catch her breath. All she could do was study the ballroom. It thrilled her—terrified her—to see how the watching crowd was muttering. Anger shaped brows. Mouths flattened. And frustration with a year of hardship boiled to the surface.

A year without goods and now bacon and apple tarts were practically tumbling from the serving trays?

The bishop may have made a mistake.

Yet as much as she wished to leave, she had no desire to destroy the entire fabric of their town. Windhaven lived and breathed the ways of the Chastry, where would they be without it? She had to convince her sister to apologize. It was only a betrothal, they'd have until the spring tyne to escape.

"Emmi, stop." Isabelle found her voice. "It will be okay. I promise."

"No, Belle." For a girl short of stature, her sister stood tall and fierce as any warrior. "I'm not letting you sacrifice yourself for me." She looked around the room, her blue eyes daring the town to support her. "You all know Belle. She helps all of you. She's always cooking or caring for young or tending your animals. And she's still in love with Thomas Marr. Jaston is an evil bastard who bullies everyone in this town and gets power from fear—"

"*Silence.*" The bishop rose from his seat. "The child is demon-touched."

"No!" Heart pounding, Isabelle threw herself in front of Emmi and faced the bishop, hands curled into fists at her sides. "She's not touched, she's scared. She thinks she's protecting me. Leave her alone!"

"Lies," Jaston countered. "She's been listening to demons."

The bishop tsked sadly. "It must be so."

He approached, and Isabelle swore the room grew colder the closer he drew. "I heard the monsters stirring this morning," he intoned, "and thought to myself, surely the Great Golden Gods would not allow the demons to taint our sacred day of harvest. This one day when the hard working people of Windhaven enjoy the fruits of their labors. But it is not so."

"Is that because of demons, or because ye've been hoarding all the meat," someone cried.

Rumbles of agreement trembled through the room.

Despite her antics, or perhaps because of them, Isabelle's sister was much loved. The people were protective of her—and, like Belle, they'd all lost too many loved ones to cries of demons. She noticed the miller and blacksmith drawing near, their expressions fierce.

"Enough!" the bishop cried. "We must rid our town of this menace."

A group of guards encircled them. Isabelle tried to fight them off, but there were too many and her fists did nothing against chainmail or plate. She couldn't keep them from getting ahold of Emmi. She begged and pleaded for mercy, but they grabbed her, shoved her into Jaston's grip.

Others formed a line between them and the townspeople, moving in sync as Emmi was dragged outside.

The squeal of the gate cut through Isabelle.

"No!" Gaze locked on her sister, she fought against Jaston's hold. "Don't do this!"

"Too late, Belle," Jaston hissed, arms tightening around her middle so much they crushed her lungs. "You should have been willing."

Unable to speak, barely able to breathe, she staggered forward in his grasp. The pain of her ribs creaking beneath the pressure was nothing compared to the horror in her heart. By the time they reached the square, the grate to the demons was already open. Guards brandished swords and shields, creating a deadly corridor, down which Emmi and Isabelle were carried.

Behind them, she could hear Mama wailing. But she was begging Emmi to repent and Belle hated her for it. Even now, with Emmi held at the edge of the pit, her mother chose the Chastry.

"You will repent," the bishop intoned, voice pitched to somehow carry over the crowd. "If you emerge, we will know you are cleansed of your sins. Thus, the Fallen Gods demand."

"Horseshit." Gods, but her sister was glorious. Head high, Emmi pointed with her free hand at the bishop. "You're an evil bastard, and so's your captain. I'd rather be with the demons that used against my sister."

"What a pity it came to this." Jaston's grip slackened.

Isabelle gulped in a breath. "No! Emmi, no! You're all I have left." She craned her neck around to look at the bishop past Jaston's shoulder. "Please, Your Eminence. I beg you. Please let her go. She's just a child. If the Chastry can't save a child, what good is it?"

The bishop didn't acknowledge her plea, didn't so much as look at her. Long, thin fingers gestured toward the pit. "The creature spouts sedition like a fish does water. Cast her back to her kind!"

"No—" Isabelle screamed as her sister was shoved through the opening. "Emmi!"

Dear Gods, it was happening again.

Her loved one was being cast below, and Isabelle was forced to watch. Jaston was holding her, just as he had the year before. All her maps and her planning and cries and she was still helpless. It was the previous year repeating, a mirror of her nightmare.

Except for one thing.

She stilled.

This time Jaston wasn't wearing his armor.

Already the guards were starting to close the grate, she must be quick.

"Oh, Jaston. I must tell you one thing..." She twisted around in his arms and waited for his head to lower toward her. Then she slammed her knee into his groin with all the force she could muster. "Go to the demons."

His arms fell from her and he doubled-over in pain with a muffled cry.

Free of his hold, she launched herself forward, racing for the pit before the grate was lowered. She threw herself forward. Her skirt caught on the door's iron spikes, yet she slid through the opening and into the darkness beyond.

Hold on, Emmi. I'm coming.

CHAPTER FOUR

I sabelle slid down angled stone into the heart of darkness beneath the Chastry.

Arms outstretched, elbows and knees scraping along the chute, she gasped when the stone suddenly vanished. Thrown into the air, she didn't have time to scream before she crashed into the ground. The impact drove the air from her lungs, though what felt like a pile of dried leaves broke her fall.

She prayed that was the case—afraid to imagine what else could lie along the tunnel's floor.

Coughing, trying to catch her breath, she tried to get her bearings. Her hand closed over a stick and she clutched it close as she got to her feet. Thank the fallen gods, she needed such a thing.

Though more than a blessing, she needed light.

The farrier would proclaim it darker than a bull's arsehole, and Belle wouldn't have argued.

It was pitch black in the tunnels.

The darkest space she'd ever seen, even darker than the cupboard she'd hidden inside as a child. She blinked, willing her eyes to adjust to the pitch, yet she couldn't even see her own hand before her face. Though... was that a lighter patch over there? She crawled toward it, and realized the faint light must mark where the grate covered the entrance above. Lighter, and it was as dark as her bedroom at night.

Still, there was enough illumination for her to see her fingers, and to pull the waxed cloth and flint from her corset.

She started to call out for Emmi. Stopped herself.

Don't make your sister a target.

She froze, listening carefully for the distinctive sound of scratching. A sound she searched for almost every day for the past year—only this time, there was no street between her and the demons. The scratch of claws reached her. Faint, but she'd swear it was growing louder with every beat of her heart.

But they are not here yet. No one had expected a sacrifice this evening, not even the demons. She had to use that advantage. Ready the supplies she'd hidden on her person and find her sister. She hurriedly wrapped the cloth around the bulbous end of the stick she'd found.

"Emmi," she whispered. "Emmi, where are you?"

No voice answered.

Her eyes were starting to adjust to the gloom, and she could make out rough shapes around her. But she couldn't find anything resembling her sister. Where was Emmi? What if her sister had landed badly, hit her head on the rock and been knocked unconscious?

She clutched her flint, hesitating to light her makeshift torch.

The waxed fabric wouldn't burn for very long, and she needed to make every moment of flame count. As far as she knew, light was the only thing that could keep the demons at bay.

Holding tight to her unlit torch, she scanned the area.

"Emmi," she called, a little louder this time. "Emmi, where are you?"

"Belle?" A shaky voice answered from a distance.

"Oh, thank the gods." A relieved breath escaped her. She squinted into the darkness, trying to find her sister. Was that a darker blot ahead? A tunnel opening perhaps...

She nearly smacked herself.

Of course, it was a tunnel. She knew it was a tunnel, because she'd marked it on her map.

Good grief, she needed to pull herself together. She'd charted every possible turn of the labyrinth beneath her town. If she'd stop to think for a moment, she'd remember how tunnels branched from the grate in the square, spreading through the town like cracks in a glass. If the grate was at her back, then the far tunnel to her left should wind north to the Keep.

"Belle?" her sister called. "Where are you?"

"Hold on, Emmi," she said. "I'm getting us out of this."

One arm outstretched before her so she didn't walk nose-first into a wall, one clutching her unlit torch, she inched toward the opening.

The space where the tunnels and the Keep collided was the largest stretch of tunnels she hadn't charted. Surely there had to be some way to escape the labyrinth. If they emerged from the tunnels, the bishop would have to declare Emmi redeemed. Then she could tell all their neighbors how to survive, and no one else would be lost to the demons.

With each step, the scratching became louder.

She hurried forward, and smacked right into a wall.

"Ouch." Wincing from the jolt, she used the wall to guide her and walked as fast as she dared. Behind her, wavering cries began to build in volume, bouncing off the walls.

Golden Gods preserve her.

Abandoning any attempt at stealth, she broke into a half run. "Emmi!"

"Belle!" Her sister, who'd stood so bravely before the bishop and his guards, sounded terrified. "Run! They're here. Run!"

To the pit of darkness with that.

Isabelle struck her flint against the wall and a hail of sparks flashed in the dark. Her torch sputtered to life, and she saw that she'd made it to the tunnel opening. She ran inside—directly toward her sister's voice.

Her feet skidded on dirt and debris and pale objects. She rounded a corner, and there was Emmi, crouched on the ground in a niche where two of the tunnel's supporting arches curved upward to join at the crest of the ceiling. Her sister's eyes were saucers, her cheeks scuffed with dirt.

And she was not alone.

Hulking shadows circled her.

The demons were huge. Massive shapes with horns, hunched beneath some kind of cloak.

"Get back!" She swung the torch at them. "Begone!"

They hissed and scuttled into the shadows. Their bodies ducked and wove around each other, so rapidly and in such great a number that it was as if the very darkness boiled around her.

Claws rattling and teeth gleaming in the dark. This close, the scratching was overwhelmed by a new sound. The slap of leather, as if a row of leather work aprons had been left outside in a storm. Flapping against themselves as the wind tossed and twisted them on the clothing line.

Throat tight with fear, she forced her way to her sister.

Placing herself between the creatures and Emmi, she faced the darkness. She kept the torch high, and crouched as low as she dared. "Emmi," she said. "Are you hurt?"

"No... no," Emmi whispered. "I'm well."

"Thank the gods," she breathed. With her free hand, she reached behind her and touched Emmi's knee. "Don't lose your nerve now. Come, take my hand. I've mapped almost every inch of this labyrinth. I can get us out of here."

Emmi fingers closed around hers. "There are so many of them, Belle..."

That there are.

Belle swallowed hard.

The creatures kept themselves just beyond the torch's light, and she was unable to distinguish where one misshapen shadow ended and the next began. But she could hear them. Chattering and scratching and flapping things, waiting for her small light to burn itself out.

How much longer did she have?

I pray long enough.

"Come." She couldn't risk the time to consult her map, she had to rely on her memory. "The Keep is this way." Without turning away from the monsters, she pulled Emmi to her feet and tucked her close against her side. "We stay together. We walk quickly. And we will get out of this place."

Together, they started walking.

The shadows churned around them, but none seemed willing to approach the torch. Thank goodness. At least that part of the bishop's claims were true: the creatures did shun the light.

She moved the torch in a careful arc, back and forth.

With each pass, the demons shifted out of reach, creating a rough path forward. She and Emmi passed beneath some small grates. Light filtered down from above, and the demons retreated further.

Was that music she heard?

Yes.

Hope shot through her.

Gripping Emmi's hand tighter, she set a faster pace. Music meant they were beneath the Keep, and the Keep had to be where the exit lay—she'd checked all the other avenues herself. "Hurry, Emmi. We're going to get out of here, and the demons can—"

Something grabbed the back of her skirts and gave a vicious tug.

The fabric wrapped tight around her knees, and she fell over her own feet. She crashed to the ground. Emmi's fingers slid from her grip.

Worse, she lost hold of the torch.

She shoved hair out of her face and scrambled toward it on all fours, but the cursed thing had bounced out of reach and fallen into a slight dip. Broken stone and what might be bone blocked some of the light. Claws sliced the air between her and the torch and she lurched back.

The demons were already closing in.

Teeth and eyes burning red surrounded her.

Unable to reach her torch, she pushed Emmi behind her and brandished her flint. "Stay back." She struck the flint against the stone floor, creating a tiny shower of sparks. "Stay away from us, beasts."

The sparks disappeared and one of the demons lunged for her.

Twisting around to shield Emmi with her body, she closed her eyes and braced for claws to score her flesh.

Except the strike never came.

Shaking like a leaf in a storm, she peeked through her lashes.

Her mouth fell open with pure shock. Another demon had appeared, only this one stood between her and the rest of the creatures. The new one roared at the mass, muscles bunching along its back from the force of the cry. Arms wide, and massive panels of what looked to be leather hanging from them.

The other demons backed up, grouping together into a snarling bunch in the narrow mouth of a smaller tunnel. She breathed a tiny sigh of relief at the increased distance—only they all now stood between her and the source of the music.

Is trading many demons for a single one better?

She had to pray it was.

"Belle..." Emmi's voice wavered.

"Hush." She tried to sound certain. "Don't look."

The massive creature stepped toward the others, and then it kicked her torch closer to the mass of demons, temporarily trapping them in the smaller space; they'd have to venture into the light to pursue.

She swallowed hard.

The creature glanced over its shoulder and tipped its head to the right. It took a few steps in that direction, then repeated the gesture.

Was it asking her to follow it?

Emmi gripped her arm and hissed, "What do we do?"

"I... ah..." Belle stared at the torch.

It was already sputtering. They didn't have much time.

Her gaze shifted between the mass of hissing demons, and the lone creature who'd driven them back. It motioned again, more urgently. Her heart stuttered at the sight of wicked talons tipping its fingers. The thing was massive, large enough to subdue its demonic kin.

Muscled and covered in dark fur and tall enough that its ears nearly brushed the tunnel's roof.

A force to be reckoned with.

She had no doubt it could dispatch a number of its brethren. But there were so many. And clearly the others wouldn't be blocked by her flickering torch for much longer. There was no way she could reach the Keep now, not with the torch on the brink of expiring and all those demons in her path. In fact, in this nest of twisting tunnels and hidden roads, there was only one path she could see.

"We follow this creature, Emmi," she said. "And pray to the fallen gods this is no trick."

CHAPTER FIVE

U p. The creature was leading them upward.

Holding tight to Emmi's hand, Isabelle kept herself slightly between her sister and the massive creature. Tricky, in the perpetual gloom of the tunnels and while navigating a narrow set of twisting stairs in her ballgown. But necessary. As much as Belle wanted to believe this demon was helping them, she had no idea where it was taking them.

Or why.

So what if she felt strangely safe around this creature? She wasn't taking any chances with her sister's life. Emmi hadn't spoken a word since they'd followed the demon out of that tunnel, and her sister still trembled.

Belle understood why.

Drawing in a breath, she squeezed Emmi's hand.

Her eyes had adjusted to the darkness, and she could finally take stock of the creature. When the bishop had spoken of the demons, she'd pictured spindly, sickly things, grasping from beneath the streets with hands like bone and faces sharp as knives—but that couldn't be further from the truth.

This creature leading her and Emmi up a curved staircase was as large as a marble statue of the golden gods, with impossibly broad shoulders covered in thick fur. What she'd thought were cloaks were in fact leather wings protruding from his back, currently clasped at his throat like a cloak.

The demons were bats—if bats were the size of orcs.

And had arms strong enough to lift a pair of oxen.

Fallen Gods of gold and scale, protect me.

Alongside a ruff of fur almost like thick human hair, huge ears swept back on its head, occasionally twitching and turning as it no doubt heard hundreds of things she couldn't. They reminded her of a fox's ears, wide for catching sounds and covered with fur so fine it resembled velvet.

She drew closer, unable to stop herself from studying its form, searching for something she couldn't explain.

Its ears stood straight up, attention fixed ahead.

Something's there.

Slowing her steps, she pushed Emmi behind her. Her demon guide didn't appear alarmed, but who knew if that was a good thing, or if they were about to walk right into its trap?

She crept around the next bend in the stairs to a small landing.

A smaller demon came into view on the stairs ahead and Isabelle froze. From behind her, Emmi squeaked.

Isabelle readied herself to run, yet the smaller demon didn't approach.

It nodded at her guide, and the enormous creature returned the gesture—the two apparently knew each other. No words were spoken, and neither creature appeared agitated. Then the smaller one disappeared from view, heading up the stairs—the same direction she and Emmi were being led.

This is either a good sign, or very, very bad.

She just wished she knew which.

Her batlike guide looked over an enormous shoulder at her, and motioned for her and Emmi to continue upward. No growls or strikes followed. Her feet wanted to follow, yet she hesitated. Was this feeling of safety a lie? What if she was being taken to a nest full of hungry young...

Dark eyes caught hers and her heart stuttered.

Brown eyes, not black. How strange for a demon.

And oddly beautiful—

"Where are we going, Belle?" Emmi whispered and clutched her arm. "And how are there stairs?"

Giving herself a shake, Belle forced her gaze away from the creature's. She searched the space behind them, relieved to find no signs of pursuit. But those other demons were down there, waiting for another chance. She had no idea how to evade them, and zero intention of facing anything until she did.

Which left up, and her brown-eyed demon.

"We keep going," she said softly, letting her gaze return to the creature's.

How was there such warmth in a demon's gaze? She couldn't understand it, and perhaps she didn't need to. Not yet. All that mattered right now was that she and Emmi had a chance to survive this place. "This one has done us no harm, and we have to believe its intentions are pure."

"But *stairs?*" Emmi hissed. "In the *tunnels?*"

Belle could only shake her head. "I can't explain it. I never mapped anything beyond the tunnels."

The creature's brows lifted and it gestured upward again.

Her lips twitched. "Our unlikely savior makes an excellent point," she said, giving Emmi a gentle tug. "The only way to discover the truth behind these stairs is to keep going."

"And I thought getting tossed in a pit was scary," Emmi grumbled.

Me too, Isabelle thought.

Hand-in-hand, they continued.

It felt like an age, but in truth it was likely only a matter of minutes before they reached the top of the staircase. She stumbled onto the landing alongside her sister. The skirts of their old-fashioned dresses had grown heavier with each turn of the stairs, and Isabelle's breaths were labored. Half-bent over her knees, Emmi didn't appear to have fared much better.

Isabelle leaned against the wall and regarded a round door set in the stone wall across the landing.

A portal to salvation, or an invitation to an untimely demise?

The creature opened it, sending the wooden circle swinging inward, and motioned for her and Emmi to enter. She couldn't see much of anything beyond, just more gloom—though there did appear to be a strangely-hued glow coming from one side.

It made her think of a fading sunset—or inhuman eyes in the darkness.

She glanced at her sister.

"Ah, Belle..." Emmi peered warily at the round portal. "Maybe we should wait here for a moment?"

Eyes fixed on the opening and its odd light, Isabelle gripped her sister's shoulders and inched away from the opening. "Perhaps we should. Yes. I rather think we should catch our breath for a moment before entering this fine creature's home..."

Faint cries wavered up the stairs.

Oh, gods.

Her entire body stiffened. Were the other demons still chasing them?

She held her breath for a moment, listening as carefully as she could. A chill snuck down her spine. No doubt about it, those wails belonged to the demons they'd left in the tunnels.

And they seemed to be getting louder.

"Gods have mercy." Eyes wide with alarm, she glanced at Emmi and found her worries reflected in her sister's gaze. "Perhaps we should go inside," she said, desperately trying to sound calm. "It would be rude to stand out here when we've been invited in."

"Y-yeah." Emmi's lip trembled. "Can't be rude."

"No. Never." Isabelle's attention shifted to their guide. "Ah, thank you. Kind —" *Demon. Creature. Terrifyingly large monster who has us at his mercy and might be feeding us to their young.* She swallowed hard and used the most neutral term she knew: "—Ser."

It inclined its head and motioned for her to enter.

"Right. Yes. Should get going..." Sharing another look with her sister, Isabelle sucked in a deep breath. Did she go first, to check things out? Or last, and stand between Emmi and their guide?

Biting her lip, she thought about the smaller creature they'd glimpsed earlier, about the host of things that could await them within that room.

First.

Definitely first.

She smiled hesitantly at the creature, then scooped up her skirts and ducked through the portal into a narrow room. Squinting into the gloom, she warily pushed past a hanging drape—and gasped.

Mouth open, she gaped at the space.

Gods. She'd been braced for tattered cloth and piles of bones and looming monsters, and what she'd gotten was a space that glowed like embers at sunset. As tall as her cottage, the room had thick wooden beams marking floors and an entire wall of colored glass.

"Holy Gods, Belle." Her sister gripped her arm. "It's beautiful."

"It is. It's..." Belle studied the glass—the stained glass—barely illuminated from light outside. It was different here, but she recognized that pattern. A swirl of rainbow, all the colors to honor their fallen gods and stand as a beacon for their return. "Golden Gods," she breathed. "We're in the belfry."

How can this be?

She turned in a slow circle, marveling at the height of the space, the growing light seeping through the glass. How could the tunnels below Windhaven stretch up into the tower?

Mind racing, she faced the creature.

It stood by the now-closed portal, its massive frame cast in soft shades of blue and pink and honey. Broad shoulders and bare-chest, aside from a coat of fine fur, it wore only a pair of loose shorts tied around narrow hips with a length of what looked to be rope.

A demon. An inhuman creature. And yet that casual stance felt more potently masculine than any of Jaston's posturing.

Perhaps she shouldn't make assumptions, but...

Her gaze dropped to its midsection and her cheeks heated. *Male. Oh, it appears to be quite male, indeed.*

She forced her eyes back to its face. "Are you..."

If they were finally safe from the other demons, then it was past time she got answers. She lifted her chin. "Do you consider yourself male? What do we call you? What are you? And why did you help us?"

The questions tumbled out of her in a rush.

"Thank you for your help," she continued, unable to stop imitating a babbling brook. "We truly are grateful. We would not have made it without you. But please. Please, I must understand—"

Movement flashed across the room.

"Belle!" Emmi jumped. "The other one is *in* here."

"Stay back!" Holding out her hand—not that her splayed fingers would do any good against such beings—Belle glanced rapidly between the pair. The second creature was the one she'd glimpsed on the stairs earlier. Noticeably smaller than their rescuer and leaner, though it wore a nearly identical pair of rough shorts.

It dropped onto the floor from a beam and regarded them quietly from beside the stained glass.

Neither of the creatures made a move toward them.

"B-belle..." Emmi's voice shook. "They're so *big*."

Her sister might stand boldly before human bullies and spit in the face of death, but she'd never dealt well with critters. When it came to evicting bats from their attic or mice from the kitchen, that was always Belle's job—one she didn't mind. She'd much rather send animals peacefully on their way than let another use cruel traps.

She pushed Emmi all the way behind her.

Shoulders back and head high, she focused on their rescuer. "Do you mean us harm?"

He shook his massive head. "No."

His deep voice trembled through her with the force of a waterfall. Her mouth formed a circle at the discovery he could *speak*. A year of studying the tunnels, and it had never once occurred to her to simply knock on the ground and ask questions. And gods, did she have questions.

"We mean you no harm," he rumbled. "You are safe here."

Her gaze flicked to the smaller one, who was bobbing his head in agreement.

"What..." She licked her lips. "What do we call you? Why did you help us? Why are we...why are we here?"

"You..." The creature's giant hand lifted, long claws gleaming in the soft glow of the stained glass.

For a moment, she thought he was going to reach for her. She tensed with worry—or was that anticipation? Before she figured out which, he'd moved a short distance away. Her shoulders sagged, though whether it was with relief or regret she couldn't quite tell.

"You have questions." His impossibly deep voice was strangely soothing. "We will answer. Later. For now, rest." He pointed to the window. "The sun rises and you have had a long night."

Dawn?

Isabelle blinked with surprise at the window.

Good grief, the light was gradually becoming brighter. She stifled a yawn, fighting a wave of fatigue. No wonder she had struggled with those stairs. Her ridiculous gown, with all its Bishop-approved layers of fabric and long sleeves, felt about as manageable as sacks of milled flour at the best of times. But after a night without sleep?

She checked on Emmi, noting the tiredness smudged below her sister's eyes and the way she listed to one side.

Their unlikely host was correct.

They'd been navigating the tunnels all night—they were exhausted. Neither of them were in any state to search for an exit. Her eyelids drooped, feeling as heavy as wet dishrags.

"Thank you," she said quietly. "We do need rest."

"Here," he rumbled, crossing the room and pulling a hanging cloth aside to reveal a nook with a layer of straw lining the floor and blankets draped overtop. "Sleep here. You're safe."

"Thank you," she repeated, stunned to discover she believed him.

Safety. Somehow, they'd found a pair of demons with a magical tower room in the middle of a dark labyrinth. And these creatures had a wonderfully cozy, comfortable corner to rest in. Belle probably should have questioned that, but the sense that she and Emmi were truly safe had sucked any remaining strength from her limbs. She'd been running on near-blind panic since throwing herself into the tunnels after her sister, and now her body was trembling.

Questions would wait.

She ushered Emmi into the nook and, with a final smile for her monstrous savior, she pulled the curtain closed. With a yawn, her sister curled into the corner, and Belle sank down to join her.

"You truly think we're safe here?" Emmi asked softly.

"I do." Isabelle wrapped an arm around her sister's shoulders. "Go to sleep. I'll keep watch."

"Liar," Emmi muttered. "You're going to fall asleep..."

Her sister's words dissolved into quiet snores, and Belle couldn't help but smile to herself. Only her sister could shift so quickly from blind fear to teasing. She was grateful Emmi was able to rest—and she knew they'd both need their strength for whatever came next.

Her eyelids drooped and her cheek rested on top of her sister's head.

The creatures had been kind, but there was no guarantee their hospitality would last. She'd just rest for a moment, then she'd study her map and figure out how to get her sister to the exit.

There had to be a way out...

CHAPTER SIX

Belle woke slowly to the scent of stone-cooked biscuits and brewing tea.

Her brow furrowed and she scrubbed her eyes with the back of her hand. Had Mama started baking without her? But her mother hated the simple recipe used by farmers in the fields... And why was it so bright out? If she'd slept in, Mama would be furious.

She blinked with confusion at the unfamiliar shape of her bed, then froze as awareness rushed back.

The ball. The tunnels.

Demons.

Oh, Gods. She wasn't at home, safe in her bed. She was in a strange tower room, with two bat-like creatures on the other side of a length of woven cotton. That fabric wouldn't stop a small dog, let alone a winged demon large enough to dwarf a warhorse.

Yet, somehow, she was certain they hadn't disturbed her while she slept.

Easing her arm out from beneath her sister—who remained fast asleep—she got to her feet. What had to be baking on the other side of the curtain smelled appealing, and gods knew she'd give blood for a cup of tea. Besides, she could hardly hide behind a curtain forever. She needed answers, and to find a way through the labyrinth of tunnels.

She started for the curtain and her skirts dragged along the floorboards in a heavy lump.

Ugh.

Enough of this.

Removing a layer of clothing might be foolish around these creatures, but she doubted her gown's thick embroidery and frustratingly long sleeves would stop a demon's claws. At least without that layer she could move more easily. With a sigh of relief, she shrugged out of the overskirt—which still left two layers of cotton covering her skin.

She stretched, appreciating her increased range of movement.

Free of the weight, able to freely roll her shoulders, she crept to the curtain and pulled it aside.

The largest of the creatures was alone in the center of the room. He was sitting awkwardly on a wooden box too small for his frame, parked before a tiny iron stove. His leathery wings were tucked together at his back, the ends resting on the floor. A thin curl of smoke drifted to the rafters above. Huge shoulders hunched forward, it stirred a cracked pot and flipped a biscuit over on a heated stone slab.

Was the monster making her *breakfast?*

A tiny gasp escaped her.

His enormous ears perked up, swiveling to her direction.

"You are awake," he rumbled quietly, without taking his gaze from the stove. "Are you hungry?"

"I..." Belle drew in a breath. "Yes, I think I am."

Straightening her shoulders, she left the relative comfort of the nook and pulled the curtain closed behind her. The longer her sister was able to rest, the better. Belle would also ensure there was food left over. For now, she'd eat and hopefully get some answers from their host.

She crossed to the stove and found a small stool positioned across the fire from the creature. She paused beside the piece, unsure if she should sit or wait for a more explicit invitation.

Was there etiquette for sharing breakfast with a demon?

"Tea?" he asked in that low rumble.

Gods, why did that tone do things to her insides?

Clearing her throat, she said, "Please." She slowly took a seat on the stool and accepted a clay mug full of steaming liquid. The vessel looked tiny in his hand, but was perfectly normal in her palm. Perhaps she was foolish to take drinks from a demon, but if this massive creature wanted to harm her, he'd hardly need to trick her with a hot beverage.

She inhaled deeply, letting the soothing scent fill her senses, and glanced at him over the rim of the cup. "How is there tea here?"

He rolled his shoulders. "There's lots of things down here."

"Or up," she said, offering a tiny smile.

His mouth flickered upward at the edges. "As the case might be."

Taking a sip, she studied her surroundings. A box of supplies sat to the side of the stove, and a small pile of books lay beside the window. The light pouring through the stained glass had grown brighter, and an almost exact replica of the pattern stretched across the floor in a straight line.

"My goodness," she gasped. "Is it noon?"

"Nearly," the creature grunted.

Gods. She'd slept for hours.

She searched the room, needing to locate the second creature. "Where... where is your smaller friend?"

"Out seeking supplies," her host rumbled. "Here."

Her gaze snapped back to the creature to find him offering her a biscuit with a make-shift pair of wooden tongs. Steam rose from the freshly-cooked piece. It might be too hot for many to touch, but her fingers were tough from years spent baking rolls

"Thank you." She took the biscuit carefully and cradled it between her hands.

It was oddly familiar, this experience of sitting beside a fire and eating stone cakes beside an enormous male. She'd made these exact biscuits with Thomas when he worked long days in the fields—and she'd been able to escape her mother's kitchen. Simple and quick to make, he'd declared the cakes ideal for a farmer and had insisted she teach him the recipe.

Memories burned the backs of her eyes, and she bowed her head against the sudden rush of grief.

Oh, Thomas.

If only you'd found refuge.

Fighting back tears, she took a small bite and chewed thoughtfully. The taste sent her straight back to the fields, into the bitter-sweet memory of the first time she'd made the cakes for Thomas. Stone-ground grain, water, yeast and a dash of salt—bound together with a few drops of lard. A common enough recipe, with easy ingredients.

Yet each baker used their own amounts.

Specific amounts, as unique to that baker as brush strokes were to a painter, or needlework to a seamstress.

Her brow furrowed, and she stared at the biscuit in her hands. This biscuit wasn't just like the ones she'd made for Thomas, it was *her* recipe.

But that was impossible.

Surely, I'm mistaken.

She missed Thomas, that was all. Sitting here, safe in the nightmare that had taken him, had brought a fresh edge to her grief and stirred the line between present and memory. Still... she didn't need to be an expert baker to recognize the ingredients—or their relative amounts. For all her failings, her mother had taught her well in this area.

She took another bite—larger this time. Her gaze flickered between the creature and the stove as she chewed, dissecting the flavors on her tongue. Years of experience in the kitchen let her gauge the ratios of flour to yeast to salt, let her test the bread's texture for proof of kneading.

Ten solid turns.

A half hour of proving.

Just enough lard to bind, without making it greasy.

"This is my recipe," she whispered, staring hard at the demon. Her chest was tight, her heart pounding. "How can you possibly know it?"

Hands poised over the fire, the creature froze in the middle of flipping another cake. The half-baked biscuit fell from wooden tongs into the flames. He didn't try to retrieve the cake or put the tongs down. He sat perfectly still, his gaze darting to hers.

She looked into his eyes—truly looked.

When they'd arrived at this space, she'd noticed they were brown and kind. Yet, her tired mind hadn't processed what that meant, hadn't really *seen*. That passing glimpse hadn't been enough.

Here, with his gaze boring into hers, she found everything she'd missed the night before. His eyes weren't the burning yellow or terrifying red that had hunted her and Emmi in the tunnels. But it was more than that. So much more. Because these eyes were the warm, rich brown of perfectly tempered chocolate that had just been taken off the heat. A color that spoke of kindness and put all manner of beasts at ease while it tended their wounds.

She'd only known one man with eyes that exact shade.

The one man she'd loved with all her heart.

The man who'd died in the tunnels.

Her heart lurched in her chest, as if it toppled off an invisible cliff. The silver ring she'd never removed grew hot against her skin. And the remaining biscuit slipped from her fingertips and fell to the floor. "Th...Thomas?"

CHAPTER SEVEN

The creature stared at Isabelle, that painfully familiar gaze boring into her very soul. "Thomas is dead."

"*No.*" Belle lurched off the stool. "That's not so."

Breath shuddering in her chest, hands flexing into fists at her sides, she looked at him in disbelief. Why was he pretending? She knew the unique recipe of those cakes, and she knew those eyes. Maybe it should have been impossible, maybe she should have been wrong.

But she wasn't.

This creature claimed that her Thomas was dead, yet he was just like him. Huge and kind and always ready to stand between her and danger. This had to be why she'd felt inexplicably safe with him. Her love was alive in this creature. Or, if not alive, then not entirely gone.

Pieces of him lingered, even if they were changed.

Fallen Gods of Gold and Scale.

This is what happened to my love.

The entire year she'd mourned him, he'd been alive beneath Windhaven. Why had she never spoken to the demons? How could she have missed this?

Her chest wanted to crack in half, her heart wailing at the unfairness of it all. And dear Gods, it hurt more than she'd imagined possible.

"I am Talos." He hunched his shoulders, ears flattening on his head and wings curving around his body. "There is no Thomas."

"No," she said again, and this time certainty threaded her voice. "You're my Thomas. Or you were."

That massive head turned away from her. "*No...*"

Good grief. That was the least convincing *no* she'd ever heard.

She marched around the tiny stove and parked her fists on her hips. With him sitting and hunched over, she had just enough height to glare down at him. "Don't you lie to me, Thomas Marr. Talos. Whatever you wish to call yourself." With a huff, she reached up and pulled on her necklace, revealing the silver ring. "I *know* you."

He regarded her from beneath a wing, eyes desperate. "*Don't.*"

How could a creature so large appear so vulnerable?

It was as if he was trying to disappear within the thick ruff of fur around his neck. The sheer pain of that pose sliced through her. She longed to bury her fingers in his fur and soothe his hurts. Except she couldn't heal this wound with a poultice and bandage, and she had no idea how he'd respond if she touched him.

Heart aching, she crouched down and willed him to meet her gaze.

"I know you," she said quietly. "Please. Please talk to me. You didn't abandon Emmi and I to our fate. Just as you looked out for me before you were thrown down here and...and..."

Realization crashed over her.

"Dear Gods." She gaped at him. "You've been watching me from the belfry. Haven't you?"

He nodded miserably. "I should not have."

Unable to stop herself, she brushed the back of his hand with her fingertips. "It gave me comfort."

"Comfort." A bitter huff escaped him. "Impossible—"

"Not so." She laid her hands on his. "I—"

"*Don't.*" The word sounded like a cry torn from his very soul. He pulled away from her and lurched to his feet, stalking over to the window. The leather wings protruding from his back rustled, the tips scraping the floor. One of those massive hands swept the air before his frame, as if to encompass his entire form. "How can *this* offer comfort?"

Over seven feet of muscled creature stood before her.

Almost more bat than human in appearance, his legs swung back like a wolf's and sharp teeth glinted when he spoke. With those ears and claws and wings and fur, he was a monster worthy of the Chastry's scariest tale.

She should probably be afraid.

But she wasn't.

Not in the least.

The only thing she feared was letting him stand there, alone and hurting, for a moment longer. Yet she couldn't throw herself into his arms as she had in the fields—the people they'd been in those sun-kissed days were gone. What they'd both become required patience. She sucked in a breath and prayed she wouldn't lose this chance. This gift.

She approached him slowly, as one might approach an injured animal.

"Don't," he warned, deep voice crackling with emotion.

Yet he didn't pull away as she drew near.

Head tipped toward the ground, his enormous body seemed to vibrate with worry—or was that anticipation? Leathery wings quivered, claws lightly tapped against the floor. Did he long for her the way she did him? She hoped so, because the pull to his side was stronger than anything she'd imagined possible. If she didn't touch him, right now, she'd fall to pieces.

She gently cupped his face.

Those gorgeous eyes flicked to hers. "I am a monster."

Her heart lurched at the pain in his words. She ran her fingers through the short fur of his cheeks, shocked by how soft it was, and held his gaze. She was close enough to feel the heat of him along every inch of her body. "I don't think you are a monster."

His snout wrinkled with frustration. "Appearances to the contrary."

Still holding his face, she stepped closer. "Indeed."

His eyes widened.

"Do you think that some fur and wings matter more than this?" She jabbed a finger into his chest, right over his heart. Careful to keep her voice low, she continued, "Because if you dare say yes, I shall defy all laws of physical ability and reason and kick your ass from here to the fields."

"Isabelle..." His expression softened. "I'm no longer human. I lost myself with the change."

"You didn't lose all of you," she whispered fiercely.

"I lost enough."

Dear Gods. He sounded so hopeless.

Was it possible for a heart to break over and over again, like a mirror that fixed itself only to be shattered once more on the floor? But no matter how much it hurt, she couldn't leave him alone with his pain. Couldn't ignore the wound gaping before her, even if it would cut them both to clean it.

"Tell me," she pleaded. "Help me understand."

His sigh shuddered through her. "I would protect you from this.""

"Please," she whispered.

"Very well," he rumbled. "Though, it will bring you no peace."

He paused, as if expecting her to suddenly throw up her hands and rescind her request. *Honestly.* Human or beast, men could be shockingly dim witted. All those days following her father's maps, and she'd never been more certain of her need to know an answer than right now.

She tipped her head to the side and waited.

He gave another sigh and rubbed the back of his neck with an enormous hand. Yet he didn't pull away, even as he began to speak, words slow and weighted with reluctance. "After we were thrown into the tunnels, we were attacked. Two of us died in those first moments. My father and I escaped with the others. We were hunted, injured. Bloodied and cut by the demons, yet determined. Those of us that lived to see morning searched for a place to hide. We found this place, hidden in the side of the belfry, thought it was salvation—"

He looked out the window.

She rested her hands on his chest, taking comfort in the steady beat of his heart beneath her touch. Her Thomas had always been strong, always broad-shouldered and steady. Whatever came next in his story, that truth would not change.

"Only our tower became a prison." He glanced at her. "We began changing."

She sucked in a breath.

Thomas and his father had made it to this place. They'd found refuge, and they'd still become monsters? Questions lodged in her throat—she refused to give them breath.

This was her love's story to tell. She had to let him.

"I don't know if we were cursed or made ill from the tunnels themselves," he rasped. "We'd all been cut by the creatures. We'd all eaten whatever food we could find—some of it in a terrible state. Yet... we thought we'd make it until we started seeing a creeping shadow at night. After it came, our wounds burned. Fever took us. And then our bodies betrayed us."

She wrapped her arms around his waist, a silent invitation to continue—and a promise that she'd stand beside him.

"The pain of it..." He sucked in a breath. "We became monsters, and escape lost all meaning. We lost hope. Each other. *Ourselves...*" The word transformed into a harsh growl. "I lost myself for a time, Belle. Did things. Lived like the beasts below. It wasn't until I chased another victim to this very tower—"

His massive body shuddered as if the memories struck a physical blow.

She tightened her grip on his waist. "You cannot blame yourself."

"Why not?" He huffed, a throaty rumble of self recrimination. "I forgot myself. I pinned a boy I considered family against this very window. And I'd have killed him if I hadn't seen you through the glass."

His lips pulled back, teeth clenched with disgust.

"Oh, Thomas," she breathed.

"*Talos.*" His gaze was fierce. "I no longer deserve that name."

"Talos, then." Unlocking her arms from his waist, she kept her body against his and once again cupped his face. She willed him to see the truth of her feelings. "I don't care what your name is or whether you have wings. All that matters is that you're here."

"Belle..." He turned away, pulling his head from her grasp. "I'm not the man you loved. I have nothing for you."

You don't want me?

Gods above, was it possible to die while breathing?

Insides reeling from his words, she slowly laid her shaking hands on his chest. His heart pounded wildly beneath her touch, the skin tensing beneath every fingertip. She frowned at the muscles dancing across his pecs. Was that the response of a man who no longer wanted her—or one who was desperately trying to save her from herself?

There was only one way to find out.

Lips trembling, she lifted her gaze. "When you gave me your ring, you swore to me I was the only woman you'd ever want. The only soul you'd ever love. Did claws or fangs change that?"

His throat worked.

She held her breath, unsure how she'd hold herself together if he'd found another in these tunnels.

"No." He sighed. "Nothing will change that."

"Thank the gods." She sagged against him with relief.

"Belle," he rumbled. "I'm no longer a man. You should not touch me..."

But even as he spoke of distance, his fingers were skimming over her hair, tracing the line of her back.

Eyes closed, she curved into his embrace. Strange, how a body could be so foreign, so strange, and yet so perfectly familiar. His chest still broad and strong, able to shield her from any danger. His steady heartbeat what she'd longed to hear every lonely night. He'd always been tall—tall enough she could rest her chin on his chest and gaze up into his eyes. An extra foot or so made no real difference to her, nor did wings or claws.

So what if he was changed or he called himself Talos?

His heart was hers.

And her prayers to the gods had been answered, because that heart had come back to her. She couldn't imagine what she'd done to deserve such a gift, but she would not shun it. Warm in his arms, wrapped in rainbow light, she couldn't ask for a better moment.

He nuzzled her hair, the gesture as sweet as it was possessive.

"Thom—I mean, Talos." She stretched up on her toes to wrap her arms around his neck.

"Belle." He rested his forehead against hers.

She gazed into his eyes, the same eyes she'd loved since she was in short skirts, and her heart stuttered. Her breasts pressed into the hard line of his muscular chest. Her thighs rested between his. Warmth spread through her, running from her heated cheeks to her toes in a heady wave, and she sucked in a breath as a rush of desire followed.

A year ago, she'd barely been bold enough to acknowledge that desire, let alone fight for it.

But that girl had disappeared when her love had been cast into the pit.

She held his gaze. "I never got to be with Thomas before he was taken from me."

His eyes widened. "Uh...Belle? Do you need to lie down?"

Well. That reaction wasn't the best start to this conversation, but she was no faint-hearted lass. "No, I'm perfect where I am." She twined her fingers through his ruff and brushed the tip of her nose against his. "But if I did decide to lie down, I was thinking—"

"No." He jerked away from her.

A gust of wind chilled her as he moved into a corner. Turning from her, he lifted a wing, as if he could shield himself from the truth of her feelings with its thin leather. "I can see what you're thinking," he rasped, voice thick with emotion. "You must extinguish those thoughts."

"I don't want to extinguish anything." She took a step toward him. "I want—"

"Please, Belle," he ground out.

This time she knew it was desire that threaded his deep voice. It sparked heat in her core, and left her knees weak with wanting even as she struggled to give that need a voice. It awed her. Thrilled her. She'd abandoned any thoughts of desire when Thomas had been cast into the tunnels. Now it felt as if those feelings were being exhumed from the past, uncovered from beneath the layers of grief.

"I'm not human," he rumbled. "I'm a *monster*. You are good and kind and pure. You deserve better."

Oh, he was not going to make this easy on her.

But damn it all, she'd survived Jaston's attentions and being hunted by demons in the tunnels. She wasn't going to wait another moment—no matter how much her cheeks burned.

They'd been given a gift, and she refused to waste it.

More importantly, she refused to waste *him*.

Be brave. Be bold.

Fight for what you love.

She straightened her spine and halved the distance between them. Then she stopped. Chasing him around the tower wasn't working. Not for this. She would find the words—she would do whatever she could and pray it was enough. "I will... I will not take another to my bed," she said, wishing her voice didn't waver. "I won't. Ever." She lifted her chin and steeled herself. "But I would gladly give myself to the memory of my love that lives on in you."

CHAPTER EIGHT

Frozen in the rainbow light of the window, the colored beams shimmering along lines of dust motes as if they were bars of a cage, Belle studied the creature concealing himself in the shadowed corner. His ears were flat against his head, shoulders hunched—he was yet to even look at her. Surely, he must also long for what had been stolen, so why hadn't he said anything?

Her breath caught in her chest, fist pressed into her stomach as she waited for the most important answer of her life. Was he going to reject her? Gods. She feared she'd fall apart if he rejected her.

A leathery wing shifted, and his eyes glinted in the dark.

She caught her breath. Even across the room, the desire in that gaze heated her skin.

He wants me. Just as I want him.

Air rushed out of her in a soft puff of relief. He didn't want to reject her, he simply thought he had to protect her. She had to convince him she wasn't some fragile creature in need of saving.

She was a woman in need of her man.

"I don't care if you're a monster." The words somehow released her from the cage of light, and suddenly her feet were moving. Head high, gaze locked on him, she slowly closed the distance between them. Perhaps she would fail. Perhaps she was wrong. But she'd be damned if she'd meekly accept defeat. "This monstrous form saved my sister and I."

"Belle..." His voice was rough with desperation, yet his eyes didn't waver from hers.

"Talos." She stopped just beyond arm's reach. Her body shuddered in protest at the space. The slice of air between them battered against her will. Yet she stood firm. As much as she longed to surround herself in his strength, she couldn't force this—he had to welcome her. So instead of reaching for him, she pushed her hands into the folds of her skirt. "If you don't want me, then I will respect your wishes. But if you still feel for me, then please—"

His massive frame shook with a bitter huff. "My feelings are not the point."

Belle battled the urge to touch him. "They should be."

"Why?" His gaze sharpened. "Do you have any idea what you're asking?"

That I'm asking to be touched? For the man I love to show our bodies we belong together? Oh, she might be fuzzy on the details, but the fire running through her veins said she knew what she wanted.

She licked her lips. "Yes. I know."

A throaty growl escaped him. "I'm enough of a creature to want you more now than when I lived as a man." He uncoiled himself from the corner, massive frame straightening until he towered over her, an inhuman mountain of muscle. His wings flexed and his gaze sharpened. "But I am not a man. I'm a creature with fangs and teeth and needs, Belle."

Oh, Gods. That should probably scare her.

Instead, heat pulsed in her core.

Because he'd finally admitted he still wanted her—that he wanted her more now than before. And that was all the permission she needed to close the final distance between them. She cupped his face and gazed up into brown eyes half-wild with desire. "Monsters aren't the only creatures with needs."

He sucked in a breath.

Stretching up on her tiptoes, she brushed her lips across his.

She felt the thrill of contact ripple from her lips all the way to those toes—the same thrill she'd felt a year ago, when she'd kissed Thomas in the field. Only stronger, as if the connection between them had strengthened like whiskey in a cask. It didn't matter what name he went by or what he looked like. Not to her.

All she cared about was his heart.

Though she certainly wasn't opposed to the package it came in.

The sheer size of him sent a thrill down her spine, and had her body thrumming with need. She leaned into him, reveling in his hardness against her thighs, how it left her knees weak and her body aching for more. Human or demon, apparently, she craved large men with shoulders broad enough to rival an ox.

Biting her lip, she glanced at the alcove—the curtain hadn't moved.

Emmi was still sleeping, and the other, smaller creature was still away. This might be the only chance she and Talos would have to be together. She'd learned a harsh lesson a year ago about letting opportunities pass her by.

No more waiting.

"If you want me," she whispered. "Take me."

"*Belle.*" Her name was a ragged plea. "What if I hurt you?"

"You won't. Not in any way I don't enjoy." Holding his gaze, she took a single step away from him and slowly removed the final layers of her gown. Remarkable, how quickly those layers came off. The laces of her short corset slid apart, as if they'd been waiting for her to ask. The buttons of her chemise came undone. She let each layer pool on the floor at her feet, until she stood naked before him.

His nostrils flared, as if drawing in the scent of her.

The thought of it drove her wild.

"I'm stronger than I look." Without taking her eyes from his, she stepped back until her body was shrouded in the colored light of the window. She'd done what she could—everything she could—now he had to come to her. "The only thing I need now is you."

"Gods, Belle." He growled. "You're all I've ever wanted."

"Good," she said.

"Gods, forgive me." For such a massive creature, he struck with almost impossible speed. His body blurred and then he'd reached her. "You're mine, Belle. *Mine.*"

Her feet left the ground as he snatched her into his arms and kept going.

Before she could catch her breath, they'd started upward. One hand kept her tight against his body, while the other used claws for purchase. She held tight as he scaled the tower room's stone wall, taking her into a private space high in the rafters above.

How was it possible to remain inside when the floor was so far below?

She blinked at him through unruly strands of hair. As grateful as she was for the distance from where her sister slept in the alcove, she was a touch concerned about how this would work. "Don't we need the ground for what comes—"

"No." He grinned at her—a smug flash of fangs against the shadows of the tower. "Now hold on." He pushed off the wall and flipped them between the beams. His wings beat the air, sending it rippling over her skin like a lover's caress. Once. Twice. Then wrapped around her as he spun them around, their bodies twining together in promise of what was to come.

The feel of her bare skin against his velvet-covered muscles was almost too much to bear. Every inch of her was a hot coal in a fire pit, a single breath away from bursting into flame.

"Talos..." She writhed against him, begging for more.

She'd spent enough time on a farm to have an idea of how this worked, but any books featuring people had been banned before she was old enough to understand them. She didn't know the words for what she needed—didn't know how to demand he touch her. "Talos, please... I... I need..."

"I know what you need," he rumbled in her ear. "It is what I need."

He flipped her around and suddenly her bare back was pressed against the ceiling. She gasped as the cool stone teased her heated flesh. Her hair fell in a pale curtain around her, and all she could see below her was Talos—his huge form almost hanging below her.

He pinned her there with his hands, his feet somehow holding them both in place.

"Now, Belle," he said. "We take."

Gone was the man she'd had to convince to touch her, and what had replaced him was a creature brimming with desire. He nuzzled her head and neck, brushing his lips across her flesh and leaving it aching for more. Teeth followed, nipping her sensitive skin.

Her body flexed and strained, desperate for more.

And why not take more?

She'd never been one to let others do all the work—or have all the enjoyment. The entire length of him was beneath her, and she wanted to explore every inch of him that she could reach. Still held firmly against the ceiling by one of his massive hands, she ran her fingers through his ruff and down his chest, her lips following her fingers just as he had done.

His skin flexed beneath her touch and she nipped his pec, reveling in the way his body shuddered with pleasure.

She reached the rope securing his shorts.

He hissed and caught her hands. "Not yet, love."

"But... but I want..." Her words dissolved into a breathy moan as something brushed the folds of her sex.

"I know what you want." His wicked grin had her quivering with anticipation. He lightly bit the swell of her breast, then drew his tongue across the mark. "But first, I taste every piece of you."

Holy Gods, how was it possible for a tongue to be as long as her forearm and agile enough to circle her breast and tease her sensitive nipple. How was he able to do this while still holding her? His grip didn't falter, and she never once feared she'd fall, even as that incredible tongue traced a line of fire across her breasts, before dipping down between her legs. Gods. Was he truly going to kiss her there? Her face heated, even as her hips bucked with wanting.

"Tal—oh!" She gasped as his tongue slid between her folds. "Oh, Gods!"

"Mmmm." He hummed with pleasure into her sex.

The sound vibrated through her, making her insides coil tighter with excitement. Then he slowly licked the length of her and sensation flooded her loins. Her eyes fluttered closed and her back arched.

Moaning softly, she rolled her hips and gripped his ruff for dear life.

Holy gods.

His tongue was long and agile and hundreds of times more talented than her fingers, when she'd thought of Thomas alone in the dark. He could reach... everything. Touch everything. And when that tongue eased into her channel, it seemed to feather, brushing every part of her. Sparks of pure bliss flooded her vision and her body shot straight into ecstasy.

The force of her release would have sent her careening off the ceiling if he hadn't had her pinned.

She shuddered, hips rolling as she drifted down to earth.

Or, up. As she was still pinned to the ceiling.

"Th—Talos..." She bit her lip and to make her eyeballs cooperate.

When she finally managed to focus, she found Talos grinning at her.

The cocky tilt of his lips reminded her of when Thomas had beaten Jaston in the winter solstice log-tossing competition. He'd been insufferable. And nearly impossible not to drag behind the barn and climb like a tree. Instead of slicing into her joy, the reminder of who he'd been only filled her heart further.

"Smug bastard." She trailed her fingers along the curve of his jaw, savoring the ability to touch him.

"Indeed." He kissed the tip of her nose. "Ready?"

She blinked at him in confusion. "Ready for—"

"This." He flipped them around.

Stone and floor and light whipped around her—or she whipped around in them—and then she was sitting astride him.

"Whoa." She flattened her palms on his chest and tightened her legs around his waist. He'd positioned them on the central beam, running across the ceiling above the stained glass window. Once again beneath her, his back was on the wood and his hands gripped her hips.

Poised high above the floor, she probably should have been terrified.

Except she wasn't. Sitting astride him on the beam, it was like she was floating, or flying. Soaring into her most sinful dreams. Her entire world was his muscled body and the ocean of colored light far below.

Confident he'd never let her fall, she spread her arms. "It's incredible."

"So are you." His wings brushed gently over her cheeks and breasts, the thin leather silky against her skin. Lips followed, and teeth and an astoundingly long tongue, kissing and scraping a delicate trail of fire across her body.

Her nipples pebbled.

With a soft moan, she bent over him and dragged her nails down his chest. She wouldn't have imagined it possible to be alight with need so quickly after release, yet her body was already coiling tight with desire.

Her core pulsed, begging to be filled.

She rocked her hips against his and started working at the knot holding his shorts closed. "I need you... I..."

"And I need you." Teeth scraped across her shoulder, then he cupped her face and searched her eyes. "Are you sure about this? I am not human. My body is different—"

She gasped as his shorts fell away, revealing an enormous member.

"I'll say—" Cheeks flushing, she clamped a hand over her mouth.

He chuckled, thumbs brushing the inside of her thighs. "My pride appreciates your awe." He flexed his hips and somehow that member swelled further, leaving her throat dry with anticipation even as she wondered how such a length was possible. "But I won't allow myself to hurt you. We'll have to take it slow, my love."

She bit her lip and nodded.

The Chastry taught her to be ashamed of the wetness of her core, yet she could find no shame in the way Talos held her, as if she were the most precious thing in all the lands. His careful caresses left her aching for more. Strong fingers circled her waist and drifted up over her breasts. Her sensitive skin reacted to the touch, hips undulating in the ancient rhythm, all of her desperate for him to take what they both wanted.

She grasped his ruff and pulled him forward. *"Talos."*

"Not yet," he groaned. "I have to ready you."

She wasn't confident that manhood would fit inside her, but she'd be damned if she wouldn't try. "Then..." She bit her lip as a rolling wave of pleasure crashed over her. "Do... it..."

"As you wish." His eyes gleamed with anticipation. Massive hands guided her hips, rubbing her slick folds along the length of his member. Its velvety softness teased her sex with every motion. At the same time, his hands slid around her thighs, his digits slipping over her honey and into her folds.

Opening her, testing her.

Tiny, desperate gasps shook her chest.

"Gods," he groaned, that deep voice adding to the pressure building within her. "I can't wait any longer."

He eased the tip of his shaft into her.

The sensation of being stretched nearly sent her over the edge. The line between pleasure and pain blurred, and yet she ached to take more of him. To feel all of him inside her.

"Easy, love." He gripped her rear, holding her still while she adjusted to him.

But she didn't want to be easy.

She wanted him. Now. She arched her back and tightened her legs around him. A ragged cry tore from his lips, then he slid inside her, piercing her to her core in one smooth motion.

The length of him stretched her. Filled her.

Her head fell back.

For a moment, she thought she'd drown in the sheer pleasure of it. Then Talos was gently pushing his hips forward, setting a languid pace, and she was rocking against his length—and being supported by it. His member wasn't the boneless sex she'd seen in cattle and heard whispered about by town wives at the well. No. Her lover's manhood was firm, stiff and secured within her.

The feeling of being so completely joined, of being held in place by that member, was an intoxicating mix of passion and protection. The slow, deep rhythm of their lovemaking beat within her, even as her body demanded more.

She wanted this moment to last forever.

She couldn't wait another minute.

As if she stood on the mountainside watching a storm approach on the horizon, the crackle of lightning seemed to build within her core. Talos increased his pace and her movements grew frenetic. She trembled with need, hovering on the edge of release.

Talos thrust within her and reared up, sinking his teeth into her neck.

The storm broke within her.

Her body snapped tight. Sensation crashed over her, shaking her with the force of thunder and leaving her ears ringing. Breath ragged from his own release, he still held her against him, his hips continuing to roll beneath her, drawing out her bliss with each thrust.

Perfectly spent, she collapsed against his chest.

"Rest, love." He kissed the top of her head and his massive leathery wings wrapped around her. Balanced on a beam high in the ceiling, and yet she felt utterly safe nestled against him.

Warm and satisfied, she let herself drift into slumber.

"Belle." A deep voice penetrated her dreams. "Wake up, my love."

"Wha..." Isabelle woke to find herself in Talos' arms. She rubbed her eyes and looked around. No longer on the ceiling, he stood on the ground, once more in the halo of the window's glow.

He nuzzled her cheek, and then placed her carefully down, holding her until her feet had steadied. "Belle. Tarn is about to return," he said, picking up her pile of dresses from the floor. "If you wish to be clothed—"

"Oh, Gods." Her eyes widened.

She snatched the wrinkled clothing out of his hands and stared at the layers of cotton and linen. There was nothing quick about lacing herself into a chemise and two underskirts. "This will take me a few minutes." She glanced from the door, to Talos. "Stall him?"

"Of course." He dropped a kiss on her forehead before slipping out the portal.

Gods of gold and scale.

Why were women's clothes such a trial? She yanked the chemise over her head and cursed the short stays as she pulled it overtop. Gripping one of the laces with her teeth, she fought with the other. It should be illegal for any garment to be this difficult to don.

As she struggled into the second underskirt, she heard low voices through the door.

A soft knock sounded. "Belle. Are you... uh."

"I'm decent," she said, unable to keep herself from smiling. A snort of laughter from the other side of the door had her smile widening. Her sister was going to tease her mercilessly about her interlude with Talos, and Isabelle would enjoy every moment.

Especially as those moments would involve Talos and her ability to kiss him whenever she wanted.

The door swung open and she brushed dust from her skirts. It was time to greet this smaller demon properly—and give her love a proper kiss. She grinned at the door, delighting in how Talos' ears were suspiciously pink when he re-entered.

His expression, however, was tight with worry. "You must wake Emmi and prepare yourselves to leave this place at once."

"Leave?" She jerked with shock. "But we...no!"

"Yes." He caught her shoulders and squeezed gently. "Tarn has been scouting the tunnels, looking for the exit my father and I couldn't find in time. He's seen what we've been dreading: the rest of the creatures gather beneath the grate."

"They're..." Her jaw opened with horror. "They're going to force their way through it?"

Mouth a grim line, he nodded.

"When the sun disappears tonight," the smaller creature said, joining them, "we fear they'll force their way through into the town."

"Gods have mercy," she breathed. "Wait—"

She frowned at the smaller demon, recognition tickling the back of her mind. That voice was familiar. But where had she heard it? Not in the bakery but... on the fields. Could it be?

Her eyes widened. "*Toby?*"

"Tarn now." Head half-scrunched into his ruff, he shrugged. "We take new names, after the change."

Her gaze darted between the two, finally processing the dynamic between the pair of males. Of course. Talos had told her how he'd chased a boy who'd been family to him into this room. That could only be Toby, the farmhand who should have taken over the Marr's holdings after they were consigned to the pit.

"Well, Tarn," she said. "I am still very glad to see you."

His eyebrows lifted and he smiled shyly. "And I you, Miss Belle. And your sister, Emmanuella. I'm very glad she's, uh, that you both are well—"

"But you won't stay that way if you remain in Windhaven," Talos cut in. "The demons grow in number with nearly every person sacrificed. There are more of them than you know—far more than you saw last night. If they emerge, the town won't stand a chance."

"Gods." Belle pressed a hand over her heart. Her thoughts were full of the miller and the blacksmith—of all her friends who hung a red cloth beside their homes and dared to dream of a better future.

None of them looked beneath the streets.

"They have no idea of the danger they're in."

"No, Miss Belle," Tarn whispered. "They don't."

"You have to warn them," Talos said. "Then you have to take Emmi and run as far and as fast as you can. For all I want the hands of darkness to shred the bishop into a thousand pieces, he doesn't understand. The demons could consume the town in a single night."

CHAPTER NINE

Isabelle stood with her sister, Talos and Tarn around a make-shift table in the center of the tower room. Spread upon that table and illuminated in all the colors of the stained glass, was her map. She laid her fingertips beside the parchment, wishing her hands didn't shake. But how could they not? Of all the uses she'd envisioned when she'd crafted those lines, it had never been to leave behind the love she'd thought dead.

And worse: To warn her town before their demons destroyed them.

The responsibility weighed her shoulders, the fear of failure tighter around her ribs than her stays. All she wanted to do was stay with Talos and rejoice in finding him again.

Instead, she had to use her hard-earned knowledge to do something terrible.

Because they had to try and stop the demons before they swept across all of Windhaven.

She glanced at Talos.

"Tell us, Belle." His eyes rested on her, a mix of pride and resignation that tore at her insides.

"My father began this map before he disappeared..." She swallowed hard and willed her voice to steady. "Having finished his work, I believe I know a way to stop the demons. But such action should not be necessary." She shifted closer to Talos, until her right shoulder rested against his side. "The bishop might be blinded by his faith, but he'll not risk the entire town. If Emmi and I can emerge from the tunnels, we can warn him and the city guard."

"So we hope." Talos wrapped a hand around her waist and peered at the map.

Oh, Papa. This isn't what you had planned... She traced her father's signature mark in the upper left corner, a compass with a heart for an arrow, then tapped a nail over the Chastry. "It is the most defensible position. We have to believe the bishop will rally the guards and—damn."

Her sleeves tried to tangle at her feet, and she kicked the over-long ends aside with her slipper. She'd have preferred to leave the gown in the tower, but if she emerged from the tower in her undergarments she wouldn't be given a chance to speak, let alone be listened to.

Of course, she'd rather be naked with Talos.

Unfortunately, that wasn't an option.

She bit her lip and looked up at him. "It is our best plan. Emmi and I will get out, and warn the bishop. If the guards are ready at the grate, surely they will be able to hold the demons back?"

"Perhaps." He let out a low rumble. "But we cannot rely on the bishop."

Her insides lurched.

No. The bishop had to see reason. Anything less put her love in greater danger.

"Belle..." His head lowered until their noses brushed. "You see another solution. There's too much at stake to hold back."

Her Thomas always put his own wellbeing last.

Talos was no different.

Curse it all. She twisted the heavy fabric of her skirts between her fingers and stared at her map. At the solution she didn't want. "If the bishop does not listen—which I'm sure isn't a worry, his commitment to punishing the demons is unmatched—I know how to stop the monsters from overwhelming the town. At least, I have an idea..."

One that will put both creatures I care for in danger.

"Go on." Talos ran a finger down her spine.

"We should know," Emmi said softly. "In case he doesn't listen to us."

Her sister's face was pale, yet she wore an expression more mature than her fifteen summers. If Emmi could stand firm in the face of such a threat, Isabelle could do no less.

Straightening her back, she pointed to three locations on her map in turn. "There is access to the tunnels through small grates. Here, beside the miller, in the eastern corner of the town. In the south, through the low grate beside the butcher. And near the blacksmith to the west."

"What good is that?" Emmi scrunched her nose. "We can't fit through those grates."

"These locations aren't about an exit," Isabelle said softly, tracing the triangle the points formed, the perfect cage in which to trap the majority of the demons. "It's about what we can put down, after we escape..."

Something awful.

Something Belle didn't want to think about.

"If we run out of options, I have an idea. But I hope it won't be necessary and honestly I'd rather not..." She glanced at her sister and gave a quiet sigh. Emmi wasn't even looking at the map anymore. Instead, she'd returned to staring at Tarn—something she'd been doing almost non-stop since learning who he'd been before the change. Any other moment, Belle would have been endlessly entertained. But today they had to face a challenge greater than both of them.

A threat that could swallow all they'd known.

"It's all right, Belle. You don't have to tell us."

She lifted her eyes to Talos.

The heat in his gaze made her knees weak. His bite burned on her shoulder, a brand she'd wear more proudly than any ring—and a promise fiercer than any Chastry ceremony.

Gods, it was so unfair.

She'd just found her love again, just taken him as hers. And now she had to leave him. Because her town and every soul she knew in Windhaven was in terrible danger.

The bishop will listen.

He will not risk all of Windhaven.

Isabelle's stomach twisted into a knot. There was so much risk—and she had so much more to lose.

But no matter how much her heart protested, her sister's safety had to come first. They had to get out of the tunnels. Belle could warn the bishop while Emmi escaped to the forest.

"You're sure I'm right?" she asked for the hundredth time. She tried to commit the lines of her map to memory, hoping that knowledge, combined with Talos and Tarn's understanding of the tunnels, would be enough. "There is an exit beneath the Keep?"

"We're certain there's an exit. It is small." Talos rolled his massive shoulders.

Her fingers ached to trace the lines of muscle. Her body crying out to climb into his arms and demand he take her back to the ceiling and—

"I do not know if the exit lies beneath the Keep," he continued, apparently oblivious to her now burning cheeks. "We found it while searching for supplies—and fighting other demons. We lost track of the location in the struggle."

"But it's there." Tarn bobbed his head. "I could almost fit."

Emmi gasped. "You'd have *left* the tunnels?"

His ears flushed. "Not to do anything terrible. But I was too big, and I couldn't leave Talos to face the others alone, anyway."

"Yeah. Because you're the muscle." Talos lightly punched his shoulder.

Tarn grinned up at him.

The affection between the two warmed Isabelle's heart.

More than an echo of the bond she'd witnessed in the fields, their time in the tunnels beneath Windhaven and their understanding of each other in their new forms had made them family in truth.

Gods, she needed them both to survive what was to come.

"You will find us before anything happens," she ordered Talos, gripping his ruff with both hands and tugging his face down to hers. "I won't take any action before I know you and Tarn are—"

"Belle." He cupped her face. "There won't be time."

"Then..." Her lip trembled. "Then you must escape before the others. Use the tower, break the glass if you must. Find us in the forest after the sun sets, when it's safe and dark..." Her words trailed and she turned to the window, still glowing bright with the afternoon sun.

Darkness.

It wasn't dark in this room at all.

"Good gods," she exclaimed. "How did I miss this?" She jabbed a finger at the window, then stared intently at each of the creatures. "This room has been full of sunlight all day, and neither of you are hiding from it. And you had a fire! How is that possible?"

"Yeah! You weren't afraid of the torch, either." Emmi sounded affronted. "What is this?"

The two creatures glanced at each other.

They shrugged in unison.

"You know..." Talos lifted a shoulder. "I've never properly thought about it. We don't know. We were both in this room when we changed. Light can be tiring, but it never bothered us as much as the others."

"Then... then this could change things," she stuttered. "Maybe we've been too hasty. Maybe the demons won't escape tonight. We can survey the tunnels and find a way to leave together when—"

"Belle." He kissed her forehead, then brushed his lips across hers. "We're not mistaken."

"We have to be," she whispered. "You need to come with us."

"There's no time." He rested his forehead against hers, brown eyes holding hers. "We have to go."

"But... but we don't know—"

"We do, my love." He gently gripped her shoulders and kissed the top of her head. "The other demons already stir, the sun is fading. Tarn is convinced the way to the exit is marked by symbols of some sort. We need time to follow those. We cannot risk waiting."

Breath shuddered in her chest.

Fear and grief sinking their claws into her heart.

She wanted to hold onto Talos forever. To bury her face in his chest and deny any danger existed. But he was right. The entire town was in danger, and she had no right to put her happiness ahead of all those lives.

No matter how much she wanted to.

"Very well." Forcing her back straight, she reached out and gripped her sister's hand. Their pockets were full of all the makings of small torches, and the map was fresh in her mind. They were as prepared as they could be. "Let us locate this exit."

D eep in the tunnels, a tiny torch sputtering in one hand, Isabelle blinked back tears and traced the shape of a tiny compass that had been carved into one of the beams supporting the tunnels. A cross, with a heart-shaped arrowhead marking north, and a small notch directing them to what she assumed was east.

"These are the marks I mentioned," Tarn said. "I've never followed them back to the exit, since we couldn't fit. But I think it's right."

"It is," Belle said softly. "They're leading to a way out."

The symbol aligned with the map in her head. But that's not why she was fighting tears. Or why she laid her palm to the carving and caught her breath.

"Belle?" Emmi nudged her. "What is it?"

"Papa made these marks," Belle whispered.

"What do you mean?" Emmi gripped her arm. "How could that be? Mama said he…"

"Disappeared in the forest?" Belle gave a sad huff. "I never quite believed that tale. Now, I know why she always turned to the belfry when she spoke of him. She knew he'd been thrown beneath, like so many of our neighbors."

"But he marked the way to safety before he died," Emmi said.

Or before he became a mindless creature.

But Belle refused to give that horror voice. "He left us a path home." Heart aching, she kissed her fingertips and pressed them to the carved symbol. "Thank you, Papa."

Following her father's path, and with Tarn and Talos' help, she led the way.

Some marks had been lost, scratched by claws or eroded by a steady drip of water from the world above. Yet between the surviving carvings, her creatures' memories and the map in her mind, she was able to piece together the puzzle and lead them through the labyrinth.

More than once, Talos and Tarn stood between them and the waking demons. Yet they miraculously avoided outright conflict. The sheer size of Talos, combined with their torches and the demons' desire to sleep through the day, seemed enough to deter any seeking a casual snack.

Though she feared their luck was coming to an end.

More were stirring, and keening wails echoed down the tunnels.

"Here," she said, pointing to what remained of a compass. "We must be close to the exit."

"Good." Ears swiveling, Talos glanced behind. "Let us walk faster."

"Oh, Gods." Emmi grabbed Isabelle's arm. "It sounds like an army waking from the dead."

"Come." Belle scooped up her skirts and hurried around the next bend.

Her heart beat in her throat—her sister wasn't wrong. If they thought they'd heard the worst on their first night in the tunnels, they'd been wrong. The volume was almost deafening, loud enough to drown out any doubts she'd had about Tarn's warning.

The demons were rising.

And they were demanding flesh.

She led them around a series of twisting passages as fast as she dared. Two markings later, the air felt lighter, fresher, and yet they'd taken too many lefts to be beneath the Keep. Rounding another corner, she gasped at the sight of a beam of white light cutting through the gloom.

She raced ahead and peered upward.

The opening was as narrow as promised and high above the ground, more of a sloping drain than anything designed for human use. Yet she was certain Emmi could fit through it, and that she would likely make it through as well.

"Boost me up?" she asked Talos.

He scooped her up by her rear, giving her a lusty wink before lifting her toward the drain. She squirmed upward on her elbows and studied the square of white light, searching for a clue as to their location. It seemed too bright for the interior of the Keep, and were those voices talking?

No. She blinked. Not just voices, *chanting.*

Gods. She knew exactly where they were—and it was where she'd least expected to find an exit.

"Pull me down," she whispered.

When Talos returned her to the ground, she faced him, Emmi and Tarn. "We traveled all the way through this labyrinth and ended up going in an almost complete circle. We're back at the square. Directly across from the Chastry—I can hear the afternoon prayers."

"Whoa," Emmi breathed. "How is that—"

"No time." Talos stepped between them. "You must go."

Gods. She needed more time. Isabelle's heart plummeted to her slippers.

"No." She wrapped her arms around his waist, and buried her face in his chest. "There must be another way. I only just found you again. I can't leave you!"

He eased away from her. "You must."

"Besides…" Tarn peered upward at the exit and scrunched his nose. "It's still daylight."

Talos nodded. "We are more comfortable with light, but we have no idea if we can survive the afternoon sun. And even if we could, even if we could fit through that narrow opening—which we can't—the people in the square would be terrified. They'd be too busy running from us to listen to any warning."

More wails rippled down the tunnel with a sudden wash of air, like the breath of an ancient demon.

"They're coming," Tarn hissed. "You have to go!"

"Belle!" Emmi squeaked.

"You both have to go," Talos said. "Now. Warn the people. Then get out."

Isabelle knew he was right. She had to get her sister to safety and warn the people of Windhaven. Yet the thought of climbing through that drain and into the world above without Talos felt like carving out her own heart. Tears streaking down her face, she threw her arms around Talos and kissed him fiercely. "Promise me you'll find us."

Talos turned away. "We'll see what we can do."

She gripped his face. "Don't you lie to me."

"Belle…" Emotions chased themselves through those brown eyes. Passion and kindness mixed with a terrible sadness. "My love. There is no place in the above-world for creatures like us."

Her fingers tightened on his cheeks. "Then we find somewhere. Together."

With a sigh, he rested his forehead on hers. "Together."

Before she could demand further promises, he boosted her up—farther this time—and she swallowed the arguments in her throat. No matter how much she wanted Talos to make promises, she needed to get her sister out of these tunnels. She wrestled off the metal grate covering the opening and wriggled into the square head first.

As soon as she was outside, she turned to help Emmi follow.

"Come." She took her sister's hand. "We must warn the bishop."

Hand-in-hand they raced across the square. For once she was glad to see Jaston standing in front of the Chastry doors in full armor. He might be a bully and an ass, but he took his guard duties seriously. "Captain!"

The people filling the square around her stopped and stared. Gasps rippled through the space.

"Belle?" Shock shaped Jaston's features. "This is not possible."

"I assure you, it is." She focused on him, but pitched her voice to carry across the square—an easier feat than usual, given the stunned silence gripping the area. "Windhaven is in terrible danger. The demons have multiplied, and their tunnels have spread below the entire town. They're gathering. They're going to force their way out tonight, and no amount of torches lining our streets will stop them."

CHAPTER TEN

"Impossible!" Jaston staggered backward, those icy eyes darting between Isabelle and her sister. "You might have been forgiven by the Gods, but you have to be mistaken by the rest. The demons cannot go beyond the reach of the Chastry, and the torches will keep them back. This we know."

"But we don't know," Isabelle said. "We thought we did. We were wrong."

"That's not the only thing that's wrong," Emmi spat. "You're—"

Isabelle stepped in front of her sister.

Keeping her eyes on Jaston, she tried to make him see sense. "I've seen the tunnels—and the demons. They are coming. The torches won't be enough—not when the skies turn to night. You haven't seen their numbers. This threat is—"

"Lies!" He shook his head. "You're confused."

She willed her voice to remain calm. "I am not."

Emmi peered around her and shouted, "We know what we saw—"

Jaston drew his sword and pointed the blade, the tip wavering, his face contorted with what might be fury—or fear. "The gods might have spared you, but that does not give you leave to spread lies."

Sunlight glinted off metal in the corners of Isabelle's vision.

A quick glance had her gulping. Armored guards were closing in from all sides.

Gods. Even knowing she'd come from the tunnels, Jaston wasn't going to hear her, which meant the bishop was their only chance—and she wouldn't risk her sister on another unreasonable man. She drew Emmi away from Jaston, into a small pocket of space created by onlookers and abandoned market wares.

The people watching them were scared—she understood, she was, too.

But they all needed to know what was happening here. How wrong they'd been about the demons, and how much danger they were truly in. If they didn't ready themselves, they'd all be killed.

Behind her back, she slid her map from its hiding place in her sleeve and clutched it in her palm.

Can I truly risk this?

Talos and Tarn remained in the tunnels.

If she gave her sister the map and the final instructions, she might be consigning them to death. Yet if she did not, if the bishop did not hear her, then she consigned her entire town to that fate. If the guards would not protect the people of Windhaven, then those people had to protect themselves.

Even if I'd rather cut out my own heart than let it come to this.

They'd listened to her sister the night of the ball.

Hopefully, they would again.

Keeping her movement hidden from Jaston's view—one benefit to her ridiculous gown—she pushed her map into her sister's hands. If she couldn't get Jaston or the bishop to see reason, then her map might be the only chance they had of surviving the night.

"Be brave," Belle whispered to her sister. "Show them."

Emmi took the map, eyes huge with worry. "Belle…"

"Tell them to use fire," Belle whispered. Then she spun away from her sister and approached Jaston, doing everything she could to keep the eyes of the guards on her. "I know what I saw!"

"You are confused," Jaston snapped.

"I am not." She felt, rather than saw, Emmi disappear into the crowd behind her, and a tiny puff of relief escaped her lips. Her sister would warn the people, help them strike against the demons and then flee for the safety of the woods.

Now it was up to her to convince their leaders to do their jobs. To lead and protect the town.

She glared at Jaston. "Take me to the bishop. Let him settle this."

"Very well." He grabbed her arm and yanked her forward, pulling her toward the elaborately carved wooden doors of the Chastry. "He will banish these thoughts from your head. Then you'll see your mistakes and take your place as my wife."

"Wife?" she yelped. "Are you mad?"

"No, Belle." He kicked open the doors. "I am furious."

He dragged her into the building and the glare of gold momentarily blinded her.

Blinking rapidly, she tried to take stock of her surroundings—while struggling not to fall over her skirts. She stumbled behind Jaston, her shoulder screaming in protest against the harsh grip. Eyes watering, the stark difference between the tunnels and this space struck almost like a blow.

The inside of the Chastry was a gleaming masterpiece of white and gold.

Carved dragons wound around every pillar, and elaborate plaster depictions of the Golden Gods traveled every wall. The entire space was blinding white plaster, broken only by lines of gold framing each panel, and gilt accenting each meticulously carved scale.

Well gold, and the massive stained glass window.

The glass framed the larger piece of the picture, above which the glass in Talos' tower merely accented. That glass had been the colored sky above, a symbolism of magic's breath. This piece told more—it depicted the Golden Gods they prayed would return.

The fading afternoon sun burned through the glass, making the curling dragon's shape seem to writhe. Belle knew it was meant to look mighty, yet something about the beast's pose spoke of torment.

Perhaps it did.

Certainly, the figure standing beneath that window at the altar claimed to know a lot about torment.

"Bishop!" Jaston called. "Isabelle DuNorde has emerged from the tunnels spouting madness."

The bishop turned as they approached. That narrow face, with its pinched features, made an eerie silhouette in the window's golden light, and his white robe with its gold embroidered trim was as pristine as when he'd cast her sister into the tunnels. Anger at this sanctimonious man who'd caused their people such harm flashed through her.

She forced it down.

This was not the moment for rage—lives were at stake.

"Your Eminence," she said, choosing her words with care. "I come to warn you—"

"Show respect." Jaston shoved her forward.

She staggered toward the altar, falling to her knees on the white woolen rug that covered the dais and the few feet of stone before the bishop. Her knees stung and the impact knocked the wind from her lungs.

"Beg forgiveness for your actions," Jaston snarled. "Repent. And I'll make a decent woman of you."

"Now, Jaston." The bishop's gaze was almost benevolent as he stood before her, a small object clutched between his weathered hands. "She might be fair, but she is hardly a fitting wife."

This time Isabelle couldn't repress the wash of anger.

All she'd done for her town, and all she was trying to do, and this wizened husk of a man deemed her unfitting? She would never be the kind of wife he'd approve of, and she'd wear that with pride. She tugged her neckline to the side, revealing Talos' bite on her shoulder. "Nor is she available."

Jaston recoiled in horror. "Demon-marked whore."

The bishop merely chuckled.

"Ah, little Isabelle." He lifted the object in his hands to the light of the window—a glass vial with a dark liquid inside. "Of all the people in Windhaven to escape the labyrinth, I had not expected it to be you. But I find myself...pleased."

"Your Eminence? What do you..." Her eyes widened as she realized it was blood in that vial.

She glanced at Jaston.

The captain's gaze seemed to be on the vial, but his expression didn't flicker.

"Normally, I refrain from excess," the bishop drawled. "But I do so enjoy admiring the fruits of my labor.

Brows furrowed, her attention returned to the bishop. "Your... labor?"

His lips curled into a terrible parody of a smile.

The afternoon light filling the Chastry seemed to flicker into shadow. The bottom of the massive stained glass window fell dark, while the top burned with a bizarre hue of red. When she blinked, the bishop's robes flashed from white to black, and an image of sharp teeth lining an impossibly wide mouth seared itself into Isabelle's mind.

A dark figure crept through the tunnels, Talos had said. *And in its wake, we changed.*

Her thoughts reeled, shreds of information pulling together like the drawing of a river, winding and flowing into a lake. How demons hunted the streets of Windhaven, but couldn't escape the tunnels. How a man who cried every day for redemption kept killing.

The lines wove together in her mind, forming a terrible map.

Because there was only one answer.

"Dear Gods, no." She lurched away from the bishop. Scrambling backward on all fours, off the white rug and onto the smooth white stone between the benches. Clutching at Thomas' ring, she stared in horror at the man who'd claimed to be a beacon of morality for her entire life. "You know exactly what's happening beneath the streets. Because you made those creatures. Didn't you?"

CHAPTER ELEVEN

"Indeed, I did." The bishop's chuckle chilled Isabelle's very bones.

As he smiled, layers of fangs filled the bishop's human mouth, growing like sharp-edged sugar crystals lining pastry in a bowl. Behind him, the light slid upward along the stained glass, the stretch of shadow growing with each heartbeat as the sun slid behind the mountains.

"No." Eyes fixed on the bishop, her feet pedaled against the polished floor. "You can't... but the people..."

Her shoulders connected with Jaston's boots.

"Captain. He's a monster. You need to..." Breath shuddering in her chest, she stared up at the Captain of Windhaven's guard. No surprise marked his features. No shock or horror. Her stomach twisted as she realized he'd known all along. "How could you? You swore to guard this town from monsters—from demons. Yet the whole time you served the vilest demon of them all!"

He shrugged. "I guard those who behave. What do I care if the sinners fall into the tunnels?"

"Sinners do keep sinning." The bishop tsked. "And their sins are so delicious."

"Sins because you declare them such!" Belle cried, the silver ring so tight in her grip that it might fuse with her skin. Her horrified gaze shifted between the Captain and the Bishop. "The only evil in Windhaven is you!"

"Ah, Belle. I do believe I see what my Captain finds appealing about you." The bishop slunk toward her, his form wavering with every step. That vial was clutched in his hand, its liquid a sickly hue, as if red blood had been burnt over a fire. "He has what he wants—the power, the prestige. All because he serves a power greater than himself. And soon so shall you."

She tried to scramble down one of the pews, but Jaston grabbed her arms and held her firm.

"No!" She kicked out, her legs tangling in her skirts.

"Behave." Jaston forced her to stand still.

"One of my creatures has already tasted you." The bishop reached her and trailed a long, cold finger down her cheek and along her neck, ending on Talos' mark. "Who am I to do less?"

Her stomach roiled.

His touch was cold as death. A soulless promise that nothing lay beyond this world—and that she'd soon be sent on her way to the worms.

Thank the gods she'd given Emmi that map.

She drew strength from the knowledge that her sister would survive—that the people of Windhaven had a chance. And gods knew the people earned that chance. Belle glared at the bishop. "The people know what you are. They're going to leave you alone with your monsters."

The bishop chuckled. "The residents are broken little sheep. Just as you will be."

His hands darted out and nails sharp as knives sliced through her gown, sending the heavy fabric crumpling to the floor. Her dress pooled at her feet, leaving her in nothing but her underclothes.

She shivered as the sun disappeared.

"Now, pretty little Isabelle," the bishop said, flashing those terrible rows of teeth again. "I intend to enjoy you before my Captain claims another prize—"

A crash sounded from outside.

Cries echoed from the square. "Fire! The streets are on fire!"

The clatter of armored guards running and the slap of thick leather boots across stone echoed through the Chastry, followed by the crackle of flame and shouts of yet more people—these cries telling residents to run.

A sliver of relief broke through the horror encasing Belle's heart.

She wouldn't be rejoining her love in the woods.

But Emmi and many others had a chance of surviving the night. Isabelle had always put her sister's life first—and this was no exception. What mattered was that Emmi had done it—she'd convinced their friends to listen. Of course she had. Those who hung red clothes already knew something was wrong, had already planned to leave—and they'd already listened to Emmi. They'd poured flammable oil through the grates Belle had marked and set fire to the tunnels, which should give them time to flee into the woods.

I'm so sorry I won't be joining you.

Tell Talos I love him.

Fighting back tears, Belle narrowed her eyes at the bishop. This twisted creature, with his false cries of sin and sanctimony, had taken her father and her love—he'd even taken her mother, sweeping her away with his lies.

She'd be damned if he took any more.

"What a shame." She curled her lip at him. "Sounds like all your sheep are about to escape your clutches—"

"Silence." He gripped her chin, boney fingers digging into her skin.

Jaston shifted behind her. "I should join my men. We will snuff this rebellion and—"

The earth rumbled beneath the Chastry.

Trembles shook the entire building and the wooden pews rattled against the polished stone floor. The panes of colored glass shook within their iron frames, vibrating fast enough to almost sing.

Then a massive crack sounded.

Inhuman wails mingled with screams, and Isabelle knew the monsters had escaped. The doors of the Chastry slammed shut and Jaston stumbled back, taking Isabelle with him.

His grip on her arms slackened. "What the—"

She kicked out. Free from her heavy overskirts, she could move faster, and strike true. Her heel connected with the bishop's chest. He stumbled back and the vial fell from his grasp.

It shattered on the stone floor, and dark blood sizzled against the white floor.

The bishop screamed with rage, and Jaston lurched for the broken pieces.

She wouldn't get another chance. While they were both distracted, she ducked between the two men. Avoiding Jaston's arms, she raced away from them and the sizzling blood to the entrance. She threw herself against the doors to the Chastry, but it was as if they'd been sealed from the outside.

Gods damn it.

"Belle!" Jaston's bellow struck like a blow.

Movement flashed behind her, and a high-pitched squeal of terror escaped her. Oh, Gods. He and the Bishop were coming for her. Whatever else happened, she wouldn't let the bishop lay those awful hands on her again. She had to get away. And if she couldn't go out—there was only one option.

Up.

She gathered her underskirts and ran up the steps to the side of the door, the twisting stairs leading to the belfry.

The last time she'd gone up the tower, it had been toward refuge alongside her sister and the man she loved. This time it was a desperate race away from the true monsters in Windhaven.

Oh Thomas—

Talos.

I wish you were here with me.

She went up the stairs as fast as she could, the sharp turns making her dizzy and her underskirts trying to tangle at her ankles. Her lungs burned and her legs screamed, yet she somehow managed to stay ahead of the monsters. Gray stone and endless steps blurred, then orange light grew.

She rounded a bend to find a window carved into an alcove.

Catching herself on the wall, she lunged for the opening and pushed open the iron window. Struggling with her underskirts, she scrambled out onto a ledge high above the square.

Below, chaos raged across Windhaven. Guards in gleaming armor faced townspeople with torches and monsters swarmed the skies. Orange flame seared lines across her city, the path of fire forming the exact shapes she'd drawn in her map in Talos' room, what felt like a lifetime ago.

They'd really done it. The tunnels had been set on fire.

Forcing her gaze beyond the square, beyond the flames, she searched the fields. Were those lights disappearing into the woods? She only caught a glimpse of movement, yet hope flared in her chest. Too bright to be embers, and all moving in the same direction.

You better be one of those lights, Emmi.

"Nowhere to run, Isabelle."

She turned around in time to see Jaston step onto the ledge, his polished armor burning with the reflected flames. He flashed that cold, heartless smile at her, the one that made her skin crawl while other ladies swooned. "Give up," he said. "Abandon this foolishness. And you'll live. You'll be my wife. We'll take what's left of Windhaven and make a new life in a new town."

She'd rather throw herself off the belfry.

"I won't make any life with you, Jaston," she said.

The bishop drifted onto the ledge behind Jaston and she shuddered. Both the man in armor and the monster in holy robes disgusted her, and she wouldn't let either lay a hand on her again.

"There is nowhere to go, little Isabelle," the bishop hissed.

She lifted her chin. Her sister had made it to the forest—that was what mattered the most. She had to believe Talos and Tarn would find her, and would make sure Emmi stayed safe. The thought gave Belle strength to step toward the edge.

"Nowhere for me—or for you." She aimed a cool smile at the bishop. "Your reign over this town is finished, demon."

Bishop hissed at her. "Then you'll pay."

"No, she won't." A deep voice announced from above.

With a beat of huge wings, Talos landed on the ledge, his massive form standing tall between her and the bishop. His hands flexed at his sides, claws gleaming in the firelight, and his voice was a low growl. "You took me from her once. I'll be damned if you'll do it again."

His wings spread wide, hind claws digging into the stone.

He stood so tall the bishop appeared as small as a child, and the roar he unleashed had Jaston staggering backward. The once-brave Captain of the Guard threw up his arms and covered.

Only the bishop didn't.

As she watched, his mouth split into one of those horrifying grins, the kind that barred the layers upon layers of sharp teeth. Then his human form dissolved into smoke, melting away as if the face she'd known for so many years had been nothing but sugar paste.

What stood before them was no longer a man but a pale, twisted creature.

All bones and teeth and glowing red eyes.

It uncoiled itself, limbs crackling like dry twigs until it stood as tall as Talos. The creature had wings and fangs, and yet was nothing like her love. Where Talos was solid and warm, this monster was twisted and vile. Faded and mottled like a piece of meat left for days in the elements, its skin sat tight and thin over a skeletal frame. A massive jaw jutting from its mouth, and she could see dark blood running through its veins like rivers of smoke.

Tipping its head to the skin, it unleashed a blood-curdling cry.

It had spent her lifetime chastising every resident about sins. And now it seemed all would pay for those sins.

With an unearthly wail, the pale demon that had masqueraded as Windhaven's Bishop threw itself at Talos. Its jaw opened to impossible proportions, its spindly limbs moving faster than should have been possible, it crashed into Talos with a shocking amount of force.

The air shook from the impact.

Her skirts and hair were blown back. Talos was driven backward and Isabelle had to drop to the ledge, barely avoiding being knocked off but a sweep of leathery wings.

Beneath her cheek, the stone trembled.

Flat on the ledge, she held on for dear life and peered up through her hair at the behemoths battling above her. With another wash of air, they took to the skies. The two creatures tangled on the ledge, almost weaving her love's dark body with the bishop's sickly pale. Fangs bared and claws outstretched, they twisted around each other.

She clutched the ledge, unable to tear her eyes off the battle unfolding above her.

Bony claws raked Talos' side, leaving a trail of red in their wake. She screamed and pushed herself to her knees on the ledge, needing to help him without having any idea how to do that. She couldn't even reach them, as they were flying above Jaston's head.

Her love struck back, his enormous fists pummeling the bishop's pale chest.

The snap of ribs sounded above the crackle of the flames below. The bishop bellowed and threw itself at Talos, and the two creatures spiraled out of sight, up the tower.

"Talos!" She staggered to her feet, searching the skies. "Be safe—"

"Give up, Belle." Jaston's cold voice sliced through her.

Stomach churning, she stared at the armored man blocking the way out. Fallen gods, how could anyone stand there so calmly in the midst of this chaos? His town was burning. His esteemed bishop was a demon. And below them, monsters murdered people and battled each other in the sky above.

How dare he wear that smug expression?

Her fingers curled into fists and she snarled at him. "You knew what he was doing. You knew and you did *nothing!*"

While his men screamed in pain in the square below, while they fell beneath claws and flames, the Captain of Windhaven's Guard simply shrugged his golden-clad shoulders. "Why should I care, when I got what I wanted?"

"Not any more," she spat. "You're finished. Talos will—"

"Your beast won't win, Belle," Jaston said. "It took me one battle in the badlands—one!—to realize nothing can stand against the spreading dark. Nothing can defeat the bishop. The mandemaggael is a fearsome creature. But if you work with it? Ah, Belle. That's where the true rewards are to be found."

She stared at him in horror.

"You killed my father," she gasped. "All those people. For *money?*"

"And power." He shrugged again and paced slowly toward her. "They challenged me. They got what they deserved."

He feels nothing.

Gods.

She was going to be sick all over the ledge.

The bishop might be a monster in his true form, but Jaston, for all he remained human, might be worse. He'd willingly consigned his men and all the people of Windhaven—all the people who trusted him—to this hell.

Her lip curled with disgust.

If anyone deserved to feel the sharp sting of justice, it was him. "You deserve to burn in—"

"*Rawrrrrr.*" Talos roared from above.

She spun around in time to see her lover and the bishop tumble through the sky above. They turned in the air, locked in a vicious struggle. A mass of leathery wings and teeth and claws. Her heart lurched, but they were out of sight before she could so much as cry out.

"See, Belle." Jaston closed the distance. "It's only a matter of time until your creature falls."

"No." She retreated to the far side of the ledge.

Back flat against the stone column that ran from the side of the front doors all the way to the top of the belfry, she searched for a weapon. A way out. Anything to stay safe until Talos could come back for her.

Gods damn it, there was nothing here.

But if she could get around the column to the next portion of the tower, she might be able to find something—or at least keep herself away from Jaston. Her gaze latched onto the carved ridge jutting out from the column. If she held tight to the dragon scales, she could climb around to the next ledge.

No time to hesitate.

With a final, panicked look at Jaston, she jumped up and took hold of the stone protrusions shaped like a dragon's spines. Her slippered toes barely fit on the ridge, but she made it work.

"Don't be stupid, Belle!" Jaston yelled. "You'll never make it."

She scrambled around the curve.

The sound of armor scraping across stone told her Jaston was pursuing her. She tried to move faster, yet fingers tugged on her skirts. Her feet slipped on the narrow ridge.

"Ah!" She lost purchase, and her legs dangled over the square as she gripped the carved dragons for dear life. "Talos!"

"Belle!" Talos dove for her from above. "Hold on—"

A wail sliced the air, and the bishop slammed into him, driving him away from her. Sending them both spiraling toward the square. Talos roared, but he couldn't break away and she lost sight of them past the stone before her nose.

Her love wasn't going to catch her.

Not this time.

Kicking off her slippers, she held tight to the carving and used her bare feet to find purchase. With her toes able to grip the shallow pattern of the stone tower, she managed to scramble back onto the ridge.

Clutching the column, she tried to catch her breath.

Gods, her love needed to focus on the fight with the bishop—not worry about her.

Fighting back tears, she pulled her skirts out of reach and kept going.

She reached the corner where the curving column met flat stone tower. Easing herself onto the next portion of ledge, she found herself looking into the hidden room she'd shared with Talos. With a soft cry, she pressed her palms to the glass and tried to draw strength from the memory.

A wail melded with a throaty roar.

She looked up to see Talos and the bishop tumbling through the air. For all her love seemed larger than the bishop, blood ran down his side. The wound gaped, revealing pale slices of bone through strips of torn fur. Gods have mercy, she couldn't tell if her love was winning—or losing.

"Hold on, Belle," he called. "I'm coming—argh!"

His words dissolved into a cry of pain as the bishop drove him downward. One of his wings snapped backward, and a long tear rent the thick leather.

They disappeared into a wash of flame. Embers swirled up in their wake like fine rain in a spring breeze, singing her skirts.

"Talos! No!" One hand gripping the wall, she leaned as far over the ledge as she dared, searching the sea of flame in the square for a sign of her love. *Where are you?* Her heart lodged in her chest, beating so hard she feared it would burst through her ribs.

Oh, Gods. Please let him be alive.

"Belle!" Jaston bellowed.

Her attention snapped to the column. Windhaven's traitorous captain was scrambling after her—tricky, in full armor, and yet his face was contorted with rage and she feared he was beyond reason. Feet slipping, armor scraping along the stone, he was still dragging himself to where she stood.

She backed away and searched the narrow space before the tower window.

The ledge here was even more narrow, barely wide enough for her bare feet to find purchase. At the far end of the ledge was a carved knight holding a stone spear. If she could break that off, it would do.

Back to the window, she slid along the ledge.

Beneath her bare toes, her town burnt. The heat of the fire blew her hair and skirts upward. She wanted to cry and rail and demand the Gods rise from the spreading dark and set everything to right—but she'd tried that when she'd lost Thomas and nothing had answered. This time, she'd fight. Then she'd search every inch of the rubble for her love.

Face tight, she took hold of the stone spire and yanked.

"There's nowhere to go, Belle," Jaston said, his metal-clad boots slipping on the narrow ledge as he stalked toward her. "No option other than me."

"You're wrong." She used her whole body and the spire broke free. Gripping the length of stone with both hands, she slowly raised it, holding it before her like a blade. "There's down."

Eyes wild, he lunged at her. "You're *mine.*"

"*Never.*" She swung the spire at him.

The length of stone caught him right across his helm, ringing like a bell and knocking off that stupid red plume. With a cry, he dropped to his knees. But his body kept coming toward her, his armored legs sliding across the stone ledge even as he teetered on the edge.

She flattened her back against the far column in an effort to escape his reach.

Half-off the ledge, he managed to grab hold of her underskirts. "Your lover is dead, Belle," he rasped. "Your town is gone. Pull me up and we'll leave this place. Start a new life—"

"Never!" Even as her heart broke for Talos, she kicked at Jaston. "I will never help you."

He bared his teeth at her. "Then we'll both die, whore."

Fist tight in her skirts, he pushed off the ledge. She dropped the spear, reaching for the column. Her fingers brushed the knight, but before she could find purchase, Jaston's full weight hit her skirts.

It yanked her off the ledge and into space.

A strange sort of acceptance washed over her as she fell. If Talos had died in that burning square, perhaps it was right she joined him. *I'm sorry, Emmi. I hope Tarn is able to find you—*

"Got you." A dark form appeared beneath her, massive wings spread wide.

"Talos!" Joy swept over her. She wrapped her arms around his neck and buried her face in his ruff. His arms closed around her and she felt them change direction. Her stomach dipped, but this time due to movement as they shot into the sky. Away from the remains of Windhaven and all the lies hidden beneath its streets. "Oh, thank the gods. I was so afraid you were dead."

"I'm never leaving you again." His lips closed over hers.

"Thank the gods," she breathed when he pulled away.

She looked down to see the entire town—the whole world she'd known—was fire and smoke and night. She'd mapped every road, every twist and turn of Windhaven, and she couldn't tell which street led to the market, and which to the blacksmith. She couldn't even identify her cottage. All she could point out was the belfry, right in the center of the flame.

"The monsters are burning," Talos said, voice a soft rumble against her cheek.

"As is our home," she whispered.

He pulled her closer. "I'm sorry."

"I should be, but I'm not." She tipped her head up to meet his gaze—that kind brown that had always melted her heart. "That town was fed by lies for too long. Twisted into a demon's garden. It is time it all ended." She brushed her mouth across his, a silent promise of what she intended to enjoy with him later. "Let's find Emmi and Tarn and leave this place."

His massive wings beat the air as he stared at her. Hope and triumph and love burning brighter in his gaze than the fires below. "You still wish to make a life with me?"

"Always," she said. "You have me. Forever."

EPILOGUE

Isabelle stood beside Talos in the shadow of their cart, watching as the convoy of survivors hitched up beasts to carts in the late afternoon sun. They had salvaged what they could from the remains of Windhaven, and now she and the survivors were almost ready to begin their new lives. They had saved what animals they could. Had searched the rubble for survivors and supplies.

It was strange, to begin a new life within the ashes of the old, yet somehow beautiful. As was her ability to stand beside her love in the fields he'd once tended, facing the remains of their past.

He had his hand at her waist.

And love filled her heart.

"Are you ready?" he asked.

"In a moment." She kissed his cheek, and leaned against his side for a moment. The steady beat of his heart, the rise and fall of his chest, gave her the strength to face what came next.

She straightened and sent him a strained smile. "Emmi and I have to do this. Then we'll be ready to leave."

Clutching a woven wreath of fir branches and winter berries, she walked to where Emmi was waiting for her at the base of the stone arch that had somehow survived the flames.

Her sister held a matching wreath in one hand. She reached out with the other, and Isabelle gripped it tight. Without a word, they walked into the remains of the town. Even now, weeks after the fire, ashes swirled around their feet and charred scraps of wood crunched underfoot. After the fires had died down and the cries of monsters had faded, until nothing remained but the soft crackle of dying embers, she and Emmi had looked for their mother.

She couldn't say whether they truly wanted to find her, but they never had the chance to discover otherwise.

Cateline DuNorde was nowhere to be found.

That hadn't surprised Belle.

Their mother had committed her life to the bishop's lies, had consigned her own children to the tunnels rather than question the acts of a monster. At the end, she likely chose to burn for those lies rather than face the truth. In the wake of the fire, she and Emmi mourned the mother they'd wanted.

But they still had to lay the one they'd known to rest.

"This way," Isabelle said quietly, leading her sister over a pile of burnt wood and brick to where a massive clay oven still stood. That oven was all that remained of their home, and the only reason she'd been able to identify it.

Together, they laid their wreaths in the opening.

"I hope you find peace, Mama," Isabelle said quietly. "I want you to know that Emmi and I are well. We are safe with those who love us." She glanced at her sister, and her lips curved into a smile. "We are starting a new life today. And we are never going to look back."

Her sister grinned. "We're going to see the world, Mama. And I'm going to bake buns with sugar and smile the whole time."

Isabelle wrapped an arm around her sister's shoulders. "Yes, we are."

Together they returned to the edge of town, where the line of carts waited to roll onto the road. Snow was falling, and the forest was coated in white, as if the gods had shaken powdered sugar across the world in celebration. Perhaps it was an odd time to set out on a journey with no set destination, but to Isabelle, it made perfect sense.

The winter solstice was when the world shifted and days stretched from darkness into light, and that was exactly what she was doing.

They couldn't settle in any town, not with Talos and Tarn.

She wouldn't leave them—neither would Emmi.

And they had all discovered that none of Windhaven's survivors had much of a taste for Chastry-led living any more. What they did have was an excellent assortment of skills and a large number of rescued animals. In the shelter of the forest, they'd crafted new homes from the remains of the old.

Her heart swelled with joy at the sight of Talos waiting for her beside the cart that had become their home.

"Are you ready?" Talos asked.

"We are." She stepped into his arms and rested her chin on his pec. "More than. Take me away."

"As you wish," Talos rumbled in her ear. His powerful hand flexed at her waist, and a contented vibration, almost like a cat's purr, enveloped her. "I'll make sure you're comfy on our journey."

Warmth flooded her body.

"I'm sure you will." She sent him a wicked grin. "But first, Emmi's and my sugar rolls must earn their keep."

Emmi snorted. "You mean *Emmi's* sugar rolls."

Isabelle made a face. But in truth, her sister was the superior baker.

Isabelle's true passion lay in mapmaking, and she intended to gain a name for herself as a purveyor of maps for local travelers. The farther afield their caravan traveled, the more she would be able to add to her knowledge—and the larger the maps she would be able to sell.

Emmi would bake. Talos and Tarn would keep them safe, protect them all from bandits. The other survivors would guard Talos and Tarn's secret, ensure they weren't hunted by Chastry zealots.

And Talos would keep her warm at night.

He lifted her onto the driver's bench of their cart, then joined her in a fluid leap. The pair of oxen they'd rescued seemed to still know him, because they never shied and set off down the road with a click and a light flick of the reins. Ahead of them, the miller led the way. Behind them, Emmi and Tarn followed in the baking cart. A convoy of sinners, setting out to create their own world.

In a strange way, it was everything she and Thomas had dreamed.

She curled into Talos' side, warm and treasured beneath his wing. She didn't know what the future held, but in this perfect moment, her life was rich with love and wonder.

The End

Want more of Dee's books? Check out:

Apex Astral Hunters
Destination Alien Bride
Destination Alien Mate
Destination Alien Treasure

Undead Miles Trilogy (Zombies, dogs and romance—oh, my!)
Three Days In Undead Shoes
Three Weeks in Undead Shoes (Pending)

The Four Houses (Complete Urban Fantasy Series)
An Inheritance of Curses
Those Curses We Had Buried
A Curse In The Dark
Those Curses That Would Rise
The Heart of All Curses

ABOUT THE AUTHOR

A Canadian author obsessed with monsters and their love lives, Dee enjoys creating rich paranormal and science fiction worlds—and always likes to play with zombies. The characters she enjoys don't sit in some narrow box and do what they're told. Whether battling supernatural forces or facing fantastical terrain on distant planets, her characters are defying expectations and finding true love.

Want to get exclusive teasers, a serial story that's free for her subscribers and hear the latest exploits of her rebellious Great Dane? Sign up for Dee's newsletter.

Join Dee Online
www.djholmes.com

 facebook.com/DJHolmesAuthor

instagram.com/dee_j_holmes

bookbub.com/profile/dee-j-holmes

THE DEN

ATLAS ROSE

BLURB

They came for me in the middle of the day when I was sick in bed. Five savage Demons invaded Crown city, ripping our homes apart, until they found what they were looking for...
Me.
I kicked and screamed, fighting the fever and them. But I was no match for their strength and their sheer numbers.
These weren't just beasts...*they were monsters.*
Glowing red eyes. Midnight black fur. Bigger than any man I'd ever seen.
They put me in chains and threw me over their backs before taking me from my home.
And bought me to a place of darkness. A place where they call...*home.*
But this *den* is not a home. It's a prison. *My* prison.
There is no Alpha to bargain with, no weakness I can find.
They told me I was theirs now.
Only I didn't know what that meant.
Now I do.

CHAPTER ONE

"You look like hell," Lia muttered, leaning in a little too close. "Christ, don't tell me you have some fatal fucking disease. I swear, A. You infect me with a zombie illness, I'm gonna come back and haunt the fuck out of you."

I winced at the sound of her voice and waved her away. "It's just a bug," I slurred.

"You said that yesterday." She straightened and took a step backwards. "And the day before that...and, come to think of it, the day before that. But fuck, you didn't look this bad."

I swallowed, nodded, and felt a sledgehammer go to town inside my head. "I'm fine." A trickle of sweat ran down my back as I whispered. "It's just so fucking hot." I yanked the collar of my shirt and looked at my best friend until she blurred. "Aren't you hot?"

"It's the middle of winter," she answered, wrapping her thick, knitted cardigan tighter around her. "And Corden's a cheap fucking bastard, so he won't turn up the heat."

"*I heard that!*" our manager called from his office in the back room.

"I wish you would!" Lia snapped, jerking her gaze upwards. "We're freezing our tits off here!"

I winced, and I didn't know if it was from her crassness or her deafening tone. I wrapped my arms around my stomach. "I think I'm going to be sick."

"You need to go to the doctor," Lia snapped.

The thud of Corden's footsteps was deafening as he came closer. "Lia." He glared at her. "I'm warning you, one more comment and I'll write you up."

"Write this up," she said, flipping him the bird, then stabbed a finger my way. "And *she* needs to go home."

He shook his head. "No, she's fine. We need that schedule by midday or it's my ass on the line."

"Then it's *your* ass, isn't it?" she snapped, turning away.

Corden leaned in, peering at me, and grimaced. "Did you eat something bad?"

I swallowed, my throat clenching at the thought. "No. I...I can't eat anything."

"Not a thing?"

I shook my head and whimpered. I hadn't been able to hold a damn thing down all week. And when I thought of food...my stomach cramped and my head spun. Lia was right, I was sick...but I just needed a good sleep, that's all.

"I think I..." I licked my lips and pushed to stand, but my knees buckled and gave way.

"Whoa." Corden stepped forward, catching me. "You can't leave...the scheduling."

"Fuck your scheduling," Lia muttered from her cubicle across from mine.

He shot a glare her way. "You want to lose your job, Lia? Keep being mouthy."

She just bared her teeth at him, then glanced my way. Concern raged in her eyes. She was worried. Hell, I was worried. I nodded and sank back to my seat. "I'll g-get it d-done, C-Corden." My teeth chattered and gnashed as I spoke.

"Good. *Thank you for being a team player, Arden,*" he said, his voice a little too damn loud just to make a point.

But he didn't need to make a point. I'd dragged myself here, and I was determined to get this done. This damn job was all I had. No goddamn bug was going to compromise it.

I winced, let out a moan, and tried to focus on the computer screen. He wanted the scheduling done, but the problem was...*I couldn't see a damn thing.* The numbers were badly blurred. I clicked, changed the formula, and added different time slots for the twenty plumbers that needed schedules for the coming week.

But the formula wasn't right. I gritted my teeth and trembled. A shudder tore through my body, making my hands shake on the desk. Lia shoved upwards, her eyes widening as she lifted her hands into the air. "Whoa...*did you feel that?*"

But I didn't feel anything as the office blurred and, in the blink of an eye, darkness descended. I caught the faint sound of my best friend screaming... before I knew no more.

"I fucking told you!"

The darkness shifted and the panicked *boom...boom...boom...*of my pulse was out of control.

"I fucking told you to send her home!"

I blinked, seeing Lia standing over me, holding something cold to my face. "W-what happened?"

"You passed the fuck out, that's what happened," Lia muttered. "Right in the middle of a damn earthquake."

"Jesus," Corden muttered.

I blinked, following his riveted gaze to the TV mounted on the wall.

"I'm taking you home." Lia grabbed my arm and hauled me up. "Say one word, Corden, and I'll kick you in the balls."

But he didn't say a word as I lurched to my feet, holding on to the desk as Lia grabbed my things and then helped me toward the door. As we left the office, the faint voice of a panicked reporter reached me. *"Some type of destructive force is tearing through the city...destroying buildings in its wake."*

"Come on." Lia dragged me into the nearly empty parking lot outside the hole-in-the-wall workforce management company we worked for. "I'm getting you the hell out of here."

Didn't she just hear the news? I tried to slow my steps, but I didn't have the strength to fight her. I just slid into the passenger seat of her old Corolla and curled myself into a ball. She was inside the car in an instant, cutting a concerned look my way before she started the engine and backed out.

We were driving before I knew it, cutting through the busy streets as Lia drove me home. "Just n-need-d to sle-eep."

"Honey, you need a hospital. You're fucking gray."

I shook my head carefully. "No. No hospital, no insurance."

She gave a sigh and turned the wheel, pulling onto back streets. "Fine, you want to go home, then I'll take you. But I'm texting you every goddamn hour and, so help me God, A, you'd better reply."

I nodded as the midday sun was smothered, plunging the car into gloom.

"What the fuck?" Lia leaned forward, staring up through the windshield as she pulled out from the back street not a block away from my small townhouse. "Is that a damn hurricane?"

Cars tore past us, tires screeching as they raced away.

"The world is going to Hell, I swear," she muttered, pulling up in front of my house. I grabbed my purse and stabbed the seatbelt release. "Thanks, L."

"Sure...just remember."

"Reply to the messages. Got it," I replied, and climbed carefully out.

I wasn't sure there was a term in the dictionary for 'worse than death'. But if there was, then it'd perfectly describe me. Lia leaned across, peering at me as I closed the door and smiled at her. I slowly walked to the door, fumbling with my key before I shoved it into the lock, opened the door, and stumbled inside.

I headed for the bedroom, dropping my things on the counter as I passed. I just wanted to sleep...

Yeah, sleep was what I needed.

I kicked off my shoes as the bed rumbled and shook. Sirens filtered faintly to my ears as I let myself fall, hitting the mattress hard, and lay there...

I was dying.

The thought hit me hard.

This is what death felt like.

My body shivered...my pulse was like a flutter in my neck.

I knew I was in trouble...knew lying there that I was probably not going to see morning. Not another sunset. Not another night. Something warm and slick slipped from the corner of my eye as the bed shook again.

Get up...

A voice inside my head commanded.

Get up, my plaything...

I cracked open my eyes and pushed upward on shaking arms. The sheets, already sodden from my sweat, stuck to my skin. Still, I had to move. That undeniable command pounded through my head, forcing me from the bedroom. I stumbled to the living room and the glass wall that looked out to the city. There, I lifted my gaze to the skyline.

Shadows descended like a tsunami against the towering glass buildings surrounding my small house. The floor trembled and the walls shook as I stared at what had to be the aftershocks of the tremor. The sound of breaking glass sounded like a roar. I couldn't move as an unseen wave of darkness slammed into the buildings, descending on me like death itself.

I stumbled backwards as daytime turned to night. That roar...grew louder until it was all I could hear. I wrenched my arm upwards, protecting my face as that darkness slammed into my house with a *boom*, shattering the glass in front of me.

Night plunged into my world.

Night stopped in front of me.

Five hulking, savage wolves stopped dead in my living room, leaving nothing but utter destruction in their wake. The wind blasted through what they'd left of my living room wall, swirling my hair. Sirens blasted like a needle inside my head. I winced as parts of the towering buildings fell in the distance. The sound was like the wake of a nuclear impact. An impact that stood in front of me with glowing eyes. Shards of glass fell from thick, midnight fur as the creatures sucked in massive breaths. I lifted my gaze, shaking as a wave of icy shudders ripped through me.

One beast took a slow step closer. The sheer size of him seemed to grow, swallowing my living room in a murky midnight blur.

Fear tore through me as I trembled, holding my hands pathetically in front of me. "D-don't k-kill m-me..."

"You..." the beast growled, his voice husky and raw.

Heat ripped through me like a blade, carving through the shudders as he took a step closer, then rose on his hind legs. I trembled in his presence, staggering backwards until I hit the kitchen counter. The *Wolf* strode forward, black nostrils flaring with every breath as he scented the air.

And me.

He lashed out, grabbing me around my neck. Calloused fingers grazed my skin, rough and worn, ending in razor-sharp claws that pressed gently against the back of my neck. This monster could kill me in an instant and not even flinch.

"You're already sick," he murmured, red flames burning in his eyes.

He lowered his head. The brush of his thick fur felt coarse against my skin before the long, wet slide of his tongue followed. I shivered in the wake of that thick muscle sliding along my throat, and my pulse skipped a beat...then raced erratically to catch up.

A growl reverberated like thunder in the back of his throat. "We found you." He closed his eyes. "Just in time, then." He pulled away, opening those pitiless eyes that looked like the pits of Hell. "You...*belong with us.*"

In the wake of his words, my phone on the counter let out a *beep.* I didn't need to look at the screen to know who it was. In the back of my mind, I replayed my fear...*I wouldn't see another sunset...or my best friend, ever again.*

"Sleep, mortal," the Wolf in front of me growled.

And the hellish creature snuffed out my light...

CHAPTER TWO

The night stayed...thudding, *booming* like a midnight storm as it unleashed inside my head. I crackled open my eyes to see the world jolting.

"No."

Thick fur under my hands...my hands that were tied. Memories slipped in, flickers of moments as the wall inside my house shattered, and those beasts...*those beasts were in my home.* Warmth moved under my body. Sleek, powerful muscles moved under me as the beast ran with me on his back. Those heavy paws met the ground with *boom...boom...booms!*

My blurred vision sharpened, watching as the city grew smaller and smaller in the distance. I knew that city...*my city.*

"No!" I shouted as I shoved upwards and slipped, falling backwards.

There was nothing but air.

Until I hit the ground *hard.*

My ass hit first before my head snapped backwards, clacking my teeth together and sending a spear of agony through my head. I screamed as the agony cleaved through my skull. Grass...dirt. The ground was hard under my body. I sucked in a deep breath. My arms shook as I pushed upward, my hands still tied in front. My vision blurred. Thick, looming shadows came closer.

Shadows that moved closer...and closer.

"Get away from me." I shoved away, but my elbows buckled, sending me crashing back to the ground.

I tried again...and again, punching my fists against ground as I shoved upwards. All I could see was black fur and enormous paws. I stared at them, and then at my hand.

It was bigger.

So much bigger.

I slowly lifted my head, taking in the beast that hunkered over me.

Heavy breaths scattered my hair. His midnight eyes were a void I lost myself in. A void that swallowed me, *consumed me*...agony raced through my body. Heat followed, blooming like a molten wave. Sweat dripped down off my chin as I stared into the soulless eyes of the beast.

"Wh-what the fuck do you want from me?"

The beast stood over me, staring me down...his tall straight ears pointing to the sky. He was bigger than any beast I'd ever seen—I glanced at the others— they all were.

"Let me go," I demanded, my body shaking as my sodden, sweatstained shirt stuck hard against my skin. "Let me g-go and I'll g-give you wh-whatever you w-want."

Agony roared through me again. My body ached, like my bones were rubbing together, splintering and fracturing until the shattering was all I could feel.

The beast didn't answer, just watched me as I stood there, trembling, my fingers gripped together. "Answer me...*ANSWER ME!*"

I stumbled backwards, until I tripped and fell, hitting the ground hard once more. But I didn't stay down. Not now when the darkness had crept from my vision, leaving cruel clarity behind. I shoved up from the ground, stumbled, then lunged.

But I didn't get far. Two of the towering beasts closed in from the sides. Their low snarls were threatening. Their heads lowered, glaring at me sideways.

I stiffened, moaned, and felt the world sway. In a blinding instant, the fight left me. I clutched my hands together, trying to understand what exactly had happened. "I hadn't finished the spreadsheet."

"What?" the Wolf behind me muttered. I let out a screech and spun, staring wide-eyed at the beast behind me. "You talk?"

"Did you want me to meow?"

"What?" I whispered.

"Did you..." He took a step closer. *"Want me to meow?"*

Did I want him to meow? Like a cat meow? "No," I said, confused, my heart hammering. "No, I don't want you to meow."

"Then stop wasting time." He took another step.

My knees trembled and a thousand ants bit along the nape of my neck. I tried to hold on, tried to trap the moan in the back of my throat. But I couldn't...

"Stay away," I whimpered, panic making me say anything to keep the beasts at bay. "There's s-something w-wrong with me...I'm-m s-sick. I'm sick."

"I know." He moved so close I could feel the heat of his breath. "Why do you think we're here?"

I lifted my gaze. His midnight eyes blurred. Black on black melted into one, and right in front of him, my knees buckled once more, sending me crashing to the ground again.

I couldn't stand, couldn't fight. Couldn't do anything but stare at the bindings around my wrists and moan with the agony.

"We can help you," the beast murmured as he looked down at me.

I flinched away, pushing my heels against the dirt as he leaned closer. He was big...*God, he was big.* The thick, coarse fur made him a midnight mountain as he towered above me. But he never let out a growl...never bared his teeth.

Fangs, you idiot.

Wolves have fangs.

But these weren't just Wolves, not like I'd ever seen before.

He bent over and lowered his head. A massive pink tongue slipped free of his mouth, catching a bead of sweat as it dripped down the side of my neck. I closed my eyes at the sensation. It was cool...so goddamn cool, like a cube of ice along my skin.

My body quaked as I unleashed a croak. "Again..." Revulsion rippled through me. Still, I pushed forward, craning my head to the side to give the monster all the access I dared. "Please, *again.*"

The tongue came again, sliding more slowly this time, long and flat, taking the salt from my skin and leaving the frigid bliss behind.

"I can take it from you." I opened my eyes at the words as he stared down at me. "Give yourself to us, and we can help you."

Give myself?

A flinch came at the corner of my eye. "What the fuck?"

Only he wasn't stopping. He leaned even closer. "Give yourself, and we can take the fever and the pain away."

He lowered his head, his black nostrils flaring as he sniffed my arm. Agony burned through me, so hot I couldn't tell which part of me hurt the most. But the moment I twisted my hands against the bindings, I saw it...

A dark mark, like a bruise.

Except this wasn't *any* bruise.

No...it was a marking in the shape of a skull.

Black, sunken eyes...a hard round head, like the most hideous tattoo.

The kind you get on a dare after a drunken night out with friends. But this was no dare. I didn't even think this was reality. No, this was a dream, one goddamn awful dream.

"No." I jerked my gaze up, finding the Wolf lifting his head, exposing his throat to me. My eyes drifted down the matted midnight fur to a faint marking that showed on his chest. One that burned through, all the way to his skin.

It was the same marking.

The same skull.

The same haunting, hollowed glare.

"What the fuck is happening to me?"

CHAPTER THREE

B ut the Wolf didn't answer, just lowered his head and stepped forward. Shoving his head underneath me, he flipped me up before I knew it. I sailed through the air like I weighed nothing at all, landing on another beast's back with an *"Oof"*.

Then the beast took off with a lunge, the hard *thud...thud...thuds* sending a fresh wave of agony through me with every brutal stride. I cried out and buried my hands in his fur, desperate to hold on.

Panic filled me as they ran. I gripped his coat and glanced over my shoulder, seeing the city slipping further and further away in the distance.

Where the fuck are they taking me?

I swallowed hard and turned back just as the beasts climbed the embankment to the freeway and raced toward the oncoming cars. Tires screeched as we ran across the double lanes and crossed through the traffic in a monstrous blur of black.

Terrified faces filled my view as the beast under me leaped, following the Alpha over a dark blue sedan as it hurtled toward us, and kept running.

I unleashed a scream as his muscles flexed underneath me. Pure power drove us skyward as the creature soared, hitting the other side of the lane with a bone-jarring *thud*.

Harsh breaths moved the ribs under my legs as I straddled the Wolf's back and clung tight. The beast looked behind at the cars as they tore past, then kept moving, tearing toward the bank of trees that stretched as far as I could see.

Lia...

She was all I thought about. My phone was somewhere in my destroyed house amongst the rubble of shattered glass and wood from where the beasts had crashed through my window.

I sucked in deep breaths, ducking my head as we plunged through the line of trees and into the darkness. *Thud...thud...thud...*the boom of paws mirrored the erratic sound of my pulse. I released a cry as a branch whipped my cheek as we ran. The beast under me slowed his stride and glanced back at me. Through the blur of my tears, I saw his gaze find my cheek before he turned back forward.

He veered, cutting through the trees into the path of the other. The Alpha let out a snarl. Anger flashed in his eyes as he bared white fangs. But then he glanced my way and something passed between them. Then the Alpha moved aside, letting the beast under me take the lead.

I didn't understand, until I glanced back at the track where we'd been running a second ago and the thick mass of trees up ahead.

He didn't want to run through them.

My breath caught. *He knew the branches would hurt me.* The thought barely rose in my mind before we were off again, racing through the darkness, heading I didn't know where. My whole body ached, my bones creaked. I clenched my jaw to keep from biting my tongue. Still, the metallic taste of my own blood was in my mouth. Sharp and sweet, making me lick my lips and groan.

Water...

I needed water. I gripped tighter as the world swayed and the darkness that had held me under threatened my vision again. Gray, that's what I saw, with darkening edges. The Alpha blurred as he ran beside me, until finally we slowed...and stopped.

It took me a moment for my body to adjust. My thighs ached from holding on, then the booming in my head eased enough to hear a rushing sound that grew louder as the Wolf moved again, more slowly this time, cautiously sniffing the air as we stepped through the trees and into a clearing.

It was a river...narrow but deep, the edge easing down to blue water. I let out a moan at the sight, not even waiting for the beast to stop before I leaned forward and swung my leg over, gripping his fur to hold on.

I looked back as my feet hit the ground. *Sorry,* the word bloomed in my head before I stumbled toward the water. My body burned, that fever stealing the moisture from my mouth until my breaths were nothing more than searing rasps.

I couldn't speak, just staggered to the water. As my bare feet hit the pointy pebbles along the edge, I fell face first into the cold flow.

My breath seized as the water rushed in, driving into my mouth and down my throat. I tried to pull back, tried to straighten, but my body wouldn't work. It just trembled and flailed.

Until I was snatched upwards, carried from the water, and dropped gently onto the grass. I heaved and retched. Frigid water came back up to splash on the ground in front of me.

"Fool." The growl came. "Could have killed yourself."

I just hung my head, my hands pushed against the grass as I wheezed and shuddered, then finally fell on my side against the ground. "Hospital."

The Alpha lowered his head.

"Take. Me...to a damn hospital."

Darkness surrounded me. His fur. His eyes. His white fangs glinted as he spoke. "We do and you'll die."

"Dying. Now."

My tears were warm, welling in the corners of my eyes. Then they spilled, meeting the rivulets of water that dripped from my hair. He came closer, that...beast. "We'll take care of you."

"No." I shook my head and pushed to sit up. "No, *you stay the hell away from me.*"

I moaned as agony ripped along my arm. That burn moved deeper, coursing along my vein until it hit the wall of my chest. My pulse thrummed, then skipped a beat. Then it skipped a lot of beats. The lack of sound in my chest was a wall of agony.

I shoved my fist against my chest as the world grayed.

"We'll...take...care...of...you." The Alpha came closer.

Darkness swallowed me. Darkness that licked my arm. His tongue was cold. Then, with another flare of cold, sound boomed in my chest once more. An ache ripped through me, the pain like a punch that had me pressing my fist against the throb and sucking in deep breaths.

The darkness eased, lightening once more until the Alpha filled my view. I stared up at him, sucking in harsh breaths until reality crashed in.

This was happening.

This was really happening.

"What is going on?" I whispered through the sawing gasps of air. "What the fuck do you want with me?"

He lowered his head, those black nostrils flaring as he sniffed, and nudged my arm. That bruise was still there, dark and ugly, making me wince when I looked at it. He came closer. "You going to trust us yet, female?"

Trust.

I jerked my gaze to his. Trust didn't come easily to me. Trust him to what? Not eat my damn face off...or trust him to keep me alive? There was a damn wide space in between there. But as I thought about that, the resounding boom in my chest screamed the answer. "Okay," I gasped, unable to do anything else.

"Then we keep moving." He lifted his gaze to the sky. "Need to move fast."

"Why?"

He just lowered his gaze, those dark eyes giving nothing away. "Ride him," he growled, and gave a jerk of his head. "Now."

Ride him?

The other Wolf came forward, and even though they looked almost identical, I knew they weren't. That drum in my head picked up a beat as those words hit me. An image bloomed...me, *him*, flesh and fur, fucking hard.

Heat flared through me as my stomach tightened. God, that was sick. *Ride him...*

Christ.

I swallowed hard and pushed upwards. "Okay. Okay, I can do this."

My ride came closer and sat with his back to me. I fell against him more than I climbed on. My fists buried into his fur as he rose and adjusted my weight, making me fall face-first against his neck.

He didn't even wait for me to settle, just took a step forward and, with one massive lunge, leaped over the river and hit the other side with a *thud!*

I let out a scream as he leaped and squeezed my eyes closed. He turned his head when we landed, glancing back at me, those dark eyes glinting as he panted. For a second, I thought he was almost...*laughing at me.*

"Cocky bastard, aren't you?" I whispered. And I swore that grin grew wider.

Then he took off along with the others, tearing another cry of alarm from my lips. Paws thudded hard against the ground as we ran, plunging back into the trees once more, until I was lost to the blur and the almost panicked pounding of their steps.

The others ran beside us, glancing at me as we cut through the trees. I didn't know where we were heading, but it was far from the city...and salvation.

In the wake of the cold rush of the river, deep shudders started tearing through me, rattling my bones. I let out a moan and lay forward, my head smacking against his neck as he ran, until he slowed, then stopped.

I closed my eyes, just holding on and shuddering.

Everywhere ached. My jaw, my joints, and I was super conscious of the panicked racing in my chest, just waiting for the sudden lack of sound once more.

"Female?" The deep growl came at my ear.

"Arden," I whispered.

"What?"

My arms trembled as I pushed upward a little. "My name is Arden."

"Arden." My name was a growl. He nudged my arm, then pressed that wet nose against my neck. "Getting weak."

"No shit," I whispered and closed my eyes. "Hospital." I tried once more.

"No hospital," he snapped, then glanced at the Wolf underneath me and gave a jerk of his head. "We need to hurry."

I held on as hard as I could. But my fingers slipped, my strength weakening as we raced through the trees. I closed my eyes, but there was no sleep...I was too terrified I'd never wake up again.

I focused on the thrumming in my chest, fixed on the sound until it was all I heard. When the trees gave way to a freeway once more, I barely flinched. I just held on, unable to care any longer.

My strength gave way. I slipped and fell sideways, tumbling toward the ground before something sharp grazed my back. I was grasped and lifted, then carried through the air. My shirt ripped, and I fell again.

But I didn't crash all the way to the ground. Instead, I landed on one of the other Wolves. We ran again, that darkness edging back into my world. I closed my eyes and held on as tightly as I could. That booming in my chest was skipping now and then, sending another surge of panic through me.

When I opened my eyes once more, the world had indeed darkened. Twilight rushed in, leaving us to race toward the last traces of light against the horizon.

There were no cars here, no houses, just more trees, until slowly even they dimmed. Reality warped, blurring until I was sure this was a dream. Trees gave way to rolling grounds that stretched out until we headed toward more trees on the other side. But instead of rushing further, we slowed.

A glow bloomed to life in the distance. I sucked in hard breaths...*boom... boom...silence*...my heart skipped again as we stopped outside a place tucked almost out of sight.

"We're here," the Alpha muttered.

Wherever here was.

CHAPTER FOUR

"What is this place?" I slipped from the back of the beast, falling hard onto my ass. I tried to catch my breath, tried to stop from falling over. But I was weak, and growing weaker by the second.

Darkness towered over me, with red inferno eyes and long, tapered fangs. The beast looked down at me before he lifted his head. "Home for the time being."

"Home?" I flinched, then my gaze found the derelict building. No central heating, no plumbing...no goddamn hospital. "No fucking way." I shook my head and tried to push to a stand. "Take me to a hospital, a doctor...*something!*"

"No hospital. No doctor," he insisted, nudging me forward. "Inside."

"Inside?" I shook my head, driving myself sideways.

"In...side."

I shook my head. "Get the fuck away from me...get the fu—"

Darkness engulfed me in an instant as the Alpha lowered his head and growled in my ear. "*Sleep.*"

No...

No!

I tried to hold on, tried to fight that consuming wave of emptiness, but it was like a tsunami, one that swelled against my weakened mind and, in my feeble state, took me down.

I woke to the faint clink of chains. The sound was grating, pulling me to the surface. I inhaled deeply, drawing in the cold and the dank and the scent of...*dog*.

Dog?

I opened my eyes to find I was surrounded by darkness. Warmth shifted at my back, and something hard was wedged against my side. I winced, fighting the panicked racing of my heart. A snore came, loud, like a growl at the back of my head. *What the fuck?*

"You're awake," a growl came behind me.

I lifted my head, to see glowing red eyes. A shudder tore through me at the sight. Agony moved deep, carving along my veins like the tip of a knife. "What the fuck..." I shoved backwards, kicking the warmth at my back.

"Watch it," the warmth snarled.

"Go back to sleep," another snapped.

My pulse stuttered as I jerked my gaze to the beasts at my back. In an instant, the past rushed back to me. My work...my sickness. The Wolves. *The Wolves...*

"Where the fuck am I?" I managed to shove upward, but I was stopped, and stood there, swaying. The massive midnight beast who'd come for me yesterday barred my every attempt to run.

Not that I could run have far.

"Home," the Alpha snarled as he stepped to the side. "Your home."

I glanced at the heavy wooden door behind him. "The fuck it is."

He lowered his head, those seething eyes fixed on mine, daring me. "Think you can run, female?" He cast his gaze to my trembling knees. "You can barely stand."

I winced at the words and forced my knees to lock. "Want to test that theory?"

He stilled, like for a second, he hadn't expected me to bite back. Maybe that was what he did? Maybe they abducted women and brought them here. I looked around the empty cabin, searching for a hint anyone else was here. But there was nothing, not that I could see, anyway.

The Alpha bent his head toward me, those black nostrils flaring. I winced, and agony flared with the movement, making me whimper. Who the fuck was I kidding...I couldn't run, I couldn't do anything but stand there and bite back more whimpers.

"Sick." The Alpha stepped closer. "Getting worse, too."

"It's just a b—" I didn't get the rest of the word out as my knees buckled again.

I hit the floor hard, landing on my hands and knees.

"You need us," the Alpha insisted as he loomed over me.

He was so close, his breath brushed my ear. I closed my eyes as that cool, slick tongue came again, licking my neck before he nuzzled my shirt. "Your pulse is too fast, too weak. Take your shirt off."

I sucked in a deep breath, curling my fingers against the filthy floor. "Fuck...you."

"You can," he urged. "It'd ease the pain."

My body clenched, fighting the waves of terror and pain. Sweat dribbled down my brow and fell into my eyes. I was burning up from the inside, on the edge of going into shock.

"Your shirt."

I forgot he was there, forgot everything was there. I lifted my head and stared into those soulless eyes.

"You want to live?"

I flinched, fear making me pathetic and weak. "Will you kill me?"

"Don't you think I would have if I wanted to?"

I sucked in another deep breath as panic pushed in. I didn't have time to think as my pulse stuttered. One more minute...one more second, and I wouldn't survive.

A whimper tore free as I rolled into a sit, drew back my arm, pulled it through the sleeve, and dragged the shirt over my head, leaving me in my bra. "There," I whispered. "Do your worst, beast."

"Beast." He nuzzled the strap of my bra, then opened his jaw, hooked it with his fang, and dragged it down.

I reached for my breasts. I'd thought he wanted to scent my skin, somehow get closer to my stuttering heart. But when he moved to my hands, pushing them aside, I suddenly realized I was wrong. One lick and I closed my eyes. The feel of his tongue was cool, perfect, easing that fire. Another came at my side. The cold nose tickled me as the Alpha let out a *chuff*, pushing my hand away.

"Take care of you," the beast murmured.

His tongue licked the peak of my breast, sending lightning tearing through my body to hit between my thighs. I released a moan, low and guttural, as his nose pressed between my thighs and sniffed.

"No." I thrashed my head from side to side.

"You need us," the Alpha repeated. "Open your eyes and see."

I opened my eyes and saw the beast lift his head from between my legs, those red eyes glowing brighter than ever before. He sniffed my arm, nudging it and drawing my focus to the mark that was deep and blue, the skull even clearer than it had been before.

The beast lifted his head, the mark on his own chest bolder and more distinct, throbbing almost. My mind swam, my senses left me as though this was a dream, almost. None of this was real. Not the sickness or me collapsing at work, or the towering, savage midnight beasts who stood before me now.

"It's not real." I lifted my head. Those red eyes blazed as the Alpha sniffed my breast and his pink tongue flicked out to lap my nipple. "It's not real at all."

Hunger consumed me with every lick of his tongue, every blast of his breath. With every tug on my clothes, I drew further and further into that emptiness.

"Let us take care of you." The Alpha nudged my leg, pushing it to the side. "In your need."

My need...

I was so hot, so unbelievably hot. A different, delicious warmth brewed under the fever, stoking between my thighs, lingering in the wake of his tongue. I could give myself over to this desire, give my...

Thud...

Thud...

Thud.

My heart.

My...heart.

Belongs to me. The whisper bloomed in my mind. The voice was familiar and strange, like the echo of a forgotten memory. A memory I wanted. No, a memory *I craved.*

"Let us take care of you," the Alpha growled again, stepping closer, his sheer size causing me to scramble backwards. Those red eyes burned in my mind and my whole body trembled. I was helpless under the spell, my will barely a thought under this hunger.

The others crowded around me. "You need us." One lowered his head, growling softly in my ear. "Your body needs us."

"We'll help with the transition." Another licked my breast, sliding his big, warm tongue across my nipple before he lowered his head and gently nipped the soft flesh at my side. He licked the tiny flare of pain away as he moved lower.

"The fever...is almost at the end." The Alpha bent low and opened his jaws.

Snap.

The button of my jeans flew through the air and clattered to the floor.

"Time to evolve...or die."

That desire thrummed inside me. I struggled to think, arching my back as he pushed apart my zipper. The beast at my side nuzzled my neck, and I had the overwhelming urge to tilt my head and expose my neck.

"Ours." The Alpha gripped one side of my jeans as another of his pack snagged the other in his jaws.

Cool air licked my thighs as they peeled my jeans down.

"Give in to me," the beast urged in my ear.

I forced my head to the side, giving him what he wanted. The Wolf's low growl vibrated along my neck, triggering the panicked rush of my pulse. I couldn't fight them...even if I wanted to.

And I didn't want to.

Not anymore.

I wanted to give in to this delicious agony. I wanted to part my thighs and let those big, thick tongues go where they wanted...

"That's it," the Alpha urged. "He's almost ready for you."

"Who?" The word left my lips before I barely realized I'd spoken.

"Your prince," the Alpha growled, and nudged my thighs apart. "He's waiting for you..."

"*Princeee...*" I whispered as he licked the edge of my panties. I writhed under their touches, pressing my neck against bared teeth as the Wolf unleashed that low, threatening thunder. "I have no prince."

"Oh, but you do." The Alpha gripped the edge of my panties in his teeth and yanked.

The fabric ripped under the force and with the savage sound, a blinding flare of clarity pushed in.

All of a sudden, I knew what was happening.

What these beasts wanted to do to me...

And I needed to stop it.

My eyes flew open. The cold spear of clarity carved through me. *"No!"* I screamed and kicked, shoving away from them. My panties were torn, leaving them as nothing more than a flap of cloth around me. They stood there, those strange mammoth beasts, staring at me while my pulse spluttered and gave a feeble *thud*.

Run...

The word came out of nowhere, only it was Lia's voice in my head. Lia, who had more spunk than anyone else I knew, came back to me now.

Run, Arden...RUN!

CHAPTER FIVE

R*un...*
I stumbled backwards, then turned. My heart gave a stutter as I lunged for the door. But desperation surged inside me, forcing me to haul ass out of there.

"Arden!" the Alpha roared my name, but I didn't stop.

I yanked the door open and ran outdoors. Trees closed in around one side, leading to some kind of hedge on the other. A hedge that had to lead somewhere. Anywhere, as long as it wasn't here.

My steps were a blur. I reached down, yanked the torn remnant of my panties free, and ran, not caring I was dressed in nothing more than a damn bra.

I ran for that hedge, tripped, stumbled, and reached a hand out to the compacted brush. But it wasn't a hedge. It was some kind of maze...no, not a maze...*a labyrinth.* I didn't waste a second, just ran while that panicked thrashing in my head stuttered.

"ARDEN!"

The howl came from behind me. Low. Growly. Sounding *very* pissed off. They'd catch up to me in no time. Then they'd take me back and...*and...*

Don't think about it. Don't think about them. Just get the hell out of here. Towering green walls closed in all around me. I turned and ran, and then turned again, until I was sure I was running in circles. Circles of hedged green. Circles that would lead me where?

"Arden, come back! You'll die out there."

It was the Alpha. I knew it. Faint thunder came from somewhere behind me. They were letting me run, playing with their goddamn food. And I was the food. Just not the kind I'd expected.

That heat welled between my legs, like a spell that refused to let go.

We can help you. Let us help you.

Their words crowded in, rebounding in my head as I put one foot in front of the other and ran. Cold moved in, a pale mist slipped in around my feet, growing thicker the deeper I moved into the labyrinth. What the hell was this place? I ran, tripping as I tried to find a way out of whatever this was.

Until I turned, running past an opening, and caught sight of a man. I stopped, backtracked, used my hands to cover myself as best I could, and stared at him. "You...can you get me out of here?"

He stared at me for a long second before he nodded and lifted his hand. "Yes. But you need to come with me."

I glanced over my shoulder. I was almost naked...and about to go somewhere with a damn stranger. A growl cut through the air, sounding close...too close. "Okay." I turned back to the stranger, but he was...gone. "What the fuck?"

He was gone...just like that.

"I told you not to run."

I spun at the sound, finding the Alpha coming closer. He wasn't even out of breath, more pissed off than anything.

"What the fuck is this place?" I demanded as I stumbled backwards. "Who are you? What the *hell* is happening to me?"

He came closer, the other four Wolves at his back, spreading out as they encircled me. "Do you want answers...or to survive?"

My knees shook. But I forced myself to remain upright as they surrounded me. "No." I shook my head, my pulse stuttering once more. "Stay away from me."

"Don't you see?" one of them growled as they flanked my side and came up behind me. "We can't."

"We're drawn to you," another at my left added.

"We can neither leave you, nor allow you to run." The Alpha drew my gaze. "Can't you see that?"

"We traveled the caverns of the Underworld to find you," the Wolf at my back murmured, his deep growl hitting me between my legs.

That hunger came roaring to the surface once more. Darkness...desire and the feeble sound of my pulse. Exhaustion made me shake my head. I couldn't fight them...couldn't fight whatever this was.

I sucked in a harsh breath as that low growl came at my back again. The vibration sent shudders along my skin and plunged down my spine. I closed my eyes. "I can't keep fighting."

"You never could," the Alpha responded.

I tracked his movement by the sound of his voice alone. *You never could.*

"Why..." I opened my eyes to find him in front of me. "Why me?"

"That's not for us to explain." He lowered his head and nudged my hand aside.

I wanted to fight him, this *beast*. But the throb of his voice called to something inside me, some darkness I'd never known existed until now. In the spluttering sound of my feeble pulse, I knew the answer. It was the same darkness that called to them.

I didn't even flinch this time when he licked my stomach, didn't even buck and fight when his warm breath blew against my core.

"Let us take care of you," the Wolf at my back urged. "Let us take away your pain."

My knees trembled as that fire rose. My heart gave a last splutter, then fell silent. Agony roared as I fell. But I didn't hit the ground, instead I hit *them*. Soft warm fur cushioned my fall.

"Give in to us, or you die right here," the Alpha's growl was warped and strange...

I whispered, "Yes."

CHAPTER SIX

The cool relief of the Alpha's tongue trailed down my neck. I cried out when that fire inside moved through my chest. Still the Alpha came closer, lowering his head to nudge my side hard enough to roll me over. This was it...this was what dying felt like.

Suspended in silence, consumed by both fire and ice, like it was lust and pain.

Power hummed along my skin as the Alpha dragged his cold, wet nose along my spine. Fur brushed the backs of my thighs as I screamed my agony.

"You've run out of time, mortal." The Alpha nuzzled my back again.

The touch was like ice along my skin. He grabbed my hips with his massive paws and yanked me backwards, dragging me along the soft green grass inside the labyrinth. I lifted my head as my ass slammed against his body. A gap in the hedge was in front of me. I knew that was the heart of all this.

Home...

The word hit me as the Alpha hunkered over me, his massive body a cage that closed me in. His cock probed my entrance. Hard, thick...*God, he was thick.*

"Told you before, you need us." His breath was a fiery blast at the back of my neck.

But I wasn't dead...not yet. Power hummed along my skin as he pushed in. Energy bloomed inside me at the connection. He stretched me more than anything I'd ever felt before, rubbing me in places that felt glorious. I shouldn't want this, shouldn't tremble in perfect agony. But my body had a need of its own, driving against him as he thrust that *thing* deeper inside me. Until I thrashed my head from side to side. "No more...*I can't take any more.*"

"You can...you can take it all," he grunted. "Take it all, Arden. Take...it...*all, and survive.*"

My body constricted around his thickening knot as he drove deeper. My core clenched, clamping tight around that bulbous hard thing as he withdrew, then drove in again.

I knew in that moment that whatever force powered this ending of it all was coming from him...this Alpha.

Another beast nuzzled my cheek as the Alpha pushed deeper inside and that hunger roared within me. I closed my eyes, giving in to the need to survive and...drove myself against him. "Who the fuck are you?" I moaned as he thrust inside me.

"Do you not know by now?" the Alpha murmured. "We are yours...yours to command...yours to control. We were created by our master to help you transition...to go to him."

Come to me, Arden. I'm waiting for you.

Was this voice in my head the man I'd seen before? The one who'd vanished when the Wolves came? I tried to think, tried to put all this together. But my mind wouldn't work. It succumbed to the unmerciful need my dying body craved.

A shudder ripped through me at the words, and something inside me howled with triumph. He drove deeper inside me, stoking that fire. "Yes." I dropped my head as shame and torment filled me.

I wanted to fight that hunger.

Wanted to run from that need.

But I couldn't. Not anymore.

The inferno in my chest seemed to cool with every slow thrust of his cock inside me. I pushed back, consumed by that ease. "Harder," I moaned, giving myself over to the delicious feeling. "For God's sake...*harder*."

"There is no God here," the Wolf at my side urged. "Only Death."

Here...that strange voice whispered with the Wolf's words. *And I'm waiting for you.*

I shoved upwards, driving my back against his thick fur.

"Mine," the Alpha growled in my ear. "No more running, Arden...no more fighting."

"*No more denying,*" the four other Wolves said in unison.

I opened my eyes, seeing the burning embers in their gazes. Pressure built in my chest, a crushing pressure. One driven by the silence. I waited for the *thud* in my chest to start once more, for the pounding of my heart to begin once more.

But it didn't, and in the silence, a new hunger roared to the surface. Agony claimed me again, tearing a shriek from my lips. The Alpha didn't stop thrusting inside me. If anything, he picked up his pace, unleashed a grunt, and drove even deeper.

"Bite me," the Wolf in front of me urged.

He lowered his massive head and his soft fur pressed against me. I grabbed him, my fingers sinking into the soft warmth, and fisted his coat.

"You need to bite, Arden," the Alpha growled.

Desire collided with agony. I wanted to stop this ride, stop the sweet agony that was building inside me. I was going to come from the Alpha, going to give myself over to the darkness inside me. As my body tightened and I pulled the beast under me, I opened my mouth. I knew there was something different about me. I knew whatever sickness claimed me had done its worst.

And as my body bucked, coming hard, I drove that desperation through me and did the only thing I knew to do...I sank my teeth through the Wolf's fur in front of me...*and bit deep.*

The Alpha gave a low, guttural grunt. Warmth spilled through me, in my pussy and into my mouth. Because it wasn't just teeth that carved through the thick fur...it was fangs. *My fangs.* Blood splashed into my mouth.

Not Wolf...

But MINE!

Hard panting came from behind me as the Alpha slowly withdrew. He was still hard and thick, skin stretched over that bulbous knot at the base of his cock. The Wolf in front of me lowered his head and brushed against my chest, shoving me backwards.

I fell...but it wasn't against the ground. It was against the Alpha.

"Tried to warn you," he growled as the two others closed in on either side, boxing me in. I threw my hands behind me, landing on the thick thighs of the Alpha.

But the Wolf in front of me didn't stop. Instead, he balanced on his hind legs, grabbed my hips, and lifted me from the ground. My legs splayed, wrapping around his thick waist. His large, pink cock slipped from the black sheath, veined and bulging. I stared at that hard knot as he neared my pussy.

The sight of that going in, pushing all the way inside, made me moan.

Fangs punched out between my lips.

But I couldn't stop this even if I wanted to.

That sickness...*was in me.*

"Ours," the Wolf growled as he drove deeper.

Those brutal thrusts claimed me over and over. There, in that consuming desire, I felt that darkness in me come to life. That power I'd felt my entire life bloomed like a deadly flower. I unleashed a moan, grabbed the Wolf, and drew him closer.

Mine...

That word roared through me. I stared into the eyes of the beast. But a beast wasn't what I saw. I saw darkness, I saw hunger...I saw five creatures who'd hunted the world for me, tearing apart buildings on their way to find me.

Now they had...

The only question was...what now?

Find out what happens next in *I Don't Kneel For Monsters,* book one of the Hell's Hounds Series.

Preorder your copy here

I might be chained, but I'm no prisoner.
They won't let me leave this pack of demonic beasts with their red glowing eyes and their pawing touch. They keep me locked up during the day and surrounded by their heat at night.
They keep me...
Confined.
Controlled.
Consumed.
Men who are monsters and monsters who look like men. Trading my fear for their sick, demented games. I hate them. Hate it when they make me run.
Hate it when they call it a 'hunt'. *But the capture.*
The capture is something I can't stop thinking about.
Fangs and claws. Their hunger is insatiable.
Until the night I saw him.
A man standing in the middle of a labyrinth where we hid.
A man dressed in white.
He's here to save me. Here to get me away from these monsters. I just know it. I'll run to him, the first chance I get. I'll get away from those demonic creatures...I'll save myself anyway I can.
Or I'll die trying.

ABOUT THE AUTHOR

Atlas Rose is a regular Aussie girl, writing wolves and witches. She loves the beach...and writing. But above all she loves her readers. Author of Chosen by the Vampire Series.

She also writes dark contemporary romance under A.K. Rose.
Loves black cats. Eats all the black jellybeans.
Yeah, she lives a wild life.

Join Atlas' mailing list for exclusive material
https://bit.ly/35m3oOv

a amazon.com/Atlas-Rose/e/Bo7SJT1R7D

BB bookbub.com/profile/atlas-rose

f facebook.com/AtlasRoseRomance

instagram.com/atlasroseromance

BLOODED LABYRINTH

S.J. SANDERS

PROLOGUE

Asterion was cursed by the gods. He didn't need to be told to know this. His entire existence was unending carnage. Those who were lost in his labyrinth were sacrificed to his monstrous appetite. An appetite that ever hungered and could not be appeased. Nothing slaked the need that burned continuously within him. Nothing save for the love of a mother who flaunted the gods themselves to see him fed rather than wasting away in Minos' prison, and a sister who comforted him whenever she came to spend a few hours in his company.

But his mother had joined the shades long ago and Ariadne, too, was no more, her lovely long limbs and sweet face nothing more than dust.

Although he knew his mother's love for her monstrous son, he knew that his existence was traded for her complete obedience to Minos. His boyhood memories of her had long since faded. But not so of Ariadne. She was the only one who descended into his shadowy realm between worlds to pass time in his company. She had been the only light in his dark life. In her company, he could find rest.

Love was cruel to have taken her from him.

It was love that persuaded her to save the Athenian sentenced to feed Asterion. It was that love that betrayed him and nearly destroyed him if the gods had not been so cruel as to preserve his life. Locked away in solitude. The terrible cruelty that had been birthed with his enslavement to the labyrinth had not ended with the Kingdom of Minos. The heart of the labyrinth was beyond the boundaries of the mortal world, and so there he remained. Starving, raving, lost in madness until even that became background noise that he learned to ignore so that he could, for a time, find some small measure of peace.

In the gloom of his labyrinth, the shrines erected within the corridors that had once been painted with the blood of his victims were festooned with flowers that grew in the boundaries of his world, offered up with his prayers for relief from his cursed existence.

The end he begged for never came.

But then something changed.

The worlds shifted, and once again prey was finding its way into the dark stone corridors as the labyrinth found new routes to the world of the living. Humans once again stumbled into his world, one at a time or in pairs. Every time he tried to resist the hunger. But it never ended.

He couldn't stop the hunger.

Blood once again was running through the labyrinth, drawing ravenous spirits back to his abode to feast on the entrails of his kills and drink from the rivers of blood.

He was cursed by the gods.

CHAPTER ONE

Vicky was lost. Oh, fuck, was she ever. Her heart plummeted as she skimmed her dim surroundings. Nothing looked familiar. Worse, the deep shadows of the forest seemed to take on an alien life of their own. She stifled a startled yelp as something moved, a darker form slinking among those that surrounded her before disappearing once again.

Nearby, an animal let out a shriek that made the fine hair on her arms stand on end, the flesh pebbling with a chill of terror. She swallowed back bile that rose up into her throat as she waited, listening intently. Her heartbeat thumped loudly in her ears, but otherwise an unnatural silence had settled once more around her, broken only by the soft whisper of leaves in the wind.

She hoped it was just the wind, at least.

Keeping her footsteps as light as possible, Vicky blazed a path through the brush, intent on getting as far away from the site where some poor creature had met its end. With every step, she cringed at the sound of the brush rustling around her and the faint snap beneath her feet. She was sure it was sending out some of sort of beacon to every predator in the area, alerting them to the easy meal walking through their territory.

Fuck. She never should have set foot inside the forest.

It wasn't like there weren't plenty of warnings to keep fools from doing just that. Although she was newer to the area, tales of the strange forests popping up everywhere had reached her long before she had arrived. She had even seen them from a distance as she wandered, vast forests appearing out of nowhere overnight where there had once been cleared farmland or brush. The sight of them had inspired a trickle of unease that had only worsened when she heard stories among the haphazard settlements that she passed through. Tales of the tricks that the forests played on unsuspecting people who wandered too far into their depths had been enough to make her avoid the creeping woods wherever possible.

Until it was not.

Vicky shivered, pulling her coat tighter, pretending that it was only due to the chill of the spring air. She stared into the deep hues of brush and leaves, illuminated only by the meager light that managed to get through the canopy.

She should have stayed at the last settlement. Although practically a ghost town, the small group of families would have at very least offered some safety. If she could have dealt with the suspicious way that they eyed her, she could have taken residence in one of the houses on the fringe of the settlement. Centered around the square of what had once probably been a quaint little southern town, there had been plenty of abandoned homes in good enough condition to make into a home. If she had been able to ignore the stony way the residents watched, all conversation falling silent, their mouths pressed in flat lines of displeasure at her mere presence. Those who had not glowered at her watched her with an open interest that made her skin crawl.

Suspicion was the norm now following the Ravening, but the unwelcoming atmosphere had been so oppressive that she had moved on again after just a scant few days of rest.

Even the trade had been miserable.

Post-Ravening, wandering through the barrens—the stretches of wild, inhospitable land between the settlements—and scavenging had become a way of life for Vicky. Typically, a few weeks of work could buy her a couple months with a comfortable bed to sleep in and a full stomach. But this time, she left the settlement with a pack of food that she doubted would last longer than a month, and a new set of clothes and boots to replace her worn items.

She had been angry, fueled by bitterness, when she had struck out in the early hours the day before. Perhaps if she had not been, she would have noticed that she had entered too far into the forest as she traveled along its edge, taking shelter beneath the trees. If she had, she would not have awoken in the depths of the ever-moving woods.

It had been a mistake. She wanted to scream that into the uncaring forest, and only just managed to stop herself by biting her tongue. Although she had not intended to enter the forest itself, she knew that even the innocent act of going near the wooded area, even its outskirts, looking for edible greens and flowers to supplement the fare traded to her, had been her downfall. Worse that she had chosen to take shelter beneath a little cluster of trees to escape an evening rain shower.

Every decision had paved her way to that moment. There was no escaping that fact, even though it seemed unfair that her misstep had landed her in a place of her nightmares.

Her fingers twisted the ribbon knotted around her neck, the small charm sliding between her fingers. The coin pendant had been a gift from her father when he returned from a business trip to Greece. Supposedly a replica of a coin from the famed city of Knossos in Crete, pressed on one side with the face of Hera and the labyrinth on the reverse, it had been the perfect gift for a ten-year-old obsessed with mythology. Back then, she spent hours dreaming up stories about where it had come from, who might have once touched it. That life, and that little girl, had disappeared with the Ravening. Her mother and siblings died in the aftermath, leaving her and her father alone in the world until he too was taken from her. Now, it was a comforting piece of her past and all that she had left from that life before.

If only the charm could do its magic now!

Vicky squinted against the gloom, looking for any semblance of a game trail that could possibly lead her back out. It was unlikely that she would end up anywhere near where she had started, but animals frequently carved distinct paths through their territory to its outer edges. If she could just find one, there was a chance of getting out. There was also a chance of going even deeper into the forest, but she quieted that fear. Seeing how she had no other resources to aid her, she had to take the chance.

The dark foliage around her didn't make it easy. It seemed to converge and blend together in a daunting mass that reached out for her with gnarled fingers. Shuddering at the thought—since, apparently, she was determined to spook herself—she continued to scan her surroundings until her breath whooshed out in relief. *There!* Among the bushes, she could see the faint passage cutting through the trees and undergrowth.

Quickening her pace in excitement, she stumbled over an uplifted edge of rock. Thrown off-balance, she instinctively stretched out a hand and was surprised when it smacked against a rough, unyielding surface. Brushing her fingers over the numerous tendrils of vines and leaves, in the gaps between them she could feel the rough scrape of stone. Curious, she peered closer, pulling out an old Zippo from her pocket. She rarely used it outside of starting campfires to preserve her scavenged fuel, but times like this made her grateful to have it. Its flame flickered as she drew it closer to the surface, and her eyebrows rose at the sight of an overgrown stone wall.

"What in the world?" she whispered.

Despite being covered in enough vines to suggest that it had been in that condition for a while, the sight of the wall, though surprising, gave her some hope that it was perhaps an outer perimeter wall of someone's property and a stone walkway. With the darkness settling even thicker through the forest, she hoped that it led to an abandoned house with four walls to protect her from whatever strange wildlife that was living in the forest.

"Please, please let there be a house." The faint sound of her voice breaking through the silence was startling to her ears, but some prayers needed to be said aloud. She flicked her Zippo shut and gave the stone surface a grim smile. "I guess there's only one way I'm going to find out."

Keeping one hand on the wall, Vicky walked along its side, relieved when it didn't immediately terminate into broken rubble. That allayed one concern. She only hoped that it would lead her to something fast. The last remnants of sunlight were fading fast, far faster than her plodding progress.

She wasn't the least bit surprised when, minutes later, she was totally encapsulated within inky darkness. She let out a frustrated sigh. She could flick on her Zippo again, but without some kind of rudimentary torch, she didn't relish the idea of burning through all her fuel for so little light. She curled her fingers slightly, feeling the tips scrape against stone reassuringly. As long as she could feel the wall, she should be okay.

Taking a fortifying breath, she continued forward, the sound of her steps on stone, interrupted and muffled in places by the overgrowth, providing disconcerting fuel for her imagination. Her fingers trailed along the rock, lifting every so often when she was forced to skirt a cluster of large rocks or heavy growth of tangled plants. Those moments left her feeling suspended in darkness—walled in by nothingness—until her hand flattened against the wall once more.

Every scuff of her boots dredged up memories of watching ghoulish *Night of the Living Dead*-type creatures rising out of ruins until she forcibly quieted them by focusing on the sound of her breathing. She was alive. She was just lost. She wasn't some wandering dead thing or spirit caught in the dark underworld. It was just the dark, unnatural silence in the forest playing with her imagination.

Unbidden, she recalled hearing that the underworld had a section that was a vast forest full of wailing spirits. She shivered and drew in a huge, gulping breath.

She was alive. She breathed, in and out. Nice and steady.

Every breath was calming, reminding her that she was alive, keeping her focused as she walked rather than feeling like some wraith gliding through nothingness. No wraith would make such gusty sounds. Was she breathing too loudly? It sounded loud. She felt certain that something was listening, tracking every breath. She gulped in a breath and held it as she came to a stop, her ears straining for any trace of sound trailing after her.

Nothing.

A weak giggle escaped her and bounced back at her at a startling volume. Vicky froze, her eyes roving helplessly in the dark.

An echo? That couldn't be right.

Stretching out her opposite hand. She slowly side-stepped until her hand flattened on another wall at her other side. Her blood chilled. Digging out her Zippo once more, Vicky ignited the flame and slowly raised her hand, her head tipping back.

Her eyes widened. Above, she could see the perfectly wedged-together blocks of stone. Lichen clung in some parts with clumps of moss, no doubt receiving meager light from some of the larger cracks between the rocks.

Some of the gaps she would even wager were cut slits to allow in air and sunlight. They were so frequent and evenly spaced that she imagined that it would be lit well enough to see by if the sun hadn't already set.

None of the gaps, however, were large enough to allow anything of any substantial size in or out. That meant that they were designed to keep dangerous creatures out... or something dangerous within.

Licking her lips, she stepped back a pace. And then another.

"I think... I think I'd better go back."

She winced. Speaking to herself was a bad habit she'd developed after her father passed, driven by some need to be reassured by the sound of her voice, but it was one that was bound to get her killed wherever she now was.

With her small light held in front of her, she spun around and raced forward several steps only to come to a skidding stop. Frustrated tears sprung to her eyes as she stared at three different branches of the corridor, each one barely visible in her weak light but enough so that her heart dropped. She had no idea which one it was. She had been forced to release her hand from the wall so many times that it could be any of them.

Tears blurred her vision as she looked from one to the other, contemplating each path until a skittering sound made her draw up short. Turning her head back toward the direction she had been heading, she turned the light that way too, her heart hammering louder in her ears as she listened. Rocks fell somewhere in the distance from the direction she had been heading and her stomach pitched.

Lifting her light to the right, the passage closest to the wall, she bolted down the corridor, the shimmer of her lighter's flame bouncing off the nearest stones, its fuel spending recklessly in her terror. Her stomach continued to roll with nausea as she plunged forward into the darkness, the vines seemingly lifting up from the walls, slowing her progress—taunting her.

From a distance, she could hear a skittering scrape of something in pursuit. The sound was an ominous combination of clicking, like something striking the stones repeatedly, layered with excited chittering and deep growling.

It didn't sound like anything she wanted to encounter in the dark tunnel. Especially as the long corridor seemed to be stretching out, continuing without end ahead of her. Her chest burned as she sprinted, dodging unfamiliar fallen stone that she hadn't recalled being in the path. Her brow furrowed at the sight of them, many coming so close to her that she would have been aware of their presence before.

Her lips parted in horror as understanding sank in.

Oh, fuck! She had gone the wrong way! This wasn't the way she came! Vicky veered right, hoping that it would empty out onto a familiar path in addition to aiding in her escape from whatever creature was pursuing her. Or creatures. There was no way of knowing what was hunting her, much less how many of its number.

As she raced down the hall, she noted the change in the vines and plant life as it became tighter and the walls narrowed. She swallowed a panicked cry. This wasn't right either. The only blessing was that the silence around her was only broken by the sound of her rapid footfall.

She drew in a ragged breath. Had she lost it—them?

Hope loosening the cold grip on her chest, she slowed her pace to a walk, her hand resting on the painful stitch in her side as she dragged in large gulps of breath. Listening.

There was a faint click and then another, sending a prickle of horror over her skin. To her dismay, the terrible sound resumed at a fiercer pace, the growls louder and far more numerous, nearly drowning out the chittering. Ducking to the left, she flew, stumbling, down another path, and then dove again down another. One twist led to another, and she sprinted for all that she was worth, praying for an end to come into view, praying that the wild sounds pursuing ever closer would quiet.

It was maddening, and, somehow, as one unfamiliar hall became another, she was certain that she was now lost in some sort of labyrinth of halls.

Jagged rocks scraped against her skin and thorned vines ripped at flesh and cloth as she battled her way past every obstacle.

A scream tore from her throat as she ripped through a thick clump of vines hanging in her path, her fear-clouded mind unable to determine if they had moved or were naturally suspended there. She didn't care; she couldn't focus with any clarity. All she knew and breathed was the instinctual need to escape. Her light flickered and died with the last bit of fuel expended, plunging her into darkness. The chittering and growling rose up behind her, getting progressively louder, drowning out her cries until it too was interrupted by a deep, ferocious bellow that rattled the hall.

Sightlessly, Vicky stared ahead, her flight down the corridor coming to a stumbling halt as the clicking silenced. The chitter-growls continued in faint, hesitant bursts, but it was as if she were not the only one pausing warily. She heard a click and another, but it didn't sound as if it were getting any closer. Instead, if she wasn't mistaken, it sounded like a slow, reluctant retreat of a predator facing a superior one.

She swallowed thickly, bile trying once again to choke her.

Gods, she was fucked. At least without fuel in her lighter, she wasn't going to be forced to witness her end. She certainly wasn't going to be able to outrun it, not with the heavy thumps that approached in a ground eating pace. Whatever it was, its stride had to be huge.

Squeezing her eyes shut may have been foolish considering how dark it was, but she did so anyway. She could feel the hot billow of its breath caress her skin, and her chest tightened as her breath seized in wait of the killing strike. Her hand raising to her charm, she gripped the coin tight.

"Daddy," she whispered, hoping that he would be waiting for her on the other side.

CHAPTER TWO

Asterion paused, staring down at the female curiously, the haze of blood lust clinging just barely to his mind. The flush of her blood roaring in her veins incited his terrible hunger, but it was dulled by another warm, seductive scent mingled with it and the startling sight of her submission, her head bowed to him.

Unlike other prey that had tried to evade him or attack him, her eyes were squeezed so tightly shut that her nose wrinkled up from the effort. Where she had desperately fled from the flesh-eating satyrs who had infested his labyrinth in recent centuries, there was a sense of surrender in her submission that gave him pause.

More than that, her single word startled him as she whispered a soft plea.

Daddy? He was oddly intrigued and... charmed by the complete submission held within that one word, yielding everything up to his whim and control. It was perplexing too that it should strike a chord within him. It made him want to dominate and consume in an entirely different fashion than his cursed nature.

He huffed and snorted, blasting back wisps of her hair from her face. He had the advantage over her that he could see her as clearly as if it were day. She couldn't hide anything, not even the tiny grimace of her full lips pressing together, in the dark. Asterion cautiously stepped back a pace, his nostrils flaring as he drew her scent deep into his olfactory glands. Sweet feminine flesh, ripe with health. Her scent was arousing, flooding his cock with blood so that it stiffened uncomfortably beneath the swath of material around his hips.

Curious.

One of his broad ears flicked in consideration.

Was this a trick or some trap designed by men to capture him. Surely the sweetness that enticed him was nothing more than a clever potion rubbed into her flesh to bait him.

A blasting gust of air left him. That had to be what it was.

His ears pricked toward the corridor ahead of him, listening for any other signs of human life as he scented the air. Outside of his unnatural hunger, he did not especially enjoy killing humans, but he would have no compunction over killing one invading his labyrinth to seek his death. He had dealt with would-be Theseus-enamored "heroes" often enough over the ages. The isolation of his labyrinth had relieved him of that particular burden, for a time. If they had returned as well, he would deal with them with ruthless efficiency. There was a time where he had once enjoyed the challenge of facing a warrior, their taste being all the more succulent for the effort, but that time had long since passed even before the labyrinth pulled away from the mortal world. Now, he was merely tired.

His eyes fell again on the female in front of him. He should cease hesitating and kill her. He could promise her a quick death at the very least before he dealt with her accomplices. Still, he had to admire the courage it took for a female to go along with such plans. He hadn't recalled a single one willingly coming into his labyrinth since the days of Ariadne's presence there.

Grunting, his gaze fell upon her hand fisted tightly around an item strung on a ribbon around her neck. *A token from the gods of some kind, no doubt.* Not that it would save her. Such things never saved anyone who entered and stirred his hunger. Yet never before had his hunger for blood and flesh warred so strongly with the carnal hunger that currently pulsed within his shaft.

He dragged his wide, flat tongue over his fangs, and silently stepped back several paces before falling into a watchful silence as he observed her, uncertain of what he wished to taste first. He knew from experience that the blood of women could be intoxicatingly sweet, and yet there seemed to be a sweeter elixir promised from the scent drifting up from her body.

One of the female's eyes pried open as she glanced sightlessly in his direction.

"Uh... are you there?" she whispered, her voice broken and trembling with obvious fear.

His stomach soured with the knowledge that his presence alone put that there. While he couldn't ignore that it was a natural part of his relationship with his human prey, he disliked the scent of her fear overwhelming the sweeter, more delicious flavors in her natural perfume.

He grunted, his ears turning toward her. "Are you so eager for death?" he rumbled out in a low, quiet voice.

His voice rasped with barely contained violence and bloodlust, and she visibly shivered at its sound. Her skin pebbling, she shook her head frantically, a pale, crystalline tear escaping from beneath her lashes.

"N... no. I... I'm sorry."

His eyes narrowed. "For what? For your part in the plan to destroy me?"

It had been so long since Asterion had conversed with anyone outside of the troublesome creatures that shared his home that his voice was raw and his throat ached, but he required answers.

Her mouth gaped, her eyes snapping open and widening in a shocked expression that was almost convincing.

"*What?* No!" She rubbed her arms as she sightlessly sought him out, her brow furrowed, the entreaty in her eyes stirring something within him best left alone. "I'm lost. I don't even know where I am, much less how to get out of here." She ran a trembling hand through her hair, her words so soft and unsteady he only heard due to the grace of his superior hearing. "I certainly wouldn't have been running blindly through this place. That's pretty damned unprepared for someone striking out to murder anyone, I would say."

Asterion snorted, pushing back his unexpected amusement at her words and the strange protective need rising beneath the desire riding underneath his flesh. The female was good. He had to give her that. No doubt, had she been born a male, she would have been as lauded as an accomplished actor in the greatest plays at Knossos. He would not be deceived so easily.

He swept a critical eye over her, noting the simple braid that framed one side of her face that bound the front part of her hair, as well as her coarse clothes, woolen coat and thick boots she wore. The pack strapped around her shoulders appeared particularly well-worn and beaten. Aside from her clean, pleasing scent, there was nothing about her appearance that suggested that she was being employed to act as any kind of seductress, and yet she was as enchanting as if she were Circe herself.

"We will see about that," he rumbled, dropping his large horned head so that he was eye-level with her. He bared his fangs in a silent warning as instinct demanded, despite her inability to witness it. "Do not tempt the monster by fighting or fleeing. Understand, little female?"

Mouth snapping shut, she paled and eyed him warily before nodding repeatedly in a gratifying affirmation. This one was intelligent, at least.

Leaning forward, his large hands nearly engulfed her small frame as he lifted her up off her feet. The moment her boots left the ground, her breath rushed out of her in a tiny, terrified squeak. Despite her reaction betraying her fear, she thankfully did not unduly struggle in his grip. In fact, her body molded against him when he pulled her up against his chest, her softness stirring his hungers higher, though he struggled to differentiate them. His claws dug against her clothing as he warred with himself to win back his control.

Although he still suspected a trap, some small part of him was aware and dismayed by the knowledge that she would not lean into him in such a manner if she were able to see him. No female would willingly surrender her care to a beast. In the past when he had attempted to control his monstrous appetite, the females he had attempted to spare had ignored his warnings and pleas. Every one of them fled, willingly choosing death when they caught a glimpse of him.

His grip tightened on the female in his arms. Although it had no less bothered him to consume the males, murdering and consuming the flesh of the females he tried to save had broken his spirit that after several years he had quit trying.

Why again now?

Why risk reopening old wounds for a female whose intoxicating scent worked to ensnare him?

There was no logic to his decision.

Grunting unhappily, Asterion strode through the winding corridors of the labyrinth, listening to the murmur of the intelligence that inhabited the structure. The voice that comforted him in his lonely youth and encouraged him to take out his rage on the race of men who imprisoned him was always present. It watched as he passed vine-covered statues of the gods who stared at him with condemning eyes, as his hooves clopped across the stone floors that led deeper to the center.

At the center he would get the answers that he sought. There would be no means for her escape there. The doors of the inner chamber into the labyrinth were concealed and sealed by his blood. Not even the satyrs, who now shared the halls at the labyrinth's welcome, could find their way in.

His body hardened and ached, his hunger twisting his belly with need as he thought of having the small warm female there in his den. All to himself without risking danger of another trying to take his prey.

That was all she was in the end—prey. He would do well to remember that.

CHAPTER THREE

Vicky leaned into the body of the creature carrying her. She had no idea what he could even be, or where she was for that matter, but he undeniably strong... and very warm. Fur brushed her nose when she snuggled her cold face into warmth as she tried to ignore the metallic odor of blood clinging to him. Beneath the blood, there was something else that drew her. Smoke and juniper. It reminded her of winter fires roaring in the hearth, with just a hint of citrus and spice.

The warmth emanating from the large, muscular body pressed up against her and the scent of his flesh worked a surprising magic, seeping deep into her bones, muscle, and tissue. By degrees, she began to relax, a lassitude falling over her that alarmed her even as she melted against her captor's fur.

The adrenaline that had saved her during her mad dash through the labyrinth was flagging fast. Even though she still trembled with residual fear, she was just too comfortable and too tired to put up any further fight.

Vicky let out a raspy sigh. It was difficult to put up a fight when, for the first time in a great many weeks, she felt warm. She couldn't fight her way out of a sack, much less fend off the gargantuan creature carrying her. Through the fog of exhaustion filling her mind she considered that if something was going to eat her in this awful place, at least he had the mercy to provide some comfort to her first. Perhaps he would even wait until she was sleeping to deal the killing stroke to save her from the worst of the terror and pain.

She had no wish to die. Far from it. She was just so damned tired. And so very warm.

The furred arms holding her tightened as the creature picked his way quickly through the corridors, taking turn after turn at a pace several times what she would have been able to walk. She could feel the cold air stinging the side of her cheek and stirring her hair from his ground-eating pace.

Other than the heavy stomp of his feet, the silence that surrounded them had an ominous weight to it that was both frightening and reassuring. The unnatural quality of the silence terrified her. Devoid of even the scurry or hum of rodents and insects, it was as if everything was still, watching the passage of the creature through the corridors. That it was also reassuring was a more complicated matter, one that veered a little too close to danger for her comfort. Everything else there, even whatever had pursued her, was afraid of the beast who had her now.

And he was a beast. From the billowing huffs of his breath to the inhumanly wide expanse of fur-covered muscle, every inch of him was of monstrous proportions. Even his rage-filled roars weren't sounds that any human could make. That he could converse like a man, however, gave her some hope that she might be able to reason with him.

Not that mankind was particularly reasonable or moved to kindness or charity in recent years. If humanity was the stick against which everything else was to be measured, then she was in a lot of trouble. With the Ravening, humankind as a whole had pitched, backsliding into madness. In her years roaming, she had seen the aftermath of enough human depravation that hadn't needed any help from the other creatures now sharing their world.

The steady beat of her captor's heart against her ear, however, lulled her into a small measure of comfort. He was not acting on excitement or aggression. Other than the grueling pace he set, she wouldn't have known that he was in any hurry at all. It certainly didn't tax him to move so quickly, and that made her wonder how fast he could race through the halls in pursuit of prey.

She shivered as her imagination picked up on that thought. She would never be able to outrun him should he decide to pursue. She could picture the walls skipping by, her feet turning down one corridor after another, as his hot breath fanned her from behind as he mercilessly gained on her, his arms coming around her, and... She shook her head, her teeth sinking into her bottom lip as a chill raced through her body that was equal measures of fear and a peculiar desire that she couldn't explain away.

D rawing in another deep breath, she turned her head just enough to notice that torches were lit, their golden-red illumination bouncing on the walls, pushing back the darkness, illuminating small patches of worn gray stone lined with vines and foliage from the darkest black to pale silver. There was little actual green to be seen. What little there was possessed a grayish tint and seemed to grow exclusively closer to the vents cut into the stone above.

Frowning, she turned her attention to the black fur that brushed her nose. Although the fur on its chest was like velvet, she noted that it was longer and thicker around the powerful shoulders and neck. A long, thin braid swayed across one pectoral just inches from her face. Bound with red thread that contained a single blue bead, it was an element that was almost human compared to the dark fur that boasted even darker splattered patches that she suspected were the source of the bitter blood perfuming the immediate air around her face.

Vicky braced her hand against the thick muscle of his chest and attempted to push back to get a look at exactly what sort of creature held her. His reaction was lightning quick, his clawed hand burrowing into her hair as he crushed her more firmly against his chest, holding her in place.

"Not yet," he rasped.

She shivered at the dark rumble of his voice and twisted subtly in his grasp. The heart beneath her ear and palm began to thump. Unsure of the reason for his quickening pulse, she froze, her breaths coming out in tiny little nervous pants.

The hand in her hair gently stroked, the claws lightly scraping her scalp in what could only be interpreted as a soothing gesture.

"Be at ease, little female. No harm will come to you as long as you obey the rules."

She shook her head, the fur buffing her cheek as tears of fear sprung to her eyes. "I don't understand. What rules? Why can't you just let me go. Please"

"I cannot," he grumbled unhappily. "I have been held within here long enough to know now that the labyrinth never again releases its prey." He huffed and at the edge of her vision just above her, the corded muscle of his thick neck taut beneath the dense fur as he seemed to turn his head one way and then the other.

A labyrinth? Vicky drew her hand across his chest and tucked it between them to finger the coin around her neck.

"B...but a labyrinth is just a stone prison," she whispered.

"Perhaps that is how it began, but it has not been that for as long as I've known it. It was old even when I was dropped within, with a reputation of its own."

The clomp of his feet on the stone lent a more ominous backdrop to his words. She cringed into him, uncertain if she wanted to know and have her hopes of escape burst, but he continued to speak, the rasp of his deep voice amplified by the walls surrounding them.

"It was said to be a path to the underworld. It is possible that there are corridors that extend into the lower world, but I refuse to search them out. I've made my refuge and survived here when I was disposed of here to die. The labyrinth nurtured me, but it never released me. Nor has it ever released anyone but one, and he had assistance from my sister. Her powerful magic that allowed her to travel the labyrinth unharmed, influenced it to release him. If only she would have done me that kindness in his stead."

The last was said with such bitter quietness that Vicky might have missed it if she weren't pressed against his chest, the rumble of his words distinct against her ear.

Moved by the pain buried beneath those words, her lips parted with the intent of asking him why his sister had not released him, but he drew in a ragged breath and began to speak again.

"The rules are simple. Never run. I will hunt that which runs, and there are other things that dwell here now that will do the same. Never struggle. That which struggles to escape is prey. I am bringing you to a safe place. None of the creatures of the labyrinth can enter my abode. Never leave the safety of the abode. No matter what you hear or see, to leave it is to court death within the labyrinth. The labyrinth yearns for blood...but it will not have yours."

She shivered against him, the tremor running through her with more strength than previously as she embraced the true horror of the situation. She was trapped inside like a hapless bug lured by the sweet sap of a carnivorous plant only to be caught within and consumed.

Helplessly caught, Vicky went limp against him, her body trembling every so often with shock, reminding her that she was still alive. The creature-hugged her tighter, a rumble echoing up from his chest as he continued to lightly scrape her scalp with his claws, as if he were attempting to soothe her. She was felt too numb to be comforted. All she could do was stare blankly at the rush of light from the torches on the wall and the light stirring of the fur on his arms as he walked.

It was only at length that she noticed when he began to slow. He hunched over her as he ducked through a series of narrow entrances, his body shifting awkwardly to slide through the barriers that felt as if he were moving through an invisible membranous substance. There was a sensation of wetness and an electric tingle that ran through her that made her skin prickle, her fingers scratching at his chest at the disconcerting feeling that made her stomach twist with nausea.

Then it was over.

She was immediately bathed in a comfortable warmth, a soft gurgle of water somewhere in the near distance. The source of the warmth, from what she could see, was a long basin that ran along one wall that was filled with fire. She stared at the fire, watching the shadows shifting around it as it danced when suddenly she was lifted away and set on her feet.

Caught off-guard, Vicky stumbled a step, her head whipping around as she took in her surroundings. An enormous platform bed dominated one part of the room covered with thick furs, and an archaic-looking stone stove was set up in one corner next to a cooking spit, glowing with the hot coals that were visible within it. There were a few small tunnels that led off from another wall, one of which she suspected was the source of the water that she heard. Although gloomy and primitive, it had a reassuring peacefulness to it as if it were undisturbed by whatever things hunted outside those walls.

That didn't necessarily mean that she was safe. There was still the elephant in the room... or rather her captor monster.

Vicky began to turn toward him just as he took a heavy step back from her.

"Do not be afraid," he whispered.

Swallowing back her nerves, she resolutely turned his way, her eyes traveling his length as he slowly came into view.

Eyes widening, her breath stuttered as her heart leapt into her throat. A clammy chill fell over her as her eyes roved over him in horror.

The massive chest that had cradled her almost appeared carved from stone, as were the hard abs that descended down toward a tapered vee disappearing beneath a swath of fabric belted around his hips, leaving bare the side of one powerfully muscled thigh and calf. From there, though, the leg twisted back into a thick hock from which descended the rest of a noticeably bovine leg that ended in a hoof.

What the hell?

It wasn't like she had never seen some of the monsters that had migrated into her world following the Ravening, but usually from a distance, and nothing quite like this. Every inch of lethal muscle was twisted into a monstrous form more beast than man.

A tufted tail flicked, and she stared at it for a moment, putting her briefly at eye level with the intimidating bulge between his thighs.

Moving on!

She jerked her eyes up, back up past his chest again, the fur thickening into a long mane of dark hair that spilled around his shoulders. She caught sight of more than one braid peeking out from within the thick mass. A long black ear flicked, and the firelight bounced off of the powerful ebony horns sprouting from the broad brow of a face that was bullish and yet not in its shape.

It was more like a demonic bull creature than anything as natural as a bull, an illusion that was reinforced by the wicked fangs she caught a glimpse of as his mouth parted.

His warning forgotten, Vicky stumbled back. She turned as to flee when his powerful hand snapped out, capturing her arm in his grip so that he could swing her back around with an incredible force that offered no room for denial or escape. He towered over her, his expression stark and terrible. He glanced down at her arm, and with a grimace he released her, allowing her to sink to the floor with a pitiful moan.

She was trapped in a labyrinth with the monster of all ancient monsters—the terrible beast of Minos, the minotaur!

He crouched, lowering himself toward the floor so that he didn't tower over her, his tail swishing around his legs. He was like a demon, waiting, biding his time to kill her if she made even one wrong move. Panting nervously, she turned her head away. From her periphery, she watched him stride over to a wall and hang a giant double-headed ax he was carrying on it, the hiss of metal on stone loud. Then he stretched his arms out from his side, palms up, his claw-tipped fingers splayed in a universal gesture of being unarmed.

Except he was armed. Those claws alone and massive hands could easily kill her in one strike.

A weak hysterical laugh escaped as she gripped her pendant tight. This eater of men and women was what promised to keep her safe? What was coming to keep her safe from his appetite?

CHAPTER FOUR

Asterion eyed the female in front of him with concern. Tears of terror shone in her eyes, and her entire body trembled where she sprawled on the floor. All things considered, she was handling the sight of him better than most and that gave him hope.

"Do not be afraid, little female," he reiterated, projecting what he hoped was some small amount of gentleness into his tone.

Not that he knew anything of gentleness. The only tenderness he had ever experienced was the little that he received from Ariadne, and that was so long ago that it was nothing more than a dim memory swathed in the pain of her betrayal. Gnashing his teeth with the anger that the memory of his sister brought, he shoved that thought away. He winced when the female in front of him scurried back as if he had just threatened violence upon her.

He lifted his hand to reassure her, and she ducked, drawing out a frustrated growl.

"Be still. I have no interest in harming you. You are safe here as long as the rules are heeded."

When she made no move to acknowledge him, he blew out an angry sigh and backed away from her. Clearly this was getting him nowhere. Perhaps with some space, she would become more comfortable with his presence. If only she did not run.

He prayed to the merciless gods who warded his prison that she did not run.

Turning away, he strode toward the spit, pulling his recent kill from the sack tied at his belt. Three rabbits dangled by the ears from his fist. Fat burrowing creatures such as these were at least plentiful in the labyrinth. Not that he had many qualms over what he ate anymore. Even the satyrs made a meal when he had the occasion to kill one. The creatures were quick and smart, and he had no interest in feeding on them unless they were foolish enough to attack him or attract his predatory instinct.

When they had first made an appearance, he had hoped that they might be companions against his loneliness and even had slaked his lust with some of their number until he realized a terrible thing about those who found their way into his prison. The satyrs did not distinguish between their hungers. Sex and food were one and the same, and they were quick to attempt to consume those that ignited their passionate hungers.

Asterion growled, tearing the hide from the rabbits' flesh. It was why he had been drawn to investigate when he heard their frenzied, gleeful hunt. There were few things that could excite them so. Being slain by him would have been far more merciful than a death at their hands.

He tipped his head in consideration and rubbed at the base of one horn.

Why had he not attempted to consume the female? She was running and acting in all the ways prey behaved, inciting his hungers... and yet, when he reached her, he hadn't been able to bear the thought of removing the light of life from her eyes. Not when she had bravely faced death and accepted it.

Not that his hunger had abated any.

His cock twitched beneath the double-belted chiton falling from his waist. He still hungered for her. He wanted to taste her flesh and blood; he wanted to indulge his every carnal lust. But he did not want her to die. He hungered for a companion as much as he did to indulge his bestial appetites.

Though those appetites were nothing if not considerable. Just holding her in his arms had been a test of his will. Every shift of her body against his made him want to devour her.

He slanted a look in her direction, noting that she still had not moved from where she had dropped. She watched him though. Her eyes tracked every movement of his claws, hands, and arms. He bit back a frustrated snarl. She was staring at him as if she expected him to strike at any moment.

Had he not proven that he would not harm her? He carried her through the dangerous corridors of the labyrinth, sheltering her with his own body. He opened the heart of the maze to her so that she could enter his abode.

Grunting, he spitted the rabbits and rubbed fresh herbs into their flesh with a practiced hand. His sister had brought in the herbs when he was still young and planted them in the smaller antechamber where they received a bit more light from the carved grating. That small gift and the chitons she offered to him, bespelled to never decay and refresh themselves over night for as long as they remained in his possession, were the only trappings that he possessed that reminded him that he was not just a beast, but a man as well.

In a matter of speaking.

Laying them over the bed of hot coals, Asterion turned his attention to stirring up the fire once more until it kissed the meat hanging over it. It didn't take long for the sizzle of hot grease hitting the coals and the scent of cooking meat to fill the room. It was only then that he heard a shuffle of movement.

Tipping his ear in the direction of the sound, he turned the rabbits, rumbling to himself. Hunger, as he knew well, was a good incentive for curiosity. Not wanting to startle her, he kept his back to her as he continued to work over their meal. Only when it was done did he straighten, pick up a large clay bowl from his crude stone table, and walk over into the light-filled antechamber. His guest may not eat if he was present and watching, but he would occupy himself in his sanctuary and give her time to eat her fill in peace.

Perhaps later, when she was feeling more confident, he would share with her his special place. He smiled at the thought as he stepped inside the antechamber and breathed deep the combined fragrances of all the plant life within. He looked around, trying to see the space how she might.

He could not imagine how she would not find it beautiful.

Light filled every inch of the space, coming through numerous flora-shaped carved vents in a natural stone-worked grating. All his life, he had tried to figure out the source of the warm sunlight and had failed. Even the seemingly delicate stone working was stronger than it appeared when he had thought in one of his youthful rebellions to attempt to break through it. He never saw the sky except glimpsed through the carved vents in the upper parts of the labyrinth, and he did not care to leave himself exposed in the hunting grounds of the other creatures for any longer than he had to.

This room, thus, had become his sanctuary. Filled with light and possessing a natural spring, it was the only source of beauty he had ever really known. And there, in the middle, a pair of peach trees grew, their limbs brushing the top of the roof above. Some of the branches disappeared entirely from sight into the grating and vents, but the labyrinth seemed to adjust around their presence.

The walls continuously reforming themselves, it was every much as alive as he had said aloud. Its sentience was not human, or like any other being caught inside, but something colder even as it took care to nurture the things that benefited it. His existence there fed it and benefited it, and so it saw that he, too, was fed and cared for. The small berry bushes, the peach trees, and the herbs kept alive in a timeless fashion were a testament to that.

Reaching up, Asterion plucked several round globes of fruit from the branches, taking care not to tangle his large horns, and he filled his bowl at a leisurely pace. He did not hear any activity coming from the main chamber, but that did not mean anything. His human was small and probably light on her feet, especially if she wanted to move with an idea of him being unaware.

Finally, he heard it, the soft brush of small human feet on the stone floors. He grinned triumphantly and turned toward the spring to refill one of the small jugs shelved on a carved-out nook in the wall off to the side of it with fresh water.

With his simple offerings in hand, he returned to the main chamber, his gaze falling on the spit where one of the rabbits was missing. He refrained from seeking out the location of his female. Instead, he walked by the spit as if nothing was amiss, carrying the fruit and water jug to the table, his fur prickling with the sense of eyes watching him.

Ignoring his companion's presence to the best of his ability—a difficult task with her delicious natural perfume thickening in the air of his abode—he attended to his meal, devouring the remaining two rabbits.

Eating his fill of meat and fruit, he eventually retreated to the antechamber to bathe in the spring to remove the grease and fruit juice from his fur, as well as the blood that had dried in uncomfortable, stiff patches all over him. Most of the blood was not his own, but there were at least a few scabs that peeled and opened a bit under his ministrations, stinging at the touch of the cool water. They bled for only a moment before washing clean.

That he healed quickly was one of the few blessings of his cursed existence. The other was his general good health. While he still questioned whether or not his immortality was a good thing, that he wasn't plagued by any manner of illness was at the very least in his favor. The gods could have been far crueler in devising his fate.

It was for that reason he did not curse them. Though at many times he felt justified in doing so. And some of that was out of respect to his sister that he still continued to visit the ancient shrines scattered through the labyrinth to pay his respects. He did not believe as she did that the gods did not hate him. Why else would he exist in the state he did? Many times, Ariadne had attempted to assure him otherwise. His birth that was a punishment to their parents had nothing to do with their decision to violate the nature of the labyrinth and seal him within it. She had been certain that unholy act had changed the labyrinth and made its thoughts toward humanity hostile.

Pouring a large jug of water over his head, thoroughly dousing his mane and horns, Asterion considered her argument for the first time in a great many years, pushing aside his pain to recall her observations. He remembered the way she had sat on the rocky ledge as he was now, bathing her feet in the water, smiling with pleasure as she spoke.

"The labyrinth was not made this way, Asterion. It has always been a mystic portal between worlds, allowing us to seek and learn the greater mysteries. That is what it was in the time of our forefathers, and theirs before them. Long before Father claimed it as his, the labyrinth drew many to experience its mysteries and to pledge themselves to the gods of the hidden road."

If she was correct and the labyrinth hated humanity as much as it seemed to love him, then he was definitely going to need to keep a careful watch on his little human. Sooner or later, it would become impatient for her blood.

That uncomfortable thought lingered in his mind, the silence from the main chamber adding to his disconcertment. Asterion rose and shook the water from his fur before hurrying back to the main chamber. He had to assure himself that she was still safe within his abode. Although aware that the thunder of his hooves hitting the rock so quickly could frighten her, he could not force himself to slow. Instead, he flew into the room, panic swelling within him as he turned around the room only to fall at last on the small feminine form slumped at the table.

Lips twitching, he walked to her side and chuckled at the grease and fruit juice smeared across her lips and cheeks, her mouth parted in a soft snore. Grabbing a rag from near his stove, he dampened it with water and gently slid it over the skin of her face and hands, washing away traces of dirt, grime, and the remaining evidence of her meal.

Only once she was clean did he carefully lift her into his arms as not to wake her, enjoying the warm stir of her breath against his chest. He indulged himself in the pleasure of holding her for several minutes as he gave his bed a long, considering glance.

There was only one place for them to sleep. As much as he did not wish to give up his only comfort, he also did not wish to see such a delicate female sleeping draped against the table or on the floor. At the same time, he did not wish for her to wake in terror at the sight of him lying beside her. As delectable as all her scents were—even the fear scent that intrigued the predator within him—he did not wish for her to look on him for much longer in a way that was plagued by that emotion.

He shook his head, annoyed by his own thoughts. Why was he even debating the matter? She would become accustomed to his presence sooner or later. Besides, there was no reason for either of them to be uncomfortable. His sleeping platform was more than big enough for them both. He would just have to take care to keep to one side so not to scare her too much or acciden-tally crush her beneath his weight in his sleep.

Laying her on his bed, he braced his weight there with one knee as he covered her with the thick furs before he too climbed in and wearily allowed himself to drift into slumber.

CHAPTER FIVE

Vicky smiled sleepily, burrowing into the warmth surrounding her. It was strange that the sun wasn't in her face, but she wasn't about to quibble over small mercies. She wasn't of the mind to move any time soon, anyway. She was so incredibly warm. And whatever she was pressed up against smelled good too. Did she spill something on her blanket? No, more like on the fur sleeping pad she used. She rubbed her cheek against the soft fur, breathing in the scent. What was that smell?

She couldn't recall having anything that smelled like that. The bit of cologne that she had found in salvage she had used sparingly, enjoying the pleasant aromas of amber and musk. But this didn't smell anything like that, and she had run out of the cologne a short while back.

Mumbling, Vicky stretched with a quiet moan of pleasure. Her pillow shuddered on her cheek, and a warm gust tousled her hair. She frowned in her sleep. That wind was unseasonably warm. Extreme changes in the weather were never a good sign from what she recalled. Best to just enjoy the simple comfort while she could, then.

Tangling her hand into thick fur, she snuggled in closer, rubbing languidly against it. She scowled again. There was an uncomfortably hard lump pressed against her belly. *Damn rocks.* She shifted against it, but when that didn't dislodge it, she began to lift her knee to shove it aside when a low, very deep moan vibrated against her. Instinctively, she froze, a cold chill suddenly sweeping up her spine when something beneath her furs shifted and a distinctive hand gripped her bottom, pressing that lump even more firmly into her.

Shying away, Vicky squeaked and attempted to wriggle free as she was enclosed even tighter against the fur, a rumbling growl filling her ears.

"You seek to escape, little female?" a voice rasped above her head as a surprisingly warm, velvety soft surface brushed against her forehead and back into her hair.

Those words and the deep growl of the masculine voice cut through the sleepy fog in her mind and Vicky bolted upright. Or would have if the arms around her didn't tighten further, pinning her helplessly in place while her heart hammered like a snared rabbit. The long, thick shaft pressed against her twitched with an excitement that made her tremble.

The minotaur!

"Please," she choked out, her words halting when she felt the slight prick of his claws.

His displeased growl shot through her, and she nearly wept at the horrific train of thoughts running through her head. There was no telling what the beast would do to her. Eat her? Rape her? Both? She had nearly worked herself into a panic when, after a stretch of silence, it was followed by a grunted sigh. She toppled over with another indignant squeak when he surged up, pushing to his feet.

Blinking up at her captor in the soft light of the torch-lit room, Vicky watched as he rubbed one horn with his large hand before dragging his fingers through his mane in a distinctly human expression of frustration. His eyes narrowed on her unhappily.

"I should not let your soft words sway me. You are mine. You are in my care and protection. My companion. I should enjoy your softness and heat as much as you enjoy my strength," he muttered with a venomous glower.

He shook his head, his massive dark horns cutting through the air, and spun away, his long legs carrying him away from her quickly. Her eyes widened fearfully as he headed toward a deeply grooved wall with the realization that he intended to leave.

He was going to leave her there—alone.

Vicky scrambled to her feet in a rush, half stumbling as she chased after him. "Wait! Don't leave me! Please!"

He tossed her an impatient look over his shoulder without so much as slowing his pace.

"I hunt," he snapped.

In the next moment, he ducked his head, angling his body to the side. There was a shift around him that blurred his edges enough that Vicky rubbed her eyes, thinking that there was something wrong with her vision, and then he was gone.

Vicky stared intently at the space for a long moment, bewildered. He had just disappeared. How was that even possible?

Approaching slowly, she continued to eye the space. There was a definite groove there, but she couldn't see any kind of doorway. Uncertain, she moved closer, waving her hand over the space in front of her until she finally flattened her hand against the stone. Nothing.

"What the hell?" she whispered.

Frantically, Vicky ran her hands over the wall, her fingernails digging into any crack or crevice in search of a mechanism or handhold that might reveal a doorway. She dipped her fingers into one particularly deep crack only to jerk her hand back at the sensation of something gripping her fingers and a tickling sensation brushing across the back of her hand. Reacting on pure instinct, she ripped her hand free and yelped in pain and then again in horror at the large black and red centipede scurrying up her wrist. With a shrieked curse, she shook it free before proceeding to stomp it beneath her boots.

"Shit! Fuck!" She continued to gasp as she rubbed the back of her hand numbly after finally stepped away from it to stare down at its pulverized remains.

She soon became aware of a stinging sensation that shot through her hand, making her wince and draw her hand up to inspect it. Even in the low light of the room she could see the trail of three deep scratches that vaguely resembled claw marks not unlike scratches she received from the neighbor's cat she tried to pet as a child. It had felt like someone—or something—had grabbed her hand.

She winced and shook her hand in an attempt to relieve the sting. It had certainly hurt enough when she had pulled free. What the hell could have grabbed her? Whatever it was, she wouldn't feel comfortable in the room unless she was certain that nothing was going to make an appearance in there with her the moment that she let her guard down.

Hoping that she wasn't doing something phenomenally stupid by investigating, though maintaining a safe distance, she crept closer to the small crevice, her brow scrunching as she peered at it. Her expression slowly morphed into a confused frown.

She couldn't see how even a whole hand would have been pushed through from the opposite of the wall. She had small hands and had only just barely been able to slip hers inside. Whatever the case, there certainly wasn't any sign that she could see now of clawed hands reaching out for her.

Vicky backed away again and shivered as she skirted around the remains of the centipede.

"Probably just got my hand stuck in a tight spot and scratched it on some sharp rocks in there. That they line up in a way that looks like claw marks is just a weird coincidence. Don't go losing your mind now, Vicky."

The pep talk didn't help.

Spinning away, she raced back toward the bed, throwing herself onto the platform and pulling her legs as she burrowed under the furs. The monsters in the walls could have them. She wasn't planning on moving from the bed at all if she could help it.

Her bladder took that moment to remind her that it was uncomfortably full. Groaning, Vicky threw her feet back over the side of the platform and slid off the bed. Keeping on her toes as if not letting her heel touch the ground would do anything to evade a potential threat, Vicky hurried off in search of a place to relieve herself.

As she scrambled around the room, she cursed the minotaur's furry hide. The very least he could have done was show her where to pee if he had planned to keep her trapped in there. Her curses turned a lot more inventive when her search turned up nothing useful, especially since she was leery about going down into the two unknown tunnels after her last experience of sticking her hand somewhere it didn't belong. With her luck, the water source would have something living in it ready to eat her. Who knew what kind of creatures her captor lived with if the centipede was anything to go by?

In a moment of sheer embarrassment, she reluctantly found a space near a wall that wasn't too dark to take care of her business, her cheeks flaming every moment that she squatted there and long after she hurried back over to the bed.

CHAPTER SIX

Asterion paused in the corridor, his fur standing on end as the sensation of being watched washed over him. His preternatural vision sharpened in the dim light as he turned his head, seeking the source of the sensation. Frustration unfurled in his gut at the delay. He had been gone far too long and was eager to return to his human, which made his mood all the fouler at being detained to deal with the creature stalking him.

"Come out now and I may not break your neck at the first opportunity," he growled, his threat amplified by the high-vaulted space of the labyrinth's torch-lit walls.

His ear twitched in response to a light scrape behind him, and he slowly turned, preferring to neither show his back nor demonstrate any unease in the face of a potential threat. His nostrils flared, drawing in a familiar musky scent.

"Barbasas, what are you doing in this part of the labyrinth?" he grunted, his eyes narrowing on the satyr that emerged from the thickness of the shadows.

The satyr was larger than a mortal man and thick with muscle that made the species skilled at pursuing their amorous hungers. Barbasas was large even among his kind but was still nothing compared to the brawn of Asterion. The male slanted a bright green gaze at him, a secretive smile playing about his lips as he brushed a lock of reddish-brown hair from his eyes.

"Is that a way to greet an old friend, Asterion?"

"A 'friend' would not have tried to devour me at first opportunity," he snapped in reply.

The satyr shrugged, his smile widening. "I admit that I got a little carried away. But that is all history, and besides, the labyrinth would have protected its favorite son." He tipped his head. "Why the threats now? You certainly have not sought out my company, and I have not offered you any harm."

"Why are you following me?" Asterion demanded bluntly.

A sly looked crossed the males face, his eyes dancing with laughter as he leaned a shoulder again the wall. "I have come to investigate an interesting rumor that has sprung up among my flock. There is talk that there is a female here... a human."

Asteron's ears flicked impatiently. "And if there were?"

"Then I would have to ask why a minotaur that we have lived peacefully with for so long would attempt to steal our prey?" Barbasa replied with a feigned casualness, his friendly words belied by the iron in his tone.

Grunting, Asterion lowered his horns subtly, which the satyr acknowledged with a faint quirk of his brows.

"From what I recall, my territory is not part of your flock's hunting grounds," he bit out. "You have your own halls and lower reaches that I do not care to traverse. I expect the same respect to be given to what is mine."

Barbasas sighed, his lips pinching. "It is not as easy as you say. Yes, prey enters our corridors, but in places where our territories converge and we pick up the scent of human flesh, it is impossible to rein in our hungers." He cocked his head n. "They also say that you did not spill her blood and that the labyrinth groans angrily for it. How did you resist the hunger, Asterion?"

"Who says that I resisted?" Asterion grumbled. "She is mine to feed *my* hungers, not the labyrinth's."

The satyr's eyes widened as he glanced around warily. "Do not say such things," he hissed. "We are granted immortal reprieve here that is sustained by the labyrinth. Because of it we do not age, we do not become sick. All our basic needs for survival are cared for by its will. Even a favorite son cannot flaunt the will of the labyrinth."

"Then it will have to be happy with the other blood I give it," Asterion replied, holding up the small roe he had found wandering the upper corridors. The deer's head hung limply, its glazed eyes staring out sightlessly. "The labyrinth shall receive more of its blood in addition to its fat and bones when I take it to my butchering room."

"And the woman?"

"Mine," Asterion reiterated. "All that the labyrinth may enjoy from her is our combined essences when she submits to me and the sounds of her pleasure. These will be offerings enough."

Barbasas frowned. "The labyrinth will have its way of getting what it wants, one way or another. When the time comes, if you cannot do what needs to be done, then allow us to satiate ourselves. It has been long since we have enjoyed a woman."

Gritting his teeth, Asterion stepped closer, his shadow falling over the satyr as his fingers of his free hand curled into a fist at his side.

"You and yours will not touch her."

A tremor ran through the satyr, but he straightened, however reluctantly, under the weight of Asterion's glare and returned it. "Then do not force us to make that choice. The labyrinth will not conceal your abode forever if you deny it."

Nostrils flaring, Asterion took another step, forcing the smaller male to crane his head back to meet his gaze. "Are you threatening me?"

Despite the bitter scent of fear filling the air, the satyr's lips curled smugly. "That would not be our intention. It would hardly serve our interest to make such an attempt. Not when it is the human that you want, and, as you can see," he nodded meaningfully at the deer, "you cannot stand guard over her perpetually."

Bellowing out his anger, Asterion swiped at Barbasas, gripping the smaller male in his brutally crushing hand. Hauling him up off of his hooves, he brought the satyr nose to nose with him so there was no possibility of the satyr mishearing his words.

"This is your only warning—one that I am only giving to sustain the long peace between us and because I do not wish an unnecessary conflict—if any of your flock come anywhere near my female, I will rend their limbs from their bodies and feed their corpses to the hunger of the labyrinth."

Barbasas curled his fingers around Asterion's hand, grinning wildly. "That would doubtlessly be quite interesting to witness. Just remember, Asterion, we all depend on the mercy of the labyrinth. Enjoy her while you can—I envy you that and would not deny you—but keep my words in mind. Sooner or later, the labyrinth will tire of your delaying tactics and demand the appropriate sacrifice. Under the madness of the labyrinth, even that carnal hunger you feel will not be able to overwhelm the bloodlust when the fog descends."

Asterion curled his lip at the satyr, lowering him again to his feet. Deep within, however, his gut clenched. He had always suspected that the labyrinth was as tainted as his sister had said but had not wanted to entirely believe that it drove its inhabitants into madness. He had thought that it was merely his imagination that the satyrs had become more vicious in their blood frenzy over the centuries. Hearing confirmation from Barbasas brought a sickening realization of just how much his human was in danger.

Nodding his head in a sharp swing of his horns, he backed away from the male, watching quietly as the satyr straightened and brushed himself off. A deadly smirk crossed Barbasas' handsome face, and he inclined his head in silent understanding before spinning away and racing back into the shadows from whence he had come.

Asterion wondered if the male truly understood how readily he would kill him despite their long span of association with each other. The wary challenge and acceptance, and an unnatural giddiness that had been in the male's eyes, suggested that he did and looked forward to it in the manner of one eager to court death and dance along the edge of danger and drown himself in feasts of blood regardless of the source. Once, Asterion would have doubted that the satyr flock would cannibalize their own, but now he wondered if Barbasas and his kin would not drink their blood as equally as any other.

Ears twitching, he stood stock still, listening as he drew in deep breaths through his nostrils to scent the air until he was satisfied that the satyr had departed. Only then did Asterion move from his spot and resume along his path back to his abode—if not at a considerably quicker pace.

Ultimately, he knew that he worried for nothing. Ariadne's magic could not be superseded by the labyrinth itself, despite what the satyr believed. Unlike the flock, his abode was not carved out and provided by the labyrinth but woven by the magic of his ancestral house that had guarded over the labyrinth and laid the first stones. His sister, disturbed by what the labyrinth had become, had woven the magic around his abode to protect him from it as she found a way to keep his fires lit and to draw the sun into his garden chamber. While it was true that the labyrinth kept him fed and had tended to his needs, his sister had been wise not to trust or depend on that generosity. Even if the labyrinth should turn against him, the satyrs would have no access. Still, it chilled his blood to even imagine what they might do to his female should they get their hands on her. It was that thought which hurried his pace.

The torches flared with his passing as he neared his destination, a comforting presence that brought to mind the ancient wanderers before his time who descended into the depths to experience the mysteries of the underworld. On some level, there was comfort to be found by those inhabitants who walked its halls despite the labyrinth's violent and deceitful nature.

His eyes sought on the carvings on the stone wall that marked the entrance to his abode. The rough-cut dancing figures gleamed within the light, but, to his surprise, he experienced only a fading echo of his usual pain at the sight of them. At the sight of his sister's likeness, carved into the stone by Ariadne when she had still been very much a girl and had helped him forge his abode with her budding magic. The girl on the stone who danced the labyrinth's crane dance of its hidden mystery, kept well-hidden his own secret—his entrance.

Tracing a claw over the complex path twined around the carved girl, Asterion's brow furrowed as the wall of the labyrinth thinned and became no more substantial than a membranous passage. It had been centuries since he had become accustomed to the peculiar sight and feeling of Ariadne's portal. That was not what bothered him. Instead, he worried that the easing of his pain meant that he was losing the last pieces of his sister that he had jealously preserved within his memory and heart.

The thought alarmed him, even as he experienced a sense of relief that he refused to acknowledge. Instead, he focused on his loss, feeding his grief with his regrets and anger at being deprived of what little he had left of her. He did not understand why this was happening, and his sorrow soon matched his growing confusion as he passed through the barrier, feeling the light touch of his sister's magic still woven after all these centuries into the stone.

What was different?

The female. *His* female.

A female that did not want him and would not love him, and yet whom he would keep anyways to stave away his loneliness. This was what was dimming his memory of Ariadne?

He snorted and coughed, the air thickening around him and in his lungs as he breathed it in. Asterion's eyes rolled back, a haze filling his mind as his lungs labored with each breath. Something insidious snaked up from where it was coiled deep within his belly, making saliva drip from his fangs as he was filled with a ravenous hunger and helpless rage that seemed to spring fully formed from his sorrow.

A bellow built up in his chest as he passed through into his abode, his eyes rolling as he attempted to look everywhere at once for the culprit. *The satyrs were right. Destroy and feed upon the female and free yourself from the female's sorcery.*

The voice seemed to come from within and outside of himself all at once. It was a familiar voice, and Asterion clung to it. At that moment, it seemed like the only thread of sanity in the overwhelming unfamiliarity of the new situation he had found himself in.

What do you know of caring for a female, anyway? Even Ariadne would not stay, choosing to be a foreigner outcast among her lover's people. She chose to die on distant shores rather than remain forever with you within the labyrinth. Your female will also seek to escape. She will not wish to be tied to you even as she steals the memory of your sister. Better to paint the corridors with her blood.

Blood. A red spring that you can drink deep from once again and keep her essence forever within you where she cannot escape. She will be a part of you forever, and a part of the labyrinth forever if you but drink and feed upon rich meat when you release her from her prison of flesh.

Shaking with the intensity of the violence filling him, he strode heavily through the room, the hunger for sweet, life-giving blood filling him. He snorted and grunted, his hot breath expelling sharply through his nostrils as his bellow worked its way up... and then died in his throat when his gaze landed on a sight that stole the breath from his lungs.

She slept.

Curled on his bed, her brown hair splayed out around her as if she were a nereid floating in wait for her lover on a placid sea, she evoked such a sharp longing through him that he fell to his knees, the sharp thump of them hitting the floor echoing in his ears, his labrys falling at his side. The roe lay a short distance away where it had tumbled to the floor unnoticed and forgotten.

Staring at her—needing her—his thoughts churned with confusion and denial even as another hunger roared through him, engulfing the mad blood-lust and driving it from him. Bile rose, burning through him as he stared at her.

He stumbled back away from the sleeping platform, his eyes rounding in horror. What was he doing? He had nearly been overwhelmed by the terrible blood hunger. He would have torn her apart with his fangs and claws, and she would have stared at him sightlessly as so many others had, her hand laying limp at her side from where she had reached out to him in entreaty just as *they* had.

On the bed, she sighed, stirring in her sleep. Although she was still nameless, it mattered little to him. He would have her name eventually. She was his.

When she stretched and turned in her sleep, the cloth of her clothing stretching tight across her breasts, his cock thickened beneath his chiton, his desire thrumming through his blood as a carnal hunger rose sharp and swift through his senses. He breathed in deep, seeking to consume her natural perfume. A pungent scent instead filled his nostrils, wilting his desire.

Despite the smell, shame filled him.

He had neglected to show her where to relieve herself. He wondered how long she waited in complete discomfort before she gave in and found a spot to empty her bladder. He was not entirely sure why she did so in the primary chamber rather than choosing one of the antechambers, but it mattered little now. He would make sure that she knew all that she needed.

Hanging his labrys in its place on the wall in passing, Asterion walked back to the garden chamber to fill yet another jug with water. The good thing was that the edges of the walls were designed with fine grooves that drained liquid so at least there wasn't a mess to sop up, and any water poured out to rinse the stones would likewise be carried off. It made cleaning in general easier for him.

As he filled the jug, a sense of purpose found root within him. He was caring for his female and protecting her. Smiling to himself, he shouldered the jug and carried it back into the main room chamber. He felt her gaze on him, and he glanced over at the sleeping platform to see her curled in the middle of it, far from any of the edges and buried under the furs, watching him warily as he strode over to the wall. Moving slowly as not to startle her, he poured out the water over the spot, washing the traces of waste away as he watched her from the corner of his eye.

Slowly, she lowered the fur pulled up to her chin, her cheeks blazing red as she openly watched him. As unnaturally red as she was, he was beginning to become concerned for her health when she surprised him by speaking.

"I'm really sorry."

CHAPTER SEVEN

Vicky cringed at her pitiful apology, shame crawling through her as she watched the minotaur wash away her mess.

How freaking embarrassing.

It didn't help that he appeared nonplussed about her apology, the only reaction being the ear that flicked at her seconds before he turned his head fully to gaze at her curiously.

"Why do you apologize?" he asked. He gestured to the draining water. "This was result of my neglect, so it is my duty to clean it." He appeared to hesitate, his expression growing thoughtful from what she could distinguish in the purse of his wide lips and the upward movement of his brows. "I am curious, though, why you did not choose another room where you would not have to suffer with the smell... unless human senses are deplorably dead."

The right corner of her mouth quirked at his observation, and a tiny chuckle escaped her that made both of his ears prick toward her. Her smile grew at unexpectedly being the center of such a powerful creature's attention. There was a thoughtful light in his eyes that hadn't been there that morning, and his focus was so absolute that it almost made her giddy to have a being so dangerous speaking softly to her and attentively listening to her.

She jerked her chin toward to the black stain that marked the ground where she had crushed the centipede. "Because of that," she admitted quietly. "I wouldn't have gotten off this bed at all after that thing if it weren't for the fact that my body didn't give me a lot of options in the matter."

Dark horns swinging impressively as he turned his head, the minotaur stared at the crushed remains and frowned as he stalked toward it. He scuffed at the edge of it with one hoof, his nose wrinkling.

"Where did this come from?"

"The wall where you disappeared. I tried to find a way through and put my hand in a crevice to see if I could find a way to open the door you used. That thing was in there." She shuddered, drawing the minotaur's concerned gaze back to her, and she rubbed the back of her hand where the scratches still stung. "It was pretty horrible."

His eyes dropped, and his brow lowered as he focused on her hand. She stilled, her heartbeat picking up as he eyed her hand. Faster than she could follow, he moved forward with a deadly speed that made her jump when he seized her arm, dragging her to him. A small scream rose from within her, but she managed to smother it when she saw the concerned way he observed the wounds, his claws hovering over them.

"What has happened?" he asked quietly.

She shuddered, remembering the feel of the pressure of something grabbing her. "I think I got my hand caught, and when I felt the centipede, this happened when I yanked my hand free. A stupid accident due to sticking my hands in holes where, of course, bugs will live."

He gave her a confused look, his head tilting as his ears tipped toward her. With his large brown eyes, there was something almost sweet about it. The moment passed, however, when he released her arm and backed away from her, leaving her feeling strangely bereft at the absence of his warm hand touching her skin.

"We need to clean and bandage this. Come this way," he murmured.

Vicky slipped from the bed and followed him through one of the tunnels. Within the first few feet, it hooked suddenly to the right before spilling out into a warmly lit room. Golden sunlight filled the entirety of the space, causing the spray from the spring to sparkle as it danced and the leaves of the abundant plants to gleam with a flush of health despite the fact that she could spy no source at all for the sun. Mouth parted in awe, she spun in place, staring at her surroundings.

"What is this place? It's beautiful!"

"The garden chamber." The minotaur's voice held a note of restrained pride as he walked to a stone table nearly entirely obscured by growth and picked up a stone bowl. He seemed to pause for a moment as if considering his words. "Like my abode, this was designed by my sister's magic. This is a safe place," he assured her. "Nothing that dwells within the labyrinth can get in here."

She shivered, rubbing her arms uncertainly. "That seems a bit impossible. The centipede got in," she reminded him.

He glanced over at her as he headed toward a thick clump of plants. "More precisely, you pulled it in."

Vicky gaped at him, affronted at being blamed for bringing the centipede in. "I did not! It crawled onto my hand!"

Bending to carefully snip off a sprig with his claws, he snorted. "It could not pass the wall. My sister's magic prevented that. It was not until you put your hand in there that provided for it a manner of access." He gave her a reproving look. "You are fortunate that it did not bite you as the labyrinth intended. Had it managed to keep its hold on you, you would not have escaped such consequences."

She shook her head, unable to wrap her head around what she was hearing. "Wait. Are you saying that it *did* grab me? That the labyrinth is somehow... alive?"

"It has always been," he explained quietly. Dropping another handful of sprigs into the bowl, he turned his head to give her a hard look. "It is why you must not leave my abode. You see now what dangers you may meet if you try to escape again."

Escape?

"What are you talking about? I wasn't trying to escape. I was afraid of being left alone in here and wanted to stay with you," she blurted out.

His right ear flicked with uncertainty. "You wished to... be with me?"

Vicky looked at him, truly looked at him, and saw the flash of vulnerability in his eyes and the parting of his wide lips and her sarcastic retort died on her lips. Although towering over her at well over seven and a half feet tall and every inch of him packed with muscle, there was something so fragile about him in that moment, as if he couldn't believe that someone actually wanted to be in his company.

She cleared her throat. "You were a bit of an ass with all this mine, mine stuff, but... I feel safe with you. I mean, look at you, you're huge. And you not only saved me but didn't hurt me like you could have."

He glanced down at himself and nodded, his expression hardening with determination as he met her eyes. "I would not seek to hurt you. I wish to protect you."

Vicky peered at him cautiously. "And this 'mine' business?"

The beast shrugged. "You are still mine, but I will not hurt what is mine." Something passed over his expression that she couldn't quite decipher, as if he were disturbed by a thought. "No matter what, I will not," he reiterated. "But I will not apologize for my desire of you. It has been long since I have known a kind touch. Not since Ariadne."

His words drifted off into silence as he stared off into the garden, like he was watching the shadows of the past that only he could see come alive.

She frowned and brushed her fingers over her pendant. "Ariadne? Not *the* Ariadne, the daughter of Minos?"

The minotaur broken free from his inward visions, glanced at her sharply. "You know of Ariadne?"

She started to shake her head but nodded with bewilderment. "I mean, kind of. It's an ancient myth. Minos built a labyrinth to cage his son whom the gods cursed with the likeness of a bull due to the love Queen Pasiphae consummated with a bull so that he might release his enemies within it to be destroyed."

His lips pulled back in a grimace, giving her a view of his fangs. "That is not quite accurate. He did not build the labyrinth, though what he did to it was a tragedy. The labyrinth was built by his ancestors as a place of mysteries. He merely rebuilt the entrance into something grander and far more terrible that instead of acting as a passage between worlds, he was able to cage them in here eternally."

He gave a miserable shake of his head. "I do not know if the souls too are trapped here as the living forever are. I hope not. If they were, that would have been a far greater crime, and I would pray that the gods saw to his punishment in Tartarus where the vilest do their penance." He huffed a sound that might have been laughter if it had contained even a drop of amusement within it. "As ill as he seems to have been remembered, my father's cruelty is understated. He took pleasure in my torment, even as he saw to it that I was educated with the best tutors as a matter of pride when I was still small enough to be controllable by his guard."

He bent and clipped off another couple of sprigs, throwing them into the bowl.

"I hate my father," he admitted. "I hated his every punishment, every condemnation that left his mouth. Even as much as I hated him, however, in some ways, my mother's transgressions against me were worse. She refused to look upon me or even speak to me except once, which she did from behind a screen when I was small. I was denied all company except those they threw to me." His hand stilled, hovering over a yellow flower. "The ancient magic of the labyrinth allowed me to know their words and understand them clearly as they begged to be set free." He shook his head violently, a shudder visibly rolling over his skin. "The words they screamed before I... killed them... haunt me."

Swallowing, Vicky stepped closer, her hand shaking as she reached out sympathetically to lay her palm against his arm, cognizant of the fact that he was a killer in every way she understood the word. Yet she couldn't help but be moved by his pain and an unease that settled in her when it came to the labyrinth. He glanced down at her hand, his body stilling. Another shudder rippled through him, and the tension eased from him, the tightened muscles relaxing under her palm.

"You are really Asterion, aren't you?"

"I am." The confession was a soft rumble that pulled at her heart.

A monster that he was, he was just as alone as she was, but unlike her he had been alone for centuries, caught in the madness of this place.

"How can that be? You've been here for centuries. And you're saying that it is the magic that makes us able to communicate?"

He nodded and clasped her hand in his, his head lowered as he looked at the difference between them. "It is necessary for the labyrinth. Even then, it was far larger than anyone knew, stretching to a number of access points that even now I cannot number. In the depths of its history, many foreigners passed through it, and even more when Minos threw his enemies within the confines of this place. As I said, it keeps us alive... those whom it sees profitable to sustain, though in my youth I did not understand it and was too young and blinded by my anger to notice how much it began to change. At first, the labyrinth was the only kindness save for my sister that I knew, but Ariadne tried to warn me. Minos twisted the spirit of the labyrinth. It became more of a monster than what you believe me to be... more than I am, anyway."

Asterion met her eyes, and she was caught by the terrible pain in those dark depths. "I do not deceive myself, female. I am a monster. I have done many terrible things within these corridors." His hide quivered with what she took as repulsion. "I hate what I have become, and I am beginning to suspect that my sister was right about another thing... the influence the labyrinth has over our appetites. It makes me want to rend and consume. The satyrs who were hunting you before, I have noted that they are growing increasingly mad and violent."

Vicky attempted to draw back, her fear rising with his confession, but he did not let her. His grip tightened as he drew her to the spring and forced her to take a seat on the rocks before releasing her. She might have sprung to her feet in an attempt to flee, except she recalled his words about not running from him and suspected that they were more of a warning. The silent plea in his eyes as he stepped away reinforced her hunch.

He gave her a grim smile, no doubt easily reading her like a book. He was ancient after all and likely had witnessed more human reactions to him than she wanted to think about. She didn't want to think about it because it stirred pity and a sort of kindred sympathy within her. How many times since the Ravening had she been looked at fearfully, as if she were potentially a cleverly disguised monster coming into the midst of a settlement? She was certain that Asterion would suffer all of that and worse if he were roaming the world, but she couldn't imagine that it could be more horrific than what he encountered within the labyrinth.

"You will not hurt me," she whispered, the affirmation more for her benefit than anything else.

"I will not hurt you," he rasped in agreement. " I cannot... When I see you, those hungers disappear. My hunger... changes."

Vicky gave him a sharp look, and heat rose along her neck and into her cheeks with the realization of what he meant. Suddenly she was uncomfortably far too aware of him. She wasn't a virgin. In the nightmarish landscape that her world had become, she believed in taking her pleasures where the opportunity presented itself. She had scratched that particular itch many times. Yet to have this huge male admit such a desire inflamed once again the kernel of interest that she had tried to ignore.

The brush of his hand as he slowly washed her wound with a flat leaf that left behind an astringent burn seemed to only exacerbate her awareness of him, and she shivered under his touch. He paused, his nostrils flaring, drawing in her scent, and she wondered if he could smell the trickle of arousal warming her core. His eyes darkened, and her breath stopped. Was he going to take that as an invitation? Did she want him to?

A pleasant tingle stirred between her legs. It had been a while since she had enjoyed intimate company. Would it be such a bad thing to mutually ease their loneliness? That feeling had been a companion long enough that she recognized it well in him. Something as simple as an intimate touch and shared pleasure could make everything more bearable.

Sadly, his mind apparently did not arrive at a similar conclusion. A gusty breath left him, and he turned away, bringing her fantasies to a screeching halt. Setting aside several long strips of leaves and some vine, he turned his attention to the task of making a poultice with the herbs that were left in the bowl.

Watching him work, her lips tipped in a self-mocking smirk. *I guess worrying about it is moot when he's hardly showing any interest.*

That he could control his reactions so well, despite his claims of how much she incited *that* hunger, relieved her as much as it disappointed her. It wasn't until he shifted closer to her, his legs spreading to make room for her so she could draw up closer against him, that she became aware of the bulge of his cock tenting the fabric around his waist.

"What do I call you, little female?" he asked quietly as he smeared a paste over her wound, the burn banking whatever desire surged through her blood at the erotic sight.

He lifted his soft brown eyes, a brow quirking at her so that she smiled self-consciously. Great. He was trying to heal her, and she was there ogling him like an inexperienced teenager. Between the burn of the medicine and her arousal, she had entirely missed the question.

"I'm sorry, what did you say?"

The corners of his mouth lifted in amusement. "Your name?"

"Oh, that." She laughed in embarrassment and shrugged. "Well, once I was Victoria Ann Marshall, but now I'm just Vicky."

"Vicky," he murmured to himself, his fingers deftly wrapping the long strips of leaves around her arm before binding it with the length of vine. His eyes warmed as they met hers, and he smiled as he gave her hand a gentle pat and he stood. "Welcome home, Vicky. Come then, let me show you our abode, and then I must prepare the meat for our meal."

A warmth curled in her chest as she rose and followed him. It had been a long time since she had a home. Even if the rest of the labyrinth wanted to kill her, that he wanted to share his home with her meant more to her in that moment than she had words to express. She had no illusions when it came to how dangerous this world was that she found herself in, but it felt good to be included and wanted there. That he offered it to her as her home as well, and not merely a guest dependent on his whims.

"All right, let's see it. But perhaps we can start with your toilets."

He gave her a confused look. "Toilets?"

She groaned miserably. "Oh, gods, no toilets. Not even an outhouse?" As he continued to look baffled at her words, she gestured onward and grimaced. "Perhaps you can share with me where I am to...uh... pee and stuff."

Comprehension crossed his face, and he nodded. "The other tunnel is bisected. The nearer path leads to the lesser spring where you can relieve yourself and wash while the further one leads to the butchering chambers." He hesitated, giving her a doubtful look. "You might want to avoid the latter. It can be... unpleasant."

She grimaced. *I'm sure it is.* "Thanks for the tip. I think I will do just that. Lead on."

Giving her what she suspected was a warm smile despite the somewhat bovine face and mouth full of sharp teeth, he led her back into the main chamber and began their tour. Although short enough, she was entirely grateful and in short order was curled beneath the furs again, her bladder once again empty as she dozed while Asterion tended to his butchering. That was something she tried not to think about, not wishing to imagine how many people he might have butchered in the past. She hoped he never actually butchered anyone, anyway.

Now that was a thought that was going to give her a sleepless night or two. She only prayed that it was all truly in the past. He was certain that he wouldn't hurt her, so surely he wouldn't... would he?

Vicky gnawed on her lip and prayed that he was able to stand up to the magic of the labyrinth as much as he claimed.

CHAPTER EIGHT

Vicky watched curiously as Asterion opened his large mitt of a hand, revealing four polished white pieces, each of them carved with delicate images.

"What's this?" she asked excitedly.

After a handful of days cooped up in the labyrinth, she was about ready to go stir crazy with boredom, especially with how often Asterion had to leave her for hours at a time to hunt. While the greens, fruits, and veggies helped vary their diet, meat was almost a daily necessity for the minotaur. Unaccustomed to staring at an enclosed space for any great length of time, anything at all new was a subject of excitement for her.

"These," he rumbled, "are astragaloi."

A soft sensation brushed her mind, producing the word he intended.

"*Dice?*"

Her eyebrows flew up as her gaze shot to the minotaur's face, seeing if he was fucking with her. He stared back blankly, but then he had the best poker face she had ever seen and managed resting beast face in a way that women with resting bitch face would envy. Unless he was moved by a strong emotion, it was anyone's guess what he was thinking, not that she didn't entertain herself frequently by trying. A game that he had not slaughtered her for, as of yet.

"No way!" she breathed. "They don't look like dice. What are these strange markings on them?"

"Dice," he repeated back slowly, his accent thick, and he nodded. "We craft them from the knucklebone of goats, and we mark our symbols on three sides as you see here." He lifted one up for her to inspect. "When we throw them, we count those that are face down without any symbols showing."

"Fascinating! And you made these? They're beautifully carved."

Both of his ears twitched. "I enjoy carving. There have been many days where there was nothing to occupy my time. I taught myself to carve centuries ago. But if you like them so much, you may have them. A gift."

Vicky breathed in as he gently cupped her hands in his large one and carefully tumbled the four dice into her hand. She stared down at them, her chest constricting even as it filled with warmth.

"I really shouldn't take them. You obviously worked hard on these," she murmured.

She glanced at him from beneath her lashes and watched as he shrugged, his head dipping with an ambivalent grunt as he examined the stone floor.

Was this great beast of a male embarrassed? He certainly looked far too intimidating for her to have ever imagined that he would have a softer side like that. As far as she had figured, his luxuriously soft, thick fur was the only thing soft about him, and even that encased deadly muscles.

She tipped her head to the side, considering him. She was starting to see that he was a lot more than what she had assumed that the minotaur of myth would be. For one, he was far less true to bull-man form. Aside from his face possessing some human qualities, in addition to its peculiar angles that lent him a shapelier face and broader muzzle than a bull's, there were other features that didn't match up with her assumptions.

With his long, thick mane that covered his shoulders and around his neck, he rather resembled a lion in that moment if she ignored his bull features. With his retractable claws and gleaming fangs, and the thick tuft of his tail and his tantalizingly soft pelt, there was a lot of lion to complement his prominent bull features. He'd been designed as a true monster, constructed to strike fear and be as a lion among men. Yet, at that moment, she saw beyond that to the stark vulnerability rising to the surface again, along with a shyness she would not have expected from a male shaped like a brute and who ordered her about like he did.

Noting his reaction, she murmured, "I haven't owned anything so pretty since we had to leave everything behind during the Ravening. I fear you've discovered my weakness—I do like pretty things, and these are amazing!" Turning the dice reverently over in her hands, she grinned down at them, totally enchanted with his thoughtfulness and her new revelations about her "beast."

His dark eyes lifted, a hint of a smile lifting the corners of his mouth. She stared at him with open surprise. She had never seen even a hint of a smile from him before.

"It pleases me that you like them. I do not have much, but what I have is yours."

Her mouth continued to hang open at his unexpected declaration. He seemed far too possessive of anything he considered his, even inaccurately, to say such a thing.

"But... why?" she stammered.

His gaze shifted away. "I tire of being alone."

She nodded, her fingers tightening around the dice as she considered the years of traveling alone and feeling no less solitary in the settlements she visited as the people actively avoided her company. Sighing, she gave him a commiserating smile. "Yeah, I think I am too."

Taking advantage of the fact that he was kneeling on the ground, bringing the formidable male down nearer to her height, Vicky stepped forward and, before she could change her mind, wrapped her arms around him. Her limbs disappeared into the thick ruff of fur, startling a delighted giggle out of her of the likes she hadn't made in years. Against her, Asterion froze, his muscles tightening to a degree that she couldn't help but be aware of it.

Vicky stiffened warily. Perhaps she misread the situation?

Embarrassed, she started to pull away when she was seized by two powerful arms that held her close, squeezing against his massive chest with a careful-ness that was endearing. Pressed against his chest, she could feel his heart thumping and felt a strange connection to him, as if something tied them together in that moment, and his soft muzzle brushed the nape of her neck bared by the ponytail she chose to wear that day. The sensation sent a shiver jolting through her, tickling her, and she chuckled as she burrowed her cheek into the fur around his collar, soaking in the warmth of actual close contact. Not human contact, but in her recent experiences, it was far sweeter and more freely given than anything she had received even from the few lovers that she had encountered.

Impulsively, she reached up and grabbed ahold of his nearest horn and gently tugged the side of his face closer to press a kiss into the fur there. It happened so quick and without thought on her part that it caught both of them by surprise. She felt him jerk slightly before cautiously leaning into the touch. She swallowed, unable to believe she had the nerve to kiss a monster like he was another human being, but she was strangely glad that she did. It seemed that the terrible monster was as skittish as a beaten creature, wary of touch while being entirely touch starved. Without drawing away, she smiled against the fur of his jawbone.

"Thank you, Asterion."

He responded with a soft rumble that vibrated against her with such strength that it nearly shook her. Stifling a laugh, she leaned into it, ignoring the shocking lick of heat it ignited within her. Given that she knew quite well that her body responded in a very healthy fashion to stimulation, she didn't put any significant weight on it and enjoyed the novelty of being hugged.

Perhaps she was more than a little touch starved herself.

He pulled away gradually, and there was something new in his expression that she couldn't quite identify. With deep, chuffing sound that might have been a chuckle, he lightly plucked the dice from her hand and held them up in front of her.

"Let me teach you how to play."

Nodding eagerly, she took her place at the opposite side of the circle he had scraped into the stone with one claw. Glancing over at her, he surprised her with a broad, sharp-toothed smile that evoked a quiver within her that was definitely not due to fear.

Okay, that was a little harder to ignore, but the fact that she was just pressed intimately against him moments ago likely had some bearing on it. She didn't know what was happening between them, but there was a certain excitement to the unknown that came with the territory of having a companion. Strange physical reactions aside, she decided in that moment that she really did want a friend for once.

Sure, whatever existed between them wasn't quite yet friendship, but it was a start.

CHAPTER NINE

Asterion's tail flicked as he tried to ignore the very naked female bathing just behind him as he worked in his garden. It wasn't like she was nude. She had her undergarments on and was using a small scrap of leather to wash herself. That she was cleansing her body just behind him should not feel as indecent as it did. He had just rinsed the blood and sweat of the hunt from himself a short time ago without any shame or compunction about her enjoying the garden nearby. Yet with her, his very presence there while she performed such an intimate task felt borderline obscene.

Days were indistinct deep within the labyrinth without any sun to track the passage of hours, so he could not rightly tell how many days had passed with her in his company. It had been at least a dozen risings now by his count. Days with his Vicky seemed to speed by. Somehow, despite the lingering awkwardness between them, that was only made worse by Asterion's inability to control his nightly reactions to her nearness and her responding arousal that perfumed the air, they had fallen into an easy rhythm that filled his days with more pleasure than any other he could remember. It shamed him to admit that it even surpassed his youthful memories from when he dotingly followed Ariadne on adventures through his prison.

Although his sister had attempted to make his abode as much a home as possible, it had never felt like more than a sheltered place to be where he could let down his guard and escape the creatures occupying the corridors. It never felt like what he vaguely understood a home should feel like. Before, unless he required rest, he never felt a need or desire to stay within the walls, preferring to hunt in his territory or pay respect to the shrines in the lower halls to pass his waking hours.

Even when Ariadne had been there with him, they had spent much of their time exploring and playing games among the twists and turns. But that was in the early days of his prison, before his father began sending victims into the halls to die, when the labyrinth had been a comforting—if somewhat dark and mysterious—place to be. But still, it had not been home then, nor in the great many years that followed.

Vicky had changed that.

With her there, he no longer felt the desire or need to wander through the corridors or to pursue his hunt as soon as he rose from bed. Some mornings, he even enjoyed lingering in bed, watching his female sleep if he happened to awaken first or sharing fruit together as they reclined comfortably in the furs for their morning meal. He still found it difficult to open up to her and was often gruffer than he ought to be, but even then he could not keep himself from watching her.

She was everything that he was not. Soft, small, delicate. She didn't belong in the labyrinth with monsters like him, and that made him not only relish his moments to enjoy her company, but he also acknowledged that it made him terribly paranoid. Even with the magics protecting his dwelling, he carefully assured himself that nothing managed to pass him whenever he entered or exited. As unlikely as it was to happen given the nature of Ariadne's spells, he could not help but worry when his female was alone there without his protection. Every moment he was away from her, he felt an unsettling dread build as each day passed that something would find a way to snuff out the bright light of her soul and beautiful laughter.

That laughter sounded behind him, stirring his cock even as it brought a delightful warmth to gather within his chest to occupy the space held by his heart.

"Asterion, you look ready to panic. This isn't exactly the first time you've been in here with me while I wash," she teased. "It's not like I'm naked and bathing. I never would have imagined you'd be so prudish."

Unbidden, he could see her very clearly in his mind's eye as she might be while bathing, her naked body reclined on the rocks beside the spring as she thoroughly washed her most intimate places. He swallowed back a groan, his cock stiffening painfully as it became fully erect with need, his hunger igniting in his belly. He was therefore startled when he heard a splash and a splatter of water suddenly doused the fur along his back, drawing an annoyed growl from him. Mostly because it did little to ease the ache between his thighs or cool the burning hunger that was rising through him like a flame upon tinder.

"Do not," he growled, closing his eyes against the haze of need burning through him.

Vicky fell silent for a moment, the gurgle of the spring the only sound in the room for several beats of his heart. He grimaced, certain that he had emotionally harmed her once again by his brutish words. He was surprised, however, that when she spoke it was with no little amount of chagrin in her voice.

"I'm sorry, Asterion. I should respect your boundaries. Please, forget I said anything."

He wanted to assure her that she was not at fault and to speak whatever she desired, but he held his tongue. He did not want to further encourage such inciting behavior when it had such quick consequences for him. She had done nothing wrong, but he did not wish to scare her with the hunger he had managed to keep contained.

His breath felt hot as it dragged in and out of his lungs, though he strove to ignore it. Although a faint haze had descended over his vision, he battled through it to focus on the bush in front of him and the small pink medicinal blooms that he was gathering to dry. Vicky had asked about pain relievers, evasively claiming that she needed something for "that time of the month." He had no clue what event occurred every lunar cycle that required pain suppressants, but that there was something like that made him feel ill.

More often than he could count, he had ripped flesh from bone, but he could not stomach the idea of his little female in pain. The irony of it all was not lost upon him, and he grunted dourly as he plucked another bloom, adding it to the pile in his basket. Unfortunately, forcing his attention to the flowers, the reason he needed them, and his task at hand did little to quell the hunger burning through him.

He wondered if perhaps he had been cast to Tartaros after all for the profanity of his existence and his terrible deeds, and some demon was solely responsible for his current torture.

Asterion sighed as Vicky's soft humming reached his ears, mingling with the soft sounds of water splashing as she returned to her ministrations. If Tartaros was where he was, he admittedly would happily remain there and be tortured indefinitely if he could keep her. That was also why he took care to not expose her to his hunger. If he yielded to her teasing and looked at her, he knew that the need would grow far beyond what he could hide. He nearly shook with it now. It was only by his will that he was remaining in place, attending to his work, rather than striding over to rip the small cloth coverings to free her breasts and sex to his pleasure.

No, he did not dare look at her. He could not risk losing even the smallest sliver of control that would make her aware of the full extent of the hunger consuming him.

With another ragged sigh, he reached out and plucked another bloom, pretending not to notice that it was the same shade of her lips... and he wondered if she possessed petals of a similar hue beneath the scrap of cloth circling her hips.

CHAPTER TEN

Vicky hated the hours that she was left alone. It was maddening, and within the complete silence of her surroundings she often thought she heard things scraping and clawing on the other side of the walls. She still had nightmares of being chased through the labyrinth, and those sounds were eerily like the ones that still haunted her in her dreams.

When Asterion was there, everything was different. There were no ungodly scratching sounds frantically trying to reach her. She was pretty sure that nothing dared to come near when he was there. But when he was not, no manner of distraction could make her unhear them.

Shivering, she climbed up on the platform bed, wrapping herself tightly in a large bear fur. She didn't even want to know how a bear was caught in the labyrinth or what else might have ended up in there. Instead, she burrowed beneath the warmth, the fur pulled up over her head, trying to block out the terrible noise assaulting her ears.

A crash echoed through the room from somewhere in the labyrinth, and she cringed at the shrill shriek that followed after it. What made the hair on her arms raise in terror, however, was the blood-curdling snarl that seemed to echo all around. It was soon joined by a booming roar that sent small pebbles clattering across the floor.

"It's okay," she whispered, squeezing her eyes shut. "Nothing can get in here. It can't get you."

Claws screeched against stone as shrieks and roars blended into a cacophony of violence that ended with one last deep, rolling growl before all was silent again. She barely dared to breathe as she strained to listen, her heart thundering in her ears. Tears leaked out from beneath her lashes, and she startled at the sensation of the rapidly cooling hot moisture as it slipped down her cheeks.

When several minutes of silence passed, Vicky drew in a shaky breath and slowly released it. Whatever it was, it was gone, likely carrying away the grisly remains of the challenger for its meal. She desperately wanted to throw up.

Burrowing her face into the furs beneath her cheek, she continued to take slow, measured breaths. She hated the labyrinth, and she had a distinct feeling that it hated her too.

No. That wasn't right. The feeling she got when she was alone, listening to the labyrinth come alive outside of the safety of their secret chambers, was too cold to be hatred. It simply wanted her dead. In the depths of her nightly nightmares, when she was lost running through the halls, she sometimes saw the stones ahead of her morph into an inhuman face filled with razor sharp teeth in a maw that gaped open, unnaturally wide just ahead. She never seemed to slow to keep herself from sliding into its terrible mouth, its black tongue eagerly lapping up her blood, its teeth tearing at her flesh until she woke screaming in Asterion's arms.

Every night he demanded to know what tormented her, and every night she brushed it off as nothing more than figments of her imagination. But it wasn't. She wasn't that imaginative, and she certainly had never been a horror fan like her older cousins were before the Ravening. It was the labyrinth itself... or rather, how it chose to show itself to her when her mind was vulnerable and open to its influence.

It was like she was caught in Rob Zombie's demented playhouse, but instead of horror icons like Freddy, Michael or Jason, it was occupied by unspeakable terrors beyond human imagination.

A fresh round of tears stung her eyes, and she sniffled into the fur.

"I want to go home," she whispered miserably to her prison and any deity who deigned to listen, her fingers clutching her pendant. She licked her lips and gave a weak laugh. "Asterion speaks of this as my home. He thinks he can keep me alive by sheer will alone, but, gods help me, he doesn't understand." She joked on another humorless laugh. "I am not going to make it here. This place is determined to kill me if it doesn't drive me mad."

At least for now there was blessed silence. She sank heavily into the furs, her body beyond weary. Her eyes drifted shut, and immediately the scratching resumed. Throwing back her head, Vicky screamed until her throat grew raw, and she collapsed back into a fit of coughing.

"Damn this fucking place," she rasped into the fur.

She might have sunk gratefully into oblivion if not for the fact that her eyes snapped open, and she bolted upright at the sudden burst of cool air that was chased by a heavy thump of hooves hitting stone.

"Vicky!"

She nearly collapsed with relief when she saw Asterion rushing toward her, his eyes rounded and wild with panic.

He dove for the platform, and she reached for him, a sob shuddering through her as he gathered her up in his arms in an uncharacteristic comforting embrace. He held her there against his chest, crooning softly to her, the rumble of his deep voice soothing against her ear. When her tremors finally ceased, he continued to stroke her hair, but it was his deep voice that finally broke the invisible wall between them.

"What is it? What has happened here?"

She shook her head against his chest. She didn't want to say and make him feel guilty that he was leaving her to be tormented by the labyrinth's sinister hunger. He couldn't stay with her even if he wanted to.

He had said before how difficult it could be to find prey, since the entrances often changed and where animals could appear within the corridors was often unpredictable. Not only that, but she was aware that he believed that slaughtering the animals he found in the labyrinth would buy her safety from its appetite. He had confided as much to her, but she had been doubtful then even before her nightmares had grown worse.

She blinked back her tears. "Just a nightmare."

His large, furred hand stroked down her back, and she could feel the weight of his concern radiating through her. "Another?"

"Yeah," she croaked. "They seem worse when I'm alone." She sniffled miserably and clung to him. "Are you sure I can't go out with you?"

His sigh was deep, but he hugged her to him, reassuring her with the small gesture of physical affection in the way that only he could. "You would not be safe out there."

Twisting in his embrace until he loosened his grip, she leaned back so that she could meet his eyes. "I'm going to be real honest right now. Mentally, I'm not okay here alone. I think I would feel safer with you than I do now."

He shook his head, baffled. "The magic of these walls can protect you far better than I could."

She shrugged. Perhaps there was something to that, but it didn't matter. "I *feel* safer with you, though," she clarified.

His ears flicked and she could see in the shift of his eyes that although he was uncomfortable with her request, he was at least considering it.

"I must think on it. I have brought down one of the deep-dwellers. We will cook what we can eat tonight, and I will smoke the rest. Its meat should give us a reprieve for a few days while I consider how best to do so that will be safest for you."

Giving him a grateful smile, she slipped from his embrace and crawled off the bed. At the same time, she tried not to watch too closely as he stepped out of their sanctuary to retrieve his prey. One look at it and, as expected, she wanted to hurl. Of course, any creature that he called "deep" would be some kind of monster!

A pale, leathery creature, it had a head armored with plating so that only a tri-serrated beak was visible. She couldn't see any eyes. Instead, it had four horns, one of which was broken, that rose up from its brow and the general area where the eyes might have been. Just above the second set of horns, a long bony crest spiked outward before flattening just above its neck and extending down in overlapping armor partially down its swollen body. From those plates, large gray spines jutted out, making it vaguely resemble a sea anemone if not for the dozens of long legs and the two thin tails dragging behind it as Asterion hauled it through the main chamber into the tunnel that led to the slaughter room.

As much as she wanted to be plastered at his side, she wrinkled her nose and sat back down on the edge of the bed. It didn't bother her to see game butchered, but there was no way she was going to be able to stomach witnessing *that* and still be able to eat. As it was, she would be lucky with however much she managed to force down if she didn't think too closely where it came from. Even from where she sat, however, Vicky could hear the sickening crunch of its natural armor being broken.

Once, when she was a child, her uncle had visited and treated the entire family to a lobster dinner. Daddy had said that he was just splashing money around, but she had been eager to try something so adult and new. Lobsters were what fancy ladies ate—the ones on the TV who dated successful boyfriends. She had been beside herself with excitement as she personally picked out her lobster from the tank before taking her place at the table in the fancy restaurant. That was until the lobsters were brought to the table, stretched across her platter looking quite like it had in the tank except very dead. She had swallowed, praying not throw up. She failed the moment her uncle had picked the big metal cracker and began to work at breaking the shell. She had thrown up all over the table, ruining everyone's dinner.

That was how she felt now as she listened to the shell cracking and popping in the distant tunnel.

Pressing a fur to her mouth, she gagged and squeezed her eyes shut. "Please, please not let cave lobsters became a regular item on the menu."

To her relief, she managed to hold down her meal without too much effort. In fact, she ate until her stomach was comfortably full under Asterion's approving eye. Unlike the lobsters of her childhood, the meat resembled grilled chicken and, true to the bizarre nature of human tastebuds, tasted like it as far as she could tell.

She couldn't believe that she actually ate it. In retrospect, it made her skin crawl, but thankfully her stomach did not rebel despite the fact. She would have hated to have thrown up all over him when he was beaming with pleasure at her appetite. She had been slow to eat bear and hadn't cared much for the gamey, half-starved deer that he had cooked for her previously. It wasn't that she was a picky eater, and she still ate her fill, but it was hard to be enthusiastic, especially when she knew that there were far tastier bunnies that scurried around through the corridors.

She hated to admit it, it seemed like this deep-dweller had even rabbits beat. She wondered if he could find any more of it instead whenever he felt the need to supplement their rabbit-heavy diet to give the population a chance to recover. Vicky chuckled to herself. He certainly could pack away roast rabbit too.

"Would you like more?" Asterion inquired, his eyes gleaming with warmth as he lifted another piece of meat to her.

Patting her belly contently, Vicky closed her eyes, waved away the meat and sighed. "Nope. I'm so full, I don't think I can move. You might have to roll me over to the bed."

A deep chuckle greeted her words that had her prying one eye open to grin over at him. It was a positive sign that he was becoming more comfortable with her. Just a couple of days ago, she could barely get a dry chuff and faint smile from him. It was definitely progress, and in that moment she felt closer to him than she had to anyone else since striking out on her own.

"I would be pleased to carry you," he rumbled. "You need not ask." With that he rose, scooping her carefully into his arms so that she didn't violently pitch, which was a good thing given how full her belly was.

Snuggling into his arms, she would have purred if she could. Her stomach comfortably full and a warm minotaur who didn't seem to mind her leeching onto him as he carried her to their shared bed was all that it took to set her world right for the time being.

She was half-asleep when he set her on the bed, the stuffed mattress dipping under his weight as he crawled in beside her. Claws plucked at her hair, lightly weaving locks together with such a tender touch that she melted into the furs beneath her. There she dozed listening to Asterion's voice as he spoke of a festival for the queen of the heavens that he once saw in his youth where so many bulls had been sacrificed that the altar had been piled high with bones, hide, and fat and the air thick with the fragrant perfume of cooking meat.

Hiding her smile in the furs, she noted that most of his best memories were food related. She filed that little bit of information away and listened contently as he spun a picture for her of how life was thousands of years ago.

If it weren't for the sheer hell of the majority of the day, she could use more that were spent exactly like this.

CHAPTER ELEVEN

Asterion smiled in his sleep as he instinctively reached for the female curled up beside him, needing that contact. Although she had clung tightly to him in the aftermath of the nightmares that terrorized her nightly, at some point she had rolled away until he sought her out again in his sleep. Curling his large frame around hers, he sighed contently as her sweet feminine heat and scent encompassed him. In the deepest night and early morning hours when his world was narrowed to only her wrapped in his arms, he could allow the moment of vulnerability to admit to himself that he loved her.

In his dreams, he whispered the words, telling her over and over every feeling trapped within his heart. In his dreams, he did not have to fear that she too would reject him and want to leave him. In the end, everyone turned away from him. His parents had at his birth. Ariadne had betrayed him and left him alone in his prison for the male she loved. The love he felt for Vicky had caught him off-guard, kindling within him so slowly that he had barely noticed until the fire had ignited and burned away everything else but his love and deep, continuous hunger for her. In his dreams, it was safe to allow himself to enjoy it. Sleepily, he nuzzled her, caught up in the stories of her world drifting through his dreams.

He often dreamed of it now, that he could leave the labyrinth with her and for the first time in centuries feel the warmth of the sun on his fur and fresh air filling his lungs. Even with the devastation of the Ravening that she told him of, he would treasure every day out in that world with her. That was a world that held a possible future rather than endless years of bleak imprisonment. Soon their shared stories of their respective worlds would dry up. As it was, his stories were few enough already. He did not recall much of the Kingdom of Minos since he was still quite young when he had been thrown into the labyrinth, and even before then, he had not been permitted out into the city. All he had to offer her were views he recalled from his window and the feast day parades of gods through the streets to holy sites and back to their temples.

For that reason, it was not the shadows of the distantly remembered past, or the echoes of his sister's laugher that he dreamed of anymore. Instead, it was Vicky's world that haunted his dreams, and along with it the hope of experiencing it with his female at his side if she should have him and be agreeable. He would no longer feel the oppressive darkness of the labyrinth surrounding him at all hours. To hunt knowing that prey hadn't been lured in to feed the labyrinth's own monstrous appetite.

In the end, he was still a monster that people would fear. But it did not matter to him what they thought. All that mattered to him was his Vicky. They would fulfill each other's lives, and he would be a protector to her out there just as much as he was here.

Asterion smiled in his sleep as he dreamed of the home they might make, one with plenty of open land around them, far from anything that would feel confining. Mountains rose in the distance in his dream, the scent of the harvest on the air, and he did not miss the walls that had been his only companion for centuries. He would make a good life for his Vicky, and in his dream, she loved him as much as his own love was growing for her.

She whispered his name, a note of longing in her voice as he dreamed of touching her body, awakening her need and stirring her desire up to rival his own. How he needed his mate. She welcomed him, her thighs parting eagerly for him. He moaned as he watched his cock slide deep into her sheath, his every thrust jiggling her breasts.

"Asterion," she panted.

Curled around his female, Asterion stirred sleepily in response, still half-caught in his dream, his cock swollen and his testicles aching as he thrust forward, his cloth-covered phallus rubbing against warm feminine heat as her bottom canted back toward him, lining his cock up more perfectly with her cunt barred from him by both his chiton and the small scrap of fabric she wore. He growled deep in his chest, needing more than anything to feel that silky heat around his sex.

Vicky let out a heated breath as she writhed against him in an instinctive dance that they had played more than once. His cock jerked against her, and a damp pearling of cum at the head of his of his cock made him moan, his body quivering against hers as his hips rutted against her bottom, his claws digging into the furs around her belly. His female wriggled, soft moans filling the air around them mingling with his own deep moans and grunts. One hand gripped her hip, dragging an excited squeak from her as he increased his speed, his mind adrift on the warm sea of lust. He wanted nothing more to yank her up on to her knees so that he could shove in hard, fast and deep.

With that last fantasy, he erupted, ropes of cum jettisoning against his chiton as she quivered and moaned, the scrap of material covering her sex soaked as she cried out. His body shook against her as he held her in place, his eyes languidly drifting shut as his cock pulsed against her mound.

His female's body shuddered against him as she came down from her own release, panting all the while. She lay still beside him, surrounded by his much larger body curling around hers, as if in shock.

"What did we... I can't believe we just did that," Vicky finally whispered hoarsely, her voice a bit patchy from all her sweet cries that had filled the air just moments before. "I thought I was dreaming again and then..." her voice trailed off in an embarrassed silence.

"If that was dreaming, then I never wish to wake," he replied, shuffling closer as he banded one large arm around her middle.

To his dismay, she twisted in his arms to give him a baleful look. His eyes closed as he settled down more comfortably, his interest turning toward getting more sleep cuddled against his female. Tiny fingers twisted his nipple, startling him while sending a fresh white wave of heat into his groin.

"That's not funny, Asterion. This is really awkward. I mean, there is a difference waking up with a bit of a...reaction, but what we did..."

He opened an eye and tipped his head to look down at her. "What we did was natural for two healthy adult beings who lay in bed together night after night to do," he interrupted. "There is no reason to be embarrassed, unless it disgusts you that much."

His stomach turned, sickening him. It was entirely possible that she regretted her responses if being intimate with him disgusted her that much.

Vicky's pointed little elbow jabbed him the gut, surprising a chuckle from him as she wiggled about until she was facing him, her dark brows drawn low over her expressive human face. Though her cheeks were still a deep pink from her blush, her brown eyes were filled with concern.

"Why would that be the first thing to come to your mind? That's not it at all."

He snorted doubtfully. "Is it not?" He swept a hand toward his body. "Is this a form that would stir desire in humans?"

Her eyes drifted over his chest and abs, her bottom lip captured between her teeth. "That would depend on who you ask. In my world, there are all manner of strange beings now that we live alongside, and while many settlements are very isolationist and keep to their own, pairings between humans and non-humans aren't unheard of. I've even seen a few cross-species couples in passing, and they seemed quite happy despite likely being whispered about everywhere they go."

"People see it as unnatural," he remarked, cutting directly to the heart of the matter.

Her wince was telling, but she sighed, her fingers stroking over the fuzz of his pelt on his chest. That gentle touch worked its magic, easing some of the tension from him.

"I don't think it's necessarily even that. I think people are afraid of change and what the mingling of species means for our world. It is no longer *our* world, you know? And that terrifies people because in the back of our minds we all know that humanity can disappear as quickly as our world did, and no one would miss us. We would just be historical curiosities that would only continue on through hybrid bloodlines."

He stroked his hand through her hair, admiring the way it slipped through his fingers. "I would miss you," he said honestly, opening himself up just a little emotionally to reassure her even as he readied himself to be rebuked.

To his surprise, her gaze softened and she leaned her cheek into his touch. The corners of her lips lifted. "Despite how we met, I believe I would miss you too," she replied.

Hiding his delight at her admission, he yawned widely and rolled onto his back to scratch an itch on his chest. He did not know what crazy impulse drove him from there, but without thought, he snaked out an arm to drag his female onto his chest. Her shriek of surprise and girlish giggle made him grin as he hugged her tightly against him and burrowed his nose in her hair.

Vicky snorted with amusement and shoved at his muzzle. "Come on. We're obviously up now."

He groaned and moved to reinforce his hold of her with his other arm only for the tiny female to slip from between his grasp with a chortle. Thwarted, Asterion opened a bleary eye and watched with interest as his female stood and pulled on the leg coverings that she called pants. He admired them, wishing that there had been such a thing in his culture. Although they would be difficult to pull on over his legs, not to mention working his tail through, having a bit more protection around his sensitive parts would have been nice. But, as much as he admired them, he preferred her without them, especially at that moment.

Peering over her shoulder, her face once again a delightful shade of pink, Vicky gave him a dirty look.

"Come on, lazy, get up. I don't know about you, but I'm hungry."

He narrowed his eyes, his need stirring again in response. "If you are hungering, then it is better to remain exactly where we are."

Laughing, she danced out of his reach and shook her head. "I think that hunger is satisfied well enough."

"Is it?" His head cocked as he regarded her speculatively. "It hardly seemed more than a taste to me that barely eases the ache."

The color in her cheeks darkened. "I'm not even one hundred percent sure we should even be doing that much when we really don't know what this is between us. For all we know, it could be... what's it called... Stockham... no, fuck, I remember hearing about this... Stockholm Syndrome."

Asterion scowled. That did not sound like anything good. "What is that, then?"

"It's a fancy term some psychiatrist came up with a long time ago to explain why people get attached to their captor."

Immediately, he bristled and pushed up into a seated position. "You still see me as your captor?"

She waved a frustrated hand. "Of course not, but that could also be part of the syndrome. I mean, you're a captive too. You have been for centuries! Maybe we're both experiencing it. I'm honestly not sure if that is how it works, but it could." At his deepening frown, she sighed, sinking onto the edge of the sleeping platform beside him. "The truth is that we don't know if what we are feeling is real, and if we ever get out of here... what if we realize that it isn't? What if we end up regretting anything that we did here?"

Growling, Asterion slipped off the bed and stalked away. He needed to change his chiton as it clung to his groin and thighs, the fabric dampened with his seed. Stalking into the garden chamber, he threw off his chiton and submersed himself in the warm pool fed by the spring and another hotter spring that trickled in from the side wall. He dropped his head back against the stone, uncaring that it thumped uncomfortably. He had a hard skull that was difficult to break, as more than one creature of the labyrinth had discovered to their own folly.

Lying there in the pool, he sighed and allowed his mind to drift to melancholy thoughts until it cleared enough for him to focus on the important part of her words that he had initially overlooked. He paused midmotion, the scrap of leathering stilling on his flesh.

She was feeling something too.

Hope sprung as a live hot flame kindling in his heart. His little female—his mate, he acknowledged—was even more cautious than he was, but this was a start.

With a new sense of happiness filling him, Asterion quickly finished washing and strapped on his best chiton, one that his sister had laughingly assured him showed his figure to its best advantage, eager to return to his mate. He was on a new hunt now, one with the goal of winning her heart even if that meant that, like the protective hide of the deep-ones, he had to pry her out of her reserved shell bit by bit.

Determined to begin his hunt, he stepped inside the main chamber, and his eyes fell on her lithe form sitting comfortably at his table just as everything around them pitched violently. The flames of the cookfire rolled up high before suddenly extinguishing as the clatter of falling objects filled the air around them. And with it, his mate's terrified scream.

Bellowing in a mixture of rage and fear, Asterion raced toward her, determined to protect her from the force of the labyrinth attacking them. Barbasas had been right. The labyrinth would not be stopped. He could hear it in the creak and fracture of the stones around them as rubble fell, destroying in its path the only testimony to the centuries of his life there.

He snarled. It could throw its fury at him all it wanted. The labyrinth would *not* have his mate!

No longer protected by the magic of his sister, there was only one thing he could do now to save Vicky. He would have to go to the deepest levels below the labyrinth to the court of the gods. The temple was the only refuge available to them now, and one he had not set foot in since Ariadne abandoned him. Worse, although it was beyond the reach of the labyrinth, it was not entirely sealed from those who knew the way. He didn't have to worry about the beasts that hunted the labyrinth, but there were others that he did.

If Barbasas even dared... well, that would be another satyr that he would gladly kill.

CHAPETER TWELVE

Turning blindly to the sound of the familiar bellowing, Vicky sobbed with relief. In her mind, images of Asterion being trapped or crushed within the tunnels fueled her terror the moment her world tilted, and walls began to crash to the ground all around her. Familiar furred arms sweep around her, pulling her safely free from the rubble piling around her. How she escaped being squashed was a miracle—or perhaps was somehow due to Ariadne's magic. Who could say?

Her face burrowed against his chest, she shook like a leaf as he picked his way through the room, his sure steps making her extremely grateful for his superior vision. As relieved as she was to be in his arms, she couldn't stop her tears as she heard the broken groan of their home falling apart all around them.

Their home. He had been right about that. As much as she had feared the labyrinth and hated it, they had been safe and found each other there. It was a part of them, and now it was crumbling around them, the life they had begun to make together slowly buried.

She wheezed against the muscle beneath her cheek, panic closing off her throat with the realization that they would now be at the mercy of the creatures that shared the labyrinth with them. She shuddered helplessly beneath the big hand that worked to calm her as it methodically stroked her back.

"Asterion," she whimpered.

"I am here. I have you in my arms. Everything will be okay," he rasped, his muzzle dipping to brush the top of her head.

She could have cried at that brief contact—in fact, she was pretty sure that she was crying, but the dust in the air was absorbing her tears, leaving streaks of grime on her cheeks—but she shook her head mutely, unable to believe it.

"It will be just another moment and then we will pass through the entrance," he rumbled. "You remember. It is a little unsettling. But we will be through it quick and you will be able to breathe clean air again."

"In the labyrinth," she moaned, shivering. "No, not there, Asterion. It wants to *eat* me."

"Does not every intelligent male desire to do so?" he teased in a strained voice.

Vicky smiled weakly into his fur, knowing exactly what he was trying to do. "It's not the same, and you know it." Her breath was coming in shallow gasps now as he talked, and she could feel the tension coiling tighter within him as she walked the line of thoroughly losing her shit.

"I will not let that happen. I swear it," he growled. "I promised that I will keep you safe and I will. Have faith in me a little longer."

Shaking her head in denial, she brought up a hand to bite down on her knuckles to resist the urge to scream. She gurgled around it, hardly able to breathe as unnatural sounds closed around her in the pitch darkness surrounding them. Asterion shifted her in his arms, and one of his hands came up and closed around hers to drag it back down so that she gasped and wheezed between her sobs.

"The walls are caving in, but the entrance is clear. Breathe deep," he ordered, and she instinctively complied, her body operating with complete trust in his will.

Parting her lips, she drew in a large gulp of air before everything shifted dizzily around her and she felt the strange membranous glide around them once again. This time, however, it felt splintered, wide cracks that threatened to cut into her and bleed her dry. Vicky moaned against him. She needed to breathe, but there was no air there in that in-between place. As she slowly choked, every muscle tightened with anticipation of the worst.

There was something wrong with the portal. They were going to die before they got through.

Unable to tolerate the burn of her lungs any longer, she opened her mouth to scream out the little air that remained in her lungs when there was a loud pop in her ears and fresh air flooded into her lungs as they emerged out into the corridor. Vicky dug her fingers into her minotaur's fur, gulping in breaths as deeply as possible, shaking like a leaf while Asterion clasped her tightly in his own arms. His body trembled against hers as they stood there for a long moment in front of the ruins of their home, pressing her against his chest with a desperation that spoke of never letting her go.

Finally, he took a deep breath and released one last shudder as he looked around, his head swinging in both direction over hers. A low, grating moan echoed through the halls like something straight out of her nightmare, and Vicky's arms prickled with fear.

"I know that. I know that sound," she whispered, her body shaking uncontrollably as her every nightmare for days came to life in reality. "It comes for me in my dreams, the wall shifting as it hunts, and it always makes that sound when it comes to feed. It's the sound of its hunger and the long bones of its teeth. It wants my flesh and my blood on its stones. It wants to drag my corpse deep within its walls so it can relish digesting every part of me."

Asterion growled angrily and spun in a direction, his hooves striking the ground with fury. It kept her sane, as did the slight prick of his claws suddenly unsheathing against her bottom. It kept her grounded in him. He became the sole focus of reality in that terrible darkness as he ran, his breath billowing mightily as he charged through one corridor and then another. There was something so exacting in the path that he picked— Vicky had to believe that it was intentional, that he was heading toward a specific destination. That she could tell from the incline that they were going lower mattered little to her. There was nothing that was safe about any of the corridors, so it ultimately mattered little what direction they ran.

A frustrated roar followed them, the extinguished torches igniting and flaring high down the hall, the walls rolling as tendrils from the vines reached out toward them in a manner that she had seen before. Her fingers tightened into his mane as she watched the walls just behind them. The vines swarmed together, reshaping their masses around the stones that dragged inward until they reformed into a terrible face that had haunted her nightly since her arrival.

Its mouth opened wide, jagged sharp teeth of milky stone opening for her, a stench of rot surrounding her from all the gore it had consumed over centuries. Whatever benevolent spirit it may have begun as, there was nothing left of it but madness and hunger.

Vines rushed toward them like hundreds of arms, and Vicky screamed, drawing Asterion's attention to what lay behind him. She heard his powerful heart stutter beneath her ear and his bellow of rage and anguish.

Readjusting her weight, he swiped out with one clawed hand, tearing through a rope of the vines hurtling toward them with the force of a honed blade. The resulting enraged scream from the labyrinth was deafening as its vines writhed with an angry buzz of hornets and its face bulged from the walls, eyes widening horrifically as its mouth opened grotesquely even wider.

There was no escaping it.

Every corridor Asterion turned into, the walls rolled and reformed into that terrible visage following close behind them, the torches flickering and roaring on the walls, casting brilliance and shadows all around them as they descended deeper and deeper into the increasingly narrow halls of what she suspected Asterion called the lower levels.

The atmosphere turned dank and musty from the water she could see dripping down the walls, in some cases running in heavy streams, wetting the floors every time the walls rolled and fractured. Torches sputtered and flared in response to the moisture, somehow kept alive by a force that Vicky didn't understand. Several nearest to them nearly died as the wet tendrils of the vines slapped at the fire in an attempt to bank the flames, while others streaked along the floor and wall, slapping and writhing in their fervor to get to them, Asterion dodging them with a sure-footedness, never once breaking his pace in their flight.

Worried that the vines would succeed and plunge them into darkness, Vicky turned her face up toward his ear and shouted, "Asterion, the torches?"

His head turned, and he chuffed out a dry chuckle. "Do not worry for the torches. Our home may have been uprooted, but my sister's magic holds and lights the way. It is just a little further now. Once the labyrinth takes form, it is limited by its own laws in this place. We are safe as long as we can stay ahead of it."

"How the fuck do you know that?" she shouted.

He just gave her a quick grin and hooked a left.

The labyrinth screamed, its maw twisting in shrieking denial. Walls surged and rolled more violently, its mouth opening to release dark vines that whipped toward her face with alarming speed. They managed to get within an inch of her face, scarlet thorns snapping at her when Asterion shifted her weight and lifted his shoulder at an angle to block it. He took a sharp turn, and the wet sound of ripping flesh was loud in her ears as flecks of something wet sprayed against her. She stared at the splattered blood just as the labyrinth gave another ferocious screech from the corridors.

Numbly, she shook her head. It wanted her. It had always wanted her, and he had defied it. For that, his home was destroyed, and now he was injured. Tears slipped down her cheeks as the raging of the labyrinth grew louder. He was going to die for her... and she couldn't bear the thought of it.

Twisting her fingers into his mane, she tugged sharply, drawing his attention. He canted his head toward her, his ear turning attentively as he took another sharp corner, nearly jostling the breath out of her in the process.

Gasping, she dragged in another breath, her fingers tightening in his fur with dread for what she was about to demand.

"Asterion, you have to put me down!" she wailed, as a barbed vine came close to biting deep into his neck, dodged only at the last moment.

His enormous chest heaved with exertion. He had to see reason.

"Please!" She choked on a sob, and his heavy arm curled tighter around her. "You can't die. Not because of me. I can't bear to see anyone else I love die. Not again."

His horns swung in denial, arching in what would have been a dangerous proximity to her face if not for the fact that he always maintained perfect control around her, cautious of his superior size and her human fragility.

"No," he growled. "You are mine. My mate, my heart. The labyrinth will have to find its own. I will not fail you," he panted. "I have no intention of dying today."

Her heart pounding in her chest, she shivered at the terrible shrieking moans of the labyrinth and breaking stones all around them, the wet leafy rattle, and the tear and snap of vines. In the midst of her nightmare, she leaned into his strength, holding her pendant tightly. It grinned at her, its blood-stained teeth gnashing. Even though his breath billowed from his lungs like a freight train, he still never slowed nor loosened his grip on her in attempt to put her down.

Gradually, its shadow rose over them, the torches dimming, dark ichor dribbled down on them and Vicky slowly lifted her gaze from the thick column of his neck to stare death in the eye. Its mouth widened, the gaping darkness filling the space behind them, the daggers of its teeth dribbling with blood.

A few more breaths and it would have them. She could feel the strain in Asterion's muscles, his massive chest heaving against her. His great strength was failing, and there was nothing she could do to help.

Vicky ripped the pendant from her neck, her eyes falling on the labyrinth carved on the opposite side, before turning the coin in her fingers so that the worn face of Hera in profile stared back at her.

"If this labyrinth is yours," she whispered to the goddess's visage, "then you own all the pain it has caused. I beg you then, if ever you loved humanity, help me now."

The icy breath of the labyrinth fanned back her hair, Asterion's mane blowing forward, and Vicky pulled back her arm as the mouth began to descend, closing around them. Her love's helpless, enraged roar echoed around them as the coin spun from her fingers, the dim torch light gleaming off of it golden as it flew through the air and disappeared into the dark void.

The stones around them suddenly exploded forward, the torches flaring high and bright as the mouth drew back and twisted on itself, rippling away from them with a hideous shriek, vines falling limp to the floor.

Asterion, his body shaking with exertion, turned to look back as his pace slowed to a trot. The face of the labyrinth was gone, the distant echo of its cries all that remained of its presence.

"What has happened?" His voice was thin and ragged with exhaustion, but she could still feel the tension in his body, prepared to face anything despite his weariness.

"It's gone," she whispered in disbelief. "My good luck charm, the coin with Hera and the labyrinth... I was so angry and frightened... I begged the goddess for help and just threw it, and it swallowed it." She blinked slowly, turning her face up to him. "Do you think I killed it?"

His ears flicked, listening, and he shook his head, squeezing her tight against his chest. "No. Whatever you did, the merciful goddess heard you. Your charm has merely hurt it. Though it will not put it off for long, it grants us some time."

With an unexpected burst of strength, Asterion's pace picked up again, moving through the narrowing corridors until he reached a level room painted with the same symbol of the labyrinth that she had seen on her coin. The room was lit with torches lining the walls, and all around stood statues of the gods, their heads bowed as if staring at the staircase that descended at the center of the painted labyrinth. A soft sigh escaped him as he stopped, looking around the room. Vicky watched him, taking in the sadness on his face.

"This is Ariadne's dancing floor," he whispered. "It was her favorite place in the labyrinth. She would say, 'Brother, come dance the labyrinth with me,' and I would follow along the winding path, dancing the crane dance."

Lifting a hand, she stroked his jaw. "You miss your sister very much. It's okay to miss her."

"I should not. She abandoned me, left me here alone." His tone was so sad, so desolate that Vicky's eyes pricked with tears.

Vicky swallowed. She understood all too well. "I know how that feels. I've been very angry with my father for years. He died—killed himself—when he was certain I was old enough to take care of myself. He wanted to rejoin my mother who died during the Ravening, but I felt like he abandoned me. That he chose his love for her over me." She sniffed back the sob that rose. "Sometimes, there's no right choice we can make when it comes to love."

His head lowered so that his grief-filled dark brown eyes could meet hers in their mutual sharing of pain and loss. Asterion's soft nose brushed her cheek and he nuzzled her, his breath warming her neck.

"I have not come to this place since she left. I have been too angry. But perhaps you are right and I can find a place within myself to begin healing.

Hopefully, this will be the first step," he murmured. "Come. Let me take you home."

Cupping his jaw with one hand, Vicky smiled and nodded, her heart filling with love as he pulled his head back and turned toward the stairs. She rested her head against his chest, trusting him, her body swaying lightly with his every step as he began their descent into what, she couldn't imagine.

CHAPTER THIRTEEN

The bright false sunlight poured over him, blinding him briefly as he exited the darkness of the stairs, and he breathed deep of the fresh, clean air perfumed with life. He had forgotten how different this place was from the labyrinth in which he had been imprisoned. It was a holy place, and though part of him was hesitant to take refuge there when it was a place of the gods, he had little choice in the matter.

Vicky turned in his arms, eyes wide with wonder. "Asterion, what... how is this place possible?"

He shrugged. "How was the magic that filled my home possible? Ariadne fueled it from here, the well of the gods. The magic that she established there for my comfort and to keep the torches lit for me were linked to the force of this place so that it would never weaken or pass with age. I do not know much about the things of magic, but this place is the source of everything. That I do know."

He closed his eyes, dragging in another breath, allowing the peace to flow into him before opening them to look out over the flower-filled meadow. Insects hummed that existed nowhere on Earth as far as he knew, and in the grasses, he could see the quaking paths of rabbits as they fled before him at his first steps in the soft, eternal spring. He snorted with amusement. Of course. Of all creatures, rabbits would have found a way to occupy this place beyond. It was no wonder that there was an unending supply of them that found their way into the labyrinth above.

He could not even say for sure from where they came. Most things entered the labyrinth through the tunnels that connected to the mortal world, but there was another entrance here that his sister had mentioned as they played at the edge of the silvered lavender forest bordering the high walls of the valley's perimeter. The forest there belonged to the gods and could be a portal itself at their will, but it was one that only flowed one way—into the holy well. There was no escape for him or Vicky through there, but it guaranteed a level of safety unlike anywhere else. The deep-ones, efficient and dangerous predators that they were, could not attack them there. That alone alleviated much of his concern.

This would be a good home, he decided as he walked through the grasses, enjoying the brush of the long green leaves against his fur. The give of the soil beneath his hooves was pleasant after so many years of hard stone. His head lowered as the tension from his body melted away. Although there was a chance that he would have to deal with the satyrs and any of the other occupants of the labyrinth should they find their way to this place, he considered the likelihood of that happening minimal. Spells hid the dancing floor from the eyes of those unworthy of entrance. It always had. That was part of the ancient test of the labyrinth.

A small hand tapped impatiently his chest, and he chuckled as she wiggled in his arms.

"You know you can let me down now, right?" she said as her head swung this way and that trying to see around his bulk.

"Maybe I like you where you are," he replied complacently, rubbing his jaw against the top of her head.

She squinted up at him, her nose wrinkling as she attempted to scowl at him despite the humor lighting her eyes. She was coming to understand his playfulness, as subtle as it could be at times.

"Come on, bully, put me down. This place is great!" She squinted across the distance where the temple loomed on a hill. "Is that a temple over there?"

He inclined his head as he set her on her feet despite his own silent objections on the matter. He preferred to carry his mate, if truth be told, but he understood her desire to explore her new surroundings. The well of the gods was a magical place.

"Come with me. I will have to return to dig out supplies, but behind the temple there is a resting house where those who came here were provided lodgings. There will not be much, but it will provide shelter until I can return with whatever furs and supplies."

Vicky spun around to gape at him. "Go back? You can't be serious. No! Have you already forgotten the walls tried to *eat* us, Asterion!"

"I have not forgotten," he replied dryly. "To be more accurate, it was trying to eat you. It does not enjoy the blood of the immortals caught here and will only consume us in a fit of rage as I once witnessed with one unfortunate creature, or to eat what it really wants."

"And you don't think it wouldn't try to do just that?"

"Oh, it would want to, except without me carrying you, it would have a very difficult time. There is a reason that I survived long in the labyrinth, and it is because of this." He pointed to the gold cuff banding his wrist. He knew it looked identical to the cuff on his other wrist if not for the symbols etched into it. "The glamour here allows me to pass through the corridors unde-tected. It makes me a superior hunter despite the shortcomings of my height and bulk."

His mate's eyebrows flew up as she inspected the cuff, her fingers brushing against the engraved symbols.

"Another gift from your sister?"

He nodded. "Her last gift, the day before she left. She gave its match to Theseus." To his surprise, he felt no bitterness speaking the name of the male he hated most. "It was how he passed through safely and could exit again when no others could." He scowled. "Not even I can manage to exit as he did. The labyrinth will not detect my passing through the corridors, but I was cursed to reside here. It will notice if I attempt to break free into the upper corridors."

A sad smile crossed her lips. "She wanted to make sure you were protected when she could no longer be here."

Asterion's heart grew heavy with love for his mate... and for his sister whom he spent so many centuries resenting and mourning. She had loved him and showed him the only way she could when confronted with an impossible choice. Knowing Vicky, he understood how difficult that decision had to have been to make.

"Come," he murmured gruffly. "Enough talk of sad things and worries. I will be fine. Let me show you where we will be staying. From what I recall, our new home is quite comfortable. There is even a vast garden to supply offerings for pilgrims and for the temple." He hesitated thoughtfully. "It is possible that some of the wildlife here has been established for offerings and to feed pilgrims as well. I recall seeing hens and quail among the grasses here in my youth, and now there appears to be rabbits that are well established. I may still hunt in the lower halls from time to time to not overtax the animals here, but the food here is plentiful."

Taking her small hand in his, they walked across the meadow and climbed the marble steps that led up the rise to the temple. Just within, he could see the statues of the gods and more who had occupied the chamber of the dancing floor, but he did not enter. He would not until he was properly cleaned. Instead, he tugged his mate along with him, circling its perimeter, passing by the cool and hot springs that fed into the pools on a lower slope. Just past that was a small, elegant house that looked as it had in his youth. Its columns and walls were painted with bold stripes, red and blue with beautiful images of crocus blooms and festive scenes and men and women in celebration.

There, just within the courtyard, was another spring and pool. This one he knew was designed so that it constantly cycled, drawing anything unclean down through the far end where the mosaic floors disappeared at the edge of a crevice. Although the water returned from the ground pure through the bubbling spring, there was a second spring just behind the rear kitchens that provided water for the house. He suspected that much of what lay beneath consisted of massive reservoirs of water that helped sustain life there.

Vicky cast a longing look at the pool, and he figured it was as good of a place as any to allow his mate to rest. The water maintained a comfortable temperature, and the couches off to the side were layered with fleecy mats and soft cushions, all enchanted too by Ariadne in her tireless work before her departure so that the fabrics were as new and fresh as he remembered them.

Turning his mate to face him, he smoothed his hands down her arms and smiled. "You remain here. Bathe and rest. If you get restless or hungry, the garden and fountains are just beyond the rear down on the other side of the kitchens. I will return soon."

Her brow wrinkled with concern as she peered up at him. "You're leaving now?"

He nodded, squeezing her shoulders gently. "It is best to do so now while everything is in turmoil, and none are likely to notice me digging through the crumbled walls for supplies."

The sigh she gave him was reluctant and unhappy, but she did not argue. She cast her eyes down toward the pool, and he tucked his knuckle under her chin, lifting her head to meet his eyes.

"I will not be long," he assured her.

"What if..." she began but he silenced her, pressing his mouth against hers.

He was not capable of kissing as humans did but the simple press of mouths he could do and the responding quiver of her body as her arousal tinted the air. Drawing back, he lifted his hand, caressing the side of her cheek with the back of his knuckles.

"Nothing can keep me from returning," he assured her.

He left her there at the side of the pool, his strides quickening as they took him farther from her. As he had promised, though the halls resounded with chaotic cries from those creatures haunting the labyrinth, Asterion was able to make his way with ease back to what was left of the place that had been his home. He expected to feel rage when he looked upon it, but when his eyes fell on the broken rocks barring his entrance, he surprisingly felt nothing.

It was not home any longer. His home was nowhere else except with his mate. A smile pulled at his mouth, and he bent down to grasp the first boulder, hauling it effortlessly out of his way. Though their flight through the labyrinth had tired him, it had not completely depleted him it seemed—or his time in the well of the gods had restored him more than he thought because he made quick work digging out a passage that allowed him access into the main chamber.

As expected, everything was in ruin, but he was pleased to see that many things remained intact. He located several sacks from his storage and filled one entirely with furs before turning to fill the others with the medicines he had collected and dried. Many of the plants had managed to survive, and it would take many trips to transplant them, but he left them for the time being. He also left the bowls and utensils until he could take better stock of what the house had, but it was unlikely he would need them. Instead, he gathered his clothes and the leather tunics he had begun crafting for Vicky and, with some luck, was able to dig out her astragaloi.

Dice, he mentally corrected.

Although he was fortunate that the magic that allowed them to converse worked just as well in the well of the gods, he would need to know her language when they escaped.

And they would. The thought which had begun to take shape as a kernel in the darkness of his mind and in his nightly dreams had become fully formed after the attack of the labyrinth. He would not suffer his mate to live caged within the well of gods, regardless of how pretty of a prison it made.

One way or another, he would free her of this place.

Throwing the sacks over his shoulder, he bent to grab his labrys that had fallen from the wall, the gleam of its blade dulled with dust, and slipped back through the hole in the crumbled wall. He took no more than two steps before he felt eyes on him, and he stilled, his own gaze searching the darkness.

"You might as well show yourself, Barbasas," he called out.

There was a shuffle and scatter of stones before slowly the satyr stepped out from the shadows, his expression grim. He glanced toward the ruins behind Asterion and inclined his head toward them.

"This was the price you wished to pay keeping that female?"

"It is a small one."

The male's expression darkened. "Our home likewise suffered much damage and we lost three beloved members of our flock and many more were injured because of your 'sacrifice,' minotaur."

Asterion inclined his head in acknowledgment, sympathy stirring in his breast. For all that he had no compunction about killing satyrs who attacked him, he never wished loss on anyone.

"You will still not do what it is right and surrender the female, will you?" the satyr demanded.

"I will not sacrifice my mate," Asterion replied firmly. "I will not feed my own heart to this monster who imprisons us all."

"Not all of us have the gifts that were given to you by Ariadne," the other male rebuked, and he could not fault him in it.

"No, you do not," he agreed. "Nor are you cursed to remain here. There is a chance that you could find your way out."

"And then what?" Barbasas snarled. "None but Theseus has been able to escape, and we have no sorceress here to aid us. Your mate's prayers, while incredible, do not make her one."

"You are right. Only Ariadne could move at will by her magic. However, you may have a chance to do so while the labyrinth is injured. That you have such an opportunity is because of my mate whom you wish death upon. But I would not wait long to do so."

He walked away, ignoring the frantic clop of hooves of the male pacing back and forth behind him.

"Guard your mate well, Asterion!" Barbasas shouted after him. "Because I will not! Her blood for ours is worth any cost, even your anger. Until then, I will take your advice and pray to the uncaring gods for all of us."

Asterion closed his eyes, fighting against the anger that welled within him and tamping it down with the iron of his will. It was just words. He would let it be for now. Should any attack, however, then they would know the bite of his labrys.

CHAPTER FOURTEEN

Asterion was glad that Barbasas did not attempt to follow him. Although only the worthy would be shown the way, he wasn't entirely sure how that would work should he be followed. He would not have hesitated to kill the male to keep the way safe. As it was, only his respect for their one-time companionship kept him from slaughtering the male outright to safeguard Vicky. If the male was intelligent, he would follow his advice. Asterion hoped he did. The satyr flock needed healing as much as he did, and he did not think they would find it in the confines of the labyrinth as he had.

Although weighed down by the sacks and his weapon, it took him little time to return to the dancing floor. This time, he allowed himself a moment of peace there, the memories he thought faded rushing up, drawing tears to his eyes. His sister was there, her long dark hair trailing after her as she danced the crane dance over the painted path, her smile sweet and eyes dancing.

"Come on, Asterion. You remember the way."

His heart in his throat, he set down his load and followed the ghost of her memory through each step, the soft echo of her laughter in his ears, and he swore for a moment he could feel the touch of her fingertips against his as she turned toward him and threaded her hands with his.

"I love you, brother. Never forget."

She disappeared back into the mists of time, and he blinked away his tears. She had said that to him, and he had not paid attention. He had been reluctant that day to dance, his spirit souring from the knowledge of his bloody fate and the torments of his hunger. Though she had planned to leave, she had come to him one last time to dance the dance and remind him of her love.

He never would have had this moment—never would have been able to see Ariadne, even if in his memories, one last time—if it had not been for Vicky.

It was time to go home. His mate was waiting for him.

Asterion picked up their things and descended the dark stairs. He did not stop to admire his surroundings this time as he strode across the meadow and made his way to the little house behind the temple. Nothing tempted his eye when need and hunger rolled through him, rising rapidly as he caught his mate's fresh clean scent.

Stepping inside, he could hear Vicky moving about in another part of the house and he shivered, his body demanding that he hunt down his female. It was the filth sticking to his fur, however, that made him pause and turn instead to the bathing pool and sink gratefully into its heat. Resting his shoulders against one side, he allowed the water to soothe his aches, and he slowly and methodically washed himself. When his hand came at last to his cock, he groaned, his hips shunting helplessly against his hand.

Water lapped gently at his fur, stirred by the female stepping into the pool across from him. Even with his eyes closed, he knew she was there from the soft splashes of water as she moved through it toward him. Moaning, his eyes slid open to take in the sight of his mate, for once completely nude, her dark hair trailing in damp locks down her back and teasing the sides of her breasts.

Nothing he had ever seen was more beautiful and more precious. Nor had roused his hungers that they burned within him painfully. He thrust up into his hand and hissed.

"Vicky." The word fell from his lips in a low groan that brought a smile to her face.

As she waded toward him, the water became deeper, sliding up to cup her sex before sliding up her hips to the soft swell of her belly, and still it rose until it kissed at the bottom curve of her breasts. His hand worked his cock as he watched her come to him with all the beauty of a nymph. Soft human hands stroked down the scars of his chest concealed beneath his fur. The way she stroked them, he wondered how well she could feel them and if she knew what it did to him.

His lips peeling back from his teeth, he let his head fall back, his cock thickening further in his hand, the red haze of his hunger filling his mind. Her eyes smiled with hot pleasure as she ran her fingers lower to caress his abs and, this time, he allowed that hunger to come. Outside of the influence of the labyrinth, he did not fear it. Instead, he luxuriated in it, enjoying the primal rush of heat and blood as she explored him.

He knew the moment her eyes fell on his cock from her soft, lustful gasp and the scent of her arousal surrounding him. Under her gaze, his hand tightened around his cock, his claws biting slightly into the soft tissue, drawing forth an erotic burn as droplets of blood mixed with the precum seeping from its flat, blunt head. Every pump made his muscles quiver, yet still he did not reach for her. Not yet. He enjoyed her attentive touch too much to put an end to it just yet. But soon.

The first light touch of her fingers against his sex nearly made him cum, his balls tightening rapturously. Her lips parted at his reaction as he jerked upward in silent demand, her eyes glazing as she slipped her hand above his, stroking his length and exploring the head of his cock with interest. Her tongue slipped over her lips, and he wondered if she might take it into her mouth. His hunger clawed through his belly, and he growled. That would have to wait for another time.

Releasing his cock, his arm snaked around her, dragging her against his chest, her breasts flattening against his pectorals as the heat of her sex brushed the reddened head of his cock. His claws bit into her arms very slightly, enough to leave red lines scratched into the softness as, in one deft move, he turned and hauled her up onto the side of the pool, her legs looping over his horns as he lowered his ravenous mouth.

The wide flat of his tongue covered her entire cunt as it swept over the wet flesh. Vicky's cry of pleasure was the sweetest music, complimenting that rich honey of her cunt. Asterion lapped at it greedily, needing to capture every drop of flavor until it burst over his tongue as Vicky cried out, her legs jerking against his horns with the power of her release. Still, he continued to drink from her, enjoying every shuddering gasp and quiver of his body until he deemed that he had enough of that flavor, and it was time to satisfy the greater hunger urging through him, twisting his gut with its frenzy.

The warmth in his belly burned as if he had drunk several goblets of the best wine cultivated on Thera's fertile lands, his cock jerking against his belly.

Unhooking her legs from his horns, Asterion rose above her, anchoring her legs against his hips as he lined up with the weeping petals of her cunt. The head of his sex bumped against her slit, and a shiver of pleasure ran through him as her slick coated him in her fragrance. His eyes rolled back in his head, tongue stroking over his fangs as the hunger roared through him, its heat streaking through his veins and belly. From somewhere in the depths of his consciousness, an awareness surfaced that, in this position, he might accidentally hurt her under the full influence of the hunger.

His claws digging slightly into her hips, he flipped her, dragging her bottom up into the air so that her sex was fully presented to him at the perfect angle. Flushed dark pink with arousal, it was like a rose unfurled just for him, inviting him to enjoy its sweetest essence. His cock glided over it, every stroke coating it further with her arousal as her musk deepened with the fresh bloom of her need.

"Asterion," she panted, her bottom lifting to him, begging to be filled.

Hands slamming down on either side of her, Asterion snarled, his cock slipping into place, and with a flex of his hips it pushed through the silky embrace of her channel. Her little body quivered around him, her cunt pulsing with tiny tremors around his invasion, drawing his seed up.

His tail flicked behind him as he braced himself. His hunger raged at him to satisfy it, to ride her little body until it drew the fire from him. He labored to control his breathing, his body shaking with the way her cunt pulled at his cock at every retreat. Beneath him, his mate whimpered and moaned with each thrust, the sound ensnaring him, singing to him as his pace quickened, his hips pumping into her in an untamable rut.

Growling low in his throat, he transferred his weight to one arm, lifting the other to capture her across the shoulders to hold her in place. Her body writhed, her cries becoming louder as his cock drove into her, his testicles slapping firmly against her ass with every stroke. Her sheath convulsed repeatedly as he rutted deep, instinctively seeking with each thrust the sensitive flesh around the mouth of her womb that would open ecstatically to his seed.

So beautiful. So sweet. So tasty. The sheen of sweat on her back made her glow in the false light like a polished rare gem. His horns scraped the stone on either side of her as he bent his head, licking her back, drawing in her flavor in a manner that made her quiver, her sex clenching hard around him again as she submitted fully to his pleasure. He drove into her repeatedly, claws scraping stone and hooves digging into the tiles, as his seed rose furiously, his hunger coiling deep within, taking root just behind his pelvis.

Bellowing, he canted his hips at a new angle and quickened his pace as the first jettison left his body with a pulse of pure ecstasy followed by blast after blast of release until his cum slicked between them, dribbling around his cock from her cunt. With the last twitch of his cock, Asterion eased his hand from between her shoulders, noting the red scratches left there. The hunger finally quieted within him, he drew away, his cock slipping from her body as more of his seed escaped without his sex to trap it inside.

Vicky sprawled beneath him, a quiet moan rising from her prone body. For a moment, he worried that he had hurt after all until he heard her faintly rasped words.

"Oh my fucking gods, that was incredible."

Asterion stood, dragging his mate into his arms as he stepped easily from within the pool, cuddling her to his chest. His heart warmed when, with a happy sigh, Vicky snuggled into his embrace, her fingers playfully toying with a lock of his mane as he strode to the only floor-level bedroom. There, in the middle of the bed, he laid his mate out on it—his perfect sacrifice—before he too climbed onto the mattress, his body looming over hers with renewed predatory interest.

Vicky's eyes slowly opened, a smile curling her lips. "Hungry again?" she whispered.

"Always," he rumbled.

Her arms opened to him. "Then come let me love you."

"Always," he repeated with a moan as her legs curled around his hips and sank deep within her willing flesh. "And always I will love you equally in turn."

The End? Be on the look out for the expansion fall/winter 2022

Thank you for reading *Blooded Labyrinth*. If you want to read *the rest of the series*, then why not check out where it all began with *book Havoc of Souls*! https://books2read.com/u/mddP8W

ABOUT THE AUTHOR

S.J. Sanders is a mom of two toddlers and one adult living in Anchorage, Alaska. She has a BA degree in History, but spends most of her free time painting, sculpting, doing odd bits of historical research, and writing.

While she has more research orientated writing under another pen name, her passion is sci-fi and paranormal romance of which she is an avid reader.

After years of tinkering with the idea, and making her own stories up in her head, S.J has begun to seriously pursue writing as an author of Sci-fi Romance utilizing her interests in how cultures diversify and what they would look like on an extra-terrestrial platform with humans interacting with them and finding love.

f facebook.com/authorsjsanders

a amazon.com/S-J-Sanders/e/B07NKLYN4P

d tiktok.com/@authorsjsanders

BESPELLED BREWS

ELLE CROSS

AUTHOR'S NOTE

Hello, and thank you for reading!

This is a monster romance, reverse harem, meaning one lucky witch is the sole attention and obsession of three big orcs.

Tropes include: size difference, monster sex, fluids, found family, insatiable sex drive, graphic sex scenes with descriptive words.

Possible triggering themes: Betrayal, abduction, physical assault, deer-hunting.

CHAPTER ONE
A WITCH FOR A NIGHT

Declan Tharraka

Magic and iron clashed together at the border up ahead.

We were nearing the Gloaming District, where humans fancied a walk on the wild side. No amount of treaties would ever make humans one hundred percent comfortable being in the presence of monsters.

The thick scent of the protective wards coated the insides of my mouth. I wanted to spit out the offensive metallic taste, but I did not want to lose even this little bit of her. Her intoxicating sweetness lingered on the tip of my tongue.

I caught wind of her just as I finished my last meeting on campus. It wasn't the first time I'd smelled her either.

For months, wisps of her would cross my path. A taunting breeze—there one moment, gone the next. Every time it would happen, I swore I was losing my mind.

I was the uncontested hunting champion of my clutch. A future orc prince. Scenting a prey was one of the first lessons taught to younglings.

And yet there was one out there who had managed to evade me.

Not tonight.

Whoever she was, I would find her. And then I would know if she were truly as sweet and decadent as her scent proclaimed once I laved every inch of her with my tongue. I needed her unraveling as I tasted her, clenching around me as she devolved into mindless pleasure. She would score her nails into my flesh, and I would carry her marks with pride.

My body ached with unspent need. I needed to find her and claim her tonight.

Rothgar growled deep in his chest. "I do not like that she is out here in such an area, possibly unarmed." Disapproval quaked over his entire being. He raked his gaze over the neatly lined cottages of the gentrified businesses. The Gloaming District was one of many neighborhoods meant to look like the hamlets that the elves preferred. But without the rolling hills and ever-roaming sithen, it had an empty and soulless quality to it.

It was like walking through a cheap amusement park, as temporary and hollow as the humans that patronized them.

"You just do not want to be in this area, you mean," I countered.

Rothgar crossed his huge arms over his chest. "No, I meant what I said. Her safety means more to me. Though I can agree that I do not want to be in this area."

On that I too agreed.

As chosen blood brothers, Rothgar and Jalen were closer than kin. They, too, felt as I did. There was no doubt that if this elusive enchantress crossed our paths tonight, we would win her and claim her together.

There was a moment where I thought I lost her trail amid the dank scents wafting up from the sewer grates, but pushed on toward a familiar street where her sweetness sang to me once more. It led to a place that I knew all too well. Bespelled Brews, one of the few hidden gems in the Gloaming District.

I let myself hope. It was a popular getaway for faculty and students alike. Maybe she was catching a drink with some friends. Unwinding after a long day on campus.

That would make sense that she might be part of the university since her scent was strongest on campus.

"I think we just lucked out," I said nodding toward the pub that took up an entire corner of the block up ahead. I had not had a chance to visit this place in a while. As an orc noble, what little time I had to myself was spent hunting game to keep the store houses full in Orc Mountain. But, if this was where she was for the night, I was grateful. There were wards in place that made it impossible for the wandering mortal to cause too much upset with their pearl-clutching, prudish ways.

This had to be a sign.

Rothgar rumbled deep in his chest. It was the sound he made when he was weighing out possible outcomes in his mind. "If we find her—"

"When," Jalen interjected.

"When we find her," Rothgar amended, "if she is willing, we should take advantage of a room."

I looked up at the mainly dark windows in the upper levels of the building. They were finely-appointed suites, suitable for any number of special nights among lovers. The fact that many were vacant seemed another mark in our favor. It would be easy enough to take stock of the surroundings and secure the perimeter.

"How can we know she is here?" Jalen asked. Of the three of us, his build was leaner, his features more finely wrought. Even his ears ended in a graceful point, hearkening to a time when elves and orcs had closer relations. But he proved that he was one hundred percent orc every time he left a bloody killing circle with not a scratch on him.

"She is here," I answered.

"We have had close encounters before."

Jalen was right to doubt. After all, finding this elusive quarry had been an obsession that grew from chance for the last two years. The last month had been even more intense.

But tonight was something different. I felt it in my bones, the same way I knew when a magical wave would hit or when a herd of deer were nearby. It was a sense honed from years of hunting.

The banner that draped along the outside was further proof of our luck. "Drink Up Witches!" and "Witches Drink Free!" lit up the enchanted banner in screaming pink over the drab green cloth.

Jalen's face lit up. "Witches! Maybe there will be a true witch among them. Maybe *she* is a Witch?"

Yes, my bones told me. A Witch. She had to be.

Rothgar's growl tumbled into a soft purr. "I pray to all the old gods and ancestors that she is one. A witch for a night—"

"—Is an orcish delight," we said in unison.

Most of the students at Elfhame Academy considered themselves witches. After all, anyone with enough belief could practice witchcraft. It was a common enough religion.

But it took more than a bit of wand wielding and reciting sanitized spells to truly be a Witch, with a capital W. One descended from gods and magic.

They were legendary...and rare. My uncle spoke of his one night with a Witch in the same breath as he did his battle prowess and sagas.

That would be us tonight for I knew in both of my hearts that she was a Witch.

We would worship her as her due, and she will be ours.

CHAPTER TWO
DRINK UP, WITCHES!

CAPRICORN JADE

I stared at my phone in disbelief. My grad school prof had finally updated our class grades, and I got a C on the final. Not the worst that could have happened, but certainly not ideal.

"What is it?" Boudica asked. "What's happened?"

I didn't have the heart to say the words out loud to my roommate, so I pushed my phone in her face.

Boudica sucked her teeth, snatching my phone from my hand. "A 'C' is good, Capri! What are you going on about? It's not like you failed."

"It's basically the same thing, though, considering my assistantship." So much for creating new glyphs for my final assignment. Damned elves, always a stickler for traditionalism. Knowing that, I should have gone with the easy, straightforward answer. I couldn't afford otherwise.

My assistantship was the only way I could attend Elfhame. It was nearly a full-ride scholarship. The only thing I needed was a B GPA and my mentor's consistent progress report on me.

The only time I ever needed to be on campus was to help my mentor, Professor Snowden, do whatever he needed me to do. Apparently, as a purple-stoled, silver-robed sorcerer of the order of Merlin, the professor could not be bothered to look after his award-winning flowers. Evidently, a sorcerer's apprentice filled a dire role in dead-heading herbs and watering plants.

I couldn't complain. If that was what fulfilled the "teaching" portion of my teaching assistantship, then I would accept it for the gift it was.

It wasn't like I wanted to be a teacher, anyway. My dream was to get in with Coventry, and be part of their groundbreaking New Magics Division. Having Professor Snowden as my mentor was my foot-in-the door, since he was on the internship committee and will be crediting me as a co-author for his next paper on the labyrinth and other magical sources.

Of course, I wasn't going anywhere if they placed me out of my program.

Bo scrolled through my phone, and I was too crushed to care. "Here! Look, your final grade point average is still a B. Look! Isn't that what you need to keep your assistantship? And your overall GPA is still a B+."

I dragged my fingers through my hair, relief commingling with anxiety, setting my innards to flame. The B for the semester was the lowest B possible. It just kept me on the cusp of keeping my scholarship. Between my jobs to supplement my ability to eat and live, I barely had time to sleep, let alone study.

"I tell you, you work too hard," Bo said, crossing her arms under her sizable chest. "Your curriculum alone is already a full-time job, and you're working your assistantship and working here."

'Here' was the Bespelled Brews, our local tavern with the best home-cooked food and private label drink. It even boasted luxury accommodations, though I wouldn't know. I only saw them once, when Tia begged me to help one night when she was understaffed over the summer. It was so classy, I felt out-of-place cleaning the toilets.

Bo continued. "If you ask me, you need to blow off steam. Take time off work. Hell, get laid."

"Oh my goddess! Sex is not the answer to everything!"

"Then you're not asking the right questions!" Bo said, laughing at her own joke as I groaned.

I ordered another round of drinks to avoid every bit of this conversation. Sex and money. Two of my least favorite subjects, as they were every bit non-existent in my life.

It was one thing for my roommate and friend to treat a meal or cover a little extra every now and again. More than once, Bo had had to cover more than her share of the rent and utilities. I always paid more the next month to balance things out, even if that meant only eating meals at Bespelled Brews.

Quite another thing to let your roommate pay for everything. Boudica's family always provided above and beyond for any daughters born to her tribe, and so she didn't have to worry about stuff like finances.

And sex...

If I could find someone who just wanted to scratch some itch and not expect anything in return, then maybe. But it never turned out that way. A long list of app-based hook-ups that I'd since blocked on my contacts attested to the fact that things couldn't be casual. There were always emotional expectations, and I didn't have the capacity for that. Maybe I never would. The field I want to be in was competitive. And I didn't do the whole ultimatum well.

If a guy made me choose between them and my work, I would choose work every single time.

Thankfully, Bo didn't feel like arguing tonight, either, though she usually lived up to her warrior queen namesake, whose blood flowed through her veins.

Whatever she might have said, she washed away by knocking back the last of her drink.

I sighed and buried my face in my hands, letting the anxiety of my grades wash away from me. At least the semester was over. Just one more to go. And, if it went well, I would be on my way to Coventry.

I could do this. There was a one week break before the new term started. Maybe I could rest...

Bo nudged my shoulder. "Hey, you know I'm more the 'castrate the bastard' kind of friend. I'm no good at the 'you got this' pep talks. That's your job."

"I know, I know. I'm sorry, I'm not being very good company—"

"Drink up, witches!" Tia, the pixie who owned Bespelled Brews, dropped another round of the house special in front of Boudica and me.

"Whoa, that was fast," I said. "I just placed that order."

Tia's heart-shaped face was full of mischief. "This round's free, courtesy of those hulking brutes over there."

I followed Tia's wicked gaze toward three orcs dominating a corner of the bar. They were brutes, all right, with swagger to match. They hailed from one of the five founding families by the look of them.

I'd seen them before, but I rarely stayed on campus long enough to form any attachments to anyone. The undergrad students were completely unrelatable anyway, and I opted to take all my grad courses remotely.

The orc in the corner, who had been mostly in shadow, leaned forward so his face was in the light. His features were carved from unyielding stone, broad with prominent cheekbones and jawline. Large ropes of braids held his black hair back, which ran down the crest of his head. Silver rings graced his ears from lobe to pointed tip. Highborn orcs usually shaved down their tusks to be manageable for the modern age; his were proudly on display. His companions' tusks were also distinctive, albeit more discreet.

They must have been part of the new wave movement among the younger generations; traditional customs were all the rage among them now.

The notch of a scar in his brow gave him a rakish appeal, and it lifted when I looked in his direction. I raised my drink to him in thanks and knocked it back in one long swallow.

A near-feral gleam tinged his gaze. His companions were not so subtly checking me out as well.

Tia gave a little hoot and fanned herself with her menus. "Hot damn, all three of them look like they're about to spread you over that table and have you for dinner."

I flushed at Tia's words. I knew what I looked like, and I was nothing spectacular. Pretty in a certain light, but nothing like Bo, who was an amazon queen and goddess combined. Literally. "How do you know they're not lusting after Bo here?"

Bo snorted, a very unladylike sound. "My entire aura screams lady-loving lesbian, my friend, and those orc sons know it. Besides, I went to school with Declan Tharraka once upon a time, and trust me. He's not lusting my way."

I gulped, my foggy brain clicking together the face with the familiar name. Declan. Tharraka. That name had graced many pieces of internal forms and documents while doing my TA duties for Professor Snowden. Declan was spoken about in those stuffy academia circles as if he was the grand orc lord resurrected from myths.

What in the hell was he doing here? And why in the hell didn't he look more...scholarly? "Declan? Declan Tharraka?"

"Yup."

"From the Tharraka clan, the highest ranking, most influential clan living in Orc Mountain?"

"That be him," Bo said merrily.

Oh hell. He was my chief rival for the Coventry internship, though he probably did not know who I was. All the Elfhame faculty said that he was a shoo-in for Coventry.

The entire Tharraka clan could buy out their mountain and rule it all. The only thing stopping them from taking over their other clans were their ideas of civility and gentrification. It wouldn't be proper to continue inter-house schisms. Their ruling council worked hard to redo their image over the last few generations. It worked.

Orcs were no longer only valued for their berserker sensibilities in battle. They consistently ranked with elves and goblins for all the things that mattered: magic wielding, physical prowess, and overall bloodthirsty zeal. The Tharraka clan was accredited for that.

How in the world was I supposed to compete against his pedigree?

"Well, damn, what am I supposed to do, thank them?"

"You drank their offering, and that's enough," Bo said. "Declan has had more than enough willing pussy thrown his way. If he wants your kitty, he's gonna have to come and get it himself." An inspired gleam shone in her eyes. "Maybe he could be the one, you know? Blow off steam? I heard he's good for that sort of thing."

Bo waggled her eyebrows at me, as if her meaning was not painfully obvious.

My face flushed with renewed heat. Though I wasn't one hundred percent human—a secret I shared with no one but my adoptive parents—I grew up on the human side of the tracks, and so human sensibility was my default. We didn't talk about sex as openly as the magical community that ruled this side of town. Mating and breeding were as openly talked about as the weather.

"Oh gods, what an image," I said, willing my heart to slow down. There was no reason to think that someone like him could be interested in a nobody like me, at least not in that way.

"Oops, I forgot about their damned hearing," Bo muttered under her breath.

"What?" I asked, panic rising in my chest. Could they have heard us talking?

"Incoming." That was the only warning Bo could give before she waved her arm high in the air. "Hail, Declan, it's been a while. Rothgar. Jalen." She nodded to each orc.

"Hail, Boudica of the River tribe. Enjoying the lovely evening?" He barely paused for Bo's nod when he shifted his gaze toward me. Across the room, he was electrifying. Up close, it was like trying to stand in the path of an oncoming storm. It was both thrilling and terrifying. It took all my concentration not to squirm.

When I didn't look away first, he smiled once more. A golden light pulsed behind his eyes. It was an appraisal of respect, one that I was familiar with.

It wasn't easy for me to be a hybrid in public school, though I presented as human most of the time. I'd learned early on to stand up to bullies and earn enough respect not to be picked on. It helped that the bit of non-human that I was packing in my DNA came with a little *oomph* behind my fist.

Something told me that a move like that would do nothing against Declan.

Bo asked brightly, "What brings you down from your mountain?"

"Hunting," Declan said, his eyes still on me, his low, husky voice that bloomed with shades of meaning. "I apologize, but I do not believe we have met."

His voice melted my insides, and an embarrassing amount of liquid heat rushed between my legs. He had no right to be this overwhelming.

Boudica rolled her eyes. "You highborns," she muttered under her breath. "Declan, Rothgar, and Jalen of clan Tharraka, may I introduce my roommate, Capricorn Jade." Bo continued. "Capri and I were enjoying an end of term hang out since we so rarely spend time together anymore."

I craned my neck back, acknowledging all three of them with a nod as Bo said their names. Rothgar was an avalanche on solid legs, nearly the same height as Declan. He was an orc's orc—built for endurance and stamina. He dressed in more traditional leathers, but wore a black t-shirt that strained over his rippling muscles. Geometric tattoos graced the length of both his arms. They appeared to be moving along his skin.

I wondered if he imbued them with magic. My hands buzzed with the need to touch them, so I curled my fingers into fists so I wouldn't make a fool of myself.

Jalen was leaner, but he still filled out his shirt and jeans just as well as his other friends. Though his sharper features and ears belied an elvish ancestry, his look was all orc. His aura practically screamed at anyone to challenge his right to stand alongside his brethren.

As someone who had never fit into any community, I couldn't quite relate. If I ever do find a place where I belonged, I hoped to fight for it with that same level of pride.

Since Declan stood closest to me, I extended my hand to him. He enclosed it with both of his much larger ones. "Nice to meet you. Thank you for the drink."

"The pleasure is mine," he said in a velvety tone. "As the night is still young, the pleasure could also be yours."

Damn, he was good. Maybe Bo was right, and I should take what this guy was clearly putting out there. I'd only ever been with human males, though, and the way I've heard other girls whisper on campus about their monster lovers made me wonder if it would be physically possible...

"The fuck it will be," Bo said.

She lifted the corners of her lips into a smile that didn't quite reach her eyes. I recognized that shift in her demeanor. Her cordial mask was slipping ever so slightly—she could swing her blade and divest them of their heads in half a blink.

Declan had yet to release my hand, and so I slowly slid it away from his gentle grasp.

Anger flashed over the orcs' features. "How so, warrior?" Declan replied. He said it as a challenge to a worthy fighter rather than in a derogatory tone. That meant that he recognized Bo could hold her own against him, though he had twice the bulk and was nearly seven feet tall.

Bo wasn't the least bit concerned about Declan's demeanor. "Because she's fucking intoxicated. If I'm drunk off my ass, she's even further gone than me. She's just fantastic at hiding it."

I counted the empty glasses. Oops, I should have done a better job keeping track of my drinks. I'd never been drunk in my life, no matter how hard I tried.

Over the years, I'd gotten tired of explaining it, and so I stopped. And now Bo thought I was drunk. It was a good thing she was kind of clueless about normal human anatomy. If I were a regular human, I'd probably need a stomach pump about now.

"At any rate, she's not deciding when she's not in her right mind," Bo concluded. Then to me, she said, "When you've sobered up, then you can decide if you want to bounce on them for a bit."

Goddess, could the ground just open me up and swallow me whole now?

To my surprise, the orcs didn't bat an eye. They each spoke. "Ah, this makes sense."

"Thank you, warrior, for informing us."

"Of course, we shall agree to those terms." In a softer voice for me, Declan added, "I have noticed drink, but no food. Have you eaten?"

I shook my head. I didn't trust my voice. No one should be allowed to sound like he did. Like the promise of good sex and wishes and dreams all wrapped up in a delicious, candy-coated shell. Goddess, he could tell me to debase myself right here and now, and I would do it.

"How convenient," Rothgar exclaimed. "We can have dinner together. Jalen, pull over those chairs."

Rothgar and Jalen were already pulling chairs over while Declan swiveled the table top so it could expand and accommodate their presence.

"I'm game if you are, Capri," Bo said in a mild tone. I knew that if I said I wanted to go home, she would back me up.

Though Declan and his friends intimidated me in more ways than one, they intrigued me more. "I'm not one to turn down free food. I'm always down to feast."

"What a coincidence," Jalen said. "I'm always down to feast, too."

 The innuendo was obvious. I buried my face in my menu, even though I already had the whole thing memorized.

"For fuck's sake," Bo exclaimed, "all you guys need to pump your brakes until after the appetizers are served, at least."

All three of the orcs' dark laughter promised that they would do no such thing.

CHAPTER THREE
A WITCH IN HAND

Declan Tharraka

C apricorn was ripe and ready to be taken. I knew it as I knew my name. I offered her the best morsels of food from my plate as it was served.

She allowed me to place the food on her plate. Soon, she would feed from my hand.

Capricorn Jade. A fitting name for one so lovely, yet so practical.

Her tongue darted over her lips. Wild imaginations played vividly in my head that I barely heard a word she was saying. I forced myself to focus.

"So, you said you were hunting? What are you all hunting?"

You, I thought.

Before I could supply an answer, Rothgar spoke. "Usually, deer and other big game. Tonight, we were tracking an elusive creature," he said. His voice was rough with need. The desire to rut was strong in him. His pulse thundered for all to hear, nor did he bother to curtail the mating hum that rumbled in his chest.

"Well, that sounds like a challenge. I hope you find what it is you're looking for soon," she said.

"We always find our quarry," he promised. "In fact, we were in town to make sure we have the supplies we need. We like being thorough."

It was good that he sat farthest from Capri. He was already struggling to contain his urge to carry her off, and he was not the one seated next to her.

Capricorn was more than just a witch, though. At least to me. She was also my mate—well, potential mate, if she would have me. The dhara seeds Capricorn ingested were proof of both. They would have been detestable for any other being.

Encountering not only a true witch but my mate in this bar, of all places, was a gift from the goddess that I did not dare question. Boudica treated Capricorn as if she were an outsider. A human.

Capricorn was neither. Not that I had any problems with humans, so long as they kept the peace.

In my experience, they were loud and brutish savages, who liked to kill what didn't fit into their standards. And they had the gall to call us monsters.

We had our own stories on Orc Mountain. Cautionary tales that elders still recount to the younglings at bedtime. *Behave, or the slayers would catch you.*

Elves? They were easily accepted by the human fray, as was clear because many flung themselves crotch first onto the nearest elf they could find, female, male, it did not matter.

Did it matter that the elves would just as soon destroy a human as they would fuck them? No, because they were shiny and their damned glamour was intoxicating to the short-lived humans.

But the orc-kin are the ones that are vilified.

Humans. Weak-minded worms.

Boudica was a formidable warrior woman. Though she looked human, she was kin to the dryads. Her tribe descended from the Huntress. Divinity blessed her bloodline and spirit.

Capricorn...I could not place her lineage, but she was a witch. Even if she were human, that would not matter at all. Human, halfling, or otherwise, she was mine, and I would keep her no matter what she was.

Perhaps she kept her origins a secret because she hid from a threat? The notion that she would be a target of any evil intent infuriated me. I would destroy any who would harm her. Her enemies were my enemies now.

"How long do these hunts take?" Capricorn asked.

"You didn't come down with the supplies you already needed? " Boudica asked at the same time.

I did not like that Boudica spoke over Capricorn, but at least her interruption diverted what otherwise would have been Rothgar's ill-veiled innuendos. "We hunt in shifts, as winter is the best for certain game. Rothgar and Jalen are my chosen blood brothers. Our clutch is on rotation these next few weeks to hunt and renew the mountain's storehouses."

Capricorn's fine eyebrows lifted on her forehead. "How many are in your clutch?"

"A fair dozen, give or take," Jalen answered.

"Only a dozen to replenish an entire mountain in only a few weeks' time?" She asked. "How is that possible? And what if someone got hurt?"

The way her eyes rounded in concern warmed my hearts. She would be a fine mate and partner, and I would not allow her to be troubled. "Our caches do not dwindle down to empty. These hunts are as much for tradition as they are for genuine need."

"Yeah, and usually so they can be baptized in blood and magic for a few weeks. We have a similar ritual to keep our boundaries strong on the island," Bo said as she picked at the last of her food, brushing the crumbs from her hands. "Are you about done, Cap?"

Anger kindled in my chest once more toward the vexing female, only tempered by a grudging respect knowing that she was protecting her friend. She had a prior claim and possibly has Capricorn's loyalty, something I had yet to earn. This would not be the time to pick a needless battle.

Capricorn spied her now-empty plate, which had been full only moments before. "No, you know what? I think I'll stay." A look passed between them, one that ended in a knowing smile from Boudica.

Capricorn blushed a charming shade of burnished copper that warmed her cheeks. She would be glorious when she lost herself in pleasure, her blue hair a tangle of silk splayed atop luxurious pillows.

Hope swelled within me.

Without prompting, a server came over and swapped out the empty plate with another one laden with appetizers.

"Tia thought you might still need something," the pixie said before flitting away.

I must have looked confused because Capricorn leaned toward me and said, "Tia is the owner."

"You must be a regular if she knows you this well," I said. Tia had just secured lifetime patronage.

"You can say that. She loves to feed me, and I love to eat. So, match made in heaven."

"I should say so. I do love seeing a woman enjoying her food," I said.

Capricorn lifted one eyebrow. "Do you like seeing women enjoying anything else?"

She was one breath away from being taken on this table...

A gagging noise from across the table spoiled the mood. "Okay, please let me leave before either of you say another word. I would rather keep my delicious dinner down rather than vomit at your obvious flirtation," Bo interjected.

A growl escaped me before I could contain myself. I had half a mind to launch myself at the obnoxious woman when Capricorn giggled.

"Please don't vomit. You can leave. Don't worry about me."

Bo shifted in her seat so she could peer into Capricorn's eyes. "I don't know how you do it, but you're sober."

"And I'm also an adult," she said. It was an odd phrase, but Bo seemed to understand. There was another unspoken moment between the two that ended with Bo's retreat.

"Well, at least Tia and her crew will be here in case you need her help." Bo stood, and a wicked smile slashed across her face as she left. "Thanks for dinner, Tharraka."

"Don't worry about paying, Tia doesn't let us pay most of the time," Capricorn said, as if payment was any concern for me.

The goddess surely imbued Capricorn with her finest aspects. Her smile could disarm the most hardened of warriors. "Paying for her food is a small price to pay for a moment of your time."

"You don't have to do that anymore," she said, her mood shifting somewhat.

I studied her features, taking in her posture. She still seemed relaxed, so that was a good thing. But there was a wariness that had not been there moments ago.

I would not lose her. "Do what?"

"This," she said, waving her hand in the air. "The vibe. The act. You don't have to play this up. It's fine. You can just be yourself."

What new game is this now? "What act?"

"You know, this whole 'I'm so into you' routine. You don't have to do this. Just tell me what you want, and I can tell you if I can do it or not."

I looked to Rothgar and Jalen, who shrugged. Well, Jalen shrugged. Rothgar was a little too focused on Capricorn's every movement, licking his lips as she spoke.

I tried a different approach. "What is it you think I'm doing?"

She shrugged her shoulders, a slight movement that told me nothing. "I haven't decided yet. Nothing too crazy, or else Bo would never have introduced you to me. However, I am stuck on one tiny detail."

Her mind was fluid and quick. Just as I thought I was getting closer to her, she spoke in more riddles. "Detail?"

"Yeah, and the rest of the night kinda hinges on it."

Goddess, I had to be careful of my answer then. "Whatever it is, let me explain for you."

"Why did you slip something into my drink?"

I went still as stone. There should not have been any way for her to know that I put the dhara in her drink.

Her eyebrow quirked upward. "I know you put something in my drink, so don't bother denying it. I might not be part of your magical community, but I know when someone's being all sneaky."

She leaned an elbow against the table, the sheet of her hair tumbling down her back. How lovely it would feel wrapped around my fist. "Besides, I know every single drink that Tia serves, and what you gave me wasn't on the menu. I didn't want to ask in front of Bo because she likes to overreact, and I trust Tia not to harm her clientele, which is why I waited until now to bring it up."

For one moment, I considered redirecting the line of questioning. It wouldn't have been lying, we couldn't exactly lie anyway, but I did not want to mislead Capri. That would be dishonorable. "I did not intend to be sneaky, truly. I merely wanted to share a traditional orc brew with a lady I found attractive."

"A traditional orc brew, huh?" she said. "And the standard ale was not good enough for you?"

"Ale wouldn't have told me if we would be...compatible," I said delicately.

She took a long swallow of her drink. "Compatible. Compatible for what?"

No sense deflecting now. "Mating. I wanted to ensure that you could be mated. The dhara in your drink proved that you are." It was close enough to the truth that I hoped she didn't pick up on it.

Instead of anger or outrage as I feared, she...laughed.

"Well, you don't pull your punches, do you?" she asked.

"Why would I punch you?" She baffled me at every turn.

Capricorn burst out laughing. So I knew it was a joke, but like her, understanding was just slightly out of reach. "No, I meant figuratively. Like, you don't dance around your motives. It's refreshing. I'm too used to people skirting around what they mean. It's exhausting trying to be a mind reader."

"You read minds?" Jalen said, aghast.

Capricorn erupted into full gales of laughter. It was captivating to see her arch back like a graceful bow, her taut nipples peaking against the fabric of her shirt. I bet they were a lovely bronze shade to match her golden skin. "No, and that's the problem. It was just a figure of speech. A human habit."

Jalen's brow gathered into a furrow, and I knew that look. He was going to contradict her, and I signaled for him to stop. She wanted people to think she was human, and so I would let her. For now.

"So do you always check in with your would-be conquests to see whether they're...mateable?"

"My past bed mates were orc kin or elves, so it was a given they could take us."

She arched an elegant eyebrow at me. "But with me, you wanted to make sure?"

In more ways than you could imagine. She seemed to like my direct speech, and so I tried it on purpose this time. "It seemed efficient. No sense wasting time if that was not an option."

As before, she found it amusing.

Who would have thought that a woman would prefer such direct, unflowered language? Capricorn was turning more and more into an impossible treasure that I needed to claim and hoard.

"I can appreciate that as well, especially since I'd been wondering the same thing," she said. "So, in that respect, when exactly were you going to plan on throwing me over your shoulder and taking me upstairs to a vacant room? Like, if it's within the next ten minutes, I should probably have Tia box this food up rather than eat it—"

I needed no more prompting. Encircling Capricorn's hips, I slung her over my shoulder, anchoring my palm on her shapely backside. She laughed, the vibrations making their way into my hearts. I would keep this memory etched into my very bones.

I made my way toward the back stairs that led to the rooms above. Rothgar and Jalen would follow in our wake, I was sure of it.

"I'll box this up for you," a pixie called out from behind the bar.

"Thanks Tia! Can we have suite 17 please?" she asked.

"Honey, I will have that entire floor blocked off for you—have whatever suite you want!"

"Thank you!" And then to me, Capricorn whispered, "see, she hardly ever charges me for anything."

I made a mental note to give the pixie as much currency as she would ever need to take care of Capricorn.

A short flight of stairs later, and I saw the suite that Capricorn preferred at the end of the hall. It was a suitable location, with independent access to the street. I would have picked the same suite if I had the choice.

I set her gently on her feet and took one step back from her. Even yielding to this much space was torture. But I needed her to want me—*us*—on her own. No influence, no pressure.

She was luminous, a faint glow outlining her features. Her soft green-blue hair framed her features and delicate shoulders as it cascaded down her back. I wanted to see it splayed over the bed.

She was perfect for me. For us. I knew it. Rothgar and Jalen knew it. But did she know it?

"You tell me what you want me to do, what you want us to do, and we take you over this threshold. If you do not, we'll make sure you get a ride back to your home and ensure your safety. What will it be, little witch? Do you want to stay?"

Words were a powerful magic all their own. They kill. They heal. They bind. Especially if you meant them.

Capricorn's eyes shone like liquid flame, and her voice was clear and sure when she said, "Yes."

CHAPTER FOUR
THREE ORCS AND A GOOD LITTLE WITCH

Capricorn Jade

Declan Tharraka lived up to his reputation. I had wanted to pick his brain, maybe talk some shop about Coventry. But there was something about him...his scent, aura, charisma...whatever it was, that magically wiped all of that stuff away like none of it mattered.

He was so present and filled my awareness that there wasn't room to think about anything else.

Of course, maybe I was incredibly horny, and Bo had been right and that I just needed to get laid. Maybe, at least for tonight, sex could be the answer to my problems.

And yes, maybe, just maybe, I might have been not so secretly curious about what it would be like to have the rumored monster sex that was supposed to ruin me for all other partners.

I was not a prude. I had sex before. But being in a room with three big, hot-blooded orcs made me question my abilities—and my sanity.

Steady, Capri. He said we were mateable. Meaning, fuckable.

As soon as the door closed, any semblance of propriety ended. Declan herded me against the wall, hands planted on either side of my head. He leaned over me, inhaling my hair, a rumbling growl coming from his chest.

The sound undid something inside of me, my body temperature rising. Heat flushed over my skin, tightening my nipples until they ached against the fabric of my clothes. I clenched my fists against the need to touch them.

He took his time surveying my body. His gaze on me was tangible. "You want me, little witch. You want my hands on you."

No questions. Pure facts.

"Tell me you want my hands on you. I know your skin screams for my touch. You should not have to suffer. I can help you."

My breath came in shallow gasps. What magic is this? He hadn't even touched me yet, and I was about to come standing in front of him.

"Yes, please," I heard myself say.

A sound of approval came from him. "Those are my favorite words. I need more, little witch. You need to tell me what you want."

I sucked my bottom lip into my mouth, swallowing down a moan. A tiny whimper still escaped me.

He trailed his fingertip ever so gently over my cheek, his gaze dropping obviously to my peaked breasts. "Your body is telling me what she wants loud and clear. But what do you want, little witch?" His lips were so close to mine, we were breathing the same air. Mulled spices and honeyed mead drenched into my skin. "Tell me."

I never had to ask for what I wanted before. The (very few) sexual encounters I had were more about a shared itch that needed to be scratched, often fast.

Most of the time, I had to entertain myself.

Staring at his mouth, I knew what I wanted. "I want your mouth on me."

A growl of pleasure vibrated the air, sinking into my skin. His scent wrapped around me. "What else? Where do you want my mouth?"

I darted my tongue out to wet my lips. "Sucking on my neck, my nipples. I want to feel your teeth scrape along my skin, just a little." I step into his space and let my fingertip linger a hairsbreadth from his lip. "And I want you to fuck me with that silver tongue of yours until I come all over your face. I want your jawline drenched with my slick."

Red glazed over his eyes, and for a moment, I thought I'd gone too far. In answer, his thick tongue flicked the tip of my finger before drawing it in for a kiss. He sucked on the end. I could feel the suction tugging between my legs.

Gasping, I clenched my muscles as a fine trembling took over my body.

"Gods, is she coming just from that?"

Declan ignored them. "I will give you everything and more, my little witch. I will watch as you give yourself to Rothgar and Jalen. They will make your flesh sing and magic unfurl, preparing your sweet pussy for me. I want your lush lips around my cock while they take turns stretching your cunt. When they're done with you, then I will stuff you full. You will scream my name until your voice gives out."

I swallowed hard. The images he described painting vivid pictures in my head, every one of my nerve endings sang with sensation as if experiencing everything he promised firsthand. "I want it. All of it. Everything you just said."

The air shifted around us, filling with portent. It felt heavy, like I could choke on it.

"As you wish, little witch."

The sound of rending fabric echoed in my ears. My "Drink up, Witches" shirt hung open in the middle as Declan tore it open with his sharp claw. Reverently, he cupped my exposed breasts. Immediate relief washed over me at his touch.

His thumbs run hypnotic circles over my nipples, teasing them mercilessly. A look of focused concentration masked his face. "My only regret is that I did not file down my claws to prepare for the hunt next week. They are sharp, and I do not want to hurt your soft skin."

"Mine are still blunted," Jalen said.

"Some of mine are, too."

I glanced at Jalen and Rothgar. They had divested themselves of their shirts and stood in their loose pants. The massive tenting was obvious. They both absently stroked their impressive lengths as they watched Declan and me.

"Good," Declan responded absently. He descended upon my body, loud sucking noises at my neck before traveling down to my aching nipples. I had needed them sucked for so long. It was cruel of him to keep me waiting.

I arched into his touch, cradling him against me. I needed to be touched. My hips rocked of their own volition, but I needed something between my legs. I couldn't get off and I wanted to, needed to. The pressure building up was likely going to kill me soon.

Declan's rough, calloused hands skimmed up my legs until he cupped my backside and squeezed. "Rothgar, hold her."

I'd been leaning against the wall one moment, the next Rothgar enveloped me in his strong arms. His body was a steel vice wrapped with velvet. My back molded against his formidable chest, which rumbled in a contented purr.

I sighed.

Rothgar lifted me higher, one arm across my chest, just under my breasts, his other hand buried in my hair, tilting me so he could place a kiss on the fluttering pulse at my neck. My breaths came in shallow gasps. "Do you like how I feel against you, my beauty?"

"Yes," my answer came out in a hiss as Declan adjusted my legs, spreading them wide to accommodate his shoulders. I was on display for him. Rather than shrink from his probing gaze, I reveled in it. I had needed this for so long, but never allowed myself to *want*. To need.

And I needed it now. Desperately.

Declan trailed his fingers down my sides, his claws skimming dangerously over the surface of my skin. "I will remember this night always," he said reverently, before he plunged that charming tongue of his between my legs.

I arched against Rothgar, flinging my arms up so I could clutch at him. "That's my beauty," he said in low tones. "My good little witchling. Does his tongue feel good in your sweet pussy? Soon, he will make you come. He wants your cream all over his face. He's been waiting for so long for you. We all have."

Between Rothgar's heated words and Declan's skilled mouth, I skimmed the edge of pleasure, and tipped over to the other side without missing a beat.

A litany of wordless moans tumbled out of my mouth until the sensation became too much. I didn't know if I actually said the word stop, but the next thing I knew, Rothgar was carrying me off to the bed.

He laid me flat on my back across the corner of the bed. He shrugged off his shirt, and I was treated to a view of his well-muscled torso. His pants were next. His cock jutted out from his hips, thick and proud. Pre-cum glistened at the tip.

I reached for him, and he obliged me, allowing me to skim my hand over his length. He pumped against me slowly. Damn, I could barely wrap my grip around him all the way.

While I was entranced with Rothgar, Jalen pressed against me. He propped himself on one hand, teasing my body with the other. Gently, he caressed my leg, dragging his finger along my skin. He swiped along my seam, dipping his finger into my heated core and swirling around my tender pearl of flesh.

My breath came in eager gasps.

Declan cupped my breasts, gently teasing my nipples until they were hard. "Remember what I wanted, my little witch?" His breath was hot along my skin.

I nodded.

"Tell me with your words that you remember."

I swallowed a moan. "You want to watch as Jalen and Rothgar take turns with me."

"And?" he prompted.

"And you want my mouth."

He hummed in pleasure. "That I do, little witch. I want all of you." Declan let go of my breast and buried his hands in my hair, pulling my head back. He kissed me.

I'd never been kissed like this before. It was soft and tender, but still possessive. His tongue flicked and teased at my lips. Gently, he nipped and sucked until I opened and welcomed him inside. His tongue darted in and out of my mouth, mimicking what he had done to my pussy.

Jalen's fingers parted me, and he slid a finger deep inside, seeking my G-spot. I moaned into Declan's mouth, and it was all the encouragement he needed. He broke the kiss, but his mouth didn't leave me. Instead, he sucked on my lower lip as Jalen worked a second finger inside of me.

I gasped at the unexpected intrusion.

"Do you like how Jalen is working your pussy, sweet witchling?"

Jalen swirled his hips and ground his erection against my hip.

"Do you want to feel his hard cock inside of you?"

I couldn't form a coherent thought. "Yes, I want his cock," I moaned. I couldn't help it. I fisted my hands into the bedding, and arched my back, seeking more of the exquisite pleasure.

"My beauty likes the idea of your cock inside her, Jalen. I think she is ready for it." Rothgar's voice was strained, and he thrust into my hand. I flicked my thumb over the blunt head, and he moaned, his eyes fluttering closed.

Jalen's fingers slid all the way inside of me, and he leaned over, his body pressing me deeper into the mattress as he brushed his lips across my ear. With one strong hand, he spread my leg apart. His breath was hot as he nipped my earlobe, his short tusks scraping the delicate skin at my neck as he spoke. "Say you want me, Capricorn."

"I want you." I was desperate and aching to be filled.

"Say you want me here. You want me to fill you. You need me to. Say it."

I did, with a passion I didn't know I had inside of me.

"Good girl," he crooned, and a tremble came over me.

"Gods, save some for us, Jalen," Rothgar said.

"Be useful and hold her leg." Jalen lined himself between my legs. I felt the blunt tip of him at my entrance.

I felt a burst of magic as Jalen pushed inside of me.

I gasped at the sensation.

Declan shifted on the mattress, obviously trying to get a better look. "Gods, your pussy is beautiful. Look how well you are taking his cock. Jalen, be gentle."

"Hush," Jalen said gruffly, but then he used one hand to spread me wide and thrust a little deeper. The shallow thrusts lulled me into a sense of security, stretching me. He flirted with the line where pleasure met pain, but never crossed it.

I relaxed, opening up to him, until he thrust into me fully, filling me.

It was a heady feeling of being able to sheathe him completely.

"I knew you were made for me," Jalen growled, and then he pulled out slowly, and then slammed back into me. His hips flexed in a dance, and I followed his lead, grinding against him. I wrapped my legs around his waist, and he slid in deeper, harder.

I felt like I was being opened in two. My legs trembled with the sensation of being so full.

"Oh gods, Jalen," I moaned. He was so big.

"Fuck, you feel so good. That's it, my good girl, squeeze me. Take all of me."

"She is hungry for more," Declan murmured. "She is so wet. Do you feel it? She is all but gushing."

Jalen pulled out a little and then pushed back in, slowly. It took every ounce of willpower I had not to throw my head back and scream.

The look of ecstasy on Declan's face as I watched him through half-lidded eyes was my reward. He caressed my face. "Good little witchling."

Jalen leaned over and kissed me. I wrapped my arms around his shoulders and pulled him closer, deepening the kiss. This was a kiss that wasn't gentle or sweet. It was hard, demanding, and possessive. His tongue thrust into my mouth, sending a wanton thrill straight to my clit.

When Jalen broke the kiss, I mewled in protest.

"Relax, Capri," Jalen said, "I don't want to hurt you. I just want you to know exactly who is fucking you. Who owns you."

Jalen's hips snapped against me, his cock hitting a sensitive spot inside of me.

I moaned and realized I was tipping over the edge again.

Jalen's eyes closed in concentration, and he rasped, "She's close. Make her come."

I saw Declan's lips move as he spoke the words, "Now, little witch."

My body arched up off the bed as I came.

I wrapped my arms around Jalen, digging my nails into the flesh of his upper back as I came. Every part of me throbbed in time with my pulse.

"Fuuuck! Her pussy is milking my cock like a greedy little witch," Jalen grunted, and I felt the hot gush of his cum fill me, and I swear I could feel it mix with my own juices.

Declan moved in closer and held his cock. I felt him against my lips. The smooth head of his length pressed against my mouth.

My lips parted, and I flicked my tongue out, licking his silky skin. Gods, he tasted like all of my favorite treats rolled into one.

"That's it, my beauty. Lap him clean. You love how he tastes, don't you?" Rothgar ground out when I groaned in delight. He reached down and re-discovered my breasts and squeezed my soft flesh. He pinched and tugged my nipples, and it only added to the perfect storm of sensation.

"I want to feel your lips on me, little witch. I want you to suck on me." Declan was staring down at me intensely.

My lips closed around the tip of him, and I swirled my tongue around the head. I caressed his base, playing with the ridges there, making my way to his balls and stroking the tightening flesh.

"Fuck, yes," he moaned. "Rothgar. Go."

Jalen slipped out of me, and I ached at the empty feeling. I whined around Declan's cock.

"I am here, my beauty. Do not worry." Rothgar shifted lower on the bed and took Jalen's place. I felt the broad, blunt head of his cock nudge me. I pulled back from Declan's cock and moaned when I felt him press into me.

"That's my beauty. Take me inside of you. Take both of us." His thick cock slid into me, inch by agonizing inch. I gasped and moaned at the fullness.

Declan waited patiently for me. I licked along his sensitive underside before taking him into my mouth once more. Declan's cock twitched in my mouth, and I swallowed more of him down. I swirled my tongue around his tip, at the same time squeezing my inner muscles around Rothgar's girth.

"Fuck yes. Tighten that sweet little pussy around me, my beauty. Take all of me." Rothgar lifted my leg, angling himself for better leverage as he thrust into me with relentless energy.

And then a new sense of fullness bloomed inside of me. I felt as if I could take more, and more, and more of what they wanted to give me.

I threw my head back, and Declan's cock slipped out of my mouth as I wailed in bliss.

Rothgar knelt on the bed between my legs, and his hands slid up my thighs, raising them higher, and then he buried his face into my pussy.

I heard him groan with pleasure as he tasted me, and there was a thrill in knowing he liked what he was tasting.

His tongue laved my clit, and that was my undoing.

I must have passed out for a moment, because I came to cradled in Rothgar's arms, his contented purrs vibrating against me. The sound was more soothing than a lullaby.

"There you are, my beauty," he said, caressing my face before his intrepid fingers made their way down my body.

"How long was I asleep?"

"Not long. Only minutes." He tilted my face up, kissing me gently, at total odds to the driving pace his nimble fingers set between my legs. I gasped as I arched back in ecstasy.

"My little witch wakes." Declan's voice was low, and it was like a velvet caress that stroked me from within. He stood at the foot of the bed, back lit by the open door to the bathroom. "I am pleased. For now, it is my turn."

Declan grasped my ankle and pulled me toward where he stood at the foot of the bed.

His gentle touch soothed my tired muscles as he slid his hand up my leg. He pressed his body against mine and kissed me, careful of his tusks, his lips sliding against mine. He tasted like honey and wine, and I wanted more of him.

I pushed my fingers into his black hair, tangling in braids, and pulled his head down, directing his lips to my neck. He sucked, and licked, and nipped at my sensitive flesh until I was writhing beneath his touch. I could feel the thick length of his cock pressed against my upper thigh.

"So beautiful and responsive. Do you want more, my little witch?" His thumb circled my clit slowly, driving me insane with need.

"Yes," I moaned.

"What do you want, Capricorn? Tell me. I want to hear the words."

"I want you to fuck me," I demanded.

He smiled in approval. "Soon, my good little witch. Soon."

Declan spread my legs gently, exposing me fully to him. My heart fluttered in my chest.

This gentleness was not what I'd expected. He was not what I expected.

He brought my foot up to his lips and kissed the top of my foot. It was so intimate, so tender, that I felt my eyes burn with tears. I reached out my hand for him. He took my hand in his, and then he kissed my palm. I felt it from my pussy through to my heart.

"You are a wonder, my Capricorn," he whispered.

"Fill me," I said, reaching out for him. "Please."

He crawled up the bed, and then he eased the head of his cock into my pussy. I felt the delicious stretch, and then he thrust in, hard and deep. I gasped at the depth of him.

He captured my lips in another deep kiss, his tongue stroking against mine. He kissed a line down my jaw, and then pulled away, planting his hands on either side of me so he could thrust into me again, a steady rhythm, in and out.

He gazed down at me. A red washed over his eyes once more, but this time I knew what it meant. It was his control hitting a breaking point, and, goddess, help me, I wanted to see him break.

"Remember what I said, my little witch," he cooed at me, his gentle voice at odds with his quickening pace, at how his hips snapped against me. "What did I want?"

My mind was a blur, trying to pull together a semblance of coherent thought. I whined when he stopped fully sheathed within me. He leaned against me, grinding the soft ridges around his base against me.

Now I knew their purpose. I moaned as the ridges teased against my clit. Gods, I needed more friction.

"Answer me, and I will give you what you crave."

Damn him. I scrambled for coherence. What the hell did he want? "You would stuff me and make me scream until my voice gave out."

A savage smile slashed across face. "That is right, my little witch. And what did I want you to scream?"

"Your name."

Blessed goddess, Declan started moving again.

Red shone through his eyes. He shifted his position, so he had leverage and drove into me like an unstoppable piston. "That's my good little witch. Now scream."

Pleasure raked over me as my orgasm locked my body into an arch, and I screamed. His name spilled from my mouth like a litany, over and over, a blessing and a curse mixed in one.

Declan wasn't done.

"Yes," I encouraged him. "Harder, faster."

He growled in response, clamping one hand on my hip and wrapping the other around my neck. He fucked me. Hard. My hips bucked against him as he thrust into me over and over until the pleasure became so intense that I was almost afraid.

I cried out his name, because it was the only word I knew, the only one that existed. Pressure built up inside me until it coiled between pleasure and pain. My heart pounded as my pussy squeezed him, and when it all became too much as if I would burst apart, I felt him come deeply inside me.

He kept pounding against my body as he came, and even though I was limp and wrung out, I wanted more. It was like I couldn't get enough of him.

I felt my eyes burn with unshed tears, and I fought desperately to keep them in.

Declan's arms folded, supporting most of his weight as his hips settled on top of me. I wrapped my arms around him, burying my face against the valley between his neck and chest. I breathed in deeply, his spicy aroma mingled with a sweet scent reminded me of baking cookies. He smelled like home.

Damn him for making me feel like this. He had no business making me feel like I was falling for him. I'd never felt this way before about anyone, and I would be damned if I would be another notch in his oversized belt.

Even knowing all of that, if he wanted more from me, I would let him. Goddess save me. I'd never felt this good, and I had never felt more valued.

And dammit, I did not know how much I needed praise, how much of myself I would give for it.

He stroked my hair. "You're so beautiful."

I wasn't sure if he was just saying it, or if he was being honest. "You don't have to say that."

He laughed. "I am not saying it to be nice, little witch. I am saying it because it is the truth."

"Your truth maybe," I scoffed.

Rothgar stroked his fingers through my hair. "You would say that after three orc sons ravished you to the point of exhaustion?"

"Exhaustion? Speak for yourself, I could go again," Jalen called from the door, gripping his massive erection.

"Shut up, so can I," Rothgar shot back. "Maybe you should focus more on the privacy wards than your cock."

Jalen scoffed in mock anger. "And miss seeing Capricorn being drilled into the bed by Declan? No, thank you. Besides, the wards are plenty strong."

"See how we all want you again. And I am not done with my turn yet." To punctuate his point, Declan's cock twitched inside of me, and I couldn't help but giggle.

Rothgar took advantage of the situation by nuzzling my neck and making me laugh for real.

Declan hummed in pleasure. "I love how you grip me so possessively." His weight on me was delicious, like a living blanket. It felt good to have someone on top of me, to feel him so close to me.

Problem was, this sort of thing could get addicting. I was in a lust-fueled free fall toward emotional damage and trauma. To be wanted, needed...I could see what he—they—offered in this fantasy bubble. I could see myself being with these three. How could I not? They said all the right things. And the sex...

Dammit, I wasn't falling; I was already there. I was already picturing myself being with them. Having more of...this.

What the hell was wrong with me? I should be past the point where I go gaga for someone just because they paid me any attention.

The sex was amazing, and I was feeling giddy and light. Hell, Declan's massive cock was still inside me. That was the reason I was feeling this way, right?

I couldn't be falling for three orcs, no matter how sweet they were. That would be absurd. One-night stands were not the basis of an actual relationship.

Still, as I laid there, with Declan looking down at me, I thought I could fall for him. I wanted to want to be with him. I could see myself being with him, with them, and that scared me.

Worse...the loss of them would be devastating.

Better to keep my distance now, and protect myself before I get even more wrapped up than I already am. This was supposed to be one night, one itch that we could all scratch together. To think this could be anything more wouldn't help anyone. "So, can I ask you something?"

"Anything, my witch. Ask and it shall be yours."

Rothgar grunted his assent.

"Would I be able to use the bathroom?"

CHAPTER FIVE
THE MORNING AFTER

CAPRICORN JADE

Night blurred into morning in a tangle of limbs. I was stretched and contorted into more positions than I ever thought possible, wrenching out every morsel of pleasure imaginable.

Declan made good on my promise that I would scream his name until my voice gave out.

All the while, Declan, Rothgar, and Jalen took turns claiming me. Sometimes together, sometimes apart, always with lavish praise woven into dirty talk.

"You are close, my little witch. I can feel it. You are gripping me so well, I never want to leave you." Declan's sure thrusts hit the right spot inside of my pussy. His fingers stroked my clit faster, locking me into a familiar spiral of ecstasy.

I moaned around Rothgar's cock, swallowing him down ever deeper.

"Yes, just like that, my beauty," Rothgar crooned. He pulled against the knot of my hair, positioning me as he needed. His breaths came in shallow gasps as he grew impossibly hard. With a deep growl, he spilled deep against the back of my throat, his powerful hands securing me as he emptied every last bit of himself with a final shudder.

Declan was next. His hand clamped on my hip while he drove into me harder. Faster.

I dug my fingers into Rothgar's thighs as pleasure rolled over my body. My hips rocked back as I wailed, nonsense words tumbling from my mouth as my orgasm overtook me.

Even so, Declan plowed on until he was finally, finally spent.

My limbs trembled with exertion as I collapsed in a heap where I'd been stretched out over a chair. I didn't care that I was sticky with sweat, slick, and seed. The weight of my academic future could have crashed down upon me, and I would have taken it without flinching.

A male chuckle rumbled against my cheek. Jalen had scooped me up in his arms and I hadn't realized it until now. I wanted to stare at his beautiful face, but I couldn't quite lift my head. "Where are we going?" I asked, my voice husky.

He shifted me up so he could kiss my temple. "We are going to wash a good little witch before we feed her." He turned on the shower without jostling me.

"Are you joining me?" I asked.

"I can if you would like."

"I didn't want you to feel left out."

A reddish gleam tinged his eye, promising wickedness. Instead, he traced a gentle finger along my cheek and over my lips. "Do not worry, my Capricorn. I plundered you plenty over the course of the night, if you recall."

My cheeks bloomed with heat, as I did indeed recall. His words, his touch, the way he gripped my neck...

He stepped into the hot shower, still carrying me. "But I will never turn down an invitation from you."

A thorough shower later, and I was towel-dried and clothed in one of the tavern's robes. The fabric was as airy and light as clouds. I sighed as Declan wrapped it around me.

Beyond him, I saw a neat stack of clothes folded on the foot of the bed.

"Your Tia has provided these clothes from her store rooms," Declan said, "but you shall not need them for the moment."

Without further comment, he swept me off my feet and carried me to the breakfast table which was laden with silver-domed dishes.

"These had been delivered a few moments before," Declan said. "If Jalen was going to take any longer with you in the shower, we would have had to speed up matters a bit.

Jalen snorted. "I would have loved to see you try."

In that moment, it was as if the air was sucked out of the room. Pressure as if from a coming storm pushed against me. I didn't like it. It felt like some kind of dominance game, and I wouldn't participate in it.

Especially within a close-knit clutch. A one-night stand with a stranger shouldn't trump a relationship like that. Not over me, at least.

"So what did we order?" I said.

Like rainfall, the immediately dissolved the tension in the room.

Declan sat me down on his lap as Rothgar uncovered the dishes, revealing all my favorite breakfast foods. As delectable as it all looked, I reached for the coffee decanter first. Tia's coffee was to die for. The source of her coffee beans and roaster were strictly confidential, and I understood why.

I savored my first sip with a deep and low moan.

Declan's hand ranged all over my back. "We will need to keep this on tap, given how much you love it."

"No worries about that. Tia's already given me free reign with this." I leaned against Declan's formidable chest and he fed me choice pieces of the breakfast meats and eggs. Rothgar slathered the appropriate amount of butter and whipped cream all over the waffles which was to say that the waffle was barely visible after he was done.

Salacious sex followed by my favorite breakfast and coffee? All in all, this was the best morning I could possibly have envisioned, and went a long way to renew my outlook on my final term of the academic semester.

They asked about my plans for the rest of the school year, and if I had any plans afterward. I didn't want to mention Coventry, as it was such a gigantic leap. So I deferred to other

"So I am assuming that since you are doing all of this that means you are not staying for too much longer," I said.

Rothgar's leathers were already on and even as I ate, somehow Jalen went from wearing his loose pants and top to his full gear including a utility belt that slung across his hips. There were also leather harnesses that wrapped around his shoulders and though they were empty I could see where he would have been able to stash various weapons including a sword or rod of some sort that could be hidden within a spine sheath.

"Yes unfortunately our hunt cannot be delayed any longer. Plus we have an errand that an elder at Elfhame wants us to look into."

Elfhame? It was on the tip of my tongue to mention that I went there too and to ask which elder and possibly, which assignment. After all, the faculty loved him or at the very least loved his family's name. Maybe he knew about Coventry or maybe this assignment had something to do with that anyway.

Though curiosity ignited within me, it didn't feel right asking about that sort of stuff now. It still felt very real, and I wanted to keep this fantasy bubble just a while longer. I would be back in the academic fray soon enough and for once in my life I was just going to let myself enjoy the present and not worry about what might happen in the future.

And so I let myself be charmed by the three orcs, as we swapped stories about neutral subjects like class work and professors and allowed Declan to feed me from his hand. When I had my fill, which was embarrassingly a lot, I realized that Declan hadn't eaten more than a few bites.

"You are supposed to leave soon and you barely ate anything," I told him.

A devilish claim sparkle in his eye. "That is because I wished to keep your taste on my tongue." He had me on the table where my plate had been. Somehow the remnants of our breakfast disappeared, and I was sprawled on top of it.

He tugged on the belt that held my robe closed. It parted easily, revealing my naked body to him. He descended on me like a man starved.

No wonder he had wanted to keep this robe on me.

Sometime later when I was finally dressed and thoroughly satisfied in every way possible, they took their leave of me. They went to the terrace entrance so they didn't have to go through the tavern. Evidently something that they were tracing or that errand that they needed to accomplish first had them going in this direction.

"You don't need to make any promises."

Declan gripped my chin tilting my head up so he could stare deep into my eyes. In that gaze, echoes of heart beats thrummed over my skin.

What magic was this? My flesh wanted so much to stay connected to him. This couldn't be. This was a one-night stand, nothing more.

Right?

Anything I might have said was taken away as he kissed me. He swept away my rationalizations with a sweep of his magical tongue. "You are ours now, little witch. Remember that. We will return from our hunt and finish this conversation. Be our good witchling and say that you understand."

The words he wanted left my mouth before I could guard them. The power he wielded.

"The room is yours until the end of the month when we return. You will use it so I know you are protected and fed."

I had a feeling that Declan would never leave unless he had the last word, and so I kept my thoughts to myself. Next week would be soon enough to establish my boundaries and tell him where to stick his overbearing head.

CHAPTER SIX
ORC NET INTERFERENCE

CAPRICORN JADE

When they left, I finally turned my phone on and saw messages from Bo.

She had been having a delightfully one-sided conversation and in it she proclaimed that the only reason why she didn't launch a search party for me was because Tia and her pixie net work have been keeping her updated on all the latest gossip including the various sounds that were unholy and demonic and thoroughly frightening that had been coming out of the suite.

My face flames with heat not necessarily because of the sex but because people had heard her.

Since I was going to stay here I might as well get ready and help Tia out downstairs. It would be fun knowing that I could work a shift that was purely optional. Besides, Bo would most likely be here soon, and she would want to know everything.

Afternoon rush was nice and steady. Not too crazy where I felt like I would want to kill some entitled customers. And not too slow where I felt like I was wasting my time. At least Tia paid her staff a fair wage, unlike my previous gig as a bartender on the other side of the tracks. The servers made a pittance and had to tolerate the attention of the bottom of the barrel for tips.

Bo had come in some time during the rush and sat in her usual corner of the Tavern. She was there for people-watching and tea-spilling, specifically my tea from last night. I would drop a cliff hanging teaser between rounds and at one point, she helped me bus tables just so she could hear the orcish play-by-play. I tried to be discreet and leave off the details, but Bo wasn't the chief huntress of her generation for nothing. She knew when I was trying to hide details and took a near-sadistic pleasure in skewering me trying to get them.

Dinner rush was steady, so I stayed and help despite Tia shooing me away. "Girl, that Declan is going to be on me for making you work too hard."

"You don't have to worry about that Tia. It's not as if he's my you know boyfriend or anything like that. It was just a one-night stand."

She arched a finely sculpted eyebrow at me. "There have been many couples who have come and gone through my hallowed rooms. Not one of them had the night that you had. That ain't no 'one-night stand,' my dear."

Bo simply nodded with a smug look on her face, agreeing with everything that Tia said. I rolled my eyes and took my tray. It was one more round of bussing and then I was supposed to clock out and head back upstairs. Declan hadn't been exaggerating. He paid for accommodations for me through a Sunday evening with a retainer in case I needed to stay longer.

It was such a short walk to campus from here; I wanted to give in to Declan's offer. For convenience, of course.

Who was I kidding? I was secretly hoping that it would be convenient for them to find me here and maybe pick up where we had left off.

My face flamed at the thought. I made a last lap around the tavern to make sure my customers had everything they needed. Scanning the tabs at the bar, I tallied all the receipts for Tia so she wouldn't have to, before turning my apron in for the evening.

My last table checked out. As I cleared it, a group of orc ladies came through. They were enviably statuesque, tall and fit, with finely honed muscles. They caught Bo's attention, who promptly rolled her eyes when it seemed she recognized them. She must have known them from her past, like she did Declan, Rothgar, and Jalen.

My heart raced just thinking of them.

The hostess seated the ladies in a nearby section. With a satisfied sigh, I pulled at my apron strings as I walked to the back.

"Excuse me, miss?" One of the orc ladies waved me down and asked me for a round of their honey mead.

"I'll tell your server," I said, and saw that the server in question was busy handling a huge order. I went to the bar to fill the orcs' order myself, and when I returned, they were all in high spirits gabbing about certain males in their lives.

I tried to keep my face neutral. Guests didn't like it when they thought you were eavesdropping on their conversation. Even as I placed their drinks around, I couldn't help but feel a sense of feminine camaraderie as they bemoan the various males in their lives.

Task nearly done, their server was finally able to make her way over to relieve me, mouthing a grateful 'thank you' at me. I winked in solidarity. Sometimes, that was the job.

I backed away when I heard the name Tharraka. I was sure that the Tharraka clan was a popular one on Orc Mountain. After all, they were one of the five founding families. Still, I busied myself arranging the condiment tray at the next table.

"He should be back from the hunt soon, and then he can explain himself in person," the one called Naz said with a shake of her head. "The update that he left on the orc net was appalling. But what can you expect from males?"

"Exactly," said another girl. "At least we know he is hale and hearty. That endurance and stamina isn't just gossip."

Naz smirked. "Haven't I told you already it isn't gossip?"

The girls erupted in laughter once more. Naz was clearly the queen bee among their ranks. Her braids, wrapped and twisted in an intricate pattern, showcased her higher status. Bo's braids were similar when she wore hers. Unique patterns, but the same meaning. Namely, that she was a high-ranking warrior who could kick ass in battle. Bo's words.

The way these orc ladies chatted, teetering and gossiping, made me conclude they were in the same class. Privileged, wealthy, and kick ass.

Which was a sobering reminder that proximity did not equate to having the same access.

Speaking of which, I should probably take myself back to my room, where I could get a head start on my capstone project for next term.

I might not come from money or privilege, but I was making moves. I knew how to work hard and save money. Eventually, I could get the hang of the networking thing and get myself in front of the right faculty at Elfhame. Coventry was well within reach. And, once there, it wouldn't matter where I came from, only what new magicks I could help discover.

"Gods, you have so much patience, Naz, I tell you. If my betrothed was fucking some whore with his blood brothers and posted about it on the orc net for all to see, I would gather my own hunt—tracking all of them down!"

Naz threw her elegant head back in a laugh. "Please. I don't mind. It's not like he's the only one getting some skin," she said, to her friends' approval. "Let him get all this seed-sowing stuff out of the way. Once I get my family's mating cuffs on Declan, though, that's another story."

The name Declan made me pause. Surely, that was a mistake. Declan isn't common, but it's not uncommon, either. Maybe there were many Declan Tharrakas...who was currently on a hunt with brothers-in-arms that also fucked around last night...

"We just have to wait until he comes back," Naz decided. "His elders are being very picky regarding tradition, and so there has been little headway in the negotiations."

"Your mother can be very persuasive," the other girl pointed out.

"Yes, between my mother and father, I'm sure they can negotiate something and all the barriers between Declan and me finally knotting will go away. Once that happens, Rothgar and Jalen will also fall in line. They're inseparable, after all."

"Thank the gods for that," someone else said in a suggestive tone that they all knew what she meant.

Sex. Lots of crazy, mind-blowing, orcish sex.

My hands went numb. It was only my server friend's quick fingers and my automatic reaction that could save my dignity and Tia's customer service reputation for taking a tumble.

With barely a nod of thanks to my co-worker, I dashed away.

Bo somehow intercepted my path and got me to a bathroom. She locked the door and, for an extra level of protection, she spell-locked it from prying ears.

"What were they talking about?" she said. "Out with it, I could tell you were upset from across the room, and knowing those bitches, I have a fair guess it was them. What did they say to you?"

I gave Bo a watery half-smile at the way she was ready to rip apart the orcs merrily laughing over my quietly crumbling heart and ego. "At first, it all seemed fun enough. Girls' night out. Trash talk guys. Same old, same old." I took a steadying breath. "But then, they mentioned something about a thing that was posted to the orc net."

Bo's eyes widened. "The orc net? That can't be good."

"What's 'the orc-net'? Is it like the Internet? Are you able to get in on that?" Bo pulled out a mobile device that I hadn't seen before. "What's that?"

"This is what I have to use when I'm home. You know, since magic and technology don't work well together most of the time."

That was an understatement. It was why I spent most of my time on campus so I could work on my assignments there without having to worry about huge glitches eating my work.

She looked at me blandly. "Of course I can. It's like one of your virtual private network type deals. You know the types that corporations have to keep their company stuff private, but you can still log in remotely. In fact... hold on a sec." A few finger taps later, and she was in. "Boom! Got it!"

Her look of triumph melted away and a gray pallor went over her face. "Are you fucking kidding me?"

My stomach clenched. "What is it?"

She looked at me, frozen, as if she realized I was still standing there. I reached for her device, which she held away from me at arm's length.

"Hey, that's not fair!" I jumped up to grab it, but I was no match for her Amazonian height.

"Capri, this is not what you want to see. You...it would be devastating."

Bo, being serious and showing this level of empathy, ratcheted up my anxiety by a factor of ten. "It's already killing me now, not knowing what it is, so you might as well just show me."

After a long moment of silently glaring at me, Bo closed her eyes in defeat. "Okay, you win. You're an adult, and you deserve to know."

She handed me her mobile, and tapped 'play' on the screen before moving away and leaning against the door.

It was definitely worse than I thought.

"It's been over a millennium since the river tribe hunted Orcs, but we still have a few heirlooms made from orc skin. I'm sure no one would notice if I added to that collection bit by bit."

I knew she joked, but I couldn't wrap my mind around what I was seeing. It looked like your average homemade porn video. Except instead of random strangers, I knew the stars. And one of them was me.

"I don't even know why I'm crying," I said. "It was just a one-night stand. I should have known better."

Bo tore the unit from my hand, her eyes flashing with rage. "One-night stand does not equate to a secret recording that was publicly broadcast without your permission!" She paced, clenching and unclenching her fists. "And what gets me is the whole host of aftercare and food. Like the entire 'boyfriend' experience...and then he does this. That's a level of emotional manipulation that I did not think Declan would be capable of."

The funny thing was, I was more upset about the fact that he already had a sworn mate. He had turned me into *that girl*. The other woman. The mistress.

My face twisted in disgust. The secret recording was despicable, but at least there were no identifying markings of me. And since I didn't make it a habit to walk around naked, no one else would recognize me from that dimly-lit body shot.

Hell, I doubted even my previous sexual partners would have even recognized me. The few encoutners I had only cared about their dick and barely touched me otherwise.

No, the truly offensive thing was being party to unfaithfulness. Cheating, low-level, douche canoe behavior. "I would never have thought Declan would be the type. Or any of them. They seemed so...honorable."

Bo snorted. "Oh, that's just the thing, sweetie. We never think that men could get any lower. Like, how is it possible for them to conceive of such things and yet here we are with another level of fuckery?"

The thought of their betrayal stung my eyes. Not that my body was out there on display or the fact that I even gave myself over to them. It was the fact that I allowed myself to trust them with something that was so powerful and emotional.

I had actually thought the night meant something, and they made me feel safe and cherished and turned out that I was just a prop for them.

So stupid.

"You should go home," Bo said. "I'll talk to Tia. Just go home."

"No," I said vehemently. "No one knows that's me. You obviously know, but no one else knows." I fought hard for my voice not to break, but I was failing. I took several calming, deep breaths.

"Besides, if I leave now, I don't want it to look suspicious. Not that they would anyway. They don't know me. For all they know, there could be a whole other heart-crushing reason I'm crying."

I couldn't finish because I was too busy sobbing and Bo was awkwardly trying to pat my back.

"Please let me kill him," she pleaded. "I already told you I am not good at this comforting stuff. I'm so much better at the hunting-down-and-skinning-them-alive stuff. You'll see. I swear."

I finally quieted. It took up almost all the tissues in the bathroom, but I dried up somewhat.

"What are you gonna do now?" Bo asked.

"If it's all right with you, I'm just going to crash on campus," I said. I practically lived there anyway. "Besides, it will give me a chance to solve more of Snowden's Labyrinth hypothesis. If I finish it early, maybe I'll have a better chance at that internship."

"I'm going to miss having a roommate," Bo said

"I don't want to abandon you. But he knows you are my roommate, and he knows how to find you. And therefore, me, and I don't want to be found anytime soon."

Bo sighed, anger still shining in her eyes. "No problem. He won't find you. And you'll always have a place with me or my tribe. Just remember that. They don't get back from their hunt for another week. So at least we have time. You don't have to run right this minute. At least for tonight, let's watch some movies and eat popcorn until we pass out on the couch," she said.

I nodded and washed my face. With a few more jokes, she pepped me up so my smile looked less watery. Not that it mattered any longer. By the time we left the bathroom, the orc ladies had left.

At least I didn't have to be reminded about Declan's perfect future mate.

CHAPTER SEVEN
LOST IN TRANSLATION

DECLAN THARRAKA

The hunting party was in high spirits tonight in the cabin. Thanks to Rothgar and Jalen, we led our clutch to a good hunting ground. All together, we had record kills. We left a generous portion as tithes to the Goddess and the old ones in the forest, and headed toward the hunting cabin to our much deserved rest. We would return to the mountain in the morning.

The captain stated we should find our heart mate more frequently, as it clearly did wonders to our focus and thus, productivity. I could not disagree with him.

At the cabin, the central fires brought out the storytellers even among the first-timers. I was not in the mood, so I watched from afar in a comfortable corner where I would not be pulled in to participate. An orc's first big hunt was always fuel for the ego, and I would not spoil their moment when thoughts of Capricorn consumed me.

I wanted to get back to her. It was not right to leave her when the dhara bonds between us were new and delicate, especially since our claim on her was not properly acknowledged. At least, the tedious rites of announcing my new intended mate had begun. I informed the clan leaders, including my Uncle Kharag, head of Clan Tharraka, that Rothgar, Jalen, and I had found ourselves a witch for a mate, so he must ready the contracts.

He had not believed us, and so Jalen shared with the clan leaders our night with Capricorn. They had been most pleased with how she had taken all three of us, especially commenting over her lusty cries. Kharag and House Tharraka's esteem rose among the five families at that moment, and my hearts soared to hear their unanimous support in acknowledging Capricorn as our intended mate–if she would have us.

Her consent and acknowledgment would be the next step, and I was eager to get that started.

Kharag himself volunteered to be present at the council meeting of elders at Elfhame Academy in order to see to her protection and care until we could return. I was relieved until he sent word this evening that he could not locate her.

He had asked about her at the tavern, and every single employee, including Tia, pretended not to know the name 'Capricorn Jade.' There were those in the community who should have been able to see her on campus or at the Bespelled Brews. Unless there was some elaborate prank, for which heads would roll, Capricorn had vanished.

"You worry too much, Declan," Rothgar said.

I glared at him, which did little good as he was watching Jalen's video of our night with Capricorn yet again. "And you do not worry enough. There would be no reason for her to leave the Tavern."

"Perhaps she had projects she wanted to get started," Jalen offered. "After all, she seemed to be very concerned with her academic performance. She probably wanted to get a head start. Which would be good."

It was true; her academics were important to her, and it showed as she was one of the best in her class. She studied under Professor Snowden, who was known for the high rate of turnover among student aides. That she had been his aide for almost two years was notable.

Two years...that was another mystery I intended to unravel. How she had evaded me for so long...

Rothgar's mating hum buzzed in his chest. "Yes, she can study all she wants while we are away. You should rejoice in that. The more she works now, the more time she has for us when we return."

Whatever he watched must have tipped him over the edge. With a rumbling growl, he plunged his hand into his pants. He fisted his cock as his gaze hungrily devoured whatever was on screen.

I rolled my eyes. "You will chafe yourself at this rate."

"More time for me with Capricorn," Jalen teased softly. Rothgar was too lost in the video to hear. I shifted my attention back to Jalen, who seemed to research something on his device.

"Have you found out anything else about her, Jalen?"

Jalen was on his tracker, which he hijacked so that he could get on the orc net.

"She is focusing on New Magics and Esoteric Spells."

Those were very hard subjects. Perhaps she was preparing her path to join Coventry. Pride spread through my chest, thinking of her ambitions. Her agile mind would be an asset to that team. I made a mental note to reach out to the Director in case he needed more recruits for the Department of New Magics Division.

Imagining her safe in her study, surrounded by piles of notebooks, pens, and midnight snacks, calmed me a little. At least, enough that I did not tear off a newly blooded orc's head when he approached me from behind to ask for help with the recent kills.

Knowing my duty as an elder to this new generation, I agreed to help. "Continue your research, Jalen. I wish to know all we can about our mate." I moved away from my brothers, even as Jalen muttered under his breath about slow connection speeds and other technologicall ills.

When I returned home and dissolved the old contracts with House Gorgo, I could publicly claim Capricorn as she should be. The other clan will not be happy. However, they would listen to reason, especially with the promise that magic would flow in the mountain once more.

I joined the ranks of the first-years buzzing with their new roles as blooded orcs. Demonstrating how I would prepare and store our kills for travel, I pried open the massive rib cage with barely a grunt. I cut out the prized organs, displaying each one to the young hunters.

I paused when I encountered the deer's heart. It was unusually large. Upon closer inspection, I saw there were two hearts, not just one. Even the captain cheered at that.

Twin hearts. This was a good omen. I called out to the rest of the clutch to finish what I'd started. Many eager hands made the work quick.

I cleaned and wrapped the hearts carefully. These would make a lovely gift. The sooner we were done, the sooner I could give these to Capricorn.

I had to be patient for an extra few days while we detoured around rock slides and impasses along the trail. These inconveniences had nullified the quick work of the hunt, but at least we would still be back before the start of term.

Imagining Capricorn's face kept me going. Needing her near me had allowed me to set and keep a brutal pace for the rest of the hunting party. No one dared complain.

Everything had reminded me of her. Her laugh. Her scent. Her wicked tongue.

A rival team had nearly ambushed me as I was thinking about her soft, creamy center, and how she tightened around my tongue.

Gods, the taste of her sweet cream down my throat was a delicacy I would hoard.

Though it felt like an entire century, Rothgar, Jalen, and I broke from the rest of the party with the captain's blessing. After a stop at one of our cabins in the foothills to clean the week's hunt from our bodies, we finally made our way back to the Gloaming District.

Something was very wrong.

I could feel it in the air as soon as I moved through the village.

Capricorn's scent was gone completely. Even though days had passed, her scent would not disappear as if she had never been here. I did not detect the subtle flavor that had haunted me for months on the campus grounds.

Her presence still called to me. The bit of her that twined with the dhara's essence still thrummed within me. At least I knew she lived. That feeling alone was the only reason I did not wage an open war upon the damned pixie who refused to even speak to me when we stopped at the tavern. Capricorn's scent was absent here, too, though it had been layered into the very essence of this establishment one week prior.

When I had reminded Tia the pixie of the retainer I had given her, she winked away from me in a flash of light, only to reappear with the bag of gold, which she hurled at me.

Though she was little, she was fierce.

I did not want to go to Capricorn's home with Boudica, at least not like this—frustrated and enraged. I would have preferred for her to invite us. However, with this sudden and strange disappearance, I had no choice.

Boudica of the River Tribe had scent markers that were easy enough to follow, and soon we were at her doorstep. It was a comfortably sized, bungalow-style town house in a quiet section of town. A little farther off campus, but closer to downtown and Bespelled Brews.

I did not like the idea of all these darkened pathways that Capricorn would have to walk to and from her classes. I would need to provide a better solution for her.

I pressed the buzzer at the door. Resonant doorbells echoed within. When the silence stretched with no answer, I tried the door once more.

"Perhaps there are other ways to enter," Jalen suggested. He looked at the entryways and scoped the windows.

"Tempting, but I do not want to disturb any wards," I said.

"This is beyond troubling," Rothgar growled. He paced the length of the front porch, scanning the streets for any sign of her. "She should be here."

"Perhaps she is back on campus, and we have just missed her," Jalen said.

"You should have planted a tracker on her," Rothgar muttered.

MONSTERS IN LOVE 559

That wasn't a bad idea, considering.

"Maybe it would be worth going in and doing a welfare check?" Jalen offered. "I could go in and out and make sure her wards are intact."

Rothgar jumped on that idea. "Yes, do that! What if she's hurt and immobilized and cannot call out?"

"Because I do not want her first impression of us at her home to be one where we barged in, uninvited."

"Don't worry, if you do, we spelled the entryway to knock any intruders back to the street anyway," a familiar voice called out from behind the door.

"Boudica?" How long had she been standing there? I hadn't heard her, and from the look on Rothgar and Jalen's faces, neither did they.

Her sharp-edged voice confirmed her identity. "Feel free to leave anytime you want. You're not welcome inside."

"What does Capricorn have to say about that?" I challenged the warrior.

"I wouldn't know. She's not here. But if she were, I could guarantee you she would repeat what I said."

Capricorn wasn't here. "Wait, if she is not here, where is she? And dammit, Boudica, open the door so I can speak to you properly."

"Hm, let me think about that. Oh, wait—No! Leave, Tharraka. You are not invited here, and I, for one, cannot be charmed by you. So take you, your friends, and your silver tongue off my property."

The warrior woman did not want propriety, fine. Bracing my hands on the threshold, I speak slowly so there would be no misunderstanding. "Capricorn was staying at the tavern, but she is no longer there, and that blasted pixie would not speak to me, and neither are you. What has happened?"

Silence. "Are you serious right now?" She threw the door open. Boudica was clothed in her leathers, her hair braided back, a weapon strapped to her back. A sheen of sweat glistened from her skin. If it hadn't been for the evidence that we had interrupted a training workout, I would have believed that Boudica armed herself before greeting us purposefully.

"You don't know why she wouldn't want to see you right now?"

I froze at her words. "I must be misunderstanding you," I said. "Your words seem to imply that Capricorn hides herself from us purposely."

"Implying it? I'm damn well saying it."

Rothgar swallowed down a roar. "I do not believe you. She wants us. All of us. She wanted to celebrate our return."

"Celebrate what, you disgusting pig? Everyone has seen that video that you and your little friends recorded, guest starring Capri without her knowledge or consent. Ev-ery-one."

Boudica's eyes narrowed as she enunciated that last word. The meaning in her gaze was clear. There was only one video that involved all of us, but how in the world did she know about it? When I asked her the question, she replied, "Does it matter?"

"Yes, it matters. It was supposed to just be for family."

"Family? Are you joking? That is something that you guys celebrate as a family?"

"Yes, because it is a mating bond that was started."

"Are you joking?" Bo fists her hair. "You just met her. Why are you starting a mating bond?"

I did not have to explain myself to this one, warrior or no, female or no. She would not understand the mysteries we held, how we knew who was ours.

Were she anyone else but Capri's roommate and friend, I would have torn her ribcage open. She was standing in the way of me claiming my mate.

Somewhere deep down in the recesses of mind, I could remind myself that Capri would be less than pleased that her friend's blood decorated her furniture.

The warrior-witch looked at me as if waiting for an answer. I ground my teeth.

"Because she is our mate, and I decided to? I don't need to explain myself to you, warrior witch."

"You do when you fuck up and share my friend's naked body without her consent to strangers."

Her words confused me, and by the looks on Rothgar and Jalen's face, they were, too. I did not let on that I was ignorant of her statement. "Explain."

She rolled her eyes and grabbed her device, tapping so hard that it threatened the integrity of the screen. "Here."

She played a very familiar video. Ah yes, there was the pretty cunt that ruled my mind, taking me so well.

My mouth watered at the sight. My already hard cock strained against my leathers, seeking relief. The growl at my back told me Rothgar and Jalen were equally affected.

"Yes, she is beautiful. I already know this."

"You are not on Orc mountain, you dumb ass. Capri is practically *human* with human sensibilities."

It was my turn to growl. "She is more than human. My dhar has told me."

She snorted. "And oh, the great orc prince would dare be with a common halfling? A hybrid?"

I raged at her accusation. How dare she question my commitment? Those things did not matter. "My dhar would not have activated with a mere human, but if it did, I would still claim her. As it is, I know she is more. I have tasted it."

Boudica sneered. "Everyone saw that, didn't they?" she said. "Anyway, she's mortified, and now disrespected."

"How so? We have displayed her pleasure and shown how well she can take my—"

Bo held her hand up. "Stop talking. Remember. Human. And don't give me that not-human crap, because even if I believed you, for all intents and purposes, she is human. Remember, human sensibilities. Not fae. Not witch. And especially not orc. Human. Like, if someone called you a cheater...or back stabber—"

Jalen snarled. "Never. We slaughter from the front."

"Yes, that. That same energy is what Capri is feeling. She's feeling like she can't show her face in public because she feels like a whore or slut or whatever. I don't pretend to understand, but what I know is that you have made her feel shame. *That* part I understand."

Shame? For what? That she can experience pleasure? There are females in the mountain who cannot.

"Well, that was a mistake, and I will let her know."

"She is practically human, despite her hybrid upbringing. She is basically a human and knows more about those cultures than she does about any other races. I don't even know your culture and we grew up hunting your kind up to a mere few hundred years ago. Some of my house's relics are still wrapped in orc skin."

I snarled. "As we have fae skin and elvish runes." I reined in the anger that coated my tongue. "Do you know where she is? Can you at least confirm that she is alive? Safe?"

Boudica narrowed her eyes at me. "Of course she's safe."

That news tempered my rage. Somewhat. "First, we will fix this and we will find her and we will figure out how to win her over."

"Good luck with that, since she has basically sworn off all of you. Besides, she is currently entering an intensive right now and can't be bothered by dumb ass orcs who think with their cocks first."

"An intensive. What does that mean?" I asked.

"At the academy?" Jalen asked at the same time. "Is she on campus, then?"

"You figure it out. I'm done educating your asses."

And the wretched female closed the door in my face.

CHAPTER EIGHT
OFFICE HOURS

CAPRICORN JADE

I knew when Declan, Rothgar, and Jalen arrived back in town. I knew when they set foot on campus.

The knowledge troubled me, because this intuition went beyond the spell craft that I wove around me to keep me hidden. No, it was a deep knowledge, one that tugged at my heart and was as basic to me as breathing. It was the same inner knowing that told me when I was allergic to something or physically off.

I craved them. Their touch, their words, their looks...hell, even their presence. I wanted to feel them wrapped around me.

And I hated myself for that bit of weakness.

This need for them should go away in a few days. It needed to. It had been so hard to concentrate, and I rarely needed help in that department. In fact, I tend to hyper focus and spend hours consumed in work. The entire world could implode and I wouldn't notice when I was in my work-flow mode.

I stood, taking a break from yet another hour of wrestling my concentration to no avail. I paced Professor Snowden's office, willing my flagging brain and body to wake up. This was the home stretch. This term would be the culmination of the previous years' work. I just needed to power through and finish what I started.

A whole new field of research was waiting for me, but I wouldn't be able to get to it until I could understand the ancient scrolls that hinted at an ancient labyrinth and its hidden wealth of magic.

Instead of making any scholarly progress, all the plants were happily watered and dead-headed. The filing cabinets have new labels and a color-coded system. I cleaned, polished, alphabetized, or trashed every inch of this office. I left Snowden's desk last.

Might as well organize it, too, as it was now a very big eyesore in an otherwise sparkling study. I quickly sorted, filed, and tossed all the academic debris that had been allowed to pile until he had a very respectable-looking surface that befitted his scholarly pedigree.

I grabbed a microfiber rag and dusted his tchotchkes one by one. I left the Key for last. A twisted bit of metal, stone, and wood that was supposed to represent the labyrinth that he was obsessed with. To me, it looked like scraps of material that someone welded together to form a surreal sculpture.

At one point, it looked like a tetrahedron, at another, a pyramid. It was admittedly fascinating, though it still held no more interest to me than being a shiny paperweight.

"Ah, my legacy," Professor Snowden said.

I jumped, nearly dropping the thing. "Professor!" I said, a little too loud. "I didn't see you return." Placing his prized possession back on his desk, I back away. A few drops of blood appeared on my rag, and I saw a slight cut on my finger.

Great. That was going to be a good look. Stain your professor's legacy.

"I wasn't expecting you back for a few hours," I continued. I hoped he would say nothing about his desk. He was very particular.

He was a wizened old man, tall, lean with wispy white hair atop his head that reminded me of a cotton swab. His eyes disappeared into the folds of his eyelids, and his wire-rimmed glasses clung to his face with magic that defied gravity. It was the only way something so large and bulky could balance on his delicate features.

Despite that, he could see extremely well, and often devoured pages of old text for hours.

He smiled up at me, staring in my general direction. "You know me. I couldn't seem to stay away." He reached for the Key. "Plus, I have a special notification to tell me if someone is at my desk."

Cringing, I apologized. "I'm sorry. I didn't mean to touch your desk. When I clean, I can't seem to stop."

"It's all right, my dear, quite all right," he patted my hand. "I understand. If I remembered you were here, I wouldn't have worried that my work was being disturbed."

A rising anxiety twisted my stomach into knots. He didn't sound mad, and he was saying the right things. But the way his eyes zeroed in on the Key made me step away from him.

Maybe it was time to take a coffee break...

"Did you touch the Key, my dear?" He asked. His tone was innocent enough, as casual as anything else he would say to me. Yet my pulse quickened, and I suddenly felt very much like a little rabbit trapped in its den.

"Only to move it out of the way as I cleaned," I said. Maybe the reminder that I'd been cleaning and organizing would make him less...strange.

Professor Snowden picked up the artifact and held it so close to his face that every now and again, some of the edge pieces clinked against his thick lenses.

I tried to act casual. It wasn't the first time that the professor had descended into one of his moods. Usually, he would mutter to himself as he tottered around his bookshelves or scowled over delicate parchment.

Silently, I went to my desk, and searched for my small essentials kit I kept in my drawer. I took out a bandaid from amid my supplies and placed it on my finger. It was already healing, thank goddess. Papercuts along my fingers were the worst.

I turned around to sit back down at my desk when I nearly knocked into Professor Snowden again. "Professor!" I yelped, jumping back. "Uh, sorry for yelling in your face. I didn't mean it."

He stuck the artifact in my face. "Does the Key look different to you?"

I blinked at it, leaning back so I could focus on the piece properly. He wasn't making it easy to inspect it. "I'm not sure, professor. I'm not an expert on it, but I suppose it looks a little different." There was an extra piece jutting out in the middle that hadn't been there, but it still looked the same. I mentioned my observations.

He studied it once more, feeling it this time rather than trying to see it. "Yes, I suppose you're right. There is a little piece. Something new, just here, am I right?"

I nodded, trying to humor him and wondering if this find would make him happier or angrier.

"In all my years, I had never seen this Key change. Not once." He turned his attention back toward his desk. "Do you recall anything different today?"

The knot in my stomach tightened anew. "I cleaned your desk, and then dusted your paperweights–I mean, your artifacts."

Snowden's face lit up. "Oh! Did you use a special solvent or acid?"

"No, just a microfiber cloth. I didn't want to ruin any finish or polish," I said.

"Bring it here. Let's have a look." His voice held the excitement of a child on Yule's morning. He took the cloth from me, and cleaned the Key, asking if he was doing it right.

"I guess," I said. "I wasn't doing anything special, just being careful while dusting it."

"Of course, of course," he mumbles. I probably no longer existed to him at this point. His entire world revolved around that damned labyrinth project. This was the first time I saw him interested in the Key.

Maybe because he had given up on it? I could understand that.

I went back to my desk, using this opportunity to pull up my portion of his study, and have him sign off on this as my capstone assignment. And, if he was in an especially good mood, have him sign off on my application for the Coventry internship this summer.

Professor Snowden cheered in triumph at something, and he was at my side. I'd never seen him walk so quickly. And his eyes were brighter than I'd ever seen. Was this what he looked like as a happy person?

"Look, it has moved once more! Another bit of thorn has appeared here," he said, pointing to another new addition, "and the metal here is smoother than before, with a bit of engraving on this stone." He offered it to me to look at it.

As I turned it in my hand, the stone portion of the Key shifted somehow, adding engraving that hadn't been there earlier.

"What kind of cloth is this?" Professor Snowden asked.

I shrugged. "It's normal. I don't even have any cleaner on it."

"Fascinating," he said, motioning for the Key again. When I handed it back to him, he started polishing it once more, as if he tried to coax a genie from a lamp. He used every bit, and like he trained his students to do, observed and recorded any unusual reactions. He was rewarded when the artifact shifted again, this time into a truly beautiful configuration.

It went from a malformed piece to a spiraling art form. Like sacred geometry in action. "There must have been some kind of solution or liquid, because it responds to this part of the cloth best," he said. "There seems to be a darker stain here that feels a little damp."

Oh. My blood. "I think I know what happened. I accidentally cut myself on the corner there," I said, pointing to the Key, "and when I noticed it, I used the cloth to stop the bleeding until I found a bandaid." I held up my finger with the bandage wrapped around it.

"Interesting," Professor Snowden said. "I had tried all kinds of magical solutions, liquids, even blood. All kinds of blood. But it did nothing before, so I stopped." He focused on me now, his eyes blazing with a curiosity that made my heart drop to my stomach.

My heart hammered within me. Something wasn't right. "Well, I see you need to focus on your work, so I'll just leave you alone–"

Professor Snowden's hand gripped my wrist. He slammed the Key into my palm and forced my hand to curl around it. He squeezed my fist hard. The sharp edges of the Key bit into my soft flesh, and I cried out.

"What are you doing?" I said, trying to gain control of my hand. The frail old professor had a grip stronger than steel. "Let go of me! You're hurting me!"

"Pain is a necessary payment for such things. Death, birth, life...pain is always part of the process." As he spoke, the meek and bumbling voice gave way to something larger, something older, beyond normal human life times. This voice was primal, as if it used to rival dinosaurs and other much larger creatures.

My hand was numb where he gripped it. I was sure that it fell from my body. "Please," I begged.

The Key in my hand shifted, and bits of it unfurled like ivy, wrapping around my hand until it became a gauntlet of sorts made of an intricate lace-work of metal, stone, and wood. It should have been impossible, yet here it was.

"Yes!" Professor Snowden bellowed savagely. "The Key!"

Shadows and darkness surrounded the professor in his zeal until they settled upon his body like transparent wings. I crawled away from him, but didn't get far.

A powerful hand wrapped around my upper arm, and it dragged me up from the floor. "You're not going anywhere. As my prized student, you will finish what you started."

"But I started nothing," I said, desperately trying to make him hear reason. I planted my feet, grabbed at anything, doing my best not to go wherever he was taking me.

"You just don't know you started something. Foolish mortal flesh. It had been you this whole time, and I couldn't see it. But no matter, I see it now. Soon. Soon, I will be free from my prison."

He pulled me along, tossing his desk aside with one hand. There, under-neath his desk, was a spell engraved in a spiraling circle.

The dark energy that pulsed from it made me sick to my stomach. Whatever was down there, I didn't want to open it.

"Finally. The final missing piece that will open the source." Almost rever-ently, he placed my hand over the middle of the circle and pushed down.

The glyphs glowed a dark light. Nothing good would happen if we ever got this open.

"The entrance to the labyrinth was here this entire time?" I asked out loud. I didn't expect an answer. Professor Snowden–or whatever had been wearing him–replied, anyway.

"Not the entrance, my dear, but the exit. And you're going to help unleash me from my prison."

"Prison?"

"I needed someone able to open it. Why you? I don't know, but I will find out when I regain my powers."

"You can't kill me!" I said desperately. "Elfhame will ask questions."

He cackles. "No one cared about the other aides, and they died long, horrific deaths," he said. "It takes a lot of blood and magic to keep this mortal flesh alive. A lot."

The floor beneath us gave way, and in the next moment, I dangled on the edge of an abyss. A black nothing yawned beneath me. My heart clenched in terror and fear. I was staring at the labyrinth, and there was something here that stared back.

I cobbled together some base spells to keep me anchored to Snowden's office. "People will look for me!" I screamed at him as he stomped on my hand, trying to cast me away. Scraping what spells and craft I could, I made an anchor to keep me in this world, where I belonged.

"Let's be honest," a voice echoed in the darkness and pressed into my mind. "No one will come for you. No one has before, and no one will come now." Something cold and slimy wrapped around my ankles and pulled me down.

My fingers slipped, and I shrieked. Snowden's maniacal laughter echoed in my ears. When the crazy man was suddenly ridiculously happy, bad things were about to go down. I knew this.

My breath rushed out of me when I stopped in the middle of my free fall. The magical tether I created held, and I grit my teeth to hold on to that sliver of power. Desperately, I reach toward the ever-shrinking circle of light.

I gave everything I had to the thin line of potent energy that kept me tethered between worlds. Intention was important. Words were important. These all fueled magic, and I needed it now.

"Please," I said desperately as the labyrinth's darkness seeped itself against my skin, forming a shroud.

Memories rushed to the forefront of my mind. I clung to the ones that filled me with the most joy. Declan, Rothgar, and Jalen appeared in my mind's eye. None of the hurt, shame, and embarrassment that I had felt this past week came up. Only the way they felt, the way they held me, the words they spoke to me. All I wanted now was to feel their strength around me. Their warmth.

The darkness wanted inside of me, needed me to accept it, and I refused, still clinging to the tether, which had stretched into a filament as fine as spun gold.

Please.

As the threshold between worlds sealed, and as the darkness wrapped itself around me in ever thickening layers, Declan's face came into view. Frustration marked his face, as it looked like he searched for something.

Or someone.

Me. He was looking for me. He was here; I wasn't just hallucinating about him.

I gathered up the last bit of strength I had and poured it all into the only name in the universe that mattered.

"Declan!"

CHAPTER NINE
A SPIRAL PORTAL OF DOOM

Declan Tharraka

"What about the fact that she might not want to see us at the moment?"

I glowered at Jalen. "She only thinks she doesn't want to see us because she does not understand what had happened."

I did not fully understand what had happened, either. Females usually demanded to be viewed as desirable. It was another reminder that though she was not human, their unfortunate sensibilities have corrupted her. Yet another thing to be annoyed at them about.

What was so shameful about experiencing pleasure, especially when that pleasure was with your mates?

There were females who could not experience pleasure, and she had had an entire night of it. What was so wrong about that?

The way Boudica described it, made me believe this entire theory was a way for human males to control their females. Considering its effect on Capricorn, it was a kind of powerful spell indeed.

We returned to the faculty aide's office, the library, and finally, Professor Snowden's office. Empty once more.

"Look here." Rothgar pointed to an area on the floor where there was a peculiar arrangement of spells. "There are spells underfoot. Something to hide from tracking."

Jalen considered them further. "Based on their uniqueness, I believe Capricorn laid them down. Let's look at what he was researching."

"Whatever he is researching is under lockdown. He even spelled his damned books to be gibberish."

Gibberish? I picked up a book. Indeed, the words were formless and would not stick to my mind.

What strange lengths to protect academic research. The elves were secretive as well, but this was, to another degree.

Some of his work looked familiar. Coventry had been tracing runes that alluded to a source of magic. However, ever since the days of the sleeping one and the chaos being known only as darkness, there have always been talks of opening up portals.

That was the job for the scholars. Out of my domain, however, when I was new when we were needed for a special kind of hands-on work, we were there to deliver.

We exited the study and added another note to the pile on his door.

A young tiefling paused in the hallway when he saw us. "If you're looking for Snowden, he's like never here." The student slipped a sheaf of papers into a drop box set at Professor Snowden's door.

"Wait," I said. "You give papers to him, though. When does he arrive?"

"He won't. Hasn't in months. He teaches the class remotely from his office."

Jalen said, "We're at his office?"

"No, not this one. I mean like his office-office. Like the one at his house or something? His TA does his grunt work, comes by to pick stuff up and drop stuff off, that kind of thing."

Hope seared through my chest. "His TA?"

The tiefling's face broke into a knowing smile. "Yeah. Her name is Capricorn, and she's a top tier pile of sweetness that gives a whole new meaning to T and A. You feel me?" He licked his lips in a lascivious way.

Rothgar grabbed the young male by his shirt front and slammed him against the wall. Nearby, a professor stuck her head from her office. Her eyes rounded upon seeing us here.

I smiled at her. "Apologies, madam. Coventry business."

Without a word, she retreated into her office and locked the door.

"Watch what you say about her, boy," Rothgar snarled. "If I ever hear you disrespecting her in any way, I will skin you while you scream. Do you feel me?"

The tiefling smartly nodded.

"Now where the hell is this second office?"

"W as this where we were supposed to go?" Rothgar asked.

Jalen chuckled. "Yes, this is the way. He was barely coherent after you scared the piss out of him, but lucky for you, I can navigate fairly well."

I did not like where this house was located and thinking that it was both close to the campus while also being off radar was concerning. We should have seen this house, this street, countless times. How many times have we walked this campus, not realizing this place existed?

Usually, when there was a supposed triangulation of magic and ley lines, the elves at least would have noticed. They gobbled up magic as a fine cuisine.

"I think it's peculiar that we had never been here before," Jalen said.

"Those were exactly my thoughts." I powered ahead. There was a sense of urgency that I could not place. Something was wrong.

A sharp pain stabbed my heart. It stole my breath. I doubled over, seeing stars.

What was happening?

"Declan? Declan!" Jalen tried to see what was wrong as Rothgar became the shield.

As suddenly as the pain appeared, it was gone. I stood, feeling as normal as I had before.

"What was that?" Jalen asked.

"I'm not sure," I said, massaging the pain in the middle of my chest. "It felt like something was stabbing me, just here." Right between my hearts.

A dark look came over Jalen's features. "Stabbed? Or did it feel like something was pulling you? As in pulling at a newly formed mating bond, perhaps?"

Capricorn!

Rage filled me, but I needed to maintain focus. Capricorn was in trouble, and every second could count. "Call the team at Coventry. Anyone and everyone. Get them down here. Now!"

I rushed to the door, Rothgar fast behind me. The scent of old magic hit me, a foul taste on my tongue. Jalen shouted a spell, melting whatever barrier was in front of me. I didn't pause, trusting in my blood brother to get the job done.

He did.

I was through the front door and tearing through the house when multiple popping sounds signaled the arrival of Coventry agents. I let Jalen brief them on our situation.

Panic seized my chest. It was a pain I'd never felt before, full of longing and loss. Regret.

When we crashed through another door, Rothgar tearing through a wall when the threshold was bespelled. I could finally smell her. Capricorn. Her sweet scent wrapped in foul magic and the tang of blood.

Her blood. She was hurt. But where the hell was she?

We were clearly in a library. Capricorn's belongings scattered about. I pushed the rage back, needing to think clearly so I could find her.

And then the most heartbreaking sound echoed in my entire being, filling my soul.

Declan!

I roared her name, willing her to hear me. Willing her to show herself to me.

"Declan, move!" Jalen said. He tossed something at the space before us, and the air shivered. The Coventry agents threw their combined might together, and with one blast, the obscuring veil before us shattered like glass.

A man with an aura of shadows laughed, stabbing the air with his crooked wand. I threw myself over Rothgar and Jalen, pushing them away from the spells flying toward them.

"You're too late!" the creature that was once Professor Snowden proclaimed. "He will rise once more, reborn from the sacrifice of flesh!"

No! I could not let myself believe Capricorn was dead. Not while her soul screamed for me.

The creature stood above a spiraling scrawl of glyphs. I nudged Jalen, pointing to the portal.

A savage gleam flickered over his eyes. "There is still hope," he said. "The portal isn't closed. There's an anchor spell."

I did not know what that signified. All I cared about was the part that Capricorn was alive and we could still save her.

"The Coventry team are armed. They will draw his fire. I will tap that spell to push the portal open. You and Rothgar need to drop him through the portal instead."

"Consider it done," Rothgar promised.

Jalen communicated the strategy to the others, and we readied to go. The team drew the creature's attention at the same time Jalen focused his magic toward the anchoring spell that Capricorn left behind.

Though miniscule, it was enough of a crack to wedge the portal open once more. Rothgar and I pushed him back. It was just enough force for the darkness to snake around Snowden's body and swallow him down.

I crept slowly to the edge of what looked like a Hellmouth. Rothgar and Jalen linked to hold on to me in case I got captured by the darkness as well.

I couldn't see Capricorn, but dammit, I could feel her. She needed me. She yelled for me.

A shining spot on the edge of the portal caught my eye. Her anchor. Of course. It was an elegant spell, one I had not seen before. I covered the spot with my hand and instantly felt something like a rope grow taut beneath my hand.

I pulled on it, careful not to pull too hard, or risk breaking the tether. All the while, I imagined Capricorn, reaching for her in the place between my hearts. The place where I felt her pulling, calling for me.

The Rothgar and Jalen received help from the rest of the Coventry unit in anchoring us so we did not all plummet into the darkness.

I worried it was taking too long, that somehow this magical rope would not have been enough when I saw a wash of teal hair followed by Capricorn's tear-stained face.

I scooped her up from the black, earning a protest from the rest of the team that had anchored me. I could barely care. Capricorn was where she belonged, in my arms.

I moved her away from the abyss, crushing her to me.

"I knew you'd find me, I knew you'd find me."

Capricorn's tears wrecked me. I allowed Jalen and Rothgar to hold her as well. It was a tangle of limbs that the local emergency services crew needed to dance around. Since Capricorn refused to let go of them, then they would not let go of her.

The Director of Coventry himself, Grey Linden, a dour-faced gargoyle, arrived on scene. "What the hell happened here, Tharraka?"

"We do not know. I was here to find my mate. But I think you are close to the answer."

At his confusion, I said, "Hell, sir. I think hell tried to happen here."

A mask of cold neutrality settled over his face. "We will debrief about this in private," he said. "My office. One hour."

"No," I countered. "I have just seen my newly bonded mate nearly destroyed as a sacrifice to darkness. I will stay by her side."

"You don't have to." Capricorn's voice was husky from her ordeal, and it broke my heart knowing how long she must have screamed. "You'll be fine to go. I'll be fine. I'll just be going to the hospital, anyway. Maybe even be asleep, who knows?"

"Then I will be at the hospital," I said.

"Really, if you're needed—"

I closed the distance between us in a step. Gripping her chin, I tilted her face up so I could look into her eyes. "I will be by your side, Capricorn."

I willed her to agree. I needed her to tell me to stay with her.

"Okay," she said. I felt the relief that poured from her.

We would need to discuss a few things in the future, but today was not that day.

I pressed a kiss against her forehead. "We should get going." I wanted to carry Capricorn in my arms, but Rothgar looked like he'd have a meltdown if I flexed my claim.

"Wait," Capricorn said. "There's just one thing." She stepped away from Rothgar's hold and walked toward where the portal was. The glyphs were burnt through, so there wouldn't be any magic left in them. Still, Coventry's containment team would ensure everything was fine.

Capricorn knelt at the place where her anchor had been, the literal lifeline that kept her safe until we could fish her out of that hole. Rothgar kept his hands on her, hovering over her like a worried hen.

I understood. He didn't want to take chances, and neither did I.

"What are you doing, little witchling?" I asked.

She placed a hand that was wrapped in something I had not seen before. Was that a bandage around her hand? Jewelry?

Capricorn pressed her hand over the spot and the floor underneath glowed. The runes melted away. When she stood back up, the floor looked pristine. As if there hadn't been a spell opening into a portal of doom.

"What did you do?" I asked.

She shrugged. "He used me to open it. I thought it would only be right if I closed it." She handed a small cylinder to Linden, whose mouth opened in disbelief at what he held in his hand. "I think I'd feel better if you held onto that."

Linden looked at Capricorn in mild shock. "I see." He looked at me, then back at her. "Thank you. We would love to study it."

"Sir," Jalen said. "Capricorn Jade is one of the highest ranking students in Elfhame, and worked with Professor Snowden—well, when he was still Professor Snowden—in the field of New Magics and Esoteric Spells."

Linden rocked back on his heels. "That is my area of expertise. Did you create that anchor spell, Ms. Jade?"

"I did," she said. "I would have done a better job, but I was distracted at the time."

"Better? I thought you did a fine job with what you did."

"Thank you, sir," she said. "We aligned my coursework with Coventry's internship in mind. Of course, now, I'm not so sure."

Linden jumped on that before I could. "Not so sure? Where else would you go? If you have competing offers, I am sure I could meet them."

Capricorn's cheeks glowed with a burnished copper. It was good to see her color return after her ordeal. "I meant, since Snowden had been my mentor, my application was going through him. He was my sponsor in the program."

Jalen scoffed. "If you want into the program, you have three referrals right here. We would sponsor you gladly."

"Hell, I'm the director of the program, and I say you're in. Just send in the application whenever you're ready," Linden said.

"Okay," Capricorn said. Her smile was all I needed to see.

"Enough of this. Time to nurse our mate." Rothgar swept her off her feet to smack a loud kiss on her cheek. He and Jalen moved toward the awaiting ambulance. "Declan, you coming?" He called over his shoulder.

Impudent ass. He should remember this moment when I cock block him from Capricorn after she recovered. "Sir, if you need to debrief—"

Grey held up his hand. "I'll find you at the hospital. Go, Tharraka. Be with your family."

My hearts surged. I enjoyed hearing that, especially with Capricorn present. "Thank you," I said, and I caught up to them in a matter of strides.

Hungry for more Orcs? Read a bonus scene and epilogue here: https:// ellecrossx.com/links

If you liked the world of Bespelled Brews, sign up for my mailing list where I will send out monthly updates on my works in progress and share exclusive snippets and promotions. Plus, you will get first access to new releases, including this story once it is expanded and published as the title, *One Orcish Night*.
www.ellecrossx.com/mailing-list

ABOUT AUTHOR

Hi, I'm Elle Cross, drinker of luxury coffee, equal-opportunity eater, ex-world traveler (paused for now, thanks pandemic!), user of way too many parenthetical remarks, and a *USA Today* Bestselling Author of darkly magical tales.

I'm usually hiding in my writing cave, but I also lurk on Facebook and Instagram, and sloooowly getting into TikTok. The best way to keep up with me will be to join my Inner Circle mailing list!

https://ellecrossx.com/links

facebook.com/ellecrossx

twitter.com/ellecross_x

instagram.com/elle_cross

STALKING TAMARA

NOVA BLAKE

CHAPTER ONE

Tamara

Welcome to The Nest, your home for the next week. Enclosed, you'll find your room key and a map to your personal cabin. Inside your suite is a private bath-room and small kitchen amenities for snacks and drink making. All meals will be held in the main building or in the courtyard, weather dependent.

I read the words printed on thick card stock, and a thrill ran through me. We hadn't even gotten off the bus yet, and my expectations had already been surpassed. When the company said we were going on a team building retreat, I'd pictured a rickety set of cabins, draughty toilet blocks, and basic meals, but as I glanced out the window, I could see lush grounds and sleek buildings, all surrounded by gorgeous evergreen trees. This was as close to corporate as we'd ever afford, and even then, I had no idea who was footing the bill for this; it was next level.

I tucked the card and envelope into my pocket and waited patiently for my workmates to file off the bus. Gemma held the queue up, though, giving me her boss vibes stare. I stood up and shouldered my tote as I stepped into line ahead of her.

"This is going to be so good," Gemma whispered. "Just you wait. It'll be the holiday we've never got around to taking."

"Just, with all our co-workers," I muttered. "And my boss. That Gemma chick is something else." I fake eye rolled. She chuckled at my droll tone and smacked my ass to hurry me up. It worked.

Once we were off the bus, I let the others waste their time waiting for the luggage to be unpacked while I took in the location. There was a wide, white stoned path that led from the parking lot to the main retreat building. The huge glass windows and doors looked like they were double glazed, reflecting the blue and green of the natural environment. The walls were a combination of wood and white, the melding of nature and construction blending to create a literal piece of art.

Some serious funds had gone into creating this place, which made me wonder why we hadn't heard of it before – why it wasn't the most talked about spot in the state.

Gemma drew my attention back to the thinning crowd. I located my luggage and gripped the handle, grateful that it had wheels and that this place had good pathways crisscrossing the grounds.

The bus was still puttering behind us, no doubt ready to make the return trip as soon as

they offloaded all the baggage. I ignored the chatter around me and tried to bask in the beauty of this place.

Tall trees rose all around us. Among the trees, I could make out colored ropes and ladders for a rope course. Now that I was out of the bus, I could see a cliff face peeking from between the trees, no doubt with a zipline. The main building's roof rippled with greenery that moved in the slight wind, linking it with the grounds it sat on. Dotted throughout the landscape were the cabins, each unique in design.

"Holy shit," someone whispered beside me. I glanced over to see Gemma, eyes wide in awe.

"It's something, isn't it?" I replied, inhaling the crisp air and appreciating the beauty of the spot.

"What?" She glanced at me, and then her cheeks flushed. "I, ah, wasn't talking about The Nest," she said in a hushed voice. "That guy over there though, is drop dead gorgeous. If he asks me to jump from the top of a tree with nothing but a bungee cord, I am totally going to do it." She inclined her head to the left, where I saw the man she'd been captured by.

He was handsome enough, but looked far too refined for me. Everything about his appearance screamed executive hippy, as though he'd found the perfect way to pair the latest technology with the natural world.

I didn't trust anyone who looked like him. And for some reason, he was coming our way. His blond locks fell in waves to his shoulders, and I could swear he had it trimmed every three to four weeks just as the hairdresser prescribed to keep it so even and free of split ends.

"Welcome to The Nest! Do you need any help finding your rooms?" he asked, his voice smooth and even, his lines practiced. "We've allocated some time for you to settle in, and then there will be an early dinner in the main hall to welcome you to the retreat."

"Um, I could do with some help," Gemma said, stepping forward. She tossed a gleeful look over her shoulder as she shoved her little map into the guy's hand. I bit back my laugh and moved away from the two of them so as not to cramp her style.

She was welcome to him. I preferred my men... Well, not him. I still wasn't exactly sure what my type was, but definitely someone a little less put together, a little grittier than that guy, who more than likely had pedicures and manicures more often than I did.

I picked a path that looked like it was in the approximate direction of my cabin, and once I'd put some space between myself and the potential love birds, I reached into the envelope to pull my map out. Within a few minutes, I found myself in front of a cute wooden bungalow set amongst the trees. I wheeled my suitcase up the paved path and the ramp to my accommodation.

I flashed the key card at the door, and it beeped before sliding open soundlessly.

"Wow," I whispered. "Did not see that coming." The level of tech in this place was way beyond what I'd imagined. I stepped inside, letting the door close behind me, then let my bag slide from my shoulder as I took in the room.

It was cute as heck. The entrance was tiled in white faux marble and held a small kitchen to the left, complete with a fresh bouquet of wildflowers. To the right was carpeted in thick white, and there was a small area with a double seater sofa, a cushy footrest, and a screen that I knew was connected to the WiFi.

A printed fabric screen separated the living areas, and I peered behind it to find a queen bed perfectly tucked into a nook with a large window on the other side. My jaw dropped when I saw the view; it looked right over a cliff that fell away to the sea. I even thought I could hear the crashing of waves against the rocks far below.

Or maybe that was my imagination.

It didn't really matter. It was a stunning sight, and I could just imagine that sunsets would look sensational from here. Or sunrises? The road had been so windy that I literally had no idea which direction I was facing right now. Either way, it was going to be gorgeous, and I could not believe my luck that I was going to wake up here, nestled in this bed with a view like that.

I stashed my toiletries in the bathroom and unpacked a few things so that the place felt as much like home as it could, then kicked off my shoes and flopped onto the bed with a book.

About half an hour later, a bell chimed in the cabin. I shot up from the bed, confused by the intrusion, and then a soft feminine voice spoke into the room.

"Please make your way to the rear courtyard. We will begin our welcome ceremony in fifteen minutes."

Well, at least they were considerate with their timing. Even if I'd been in the shower, fifteen minutes would be enough to get myself presentable. I freshened up, slid my phone into my pocket, put my shoes on, and headed out. Others were emerging from their cabins as well, merging on the larger path and making their way to the main courtyard. Even though there was still daylight, little lights dotted along the path, guiding the way.

Attendants directed us around the side of the main building to a large paved area with long tables in rows. Glimmering fairy lights were strung from beautiful trees that curved around the space like necklaces between the main building and the view. The sea. It looked like you could step right into the water, even though the drop was massive. There was a thin glass barrier, almost invisible if it weren't for the way the lights sparkled on its surface.

Gemma found me as we were ushered in, and we sat close to the rest of our immediate team. All up, it looked like there were a good hundred people from the company here.

Again, I could not help but wonder just who was paying for this.

The executive hippy who we'd met earlier spoke into a mic, and Gemma nudged me in the ribs.

"So hot!" she hissed.

I shook my head with a grin and did my best to listen as he welcomed us to this space on behalf of the owner of The Nest and ran through a list of health and safety measures. It was hard to stay focused when the sheer beauty of this place was so overwhelming.

"In the cupboards of your cabin you'll find an information packet reiterating all of this, along with details about the hiking trails and other facilities, which you're welcome to make use of whenever you feel. Your timetables for the week are also in your packet, and I hope you'll agree that there is a great balance of team building exercises and free time. All meals will be served here or inside the main building behind us, weather dependent."

"We don't need to do a trust fall this week, do we?" some guy called out.

Gemma's future lover laughed and shook his head. "No, no trust falls, though there will be other activities that require building trust with your co-workers and teammates."

There was a wave of relieved sighs and then nervous chuckles as we all realized we'd really wanted to avoid any damn trust falls.

"Excuse me. I just need to-"

I heard the hushed voice and turned to see Keziah rushing toward me. Her head ducked low, gesturing frantically for me to scoot. Gemma slid down, and I made room for Keziah to join us. She huffed out a breath and shoved her handbag under the bench seat.

"Where were you?" I hissed.

"Late, you know me." Kez rolled her eyes, then dragged her hair from her face and tied it up. "I missed the fucking bus because I couldn't find my house keys."

Someone shushed her, and she let out an exasperated sigh. I grabbed her hand and gave it a little squeeze, wanting her to know that I was glad she was here.

She might always be late, but she worked hard and got her job done, and she brought some much needed levity to the office. She squeezed back, and I was relieved to see that our host had finished talking and attendants were bringing out trays of steaming food. A range of scents hit my nose, most clearly, hot roasted meat. My mouth watered, and as soon as grace had been said, everyone dug in.

I ate in silence, watching everyone around me. The food was terrific, but I never enjoyed these big get togethers. There was too much noise: the clink of cutlery on plates, liquid in glasses, and all the different conversations. So many discussions, all blending together, building the tension in my brain, reminding me just how bad I was in this kind of setting.

Gemma and Keziah were deep in conversation, but I just couldn't seem to get involved. I nibbled my food, trying to let the sounds wash over me instead of invading me. Under the table someone's foot touched mine, and I pulled it back, looking across from me to find a slightly attractive man raising his eyebrow as if asking if I'd be into something later.

No. No, I would not.

This was all too much. I couldn't do it.

"I need to get out of here," I said to Keziah, nudging her with my elbow.

"Where are you going?"

I just shook my head and stood up. It felt like all eyes swiveled toward me. I had to go. Now.

"Headache," I mumbled, and then moved away, not waiting for any more questions. I just needed to be gone. One of the attendants moved toward me, but I shook my head again, kept my eyes averted, and as soon as I was around the side of the building, I ran.

The cabin wasn't far enough away from the noise. I switched into some hiking gear, grabbed my small pack, a torch, a bottle of water and a few snacks. I'd not managed much at dinner and I knew I'd get peckish soon enough.

Finally, I shoved my head lamp onto my head. I did not want to get caught out there in the dark.

When my cabin door slid shut behind me, I wondered if this was a stupid idea and I was overreacting, but then the sounds of laughter hit my ears, and I moved down the path toward the trail head. I'd not studied much of the maps, but there was a bright orange sign on a post, with different distances and names for tracks. Right now, all that mattered was that I was out of sight and in the woods, letting the sounds of nature wash over me.

I wasn't the kind of person who went for a run or walk with music in my ears. The sounds of the natural world were what I wanted to listen to. I exhaled, letting the gentle noise of leaves rustling in the wind wash over me, letting my feet find a good pace. Not a run, because I didn't know this place, but not your average stroll either. I needed to burn off a little of the anxious energy inside me and put some distance between me and the rest of the company.

Why had I agreed to come on this retreat? I mean, aside from the fact it wasn't really a choice, so much as a strongly advised suggestion. Gemma had hinted that I wasn't as much of a team player as others in management would like, and so I'd been determined to show them that I could definitely work well in a team.

Yet here I was...

I rolled my shoulders, pushed those thoughts down, and kept moving. The sun had lowered in the sky, sending more shadows through the trees. This path wasn't the most even, and as I got further in, vines and weeds encroached until it was barely more than a thin line of dirt that probably only deer used. To give myself a little more visibility, I pulled out the head-lamp and switched it on. Technically, I should turn back, but I didn't feel like I was far enough away; I swore I could still hear laughter.

On and on I went. Watching the light dim around me, inhaling the scent of damp undergrowth and the faint tang of salt on the breeze. Each step calming my brain, taking me deeper into the wild, the place I felt the most at home.

The crack of branches somewhere to my left made me freeze, and I whipped my head around. Whatever had made the noise wasn't visible, maybe too far away to see yet. A chill juddered up my spine.

It felt like someone was watching me. My hand flew to the headlamp, shutting off the light and leaving me in darkness. The reflector strips on my stupid hiking gear caught the light from the moon, and if whatever was out here with me meant malice, they would surely find me.

Shit.

Fuck.

I was such an idiot.

Alone in unknown territory, in the dark. And no one knew where I was...

First rule of hiking, Tamara. Tell someone your plans. I'd been so in my head that it never crossed my mind I might find myself in danger. Not on this remote corporate retreat.

Yet here I was.

Another cracking branch, what sounded like footsteps, but heavy. Dragging. What the hell was out here with me? A low rumble sounded and I didn't know if that was from the sea, the sky, or the thing in the woods. It took all my willpower to choke back the scream that threatened to escape my lips.

I spun in a half circle and searched the ground for any sign of the path. It was too dark now to see it without the light. I froze, not knowing what to do. Risk the light? Risk breaking my neck?

Another rumble came, but this time it was definitely the sky. Then rain fell in fat, heavy drops that slicked down my skin and soaked through my clothes. I hadn't thought to bring anything waterproof because it hadn't looked like it was about to rain when I'd set out. *Dammit.* Damn my need for space and the temptation of a trail, damn the woods at night, and goddamn whatever was behind me. Or in front of me. I had no freaking clue right now.

But I had to risk it. Risk the light. It might all be in my head, and I'd be doing myself more damage by wandering further off the path. We were so far from civilization that it might take weeks for them to find me, and I could not go without coffee for that long.

I took a deep breath, exhaled, inhaled again, and then hit the button on the headlamp. A circle of bright white hit the ground, illuminating green and brown, but nothing that looked even vaguely path like.

Crap.

More noise; this time it wasn't thunder. It was like the rattle of bones, or maybe a snake, the scrape of claws? My anxious brain couldn't decide which it seemed most like, but it conjured all things beastly. I shut off the light and ran. It didn't matter where; just away from this place, away from that noise.

Away from whatever was chasing me.

The ground was already damp beneath my feet, and I could glimpse slivers of moon through the branches, never enough to show me where I was going, though.

Another roar.

I just wanted to close my eyes and stop, to freeze, to lie down on the ground and hope that this beast would pass me by. But if it were an animal, it would smell me here, the stench of fear sloughing off me in waves.

I didn't want to die tonight.

This was meant to be a goddamn retreat. What the hell had I been thinking, running off into the woods like that? An attempt to be alone with my thoughts, away from the reminders that I didn't really fit in wasn't worth my life.

A gust of cool air hit me from the right and I turned to see a gap in the trees. Dare I head into the open? Or would that only put me more at risk? Even a split second seemed like it was too long to make that decision, so I bolted left, keeping to the cover of the trees. The wind had picked up even here, pushing me on, pushing me away.

My feet slipped on the undergrowth and I fell, hitting my hip against the hard ground, jarring my bones. I scrabbled to stand, but my foot found only air, and I glanced over my shoulder to find that I was dangling over an edge in the ground.

I scrabbled for purchase, reaching around for roots or grass, anything to cling to as the momentum dragged me down. My knee found the lip, and then there was nothing but air and the dank spell of mouldering leaves.

CHAPTER TWO

There was a disturbance in my lair. A shudder, a rumble. Something had entered where it was not welcome.

Anything within the walls of this labyrinth was mine for the claiming, and whoever – whatever – had stepped inside had forfeited their life.

I glanced around my living space, full of old lushness from times long gone. Furniture carved from ancient wood, the weapons of a ferocious past hanging on the wall, still sharp and gleaming; I kept them ready, even though it had been a long time since anything unwelcome had invaded my halls. Longer still since my people and other races had used this place to do battle, to claim a title of honor.

As much as I did not want to live in the world above, the new world. I refused to live in the ridiculous conditions that some of those around here did. The Nest was a haven for all of us – those who wanted to live in relative safety but who might want to fight or fuck or feast without fear of human authorities catching wind. They posed no real threat to us, but it wasn't worth the time and energy to deal with. Our glory days were gone, but we refused to pass into history in the way the humans wanted us to.

Another shudder and the threads of my protections tingled, alerting me to more movement.

My gaze went to the rack of weapons, lingering on the sweeping sword blades, the axe, the daggers. No, tonight I would wield my morning star; it had been too long. We would hunt, and we would claim the spoils of our conquest.

CHAPTER THREE

Tamara

Everything hurt.

No, not *quite* everything.

I shuffled my body closer to the nearest wall, propping myself against it so that I could survey the damage. My pants were shredded along one leg. My ankle throbbed so badly I wasn't sure I'd be able to put weight on it, and while my wrist ached, I was pretty sure it wasn't broken. The headlamp had lit up when it hit the floor, and now it flickered on and off, casting rings of light against stone and dirt. It looked like I was in some kind of stone corridor, but that made no sense.

Why would there be a corridor here?

I tried to crawl onto my knees, but a sharp pain ripped through my ankle. I needed to wrap it if I was going to move from this spot – and I definitely needed to move. Trickles of water dripped down the wall I leaned against, and a sliver of moon pierced the crack in the earth that I had slid through. It didn't illuminate much, and I could only hope that whatever had been chasing me through the woods wouldn't enter.

Right now, I couldn't worry about that. My ankle was the more pressing matter.

I ripped fabric from my torn pants and bound my ankle as best I could. I didn't want to remove the shoe for fear I wouldn't be able to get it back on, but the binding worked well enough, and I was able to drag myself to the headlamp and smack it a few times. The beam of light didn't steady though; it flared and then died.

"Shit," I muttered. Just what I needed. I reached into my pack for my torch and then flicked it on; it would double as lighting and a weapon in case there were rats or bats. Or spiderwebs. Casting my light around the corridor, I could see that I was right. This place was a mess. The hall extended beyond the light of my torch, and the floor was dotted with broken stone and dirt, branches that had slipped through the crack as well.

Yet none of those things were going to help me get out of here. The gap I'd come through was too high up, and I knew my ankle wouldn't support that kind of climb. But what other option did I have?

I gripped the wall and inhaled, steeling myself. I got my good leg under me and then pushed myself up, tentatively placing weight on the twisted one. An initial spike of pain shot through me, and I hissed, closing my eyes and gritting my teeth.

Nope. I wouldn't be able to climb.

I was such a fucking idiot. I knew the guidelines for hiking; I was always out in the woods or on a trail. Yet here I was, twisted ankle, shredded clothing, in the crushing darkness of some abandoned place, and no one had a clue where I was. *Good one, Tamara. Real good.*

The throbbing in my ankle had subsided to a bearable amount, and I tested it out, walking a few steps, taking my time, working out which positions were the worst. Slowly, the ache eased enough that I could put a decent amount of weight on it. I wasn't going anywhere in a hurry, but at least I could try to find my way out of this place. Whatever it was.

That question rolled around in my brain because what *was* this place?

I trailed my free hand along the wall, feeling the stone, the crumbling mortar. Nothing in The Nest's brochure, or even the website, mentioned an older structure. And this was definitely old. Abandoned. Would anyone even think to look for me here?

I closed my eyes. I inhaled and exhaled, trying to still the panic welling in my gut, the anxious voice in my head. I was okay. I could do this. I could find a way out and get back to The Nest. Someone would notice I was missing in the morning, and it would be fine. Totally fine. I had spent nights in the woods with only a few more resources than this, and I'd eaten a little at dinner. I had water and some food.

I'm going to be okay.

Which was when a howl split the air above me, and I froze, my body unable to decide whether to curl up in a ball or try to run. The howl came again – or was it a howl from a second wolf? – and that got me moving. I flicked my gaze between each end of the corridor, then went left, hoping that I wasn't heading for a dead end. Who knew what parts of this freaking labyrinth were clear enough to move through?

Adrenaline flooded my body, and I shoved down the pain in my ankle, ignoring it in favor of not getting eaten. The way my torch light bounced off the walls made me feel a little sick, but I couldn't stop moving. I just had to keep going, leaning against one wall to give myself the extra support.

The sound faded, or the wolves stopped calling. Either way, I slowed down, needing to catch my breath. The throb in my ankle was worse now, and I scanned the ground for a good place to sit. I'd turned a few corners, and I had no more idea where I was now than before, but at least there were no gaps in the ceiling here, no way something could slip down and grab me.

I sank to the ground in a mostly rubble free spot. The wall opposite me looked like it was on a slant, but I didn't think it was going to fall over and crush me – or maybe it would, knowing my luck right now. Maybe that would be a mercy. I was going to be the laughingstock of the office after this. I just knew it.

I unzipped my pack and reached inside, groping for the water bottle and taking a small sip. It wasn't a lot, so I was going to have to make it last unless I could find another water source. And who knew? There might well be. The halls in this place seemed to extend and twist and turn like a goddamn labyrinth.

A labyrinth?

Surely, it couldn't be. That would be insane. And also, the kind of thing someone would mention, right?

And yet...

It was hard to argue with the facts: this place was definitely abandoned, there was no rhyme or reason to the way the corridors went. I'd not seen a single room or door coming off it so far. Nothing. My stomach dropped as I realized that if I was right, it was going to be a whole heck of a lot harder to escape than I'd initially thought.

Maybe I should go back to the hole in the ceiling and take my chances with the wolves?

CHAPTER FOUR

Kavi

It was a female, human, from the scent that tickled my nose. My stomach rumbled and my cock twitched, and I couldn't decide just yet whether I wanted to fuck or feast. All I knew was that she smelled delicious, and I needed to find her.

This area of my labyrinth had been unused for a long time. I'd abandoned it as the days of glory fell away, as we gave up the hunt for a quieter life, as even our gladiatorial events faded into obscurity. And yet, that urge sang in my blood right this moment, to leap into battle, to fight and win.

She had awakened that desire again.

I strode the halls, my morning star trailing behind me. I would find her sooner rather than later.

And then another scent tickled my nose; one of the lesser beasts in this area. A wave of rage swept through me, and my feet moved faster, thudding against the ground as I closed the distance.

I could not let it find her first, and I would not let it live for longer than a few moments after I laid eyes on it. A soft gasp reached my ears, and I broke into a run, a strange protective urge washing over me.

That beast could not have her. She was mine.

CHAPTER FIVE

Somewhere along the way, I'd gotten lost. There was no doubt about it. I'd not been able to find my way back to the hole in the ceiling, and this hallway looked different to the last. The walls weren't as crumbled, and not as many vines covered them or slithered their way across the ground; I wasn't walking through cobwebs as thick as walls either. The air was still somewhat stale, probably because no breeze touched this place.

I was still trying to get my head around what this labyrinth was doing here in the woods. If there had been any reception, I'd have Googled it, seen if I could find out anything more, but there was no way in hell it was going to work down here if it didn't work on the surface.

The drip, drip, drip of water hit my ears and I moved toward it. So often water showed the way out of a place; maybe I would get lucky. I sure as hell couldn't get unluckier.

My ankle ached, as did other parts of my body. My knees were no doubt skinned, my elbows too. And my wrist was tired from holding this damn torch. I just wanted to sit down and cry, but if I did that, I might not get up again, and I had no idea what else might be down here with me.

The hallway opened into a wider space and I glanced around, letting my torch disperse the shadows a little at a time. This was different. The first time I'd come across anything other than halls and junctions. A square room, and in its very center was a well.

A well. In a labyrinth. Okay. Well, there were stranger things to be found, I was sure. I just hadn't expected this.

Small purple and blue flowers dotted the floor and climbed the walls on dark green vines. My gaze followed them up, finding a small circular window through which I could glimpse the moon. I flicked off the torch, letting my eyes accustom to the darkness, and then I sucked in a breath.

The flowers were glowing in the moonlight. It was the most unexpectedly beautiful thing in this desolate space. I hobbled toward the well, which the vines had also claimed, and cupped a flower in my hand, in awe at the glow against my skin.

This was magic. There was no other word to describe it. I'd never seen anything like these flowers, and I wondered whether they would crumble and collapse if I tried to take one with me. I lifted it to my face and inhaled the sweet, tangy scent. So fresh and clean in this dank space.

Bliss!

A wave of peace washed through me, easing some of the cramps and aches in my body as I let the flower fall back to its position.

The sparkle of light on the surface of water drew my attention. I peered into the well, surprised to see that the water came almost to the top. Close enough to drink from. Close enough to wash some of the grime from my body.

My hand hovered over the surface. A frisson of fear shot through me. Something nasty had chased me in the woods; something nasty could be waiting in this water too. Something that might want to eat or poison me.

Which was probably the thing I had to be more worried about.

How was I going to make sure it was safe enough? I couldn't tell if it would make me sick, but I quickly stripped off my t-shirt and dipped the bottom of it into the well, making a shallow bowl for the water to drip through. No residue or anything else stuck to the fabric, which was a good first sign. Next, I sniffed it, but it smelled fresh, almost sweet, but not in a toxic way. Like spring water from a natural bore – not unlike the water at The Nest, come to think of it.

I dipped the hem in again, using the fabric to clean some of the grime from my face, my neck. The water was cool and delicious as it slid down my torso. A low rumble startled me and I looked around, trying to find the source. But I was alone.

Pain gnawed at me, so I cupped my hands in the water, lifting them to my lips. The water was sweet, delicious, and I groaned as it slid down my throat. This well was the single good thing that had happened to me tonight.

Then I heard a chilling howl that echoed around the room.

CHAPTER SIX

Kavi

She was not what I had expected.

Long blonde hair, a frame much smaller than mine but bigger than many females from her world. Not that I cared. Her eyes glinted brown in the light of the moon as it bounced off the water, and when she dragged the fabric of her shirt across her body my breath shuddered with want. With hunger. I had seen nothing as beautiful as her for years, and I yearned to reach out and touch her. So close, and yet, if I let myself into the light of the moon, she would run. I just knew it.

The water trickled down her abdomen, and a low growl started in my belly, moving up my throat and through my lips. Her head shot up, staring at the entrance to the room that I was hiding in. I was sure she couldn't see me. Not with her human eyes. I tamped down the sound, swallowing my lust. I did not want to scare her away, not when she was so close.

She went back to cleaning herself off before tugging her wet shirt back on. She tentatively cupped her hands in the water and lifted them to her lips. She closed her eyes and groaned in pleasure, and I just knew she was savoring the sweet taste of my well. It warmed something inside, made me almost step out from the dark.

Another noise came but from a different hallway. The same howl that had echoed through this place earlier. Damn beast. It had no place here, and no place near her.

Her head snapped around, following the sound. Had she glimpsed the creature? There was fear in her eyes, glinting in the light of the lamp she had reignited, a hint of desperation wafting off her now. I ached to step out to reveal myself, to speak with her. But that damn beast was coming. My eyes were used to the dark and I could see it now, a four-legged thing, muzzle of a wolf but with spines protruding from its hips and hocks, a crest of spines.

It grumbled low and long, a snarl that made the woman's skin shiver and prickle, the scent of her fear escalating. It did not entice me like it might have on other days. It only made my urge to protect her grow stronger. She was mine. This beast could not have her.

I coiled my muscles, lifted my morning star, and ran.

CHAPTER SEVEN

TAMARA

When before there had been all but silence, now noise filled the air. I spun around to see a gigantic beast charging from the depths of the shadows. Right at me.

I was frozen. Shock caused all of my muscles to seize up. It – he – was at least seven foot tall, though if I counted the curved double horns on his head, it was closer to eight. His chest and arms were bare, dark grey skin bulky with muscles, and he was wielding a wicked looking morning star. How? How was this reality?

And then I caught the flash of tail, hooves, and black fur peeking out from under his pants, and I think my brain stopped working entirely.

The beast emitted a thunderous roar, and then it was past me, colliding with another creature, another thing that my brain was scrambling to fathom.

What I'd assumed was a wolf or wild dog was not. Because none of the wolves I knew of had spikes coming off them. None of them had fangs that big or claws that lethal.

I braced myself against the well, unable to take my eyes off the battle before me. The meagre light of my torch didn't show everything, but it was enough. The way the tall creature, a satyr perhaps? *How were they real? How was any of this real?* The way he swung his weapon, slamming it into the side of the creature, made my heart clench.

Part of my brain was wondering what else I'd expected to find in an abandoned labyrinth, while another part had shut down entirely, and the rest of me was just fixated by the way the satyr moved. He was so big but nimble with it, swinging the morning star easily to smash against the side of the other creature, which was like nothing else I knew or could name.

Get the fuck out of here, Tamara. Run. While they are fighting. This is your chance.

But run where, exactly? I had no idea how to get out of this place. The wolf thing had followed me here, and if it made it out of this alive it could keep tracking me down.

And the satyr?

My gaze caught on the ripple of his muscles. He had lost somehow the morning star and was gripping the beast's head, forcing it to the side so the vicious fangs couldn't find a spot to clamp down on. There was blood though, probably from them both.

I'd thought the satyr was going to kill me, but he was protecting me. Saving me from certain death. I didn't expect the flutter of desire at that realization, but there was no denying it. This primal beast of a male had leapt to my defence without even having met me.

No one had ever put themselves on the line like that for me before.

CHAPTER EIGHT

Kavi

I was out of practice.

Too long had I languished in these halls unchallenged. I'd underestimated this beast, for while it might be lesser than me, it was strong, wily in the way that things above ground needed to be to survive. The thorns of its protective layer pierced through the flesh of my hands as I gripped its neck, trying to twist it, snap it, but pain shot through me, spreading.

This beast was poison. If I didn't slay it now, I might lose my chance entirely.

Maybe I deserved it. I'd let myself fall too far away from the world, lost my touch.

No. The thought roared through my head and I bellowed at the beast. If it killed me, then the woman would be next, and I would not let that happen.

The creature shoved me onto my back when I gripped its head harder. I twisted my right hand, snapping one of its thorns off before stabbing at its side. I had no idea if the poison would work on the creature too, but if nothing else I would gut the beast, let it bleed out, make sure it never breathed again.

It howled at me, snapping its teeth, unable to make contact. I rolled so that I was on top, groaning with pain, spines embedding in my chest, stomach, and legs.

But I had to win this fight.

The woman moved, distracting my gaze for a second. She was hovering, as if wanting to help but not knowing how. She was so fucking beautiful.

A sharp pain made me refocus on the beast beneath me. I punched its muzzle, feeling the grind of its teeth against my knuckles. A snarl tore free from it, then morphed into a whimper as I snapped off another thorn and stabbed it into its other side, ripping through fur and flesh. I could feel the hot slick of blood on me, knowing that some of it was mine. It gnashed out again, and this time I grabbed its jaw and tugged, tearing the bottom one out of place with a vicious snap.

I just needed it to die. Soon.

It pushed further into me, locking itself against my body with its thorns. I could feel the poison working, feel it clouding my mind, stealing the will from me.

Just a little more.

I was slumped against a wall now, breaths ragged as the beast collapsed. Its weight bore down on me as it breathed it's last breath and then lay motionless against my chest.

The flowers.

I just needed one, maybe two, to keep me going. To stave off death a little longer.

CHAPTER NINE

The satyr was propped against one wall, the thorny wolf creature was dead but impaled in the satyr's body. I could tell he was still alive. The rapid rise and fall of his chest was evidence enough. Now that they were still, I could see them better – get a feel for the vicious wolf creature. The wickedly strong satyr had basically torn its jaw in two.

There was blood everywhere, and I was thankful that the light from my torch meant I couldn't take the entire scene in at once. I didn't want to know, didn't want to see what was there. All of this was already too fucked up to be real.

I was in a labyrinth with a satyr and a dead beast which I didn't even have the words to describe. Something I'd never seen in mythology. Yet had been a very real, living thing, breathing down my neck. And now it was dead.

I leaned against the well, every limb and muscle in my body losing tension. Tonight was not the night I would die. But I was still stuck here. With him.

Inhaling deeply, I steeled myself and stood, setting my shoulders back. It felt like I was still quaking internally, but I knew I had to move. This male had protected me, had defended me at risk of his own life, and now he needed my help; besides, he might be the only way I would escape from this wretched place.

At the sound of movement, he snapped his head toward me, his gaze locking on mine. My first instinct was to look away, but I couldn't show any fear here, not if I wanted to make it out alive. His eyes burned like liquid amber, flares of orange sparking in them. Now that he was mostly still, I could see him so much better. His face was mostly humanoid, lips and nose, those brilliant eyes. The lines of his face were more angular than most humans, and of course, his horns. Something inside of me fucking purred. They were magnificent, one set curled up and away from the top of his head like a ram, while the other were higher, straighter. I wanted to reach out and touch them, wondering what sensation that might give him.

For a moment I wondered how the heck he slept – certainly not on his back – but then I shook that thought free. Wonder crept back in again. A real life satyr. Right here.

"Hi," I said, giving an awkward little wave as I took another step closer. "Um."

Yeah, this was not going well.

He emitted a low vibration, and my eyes dropped to his bare chest, that heavily muscled chest, a freaking six pack. He wore pants but I could see what looked like soft black fur poking out from beneath the fabric. His thighs were solid, so thick, and his legs ended in massive hooves. I shuddered, but it wasn't in disgust – this was a creature straight from myth, a beast of fantasy, but it was here. Real.

"Help me," it said.

He said. He was very much a male, and the way he was looking at me now, with pain dulled eyes, was more human than I could ever have guessed he would be.

"I..." I sucked in a breath, not sure what to say or do, even though he was communicating with me in English. My brain struggled to catch up to the reality that was very much here and smacking me in the face.

"If you don't, I will die."

My mouth fell open and my heart tripped over itself. I took another tentative step forward.

"Can I trust you?" I asked, my voice sounding quiet and shaky..

He gave a rough laugh. Almost a bark. "If I had wanted you dead, I'd have let the spined wolf have you."

True enough. It would have been the easier option. I moved forward again, hefting the torch in my hand, as if that would be any defence against him once he was free. As I got closer, I noticed more details. Long dark hair, tangled and knotted like he never used a brush. Did satyrs have brushes? There were too many questions, and right now, none of the answers mattered. I reached his side and heard the labored breathing, saw him wince in pain.

He'd saved me. I would have died at the fangs of that creature, and now he might.

No. I wouldn't let that happen.

"Tell me what to do," I said, steeling myself.

I didn't know where to touch, where to look. Where to start. His whole body was something different, new. Did he have the same organs as me? The same places I should be concerned about?

"Please," he hissed the word out, the pain obvious. He pointed with one hand, and I turned to follow his finger. "The flowers."

I bent to pluck some from the vines and edged closer. My body tremble, as if mere proximity to this beastly man was enough to trigger my fear response. He took the flowers from my palm and shoved them into his mouth as if they were the most delicious thing in the world.

A moment later he sighed, his body relaxing a fraction.

"I need you to free me," he said. "But be careful. Its spines are poisonous."

Right, well, that was delightful

I raised my hands, fingers twitching as I tried to decide where to start. The spined beast was embedded deep in the satyr's torso, and it was going to take a lot of effort to get it out.

"You promise you won't hurt me?" I flicked my gaze to his, winced at what I saw there. His eyes were even duller than before and I knew I had to move now or he might die, and with it, my chance of getting out of this place alive.

He sighed, looking at the ceiling as if steeling himself, fuelling his patience enough not to crack my neck then and there. His horns scraped against the walls but he didn't seem bothered by that.

Finally, I reached out and gripped the wolf beast on either side of its head, careful not to touch the thorns. Its fur was damp with blood, sticky and congealing as the body cooled. I tugged hard, cringing as the satyr groaned. He shoved with his hands, aiding my plight, but I had to move my body, press one leg against the wall of the hallway in order to get enough leverage to tug.

With the wet, sucking noise of open wounds, the creature came away and the satyr tossed it to the side, his breath coming deep and hard as he pressed his hands to the wounds in his torso. He couldn't cover them all though.

I stood up, wiping the blood onto my pants, unable to cleanse them of the gore, of the liquid that should be inside this creature before me. He was huge but vulnerable, slumped against the wall, the pain obviously threatening to overwhelm him.

"What do you need?" I asked. My voice cracked, suddenly dry. I needed more water. Needed light. Needed to wake the fuck up and get back to reality because this was too much and if I didn't find a way to keep breathing, I was going to pass out or start screaming.

This was a horror movie. A strange, surreal thing that could not be real.

"Just tell me how to get out of here and I promise I won't intrude on your place again. I just... I need..." I gasped for breath, and then all of the strength left my legs and I crumpled to the ground. Nausea roiled in my stomach, but I didn't think I'd eaten enough to actually vomit.

"You're a satyr, right?" I asked, the words spilling out of my mind and into the space between us.

He laughed, the sound so low that it vibrated through my chest. "That is what your kind have called me, yes. You may call me Kavi."

"Kavi?" The name felt softer in my mouth than I'd expected. "I'm Tamara."

"Tamara," he said, as if testing my name out as well. "Thank you."

I exhaled, some of the tension leaving my body. I think my mind was struggling to wrap itself around the fact that I was sitting here talking to a satyr. Who spoke English!

"I need you to help with this." Kavi groaned as he twisted his back slightly, showing me where another spine had pierced his side, impaling him below the ribs. The wound oozed blood and the surrounding skin had reddened as though an infection was already taking hold. But it couldn't be, not that fast.

I rubbed my face, then remembered how dirty my hand was. Focus, Tamara. You have to get this out of him while trying not to touch it. I stripped off my top, ignoring the way his body seemed to stiffen at the sight of me shirtless, a sudden tension flooding through him at the sight of my bare skin.

Maybe I was having the same effect on him as this strange creature was on me.

I pushed those thoughts aside and wrapped the cloth around my hand before gripping the spine protruding from his body. I tugged experimentally, but it barely budged.

"I think you need to lie down," I said. "So that your body is stretched out. It might help."

Kavi grunted, then moved so that he was stretched along the ground rather than propped against the wall. He turned his head so that his horns pointed away from me. I wanted to touch them, to know the texture, and feel them beneath my skin. Instead, I focused on the spine again, kneeling to pull it out.

Still, I couldn't get it free.

I heaved a sigh. There was only one way this was going to work, and it meant getting up close and personal with this strange being. "I'm going to straddle you," I said, coughing awkwardly. "Is that okay?"

"Just get it out," he barked, wincing in more pain. "I don't care how."

Fine, if that was how he felt.

I flung one leg over him and sat on his hip, planting my feet on either side. I sure as hell couldn't kneel; he was too broad for that. He was such a solid build beneath me, larger than any man I'd gotten this close to before. Hard, rigid with muscles and strength. I ran one hand along the wound. His skin was hot, firm, but buttery soft too. I didn't let my thoughts linger on the lines of his muscles but planted one hand firmly, grabbed the end of the thorn with my other hand and pulled.

The extra leverage, the pressure on the skin around his wound, it all helped. The spine shifted, slowly at first, before slipping free with a gross, sucking sound, followed by a massive bellow from Kavi as I yanked it free.

I threw it across the room, panting, planting both hands on Kavi's torso to centre myself. A thin trickle of blood oozed from the wound and I pressed my shirt against it, hoping to stem the flow.

Kavi exhaled. His body relaxed beneath me now that the spine was out. For such an enormous creature, he looked helpless now. He was bleeding in several places, weak from the fight. Poisoned, too, if his words were true, and he had no reason to lie.

"Do I need to wash the wounds?" I asked.

"Yes," he said. His words were weaker now. The bite from before had gone.

I bit my lip, knowing that right now I had the upper hand. "If I help you, will you lead me out of this place?" I asked.

"Whatever you want," he said, his eyes fluttering closed. "Help me, please."

"Promise."

He moaned but forced his eyes open and flicked his gaze to me. Those amber orbs seemed to burn through me, burn through my defences. "I promise." He said it with such force that I knew I could trust him.

CHAPTER TEN

Tamara. I rolled the name around in my mind. The feel of it like a promise in itself.

"I promise, on my life." I hoped she knew I meant it. I had shed blood for her, risked my own life. There was no way I would bring her harm now, though I wasn't sure I could let her leave this place either. Not now that she was right here with me, the feel of her hands on my body stirring my lust, despite the pain gripping my body.

I wanted to roll, turn my body so that I was flat beneath her. The thought of that did nothing to quell my desire, and I didn't want to cause her fear at the swelling of my cock, so I gestured for her to get off me, and dragged myself back to a seated position. My bulge was at least a little less obvious now.

Tamara stood up, wiping her hands on her pants. She wouldn't get clean that way, but I understood the urge. There was so much gore on me, my own and the beasts. I needed to get to the healing waters below.

"Can you walk?" she asked, as if sensing my thoughts.

"I will have to," I said, a slight smile tugging at my lips. She was small compared to me. No way could she carry me anywhere. I forced myself to stand, wincing at the pain. I would not double over. I would not die here. Not like this. Not in front of her. My breath was heavy, hard to come by, so I leaned against the wall waiting for the spinning in my head to stop, for the pain to subside, just a little.

It washed over me in waves.

"How far do we need to go?" she asked.

"Down," was all I could force out. I could feel the poison from the beast leeching into my system, slowing me down even more. "Flowers," I said again. Tamara scrambled for more, even though she could not possibly understand my need. She passed them to me, and I crushed them up, pressing them into my wounds as best I could, letting the juices from them start their work. "This way."

I dragged myself along the wall, ignoring the scraping against my skin. It would be okay soon, as long as I got to the pool.

Tamara took a few halting steps. I could practically smell her trepidation, but then she moved alongside me, slipped under my arm and took some of my weight. Her skin against mine was enough to drive my thoughts to other things, but I had to stay focused. I wanted to claim her in all senses, but I could not do that if I was dead.

"Is this okay?" Her voice was quiet, and she didn't glance at me. It was like she was keeping all of her focus on moving, one foot in front of the other.

"It is good," I said. "Thank you."

She paused then glanced up. The light from her torch didn't illuminate her face, but I could still see the glistening in her eyes. "Thank you. I'd be dead if you hadn't come along."

"And I would have died if you had not saved me. This is right." I nodded once, hoping that she understood that I meant she owed me nothing. We were equals. The slate was clear. What I would not say was that I wanted her in my bed more than anything, but not because she thought she owed it to me.

We shuffled down halls until I could smell the water below. I could have walked there in my sleep, in the pitch black, but I was grateful she had light enough for her. Our pace was glacial, and the speed with which the venom moved through my body was faster. We reached the top of the stairs and I removed my arm from around her shoulder.

"Wait, I can help you."

"And if I fall, you will too. It's okay. This won't kill me."

She looked at me with awe and a little disbelief. I must look worse than I'd assumed because she hovered near me as I picked my way down the stairs, as if she could stop me from toppling. I made it to the last steps before my legs gave out and I stumbled, hitting the stairs and sliding to the bottom landing. Tamara rushed after me, dropping to her knees beside me.

"Not far to go," I said, my voice slurring slightly. I needed to get to the pool. The quicker, the better. She tried to help me up, but she was so much smaller, not just in stature but in build. I felt like a giant next to her, and it made me want to pick her up, to protect her from anything that might threaten her. I leaned against her, trying to keep most of my weight against the wall. I wanted her nearness, the feel of her skin against mine, the warmth of her body. A shudder wracked me, and it wasn't just from the poison running through my veins.

The gentle lapping of water against rock hit my ears, and I moved faster, stumbling over my own feet. One hit the lip of the pool and I let Tamara go, falling into the cool water. The shock of it against my body made me gasp, but then I sighed, sinking into it, accepting the water into my body, drinking it down as it enveloped me.

This pool had been here for so very long, merging the water from inside my labyrinth with that of the ocean. The creatures beneath the sea gifted me with their magic in return for magic that could only be found on land. This was not just my place, but ours.

Tamara lunged into the water beside me, reaching for my head and cradling it, lifting it to the surface. She needn't have feared, but it was sweet that she wanted to care for me. Maybe... Maybe my desires would be returned and I could claim her in all the ways I wanted to.

She pushed dark hair away from my face and I gazed up into her deep brown eyes, lost in them, lost in her, all thought of the aches in my body gone. The only places that burned now were where she touched me.

"You are beautiful," I said, lifting a hand, stroking her cheek with my fingers.

I could crush her skull so easily, but the only thing I wanted to crush were my lips against hers. She tensed for just a moment, and then leaned into my palm, her eyelashes fluttering shut, and exhaled as if she knew I would be okay.

As if that mattered to her.

"And you are..." She bit her lip. "Like nothing I've ever seen before."

There was awe in her voice, wonder. Not the fear I knew she had held before. It was like she could see me for who I really was, and that rattled me to the core.

She winced then, and I realized my horns were digging into her leg where she was cradling my head. Such a fool, I was. I sat up, exhaling deeply and focusing on my wounds. The pool was doing its magic, drawing the toxins from my body. Now all that remained were the cuts themselves. I'd need to get back to my rooms and apply a poultice. Start the healing work needed, though all I could think about was her, how close she was. How I wanted her to be closer.

I stood, the water sluicing off my body, and reached a hand down to Tamara.

CHAPTER ELEVEN

H e was a giant.

I sat there in the pool, my eyes travelling from the line of the water up his body. His hand stretched toward me, and without thinking I reached out and grabbed it. His fingers dwarfed mine, his hand twice the size, it seemed. Even wounded, he was exceptionally strong, pulling me to my feet with ease.

I cried out, my ankle somehow feeling worse even though this was meant to be a healing pool, and it had certainly worked its magic on him.

Magic...

It could be real, now that I thought about it. If a male such as him existed, then it would make sense that magic did too. My world had changed drastically all in one night. If I hadn't come to this retreat, I would have known nothing outside of my mundane little life.

I hadn't exactly enjoyed being chased through the forest, or falling into a labyrinth, or the battle between Kavi and the beast. And yet...

I wouldn't change it because now I was here with him, and something about that just felt right. None of the pretty boys, bad boys, or other assorted creeps had ever taken my fancy. Yet Kavi did. I couldn't explain it. I couldn't even begin to comprehend how this beast of a man, complete with horns, furry legs, and hooves could make me want, make me ache, in ways that no one else had.

"Are you okay?" Kavi asked.

"My ankle," I said, shaking my head. "I can walk. I'll be fine." Yet as soon as I stepped from the pool I bent over, gripped with pain. I'd barely stopped moving since I'd hurt it, so I guess it made sense that it was worse now. I'd thought perhaps the healing waters would work on me too, but I looked down to find my ankle swollen and bruised. Shit. I hoped I hadn't done permanent damage to it.

"You are not fine."

I huffed out a pitiful laugh. "No, I guess I'm not."

The next thing I knew, he'd wrapped his arm around me, hooked another behind my knees and lifted me against his body, cradling me.

"Kavi!" I screeched. "Put me down! You're more wounded than me."

"I'm fine," he said. And he seemed better, at least. Capable of this.

His skin was so soft and cool from the water, his arms so strong as they held me. And now that he wasn't dying, now that nothing was chasing me, I could catch his scent and hold it, something strange and primal, earthy and spiced. I couldn't help but lean closer, inhaling him as I rested my head against his shoulder.

What the fuck is going on?

I couldn't explain the bizarre reaction I was having to him. I'd consigned myself to being eternally single because I couldn't find a man, woman, or anyone who really did it for me, but Kavi?

It wasn't just that he had saved my life. There was something about his body, the way he moved, even his goddamn horns. Who knew that was what I'd be into? I'd been looking at entirely the wrong species all along.

Kavi strode to the stairs and carried me up, up, up. I closed my eyes and savored the feel of his body, trying to ignore the way my nipples tightened at the sensation of skin against skin. Wanting more.

That need was confusing, so much so that my brain skittered away from looking at it too closely. Maybe this really was some warped imagining, maybe the well had been tainted with hallucinogenics and this was all a drug fueled dream.

My head felt a little groggy. I couldn't keep track of the turns we took, aware that we were moving ever deeper into this forsaken labyrinth. Aware that there was no way I was getting out unless he helped me leave.

Would he?

CHAPTER TWELVE

KAVI

She was so small in my arms, the size difference between us more obvious when she was cradled against my chest. Water dripped from her clothing, trickling down my arm, seeping into my pants, wetting my fur.

I bit back a growl as I thought of her dampness, the wetness inside her, and how that might feel. The very fact she was letting me hold her assured me she did not find me horrific, and I could smell her desire, her wanting. Felt my own desperate to respond.

But not yet.

We were still damaged. The poison was gone from my body, but I needed to apply a poultice to my wounds to stave off further infection. I needed to do the same to her cuts and ankle, which was purple and swollen. It made my chest ache to see her hurt. I would do anything to prevent that from happening again. Anything to stop her from experiencing pain. I clutched her tighter, and instead of pushing against it, Tamara leaned in rested her head on my shoulder. She inhaled.

My knees went weak, but I didn't falter. I could sense her curiosity about me, and my skin tingled when she traced a finger across my chest before pressing her palm against it as if she hadn't been feeling the lines of my muscles.

Finally, we made it to my chambers. I pushed open the door and strode in, gently laying her on my bed. She scrambled to a seated position, eyes wide and darting around the room as if she couldn't quite take it all in.

Was it a surprise to her, the way I lived?

I glanced around the space, trying to view it as a stranger might. It was sparse in some ways, an entire wall dedicated to weapons, but the bed was sumptuous, the blankets lush. Beautiful rugs covered the floor, paintings of strange and mystical things adorned the walls, and ornate wooden furniture created a living space. I had other rooms, of course, but this was where I spent most of my time.

I returned to close the door and bolt it, hoping she knew it was only a precaution, and then I lit more lanterns so that the room was illuminated by more than the fire in the hearth.

"Kavi?" her voice wavering. "How did you get all this in here?"

I turned to look at her, mindful of how my horns cast dancing shadows on the walls. I hoped she didn't see me as a devil, wouldn't scorn me the way others had. Maybe if I could show her who I truly was, I could claim her in every way I wanted to. My cock twitched at the thought, threatening to tent my pants and reveal my lust. Pushing that down, I inhaled and moved to a workbench, pulling down the jars of herbs to mix the salve.

"Once, this place had another purpose. A hunting ground for beasts. A place of trials and competition. But it was always mine." I swallowed hard and turned my head so I could look at her from the corner of my eyes. "I've had many years to accrue these items. I may be a monster to you, but I'm a monster who likes his comfort."

"I..." She exhaled a ragged breath. "I don't think you're a monster, not a bad one, anyway. I..." There was a pause, and I resisted the urge to face her directly. I desperately wanted to know what she was going to say. There was a sound from the bed, and then she groaned. I spun to see that she had tried to get up. Had tried to walk toward me. I scooped the salve from the bench and marched across the room, scooping her up with ease and planting her back on the bed.

Her breath came in ragged gasps as our eyes met.

"Are you afraid of me?" I demanded.

"No!" she said. "Yes. Maybe?" The tension in her body fled, and she sank against the mattress, gaze fixed on the ceiling. "I'm afraid of the way you make me feel," she whispered.

It felt like the stars exploded, and it took all of my willpower not to claim her then, not to drag my tongue up her body, taste her, take her mouth in mine, kiss her deeply and bury my cock inside her.

Instead, I picked her foot up and placed it against my thigh, scooping some of the salve with my other hand. I rubbed it gently on her ankle, trying my hardest not to let the rough pads of my fingers graze her body, not wanting to do her any further harm. She tensed, and then relaxed as I tended to her, only the slightest of whimpers escaping her lips.

"What's in that?" she asked. "It feels so good, warm and cold at the same time."

"My own mixture," I replied, pushing my fingers up from her ankle, circling her calf. "You have other wounds?"

"Just small cuts," she said with a shake of her head.

I ignored her. No queen in my home would go untended. She was still shirtless, her flimsy bra covering only her breasts. I moved her ankle off my thigh and knelt beside the bed, gently applying more salve to the cuts on her stomach, her arms. She gasped at my touch, but she didn't recoil, and then she moved so that she was sitting, her legs dangling off the bed between my thighs.

Tamara indicated for the small tub. I passed it over and watched as she dipped her fingers into the salve and reached for my body, running her fingers over the cut on my side. I winced at the pain, at the feel of it, but as she flattened her palm, cupped my side, stroked my unwounded flesh, I couldn't help but groan.

"Too sore?" she asked, freezing.

"No. Your touch is what I need," I growled and I leaned toward her as she moved to the other wounds, dabbing salve over them. I inhaled her scent, sweat and sweetness, damp and desire. I stroked the sensitive skin of her neck, watched her mouth part, full lips opening as a moan escaped as I tilted her chin, forcing her to look at me.

CHAPTER THIRTEEN

Tamara

Every cell of my body was on fire; and it wasn't because of my stupid ankle. This man, beast, monster had woken me from the slumber I'd been in for my whole damn life. I looked him dead in the eyes, saw those amber orbs blazing at me, his mostly human face showing all the signs of lust that I knew.

I put the tub of salve down and smoothed my hand across his skin to rub in the excess, turning the motion into something more.

To hell with it.

I hooked my good ankle around his body and pulled him to me.

Kavi didn't resist. He slotted between my legs, his broad chest spreading them wide as I bent my head and took his mouth with mine.

His lips were firm but lush, and when his tongue slipped into my mouth I gasped in surprise at the delicious point of the tip.

I had a feeling there were many other things he could do with that tongue, and I hoped I would get to experience them all. But for now, this was what I wanted.

I kissed him like he was the sustenance I needed, like he was the sun, the moon, the source of all life. Utterly losing myself in the sensation of his mouth, of his chest pressed against my body, of his hand tangling in my hair. My whole body tingled with sensation, and when he dragged the tips of his clawed fingers across my skin, I gasped.

He groaned as he pushed against me, and right then, I wanted nothing more than to feel the press of his bulge against my core.

"I want to taste you," he murmured against my lips. Before I could respond he had pushed me back onto the bed and dragged what remained of my pants off. He leaned in, nose tracing up my inner thigh, tongue flicking out to taste my skin.

"May I?" His eyes closed, and he growled with lust as he inhaled the scent of my desire.

"Yes." I choked the single word out, my core clenching in anticipation. With that word, he ripped the fabric of my panties, tossing them aside, his tongue flickering across my slit, his fingers carefully opening my lips, his thumb pressing a circle into my clit.

"Kavi," I moaned, writhing on the bed. I tried to reach for him, but he was too clever, too strong. There was nothing I could do as I lay there, exposed, as he pressed against my sensitive nub, as he slid that pointed tongue into my entrance.

I screamed, hand moving to my mouth to dampen the sound, and then I realized it didn't matter. We were alone and I could scream as loud as I wanted.

Kavi lifted my hips and dragged me closer. I hooked my legs over his strong shoulders, not for one second worried about whether he could take my weight. He tongued me harder, the pointed tip penetrating me rhythmically, the slight roughness of it grazing me until I was a quivering ball of nerves, until my voice was hoarse from my cries of pleasure.

He increased the pressure on my clit, expertly rubbing, and I shot up, too much tension in my body to stay lying down. I gripped his horns, the ridges of them giving me purchase so I could thrust against him, ride his mouth, drive him deeper inside me.

He responded to my frantic movements, pushing harder, faster until I lost all rhythm, my orgasm crashing through me like an avalanche.

I froze, pressed hard against his face, riding the last waves as he gently stroked inside me, licked me clean, groaning in pleasure at the taste of me.

I had never felt more desirable, sexier, than right in that moment.

"You taste amazing," Kavi said, licking me again. "I could dine on you daily," Kavi murmured in pleasure, trailing kisses from my sex to my thighs and then up my belly.

I shuffled back, just far enough so that I could bend to kiss him. I wanted to taste my pleasure on his lips, taste the way he'd made me cum.

"You're amazing too. I..." I chuckled against his lips, grinning stupidly. "And that was only your tongue. You're going to fucking kill me with pleasure."

"And then I will resurrect you for more," he promised.

He stood up then, the bulge in his pants impossible to ignore. My greedy hands reached for his buttons, making quick work of them. Kavi took over, shoving his pants down thick thighs, revealing a dark thick cock ringed with ridges in the same way that his horns were.

I practically salivated, and my mouth wasn't the only thing getting wetter. Which was just as well. I was going to need to be slick if there was any chance of getting that inside me.

I reached out, planting one hand on the soft fur of his groin, spreading my fingers through the thickness of it. It most definitely wasn't hair like a human man would have. It was thick and glorious and covered him all the way to his hooves.

If it wasn't for his huge cock, he could totally get away without wearing any pants. But his member was impossible to hide or ignore.

I gripped it with my free hand, and when that failed, I used both, gripping him firmly, the feel of those ridges making my insides clench in anticipation.

I wanted him inside me.

But first, I wanted to at least try to return the favor. I leaned into him, flicked my tongue out to caress his cock, exhaling so that the heat of my breath made him tremble. I slid my hands up the length of him and took the tip of his member in my mouth. Unable to take much more than that, I worked him until his hips rocked against me and his big hands cradled my head.

"Enough," the word snapped out of him. He picked me up and practically threw me up the bed before kneeling on it and stalking after me.

Anticipation, desire, nerves, all of those feelings washed through me as I sunk into his pillows and spread my legs wide, moaning as he reconnected with me. His skin, his weight, were everything I needed.

"You have no idea how much I want you, woman," Kavi growled. He hovered above me, the tip of his cock grazing my slit, making me tilt my body into him, desperate for everything he could give me.

"Get inside me," I hissed. "Now."

But he waited, just a little longer, stroking along my slit, the sensation almost too much to bear.

I gripped his arm, digging ragged broken nails into his skin, tugging on his bulk. I wasn't strong enough to shift him, but he moved anyway, submissive to my need.

His cock breached my lips, stretching me already. Kavi held himself steady, rocking back and forth, one ridge entering, exciting me, the sheer width of him enough to make me moan. He eased further in, each ridge stretching me deliciously, each small reprieve allowing me to breathe, my moans growing in intensity. Moan's which Kavi echoed.

I thought he wouldn't fit, thought that this was all I could take, until he slid his large hands beneath me and tilted my body. I gripped his arms for support and panted out a single word. "More."

And he gave it to me, the full length of his thick shaft filling me until I could feel the tickle of his fur on my ass and my inner thighs.

I screamed, ecstasy just about ready to push me over the edge already, but Kavi stayed there, filling me completely, waiting for me to catch my breath.

"Tamara," he rasped. "Look at me." His hand cupped my face, his thumb trailing over my lips. I drew it into my mouth, sucked on it hard, my muscles clenching around his cock as he closed his eyes and groaned, rocking inside me.

His eyes flashed open, locking with mine, the amber in them flaring with orange as he pulled back, ridge by ridge, the slow sensation of it making me moan and bite down on his thumb.

That drove him over the edge, all his slow control gone as he thrust inside me.

It was too much to handle – an overload of sensations that rippled through my body. I clamped down on his thumb, unable to do anything to slow the waves of pleasure, the tightening of my core.

I was going to explode – any second.

Kavi tore his thumb from my mouth, crushing a kiss to my lips, swallowing my moans of pleasure as he picked up his tempo.

"Kavi," I gasped. "I can't—" I moaned against him as he slammed into me, my head tipped back, eyes closed, stars imploding behind my eyelids.

"Can I bite you?" his voice was rough with need, and right then I would deny him nothing. "I want to be yours."

"Yes. Yes. Oh my god, yes!" I screamed, then his sharp teeth bit into my shoulder and clamped down. As he pierced the skin my orgasm detonated. My muscles clenched around his cock and he thrust inside me like a wild, frantic beast, his own moans of ecstasy joining mine.

Kavi's seed filled me. I could literally feel it, and for a split second concern over birth control and whether our species could breed flashed across my mind, only to be erased by another wave of pleasure and soft kisses along my shoulder, neck, and jaw before he found my mouth and gave me a long, lingering kiss.

"Are you satisfied?" he asked, genuine concern darkening his eyes. "I did not hurt you?"

"Only in the best kind of ways," I said, a deeply satisfied smile stretching my lips.

"Good." He rocked once more inside me, and then withdrew, each damn ridge giving me another wave of pleasure. I was overstimulated, sensitive as heck, and I swear by the time he was all the way out of me I'd shuddered myself into exhaustion from the soft aftershock orgasms that washed over me.

I had never been so fully sated in my life, so completed by another.

Kavi kissed my shoulder again, his tongue lapping gently. I glanced down to see that he'd broken my skin, but rather than bothering me, the idea of him consuming my blood gave a warmth in my chest that I didn't understand.

He rolled off me, curving his body around mine, one large arm draping around my waist.

I felt so small there. So safe.

"I am yours, Tamara. Always," he whispered into my hair. "I claim you. You're my one."

I didn't know what to say to that. What was the right response?

For all intents and purposes, we had not long met, but I knew him. Trusted him. Felt more alive with him than I ever had before.

I woke to darkness, my body aching all over, a combination of the trials of the night before and the exertions with Kavi. To say that I had never been fucked like that before was the understatement of a lifetime.

As if sensing that I was thinking about him, his arms tightened around me, drawing me hard against his chest. The fur of his legs tickled the backs of mine, and I suppressed a giggle.

"That's going to take some getting used to," I murmured, turning to look over my shoulder at him. The flames from the fire still lit the room and I could tell that he was smiling, his sharp teeth showing. His ear twitched and I turned further, reaching out and running my fingers over it.

"Stop that," Kavi said, twitching more. Then a strange bark erupted from him, making me jump in surprise until I realized it was a laugh.

"The big bad monster is ticklish?" I asked playfully, arching an eyebrow as I let my fingers slip to his neck, then down his chest. He relaxed under my touch until I went for his armpit. He growled and pinned my hand between his arm and body, quickly releasing me when I squeaked in pain.

"Sorry," he said, bringing my hand to his lips, pressing a kiss against each finger, then my palm. "I did not mean to hurt you."

"I know." I nodded. I sucked in a breath as the reality of the situation really sank in. After the most surreal night of my life, I was lying naked in a satyr's bed. Trying to tickle him.

Nope. It did not compute. This was perhaps even weirder than falling into a labyrinth in the first place.

I bit my lip and gazed into his amber eyes. I'd thought them full of fire initially or rage. Hunger. And it turned out he had been hungry, just not in the way I'd imagined. There was so much warmth in his eyes now. Warmth that promised to wrap me up, to never let me go, to spend each moment of my life adoring me. And I said that because I sensed he was far older than I and would live long after I was dead.

"What do we do now?" The words came out as a whisper. I barely knew him and yet this felt so right. I didn't think I could go back to the mundanity of my regular life. I did not want to be hit on by normal men or have regular conversations. I just wanted to be here with him. My family were assholes. I just wanted him to tell me I could stay. Because I would. In a heartbeat.

His lips curved into a smile, his fingers tracing down my spine to splay against my hip, pressing me closer again. I could feel him harden, ready for me. The ache in my core reminded me of every tremor of pleasure he'd drawn from me. I hooked a leg over his hip, letting his member trace my slit, moaning softly in pleasure.

"That wasn't what I meant," I said, tilting my body to feel more of him pressed there.

"You do not seem to be complaining." His throaty laugh tickled my neck where he pressed his lips, grazed me with those sharp teeth. Nipped at me deliciously. Oh gods, but I wanted him again, as much as I could feel he wanted me.

"Roll over," I said, trying to push him with my body. He was so heavy that I didn't have a chance in hell without his cooperation.

Finally, he conceded, moving slightly so that his horns stuck off the edge of the bed and he could lie flat. I straddled him, but my knees didn't touch the bed, so I had to switch tactics and plant my feet on either side of him.

From this angle he was huge, the expanse of his chest laid out in front of me, his long legs hanging off the other side of the bed. And that cock... I squirmed just thinking about having him inside me again.

Ribbed for my pleasure. How the fuck did I get so lucky?

Kavi's body stiffened under me, and not in the good way. A preternatural chill flooded the room as he rolled me off him and stood, the fur on his legs bristling, the muscles in his arm rippling as he assumed a fighting stance.

CHAPTER FOURTEEN

CHAPTER FOURTEEN

N*ico.*

My lip curled in a snarl as I turned to face the monster who owned The Nest. I slid my feet further apart to brace against whatever force he delivered. It was unlike him to come barging in unannounced.

"Kavi. I should have known she'd be here." Nico's dark skin blended into the shadows, the feathers of his wings rustling like whispers.

"I didn't lure her, if that's what you're insinuating." I sneered at him. This winged creature had been both my savior and my jailer in a sense. While he had purchased the lands around here, created The Nest, a haven for those like us, he'd also made sure that no monster who entered left again.

"So defensive." Nico stalked closer to me, letting his wings drop so that they shrouded him, morphing into a thick cloak. His skin was still that sleek black of his original form, making him seem like he was one with the shadows.

There was movement behind me and I glanced over my shoulder to see Tamara twisting the sheet around her body to cover her nakedness.

"Oh." Nico raising an eyebrow. "You move quickly, old friend."

I stepped to the side, blocking Tamara from his view until she was ready.

"Well, you've had your fun now. She must return with me to the retreat. Her people are looking for her."

As he said those words, I could practically hear them above us, though I knew it was nothing but his magic.

"They are searching the woods, and we wouldn't want them to find this place, would we?" One eyebrow arched, the rest of his face remaining impassive. He knew he had the power here, but what he didn't know was that I couldn't let her leave. Without her I would grow heartsick.

"Find an explanation," I growled. "She stays."

Nico's wings twitched, morphing from coat to feathers and then back again, the only sign that my demand even slightly ruffled him.

"You know the rules," he hissed. "You know how we stay hidden."

I could feel Tamara behind me now. She reached out and slid an arm around my waist, ducking under my arm so that we were side by side, connected. I glanced down at her, saw her force her breath in, long and slow, before exhaling in the same way. At least in this form Nico wasn't as intimidating as his monster self.

"You're the guy from The Nest. The owner," her voice wavered slightly, the dig of her nails into my skin the only other sign of her nerves. She was so damn brave. So fucking beautiful. I had to tamp down the urge to fight Nico right here for her because I could tell she didn't want to go either.

Nico inclined his head. "And you need to return to your own kind."

"What happens if I don't want to?"

Nico's fingers twitched as though they would revert to claws any moment, then he forcibly relaxed them.

"Then you put Kavi at risk. You put me at risk, not to mention the countless others reliant on this safe space. I cannot allow that to happen."

The threat was quiet but clear, and it reverberated in my brain. The fur on my legs bristled, and my ears twitched, my tail flicking violently. It took everything in me not to lunge at him, to find a weapon, to cleave, to claw.

Tamara circled to look at me, her hair still tousled from sleep, the sheet clinging to her perfect body. She placed a palm against my bare chest and I could feel the warmth of her. The strength of her.

"Kavi," she said.

My heart shattered with the pain in that one word. The tension in my name.

"No," I said, gripping her hand, drawing her to me with the other. "You cannot go."

"I don't want to," she whispered. "But I have to. I can't risk anything happening to you. I'll come back. I'll find a way. This is where I want to be. With you."

My breath was ragged in my chest, and I shook my head.

"I promise," she said with so much strength that I had to believe her. She rose on her tiptoes and placed a hand on each of my cheeks, kissing me long and slow, not caring that Nico was there. I claimed her with my lips, crushed against her, tasting a drop of blood from her mouth or mine I didn't know, didn't care. We were bonded, and I just had to trust in that.

Trust in her.

I ducked my head as she retreated, pressing my forehead to hers. "I will see you soon."

"You will," she said.

And then she stepped away from me, reaching for what remained of her clothes.

CHAPTER FIFTEEN

TAMARA

It wasn't that I wanted to go. Because I didn't. My heart ached as I left Kavi behind, and I could practically feel his anger at Nico, his loss at my decision. I just hoped he knew my promise was true. I would come back. Nothing would stop me from doing so.

"You understand that if you speak a word about this to anyone else, I will be forced to discredit you or silence you?" Nico didn't bother to look at me. Clearly he expected to be obeyed without question; and truthfully, I had no desire to go against it. No one would believe me anyway.

How was the retreat, Tamara? Oh, you know, went for a walk, fell into an abandoned labyrinth and fell for a satyr. How was your week?

Yeah, that was going to end with me in forced therapy, and I had no desire for that.

"I'll keep my mouth shut, but I meant what I told Kavi. I'm coming back to him. You can't stop me."

Nico spun and faced me, his cloak twitching into feathers and then back to its fabric appearance. It was some kind of magic, I knew, but what was the point in questioning it at this point?

"I could stop you, if I wanted to." He dropped his shoulders, forced some of the tension from his frame. "But I don't want to. He deserves happiness, just like the rest of us."

"And you don't have a problem with the fact I'm human?"

Nico snickered. "My own lover is human, though she spent a long time trying to put me in my grave before she ended up in my bed."

"Oh." My mouth hanging open. I had not been expecting that. "Right. Okay."

"You are new here, and have much to learn, but if Kavi has chosen you, then you come under my protection. I wish only to keep this place safe, for all of us."

I was going to have to rapidly change my approach to this monster. I thought his breaching our love nest meant we would have to fight to be together, but the opposite was true. He turned again and kept walking. Despite the darkness of these halls, he seemed to have no problem navigating the space.

"If you can limp, this will go easier. I'll have one of my staff return you to the city on the premise of getting you checked out. Then it's up to you. If you wish to return, you can call my assistant and you'll be collected, but you have to tidy away your life first. You'll be given a fake job here at The Nest for as long as you wish to remain."

I pulled to a stop. "What?"

Nico sighed, then turned to me again. The shadows obscured his expression, but that was probably a good thing for me.

"As I said before." His patience clearly fraying. "This place must be protected at all costs. If you choose to be here, you need a reason. I will not fake your death and deny you your life; that would be harmful to you, and my lover requires that even the humans who live with us are protected." I could practically hear the way his teeth ground together. "Can we get out of here now? As much as you might like this place, I dislike being underground."

I pressed my lips together, suppressing the chuckle that threatened to escape. This beast, the one in control of everything here, and he was afraid of being in the labyrinth. A creature of the sky, clearly. We got moving again, and Nico led me to a nearby set of stairs that exited into fresh air, and a small, high-walled garden.

"Where are we?" I asked, spinning on the spot. There were a few flower beds and a double-glazed door. Nico approached it and turned the key, locking it behind us, and drawing the curtain to cover it. We were inside a small antechamber, and beyond that there was another room, what looked like a large, luxurious living area, complete with kitchenette.

"This is a gathering space for those who live on the grounds, of the non-human variety. It's kept away from the main complex to avoid any...run-ins. But it serves its purpose."

He walked to a set of double-glazed doors, one of which he slid open, showing an expansive garden full of wildflowers and trees. He pointed to the left.

"Go that way, through the gate – the code is 2945 – then keep going left, you'll find the main complex. Hopefully one of the searchers will find you before you get there. And make sure you limp."

My head was still reeling with the information as I stepped outside and walked across the garden toward the high fence surrounding it. Higher than your regular six-foot ones, though if someone came out here with a drone, they'd still be able to spy.

Unless there was some kind of magic preventing that too? My brain couldn't think about that now.

I found the gate, entered the code and stepped through. The gate automatically closed behind me with a loud *thunk*, and I wondered whether the same code would get me back in. Pushing those thoughts aside I got moving, remembering to limp and look as bedraggled and sore as I should have after a few nights in the woods. My clothes – or rather, the damage to them – were doing the bulk of that job.

The reality was that I felt rested, satiated in ways I'd never been before, and the only aches remaining in my body were from making love with Kavi. My core clenched at the thought of his impressive member and the way he'd used his tongue to work magic on me.

"I see her!" someone yelled. "Tamara!"

I stopped moving, glancing around for the voice, and then she came closer. It was Keziah, and my relief at seeing her face surprised me. We were work friends, not really hang outside work friends. But she was someone I knew, someone I liked, and that felt so damn good. I had a sudden urge to tell her all of the crazy things that had happened since I'd sat beside her at dinner. To warn her not to go off the trails, not to go too far from the retreat.

I wouldn't take back what I'd learned; would never give up having met Kavi, but I wasn't sure I'd wish this life shattering revelation on anyone else. My brain was still struggling to comprehend it all.

I hobbled toward her, making it clear that my ankle hurt, wishing it was a whole lot worse because the desire to run was overwhelming. She crushed me into a hug and then pulled back to look at me. There were a few cuts and scrapes still, and my clothing was dirty and torn. Her face creased in concern.

"I'm fine. I swear. I'm just so happy to see you," I surprised myself with the honesty in those words. Because it hit me then that if I was to do this – leave everything I knew and come here – I would miss her. I would miss my family. Those day-to-day things that I was so accustomed to.

Could I?

His face filled my mind along with that feeling of rightness that I'd never had with anyone else. The feel of his arms around me, the safety I'd felt cocooned with him in his lair.

Yes. I would. I'd do it all for him, for us, even if it meant giving up everything else. Even though I didn't have to.

"Come on, I'd kill for some fresh water," I said, wrapping an arm around her shoulder. She supported me back to the complex, where someone found a wheelchair of all things and pushed me through to the medical bay. It felt like half a dozen people hovered in the room as my cuts were cleaned and medicated, my ankle wrapped. They were all asking questions, questions I didn't know how to answer and then Nico came in, looking far more human than before. No trace of the monster I knew he was.

"I'm Nico, the owner of the retreat," he said, holding out a hand for me to shake. I took it, head too full of thoughts and questions that I didn't trust myself to actually speak.

Everything here was so normal, so mundane, as well as being a hive of activity. Gemma bustled in then, eyes going wide at the state of me. I wished everyone would just leave me alone. I was fine and the fuss was overwhelming me, the same way it had on the night we'd arrived. I needed out.

"Clear the room," Nico commanded. "I think Tamara needs a moment. If you'd step outside with me." He directed this at Gemma, who conceded with a concerned nod.

And then they were gone and I was alone, and I could breathe again.

I inhaled a long, shaky breath and leaned back in the chair, forcing my body to relax. I wanted to be outside again, on the trails, or back in the labyrinth with Kavi. It hit me right then that he gave me the same feeling I had when I was alone; only better. I'd barely been hanging on at work – was on the verge of quitting anyway. I had nothing to lose by taking Nico's offer. This mad return to reality was showing me that. I needed to go. To get away from here and tidy up my life so I could get back.

Nico entered then, closing the door firmly behind him. "One of the staff will take you back to your apartment. You have two weeks to tidy your affairs and return." He handed me a business card along with a small vial. "Drink it."

"What is it?" I asked, turning it over in my hands. The glass was clear, and a deep blue liquid was flecked with silver.

"A vial of forgetting. If you haven't called me before the two weeks are up, you'll forget this place. Each day it takes you, a little more will fade."

I shook my head violently and held it out to him. "I don't want to forget."

"This is non-negotiable." His eyes narrowed. He stared, as if he could make me drink the liquid just with the force of his eyes. "I must protect The Nest at all costs. This is my insurance policy."

My hand shook as he reached out and removed the cap from the bottle. He pushed my arm back toward me, his dark eyes boring into me the whole time.

"No," I said, even as I raised that bottle to my lips. Tears spilled down my face as I drank the bitter liquid down. What if I forgot earlier? What if it wasn't enough time?

I closed my eyes, letting the empty vial fall to the floor, the bitter taste still on my lips.

"I hate you," I whispered.

"Sometimes, I hate me too," Nico's voice was softer now. "But when you arrive, I'll give you the antidote, and everything will be reversed. And you'll understand just why I have to be the asshole."

I hoped so.

After all, he was going to be my new 'boss'.

CHAPTER SIXTEEN

Kavi

Time seemed to pass so slowly now. I roamed my corridors in a fury, smashing the walls with my hammer, and then feeling the need to clean up the messes, to make the space tidy and clean for when Tamara returned.

If.

I hated Nico; though I understood him too. We had rules here, and I had been stupid to think that I was exempt. That he wouldn't realize exactly where she was. That he wouldn't come.

But I had been so wrapped up in her; her skin, her laugh, her body. Everything else had faded for those precious hours when she had been mine.

Now I had nothing to do but wait. And prepare for her return.

And if she didn't, I would have to go and get her.

My body ached, tired, sore, as if the loss of her damaged more than my heart.

I had claimed her, but she hadn't claimed me. Until that connection was complete, I would weaken further.

Without her, I was nothing.

CHAPTER SEVENTEEN

Tamara

It was all taking too long.

I'd given my notice. I'd tried to continue with the daily grind, returning to work only to leave immediately. No one else was home yet anyway, and the skeleton crew in the office had everything under control. I could not handle it. My skin practically itched to leave this place, and it felt like every moment I was away from Kavi and The Nest, I was losing something. Even if I couldn't put my finger on what, exactly.

It had only been three days and I didn't think I could wait any longer. In fact, I was packing my main bag when a jolt shot through me. My heart literally ached, and I clutched my chest, trying to take deep breaths and failing miserably.

My arm and shoulder didn't hurt. I wasn't having any other heart attack symptoms, and I was hopefully far too young and healthy for that anyway. So what the hell was going on with me?

My heart felt like it was throbbing instead of beating, but I managed to slow my breathing enough to think.

But it wasn't thinking that I needed to do right now. It was feeling, and I *felt* like there was something wrong with Kavi. The lethargy that had been weighing me down with each day I was away from him vanished, and I finished throwing items in my bag, zipped it closed and grabbed my keys.

I had to go. *Now.*

There was no time to waste. I wouldn't call Nico and wait for someone to pick me up. The urgency was overwhelming as I threw my bag into the back seat of my car and slid behind the wheel, punching The Nest into my map app and leaving the directions up to my phone, which right now was much more capable of rational thought than I was.

I raced out of town and down the highway, and it struck me that I had no regrets right now. Kavi needed me; I knew it. And that was all that mattered. He was all that mattered. I had to work hard to keep to the speed limit or as close as possible. Being pulled over would only delay me and I didn't think I could cope with that right now.

By the time I finally arrived, that ache in my chest was all I could feel, and the voice of the map woman was driving me absolutely nuts. I pulled into the long driveway for The Nest and followed it to the main retreat, then kept going past the sign that said, 'Private. Do not enter.' I didn't want to see any of my co-workers, didn't want to see anyone but Nico and for him to give me the antidote and let me back into the labyrinth.

I needed Kavi.

Kavi needed me.

Blood whooshing in my ears, I got out of the car and didn't even bother to shut the door. I ran across the lawn and pounded on the main door.

It took a minute, but then a red headed woman opened the door and looked at me curiously.

"Wait. Tamara?" Her brow creased in confusion. "How did you get here?" She looked out the door and spotted my car. "Are you okay?"

"Kavi. I need to see him."

"I-"

I didn't wait, just pushed inside the house and heard her close the door behind me.

"Can you let me in? I can feel... something. I just-" My hand went to my chest again, the ache worse, the lethargy creeping back into my body now that I was here. I scanned the room, trying to find something that I recognised, some way down. "I need the antidote. Now." I spun to look at the woman, who appeared quite concerned about the state of me.

"Sure, yeah. Come on." She shook her head and focused on what I'd asked, leading me through to another room and then opening a small drawer that contained a bunch of vials like the one Nico had made me take. She selected one with a red liquid inside, and I wasted no time snapping off the lid and downing it. The small burn that traced my throat all the way to my belly felt like an assurance that things would be okay.

"Now, let me into the labyrinth," I said, tossing the vial into a waste bin.

"Are you sure you want that?" The woman planted her hands on her waist, and raised an eyebrow.

"Look, I assume you're Nico's human lover. Well, I'm Kavi's. This is what I want. *He* is what I want. Now open the damn door."

She quickly moved to another door, and when I followed, I could see that this was the place Nico had brought me to. The double doors were there, waiting. I rushed across the room and tried the handle, but it was locked.

"Hold on," the woman said, grabbing some keys and inserting the right one into the door. As soon as she slid it open, I was through and rushing for the stairs. Whatever words she might have spoken lost to me as I plunged into the gloom of the labyrinth.

The air was immediately cooler here, closer. But it wasn't claustrophobic for me now. It felt like home.

It struck me then that I actually had no idea how to make my way back to him. I'd been lost in the labyrinth when we met. He'd carried me back to his rooms; I'd been too focused on his arms holding me against his muscled chest to notice which turns we were making.

I cupped my hands around my mouth and yelled, "Kavi!" and then waited.

Nothing but the sound of my own voice echoed back to me.

"Kavi!" I set off down the hallway, feeling like this was familiar enough, but then a sharp jolt tore through my chest, and I *knew* it wasn't the right direction. I spun and ran back the other way, trusting my instincts, that tug in my body that told me when I was right or wrong until I finally laid eyes on the door to his chambers.

I slowed to a walk, catching my breath, afraid of what I might find on the other side. Everything in my body was aching now, weary, trembling. I pushed open the door and stepped into his room.

He was lying on the bed, still as the dead, his chest rising and falling in shaky, shallow breaths.

"No," the word came out so choked that I wasn't sure I'd even made a sound. I ran across the room and threw myself onto the bed.

"Kavi?" I ran my hands over his face, his horns. His eyes were closed, but they squinted open at my voice.

"Tamara." My name came out on a sigh, wistful, as though he thought he was dreaming me.

"I'm here. You fool, what did you do?"

He tried to shake his head, but he could barely move.

"What happened?" I spoke louder, hoping to shake him from whatever was going on.

I pressed my lips against his, kissing him like I'd been dreaming of for the last few days, running my hands over his chest, threading one through his hair and up to his horns, stroking them the way I wanted to stroke his thick member, though now was not the time or the place.

He seemed to come alive beneath me, his mouth responding, his tongue searching for mine. One of his big hands dragged me closer so that I was lying against him.

When we pulled apart, breathless, it felt like life had returned to flush his dark skin. His eyes fluttered open, locking onto mine.

"You're here." Awe filled his voice.

"Yes," I shot back with a stupid grin. "You're sick. I could feel it. Here." I pressed a hand to my chest or tried.

"I am. I was." He clutched me tighter to him.

"What happened?" I asked. "I wish I'd known sooner. I'd have come."

Kavi swallowed hard. Like his throat was dry. I looked around and found some water, lifting the cup to his lips and gently pouring some of the liquid into his mouth. He drank it, sighing in relief.

"Tell me, Kavi." I stared down at him, needing to know. Wanting to make this better and having this strange sense that somehow, I could.

His amber eyes locked on mine and they were lined with sorrow. Regret? I couldn't tell for sure. "You need to claim me."

"Claim?" I rocked back on my heels, confusion clouding my mind. "I do. I did. I want to be with you and only you. I'm here with you, now."

He shook his head, though I could see it took some effort. He grasped my hand and brought it to his chest. I could feel the thump of his heart beneath my fingers. "Do you remember when I bit you? Hard enough to make you bleed?"

My free hand went to my shoulder. He'd asked first, clamped down so damn hard but it had felt amazing, flooding my body with a pleasure I'd never expected. "How could I forget?" I said with a smile.

"I *claimed* you then. I wanted you as mine from the moment I saw you, hell from the moment that I scented you in my hallways." He swallowed hard, and I realized that it wasn't a dry throat causing his nerves. "I need you, Tamara. I need you to need me too. I'm lovesick."

I flung myself at his chest, knowing that I wasn't going to hurt him with my touch. He wasn't sick with a physical illness, but from his big dumb heart. "Why? You must have known this would happen," I demanded.

"I couldn't help myself," he whispered in my ear. His hands caressed my back. "I don't want you to do it, if you don't want to. Just having you here with me is enough."

His voice was so soft, his hands so gentle. I couldn't understand the compulsion behind this claim, but clearly it was important to him, his people, and it meant the difference between a life fully lived and a shadow of himself. I had a choice to make, and it was clear. I moved up his body, kissing a trail to his neck. The skin there was tough, and I wasn't sure my measly human teeth would be able to get through.

"Does it have to be the neck?" my voice hoarse, raspy with want, desire, and anticipation. What would it feel like? What would he taste like on my tongue? Would there be any change in me afterwards?

"No." His voice was ragged and his hands were on my back, urging me on but not pressuring me. "Is this really what you want?"

I didn't answer with words. I licked the lobe of his ear instead, the shudder of his body under mine a drug all of its own, and then I bit down, knowing that this was one of the most sensitive spots on his body. It took a few seconds, but then I tasted the tang of blood on my tongue.

Kavi stiffened beneath me, his whole body going rigid and his fingers digging into my back, holding me there as he rode whatever was flooding his system. I lapped at the blood, swallowing it down, feeling a tingle I didn't expect.

Something was shifting inside me. I gasped in awe at the sensation, understanding now what I had done.

This was a connection unlike any other. I could sense Kavi on new levels, and my heart swelled, my yearning to be close to him strengthening. I pressed a hand to my lips, eyes widening in shock as I sat up.

"Are you okay?" His voice was already stronger, the color returning to his skin. His eyes searched mine as if he was looking for a flicker of regret.

But all they contained was wonder. I knew this; because it was the feeling overwhelming me right now. I nodded, unable to form words. A smile split Kavi's lips, and then he sat up, pulled me into his lap and kissed me hard.

I chuckled against Kavi's mouth, then nestled my head against his shoulder.

This was my new life.

Our new life.

"Better?" I asked.

"The best," Kavi replied.

THE END

Thank you for reading *Stalking Tamara*. If you want to find out more about Nico, and how The Nest began, then why not check out *Run Red!*

* * *

Join my mailing list to stay up-to-date on my works in progress and get access to exclusive promotions.
Click HERE or paste this link into your favorite browser:
https://linktr.ee/novablake

ABOUT THE AUTHOR

Nova is a lover of pizza, coffee, and zombies (in no particular order). She was raised on a healthy diet of fantasy, horror, and science fiction, and despite many attempts by various English teachers, has refused to budge on her position that these are the best genres ever. When she's not busy raising her wonderfully creepy children, or dreaming of the day she'll have an army of ninja kittens, she is writing, reading, or playing games.

She writes a whole range of subgenres, but for now her one true love is MONSTERS. She always enjoys a bit of darkness in her tales, as well as a chuckle here and there, so you can expect all of her books to be some combination of magical, spooky, sexy, and fun.

facebook.com/novablakewrites

instagram.com/novablakewrites

tiktok.com/@novablakewrites

MY VEILED PURSUER

OPAL FAIRCHILD

CHAPTER ONE
INTO THE LABYRINTH

T he way my skirts feel around my ankles as they swish to the music coming from outside makes me feel delicate. It's been so long since I've seen myself in anything other than my old, ratty gray Imperium uniform.

"Echo! You look gorgeous; look at you," Jetta says, taking a piece of my coiled tawny hair into her fingers.

Her face is rosy around the edges from drinking mead. I can smell the sweetness of it on her breath. Still, I'll accept the compliment. We deserve to have fun tonight after days of setting up the camp.

I look down at my skirt, loving the brighter periwinkle, especially with the way the bioluminescent lights from the planet glimmer off the satin.

"Thank you. I'm glad the commander is giving us at least tonight to let loose." I giggle, thinking about how hard our work has been getting to this point. We've been in space for over a year. I do miss my cabin on ship because the ratty tents are disgusting and smell musty.

"It will thrill Kane to see you looking like this." Jetta's hand falls from my hair, giving me a saucy wink. "You're not wearing your glasses, are you? Don't cover up your eyes; I'd kill to have those."

Peering into the holo mirror, I sigh. I wish I didn't need them, but unfortunately, I don't have enough credits to get surgery. Instead, the large coke-bottle lenses make my stormy gray eyes bug-like.

"I don't care what he thinks; you know that." It's a lie that tastes sour on my tongue because I've had a crush on my boss for years now.

Working side by side in the lab has made it easy to grow fond of him, and he and I worked seamlessly together. Still, it's something he doesn't know, and I'll never tell him.

Jetta shakes her head, making her blonde hair fall free. She pats my arm with a tinkling laugh before patting my shoulder. "Come on, let's hurry. We only have a few hours until we'll have to pretend this was all a dream."

Jetta leaves my tent in a flurry of her yellow dress, leaving my heart racing as I follow. Once we're both outside, the sound of music fills the air, and I peer up through the trees that glow a brilliant purple and pink. I allow myself only the briefest moment to look at life on the other side, excited at the prospect of finally seeing it up close.

A hand reaches out to pull me away, reminding me that soon enough, we'll be out there seeing the world, beginning life anew for all of us. "Come on, girl. Your plants will wait for you tomorrow!"

The flicker of something in the distance catches my attention again.

Azgul lives in nothing but darkness, but there's bright light among the array of swaying trees. The trees of this planet tower like skyscrapers; each limb and flower shine in a multitude of brilliant bioluminescence. They are varying ranges of purples, pinks, bright blue, and all of them shimmering as brightly as the moon.

A few of the trees appear to have bulbous lanterns attached to their bark, and in a flurry of wings, there are bird-like creatures that perch in the higher branches. Some trees have long, slender tentacle-like branches that waver in the wind, while others appear more like trees I've seen before, standing tall and strong with leaves that glow.

Yet there is a flicker of light far in the distance that reminds me of fire. "Jetta, there's something out there," I whisper, jerking her hand to pull her closer.

"Nothing is out there; this planet is entirely void of sentient life. There's no boogeyman to get you." Jetta sighs, dropping my hand. "You need to loosen up."

A loud trilling battle cry cuts through the air, and a spear hits the side of one of the tents, cutting through it like butter ripping the fabric.

Jetta screams immediately, rushing off into one of the tents, likely for a weapon, but I can't move. My feet are planted into the grass as I see the monstrous beings on four legs. They have large scorpion-like tails that curl up from their backs with humanoid torsos. Each one has a spear with a glowing fire-like light at its end.

"Echo, move!" I hear my name just as the beasts enter the camp.

My feet swivel, and all at once, I react. My heart is hammering in my chest, but I hear the skittering of their legs behind me.

The crew from the Peony rushes out of the tent, many too inebriated to run, many falling down just as a spear cuts through the air toward the group.

I'm jerked backward immediately by a tug on my scalp as rough hands pull at my hair. I scream out in pain as tears well in my eyes, forcing them closed. "Let me go!"

Gunfire ricochets around the camp as do the shrieks of pain. As I'm pulled backward, I dig my heels into the dirt, hoping beyond hope that it might deter the absolute strength that holds me.

Another shot is fired, and the grip of the beast that holds goes slack. I can't see where it came from, but on instinct, my legs move. There are so many bodies, theirs and ours, that I choose to maneuver through the tents. Sweat laces my brow, but I shove through until I'm on the opposite side.

"No!" I hear someone yell.

Then there's choking and a deep, grotesque laugh in reply.

So I run. I run so fast, not thinking about where I'm headed. Deep into the darkness of the woods I go, not stopping until I can't hear the sounds anymore.

My chest aches and constricts with exertion, and I finally stop to catch my breath. Doubled over, I inhale through my nose until finally my breathing evens out. When I settle, feeling the welling of tears in my throat, I glance at where I am.

There's at least twenty feet in a circle where the trees have chosen not to grow, a huge clearing with forest on either side. The moss here glows with each step of my foot, my shoes long gone. It's as if the moss is electric.

I can't hear screaming. There's nothing but the tittering of birds and wildlife around me, along with the rapid beating of my heart.

A great glowing antlered beast walks through the trees. There are six subsections on two of its heads with four legs, and its body is a solid black with bright piercing blue eyes. It's unlike anything I've ever witnessed. What's more amazing is that it's as large as a car and doesn't stop at all to look at me before it heads off in the direction it intended.

This must be where animals graze, and I was in that deer-thing's territory. A breaking of a twig has me going rigid, and another has me running again.

The trees narrow the farther I go, and soon enough I'm walking a straight narrow line between them. Their bark is strangely normal-looking, though some have swirling bioluminescent markings that travel up in a pattern I can't discern. Tighter and tighter they grow until there's just a hair's breadth between me and them.

I reach out a hand to stroke the bark, wondering if my hand might create a light show just as my feet do on the ground. My fingers collide with the rough texture of it, and it lights up as if on command.

"Amazing–" Just when I speak, the tree moves and takes another shape. A long snake-like vine twists and curls in my periphery, but I'm too entranced in the beauty to care.

Fingers form where my hand lies flat, and then two eyes just above them. The forest hushes; the birds and wildlife cease their noises as the hand closes roughly on my arm. It jerks me forward, and the tendril behind me comes closer to my face.

"Fuck!" I scream, but there's no one here to hear me.

My yell creates a chain reaction, and the trees all move in the same way. Each one grows eyes, and their hands move, reaching out, and every tendril writhes closer to the sound.

Suddenly, the feeling of rough vine gathers against my throat, coiling around my neck until I can't breathe. I gasp the last of my breath away as the tendril wraps once more around me, and another slithers around my torso while the tree's hands grab at me closer.

One tugs at my clothes, yanks at my shirt and skirt. The sound of fabric shredding is all I hear over my heart beating in my ears. I try to wriggle, but the strength of this tree is far too much.

I'm going to die.

My eyes squeeze shut while I groan through the pain of my windpipe being crushed.

A guttural cry cuts through the sound of my heart hammering in my ears, and suddenly the tendril wound around my throat falls away. Then my body is yanked from the tree's grip, ripping the vines away. I don't have time to feel gratitude as powerful arms wrap around my middle, and then I'm jerked upwards.

The ground disappears, and the feeling of air forces a scream from my throat. My glasses nearly slide from my face, and I kick my legs. "Let me down!"

"*Hiljaen likva!*"

My eyes pan upward to the thing carrying me, and I suck in a breath.

Large pale green wings sprout from this being's back, and they have two sets of arms. Settled between a delicate aquiline nose are bright white eyes and a long antenna sprouting from its head. His body and face are entirely white, and around his neck is a thick ruff of fur. In one of his hands is a long, slender blade, dripping with a brightly glowing sap from the vines.

"Set me down!" I scream again when we dip under a limb, spiraling upward again with abandon. I think I'm going to hurl because this creature doesn't care how much my legs dangle or how close we get to the monster tree, or even that he's flying like a bat out of hell.

The thing curses under its breath, or at least I assume that's what it's doing, because we stop blissfully a moment later on a limb thick enough to stand on. It sets me on my feet, sneering at me as my legs tremble and I try to catch my breath.

"Not up here!" I screech out, peering over the side of the limb, immediately squeezing my eyes shut again. We have to be twelve stories high. I can't even see the ground at this point, and I'm with a weird butterfly thing.

"*Hiljaen itsei! O'lena kunnosi,*" it says, shaking its head. The sound of its voice is a deep baritone, and I realize now this creature is male.

I look him up and down while I try catching my breath. He has no shoes on, but his feet are two toes with a third on the ball of the foot. He has five fingers on each of his four hands. His thick biceps look as though he's of the working class.

The small green designs on his arms match the long, slender forewings on his back, and they trail up his muscular bare torso. His hind-wings are the same color, though much longer, with little designs that look like eyes on them. In my studies of old Earth insects, I recall an insect like this. It reminds me of one that fascinated me called the Luna moth.

He's clothed in nothing but a leather-looking loincloth that drapes over his front. I don't see the outline of any sort of genitalia, so maybe he has a pouch?

"What are you?" I look him up and down, realizing just how humanoid the face is. There's a delicate set of lips, but when he opens them, the lips cut across his chiseled jaw, opening further than it should.

He shakes his head, heaving an almost irritated sigh as he tilts his head down at me with a sense of superiority. "*Ekna.*" He points at the limb and pins me with his stare. "*Jah?*"

Now that I'm closer to him, I can smell something strangely tempting from him. It's sweet, almost like the baked bread from Tarsil. I've not had anything like that in ages because we eat the same thing nearly every day on the Peony. There's even a mild hint of something spicy. Why does he smell so fucking delicious?

Why would a creature like this need to smell nice? Is it a pheromone used in finding mates or a deterrent from being eaten?

I don't know what he keeps saying, but it isn't like I could comprehend his language now. Still, the sound of his voice is pleasant to listen to, and honestly, he could call me hideous. At this point, I like the way it sounds. From this height, the trees don't seem to be able to get us, which I'm highly thankful for.

At least for now.

CHAPTER TWO
SWEET LIKE HONEY

This hideous creature nearly got itself killed. It has no wings nor exo to keep it safe from the Amae'sil. We heard the loud, thunderous noises from our position in the grove, and, of course, I could not keep myself from investigating. Curiosity has always put me in detrimental situations before, but it's who I am. My hunting party knows me well enough at this point not to question my desire to find trouble.

I barely had a moment to do a single thing before I heard the scream cut through the forest. The *Amae'sil* had wrapped its vines around this tiny thing's throat, and its maw was already open, waiting to consume it.

Such a funny-looking thing. The more she screamed, the angrier she made the forest, and now that we are in a better position, I can finally take in her appearance. Two legs and arms hidden by shredded garb offering no protection. Two tiny eyes with black balls inside of a slate-colored circle. There is a high bridged snout to her face, and her russet hair is wild and untamed. Her body has a curvy shape, and she's so very short that she comes to my middle. She has no *tunsajk* either, so it's no wonder she appears clumsy on her feet. How has she survived?

"Ken yu lek me dwun?" Her legs continue to tremble as she peers down at the ground.

She has not stopped speaking since I picked her up, but if she is sentient, then I cannot in good conscience leave her to die.

The *Kugitauri* will know what to do, especially if there are more of these creatures. They clearly cannot mean us any harm the way they are now.

"Settle yourself, *otoki*; there is nowhere you can go." Even if she wanted, there is no way down from here without me.

She shakes her head. "Icnt undrsztd yyuu."

When the thing steps forward once again, I snort. The legs she stands on still tremble, and I swear she looks down every few ticks to see if the ground has gotten closer before she will swallow loudly and look at me again.

"It will do you no good to look down." Trying to hide my snicker, I force myself to swallow it down. I will need to take us to the swamp lands to find *verjima* so we can communicate, because I will be damned if I am forced to hear her speak gibberish.

A noise sounds in the distance and catches my attention. It's a light beating of wings and feet hitting the tree branches. We are too close to the Sagath boundary for my liking, and with this imbecile screaming, catching every-one's attention, then they will come bloodthirsty as ever to investigate.

While my back is turned, I feel a brief caress against my wing, enough that it sends a shiver through my entire body. Tender fingers brush against it one final time, delicate and soft, before I hear her say, "Iz so sft." I shudder, releasing a tense breath as my body tingles at the touch.

Turning on my heels, I wrench her hand away, hissing like a mad beast. Grasping her small wrist in my hands, looking down into her deep eyes, I realize she has no clue what she's just done. Does she not understand how indecent it is to touch me there? Of course not, but the feeling of tiny fingers brushing against my scales has my heart racing.

"Do not touch." I speak to her as if she is a child, enunciating every word and syllable so she might understand.

All it seems to do is cause her mouth to gape open and her eyes to blink up at me. Being this close to her, I can taste her scent on the wind. She is like nectar, though there is a hint of something akin to *lampfyr*.

My tongue darts out of my mouth to get a taste, finding the shell of her ear. A tiny little flick, just enough for me to know. It's amazing. Like flowers and sweetness. I want so badly to give in to the desire that now has my *tirska* extruding and take her against my aching body. She shudders, batting my tongue away, and her face contorts into confusion.

It's been so long since I've been touched this intimately, I forget my manners and how rude I'm behaving. I battle with all my strength to force the indecent thoughts away.

Her hands fall away with one final hiss of annoyance before I hear a Sagath battle cry. "*Vittar!*"

I grab her in my arms and press her closely. "We need to leave."

Leaping off the tree limb, I manage to dive just in time to see one of them out of the corner of my eye. The long white wings and swirling horns over his head prove this is a warrior. He's decorated in full war gear, which is nothing but *yuanji* skins and bone chest plates.

A shrill scream sounds through the air as I dive even closer to the ground, so close that the *Amae'sil* come to life. Their bright blue and pink flowers begin to light up, and their vines slowly begin to unfurl.

"That is it! Scream again, *otoki!*" The louder she is, the more they will wake from their slumber, and the Sagath will fall into the trap I'm setting. They are far too bloodthirsty for rational thought.

I dive again, and when I do, she lets out a loud yell. All at once the forest glows brighter. My arms are close enough to the ground that if I reach out, I can touch it, but I don't. I wait until I hear our pursuers behind me, then I zip up into the air.

Looking down, I see a Sagath with its larger wingspan and horned head barreling upward with sheer determination. Unfortunately for it, the tendrils of vine lash out, grasping it. I pause for a brief moment to watch as two of the vines rip the beast's arm off, feeding it into its waiting mouth.

The sound of the warriors' scream is drowned out by the trees' leaves rustling, but the small thing in my arms clutches on to me tighter with a whimper.

My fingers grip her hair, loving the way my fingers filter through it. "Shh, quiet. Now we must go."

CHAPTER THREE
TOUCHES

The mothman clutches me to his chest, holding my head against him so I can't see anything. Horrifying screams of pain ricochet through the forest. It's brutal and terrifying to hear, but it's over so quickly, I hardly have time to register anything is wrong before we're flying through the air again.

Eventually it all stops. We land, but I'm still clutched in his arms. His chest heaves with exertion. *"Mejan pitas turzassa nyit,"* he whispers as he pats the back of my head.

I can't tell what he's saying, but curiosity gets the better of me again. Earlier I touched his wing, and it was like nothing I've ever felt before. Now there's a section of his wing just under his arms that I can reach with a finger. It's only a gentle poke, but his grip on me tightens, and his back straightens before his wings draw closer to his body.

He sucks in a breath before a set of hands jerks my head back by the pony-tail. *"Vittar otoki. Aalkos miniesla!"* His eyes bore into mine. They are entirely white, but they shimmer with the bright colors of the forest.

The smell I noticed earlier grows stronger as he bends down toward my neck. He inhales a deep breath of me and hums a low sound in his throat. What he says is unintelligible as one of his arms lowers to my ass, gripping me with such ferocity that I gasp.

"Wait—I—" I barely get out what I want to say before I feel a simple flick of his tongue against my neck.

I moan, and my pussy throbs, a reaction I can't explain. The mothman's deep, desperate groan as his hands tighten their grip should concern me; instead it seems to simmer just under my skin.

One of his free hands splays against my ass under my skirt, slowly inching toward the ache that has started just between my thighs. When he finds my underwear, he roughly tugs them aside, until a finger runs along my slit, coating it in my wetness.

"*Halako sin mina otoki?*" His rich voice purrs against my neck, and I whimper.

I don't even know what he's saying, but I don't care. I just want him to touch me. Something grips at the front of my hips, clutching me to him until I feel feathers at the bare skin of my stomach. It tickles, and yet when it touches my skin, it leaves behind warmth.

His tongue and mouth pepper against my collarbone while his finger presses against my waiting core. The scent of sweetness is so strong that I can taste it on my tongue as if I'm eating it. When his finger finally enters me, I keen out a depraved sound that has me canting my hips forward against something long and wet.

Glancing down, I can hardly see between our bodies, but I don't miss the long frilled-looking tentacles that still dance around my waist. It looks like little feather dusters, and there are four of them that have gripped hold of me.

"Please." I whisper as the finger inside fills me up.

The mothman grumbles something unintelligible before pulling his finger out of my throbbing pussy. I whine at the loss of him, especially because all of his hands that were holding me let go.

He's panting when he stands back upright. I watch as the long white feather-like tendrils recede back inside his pouch, along with the tip of something bright green.

The mothman runs a hand down his face, shaking his head at me. "*En voa, ien vila.*"

With a sigh of disappointment, I shuffle my skirt back around me, covering my body, moving my shirt back over my shoulder.

I look up at his face. There's a pained expression there pulling his lips down and his brows together. *"Et todellaken teida milla peela,"* he says, patting my head once more.

"I wish I could understand what you're saying."

Instead I'm answered with him pulling me back into his arms, and he steps off the branch, taking flight again.

CHAPTER FOUR
THE BOG

We fly for a long time, but slower than before. It's almost a leisurely pace, which helps the somersault my stomach gives every time he dives or moves quickly. Eventually we settle somewhere, but I can smell it long before I see it. There's an almost sour, rank smell that reminds me of the trash compactor on the ship. It lingers in my nose, making my nose wrinkle up. God, it's horrible.

The moth lets me down on a more slender limb this time. It barely has enough space for both my feet, and when I look down, it's covered in moss. Below us, a large swamp shimmers like the stars, and the roots of tall grass shimmer under the water. Skinny pale pink trees with large spines grow from inside the water. A large tree in its center has long tendrils that dip into the water, and there are large lily pads everywhere.

Staring at the gorgeous scene before me has excitement tickling at my nerves. This place is beautiful. Everything about this planet is gorgeous and dangerous. That goes for the mothman too.

He slides off the branch onto one of the large lily pads, but the way he moves is like a dance. Every step he takes is calculated as I shimmy off the branch to follow. When my boot touches the lily pad, I'm shocked at how solid it feels. It's as strong as any flooring, holding my weight with ease.

"*Pysi siela.*" The moth's hands come out in a halt motion, pinning me with his gaze. "*Psyi.*" He points at the limb, and I shake my head.

"I don't want to stay by myself. What if one of those things comes back?" I cross my arms over my chest. "I don't even have a gun." Not like it would matter because I hardly know how to use one. It's standard for some of the personnel to carry them, but I stay in the lab, so it isn't as if I've ever had a use for one.

He shakes his head, almost exasperated with me, before turning to start his weird dance across the pads. The further away he gets, the more nervous I feel. He's only a few feet away, close enough, if I needed to, I could get to him, but why I feel safety with this moth creature I can't understand. At least he hasn't tried to eat me yet, so that's something.

Eventually he gets across the swamp to the large tree in the center, but I can't figure out why he walked at all when he could fly. The closer to the tree's tendrils he gets, the more they begin to sway, but he moves so slowly. When he's close enough, he steps onto one of the large upturned roots before bending down near its base. His hands slowly and methodically lift a section of reeds, shoving one of his hands into the water.

Why he had to go that far to get into the water doesn't make sense because couldn't he have done it here where I am?

Suddenly the water breaks around him as something leaps up at his hand. He doesn't move, but I see the way his wings and back go rigid. Is everything on this planet out to eat you?

I gasp as the thing beneath the water comes up a second time, this time leaping enough that I have a chance to see it. It's bright orange with serrated teeth and large fan-like fins as large as my arm. It doesn't bite the mothman. Instead it seems to be angry that he's messed up where he was living.

When the fish goes back beneath the waves, the mothman pulls his fist out of the water. I'm not sure what he has, but he doesn't open his fist. Instead he slowly begins to move in that same dancing way back toward me.

Once he's standing in front of me, one of his other hands beckons me closer, and I shake my head. "What, why?"

He sighs, almost annoyed with me, but I can't tell what he wants.

Then he steps closer on the same lily pad I'm on and waits a moment so it can settle with both of our weight. With one step, he's right in front of me, and one of his hands reaches out to pull me closer. I'm so used to it that I don't move, thinking we're going to fly again. One arm is around my waist while another immediately grabs my head, wrenching my neck to the side.

"Hey, what the fuck?" I push at his chest, immediately taking a step back, but there's nowhere to go.

His hands are tender as they touch the side of my neck. "*Se onki.*" He shushes me after that. My breathing hitches as I lean into that touch, unsure why it feels so comforting when I should be worried this moth might eat me.

The hand that was in the swamp comes closer to my ear; the water drips on my cheek and slides down my neck. His deep voice rattles off more words before I feel something slimy against the entrance of my ear. "Get the fuck off me!"

Digging my fingers into his skin, I try to squirm away, but his grip is far too tight as his massive body pulls mine flush with his. The slimy feeling ebbs into nothing but blood-boiling pain. Something digs inside my ear canal, worming its way into my skull.

My scream rattles through me as the white-hot feeling of something maneuvering inside of me takes over my body. My spine is rigid, sweat breaking out all over my skin. Immediately a large hand covers my mouth to silence me as more whispered words are spoken as if to keep me calm.

My knees knock together, and the mothman holds me up so I don't fall over. Eventually the pain stops, but I'm laced with sweat and panting as I'm held up by his arms.

"*Otoki,* are you well?" Gingerly he pushes the hair that's stuck to the side of my face away.

The sound of his deep, sultry voice shocks me because for once I understand him. I have no energy to move, but I lift my head enough now that his hand has moved away. "I understood you..."

"Mm...yes, that was the point of coming to collect a *verjima.*" He sounds so annoyed with me, but his hands continue to hold me up and stroke my hair regardless of his tone.

"You put something inside my head!" I finally wriggle from his arms, but he doesn't allow me much movement. "You didn't ask me if I wanted that thing in there."

His broad hands don't cease their tender touches. "Did you want to continue to misunderstand one another? Unfortunately, now that it has made home inside your head, nothing can be done. I am truly glad to speak with you now."

The mothman rubs one of his fingers over my bottom lip, caressing it as he studies my reaction to him. My breath catches because why does he have the ability to make me forget how angry I am? His fingers are just as soft as his wings were, like velvet. I wonder what that would feel like all over my body?

A shiver runs up my spine despite myself. "You mean to tell me, thanks to you, I have a worm inside my head forever now?"

"For as long as you live, *kilaa*." He pauses his touches, opening his mouth to allow his long proboscis-like tongue to unfurl. It's a rich navy blue, and as it unfurls, I realize it's twice as long as mine is. It moves in the air a few moments before retreating back into his mouth. "Now that we understand one another, and you have been intimate with me twice already, it is only fair that I have the same ability, is it not?"

"What do you mean?" My voice is a breathy sound until his fingers clutch the bottom of my chin. The smell of freshly baked food is stronger than ever, and I find myself inhaling just to taste it. "I wasn't intimate with you..."

A rich, deep-sounding chuckle is all I hear before his face is inches from mine. His blank white eyes are so captivating as they shimmer in all the glowing lights the forest provides. He's so beautiful, I don't know if I can or want to look away from him. "The lust you have unleashed inside me is a river overflowing."

My breathing halts, and I blink up at him. "I don't under—"

His breath tickles over my lips, and when I feel it, my mouth parts lusting for something, anything to touch me. What I didn't expect was for his long, slender tongue to dart from his mouth into mine. His mouth collides after it, but not in a soft, simple kiss. No, it's full of power, lust and desire.

One of his hands grips me around my back, folding me into him as his tongue runs along the inside of my mouth. At first it's slow flicks, easy and measured so I can tease it with mine. It feels like any tongue would, though it's a little narrower than a human's. My fingers twine around his neck, moaning into his mouth as the sweet smell of him envelops me. The little ruff of fur around his neck is so easy to bury my hands in.

Deeper his tongue goes until I feel it against the back of my throat. Immediately I gag, and he moves it back to an easier position.

It's then he picks up the pace, and his long tongue starts to nearly vibrate inside my mouth. It seeps into every fiber of my body. He's tasting every single nook and cranny, and the vibration is uncomfortable enough that my eyes begin to water. When his tongue dips into the back of my throat, I push at his shoulders. His other hands begin to knead at my ass while he holds me steady against him.

My body throbs as the vibrations increase, and a liquid heat begins growing between my legs. I want to feel it on my pussy, not in my throat, so badly. My gagging doesn't stop, but the saliva in my mouth starts to pool, and that's when he finally stops.

He pulls his tongue out with one farewell flick against mine. With a final peck against my lips, it's all over. "We will finish this later, *otoki*.

I hardly hear him over my rough panting. As my fingers leave the soft, downy ruff of his neck, I pretend not to notice the captivating smile on his face. I wipe away the drool on my chin, trying and partially failing to put myself back together.

CHAPTER FIVE
PAYBACK

The dazed expression that lingers across her now rosy-toned face is a sight to behold. I find it excruciatingly hard to remain composed now that I can understand her sweet voice. I'm completely enthralled by this tiny little bug. My *tirska* is pressing against my seam, begging to be touched. Yet I cannot, not yet.

"What was that about?" She continues to wipe her saliva from her chin.

Surely she knows. "As I said you were intimate with me, so I have repaid the favor, *otoki*."

I tip her chin with one of my nails, forcing her to finally gaze at me. Her face blossoms into a richer shade of red and she bites her bottom lip. "Why do you keep saying that to me? Are you cussing me out?" Her brows knit together.

I cannot help it; I bark out a laugh. "Oh no, it is but a name to call you as I did not know yours."

"My name's Echo, not otokee?" She completely butchers the word, forcing me to swallow another laugh to spare her the embarrassment.

"Eu-toh-ki," I pronounce for her.

Her eyes roll in her head, showing me the whites of her eyes. Is she intending to show fear? "What's your name, if we're going to be giving them? It's better than calling you 'Moth.'"

"Xakiras."

She hums a little. "Can you take me back to my camp? My people were attacked, and I need to find my crew." She hesitates a moment, chewing at the bottom of her lip. "Please, Xakiras?"

I should lie, tell her I will take her to wherever she needs, but I know it will be of no use to give her false hope. "I cannot. Not yet."

I feel saddened by the defeated look she takes on because I cannot take her anywhere but to the capital. We cannot allow *ukolist* alone to die or perhaps destroy our lands.

"What is your plan then? I'm only trusting you because you haven't tried to eat me yet. You did kiss me—" Echo pauses, and her eyes dart away again. "I've been with aliens before, but they usually ask me first."

She speaks so quickly that I find it hard to follow her train of thought. "I am taking you to the *Kugitauri*. As for the rest, you touched me without my consent first, so, I have every intention of finishing what we started."

My fingers trace the edges of Echo's face again, but her hand slaps it away.

"Nothing will happen from this point on between us. You can take me back to the camp right this second. I need to find my crew as soon as possible, and the Imperium needs to know where I am." Echo's lip pokes out in a pout, and she crosses her arms. There is a simmering fury lingering behind her eyes that flickers like *lampfyr*. She will be stubborn about this, I see.

"I have been flying much of the day and need rest. We will speak more on the matter of taking you back the way we came then. For now we should seek shelter."

Echo sighs, those stormy eyes of hers downcast. "There were large scorpions that attacked us. I don't know what they were; they had four legs and exoskeletons, but the upper half of them were humanoid. I need to go back."

Then it is too late for them. The Krel leave nothing alive; how did Echo make it out alive?

When I am to my feet, I finally answer her. I keep the information to myself, knowing that for now, we are far too out in the open. She will be inconsolable when she realizes they are all likely gone. "We will continue this conversation when we are in shelter. I am certain you do not wish to smell the bog any longer than necessary."

Echo shakes her head, her brows knitting together. "How long will we be gone? Just take me back." She crosses her arms, widening her stance. "I refuse to go with you."

Echo is trapped here, unable to keep herself safe unless she is with me—with all of the Nocris.

"*Otoki*...you will go back when I say you may go back." I step closer to her, looming over her, and yet she doesn't back away. The defiance sparkles anew, and I wish things could be different than they are. "Now do you wish to be taken against your will, or shall you come with me willingly?"

Echo's lip pokes out a little bit further than usual, and she looks up at me defiantly. "You wouldn't dare!"

I snort, unperturbed by her because I will take her to safety whether she wants it or not. I will try to be kind, however. She is, after all, in a new place, where she clearly does not understand anything.

"Echo, I will do what I must to ensure your safety. Please do not make me treat you like I would a child." My patience is growing thin with her. I grab her, pulling her small body to mine as I have multiple times.

"Let me go! I don't want to go with you; I need to get back to my camp!" Echo pushes against my chest, wriggling to get free. The more she struggles and screams, the harder I hold her.

"Quiet! Do you want the Sagath to hear you?" I grit through my teeth, jerking her up closer to me.

"Go fuck yourself." She brings her foot down on mine, sending a wave of pain through my body.

I hiss in pain, grunting and baring my teeth at her assault on me. My anger boils, and without warning, I grip her tighter and rise into the air. Taking care to miss the tendrils from the great tree, I fly faster and harder than I have before. I intentionally refuse to speak, and the faster I go, the more she screams.

"*Otoki,* quiet! Do you want every predator in this forest after us?" I lean in closer to her, close enough to smell her. I really do not understand why she smells so delicious when, by all rights, she is the most hideous and annoying creature I have ever come across. Tempted by her scent, I lick at the strange little nubs on the side of her head. Her perspiration is salty and sweet.

Her body tenses, and finally she quiets. I can hear a noise gather in the back of her throat. "Stop that," she says with defiance as she squirms.

"Then stay silent." My breath ghosts over the shell of her ear, and I force down the need to inhale. "We are close to the Sagath territory. We must be quick and quiet."

My hand comes up over her mouth, pressing it closed. My *tirska* throbs again at the sight of her eyes widening and the feeling of her soft lips against my skin.

I want her so desperately, and the moment I find us shelter, I'm taking what's mine.

CHAPTER SIX
MY FLOWER

As one moon slowly sets, the other rises, casting the reddish hue along the trees. My body throbs as Echo's soft, plush body presses against mine. The need overwhelms me entirely. My mind swirls with thoughts of her caressing my wings and of how my *tirska*, extruded wetting the front of her pretty skirts.

My hunting party will search for me, and yet I fly through the Amae'*sil* in the opposite direction. The forest holds no room for rest. Everything that lives in it will come to harm Echo, so I press myself harder than I should, waiting until I reach the end of my strength to stop.

There are dead *Amae'sil* here that were once home for the Volese, their stumps hollowed out into cabins. Once the Krel and Sagath edged into their territory, it forced them to live closer to the Caliphate.

This will be the perfect place to stop. I fly, finding the largest house built into the top branches with rows of swirling blossoms and vine.

"We will rest here," I say, setting her down just in front of the large open doorway.

Echo makes a noise in the back of her throat, something akin to awe.

"Wow...what is this place?" She turns on her heel and searches through the rows and rows of homes. "Do people live here?"

"They did in the past." A hand finds the center of her back, pressing her forward to the door. "Many things have changed since then."

She turns to look up at me, worry etched on her face, pulling her brows together as her lips twist downward. "Everything in this place is trying to kill you, huh?"

If she only knew just how true that statement is.

I push her forward again until she finally relinquishes control, edging inside the darkened home. Her steps are unsure as I find the edges of a moss-covered door, sealing us inside.

My body towers over her in the small space of the home, forcing me to tuck my wings in closer to me so she has room. I step to her with a single-minded purpose, so eager to press her to me. Grabbing her around her waist, loving the little hitch of her breath as skin touches skin, drives me wild. "I desire your hands on me, *otoki*..." I whisper into the edge of her neck.

She swirls around facing me, chewing on the bottom of her lip. "Xakiras?"

What can I say? Since the moment I felt her hands and tasted her mouth, I have wanted nothing else. Hearing the sweetness of my name from her lips has my body trembling. I should not want a *ukolist*—an outsider—to touch me; still I cannot get the thought from my mind.

"I told you I would finish what was started." My hands splay against her back, tangling in the long tresses of her flax-colored hair before I wrap it around one of my hands.

"Why?" Her voice has a breathless quality to it, which only fuels the yearning I feel.

Why indeed.

A rough tug pulls her head backward to show me the column of her neck, and the gasp that gusts from her lips is like music to my ears. I want to taste it from her lips as she whispers my name. Instead, I hold back my lust, realizing she needs an explanation of what brought this on more.

My lips graze the delicate skin behind her ear. "*Otoki*, in my culture, wings are only stroked during intercourse. It is a highly erogenous place, and yet you have touched mine twice now."

I wait for the moment it dawns on her. "Oh, no...I didn't mean to."

"I know, and yet when I tasted your mouth, you clung to me as though I was your very breath." I lick the bottom of her ear as another of my hands feels up the bottom of her thigh underneath her skirts.

Echo's moan and the scent of her arousal make it clear she likes what I'm doing, but I desire more; if she begs me, then I will act, but only then. "What about taking me back to my camp?"

"As soon as I am allowed, I will, but first, we will need to tell the *Kugitauri* and Caliphate of what transpired." I kiss the crux of her neck and shoulder.

"This won't mean anything else to you, then? I know certain species take sex very seriously."

Nocris choose their mates very seriously, but this will not be that. We would dance under the starlight, touching one another's wings, and our *tunsavri* would tangle together. Echo has none of those, and so there will be no choosing her.

"Nothing else besides making your knees quake and hearing your sweet keening sounds as I ravage you like the delicious little thing you are, *otoki.*" My hand on her thigh finally reaches the edges of her mound, and I press against her undergarment, leaving my finger damp.

Curiously, these creatures self-lubricate. That may make her pleasure easier than Nocris females are used to. Interesting...

Her hips cant toward my finger, and she sighs out, "What if we don't fit?"

"Do not be concerned; Nocris males are designed with females' pleasure in mind." She nods, and I feel a renewed sense of excitement at her eagerness. "Your tongue felt amazing. Will you use it on me now?"

I find myself entirely unable to answer. It is as if she has taken my tongue and tied it in a knot. My hands leave her aching wetness, and the one in her hair lets it free. She sighs out a breath, and I kneel, slowly kissing down the front of her body, even through the clothing she wears. Each press of my lips makes her create tiny little noises in the back of her throat until I shove the hem of her skirt upward over my head.

"Ah!" Echo's fingers grab at the ruff of my neck, pulling me closer to her as she cries out, and I realize she's so eager for me too.

I take my time kissing the insides of her thighs, waiting for the subtle moment I hear her breathing pick up and her scent grow headier. Two of my hands are holding her thighs apart for me while I make my way to the place she wants me most. One slow, languid lick against the wet fabric has her hands clutching on to me, and I instinctively know she's ready.

"Take these off so your sweetness drips onto my face." I stop everything, waiting for her trembling hands to leave my neck.

Slowly, Echo lifts her skirt until her hands brush the top of mine. I glance up, and she's biting the bottom of her lip with rosy cheeks, but those stormy eyes of hers bore into mine. "You're decidedly dirty for someone I just learned could speak."

I snort through my nose at her comment because I could always speak. She just did not understand it. "Now, *otoki*."

Her hands grab at the top of the fabric, pulling it until it is just on top of my hand. I rub tenderly at the skin of her fingers and then yank the offending clothing down.

The little "oh" Echo makes in response makes a groan escape from my lips. Now that the garment has freed her, I see the delicate little mound with fur that is darker than the hair on her head. That lovely scent I associate with her permeates the air, and I inhale, drinking it deeply.

"You are to stand here and allow me to devour you. If you so much as move, I will make you regret it." I stare up at her, watching as realization dawns on her.

Her tiny pink tongue darts out of her mouth and wets her lips. It makes me wish I had multiple mouths so I could both lick her and taste her mouth at the same time. Echo's lips twist, but she gives me a single nod in reply.

That is all it takes for me to grab her by her back, pulling her to me so I can finally have a taste of her. The yearning inside me swirls just as my tongue snakes out to nestle between her folds.

The immediate connection has her hips locking, but she doesn't move. "Oh fuck," she hisses through her teeth.

I grab on to her backside with two of my hands, while the other two spread the folds of her mound apart for me to see. She is the same lovely shade as the blossoms that grow just outside this door. Echo is so soft, pink, and the dew she is creating glistens as if ready for me.

There is a little pink bud peeking out between her folds, and I realize this little creature is no bug at all but a flower ripe for picking. My tongue darts out eagerly, wrapping around the small bud, flicking at it, curious as to what it might taste like.

Echo doesn't move, just as instructed, though I'm not disappointed to hear her little whimper as I move around exploring. She tastes like nothing I can describe, and yet at the same time, it is delectable.

I cannot wait to hear her crying my name with weak knees.

This little flower will be mine.

CHAPTER SEVEN
POWER PLAY

Xakiras's hands on my thighs and ass make me so nervous. He says I can't move, but the feel of his tongue on my clit makes my hands ball at my side. I should have grabbed hold of him before his demands because now, knowing I can't move, only makes me want to more.

Once again his tongue lashes out, finding my clit, and every nerve in my body zings with the awareness.

"*Kukali*...you taste divine." Xakiras looks up at me, and I see deep in those eyes of his a flash of lust.

Biting at my lip, I hold back the whimper that tickles at the back of my throat. It's at that moment his long tongue twirls around my clit, gripping it tightly as if it's in a vise. Then his entire mouth covers me, and I feel the tongue release before sliding through my folds into me.

I whine when I feel the snakelike thing swirl around, finding every inch of me as if dedicating it to memory. My fingers itch to grab him as they ball at my side.

"Xakiras!" When I speak his name, his tongue pulls out of me only for his hands to leave me entirely, just for a second.

He glances up at me, a daring smirk across his face. "I need more space to devour you. Lie on the ground."

I hesitate, but the way he looks at me makes me so excited that my knees knock. The floor here is just the knobby bits of tree limb. It isn't going to be comfortable, and yet I just don't care.

Sliding onto my knees, I slowly get to my back. I hardly have time to adjust before I feel his body hovering over mine. A set of his hands grabs my legs, jerking them apart while the others snake up my shirt. His bright white eyes never once leave mine either.

"Make no noises, do you understand? I will allow you to scream when I tell you so." His tongue flicks out of his mouth, and I shudder.

I want to tell him no, that there's no way I can stay quiet with his vibrating tongue working me over. Instead of the no that burns on my tongue, I swallow roughly. "I—I don't know if I can."

"You will for me."

It isn't a question in the least. Xakiras bends his head down to my stomach as one of his hands lifts my shirt, exposing the soft planes of my stomach to him. His lips graze over it while a set of his hands roughly digs into my thighs.

I don't think I'll ever get used to four sets of hands touching me at all times. Thankfully I won't need to.

"Say yes, Echo," he says as a finger rubs along my slit, and I sigh.

My body throbs, and I finally decide to give in fully. I don't know why I want him so badly or why I'm giving in. It doesn't matter, does it?

"Yes." My head falls backward, and just as it does, Xakiras's tongue reaches back out to my pussy. He swirls it around before once again covering his mouth over me.

Two of his fingers dip into me simultaneously while his tongue and lips work me over. I bite my cheek to keep from groaning, squeezing my eyes shut at the various sensations.

While his fingers fill me, Xakiras groans against me, picking up his pace. The flicking of his tongue becomes a violent vibration until my hips buck upward and I'm swallowing every moan.

A set of hands holds my hips down so I can't get my pleasure faster. I grunt at the abruptness, but it's so quiet, I hope he didn't hear me.

I'm not that lucky. Xakiras's tongue halts as do his fingers, and he glances up at me with my own fluid coating his chin.

"What did I just hear?" His tone of voice is a sultry velvet, making me instantly gulp down saliva that had pooled in my mouth. When I don't answer right away, he jerks my body closer to his chest. "Answer me, *otoki*."

"It shocked me when you held me down." It's the truth, and my tone is so breathy that I hate the way I sound.

"Did it harm you?" Xakiras looks at me softly, and one of his fingers rubs a circle on the inside of my thigh.

It's a tenderness I didn't anticipate from someone who wants to fuck me.

"No, it didn't." I sigh out a breath.

His mouth twists into what I can only describe as a smirk, but on him it looks menacing as well as sexy. "Good, then stay silent."

Xakiras's head dips back between my held-open thighs, and I feel his tongue once again. The pace isn't slow like before; instead he's vibrating so quickly, I bite my lip to keep from moaning. His fingers are just as quick while one of his other hands slides up under my blouse to grab at my breast.

He pumps into me viciously with two fingers while his tongue works over my clit. I'm still pinned to the floor, and even though my hips buck upward, he shoves me right down.

I bite at my lips until I taste the tang of blood, but he doesn't stop. The electricity he creates with his tongue sends shivers up my spine, and I start to writhe around, locking his head with my knees.

"Scream now." He ceases his touches long enough to command me and goes right back to the same pace.

My orgasm, which had been building—I shoved it deep down inside me so I made no noise at all—erupts at the sound of his voice. It's earth-shattering as it washes over me. My voice is so loud, I worry about giving away where we are.

"Fuck! Holy shit!" I scream over and over as his tongue continues until I feel like I might die. Every nerve and fiber of my being feel frayed at the edges, and I can hardly breathe, but he doesn't stop.

Closing my eyes and tilting my head backwards, I let out another scream when another wave rolls over me. It morphs into laughter as the sensitivity turns into pain and pleasure. I've never had someone lick my pussy so hard or with so much dedication before.

"Please—it's too much!" I squirm, thrashing my hips so he might stop.

Xakiras finally lets his tongue leave my clit, and when he does, I sigh with relief, but his fingers stay where they are seated inside me.

"Look at how gorgeous you are, *Kukali*," he says, slowly pulling his fingers out of my channel. When he does, I watch as his blue tongue flicks out, licking my juices while he closes his eyes with a hum of delight.

The longer I look at him, I now see long frills that have come out of the sides of his pouch. They match the white color of his neck ruff, though he hasn't touched me with them. What's more intriguing is that I now see his cock has extruded too. It's slender, bright green and pointed. I want to see more of it.

"Xakiras, I want you to fuck me." I can't believe how forward I'm being. I shouldn't want him so badly, but the smell of sweetness has grown so strong that I'm salivating.

The throbbing of my pussy has started up again in a rhythm that matches my heartbeat. I want him so much that I can't think of anything else.

I don't get an answer as Xakiras lets out a grumbling from somewhere deep inside his chest.

He leans down over me, looking deeply into my eyes, and a single hand comes up under my chin, tilting my face. "Oh, *otoki,* I will do more than that. I will ravage your body until you cannot stand without my help. Your body will be clay in my hands to mold and shape. Do not worry about the pain, little one, I will take care of everything."

Oh fuck, please take care of me.

CHAPTER EIGHT
FLYING HIGH

Immediately I'm scooped up into two of his broad arms as if I'm nothing more than a rag doll. Face to face, the gust of his breath sends shivers over my arms, and I blink up at him awkwardly. I don't know what he intends to do. This room is so small, I'm unsure if he can even find a position comfortable enough for us both.

"What sort of pain?" I finally find myself curious about that as I feel his leaking cock against my thigh.

Xakiras's tongue moves like a snake being charmed out of his mouth to lick the side of my cheek. "You are equipped with enough lubrication that there will be none. Your kind is very blessed."

Oh...oh, shit. That does make sense.

"Your species doesn't have that? Then how—" The scientist part of me wants to know everything, but he gives me a look before his tongue trails lower to my collarbone. It renders me speechless. A low groan leaves my mouth, and I tip my head backward to give him more access to my neck.

"Will it make you more comfortable if we speak of it?" His licking stops, and his lips ghost over my skin.

"That's really sweet of you, but, no, I think I'll be fine." The words come out of my mouth, and a moment later, his hands are all over me.

Xakiras pulls my ripped blouse over my head while another set of hands travels up my skirt and thighs. He's efficient with his four arms, making short work of both undressing me and foreplay. While he kisses my neck down my collarbone, I clutch him, searching between us for the thing I desire most, which is his cock. I want so badly to see it, to touch it and hear the noises he might make.

When I finally find his cock between us, and my fingers trail along it, I'm surprised to find it's entirely coated in something wet. I want to ask him what it is, but he moans against my neck, then it's all forgotten.

The feeling of his cock in my hands sends my pulse racing, especially with the way his eyes close. Xakiras groans deeply just from the grip I have on him, and I feel so powerful with the knowledge that I might make this huge, terrifying monster weak in the knees.

The frills I felt earlier have wrapped their soft, feather-like tendrils around my thighs as if they are nearly sentient themselves. One pump of my hand and Xakiras shudders a breath, the movement of his hands on me halting like he can't do more than one thing at a time.

"*Otoki*...stars above, that feels amazing." One of his hands grips my breast tighter as I give him another slow movement, but the amazing part is, the more I touch him, the wetter he grows.

The image of him panting, begging me to let him come, washes over me. I'd love so much for it to be real. Instead, I lean forward to his neck, planting a kiss.

"I need you to fuck me, Xakiras." I tilt my hips, and his eyes fly open at the sensation.

A lusty fire burns behind his eyes, and he grabs me so swiftly into his arms that I gasp, letting out a little laugh.

He has to duck his head so he doesn't reach the ceiling, then he swings open the small door we came in. Back in the night air, I realize one moon has entirely set, and now the entire forest is glowing a very eerie red, casting a shadow over all the lush, glowing trees. Even they have dimmed as if they need sleep too, which I find fascinating.

"Without wings, this will be truly difficult for us." He doesn't even look at me, but everywhere else, as if he's trying to navigate just how he might perform the act he wants to. "We will make do."

Oh, just how does his kind have sex? I wonder. I don't have time to even think about it before he's ascending into the air with his frills wrapping around my thighs. Xakiras lifts me just over his leaking cock, looking at me in the eyes before his tongue darts out to lick at my lips. It makes me forget I'm in the air. The fear of falling from his arms has long passed after everything I've been through today.

"You won't drop me?" I bite at my lip for a moment, feeling my need throb between my legs.

Xakiras holds my gaze before pressing his lips to mine in a sweet peck. "I will never drop you."

I smile and lift my hips, gliding myself over his cock, wanting so badly to see it, but more so now to actually feel it. One of his hands is between my legs, taking his cock and sliding it through my folds, while the others are holding me tightly. I'll never be able to get with a man with fewer than four arms after this.

He presses his length inside me, and I whimper in delight. "Yes, please."

Xakiras takes that as an invitation, nudging himself deeper, and the sensation is glorious. The frills on the sides of him hold my thighs open for him, while his large cock fills me full inch by inch. The texture feels nothing like his hands. Instead, it feels like a very lubed-up toy with spiraled ridges that rub at my walls. It takes my breath away, because I'd imagined, with us both being so wet, that I'd hardly feel a thing.

"Oh, Echo, you feel so warm." His voice has taken on a husky quality, and his eyes have glazed over. "And you hug me so tightly."

I groan at the sound of his voice. "I want you." It doesn't feel like enough, but it's all I think of saying because, now that he's seated fully, I need more. I want all of him.

With a snarl, Xakiras takes us higher into the air, and while he does, his hands move me up and down on his length. Flying and his thrusts have my senses entirely scattered. I'm unsure what to do other than hook my ankles around his back and my arms around his neck to hold on for dear life.

His tongue snakes out of his mouth, and when it does, I open mine, welcoming him inside, wanting all of him. If Xakiras gives me every single blessed inch of him, it wouldn't be enough. Once inside my mouth, he plays with my tongue, moving me up and down on his cock like I'm nothing but a doll to control. Everything is messy; there's no rhythm to anything, and yet the feeling of his cock as he moves and his tongue as it vibrates makes my entire core turn molten.

I grind my hips in tandem with him, but there's no way for me to keep up with him. After my last orgasm, I'm so keyed up that my body is thrumming. I scream into his mouth when I feel our trajectory drop, and he pulls his wings in toward us both, allowing my fingers to graze the inside of them.

One stroke of his wings and Xakiras's mouth leaves mine, a slew of curses flying from his lips. My fingers make patterns on the soft feathers until his motions are erratic and his breathing just as much. I'm whining and writhing while touching him, but I can't find my fear as we plummet to the earth.

Deep inside my brain, I know he has me. I'm safe here. I grab his wing and yank when his hips piston deeper, hitting my cervix until I'm keening out in both pain and pleasure. He's gripping me so tightly, I think I might bruise, but I don't care.

"Fuck!" I finally find my voice as his cock once again hits that spot deep inside that has my body spiking with electricity.

Xakiras's rhythm is uncontrollable, as my fingers and hips work in tandem. He holds me tighter, whispering over and over, "Just like that; don't stop."

The sound of his voice makes my hips grind in larger circles just to satisfy him. His body begins to spiral around, and a second orgasm begins to work itself from the pit of my belly. Just as I feel it, Xakiras clings to me, and his tongue finds the shell of my ear as a low growl rumbles from his throat.

We shoot upward suddenly, his wings leaving the safety of my fingers, and he slides his cock out of me so fast, I swear I might have whiplash. A hand goes between my aching body, wanting so much more than this. He strokes against my stomach. The slick appendage glides against my skin, making me moan. When I look at him, his eyes close, his mouth opens, and he speeds up his touches until he's a groaning mess.

I want to touch myself, but I don't want to move my hands. Xakiras bends down with his mouth near my ear. "I am going to paint your pretty skin with my seed, little bug."

When I whimper with excitement, he jerks, and his panting turns to grunting. Xakiras grips my body tighter, and finally his release comes with a roar. My stomach grows wet, and as it soaks into my skin, I feel a tingling sensation I can't describe.

Xakiras pants against my ear, and I want so badly to come again, but this time while we aren't in the air. I want to feel him against the bark of a tree, hilt deep or riding him so I see the look on his face as he comes again.

"I want more." I'm shocked that I say it, but there's no blush on my face. "On the ground this time."

The way he looks at me, pulling himself together is comical. He blinks several times but nods. "My pleasure."

Fuck yeah, it is.

He flies so fast that I grip his neck, squeezing my eyes shut to keep from feeling sick. At least he's just as excited as I am.

Once his feet touch back down onto something solid, he grips the bottom of my ass in two hands.

"On your back, Xakiras. I want to see your face." I take my hand and run it along his wing.

He shivers at the touch, which makes that powerful feeling of making him melt beneath my hands return.

We are nestled on a long, wide limb near the side of the house I think we were in before. These trees are still so large that I know, if I look down, we will be stories high. Xakiras sets me on my feet, giving me free rein for the first time in hours. He slowly kneels in front of me, his hands still touching me as he goes.

I take my fingers and stroke the side of his face, bending down just enough to kiss him on the lips. "All the way down please."

He inhales a sharp breath but slowly begins the task of lying flat. Now I can see the large cock between his legs. It has two long, frilled, white tendrils that come out from each side and is a bright green just like his wings. The tip of it is pointed, and along the top there are swirling ridges that grow larger until you reach the base. His testicles are tucked closely to the pouch his cock extrudes from and are a richer, deeper green. Its slick coating has a shimmering quality to it, and when I look down at my shirt, it's glittery. The skin it touches has a tingling numb sensation, and I realize just how amazing his species is.

The females produce no lubrication, so in order to help, the males create the lubrication themselves, and their semen numbs the female so they aren't in any pain.

That's kind of adorable.

I hike up my skirt and straddle his large hips, taking him in my hands to slide him inside me again. As I sit on his cock, his head tilts backward, and he groans. His hands grab hold of my hips, while another set takes my arms.

"You feel so amazing," Xakiras hisses between his teeth.

In this position, he's nearly too deep, and I whine taking him all. I swear he feels larger than before, stretching me wide until I finally acclimate to his size. I use my thighs on the tree to lift myself while my hands are in the ruff of fur around his neck. I glide off him so easily that when I come back down, the tip of him hits me so hard that I close my eyes.

"So deep," I whine but I continue my rhythm.

Opening my eyes, I move, slowly watching as his face changes. My hands go around his throat, gripping the sides of it, though pathetically with how much larger he is. Then I pick up speed.

Each thrust I take with my hand around his neck has his hips moving to meet me. One of his hands plays with my nipple while another finds my clit. It's then the set of hands on my hips wraps around me, pinning me to him as he quickly thrusts into me.

The power exchange lasted all of two minutes.

Xakiras's speed is far too quick, making our bodies slap together. Each thrust takes him deeper to a painful place, but I can't stop. The look on his face is pure desire, and his tongue has several times flicked out at his lips.

His finger on my clit furiously rubs in tandem with our movements, and I squirm on top of him. Every circled movement he makes takes my pleasure higher. My stomach gives a twinge; my pussy throbs, but I want more.

"Please! Please," I whine.

I grind against him, the pain and pleasure so much that my body cranes forward against his chest. He pounds into me harder, clutching me to him.

Every single time he bottoms out, I whimper, but he doesn't stop. Instead, now that I'm near his mouth, he groans into my ear, "That's it; take all of me."

My orgasm crashes over me at the gust of his breath over my skin. I scream so loudly that one of his hands comes up and covers my mouth as he continues to thrust up into me.

I'm so sensitive that I can't keep quiet, and drool starts to pool between his fingers. Xakiras licks the side of my ear. "I am going to paint your insides, sweet *otoki*."

He grunts, speeding up his thrusts until I hear him groan and twitch inside me. The jet of his spend hits me in hot ropes, and I sigh into him as the tingle begins to take over.

Its numbing agent quickly overtakes me, and I sigh a breath of relief as he pulls himself out.

"Beautiful," he says, brushing my sweaty hair from my face.

I breathe in, trying to catch my breath, smiling at him, perfectly sated. "Holy shit...that was amazing."

Xakiras smiles back at me, letting my body go limp against him. We fall into an easy silence after that, watching as the forest once again seems to come to life.

I could really get used to this.

CHAPTER NINE
AT OUR DOOR

My body feels lighter than I can ever dare describe. Echo's body is still lying on top of mine; her breathing has evened out into a slumber. I wanted to take her several more times over, but she is so tired that I dare not wake her.

My fingers brush through her hair, loving the way the silky strands move and the little happy noises she makes when I do it. A snapping twig brings me back to awareness, and I glance toward the sound. We should not be so unsheltered, but I do not move. I wait.

My breathing halts in my chest, and as another twig snaps, I grab hold of Echo as the sound of an arrow zings through the air. I scoop her into my arms. My sword is no longer sheathed at my side; instead I left it inside the cabin.

"*Vittar!*" I have no choice. I will need to grab it.

Another arrow hurls at us both, and Echo screams a blood-curdling sound. I take off running, holding her closely, but behind me I can hear the sounds of screaming.

"Sagath are here. Echo, stay close; do you understand?" I shove open the door just in time for another arrow to whiz by our heads, but it grazes the side of her arm.

"Fuck!" she screams, and the metallic scent of her blood permeates the small cabin room.

There's no time to look at it as I grab my scabbard on the ground and her shirt, tossing it to her. I curse being an *Arcanil* because in this moment I could use the added protection of magick—though I have never needed it. Being alone in the *Amae'sil* forest is something that is never done. I should have never attempted it.

I curse under my breath, whirling around until we face the door once more. "Echo, I do not have time to tend to your wound. The Sagath are blood-thirsty creatures that will tear your limbs from your body to consume while violating you in every possible way. Do not scream; do you hear me? Stay silent and cling to me."

Echo's crying has grown, but I feel the small nod of her head. "I'll try."

"There is no trying, *otoki*; you must."

I brandish my sword and hold steadfast at the door, knowing they will be waiting. Just how many will have come?

We have to leave the cabin. Leaving through the front door is risky, and, though there are windows, it's much tougher to get through them with my size. But Echo would fit. I hesitate before swallowing down my fear. We will do what we must.

I kick the door open and bolt for the nearest limb. The Sagath are standing on a large tree just across from us with their weapons drawn. I make it just in time to dive but a slew of arrows follows.

The high-pitched shriek of their battle cries follows behind us as I zip through the air. My heart rackets in my chest, but I pray I can find us safety. I fly as hard as I possibly can, zig-zagging through the trees. We are one hundred clicks away from the safety of the living *Amae'sil,* and I still have yet to rest. The fatigue of my body burns as I zip upward into the tree line.

I feel them encroaching behind us, pressing me further into the wood. They are faster and more agile than I am. Swiveling my head around, I try to count their numbers. I see three following, which means there must be others who are trying to cut us off.

I turn my head just in time to see the other two I knew were waiting. They aim an arrow, pulling it back just in time for me to dive. I zigzag through the trees, and just when I fear I'll be overrun, I hear yelling.

Clicks in front of us is my hunting party. Red flames lick beside us, and I barrel roll to the side.

"Xakiras, there you are!" I hear one of them yell.

My heart swells with gratitude that they have found me, but I am far too late. Just when I feel as though we've been saved, I see them: three more Sagath warriors behind my hunters, all poised and ready for attack.

"Behind you!" I hold Echo tighter as I halt in the air.

Our magick user turns; the flames explode, and before I have a chance to do anything but watch, pain lances through my body. My shoulder throbs, but I dare not look at the wound. I know what I might see when I do.

"Oh my god!" Echo gasps, grabbing on to my chest, but I cannot stop. Her safety needs to come first.

She cannot be left alone in the trees because she cannot fly away. The only option for her is the ground, so I dive, ignoring the scent of my blood and the sting of my body. I can hear Sagath following behind, but once I have her on the ground, she might be able to hide.

My legs touch down on the plush moss. "*Otoki*, find a place to hide. Do not touch the *Amae'sil*; they will consume you. I will return for you."

"Are you kidding me?! You can't just leave me!" She hesitates to let me free, but I shove her from my arms.

"Do not argue with me." I pin her with a stern look. "I will find you. Now run!"

Then I swivel around, ignoring the sounds of her feet behind me as she retreats.

I will come back for her if I die trying.

CHAPTER TEN
INTO THE FRAY

I run like my life depends on it, forcing myself not to go too far into the horrible labyrinth of this wood. I can hear the sounds of their fighting, but I'm inept to do anything about it other than hide like a coward.

It's times like this I wish I had a gun with me. I worked in a lab studying plant life for terraforming this planet—I wasn't in the military in that capacity—so it wasn't standard practice for me to have a weapon.

There's a dead tree similar to the one the cabin was created from, and while Xakiras told me not to touch the Ama-whosits, which I guess meant the trees, I'm going to assume the dead ones will be safe.

I crawl inside of it, my skirts growing moist from the detritus on the ground, but I hardly care. I'm hoping those creatures won't find me. There was hardly time to get a significant look at them because Xakiras held me to his chest, but they remind me of horned owls. We've fought against them several times now, but each time, they move far too quickly to get a good look.

This time I saw large swirling horns on top of their heads and pale skin with long, white feathered wings. They were definitely more bird-like compared to Xakiras's insect appearance.

My heart rackets in my ears as the brutality continues to ricochet through the forest. The screaming is blood-curdling, and every time I think it's Xakiras, holding my breath for his voice. When it never comes, I finally breathe until the next set of screams begins.

I hear twigs breaking behind me. Taking my legs to my chest, I squeeze myself tighter into the hollow of the tree to become smaller. A mantra of "please don't find me, please..." roars in my head.

There's a sound of sniffing and a deep hum of a male voice. My armpits start to sweat, and I hold my breath just in case the creature can hear my breathing.

Something hits the side of the tree—*thwack, thwack*—before I hear them say, "Come out, little morsel..."

I hold back my whimper as fear latches onto my body, and I swallow down the desire to run. When bird-like feet come into view, I decide I have to fight. The creature is covered in leather armor with a spear in one hand. It bends down, and when I see its face, I'm shocked to find deep, curious eyes, a blunt nose and sharp teeth.

I gasp, flattening myself to the back of the tree, but it gives me a wide smile. "Hiding will do you no good."

A hand reaches out, grabbing at me, and I bat it away. "Go fuck yourself."

The creature's dark chuckle makes my blood run cold. A hand yanks at my arm, pulling me forward. I dig my thighs into the moss to keep myself from tumbling. The grip is crushing, and I scream, trying to wriggle free.

"Do not fight me," it says, giving one final jerk to my arm until I tumble out of the hole.

I scream and thrash around, but the owl-man grabs hold of my hair, yanking me upward. There's no malice in his eyes, but what I assume is ambivalence about what to do with me.

Kicking out my legs, I try to get one shot in, but his grip on me is too tight. "Xakiras!" I scream his name, not knowing if he'll ever hear me or not. But there's a glimmer of hope that he'll crash through the sky to my rescue.

The owl-man wrenches me upward, wrapping his arm around my waist as he grins, showing sharp rows of serrated teeth. "Little prey, silence yourself; there is no one coming."

"Help!"

A hand reaches out, smacking me across the face. My neck whips sideways with a crack from the force of his slap.

"Silence!"

I swallow back the tears, allowing defiance to bloom along with the aching bruise I know is forming on my cheek.

Suddenly, I hear a loud cry from behind us. There's a swing of metal over the owl's shoulder, and I'm splashed with fresh blood. I squeeze my eyes shut, and the owl turns around as though it didn't hurt him at all.

"Let her go!" I hear his voice, and it's rougher than I've ever heard it before. Still, I recognize it right away. Xakiras came to me.

The owl takes his spear and twirls it outward, the gushing of his blood clearly less important than Xakiras is.

I'm still clutched to his chest, but in that instant, the owl throws me to the side. As I fall onto the ground, my teeth rattle, and my back jars. The soft moss doesn't help break my fall in the slightest.

I groan as I turn to face the two men fighting. Xakiras has already torn the arrow from earlier out of his shoulder, and it's still bleeding all over his wings and back. He's covered in gore from head to toe.

The owl lunges forward, and Xakiras uses his sword to knock it out of the way. It's an unfair fight with one being so close-ranged while the other isn't, but Xakiras waves the owl closer anyway. It's almost like he couldn't care less if he's run through with the spear.

They clash weapons one more time, and Xakiras tries to dance away, only to get nicked in the back. The tip slices through one of his wings, tearing it across the edges like it's little more than tissue paper. Xakiras makes absolutely no noise, but I gasp, covering my mouth with my hand. It has to be painful with how sensitive his wings are. The look of determination on his face doesn't hide the sweat that gathers on his brow.

While the owl is recovering from his thrust, Xakiras screams, taking a running start at him from the side. The owl doesn't have time to correct, spinning on his heel only to have a blade shoved through his stomach. It collides with the wing, spraying blood and feathers all over the ground.

Xakiras doesn't stop. He pulls the sword from the owl's gut, thrusting once more before the owl falls to his knees. The last thing I see is the sword connecting with his neck, cutting the owl's head entirely off, throwing it across the ground.

As soon as the threat is over, I stagger to my feet. "Are you okay?"

Xakiras gives me a tense look before dropping to one knee. His breathing is heavy, and the sweat on his brow glistens in the lights of the forest.

"I am fine." He wheezes out another breath, and I know better. He's putting on a tough act for me, maybe so I don't worry about him.

Once I get to him, I shake my head. "You're not. What about your people? Should we call them to help?"

He emits a low groan, looking up at me with a down-turned lip. "They were overrun, but I cannot fly to them in this condition. I need rest, and we will find them after."

"Is there somewhere you can rest nearby that would keep us hidden?" I chew on my bottom lip as he stands to his feet. He leans against my shoulder, forcing me to wrap an arm around his waist to keep him upright.

Xakiras nods and points in the opposite direction, where I think we came from in the first place. "There is a cave here with an indoor mineral spring the Volese use to farm. We can stay there for now."

CHAPTER ELEVEN
FIREFLIES AND PAIN

When we finally get to the entrance of the cave, the eggy scent of sulfur fills my nose. The cave's mouth is smaller than I anticipated. Glowing ivy has grown over the entrance, and even though he said there was someone who came to live here, I didn't think it'd be so lively inside.

"Do people live here?" I finally pull him to the entrance, pullinghim up straighter on his feet.

"No, they do not live here permanently. They might stay during harvesting," Xakiras explains as we push back the ivy. It makes a strange noise, like tinkling bells, and the entire cave quiets.

In a hush of whispers, we enter the cave, and I'm amazed by what I see. There are twenty tiny people with auburn skin, large eyes and round bodies. They glow a bright neon green from the tops of their chests to the bottom of their torsos.

Most of them have very little clothing, and what they do wear is in tatters. Some of them have instruments in their hands.

The entire cave is warm, inviting, with steam rising from the backmost portion of the cave. Tiny twinkling ivy is everywhere, and there are large, upright torches with flickering blue light inside them.

Xakiras acts as though he owns the place. However. Once we're inside, he quickly says, "I need the bath."

One of them stands, immediately rushing to our side. "Of course! Right away. Will you desire anything else?"

"Food for her, if you please."

I'm shocked entirely by the way all the fireflies stop their lounging to jump into action. All of them begin flitting around the cave, and the one in front ushers us down a long corridor.

Stalactites drip water above us, and the farther in we go, the darker the cave becomes. The plant life from the mouth is scarce until we enter a cavern with more of the blue torches, as well as little red and pink lanterns that float in the large steaming pool.

"We will bring miss some of the fruits from luo shortly," the tiny creature says. He gives a low bow before leaving us alone again.

I can't understand what's happening. Why are they treating Xakiras like he's royalty?

"Otoki, will you help me into the pool?" His deep, rich voice breaks me free of my thoughts immediately. There is a slight hint of exertion there that breaks my heart.

"Of course, but, Xakiras, why are they treating you like that?" Slowly we walk to the pool's edge, and he bends down with my help to sit on the edge, dipping his feet in.

"The Volese are the *maaorji*. They farm for us and are our servants." He doesn't seem to care about the implications of that. Instead Xakiras eases into the waters with a grunt.

I hesitate at the edge, worrying at the bottom of my lip. So, they have slavery here? When I dip my toes into the water, I'm shocked by how warm it is, and how it tingles at the bottoms of my feet. Xakiras moves to the back end of the pool, leaning against one of the larger rocks, forcing me to squint to see him.

"Come in, *otoki;* it will help." He beckons me closer with a wave of his hand, but I can't see the look on his face from here.

With a sigh, I slide my ripped and disgusting come-covered shirt over my head, only to pull my legs out of the water to shimmy my skirt down. "It does feel really good."

"The bruise on your face, *otoki*, did he hurt you anywhere else?" Xakiras moves through the water, back toward my end of the pool, until I can finally see his face.

"No, I'm fine." It isn't a lie, but I'm not sure my racing heart has slowed yet.

The glowing lights make him appear ethereal. With the shimmering blue lamps, it makes his eyes brighter, and the subtle glint of mischief there isn't unnoticed. Once my feet are back in the pool, his hands are on my thighs, holding me like I'm an anchor.

"If I were not *arcanil*, I could have protected you." He lets out a rush of air from his nostrils before his lips find the inside of my left thigh.

My hands find the tops of his shoulders, and I settle them there, playing in the little ruff around his neck. "What does that mean?"

Xakiras looks up at me, closing his eyes momentarily. "An *arcanil* is someone without magick. I was born without the gift, which does not allow me many comforts, but I do own my own home."

"So you are in a caste system here on this planet? Does this mean you have kings and queens?"

I'm enraptured by the history surrounding it, but Xakiras seems so saddened by his lack of magical prowess. How hard could it be for *arcanil* here?

"We have the the *kunisket*; they are a family who rules us alongside the caliphate. Why do you ask, Echo?" His hands continue to trail my legs, and I narrow my eyes.

"Stop distracting me. I have a lot of questions. Like the Volese, they are a slave class?" I kick my leg at him, and he grabs it with another hand.

"They are not slaves. They work for our protection. Without us, they would have been murdered by the Sagath when they took their territory. This forest is very unsafe for most of our people. Only hunters and the Volese farmers come here. It is far too easy to get lost or lose your life in the forest. This area especially is a labyrinth. The *Amae'sil* shift and move. One area may look entirely different the next time you venture inside. It is very easy to die in the forest." His fingers rub small circles on my leg with a tender look on his face.

I'm flabbergasted by how adorable he looks.

"I'm glad you rescued me, then. I would have hated being eaten by those trees or potentially being lost forever." I finally slide into the water in front of him.

Xakiras's hands come up to brush away my hair that has stuck to my face. "I would not allow you to die regardless of our differences. I hope the caliphate will allow you to find your people soon."

"We were supposed to be here to terraform your planet for us to live on. We had no idea there was sentient life here, but I worry that they're gone for good. What if all of them are dead?" I bite at the edges of my lips and look up into his eyes, finding that he's turned away from me.

"*Otoki,* they are likely all dead. The Krel leave nothing alive, and if they do, then it will not be a pleasant experience for them."

I can feel the tears sting at my eyes, and the weight in my stomach overrides the lump in my throat. "They can't all be dead. Someone has to be alive—"

Finally Xakiras looks back at me, shaking his head. "They are gone."

"If I tell the Imperium about this, they will go to war with whoever murdered my crew. Your planet will never be the same." I try to swallow back the tears, instead replacing them with actionable plans for what might be coming for us. I can't cry. If I cry, then I'll have given up.

Xakiras sighs, folding me into his large, strong arms. "Echo, do not ever say that to the *Kugitauri* when you meet them. We will never speak of that again."

His grip on me forces those emotions to come all at once. "It's unfair; we had no idea there was sentient life here."

The tears come full force, and I clutch Xakiras more tightly while he strokes my back and hair. I'll never be able to live with myself if the Imperium comes here to destroy this place.

E cho clings to me in the waters, her body melded to mine. Stars, all I can think about is never letting her go. As her shoulders shake with her tears, I continue to stroke her hair, telling her things will be alright, though I do not really know if that is true.

While we are holding one another, the sound of tiny feet pitter-patter on the cave floor, signaling the Volese are back with the food as promised. They are kind enough not to announce themselves and set it near the edge of the pool before leaving.

"*Otoki,* you must eat, then with the waters, you will heal. After rest, we will go find my men. The waters will heal my wings, but I will need time to dry them." I kiss the top of her head.

She shakes her head no and sniffles. "I don't feel like I can."

Something inside me snaps, and I pull her from my hold. "You will eat." I put as much assertion and dominance as I can into my voice, tipping her chin upward with my finger. "Do you understand?"

Echo's eyes narrow, and indignation flares in her eyes. "Are you fucking serious?"

"Yes, I am quite serious. You have to eat, and if I must feed you, I will."

The tears are still wet on her face, and her lips turn down into a grimace that sets my temper on edge. She is going to intentionally go against what I demand of her.

"Don't tell me what to do, Xakiras. I'm very capable of taking care of myself, so save your alpha male bullshit for someone else," she says, pushing my chest.

That only has me holding her harder. I back us both against the pool's edge, shoving my legs between hers. "You will eat, *Otoki*. Once you have, like the good little girl you are, I intend to show you just how good you can be."

She doesn't give in; instead Echo smirks, tilting her head upward at me. "You think that's going to work on me?"

I have no idea what I intended, only to prove to her that she must take care of herself. We both have been going nonstop; she needs to eat and rest. "I would never clip your wings, but I need you to stay alive and healthy."

I reach behind her and grab a piece of fruit from the plate, putting it to her lips. The juices run down my hand, but before it falls, I flick my tongue out to lick it from my skin. The flavor of it makes me buzz, wishing to taste it from her mouth.

She doesn't open her mouth, but she doesn't need to because I take my other hand, grasping at the edges of her jaw to hinge it open. Echo shakes her head, but I trail the fruit over her lips instead of forcing it inside. "Eat for me, baby."

Echo snarls, but her tongue comes out of her pretty pink mouth to lick the juices that have gathered there. She moans, and her eyes close, which only furthers the problem growing tight against my pouch.

Slowly I finger the fruit into her mouth, letting her cheeks go so she can chew properly. She does not disappoint me as her mouth closes and she chews, swallowing it down without a fight.

Once it's entirely swallowed down, she glares one final time. "Don't ever do that again."

I say nothing because we both know I will do it again, but I uncage her from my body so she can move freely. Like the good girl she is, she takes another piece of the fruit into her hands.

"You're eating too, right?" She raises one of her eyes up at me, and I smile.

A devious thought enters my mind, and I truly wonder just how far I can take things with her. "Feed me."

I am already enthralled by her body, which I once felt was entirely ugly, though now I realize I love it. The softness of her skin, the way her breasts look in the lampfyre. She inhales a breath, blinking a few times before her lips tip up into a smile.

My little bug.

When she has a piece in her hands, the music from earlier starts back up. The twinkling melody echoes through the cavern. It's a beautiful song that tells of love lost.

"That's so beautiful..." Echo puts the fruit up to my lips, and I open happily for it. I want to tell her she's the beautiful one, but instead I stay silent, eating fruit from her fingers, suddenly far too shy to speak up.

When her hand pulls back, I grasp it by the wrist, pulling it to my lips to lick the juices from her palm. I do not miss the inhale of breath or the subtle way she stops breathing entirely.

The flavor of her skin and the fruit juices mixed together create a blend of something so dangerously sweet and tantalizing that I pull her closer to me.

"What are you doing?" She chews on the bottom of her lip, pulling the skin off of it.

How can I answer her?

"We should sleep," I tell her, letting her arms fall free.

Why suddenly am I lost for words like a small child? It frustrates me, and while she climbs out of the pool, I look at the soft globes of her ass and curse myself for being weak. I have already fucked her twice. Why does telling her my feelings feel like a weight I cannot carry?

CHAPTER THIRTEEN
DANCE WITH MY DEVIL

Once we've put our clothes back on, Xakiras leads us back into the large open cavern where the Volese are still playing music. There are several of them dancing, while the others strum and pluck at various instruments.

They all seem so happy, so carefree, considering they are little more than slaves. The music grows more upbeat, and one of the Volese comes to our side. I think it's the same one from before, but I can get a much better look now that they are here.

"Is there something else I can get for you both?" He glances up at Xakiras, and I shake my head.

"No, we're perfectly fine. What is the name of this song?" I try to redirect the conversation so nobody orders anyone around. I know it's not my place, but I feel badly that they're taking care of us. We're capable of doing it on our own.

The little firefly looks at me, confused, but a small smile grows over his tiny face, showing sharp teeth. "This song has no name. Havita made it up herself."

"Whoa, that's amazing!" I look at the person who's playing the larger instrument, realizing they have a white ball of downy fluff for hair. "Would it be okay if I join for a while?"

"Of course. Do you know how to play?"

I shake my head. "No, but I can dance a little."

"*Otoki*, what about resting?" Xakiras tilts his head down to me, pinning me with stern eyes.

I sigh, reaching out to pat at his arm. "One dance, then I'll sleep. We can't just let this music go to waste, right?"

The firefly looks afraid to agree until he hears Xakiras mumble a reluctant "alright" under his breath. Once that's uttered, the creature grabs my hand in their tiny one, jerking me forward. They're stronger than they look, making me yelp at their strength.

They tug me along until we're in the circle of other Volese who are swaying along with the rhythm. "What's your name?"

My new dance partner beams proudly. "I am Jati, and you?"

"Echo," I say, shaking its little hand.

The tempo changes again with a new song, and at first I watch as the others shift their movements to match, but once they have and Jati dances along, I find my rhythm. My hips slowly sway, and I close my eyes, listening to the beat created by someone's subtle slaps on their legs.

Eventually I let loose, moving along the dance floor until I feel hands against my waist pulling me toward a strong, broad chest. The scent of sweetness floods my senses, and my eyes immediately open as I'm twirled around to face my partner.

"I didn't know you danced?" I laugh at the thought of this very severe man actually allowing himself to relax enough to enjoy anything at all.

Xakiras doesn't answer. Instead, he moves his hips in tandem with mine until he twirls me around in a circle. The laughter bubbles out of my chest until I'm pulled back to him, where immediately I see the look on his face that says this is not just a dance to him. Behind his eyes is a simmering carnal look of desire.

He holds me tightly to him, grinding our hips together, and the smell of him grows so heady and strong that a moan gathers in the back of my throat. Can the others smell it too? Do they know how good he smells?

"*Otoki*, you came from the stars and, out of all the constellations in the sky, to me you shine the brightest of them all." He tilts my chin upward, leaning down to press his lips to mine in the sweetest, most chaste kiss he's ever given me.

I'm at a loss for words. My heart beats out of rhythm with the music, but instead of running away, or telling him off, I put my head to his chest. "You're a good dancer."

Xakiras chuckles, and the rumble vibrates against my head. "I have practiced."

"Why would you need to?" I look up at him and see the worry etching his features, but he doesn't immediately tell me. Instead, he pauses our dance, pulling me off the dance floor. Nobody says anything about our departure as he leads me down another dark corridor, out of the view of everyone else.

Immediately he pulls me up so I'm straddling him, and his tongue is in my mouth. I moan, grinding my hips against him, feeling the wetness of his cock already soaking through my clothes.

He doesn't speak at all, and I feel his fingers glide between us, touching between my legs to find my clit. Xakiras kisses me with such intensity that I'm breathless, while his fingers touch me in just the right way. My hands grasp at his neck, and I tighten my thighs around his waist while he rubs circles there until I'm grinding back, moaning into his mouth.

The tight coil of my orgasm grows in my belly as his fingers pick up speed and his tongue begins to move around my mouth in the way I know means he's going to go deeper. He pulls away and grabs hold of his cock in one hand, slowly lining it up with my entrance. The tendrils wrap around my thighs, and as his cock enters me, every spiral rubs deliciously inside me.

"I will never clip your wings, little bug, but know I want you as my mate. I desire you like no other, and no matter what happens from this moment on, I want you ruined for anyone else."

With that said, he immediately presses into me, and I groan, shutting my eyes. He's not as gentle as the last time. Once he's inside me, he pushes me onto his cock until I dig my nails into his back. "Fuck!"

I can't find any other words because he shifts us so my back is against the cold, wet cave wall and his lips are on my throat. When he thrusts into me, I feel every nerve ending in my body grow taut.

The scent of sweetness grows even stronger, and the heat pools between my legs. Every thrust Xakiras takes makes me wetter until I hardly feel him at all, at least until his cock engorges. It grows thicker, longer inside me, until I'm writhing against it, bucking my hips in tandem with him.

"That is my sweet girl; take all of it," he says against my throat as he continues to pound into my body.

His cock continues to grow inside me until I feel so full that I can't breathe, but there's no pain just as he promised me. When he pulls back out only to dive back inside me, my stomach knots and feels tight, but I still want him.

Xakiras's hand continue to rub my clit while his tongue tickles my neck. It's too many sensations at once. My moans grow needier, and the coil in my gut starts to tighten until I feel ready to snap.

The louder I get, the needier his thrusts grow until I'm screaming, writhing against him. A thread inside me snaps, and the rush of my orgasm floods my senses. I dig my nails into Xakiras's back because he doesn't stop, even after I've come. His finger continues to rub at my clit, and he pounds into me over and over until I can't breathe anymore.

"I am going to fill your pretty little cunt up, Echo," he says as his thrusts take on a more impassioned speed.

My response is a whine; I'm unable to formulate thoughts as another orgasm builds beyond my control. I'm beyond overstimulated, but I can't seem to tell him to stop. His hands grip at my body tighter, wrapping around my back, pulling me against him as he growls into my ear. His seed releases, and he digs his fingers in, painting my insides in hot, thick cum.

"Oh, my god!" I cry out when I feel its warmth, and my orgasm finally collides over me while the two of us breathe in rough pants into one another's skin.

As we come down from our bliss, Xakiras cradles me in his arms. "I wish you would stay with me."

I don't want to answer him, not now as I feel him running down my legs, but I can't help wondering what he meant earlier about choosing me as his mate. I'm far too tired to question it. Instead I hum into his neck while a sluggish feeling overtakes my eyelids.

I'll ask him later.

CHAPTER FOURTEEN
NO WAY HOME

When I roll over on my side, I'm surprised to find powerful arms holding on to me. I fell asleep so quickly, I can't really remember how we got into this section of the cave. My body feels like a wrung-out rag, and even my inner thighs ache.

"Xakiras, are you awake?" I try to wriggle to my side to face him, but he holds me closer, rubbing his face into my neck.

"I am. We will leave soon." His lips graze my skin, pressing a gentle peck there.

I sigh, loving the way it feels and recalling immediately the intimacy we shared earlier. He really fucked me against the cave wall, and his cock grew sizes larger than it had the last time.

I realize he's taking me back to his people today, but the lingering ache of my crewmates is still in the recesses of my mind. I've been a little distracted recently with Xakiras and his absolutely amazing ability to fuck me. Still, once I meet his leader, I'll have to tell them the truth. I'm not sure I want to because once I do, things will never be the same.

Xakiras's hands roam across my body, slowly making their way under my soiled, ripped shirt. "We should get up then; it'll be a long day."

"I have decided to take you back to your camp. I would like more information about what the Krel are up to before I tell the caliphate." Xakiras presses another kiss to the inside of my neck near my shoulder before releasing me from his hold. "I hope we will run into my hunting party on the way."

I roll onto my side to face him, seeing the serene look on his face as if he's completely sated and comfortable here beside me. He looks so relaxed. "About last night. What did you mean about being your mate?" The question burns on my tongue.

Xakiras's face doesn't change in the slightest. He only pulls me closer, pressing my chest against his. "Nocris choose their mates by dancing together. Last night when we danced together, I decided I wanted to see how it might feel." He smiles, and a hand comes up between us to brush hair from my face. "I choose you, not a Nocris, as my mate, Echo."

"I can't stay here when the Imperium knows they'll come here to start a war with the Krel," I say, wrapping my arms around him. "I'm sorry."

"Do not be, *otoki*. However, you are mine, regardless of what may come later." He takes a fistful of my hair in his hand, jerking my head backwards. "I always protect what belongs to me."

I hate the way my pussy throbs and the way my mouth parts because I know he means what he says. There's a tiny part of me thrilled at the idea of being his and staying by his side, even though we hardly know one another. I know I'd be safe with him.

"I want that too."

The look on his face says it all. His eyes widen, and a smile grows on his lips, showing me his rows of teeth.

Xakiras's lips crash into mine with such ferocity, my teeth bite into his skin.

Before we leave for the day, we have sex together one more time. This time he holds me close, whispering sweet nothings into my ear as if I'm the best thing to come into his life.

When we finally leave the cave system, it feels as if not a single day has passed. The forest looks nearly the same, though I realize Xakiras was right. This morning, trees I remember are gone entirely. A large swirling tree with great big violet blossoms is now in front of the cave instead of smaller spindly-looking trees.

"We should find your camp fairly quickly, but remember, Echo, you must remain quiet. The Sagath may still be in the forest." Xakiras picks me up bridal style, and I wrap my arms around his neck.

"I understand. I'll stay quiet. You have me, so I'm a lot less afraid of flying now." I pat his cheek and smile at him. "I'll be a good girl."

Those words ignite a fire behind his eyes, and a deep rumble comes from his throat. "Yes, you are and distracting as well."

CHAPTER FIFTEEN
NOTHING LEFT

We fly for hours, until my arms feel like Jello and my ass has a cramp in the left cheek. As we approach the camp from the sky, I see the tents crumpled in heaps, some with holes in the sides and the small shuttle we used to get here still sitting relatively untouched. The Peony would be coming back for us in six weeks with more men and rations for us, and now there was nothing left.

When Xakiras touches down, I want to leap from his arms, hoping to find Jetta in her buttercup-yellow dress, drinking the gross coffee from the canteen. I know it's a fantasy, but there's a tinge of hope that bubbles in the center of my chest that they're not all dead. That at least a few of them survived.

"Let me down. I want to see." I squirm from his tight grip on me.

Xakiras doesn't immediately let me down; instead one of his hands comes up and holds my chin in place so I'm forced to give him eye contact. "Echo, do not stray too far from me. The Krel may be nearby; they enjoy the thrill of luring their prey into a false sense of security."

"Don't tell me what to do, Xakiras. I'm going to be safe. I'm not a baby." I narrow my eyes at him, hating the way he thinks he can just tell me what to do.

He gives me a smirk, jerking my chin forward until I'm in front of his face. The gust of his breath tickles my lips. "*Kukali,* do not tempt me in punishing that sweet body of yours for misbehaving. I have kept myself from touching you since we woke, but do not think I will not choke you while I fuck you senseless, just to prove who controls whom."

My body tingles at the promise, and I swallow loud enough that I hear my throat bob. I force myself to only lick my lips and nod. "That sounds less like a punishment and more like fun to me."

Xakiras smiles. "You may think that, but my stamina will outlast yours. How many times might I bring you to bliss before you beg me to stop?"

A throbbing in my core has my breath hitching. "Later, after we've looked around."

"Mm...yes, later."

Finally he sets me on my feet, and already I feel woozy and weak. I want so badly the "punishment" he promised me, but he's right; I should stay close to him. The Krel were huge, much larger than Xakiras is, and he's seven feet tall and full of muscle.

I think I recall them as being taller than that, and they have a thick exoskeleton that would be hard to shatter without a weapon. They also have strange spears with the same fire from the caves.

Was that the magick Xakiras mentioned?

As we move through the camp through the broken and ripped tents, I see blood everywhere on the ground. The bright green grass that glitters as I step is covered in it, but there are no bodies.

"Where are the bodies?" We have barely walked through the main stretch of camp, but there isn't a solitary shred of evidence that anyone died here other than the blood on the ground.

I stop walking as Xakiras does. One of his hands reaches down to grab hold of mine. "Echo, they were consumed."

My heart halts as I gasp. "No, they wouldn't have done that."

No, no, no.

Xakiras squeezes my hand, and it pulls me back to the moment as tears leak down my cheeks. I want to float away to a place far from here, but he's there keeping me on the ground.

"Echo?" His voice is so tender and so full of grief for me, and he pulls me closer to his side. "I will keep you safe."

My shoulders shake with sobs, and I turn around just to bury my head in his chest, knowing and trusting he's telling the truth. He would keep me safe.

"Why, why would they do that?"

Xakiras grips me tightly, running his hands through my hair. "Both the Sagath and Krel are predators. They are unable to feel true remorse for their actions and are unintelligent, acting only on their urges."

I sob harder, holding on to him like he is my lifeline in this world. I suppose he is, and for once the fears of what might come when I tell the Imperium what happened here settles like a weight in my chest.

Just how much should I actually share?

CHAPTER SIXTEEN
VENOM

Echo sobs for a long while, held to my chest while I whisper pretty little lies that might make us both feel safer. I know there will be no peace when the *Kugitauri* and caliphate know of the brutality here. We have been without war for so long, but things will only get worse now.

"Echo, we should continue searching the camp. Will you be alright?" I pet her hair, and she sniffles and nods.

"I'll be okay. I need to find the comms unit." Her voice is so strained and tight, and it hurts my heart to know her coming here might have been the best thing to happen to me, yet it is the worst to happen to her.

Her arms untwine from my waist, and she peels herself away from me, using the side of her arm to wipe the mucus from her nostrils. Echo's face is red and splotchy, and yet there is a tiny fake smile she puts on her face just for me.

We move through the camp again, her hand tightly gripped in mine until we find a large tent that is falling on one side. It smells like decay, though I know the bodies have long since been disposed of.

"This is the one. I'm going to go inside. Will you follow me?" Echo looks at me, appearing so small, holding her arms around her chest, protecting her vital organs.

I grip her hand. "Of course I will. I will always take care of you, Echo; you are mine, remember?"

The words tumble from my lips, though I know we haven't truly spoken about what happened last night.

Echo nods, another fake smile on her lips showing a tiny fraction of her teeth. "I know you'll take care of me."

With one final squeeze to my hand, we go inside the tent. I have to bend my head down to fit, pulling my wings closer to my body so there is space.

Everything inside is in disarray. Several large, shiny objects are broken and smoking, and tables have been flipped on end. Echo takes small steps as she walks through the wreckage, finally letting our hands drop between us.

"This was where the commander slept. He was a great man," she says somberly.

Her shoulders slump down for a brief moment, but then she straightens back up as though she cannot possibly show me her despair.

It is not weakness to show your sadness, though I do not tell her that. I allow her to grieve in the way she needs.

"How will you communicate with your leaders?" I follow her as she begins to peel through metal wreckage on the floor near an upturned cot.

Echo stops a moment, her nose wrinkling upward. "Well, there's tech here that I can contact them with if it's not broken."

I hear a tapping then, strong and steady as if something is creating a rhythm in the earth. My head swivels to the sound as it continues a rapid pounding tempo. I know that sound; it is the beginning of a warriors' cant.

"Echo, hide. Now." I turn on my heel, grabbing my sword from the sheath on my side.

She looks at me wide-eyed. "What? Why?"

"Now!" I grit through my teeth before holding the flap of the tent upward and heading out into the open where I know a Krel will be waiting.

As soon as I am outside, I see the *lampfyre* glimmering from a solitary spear. Why would one be alone?

I should have searched for my hunting party before coming here alone. Echo has made me so irresponsible, but I would do it again and again for her.

I rise to the air, and as I do, I see why this Krel was left alone. One of its legs is broken, and it has been hiding in one of the tents to save itself. They care very little for wounded brothers and typically leave them behind if their injury is too great and may cause them to lag behind. Once he heals, he would be able to return on his own.

He stands proudly, however, holding his spear, pounding it into the earth as though he intends to scare us off. This Krel is a large red beast with long, matted, ink-colored hair. Bits of his exo are torn, showing the flesh underneath. His left arm is bruised, while the leg on the back side is splintered very poorly with twine on a limb.

"I will show you no mercy, Nocris!" He beats at his chest with a roar.

No matter how injured he is, it will be a difficult fight to win. I will have to be very clever in how I attack. "You are wounded. You cannot last."

He charges immediately, likely angry that I exposed him as weakened. His tail goes upright and his spear outward, but I dive at just the right time to slice him along his bare back. There is no scream of pain. Instead his tail flicks toward me, nearly missing me by a hair's breadth.

Its poison would render me unconscious immediately, so their tail is the most dangerous part of them.

He points the spear upward, and a flash of blue flies from it as he casts some form of magick from its end. The flame hits the tip of my shoulder and part of my wing. I scream, twirling in the air. The flames do not catch entirely, only scalding the skin, but it's enough to have me off-guard.

The warrior takes this instance to stab with his tail toward me, and I force myself to roll out of the way. "I smell a female with you, Nocris, and when I find her, I will make you watch as I eat her."

Rage burns inside my body until I am consumed by it. I charge at his head, immediately swinging at his broad neck. He's faster on his feet than I give him credit for as his spear comes out to stab before I can get at his neck with my sword.

"Why are you here? This is not your land!" I scream as I twirl away.

The warrior's booming laugh does nothing to temper my growing rage. "We will take this land as ours! The badlands are unfertile, and we desire to thrive without your measly *Kugitauri's* aid!"

Ah, so it's like that. They do not wish to be under our thumb any longer. We have kept them in the badlands since the last war, only giving them minor aid during the harsher months. But their leader has grown older, and perhaps with this show of strength has passed down his leadership to someone new.

"We will never allow you take this land!" I scream as I rise into the air. I look down upon him and weak, inferior warriors of his kind.

He already has sweat on his brow, and he's done nothing but defensive maneuvers now. The warrior will eventually wear down.

The tail lashes one more time upward as he casts another fire ball my direction, but it's too slow. I dive when I see the muscles in his neck twitch. With a scream, I come down with a backhanded swing. Nocris are stronger than Krel because we are faster, more agile and have the high ground. Though they have a greater affinity for magick than we do now, this one is far too weak to cast properly.

I swing the sword across his neck while my legs kick him in the face. His tail flicks at the same time, and as my sword cuts his head off, his tail stabs me.

The venom courses through my body, but I know I will not die. It will only render me unconscious for a time. "ECHO!" I scream as my body goes rigid, and I fall from the sky to the ground below.

CHAPTER SEVENTEEN
COME BACK TO ME

I hear my name, and from my hiding place under a fallen cot, I know without a doubt, it's Xakiras's voice. My heart leaps in my throat, and I pull myself out from underneath it, slipping on the floor as I scramble. Before hiding, I found one of the blasters underneath the cot. In my hands, it feels cool, sleek, and I worry I won't know how to use it. I was never trained, but I know all I need to do is point and fire.

When I'm outside, I don't see him right away and call out, "Xakiras? Where are you?"

There's no answer.

My pulse races in my neck, and my underarms begin to sweat. I point the gun outward from my chest as I walk through the rows of tents. "Xakiras?" I continue to call for him, and the longer there is no reply, the more tears well in my eyes.

I start running through the tents until I find the large Krel's head feet away from his body and the bright green color of Xakiras's wings.

He's on his face on the ground with his wings spread behind him, and his body is rigid as stone. I can see the sword still gripped tightly in his hand.

"Xakiras!" I run to his side, sliding onto the grass until I'm beside him. My hands wander over his body, searching for a wound. I see nothing at all on his back, though, and there's no blood anywhere.

"Honey, please talk to me. What's wrong?" fear echoes in my voice, and my eyes blur with unshed tears.

He doesn't answer or move.

Immediately my fingers fly to the side of his neck to check for a pulse. His skin is still warm, and there, underneath the pad of my index finger, I can feel a faint, subtle little thump.

He's alive!

"I'm going to roll you over, okay, baby? I need to check you for wounds and treat them," I say, though I'm talking to myself at this point. It calms me to keep speaking because the forest is so quiet that I'm afraid to hear my own thoughts.

My hands go under his waist, but I don't know how to roll him without hurting his wings. If I break them, would he despise me?

Still, I have to know if he's okay, and if that means he might need time to heal, then that's fine.

I grunt as I try to turn him, but as his body is so stiff, it's like moving a boulder. Eventually I get him on his side, not wanting to break his wings or fold them entirely. There on his stomach is a large, throbbing wound with bright red veins reaching out through his skin.

Xakiras's eyes are wide open, as is his mouth, and he's breathing. I can tell by the shallow way his chest rises and falls. "Oh my gosh."

My mind flips pages of a book inside my mind that remembers details of scorpions from distant Earth. We no longer have any of their DNA to recreate them, but I know I've seen them when I studied in university.

The venom, if left untreated, would usually kill them. My tears finally begin to trail down my face. He's going to die here on the ground alone.

Pulling him to me, I hold him in my lap, stroking his neck ruff and hair. "I'll stay with you," I say, though the words are followed by sobbing.

I hold him like that in my lap for over an hour as I sob and promise he won't die alone. The longer we sit, the more I realize the venom isn't as fast-acting as I expected. He doesn't have any change to him, and he doesn't die. His breathing stays the same even though he can't move.

My legs are asleep, and my eyes ache from all the crying, but I continue to talk to Xakiras until I hear the subtle sounds of wings in the air.

I look upward into the glowing pink of the moon, and there I see several Nocris with various-colored wings flying in a formation over us.

"Help!" I scream, waving an arm upward into the air. "Please!"

They wouldn't hurt him. Maybe they are the hunting party from before, coming to investigate the place the Krel murdered my crew.

"Ho!" one of them calls, and he pauses in the formation with a hand upward to halt everyone else.

"Please help!" I call again, squeezing Xakiras's shoulder. Leaning down, I whisper to him, "They'll help you, sweetheart. It'll be better soon."

Within minutes, the entire five Nocris men have settled onto the ground near the dead carcass. One of them has bright pink wings, and another dark brown with eyes that look bright orange.

"Xakiras?" the pink one says, stepping forward, hesitating as I look at them with sad, begging eyes.

I swallow down the desire to cry. "He was hurt by the Krel. He can't move. Please help him."

Immediately the one stepping to me laughs. "Ah, is that all? He'll be fine. We are all dosed with the venom early. He's only paralyzed and unconscious. He won't die."

The others all start to laugh, and I shake my head. "Why are you laughing?!"

"We aren't laughing at you. My apologies. It is just very like him to go off on his own and get hurt in the process. I assure you he will live."

I feel delirious, there are so many emotions swirling in my head—fear, anger, elation, guilt—that I start to laugh along with them. "He'll be okay!"

CHAPTER EIGHTEEN
LOVE IS REAL

They were right. Within hours Xakiras is back to himself, though frustrated and embarrassed. We've all nestled near a fire that one of the men created, eating some sort of meat from sticks.

Xakiras is constantly at my side, holding me close as if he doesn't want a single inch of air between us.

"When will you learn not to go off on your own?" the pink one, whose name I now know is Paki, asks between chewing.

Xakiras grumbles, and I chew on my lip to keep myself from laughing. "I saved Echo from *Amae'sil* and the Krel in the process. It is truly worth it that I broke protocol."

"Who is she to you?" another asks, and I feel the blush creeping along my neck and cheeks.

There is no hesitation as Xakiras proudly looks at his men, pulling me even tighter to his side. "This is my mate, Echo."

Everyone stops their chewing, and silence falls over all of them. There's no more side conversations at all. "Mate?"

Xakiras nods. "Yes, she is my mate. We will go to the caliphate and explain the situation shortly."

"Well, congratulations, then. I truly hope you know what you're doing." Paki shoves a bite of food into his mouth.

I sure hope so too.

Later after we've eaten and discussed the future, Xakiras and I head back to the my commander's tent. There's a cot there that I'd much prefer to sleep on than the floor.

"Echo, my sweet beautiful flower. I am so sorry I worried you." His hands tenderly rub against my cheeks, pulling me closer to him once we're inside, away from prying eyes.

"It's okay. You didn't mean to. I'm just glad you're alive." I tightly embrace him. "Please don't ever fucking do that again, do you hear me? I was terrified!"

Xakiras lifts my chin, running a thumb over my bottom lip. "I am a hunter. I am always in danger, but I assure you that I will never go off on my own again. I will always return to you."

"You swear?" I pin him with my eyes, narrowing them, itching for his promise.

His navy tongue darts out of his lips, wetting them. "I swear to you on my life, I will never leave you. I love you, otoki, my little bug."

My god, I love the sound of that. Tiny little goosebumps rise on my arms, and I smile up at him. "Why am I a bug?"

Xakiras smirks deviously as he ghosts his lips over mine. "Because I eat them, and I will eat you too. Now get on the cot."

I don't hesitate at all as my heart thunders in my chest and heat pools between my legs. The scent of sweetness swells around me, and instantly I'm yearning to have him.

Once I'm on the cot, I spread my legs wide for him, and like a beast, Xakiras is immediately between them.

His tongue laves down the sides of my thighs, kissing along the skin. "I am going to fuck you senseless. Are you ready for me?"

I barely nod as he pulls my waist, forcing me closer to him. His tongue finds my clit, licking it slowly enough that my head tilts backwards in ecstasy.

Xakiras holds my hips while another set of hands roves under my blouse. I squirm, shuffling it over my head for him to get better access to me.

A purring sound comes from his mouth when he can touch my skin more easily. He glances up at me, only to stop licking. "I want you to watch me as I taste you. If your eyes close for even a moment, I will make you pay for it. Do you understand me?"

I whimper with excitement, feeling my body throb at the delicious temptation of his punishment. "Yes, I understand."

He kisses my thigh as two of his thick fingers enter me, forcing me to fight against the desire to close my eyes with pleasure. Xakiras goes back below to lick at my clit, this time much faster than before. The way his tongue moves makes my hips rise and grind against his face, but the entire time, he's looking at me. The fire and lust in his eyes take my own to new heights.

It builds slowly, simmering like a tiny flame, and with each thrust of his fingers and flick of his tongue, I writhe under his attentions.

"Please!" I don't know why I'm begging; it flies out of my mouth anyway.

Xakiras doesn't allow me to come. He stops hooking his fingers inside me while his tongue goes back inside his mouth. "On your stomach. Now."

His fingers disappear, and I curse at the loss of him. "What? Why?"

I blink in a daze, searching up into his bright white eyes, finding him entirely stone-faced. "Did I ask? I am fairly certain I told you to get on your stomach."

Sitting up, I roll onto my stomach for him, making sure to do it slowly. The cot digs into my chest because it's made of coarse plastic, but I want what's coming next.

Xakiras's hands roam over my body, finding the edge of my skirt that I forgot to take off. He doesn't wait, flipping it upward onto my back and digging his fingers into the globes of my ass.

"Mm...look at you," he purrs, grabbing hold of my hips.

He jerks my hips upward so my ass is in the air while another set of his hands grabs my hair, yanking my head backward.

I whine, and my pussy throbs. I'm so wet that I swear it could be dripping down my thighs. When something wet rubs itself between my folds, I groan and arch toward it. "Please, Xakiras, I want you."

He lines himself up, pressing in while forcing my head backward. "You feel so amazing." His voice is breathy and deeper than usual which makes me feel like I'm a goddess.

Once Xakiras is seated all the way inside me, he says, "I do not want you to come until I say so. Can you do that for me?"

He drags himself out of me, only to thrust into me so roughly that my breath catches. His fingers dig into my hips, and the one in my hair grips my head tighter as he pounds into me with abandon. Every flick of his hips spirals me higher, and the long tendrils of feathers reach out to play with the skin on my thighs.

As they tickle and he thrusts, my hands grip on to the side of the cot. I can feel every inch of him, and as he swells inside me, my moans grow louder. The hand on my hair disappears, and I let my neck fall limp with a sigh.

Xakiras's hand moves between my legs, and I whine as I feel him touch my clit. "No, don't, please, I'll come!"

My body is already so wound tight that if he gives me the friction I need, I'll combust. His response is nothing but a smack on my ass. "Do not, not until I tell you."

His fingers touch me in tandem with each rough grind, and my moans turn into nothing but sobbing, begging as the sensation builds in my core.

He grasps my hips harder, digging into the skin so deep that I cry out with pleasure. Everything inside me feels too much, like I'm in a whirlpool swimming against a mighty current.

I have to bear down, going into a space where I feel hollow so I don't come. "Please, please, please let me!" I chant, and Xakiras's hands shove me back down onto the cot, grinding into my ass with rough, brutal grunts.

"No, not yet." His hands go to my neck, holding at the sides, making each breath a trial.

This new sensation makes the wave I'm in roar higher. "Please! Fuck!"

Xakiras's hips continue to pound into me, using me fully. "Come for me, my sweet flower."

All at once, with his permission, it washes over me. My body goes rigid; my toes crack, and I scream out in pleasure as my pussy throbs against his cock.

He leans his body against my back, holding me against him as he thrusts into me. The sweat that coats his body in a sheen feels cool against my hot skin, and I think about how much I want to lick it off him.

Xakiras's tongue flicks out at my ear, and I hear the strain in his voice as he grunts, "I love you."

It's as if the words are his undoing. He throbs inside me, and a tight whine comes from him as his hot cum fills me up. I whine at the feeling, loving the way it tingles while it numbs me from any and all pain.

"I love you too."

His hand comes up and holds mine as he presses a kiss to the side of my face.

"Good girl."

CHAPTER NINETEEN
MORE TO COME

There's a faint beeping that wakes me from a deep sleep.

"What is that?" I wonder aloud as I tilt my head toward the noise. It trills louder and louder, and Xakiras beside me grumbles in annoyance.

"Make it stop."

My eyes fight to stay open from being fucked into oblivion. We had sex three more times that night, and I've never been so thankful for his magical cum. For once the feeling between my legs doesn't leave me raw and in pain.

I roll off the cot, allowing Xakiras's arm to fall away. "It has to be one of the comms units."

The entire tent is a mess, but the sound continues from the lefthand side of the tent, far in the corner. Padding over, I see underneath a pile of books something shining underneath. Moving them aside without caring if I bend the spines, a holo blessedly lights up in bright blue lights.

On the screen it says "Peony." As I hold it in my hands, they tremble, not knowing just what I should say. "It's my ship..."

I know my voice likely gives away my feelings on the subject, but Xakiras sits up on the cot. "It will work out for the best. You must tell your people."

"What if things are worse?" I chew at my bottom lip, tugging at the skin until the tang of blood fills my mouth.

My nerves are shot as I fidget with the holo in my hands.

The cot gives a groan, and strong arms wrap around my back, encasing me in comfort. "I am here, Echo. Tell them what you must."

I exhale a rattling breath and nod. "You're right. I need to, for their families at least."

My fingers slide across the holo's screen until it asks for a passcode, and I enter mine. From the day my contract started, it was what I always used because it was simple and easy.

"Hello, this is Echo from Crew J9876," I say, willing my voice stronger.

The voice sounds so pleasant, one I've heard a hundred times. It's Jetta's mother, Hirana, and my throat closes. Tears well in my eyes, and I try to hold back the sobs as she kindly asks, "Where is your commander, Echo?"

"Ma'am, there has been a massacre." I swallow roughly, and my hands tremble, but Xakiras continues to hold me tightly in his arms, giving a kiss to my cheek.

"Where is Jetta?" Her voice is strained, and I can hear the fear in her tone.

That's when the dam of my grief breaks free. "Ma'am, everyone is gone. There are sentient species, and one of them came into the camp." I sniffle and try to maintain some semblance of calm. "I—I think I'm the only one left."

She breaks for only a moment as I hear her groan down the emotions she so very much wants to release. However, we have to maintain decorum, and Hirana is a lieutenant. She must keep herself in check.

"I will contact the Imperium and have you relay what happened. Are you safe?" I wipe at my nose and inhale a ragged breath. "Yes, I am with one of the peaceful species called the Nocris. They want me to speak with their leader as well."

"Echo, we will be back to you in six weeks. Are you sure you will be okay?" Hirana's tone is more sincere and motherly now. "Do not tell them anything until the Imperium has been debriefed; do you understand?"

They want me to wait? What would they do, have me lie?

"Yes, ma'am. I'll be fine until then."

There's a noise, and she quickly says, "Do not tell them anything; do you hear me?"

My blood runs cold because I'm not sure what they need to hide from the Nocris. They've helped me so much already.

Xakiras's arms squeeze me tighter, and I realize he's hearing my people ask me to lie. "When will they contact me?"

Hirana sighs on the other end, going silent for a few seconds. "I will send them a transmission now. You should hear back by the end of business. Keep yourself safe, and, Echo, if you find Jetta, will you—" She pauses, and I hear a sniffle from the other end. "If you find her body, please keep it until we return."

I don't have the heart to tell her that they've been eaten, that there will be no bodies to bury. Instead I lie, telling her I will.

When the holo goes dark, I slump forward, and the tears run down my face. "Nothing good will come of this. What do I do?"

Xakiras kisses my neck. "Echo, we may only do what we can. We cannot control the actions of those who are above us. We must only hope they will take care of us."

I hate that he's right because I know now he's not in a high caste position, so I won't be either. Not to mention that if the imperium decides to come here and cause war, how much destruction will take place?

"I know you're right. I just can't help feeling like it'll be my fault if something happens."

"Nothing will be anyone's fault, my love, other than the Krel who came here to take our lands. They will have to pay for what they've done, one way or the other. All we can do is pray things work the way they are intended."

I know he's right, and yet I've never been more worried. At least I have him in my arms, holding me and giving me love.

We can make it through this together.

Thank you so much for reading this story!
I have had this idea in my head since the beginning of 2021 and I wanted so much for it to come to life. I wanted to create a world completely at night with hard fantasy elements and SCIFI elements.

So, in true Opal style, I went why not both?

There will be more to come with this world, and I'm so eager to share it with you. So, keep a lookout for it.

Volxek Shifters
An omegaverse alien shifter series
Claimed in the Chaos Book 1
Taken in the Chaos Book 2

Other Books:

Thieves and Monsters: Three fates Mafia with Clio Evans

ABOUT THE AUTHOR

Opal Fairchild has always loved monsters and thought, 'hey why does the Beast look better as a monster than he does as a human'. Alpha males who can both be aggressive, but a cinnamon roll is her ultimate favorite, so she decided why not write about them? Fantasy worlds in distant places filled with strange magic and tech she loves writing about things that get you feeling.

Opal is living in North Carolina with her two cats who drive her nuts. When she isn't a gremlin hunched over her keyboard, she loves hanging out with squirrels, sitting with trees, collecting animal skulls and playing video games.

Want to connect? Find me on Tiktok and Instagram the most!

My website where you can find me: Here

amazon.com/Opal-Fairchild

tiktok.com/@opalfairchild

instagram.com/opalfairchild.author

facebook.com/Opalfairchild.Author

twitter.com/opalfairchild.a

THE MINOAN BRIDE

C.M. NASCOSTA

CHAPTER ONE

"Can we go through the labyrinth in the garden after our tour?"

A chorus of little voices chimed in, agreeing with the speaker, a small satyr who looked incredibly pleased with himself for being brave enough to ask the question all of his classmates were thinking. Madoc grinned, and Gwen felt her own mouth turn up at the sight, already knowing what was coming.

"Well, you can, but the hedge maze we have here is different from the labyrinth of Crete. *Our* labyrinth is unicursal, and the Cretan labyrinth we've talked about today was *multicursal*. Can anyone tell me what the difference is?"

She smiled again when several small hands shot up, as Madoc led the group of visiting schoolchildren out of earshot, their teacher and parent chaperone shepherding the back, ensuring no one dawdled or strayed. *He's going to be a great dad.* The thought made her breath catch and her stomach flip; their recent conversation still fresh and full in her mind.

They'd already picked out the braided circlet she would wear on her wrist after their summer nuptials—white gold and delicate, inlaid with diamond chips that caught the light and sent a splash of rainbow color on the jewelry shop's wall on the day she'd first tried it on, a twin of the heavier version that would go through his nose. The variety of wedding jewelry carried in the shop had made her head spin, a sign of the varied community she would soon call home. Orcish cuffs and minotaurean circlets rested in the case beside all manner of rings worn on fingers and toes, necklaces and torques and hairpins, goblins and harpies and trolls all having their respective cultures represented in a limited selection within the cases, a reminder that she'd soon be living amongst them. They both wanted children, and during a giddy conversation in the pre-dawn hours several days earlier—pressed to his front in bed, in the house she'd soon be moving into—they agreed not to wait.

"We've done our waiting," he'd reminded her, huffing against her hair as she agreed. Grad school and PhDs, postdoc research and dig sites, endless time away, endless time apart. "I don't want to be the same age as the grandfathers on graduation day. Time to start actually living before our knees give out."

"*With* the living," she'd agreed, squealing as he rolled her. "The mummies can wait."

"They'll still be dead," he'd assured her, blunt teeth nipping at her throat, her gasp as he pushed into her swallowed by his lips.

"So how did you two meet?"

The voice of his co-worker, an amphibious woman with blue-green skin and glossy black eyes, who had been extremely welcoming when Madoc had introduced her around to the museum staff that morning broke her reverie. *Sleeva, that's her name.*

"It was on a dig," Gwen laughed ruefully, thinking back to that sun-baked summer after her graduation. "A village settlement, Fort Meridian selkies. I had just graduated, he was already in grad school. The student volunteers were paired off alphabetically and we have the same last name."

"Ha! That was fate, wasn't it?" the amphibious woman smiled broadly. "You kept in touch afterward and it just went from there?"

"It was definitely fate," she agreed, not mentioning the fact that it had only taken a few days of sweating their asses off side-by-side on the dig site to work up a sweat together at night in a barely-big-enough bed in the makeshift quarters. Despite being Minotaurean herself, she'd been raised by her human-presenting mother in a predominantly human suburb, and Madoc had been the first male of her kind she'd been with. She'd had a handful of sexual partners at that point, but the mouthwatering sight of his thick cock and its first subsequent press within her had sent fireworks shooting behind her eyes, her body designed to accommodate his girth and length with ease. Moving with him in the small bed—the grit and dust of the dig site still hanging in the air, the close confines, the ruins and history surrounding them—it had felt magical. Magical and fateful, and when she'd cried out, climaxing around him, Gwen had been certain she could hear the echoes of lovers across two thousand years, living and loving and dying right there, a touch of eternity. "After that, we were always a few steps apart. I wound up going to his school for my grad degree. We were there for a year together before he left to do his doctorate, then I did a fellowship in the same city before he left for postdoc research...and that's how we've lived for the better part of the last decade."

She similarly neglected to mention the way they grocery shopped over the phone together every week, did laundry at the same time, watched movies and listened to audiobooks, anything they could do to make the distance chafe a little less...but his co-worker didn't need to know that. The sight of him sitting before his laptop screen, legs splayed open and hard cock in hand was one she saw weekly, long-distance sex that paled in comparison to the real thing, but the best they could manage. She knew exactly in which direction his horns would slice through the air and the way his cock would jerk as he came to her encouragement; knew precisely where the thick white ropes of his release would splatter against his chest and belly. She knew the way his stomach muscles would tighten and contract, the way his heavy balls would rise and pulse as he emptied for her watchful eyes. Gwen knew he would be able to say the exact same thing, having watched her own climaxes weekly for longer than either of them cared to count, and his co-worker *certainly* didn't need to know that. She didn't bring up the fact that the odd collection of time they actually spent in one place—cobbled together weeks that sometimes turned into short, blissful months—were seamless and easy; that falling into step with each other was as natural as breathing, which only made the inevitable parting feel as if her heart was being slowly poked apart, bleeding her dry until she had nothing left.

"It's okay though," she went on, "because we always knew where we stood. Being apart wasn't ideal, but there wasn't any resentment or anything, because we were doing the exact same thing. All the same degrees, the same digs, the same fieldwork. I get to nerd out over bronze age pottery with my best friend, how many people get to say that? I was a few steps behind him, but we both knew where we would wind up."

"And I'm so glad it's here!" the other woman squealed. "We're so thrilled to have him, you have no idea. This collection he's put together...it's remarkable stuff. The minotaur community here is so proud to have this sort of representation. And how amazing that you were able to find a position so close! My kids love the history museum in Bridgeton, we're not big enough to have any cool dinosaurs here. You'll have to let us know when your exhibit opens, and don't listen to what anyone tells you, you're not even going to notice the drive! It's a straight shot into the city. He said you'll be moving in soon?"

Gwen nodded, feeling a flutter of butterfly wings move through her. "Next week. I'm flying back just for the day to turn the key in and make sure nothing is left behind, but the movers will already have everything packed and loaded." It was a rental house, the only thing that had been available when he'd taken the job at the small, private museum in Cambric Creek, simultaneously terrifying to contemplate and a relief that they'd be able to pick out their forever home together.

"We'll keep an eye on things," he'd assured her the first weekend she'd spent visiting in Cambric Creek after he'd moved. "I already found an agent who will let us know when things hit the market so we can see them as soon as they're available. As far as rentals go, this one is pretty great. Look, we have a yard! Real grass! Can you even believe it?!"

"Perfect for kids," she'd murmured, stretching her toes out to brush the grass beyond the edge of the flagstone terrace where she'd sat across his lap. "And the schools here are good you said?"

"The schools here are great," the amphibian woman continued, almost as if she were able to hear the conversation Gwen replayed in her head. "It's the public system, but you'll feel like you're getting the benefits of private tuition. The classrooms all have aids and specialists, tons of one-on-one attention. My youngest, Finny, he's at the primary school right now, and he cries on Saturday mornings when I tell him he's stuck with me all weekend." Gwen joined her chuckle, trying to envision a little boy with blue-green skin and webbed fingers. "Our property taxes are through the roof, of course, but it's worth it. That is, if you're even thinking about kids," she added hastily. "I don't want to sound like a pushy great-aunt."

"We are. And the schools were a big draw, believe me. I grew up in an all-human town, so the thought of our kids growing up in a diverse place is important to us."

Sleeva's dark eyes darted to the side to take her in, a quick up-and-down that Gwen felt like the slide of a hand. "Sooo...a girl will look like you, and a boy..."

"A boy would look like this handsome lug," Gwen finished, as Madoc turned the corner back into the room. "Although hopefully with better dress sense."

"And what's wrong with what I have on?" His wide, dappled nose wrinkled with his words, and she beamed, envisioning what it would look like in a few months, cinched in white gold. He was the most handsome minotaur she'd ever met, and unlike most academics, he was *actually* good with people. She had no doubt his co-worker's words were true—people loved Madoc wherever he went.

"He's had this sweater since grad school, Sleeva,"

The amphibian woman hid her laughter in webbed hands at the scowl Madoc pulled, her slender shoulders shaking.

"Go on, get out of here," she wheezed out, waving her hand at the towering minotaur. "That was the last group for the day, I'm closing up the gift shop. Go be young and in love somewhere, Doctors Bowman."

"Oh, I'm getting a private tour of the exhibit! That's actually what counts as romance for us," Gwen called out to Sleeva's retreating back, the other woman's renewed laughter echoing through the marble hallway as she left them alone. "She seems nice. They all love you here."

"She's very nice and I'm supremely loveable, so that checks out." He grinned as she swiped at his chest, capturing her arm easily and pulling her flush against him. "One more week, Dr. Bowman." His voice was low, barely a whisper, and tears pricked at her eyes at the nearness of the date, an end to the separation once and for all. She hadn't lied to his co-worker—there had never been any resentment or bad feelings over their separation, but Gwen felt as if she'd woken up one day to mysteriously find herself on the other side of thirty, and the last year had been harder than the entire decade that had preceded it.

"One more week," she agreed, smiling when he ruffled her hair. "Dr. Bowman."

"Let me lock up the west entrance and close off the exhibit, and then we'll start. You enter from there," he pointed to the doorway behind them, "at that first vitrine, and then move clockwise into the walls. But wait for me!"

She watched his retreating back, heart quivering with fear and excitement and more love than she'd once thought it was possible to feel. *One more week.* One more week before she left her apartment and the city that had been home for several years; one more week until she settled into life in suburbia, far from a classroom or field office or dig site, far from everything that had been normal for the last ten years. They would be together, but she was still sailing into the unknown, uncertain of how she would adjust to life outside of academia, life with him, side-by-side and not separated by miles and cities and time zones. The whole world felt possible, Gwen thought, but it didn't change the way her heart trembled. One more week, and everything would change.

CHAPTER TWO

The sea was wild and angry the day the bireme left Salamis. It has been that way since we sailed west from Athens, stopping to feast and drink one last time before the princess boarded the ship and we sailed south. Periboea thinks herself better than the rest of us, I can tell, but today she is afraid. Earlier, she held my hand and wept as we stared out at the black waves, crashing against the oars like an omen of what is to come, as if Poseidon himself is following to announce our arrival. We are close to the palace at Knossos, very close the guards tell us. It will only be a few nights more until we arrive at our final destination; until we leave the bireme in chains to be presented before the King. Periboea held my hand and wept, and the tribute from Melos has not stopped sobbing since we left her island behind, but my eyes are dry today.

I will not pretend that I am unafraid. I am **very** afraid. The men on the ship have told us stories, whether to warn or frighten us, I do not know. They have accomplished both, and are all the crueler for it.

The beast will devour the men first, they say, leaving us unprotected. He has sharp teeth, they claim, for tearing our flesh and eating us alive, and the body of a man, for raping those he does not immediately kill. I questioned one of the men about how they knew such things, for no survivors had ever escaped, but they only laughed and said I would soon learn. We will arrive soon in Knossos, and learn we will, and the sea god is as cruel as the men with their stories, *but today my eyes are still dry. The princess is afraid and I am as well, but I have looked into the oracle fires and have seen the truth that will come to pass. I am Melita of Korinthos, and my name will not be lost to Minos's maze. We will arrive soon in Knossos and the labyrinth beneath the palace and I am sailing to my death, but today my eyes are dry.*

CHAPTER THREE

The first vitrine held a single set of manacles. Gwen paused before the glass, the bronze restraints within seeming too small to have bound anything but a child. The walls behind the display cases had been wrapped floor-to-ceiling with a stylized map of the Aegean Sea and all of her islands, red dashes dotting the blue water, marking the path the sacrifices sailed to their final destination at Crete. She tried to imagine what it must have been like for the young men and women—drawn by lots, their fate a simple luck of the draw.

Around the wrist cuffs, the preservation team had done exemplary work revealing the classical labyrinth design, a seven-course block that showed up repeatedly on coins and rings and vases, repeatedly throughout history. *Unicursal*, she smirked, knowing the misrepresentation in artifacts was one of Madoc's biggest pet peeves. She tried to imagine the small-statured prisoner these manacles had once held as she rounded the case, examining the restraints from every side. Not a prisoner, she mentally corrected, reminding herself of the exhibit's theme.

A tribute. A bride.

"They must have been very afraid," she said suddenly, listening to his tread on the marble flooring crossing back to her, the click of his wide hooves silenced by the silicone gaiters he wore. Seven young men and seven young women, given in tribute to Crete, to the labyrinth. Gwen closed her eyes and let her mind paint a picture of the young people ferried across the sea, far from their homes, traveling into the unknown. *The unknown and a minotaur*, she thought, her breath catching at how similar her situation was to whoever had worn these manacles.

"I'm sure they were," Madoc agreed, his huge hands dropping lightly to her shoulders. The overhead light cast his shadow on the ground before her, his horns cutting an impressive silhouette, absorbing her completely, her and the case holding the manacles, and Gwen wondered if the labyrinth minotaur's silhouette had been nearly as impressive as this diminutive sacrifice stood before him. "But you know what happened to them. They weren't afraid for long."

"Pfffttt, says you. You have no idea what it's like being a sheltered young woman leaving home for the first time. I loved undergrad! I loved my room-mates and our quad and all of my friends, I loved my classes. I loved being independent and trying all the things my family kept me from. And I *still* went into the showers and cried every single week because I missed my mom and my room and everything that was familiar. I can promise you, they were fucking terrified, and that doesn't just turn off like a switch."

Gwen twisted her head back, eying him defiantly. She didn't bother reminding him that she had been nearly sick with nerves on that first dig site as well; that she likely never would have fallen into bed with him at all if he hadn't gone out of his way to make her feel comfortable and lessen the clenching homesickness she'd felt. That initial terror of the unknown had never gone away, following her into adulthood—every new city, new job; each new department and school and field office always felt like entering a black cave where anything might be waiting to swallow her up. She *still* cried in the shower with every terrifying new beginning and knew she would undoubtedly do so again in a week's time, after her move to Cambric Creek.

"*Fine*," he huffed, "they were probably very afraid. These were nobles, so—"

"Priestesses, temple attendants. Keybearers to shrines."

"Exactly," he smiled, nodding. "Most of them had never left the cities where they were born, not the women. They were manacled to be presented to the king as a show of Minoan power, but it's likely that they were not bound on the sea crossing and did not go down to the maze in chains. These and the others like them were discovered at the base of the platform that lowered the tributes in, indicative of them being—"

"Cast off once they left the platform."

Gwen moved away from the manacles, not liking the way they made her stomach flip, and instead raised a hand to the wall wrap around the room.

"What are all of these different colors meant to denote? You know they only talk about the Athenian sacrifices in school."

Madoc huffed again. "Of course they did, just like they taught you that all of the tributes were eaten. Human schools are so revisionist, it's a wonder you even learned to read." She laughed in outrage but was hard-pressed to see the fault in his words.

"Sleeva said the schools here are really great," she added, glancing over her shoulder to see his reaction to her words. "So that's one less thing to worry about, I guess." He gave her a knowing smile at her words, catching her around the waist, pulling her to his hip.

"You know," he murmured, "we're not on anyone's time timetable. We can settle in, enjoy being newlyweds...no one gets a say about this other than us. And yes, Athens sent the lion's share of the tributes as a part of their agreement with Crete, but...well, once word got out, the other kings wanted their own warriors. Melos, Mycenae, Korinthos, Thebes...they all sent tributes of their own. Now, are you going to keep interrupting and finishing my sentences?"

"You know that I am," she laughed. "That's what makes us such a good team." She didn't quite understand the meaning of his words, but if the years together had taught her anything, she knew her big minotaur loved show-manship. Reconstruction was the discipline in which he excelled, whereas she had specialized in the human element, particularly the role of women in society. One of the most fascinating things about studying ancient cultures and civilizations, she had always thought, was finding the proof that people never really changed. Road rage and warnings against dishonest merchants, property disputes...it was always the same. Regardless of the species, regard-less of where they had come from and when they had lived, there would always be evidence of living and loving and dying; of people fighting to get ahead and fighting harder still to keep what they had already gained, of neighbors helping neighbors, and parents loving their children. She knew he would make his point when he was good and ready, in the most dramatic way. The museum collection would have been curated and displayed in such a way to elicit an emotional reaction from the viewers, this she knew from her own work. Knowing her fiancé as she did, Gwen had no doubt that she would be in tears at some point during her tour.

"So they were presented to Minos in chains because he was a real dick, got it. What's next?"

Following the pathway, she came to a long display case of helmets from Minoan and Mycenaean kingdoms, several tablets, coinage, and other bits of bronze age ephemera. Madoc swept his hand over the case, drawing her attention to the tablets first.

"Minoan relics found all over the Aegean. We know from Linear A that these tablets are an accounting of purchases made, with names attached. Once they were presented to Minos, the men were sold. Fighters, rowers —"

"Slaves," Gwen finished for him. "The men were never sent into the labyrinth?"

"The labyrinth had no need of any men. The palace already had its own slaves and servants. The women were given as brides, and the men were sold away."

"Mhm...King Minos was a dick and here's the evidence, part two." She listened as he spoke excitedly over the designs of the helmets, the minuscule detailing of the coins, but her mind wandered to her own upcoming *presentation*. She had already met his family, of course, numerous times, but they'd not gotten together with their respective clans since announcing their engagement, and Gwen knew from her own family's reaction to the news that there was a world of difference between him introducing her as his girl-friend and introducing her as the woman for whom he planned on putting a ring through his nose. *They should have seen it coming, right?* She had no doubt his grandmother might very well pull out a measuring tape to gauge the width of her hips, determining her ability to carry bullish sons before giving her blessing over their nuptials.

"I got an email from the caterer this morning," he said suddenly, his mind seeming to wander in the same direction as her own. "Just confirming everything we sent over...are you sure we shouldn't put more meat options on the menu? Just as a precaution? We could always—"

"We're giving them a chicken dish," she cut in with a smile. He fretted endlessly over impressing the human side of her family, and it didn't seem to matter how often she told him he had nothing to worry about. "If they're not happy with that, they're more than welcome to eat before they come. No, we don't need to add more meat. More than half the guest list is vegetarians, it's fine as it is."

"Your Aunt Simone is a big gossip, by your own admission. I don't want your family thinking I'm overly controlling..."

She spun, the ancient coins forgotten, for the moment. Her smile at the sight of him wasn't one she could help—he was the exact same slightly rumpled academic he'd been when they'd met, confident and forthright, but he'd always had a bit of insecurity when it came to impressing humans. Professors, site managers, other anthropologists...and now her family. She stretched up onto her toes, wrapping her arms around his thick neck, pressing herself to his solid heat.

"My Aunt Simone is going to find something to gossip about whether or not we give her cause for it, so I say let's do things our way and not worry about it." His teeth caught at her ear as she nuzzled the thick hide against the side of his neck. "Okay, no more wedding talk. From either of us. We're just getting ourselves stressed out." Dropping from her toes, she spun again, pulling him by the hand. "No more wedding talk! Show me what's next."

Her breath caught as her feet turned inward, following the exhibit's pathway, coming face-to-face with their joint preoccupation. The chiton on the mannequin was dyed a rich, vibrant purple, definitely not an everyday color, and the dark wig was crowned with a wreath of small, white flowers.

"This is how they were dressed for their presentation at the palace," he murmured in a low voice. "The Minoan Brides. The color was a symbol of...well, you already know that."

She sucked in a long breath, leaning back against the solidity of his form as an arm came around her. She'd already picked out her own dress, a frothy summertime confection of royal purple chiffon with a draped bodice and cinched waist, not altogether that different from the chiton the mannequin wore. *A touch of eternity.* "This is a reproduction, of course, based on what we know from pottery and frescos. The tributes were washed and anointed with oils, dressed as brides. Presented in chains. There was a great feast, we know from the frescos there were musicians, and they were well fed. It was quite the party."

"It sounds like a typical wedding," she said ruefully, leaning against him as strong arms came around her. "Speaking of which, we need to book the music soon. We need to decide if we want a DJ or a band, or maybe both..." They had dozens of friends and colleagues, former classmates and room-mates and lab mates, research partners and professors, mentors and students. She'd not initially wanted a big wedding, but they'd quickly agreed that *big* was an inevitability, unless they had a private ceremony.

"I'm going to say both every time it's an option because it's one less decision to make. And what happened to no more wedding talk?"

She stretched up to reach his mouth, sighing into the heat of his rough tongue, wanting to lay her cheek against his chest and not move any further —not into the exhibit, not into her move, not into life. Frozen there, together, like the mummified remains of a dig site...alas, she sighed, that wasn't an option, and the next exhibit display was yet around another corner.

"Yes, right. No more wedding talk. So we're coming from all over the Aegean on a Minoan ship. I'm getting a bath and a post-sailing glow up, flowers in my hair, a pretty purple wedding chiton...now what?"

His fingers, long and thick, laced with hers, squeezing her hand as he winked, and she decided at that moment that he was going to be the most handsome minotaur in the world once his nose was cinched.

"Well, you know what they say. The best part of any wedding is the wedding night."

CHAPTER FOUR

W e hear the screams first. It is a girl's voice, rising and falling with greater and greater fervor, and we hear her before our eyes have a chance to adjust to the darkness.

The darkness of the pit is all-consuming. The sweet smell of orange blossoms in the wreaths that each of us wears upon our hair is nearly overpowering as the light above slowly recedes, as we are lowered into the maze. It is almost a shock when our manacles are removed. We huddle together beneath the hole where the platform rose up, leaving us behind, when one of the other girls begins to shepherd the others down a black corridor. None of us want to move, for it seems smarter and safer to remain stationary and huddled together, but it is almost as if our wills are not our own and we have been left stricken dumb and mute and mindless as worms. We are sheep, and we go where our shepherd moves us. When a corner is turned, the darkness is broken by torch-light. There are torches dotting the pathway we are on breaking up the impenetrable blackness in small glowing pockets. A first, it is a relief to be able to see what is in front of us, but I have quickly realized that the torchlight's meager illumination creates a false sense of security, and the pockets of darkness in between the torches seems more ominous and filled with dangers than the black corridor had.

We have turned several times before we truly realize we are being shepherded. The girl who guides us is not wearing sweet-smelling flowers in her hair, there *is nothing sweet-smelling about her. Her face is streaked with dust and dirt, her hair a matted, snarled nest for birds. Her chiton, what is left of it, is faded and in tatters. It is then that we hear the screams.*

We hear the screams and then one of our own begins to scream as well, and like sheep, when one starts bleating, the entire herd soon follows. We are running now, running in a mindless panic, trying to close the distance on each of the torches and remain in the meager circles of light they throw, but the screaming girl is getting louder, and I realize we are being herded to the center of the maze where the beast resides.

Another turn, and then suddenly there is more than one dirt-streaked girl at our backs, pushing us further down the corridor until we have spilled into the center of the maze, ringed in torches, firelight banishing the darkness so that we might see every bit of the scene before us. We have discovered the source of the screaming. The girl is not screaming in pain or terror, we see immediately. I expected to see carnage, but instead, a scene of carnality greets us. The girl is held aloft, her bare toes scraping the air above the labyrinth's dirt floor, impaled on the beast's cock. A rising, frenzied pleasure seems to grip her as thrusts, and the ring of onlookers—the other brides, whose numbers we are there to bolster—are equally as affected, each one begging for their turn; begging, begging, to be taken next. The girl's cries reach a crescendo in a long, broken wail, and as we watch, her belly distends as if she is an overfilled wine-skin, brimming with the monster's seed. I am not ignorant as to the shape of a man, but nothing in any oracle fire could have prepared me for the sight of the rigid rod of flesh that speared the girl, still proud and erect, even as she is dropped in a gush of fluid.

When the girl is deposited, several of the others rush forward—not to help her, but to offer themselves in her place, begging to be ravished in the same way. She is eventually pulled aside by several sets of hands, all belonging to women who are swollen with child, her body rolled with them to the edge of the torch-light where they squat and watch the others. Another of the brides has been selected by the beast, moaning already as she is similarly speared, but I am unable to pull my eyes from the girl laying in the dirt, and the way she whimpers. One of the young women from the circle surrounding Minos's monster has pushed her way to the back of the press of bodies, where the fecund women squat. Dropping to her knees before the newly used bride, she begins to bite at her thighs like an animal. She is quickly joined by another from the circle, then another, and soon they are fighting; pushing each other and pulling hair to ensure each of themselves the best position to bite the girl. I cry out at the barbarism, shrieking for someone to help her, and then I realize she is not being bitten at all. She moans feebly, her legs twitching, and I see that what they fight over is the minotaur's seed, licking it from her legs and directly from her sex, pushing each other for the privilege, and I despair over what depravity lies in store for us here.

CHAPTER FIVE

"Did I tell you there's one of those milking places right by the museum? It's literally right there, right on the corner! Just think, you can visit me at work in the city after I move, get a little vacuum sucky-sucky, and get paid for the day."

Madoc gave a sharp bark of laughter, his hand landing on her hip. "I haven't been to one of those since I was doing postdoc...honestly, it's not a bad idea. We can pay for the caterer in cash. A bigger down payment once a house comes up would be good to have, and we should probably start saving now for college funds...what does the place look like from the outside? You know some of them are kind of skeevy."

"I have no idea, I didn't go inside. It's in the building on the corner, it looks like every other grey high rise in the city. You'll have to scope it out after I start. It's not like you have a shortage of *organic specimen*, after all."

"Vacuum sucky-sucky," he repeated, shaking his head in disgust. "Why do you always come up with the worst names? What did you call that one by our apartment, before I left for that dig in Croatia? The sploogey—"

"The Splooge Sucker Emporium!" she crowed, his rich laughter echoing around the marble space. "That place was great, we didn't have to spend any of our stipends on rent the whole time we lived there! Okay, yes, you're definitely checking out the place by the museum. Now, no more splooge talk!

No more splooge talk or wedding talk, this is a very serious cultural exhibit and I want to give it my full academic attention, stop distracting me."

"Mhm," he hummed, trying and failing to conceal his wide smile. "Famous last words." Motioning to the next turn, he ducked his head, shoulders shaking in suppressed laughter. "After you, Dr. Bowman."

It took her several minutes to collect herself enough to form words. The next turn within the exhibit brought them to the meat of the collection, and Gwen stopped short before it. It was the main event, meant to elicit the exact stupefied reaction she displayed, but the knowledge that the shock she felt was by design didn't prevent her cheeks from heating.

Her stomach swooped and flipped at the sight of the carved minotaur positioned at the entrance, its body curled over the figure beneath it. Despite its age, the anatomy was still clearly defined, depicted in a way that left no room for debate over what exactly the two forms were meant to be doing. As a prelude, the piece was impactful. She imagined how the average museum guest might react, what an elf or a werewolf would think, seeing the centuries-old proof of the carnality that had taken place within the labyrinth, certain they would blush or exclaim in outrage, perhaps question the docents over the appropriateness of such a display. As someone who regularly enjoyed the very position being depicted, however...Gwen shifted, squeezing her thighs together at the mere thought. She loved being taken by her bull in such a way—up on her knees, ass high in the air as he rutted into her, his elbows on either side of her shoulders, bracing him as his hooves scraped the ground, his breath hot at her back.

"The Splooge Sucker Emporium had a Minoan outpost," she mumbled, scanning the room slowly. "Dr. Bowman, this is the horniest exhibit I've ever seen." On the other side of the statue, the exhibit opened up into a large, square room. The rows of pottery were endless, the pieced together frescoes like giant jigsaw puzzles from another age, threadbare tapestries that had been painstakingly re-created, and everywhere she turned: the Minotaur and his brides. Gwen felt a ripple of pride move through her, surveying the extensiveness of the display, giddy that he did this, that *he* made this collection a reality. *Smart, sexy, passionate. He's your best friend, and you're going to spend the rest of your lives together. And,* she mentally added with a sly smile, *he's fucking amazing in bed.*

Madoc spoke from behind her as she stood frozen before the pillar. "This is the heart of the maze," he murmured, the finger he stroked at the back of her neck making her shiver. "This is where the Minotaur resided with his brides." The first row of pottery portrayed a line of women with heads bowed low, kneeling before the king. From vessel to vessel, she examined the progression of the tributes' journey to the labyrinth, from a vase circled with dark-haired, wide-eyed girls to a tablet inlaid with the classical unicursal labyrinth design. The shelves of pottery were broken by a fresco hung in the center of the aisle, a visual pause point that took her breath away—her first glimpse of the horned Cretan prince, standing before a long line of the women sent into the maze.

He was depicted as an ivory bull in this particular piece, matching the myth she'd always heard growing up, and the sight of him on the fresco, crowned in golden laurel, wearing a short chiton, banded with red and black, sent a shiver up her back, her eyes sliding to her fiancé. Madoc was also an ivory bull, his hide dappled with golden spots and a spray of brown freckles across the pink of his nose. He was tall and broad, as the original minotaur surely was, she thought, with his ivory horns tipped in black. She tried to envision him crowned in the same manner, how regal he would look, just as handsome as he would look that summer for their ceremony; imagined herself kneeling before him in her purple wedding dress, a tribute to the labyrinth, there to be devoured by the ravenous minotaur within...she bit her lip, breath quickening. *Your wedding night is going to be a cosplay at this rate if you don't get ahold of yourself.*

Her cheeks heated, thinking again of that very first dig site, all those years ago. Several of the student volunteers had dinner together at a small restaurant in the village, towards the end of their first week, and the smell of that harbor still lived in her nose, the bite of the local wine dry on her tongue. She had gone out of her way to touch him throughout the evening—her bare toes grazing the short hide of his lower leg, her hands brushing against and lingering at his arms until his fingers had laced with her own beneath the table. When they'd headed back to the makeshift dormitories, his fingers had remained threaded with hers, leading her to his room and his bed. There had been an aura of something larger than either in the air, licking up her back as she laid against his chest, trying to catch her breath and listening to the thunder of his heartbeat. Standing beside him now, surrounded by the relics of their shared heritage, Gwen felt the same shiver.

"Was there a mating ritual?"

"That, we don't know," he chuckled. "It's unclear whether there was a hierarchy of the brides, or how soon they were invited to take part in the...let's say the physical relationship."

"'The physical relationship'. You are so cute when you try to be professional and shit." He snorted at her words, arms coming around her as she stared up at a trio of vases, each depicting a different sex act between a minotaur and a human woman. Tracing her nails over the sinew of his forearms, she dropped her head back as he continued his recitation. She realized, as she took in the details, that each vase depicted a different woman, despite being from the same series by the same artist. The differences were subtle, but clear, once she noticed them, an indicator of the procession women in the maze. The first showed the minotaur—depicted as black in this series—with a jutting erection, the kneeling woman before him holding it in her hand, guiding it towards her mouth. The second showed a different woman, held in the bullman's arms, facing him, the top of the black-painted cock disappearing into her. The third portrayed yet another woman being taken on her hands and knees, much in the same way as the statue at the entrance of the room. "Is there provenance for all of these?"

"Most of them, yeah." His voice echoed around the vases as he gestured beside her. "That one there is a part of a series from Corinth. 'Melita' and 'Korinthos' is what that script forms, but we're not sure if that's the artist's name or who the vase was cast for possibly? The artist favored the white bull motif, there are several in this set, all with the same female figure."

She eyed the minotaur on the vase, hips drawn back, ready to penetrate the waiting woman. "Is that where you get your libido?" she asked cheekily, squeezing her thighs again. He'd had her that way just two nights prior, over the marble-topped kitchen island, thrusting into her from behind until he came with a grunt, and she'd pointed out that one of the perks of the new rental were the easy-to-clean floors, as a gush of fluid hit the tiles with a splash as soon as his softened cock slipped from her body.

"*Me?*! Are you asking that question to a mirror? I had to stop at the pharmacy for eyedrops this morning, you've been here a week and my whole body feels dried out. I don't think I'd be able to handle more than one of you, he was a fucking champ."

She pushed back against him in response, the curve of her ass bumping into his crotch. She knew just how to shift her hips to press into his cock behind her, knew the exact spot against his thick thigh where it would be resting, and she smiled in triumph when he grunted. He wasn't wrong, of course. She looked like a human and she'd dated plenty of human men over the years, but none of them could keep up with her the way he could; none of their cocks had stretched her open the same way, had filled her the way her body was meant to be filled. Despite looking human, being the product of minotaurean parents meant her body was designed to be bred by a bullish man, designed to carry bullish sons, and although she thought she'd been in love a handful of times before being paired with him on that dig site, none of her other lovers had ever satisfied her the way Madoc did. She felt a queer camaraderie with these ancient brides, glad that she could boast a minotaur in her bed.

"Mmhm, whatever. Sounds to me like you should be drinking more water. *And* they were all humans. That's not the same and you know it. So...we have no way of knowing what the mating selection looked like, only that everyone was getting dicked down. I had no idea this exhibit was so porntastic, I can't believe you're showing this to kids!"

"The less explicit stuff is against that far wall," he admitted sheepishly, nodding to the far wall where dark blue velvet ropes stanchioned off the corridor, leading out of the big room. "That's where we take the kids. They don't have the attention span for all of this anyway. The stanchions are pulled back two more rows for the older kids."

"I can't help but notice you brought me right to the hardcore fucking," she laughed. "I see what you're doing here...fortunately for you, I want to see more of the pre-Hellenistic lewds on vases. This is hotter than I expected. Lead on, Dr. Bowman."

CHAPTER SIX

The first time I am had by him, it is the middle of the night. Sleep does not come easy in this place. The darkness of the labyrinth is unending, and so my body finds acclamation impossible. I sleep during the hours which must surely be daylight, and find myself unable to rest when the others huddle together in slumber.

I am wandering through the maze on one of those sleepless nights, the first time he finds me alone. I expected there to be hidden dangers throughout the twisting corridors of Daedalus's creation, but I soon realize that the maze itself is the trap. The Minotaur dwells in its heart, but the winding passageways are the true threat, for it does not matter how long one wanders—each corridor is identical to the last, each turn no different than the previous two or ten or twenty taken. I quickly learn that to wander the halls of the labyrinth is to find freedom from one's sanity, because there is none to be found here. Turn after turn, corridor after corridor, darkness broken by torches broken by darkness, an unending sameness no matter how far my feet walk. I wonder if the lost souls in Tartarus walk a similar endless maze, each twist and turn bearing no change, no hope, no hint of freedom to be found. I had been wandering that night for what could have been minutes or hours, there is no way to tell, and it is almost a relief when he finds me.

At first, I am terrified. I have never been this close to him, and he had never set his beady gaze upon mine. In the heart, it is easy to shrink and hide behind the *other, more eager brides, but now there is no one else, only me and the Mino-taur. He approaches me with a lighter tread than I would have anticipated for a monster his size. It is the first opportunity I have had to take in his form truly, without distraction, and I am surprised by the elegance of his figure. His head, of course, is that of a bull's—flaring nostrils, glossy dark eyes, and horns tipped into sharp points. Unlike any bull I've ever seen, there is a curly thatch of dark hair between the great horns that tumbles in between his eyes. His body is as impressive as any warrior who has inspired songs. He is covered in a short, coarse hide, white like the beast that sired him, and thick with muscle; broad and barrel-chested, his arms long and heavy looking. There is nowhere to run, nowhere to hide, and I am helpless before him. He has the hands of a man, which somehow makes him less terrifying and even more strange to contemplate, for when he reaches for me and long fingers wrap around my arm, I can persuade myself that he is any stranger I might encounter in the marketplace.*

It is the first time I am seeing him without one of the brides pushing and shoving to reach his hard cock. He is always hard, always ready to mate one of the pleading women that surround him, and I have watched him spill his seed more times than I am able to recount in the days since my arrival. No amount of our flesh can satisfy his lust, his constant hunger; yet as he hungers for us, I have watched the frenzied need of my companions grow. Desperation is not something he needs to feel, for his lust is easily slaked, but desperation is some-thing I witness often enough in the eyes of my fellow brides. Being had by him once awakens something, they tell me. Once I am filled with his seed, they say, I will understand. Once my body knows the shape of him, the pleasure brought by being filled by him, the emptiness of the times without will drive me to madness. I look at them with pity, for I cannot understand. I can think of nothing but the sun, as I walk the labyrinth halls, and I cannot imagine a time when my mind will be eclipsed by the carnal obsession the other brides share, but as I stare at the fat testicles swinging low and loose beneath his sheath, the thick, pink spear it conceals already beginning its ascent upon the sight of me, I realize I am about to learn if their words had the shape of the truth.

I freeze in fear when he lifts me, as easily as one might lift a flower, his wide nose pressing to the side of my neck. His breath is hot, and he snuffles against my skin as though he were searching for something; down my neck and over my clothed breasts, he does not stop until he finds the prize he seeks—the quiv-ering heat between my thighs. His tongue is rough and textured, wide and hot, and it drags up my exposed legs as my chiton is pulled away. I've never before known the shape of a man within me or the touch of one against my sex, and the drag of his tongue is the first experience I have ever had with such things, hot and wet and rough. It never occurs to me to struggle or to attempt escape, for I have walked these labyrinth halls and I know there is no escape, and so I submit. After all, I am a bride.

*I remind myself, as he tastes my skin with his tongue, that in the days I have spent here, I have witnessed no cruelty enacted upon my fellow brides, no violence, and no rape. The debauchery I have witnessed has been consensual for all involved, and it no longer matters if we were brought here against our will. This is our destiny, decided by the gods, and we would have been similarly shipped away by our fathers, given to husbands with cruel hands. I do not thrash, and I do not kick. I surprise myself when my thighs part willingly to take the lashes of his tongue. I do not **want** it to feel good. I do not want to admit that my head drops back, or that my voice echoes off the stone walls in a sigh of pleasure. I do not want my pelvis to lift, seeking out the friction of that wide tongue when he draws back momentarily, nor do I want to know the girl who moans when he re-doubles his efforts, but I am unable to pretend pleasure I feel vibrating up my spine belongs to anyone but me. When I cry out, the stones of the corridor swallow the sound. There is no one to witness my submission; no one to watch as I tremble and shake, the pressure of his tongue causing a fit to ripple through my body. There is no one to see, and so I tell myself it did not happen, for pleasure was not a part of the stories we were told. When my ankles are hitched over his elbows, opening me to receive his cock, I remind myself there will be no witness to this moment either; only me, my bullish husband, and the gods, if they watch.*

The first press of him within me leaves me breathless, the sheer size of him feeling as though it will cleave me in two as he lowers me onto his rigid spear. The pleasure I had felt is supplanted by fire and with every thrust into my body, the inferno burns. I am stretched too wide, too far, and he batters my core until I cry out in pain, which causes him to still.

The burning ceases when he abruptly pulls me from him, dropping me to the floor, not ungently. His body covers mine as I am pulled to my knees and mounted from behind. His size is just as overwhelming as it was a moment ago when he held me upright, but there is something about this new position, this new angle that leaves me breathless in a different way. Rather than clenching my muscles against the intrusion of him, I find myself pressing back to take him in further. When the pleasure returns, I understand why the other brides circle around and beg to be next. There is little else here for us, after all. We have no vocation, no purpose, no role to fill other than the role of bride. When my body seizes, overtaken by clenching contractions that make my core pulse, it is as though I were being hurled from the highest mountain top, thrown out to the sparkling sea. There is no darkness as my body sails through the air, no chains or cruel king to imprison me. Only pleasure and the shape of my husband within me, the sparkling waves and the free air, and I realize the truth of the words the others have spoken.

Submitting to him, being one with him, is the only way to ever see the sun.

CHAPTER SEVEN

"I love fucking you this way."

His voice was a low rumble against her hair, his hands snug around her waist, and Gwen whimpered. Pulsing her thighs together excited the tingle between her thighs, but there was no friction, no pressure, nothing her clit desperately wanted, and his words were not helping in the slightest.

The vase was another depiction of a bride on her knees, being taken from behind by the crouching minotaur. She *did* love when he fucked her this way—the swell of his shaft making her cry out on every thrust, dragging over her g-spot, the angle allowing him to plumb her deeply, bumping the edge of her cervix in a way that made her back arch. It was harder for him to find the right angle with her on her back, and she'd taken the full brunt of his cock-head against her cervix before, always painful, and he was always sheepish and apologetic when she cried out in pain. *This* position, however...there were no downsides. If she pressed her shoulders to the mattress and kept her ass high, his balls slapped into her clit, fat and full and low-hanging, and she always, always came quickly this way.

"You're *really* not making this easy to get through," she grumbled, shifting purposefully against him until he hissed. "The horniness of this exhibit is an intentional attack on my self-control."

There was a primal energy to the images, and as they moved in a circuit around the room, it awoke something deep inside of her. Gwen wasn't sure if she ought to be as turned on as she was by the sight of the Minotaur on the vases and frescoes engaged in non-stop intercourse with the tributes that were sent to him, but with every piece of artwork that showed the bullman in a similar position to the ones she enjoyed with Madoc, she found the press of her thighs moved a bit easier, an increasing slickness aiding the movement. When the painted figures depicted one of the women on their knees, Gwen couldn't help pushing her own rear end back, bumping into the growing hardness she found behind her. At one point, he gripped her hips with both hands, pulling her hard into him, the action mirrored by the human and Minotaur in the fresco before them. She could feel the shape of him, straining against the front of his pants, opening her thighs in an effort to trap the bulging outline in her cleft. The swingy skirt of her a-line dress could be easily flipped up, the strained zipper on his pants given relief, and the fat firehose of his cock allowed loose...the thought of balancing over one of the marble plinths made her whine, and she was almost able to feel the roughness of his belt and the rasp of his zipper against the curve of her ass, the stretch of his head and thick, mid-shaft swell within her and the slide of his fingers against her clit...she pushed back again, certain she could feel his cock jump.

"You're going to get me fired before you even move," he groaned, grinding against her. There were cameras everywhere, she knew that without needing him to say it, and no matter how hot and bothered the display was making her, she didn't actually want to be arrested for public indecency, or to have him fired from his new job before she'd unpacked her toothbrush in the rental house. Gwen squirmed, bumping her ass into him one last time before they moved onto the next row. Surely, she thought, the distance hadn't made her this pathetically needy. *You can get through one exhibit. If school kids can do it, you can do it. It's history. Anthropological. Educational. Get a grip.*

CHAPTER EIGHT

After that night, it becomes a routine we have, my husband and I. I'm still unable to sleep when the time for sleeping comes, and so my feet wander the corridors of the maze. The first time he finds me after that first night, he seems angry. I do not know how long I had been away from the group, only that I noticed the torches burn brighter at the heart, spread further and further the wider I roam. At first, I think it to be a clue on how one might escape, but I soon realize that the darkness is uniform beyond the center of the maze. There is comfort in the darkness. At the heart where we dwell, the torches burn bright, always lit, always burning. The outer rings of the labyrinth are dimmer and those long stretches of darkness that frightened me so much on the night we arrived hold a measure of tranquility now, a peacefulness that reminds me of the temple where I had served. I linger long in the shadows, stopping in between torches to rest against the stone and sink into the blackness that resides there in between. It is not the sun, but the familiarity is a small comfort, and those are in short supply.

I am languishing in the shadows when he finds me. That first night I assumed he had stumbled upon me by happenstance, perhaps out wandering the maze himself, searching for a way out, but when he finds me in between the torches, he stops and huffs, snorting from his wide nostrils and grunting deep in his throat. When his hands—hands so like mine—wrap around my arm and tug me back to the torchlight, I realize he was looking for me. It is silly and foolish *to admit, but my heart thrills at the notion. We have turned several times, still within the dimmer outer corridors when I pause.*

I am still not convinced the others speak truly, for I have not been consumed with lust since our coupling. I have not pushed and shoved before the brazier amongst the other brides, fighting for position to be taken by him, I do not rock in corners when I am not chosen. Instead, I walk, and put distance between myself and the debauchery...but I would be branded a liar if I were to say I had not thought of that night more than once. When I stop in the darkness between the torches, he grunts, tugging my arm to follow. Instead, I lay my hand over his, my fingers that are so like his, sliding up his arm until I am able to drag them down his chest. The broad plain of his body is familiar to my hands, in the way a sheath is familiar to a sword. Despite the silky-coarse hair that covers him like a pelt, his body is that of a man's, and the curves of my own form fit against him as if they were carved in stone to do exactly that. My fingers—small, but so like his—trace the shape of him, the line of his throat and the hollow of his chest, learning him. There is a bubble of fear in my chest, but it has been eclipsed by a mad bravery, like Apollo's chariot covering the darkness of the sky with his light. In this darkness, my husband is the only sun, and I am eager to be warmed by his light.

It does not take much to prod him to arousal. He grunts again, deep in his throat, a much different sound than the one he made when he found me. His manhood is a thick, shining rod, and for the first time, I am able to take a long look at it. As it rises from the furred sheath above his heavy testicles, I am able to see the pink of it is yet another sheath, pulling back slowly to reveal the winking tip, already leaking a viscous stream of his seed. My observance is short, for his hand lands at my waist, and I am lifted once more.

I am taken on hands and knees once more, and once again I find myself opening for him eagerly. I do not wish to be one of the desperate, scrabbling women who push and shove for the privilege of his cock, but I am unable to pretend I do not enjoy it when he ruts me against the labyrinth floor. When he empties inside of me with what is nearly a growl, I am once again sailing through the sky, sailing on wings into Apollo's bright sun. My belly bulges with the shape of him, and his copious release puddles on the floor even before he has withdrawn. When I am pulled back to my feet, it is not without gentleness, and I cling to his strong arm until I regain my balance.

"Are you able to speak?" Since arriving, I have not heard him utter a word to any of us, and it is easy to think him a mindless beast without speech. When

his hands motion to his throat, I am able to see the scars, buried deep beneath his thick hide. I understand then, that he is a prisoner here, just as we all are, and my heart quivers at the thought. I wonder of the life he has lived; if he has ever known the warmth of the mountainside and the wind blowing free across his face; if he has ever looked out to the sparkling sea.

He knows the way back to the heart, that he knows how to find me when I wander too far, an indication that he has walked the same halls over and over and over again. I wonder if he too misses the sun; if he knows the same absence of hope I have felt wandering these endless corridors. There is nothing cruel in the way he grips my arm, leading me back to where the torches are tightly aligned on the walls, and the way he looks back to me whenever we pass beneath the flickering flames leads me to believe he is not without intelligence. If he could speak like a man, it might have forced those topside to treat him like one, and I remember for the very first time since my lot was drawn as a tribute that he is a prince. A prince of Crete, born to the Queen herself, and if he is a prince, then I am a princess. There is no throne to which my husband leads me back, but I follow him willingly, allowing him to grip me tightly.

T he next time he finds me, there is almost a hint of a smile playing at his wide mouth, as if this has become a game. I put my hands around the great spear of his cock as it rises from its sheath upon finding me, stroking up the pink skin, feeling the way it swells, and closing my small hand around the fist-sized head that graces the tip. The sheath of skin covering him moves easily, and he grunts as I pull it up to cover his cocktip completely, before moving my hand down once more, exposing the moisture he leaks. He takes me against the wall, and it is the first time I face him as he mates me. My hands are free, and I am able to grip his wide shoulders and feel the strength in his arms and chest, drag my fingertips over the scars at his throat and gently touch his face.

The next time I go wondering, he very nearly manages to take me by surprise. I had turned a corner paying more attention to the torchlight flickering ahead than I did to the shadows beyond, and when he hooked me around the waist, swinging me into the air, I shrieked. It is only when I realize they are his broad arms encircling me that I'm able to relax, melting into the warmth of his skin. His tongue is just as rough and wide as I remembered from the first time, when it strokes up my legs, parting my thighs. I hold onto his horns as he spreads me open, and for the first time since I watched the frenzy of brides encircling him, my own voice rises in a hitching, gasping moan. If new brides were to arrive at that moment, it would be my voice they followed, my screams that caused their own, and when they found me, I would be on my knees in the dirt, carried on the tide of ecstasy as my husband took me from behind. They would see my belly swell like a wineskin as he filled me, would see his seed dripping from me as he thrust through his release, and it would be my body they pulled aside to clean with their tongues, every drop of his essence a feast not to be wasted.

I understand now, that scene I first saw on arriving in the maze. I am able to feel him inside me even when he is not; able to feel the shape of him pushing through my skin and stretching me wide, and when I realize it is a dream and I am alone, the maze is darker than ever.

When he holds me aloft in his arms, thrusting relentlessly into me, I can see the sun's glow and feel its warmth. It is the warmth of his breath, I come to realize, and he is the only sun I will ever need again. When he releases into me, filling me with his seed in great spurts that I am able to feel shaking up my spine, I am able to see across the sea, to the very gates of Mycenae, to the top of the Acropolis, to the fires of the great oracle. It is the freedom of being his that I feel, and this is the only independence I will ever need again. Topside, my behavior would probably be viewed as concupiscent, but here there is no shame in desiring to lie with my husband, to feel the freedom and hate of being filled by him, the shape of him within me breathing new life into my indentured soul.

I do not know if he engages in these private assignations with any of the others, and I do not like to dwell on the thought. The time we spend together in the shadows between the torches belongs to us alone. I belong to him, and I was fated to be his bride. I realize when we arrive back in the heart where the others are, I will likely never join in their hysteria-fueled bacchanal. The temple where I served had no such ritual; I have never witnessed the ecstasy of the maenads, nor have I desired to join their ranks. I do not begrudge the others though, if this is their way of celebrating their marital rite with him. It is not for me, will never be for me, but as long as I wander I have the security of knowing he will always find me. If I am to end my days in this maze, at least I know there is someone here who will notice when I am gone.

CHAPTER NINE

"I think we need to take a break," she gasped. His hand had moved up the back of her thigh, finding its way beneath the edge of her skirt in such a way that it would not have been immediately evident on the fish-eyed camera lenses around the room. He'd moved beneath the edge of her panties, working a thick finger into her.

"You're dripping, Dr. Bowman." While she normally prided herself on her poker face, Gwen was finding it increasingly difficult to keep her knees from buckling as he fingered her, giving her clit the friction it needed at last and stroking her inner walls. She could feel his cock against her, swollen like a club, and she wasn't sure if they'd be able to wait to get home before finding relief.

"Your office doesn't have cameras, right? You *do* have your own office, don't you?"

"It's like a broom closet," he chuckled, cutting off on a groan when she tightened around the finger he'd worked into her, reminding him of the way she'd squeeze his cock, given the chance. "But it *is* a camera-free broom closet. I'm a little disappointed to hear the exhibit isn't holding your attention."

"I love the exhibit, babe, I do...but I *really* need you to fuck me. I don't think I can look at one more minotaur cock painting without pulling yours out."

His low laugh was a rumble of thunder against her, the pressure against her clit increasing, the other arm around her doing the bulk of the work holding her up.

"You seem a little on edge," he hummed. "Are you going to come on my fingers, right here in the middle of the exhibit? Or would you rather I leaned you over one of these plinths and filled your pussy the right way? I'm not sure this is academically appropriate, Dr. Bowman."

Gwen whimpered, wanting exactly what he described. She wanted to feel like one of these ancient brides, being bred by her big bull with her ass in the air, wanted him to pump her full...but she knew the security made such a scenario impossible.

"I'm going to pull your cock out if you don't take me somewhere to fuck me right now, Madoc. Is that what you want to happen? I'll stroke you right here in the middle of the exhibit, I'll get down on my knees and suck until you empty those big balls all over one of these frescoes. Will you be able to live with yourself knowing you came all over a priceless artifact? The janitor will clog up their shop-vac trying to clean up a lake of cum, and you'll be known all over town as the minotaur who splooged all over the museum."

"Enough!" She smiled in triumph as his shoulders shook in laughter, breath hitching when he sucked clean the finger that had just been inside her. "Fine! We'll take a fuck break. You can't even get through the same exhibit school children have been looking at all week because you can't control your horny, I hope you're proud of yourself. Don't blame me when you're finishing the exhibit bow-legged."

She squealed as he led out the way they'd come in, her heart flip-flopping briefly again as they passed the case containing the iron manacles. His office *was* a broom closet, probably hastily cleaned out and requisitioned once he'd been hired, but its lack of spaciousness didn't stop him from dropping his ass on the edge of the cluttered desk, hooves planting wide on the tiles as he opened his pants.

"I was promised someone dropping to their knees to suck," he reminded her, pulling his cock free.

She wasted no time following the directive. His balls were fat and full, hanging heavily in a soft pink sac, and she focused her attention on them first. Gwen loved the nearly-transparent fuzz that covered them, feeling like she was mouthing at plump, juicy peaches as he groaned, licking and nipping at the soft skin, pressing her tongue into the seam that separated them until they lifted and bobbed. His cock had already swelled out of its ivory sheath, dark pink and riddled with veins, and as her hand pulled up its length, she twisted, giving him the friction over his head that knew he enjoyed, gratified by his groan.

"Sounds like you're enjoying the effects of my horny," she pointed out, twisting her wrist again. "Or at least, your cock sure is. Do you think the original brides stroked their minotaur this way? Do you think they lined up to take their turn on his cock? Or was it a free-for-all? Do you want to go back out and look at more vases, or do you want to show me how the minotaur fucked his brides?" He'd already teased her cunt into readiness, and she clenched as his dome-topped cockhead was exposed, one pump after another, squeezing him over his swell until pre-come oozed over the edge of his foreskin.

She yipped in surprise when his big hands tugged on her arms, lifting and spinning her, reversing their positions. Gwen sucked in a breath, clutching the edge of the desk as he loomed over her. She was tall, taller than most human women, her own minotaur blood seeing to that. Her mother was the daughter of a bull herself, and despite stressing over the years that Gwen could fall in love with whomever she wanted, there had been something in her bones that echoed when she'd met Madoc, an undeniable attraction that owed, she thought now, to those dutiful first brides. "Are you going to devour me?"

Madoc smiled, his hands closing over her wrists as she backed up into the desk. His arms were solid with muscle, tenting around her until she was trapped, as helpless as the tributes of old. She already knew every corner of his body, had mapped every inch of his skin with her lips; knew how he took his eggs and preferred brand of detergent and that he hated talking on the phone...but there was something about this game of pretend, something primal that quickened her pulse.

"I am," he confirmed, horns cutting through the air as he leaned over her, pushing the mountain of papers back and sliding her to the center of the desk. "You belong to me. A sacrifice. A supplicant. Mine to devour."

She mentally cataloged the direction in which her panties were thrown as his head lowered, his wide, rough tongue licking a broad stripe up her sex, dragging against her clit in a way that made her toes curl. She understood how the myth of the tributes being eaten was started, she thought, for if the labyrinth's minotaur ate out his brides half as well, they probably bragged to anyone who would listen. The texture of his tongue against her clit made her writhe; the way he sucked on it made her vision go fuzzy. Gwen gripped his horns as he devoured her, her hitching breaths cresting into a moan when she tightened and released against his mouth, his hum of pleasure at her gush on his tongue vibrating through her.

She barely had time to recover before she was being lifted, her legs over his arms as she was lowered onto the glistening head of his cock. She was built to take him, her anatomy designed to be bred by a big, well-hung bull...but every time was like the first time when he speared her, stretching her open, his mid-shaft swell pulling a strangled moan from her throat. Gwen closed her eyes, imagining the purple dress she would wear, the way he would lift her on their wedding night, filling her until she bulged with the shape of him, coming inside of her over and over until she dripped in his seed. Her clit rubbed against his front in this position, his cock dragging against her inner walls, and she could feel the curling pressure within her beginning to give way to a spine-rattling orgasm, so close...when he pulled out of her, she nearly sobbed.

"I'm going to come," he groaned, setting her back on the edge of the desk, ignoring the way she clawed furiously at his arms, "and in case you were unaware, we're not at home. The night janitor isn't a splooge mopper and the museum doesn't have a sucky-sucky machine. I don't want it running under the door."

"Why do you have condoms at *work?!*" she exclaimed in wonder when he produced a large, gold-foiled square from his desk drawer.

"I bought them when I picked up the eye drops. I don't know how careful you want to be before the wedding, and I just thought..." His voice trailed off as her shoulders shook with laughter, watching him unwrap the prophylactic. The condom rolled over his thick shaft swell, the reservoir at the tip resembling an empty sandwich baggie. He was right, they should be a bit careful before the wedding ... but she hated the way the huge reservoirs felt within her, and would rather take her chances. After all, they were looking forward to children ... but he had a point, she conceded, not wanting to have to run to the ladies' room for paper towels to prevent the rivers of his release from running under the door once it poured out of her.

When he turned her to lean over the desk, bracing his body over hers, Gwen was certain she knew exactly how the women in the maze must have felt. Even if they were terrified upon their arrival, which she was certain they were; and even if they were uncertain in their futures, which they certainly couldn't have known—there was safety in *this*. The familiar, comfortable weight of him atop her, the heaving breaths, the eye-crossing pleasure...Gwen was positive they felt safe when they were with their Minoan prince, for there was nowhere else in the world that felt safer than Madoc's arms, and nowhere else she'd rather be.

When he came, the pressure of the condom filling was enough to tip her over the edge, inflating like a balloon, and she clenched, clenched around the shape of him hard enough that it was a wonder the condom did not pop within her. His deep groan seemed to rattle the desk beneath her, not as exciting as a marble plinth on the exhibit floor, but more than satisfactory for an evening tryst. She continued to clench around him as he poured into her, her own orgasm extended by the way the condom inflated with every pump of his big balls into it. She felt the moment he finished—a slight slump of his shoulders and a drop of his weight, his deep sigh warming her like a comfortable, familiar blanket. The pull-out sent a ripple up her back, the sloshing condom tied off, like a particularly threatening water balloon.

"Now what?" she whispered against his chest once her panties had been pulled back on and his softened cock tucked back into his pants, his clothing adjusted and her hair unmussed, restoring a modicum of respectability to their persons.

"Now we finish the exhibit," he murmured, lacing her fingers with his own. "I have a feeling you're not going to like the rest of it, but...well, perspective is necessary. You'll see. First though, can you please sneak this into the ladies' room? I don't want to leave an evidence trail." She didn't like his words, didn't like the uncomfortable twinge she felt, so similar to the way her stomach twisted the sight of the manacles, but she wrapped her arm around his, nodding. After all, Gwen reminded herself, she'd follow him anywhere.

"Let's get it over with then. If it makes me cry, you have to buy me ice cream on the way home."

"There's already a triple fudge sundae waiting for you," he chuckled. "The tears are inevitable, and I came prepared."

CHAPTER TEN

I have given birth to a son.

    I thought his birth would kill me. Bringing him into the world was a pain I never could have imagined, but I am grateful to the others who helped, who held me up and wiped my brow as I pushed and writhed, and holding him in my arms was a balm to all of the screaming agonies that preceded his first breath. He has the features of his father, a fact which brought me immeasurable joy the first time I gazed down upon his small, squalling face. His nose is pink and the hide that covers him is the same color as the milk he drinks at my breast. For the first week after his arrival, I am unable to stop kissing him—his small nose and the curly thatch of dark hair between the velvet buttons where his horns will sprout, each of his eyelids, which are closed in sleep for much of the time. I sing him the songs of Korinthos and tell him of my life there and the people he was from, keeping him warm near the brazier, always in my arms.

I do not remember when they took him, only that one day he was there, suckling at my breast, and the next he was gone. I do not know how long he was with me. That thing we once called time has ceased to exist here, at the heart of the maze. The only light comes from the torches and from the trap door, which lowers several times a day with food and supplies, the only reminder that the outside world still exists. There is no sun, and so the marking of its *passage across the sky is meaningless here. There is no sunrise, no sunset, and thus, there is no time. In this world of endless darkness, time is fractured into only two halves: the time spent being filled by my husband—filled and fulfilled—and the agony of emptiness. The only time I am whole is when I am filled with his cock; the only time with meaning is when I am joined to him, and every minute spent empty and alone and waiting is borne with a heavy heart. What use have I for the sun in a place like this? What use have I for a child?*

He has gone on to become a great warrior, that is what I am told. The brides who have borne children before me speak assurances, and I have no choice but to believe them. At length, I accept it is for the best. My only purpose is to serve my husband and be served in return. The cost of devotion in his temple has cost me my son, but the pleasure I receive in payment for my veneration is well worth the sacrifice. The trapdoor's platform is large enough to lower us all into the maze on the day we arrived, and I am certain it would be large enough to raise us all back to the surface, back to the light, but I have no wish to leave my temple. There is nothing left for me topside, and the life I may have led, the girl I once was, is gone. Outside of this place, in a world of light, my son will be a warrior, and may someday become a king. I gave him the gift of life, and I nourished him from mine own breast. If the last gift I give him is a life in the sunshine, then I have served him just as admirably.

I am wandering when I hear the shouts. At first, I think it is an issue with the trapdoor. The platform lowers each day and the guards atop it unload the baskets of food they carry without sound, most days. There are always four of them—two to unload the food, and two to stand guard with spears, an unnecessary precaution, for none of us have ever charged the platform, and it is well away from the heart.

The shouts, I realize are not coming from the direction of the trapdoor, nor are the voices I hear those belonging to any of my fellow brides. They are low and coarse, loud and echoing across the tall walls of the maze. Men. The realization fills me with a clenching fear, for nothing good can come from men, certainly not here. I think of the boastful boy on the brieme, the one they said was a prince. He loudly proclaimed his intention to rescue us from the maze, *insisting he could find a way, either by cleverness or by force...I begin to run away from the voices, pressing myself into the long stretches of darkness between the torches. I know it does not matter how far I go or how lost my feet become. I will hide from these men, for the maze will swallow them up as it swallows all, and no matter how far I wander, my husband will always find me.*

CHAPTER ELEVEN

"So they really weren't eaten. But why so many? He couldn't be happy getting it on with one tribute at a time? And why the replacements every few years? Are you *sure* they weren't eaten?"

His laughter was a rich, deep rumble, and her back arched to hear it. She wondered how long it would take, for the newness of him being there all the time to wear off; wondered when the solid heat of him beside her in bed would no longer leave her giddy upon waking. *Hopefully never.*

"You're making me spoil the exhibit, but I know you won't let it go and just be patient."

"Nope," she agreed, giving him her cheekiest wink. "You already have me walking like I just spent a week on a centaur's back, now I want all the spoilers. You know I always read ahead to the end of books first."

Madoc rolled his eyes, giving her a put-upon sigh.

"If you absolutely have to know now...they were there to be bred. He was able to mate constantly, and no, we don't know how. Maybe he suffered from a form of priapism, maybe it really was a curse from the gods, who knows. 'Inheriting Pasiphaë's lust, the son bore the curse of the mother,'" he recited, nodding at the inscription on one of the plinths. "What we do know is that he mated them continuously, with the goal of the palace, of course, being conception. The resulting offspring were sent back to their mother's home-lands. Sons were trained as warriors, and every king in the region wanted to boast minotaurs in their armies. That's why the tributes were sent."

The implication of his words took several beats to fully sink in. It wasn't much different than the arranged marriages of women of every species throughout history, she reminded herself. Daughters sold in marriage to build alliances for their fathers, to have sons who would inherit empires...

"And the daughters?" she demanded, spinning in his arms, her stomach flipping the same way it had at the sight of the manacles. "What happened to them?" Madoc lifted a broad shoulder in a beseeching shrug, the corners of his mouth lifting slightly in a sad smile, resignation tingeing his eyes. Pulling her flush to him once more, she let him wrap her in his arms. "Slaves," she answered her own question woodenly, already knowing it was true.

"You have to look at the big picture," he murmured after a long moment. "What happened to these girls was terrible, yes. They were sent from their homes, and you're right, they were probably terrified. They were made to have children over and over, and every few years they were replaced with fresher candidates. But," he turned her, lifting her chin to look up at him, "we know that plenty of those sons and daughters survived whatever fates they went on to. You and I wouldn't be standing here if they hadn't. We wouldn't be planning our wedding and talking about having our own kids if they hadn't. That's why exhibits like this are so important. We took back the rings the humans placed on us and made them our own symbol of commitment."

It was a relief he held her so tightly, for her legs surely would have failed her then. He was right, of course. Finding the thread from the past to their current time was her job, after all. Loving and living and dying. Madoc could have been a direct descendent from that Minoan prince, after all, and their children would carry those genes forward into the future.

A touch of eternity.

"If we have a daughter, she is going to be *so* spoiled, do you understand?"

"The most spoiled princess in all of Cambric Creek," he agreed, using his sleeve to mop at the tears tracking down her cheek.

"Tell me we're going to be okay," she mumbled against his chest. "Everything is going to change now. Promise me you're not going to get tired of the way I chew or my morning breath or if I'm really bad at being pregnant. What if I'm invited to a dig on the other side of the world? Or if some university wants you as a guest lecturer? How are we going to manage this with kids?"

"You are getting ridiculously ahead of yourself," he cut her off. "We are going to be fine. I'm not interested in any job that takes me away from you, and I love the way you chew. My grandmother is going to love you, and if your Aunt Simone wants to start a rumor that I splooged all over the museum, we'll just have to prove her right. If you want to pick up and move across the world, we'll go with you. It doesn't matter how far you wander, because I'll always find you. Isn't that what we've always done? Nothing is going to change."

He was wrong, she knew, for everything was about to change, but he was right about the rest. It was what they'd always done, and they'd be fine. Living and loving, and the whole world was possible.

"Let's go home. We have four months before the wedding, and I want to see if we can use your bracelet as a cock ring before it goes on your wrist. That thing's gotta pay for itself somehow."

She squealed in laughter, giving the thick shape of him a squeeze through the front of his rumpled pants, heedless of the cameras that tracked them. "You're gonna go to the sucky-sucky vacuum place, that's how it's going to pay for itself. I'm going to make you an appointment right now!" She pulled out her phone as he moved the velvet cords into place at the exit of the exhibit, their very own labyrinth. She was looking forward to visiting him at work, again and again, examining each vase and fresco from every angle, learning the details of the different women depicted. "You're not going to believe this," she announced as he turned out of his office, work bag over his shoulder, the silhouette of his horns cutting across the floor, "there's one of the sucky-sucky vacuum places right here in town! We can make an appointment right online."

"First home," he insisted, setting the alarm at the exit, once she was on the other side of the double-paned door. "Then cock ring. You can make an appointment later."

"First ice cream," Gwen corrected, feeling a kiss of the past at her neck as they walked away from the museum and the display, the evidence of all who'd come before them. "Then appointment. Then cock ring, and that's a maybe. Don't you go getting splooge all over my bracelet, I have to wear that thing forever."

"Forever," he agreed, leaning down to kiss the top of her head, opening her car door.

She was going to like this place, she decided as Madoc walked around the car in the growing twilight. They were going to raise a family here, were going to live and love and they were going to be fine.

"Forever," she confirmed, lacing her fingers with his.

Thirsty for more sweet and steamy monster romance? You can find more stories from Cambric Creek HERE.

ABOUT THE AUTHOR

C.M. Nascosta is an author and professional procrastinator from Cleveland, Ohio. She's always preferred beasts to boys, the macabre to the milquetoast, the unknown darkness in the shadows to the Chad next door.

She lives in a crumbling old Victorian with a scaredy-cat dachshund, where she writes nontraditional romances featuring beastly boys with equal parts heart and heat, and is waiting for the Hallmark Channel to get with the program and start a paranormal lovers series.

Want updates on when new books release? Do you love exclusive shorts? Sign up for my newsletter at: http://cmnascosta.com and receive an exclusive short once a quarter.

Patrons receive a monthly short story and more. Find me on social media—I love to chat with fans!

 patreon.com/Monster_Bait

 instagram.com/CMNascosta

twitter.com/cmnascosta

facebook.com/authorcmnascosta

AFTERWORD

Thank you for reading!
If you enjoyed the anthology, please consider leaving a review on Amazon
here: http://Amazon.com/review/create-review?&asin=B09L775XHV

Please consider supporting more monster romance tales by preordering our
other anthologies.

MONSTERS IN LOVE VOL 2: LOST IN THE DARK
{BOOKS2READ.COM/MONSTERSINLOVE2}
RELEASING SEPTEMBER 2022

MONSTERS IN LOVE VOL 3: LOST IN THE FOREST
{BOOKS2READ.COM/MONSTERSINLOVE3}
RELEASING MARCH 2023

MONSTERS IN LOVE: A MONSTER PARANORMAL ROMANCE ANTHOLOGY
{BOOKS2READ.COM/MONSTERSINLOVESET}

(Wicked Tales and Monstrous Ever Afters)
(Proceeds will be donated to benefit best friends Animal Society)
Releasing March 7, 2023